Richard Corbden

**Speeches on Questions of Public Policy by Richard Cobden**

Richard Corbden

**Speeches on Questions of Public Policy by Richard Cobden**

ISBN/EAN: 9783742844286

Manufactured in Europe, USA, Canada, Australia, Japa

Cover: Foto ©Andreas Hilbeck / pixelio.de

Manufactured and distributed by brebook publishing software
(www.brebook.com)

Richard Corbden

# Speeches on Questions of Public Policy by Richard Cobden

# SPEECHES

BY

# RICHARD COBDEN, M.P.

# SPEECHES

## ON QUESTIONS OF PUBLIC POLICY

BY

# RICHARD COBDEN, M.P.

EDITED BY

### JOHN BRIGHT

AND

### JAMES E. THOROLD ROGERS

IN TWO VOLUMES

## VOL. II.

FREE TRADE, PEACE, GOOD WILL AMONG NATIONS

### London
## MACMILLAN AND CO.
### 1870

OXFORD:

BY T. COMBE, M.A., E. B. GARDNER, E. P. HALL, AND H. LATHAM, M.A.,

PRINTERS TO THE UNIVERSITY.

# CONTENTS OF VOL. II.

## WAR.

## FOREIGN POLICY.

## INDIA.

## PEACE.

## POLICY OF THE WHIG GOVERNMENT.

## PARLIAMENTARY REFORM.

## EDUCATION.

# W A R.

# RUSSIAN WAR.

## I.

### HOUSE OF COMMONS, DECEMBER 22, 1854.

[On Dec. 12, the Duke of Newcastle (War Secretary), introduced a Bill, the object of which was to raise a force of 15,000 foreigners, who were to be drilled in this country. The Bill was opposed by the Conservative party, as impolitic and dangerous, but was finally carried, with very little alteration, by 38 votes, on Dec. 22 (163 to 135). Little more than a month after this, the Aberdeen Government resigned, in consequence of an adverse vote of the House of Commons on Mr. Roebuck's motion of Jan. 29.]

If I ask permission to enlarge a little the scope of our discussion, I have, at all events, this excuse, that the subject-matter more technically before the House has been very ably and fully discussed. There is another reason why the question may be viewed in a more general way, as affecting the conduct of the Government in carrying on the war and conducting negotiations, namely, that we have heard several hon. Members publicly declare that they refuse to entertain the matter now before the House on its merits, but persist in voting, in respect to it, contrary to their own opinions, and simply as a question of confidence in the Government. I must say, among all the evils which I attach to a state of war, not the least considerable is, that it has so demoralising a tendency as this on the

B 2

representative system. We are called on to give votes contrary
to our conscience, and to allow those votes to be recorded
where the explanation would not often appear to account for
them. It was stated the other night, by the noble Lord
(John Russell) the Member for the City of London, that proposals for peace had been made on the part of Russia, through
Vienna, upon certain bases, which have been pretty frequently
before the world under the term of the ' Four Points.' Now, I
wish to draw attention to that subject; but, before I do so, let
me premise, that I do not intend to say one word with respect to the origin of this unhappy war. I intend to start
from the situation in which we now find ourselves, and I
think it behoves this House to express an opinion upon that
situation.

I avow myself in favour of peace on the terms announced
by Her Majesty's Ministers. At all events, hon. Members
will see the absolute necessity, if the war is to go on, and if
we are to have a war of invasion by land against Russia, of
carrying it on in a different spirit and on a different scale from
that in which the operations have hitherto been conducted.
I think both sides of the House occupy common ground in
this respect; for we shall all recognise the propriety and
necessity of discussing this important and critical question.
Before I offer an opinion on the desirability of concluding
peace on these four points, it will be necessary to ask, what was
the object contemplated by the war? I merely ask this as a
matter of fact, and not with a view of arguing the question.
It has been one of my difficulties, in arguing this question out
of doors with friends or strangers, that I rarely find any intelligible agreement as to the object of the war. I have met
with very respectable and well-educated men, who have told
me that the object of the war was to open the Black Sea to all
merchant-vessels. That, certainly, could not be the object,
for the Black Sea was already as free to all merchant-vessels
as the Baltic. I have met with officers who said that the

object was to open the Danube, and to allow the ships of all nations to go up that river.  The object, certainly, could not be that, for the traffic in the Danube has, during the last twenty years, multiplied nearly tenfold, and the ships of all nations have free access there.  I have heard it stated and applauded at public meetings, that we are at war because we have a treaty with the Sultan, binding us to defend the integrity and independence of his empire.  I remember that, at a most excited public meeting at Leicester, the first resolution, moved by a very intelligent gentleman, declared that we were bound by the most solemn treaties with the Sultan to defend the integrity and independence of the Turkish empire.  Now, Lord Aberdeen has even ostentatiously announced in the House of Lords—for the instruction, I suppose, of such gentlemen as I have referred to—that we had no treaty before the present war binding us to defend the Sultan or his dominions. Another and greater cause of the popularity of the war out of doors has been, no doubt, the idea that it is for the freedom and independence of nations.  There has been a strong feeling that Russia has not only absorbed and oppressed certain nationalities, but is the prime agent by which Austria perpetuates her dominion over communities averse to her rule. I should say that this class was fairly represented by my lamented and noble Friend the late Member for Marylebone, from whom I differed entirely in reference to his views on the question of interference with foreign countries, but for whose private virtues and disinterested conduct and boundless generosity I have always entertained the greatest veneration and respect.  The late Lord Dudley Stuart for twenty years fairly represented the popular feeling out of doors, which was directed especially against the Emperor of Russia, and the popular sympathies, which were centred mainly on those territories which lie contiguous to the Russian empire.  I used sometimes to tell that noble Lord, jocularly, that his sympathies were geographical — that they extended to all

countries, from the Baltic to the Black Sea, bordering on
Russia—that if the Poles, Hungarians, Moldavians, or Wal-
lachians were in trouble or distress, he was sure to be, in this
House, the representative of their wrongs; or if any unhappy
individuals from those countries were refugees from oppres-
sion in this country, they were sure to go instantly to him for
relief and protection. Lord Dudley Stuart represented a great
amount of public sympathy in this country with respect to
nationalities, as it is termed; but I ask, whether the ground
on which the public impression is founded—that we are going
to war to aid the Poles, Hungarians, Moldavians, or Walla-
chians—has not been entirely delusive; and whether it may
not be ranked with the other notions about opening the Black
Sea, or a treaty with the Sultan, and about the Danube not
being free to the flags of all nations?

I ask, whether all these grounds have not been equally
delusive? The first three grounds never had an existence at
all; and, as to setting up oppressed nationalities, the Government certainly never intended to go to war for that object.
To set myself right with those hon. Gentlemen who profess
to have great regard for liberty everywhere, I beg to state
that I yield to no one in sympathy for those who are struggling for freedom in any part of the world; but I will never
sanction an interference which shall go to establish this or
that nationality by force of arms, because that invades a principle which I wish to carry out in the other direction—the
prevention of all foreign interference with nationalities for the
sake of putting them down. Therefore, while I respect the
motives of those gentlemen, I cannot act with them. This
admission, however, I freely make, that, were it likely to advance the cause of liberty, of constitutional freedom, and
national independence, it would be a great inducement to me
to acquiesce in the war, or, at all events, I should see in it
something like a compensation for the multiplied evils which
attend a state of war.

And now we come to what is called the statesman's ground for this war: which is, that it is undertaken to defend the Turkish empire against the encroachments of Russia—as a part of the scheme, in fact, for keeping the several States of Europe within those limits in which they are at present circumscribed. This has been stated as a ground for carrying on the present war with Russia; but, I must say, this view of the case has been very much mixed up with magniloquent phraseology, which has tended greatly to embarrass the question. The noble Lord the Member for the City of London was the first, I think, to commence these magniloquent phrases, in a speech at Greenock about last August twelvemonths, in which he spoke of our duties to mankind, and to the whole world; and he has often talked since of this war as one intended to protect the liberties of all Europe and of the civilised world. I remember, too, the phrases which the noble Lord made use of at a City meeting, where he spoke of our being 'engaged in a just and necessary war, for no immediate advantage, but for the defence of our ancient ally, and for the maintenance of the independence of Europe.' Well, I have a word to say to the noble Lord on that subject. Now, we are placed to the extreme west of a continent, numbering some 200,000,000 inhabitants; and the theory is, that there is great danger from a growing eastern Power, which threatens to overrun the Continent, to inflict upon it another deluge like that of the Goths and Vandals, and to eclipse the light of civilisation in the darkness of barbarism. But, if that theory be correct, does it not behove the people of the Continent to take some part in pushing back that deluge of barbarism? I presume it is not intended that England should be the Anacharsis Clootz of Europe; but that, at all events, if we are to fight for everybody, those, at least, who are in the greatest danger, will join with us in resisting the common enemy. I am convinced, however, that all this declamation about the independence of Europe and the defence of civilisation will by-and-by disappear. I take it for granted, then, that the statesman's object in this war is to defend Turkey against the encroachments of Russia, and so to set a barrier against the aggressive ambition of that great empire. That is the language of the Queen's Speech. But have we not accomplished that object? I would ask, have we not arrived at that point? Have we not effected all that was proposed in the Queen's Speech? Russia is now no longer within the Turkish territory; she has renounced all idea of invading Turkey; and now, as we are told by the noble Lord, there have been put forward certain proposals from Russia, which are to serve as the bases of peace.

What are those proposals? In the first place, there is to be a joint protectorate over the Christians by the five great Powers; there is to be a joint guarantee for the rights and privileges of the Principalities; there is to be a revision of the rule laid down in 1841 with regard to the entrance of ships-of-war into the Bosphorus, and the Danube is to be free to all nations. These are the propositions that are made for peace, as we are told by the noble Lord; and it is competent for us, I think, as a House of Commons, to offer an opinion as to the desirability of a treaty on those terms.

My first reason for urging that we should entertain those proposals is, that we are told that Austria and Prussia have agreed to them. Those two Powers are more interested in this quarrel than England and France can be. Upon that subject I will quote the words of the noble Lord the Member for Tiverton, uttered in February last. The noble Lord said,—

‘ We know that Austria and Prussia had an interest in the matter more direct and greater than had either France or England. To Austria and Prussia it is a vital matter—a matter of existence—because, if Russia were either to appropriate any large portion of the Turkish territory, or even to reduce Turkey to the condition of a mere dependent State, it must be manifest to any man who casts a glance over the map of Europe, and who looks at the geographical position of these two Powers with regard to Russia and Turkey, that any considerable accession of power on the part of Russia in that quarter must be fatal to the independence of action of both Austria and Prussia.'

I entirely concur with the noble Lord in his view of the interest which Austria and Prussia have in this quarrel, and what I want to ask is this—Why should we seek greater guarantees and stricter engagements from Russia than those with which Austria and Prussia are content? They lie on the frontier of this great empire, and they have more to fear from its power than we can have; no Russian invasion can touch us until it has passed over them ; and is it likely, if we fear, as we say we do, that Western Europe will be overrun by Russian barbarism—is it likely, I say, that since Austria and Prussia will be the first to suffer, they will not be as sensible to that danger as we can be? Ought we not rather to take it as a proof that we have somewhat exaggerated the danger which threatens Western Europe, when we find that Austria and Prussia are not so alarmed at it as we are? They are not greatly concerned about the danger, I think, or else they would join with England and France in a great battle to push it back. If, then, Austria and Prussia are ready to accept these proposals, why should not we be? Do you suppose that, if Russia really meditated an attack upon Germany—that if she had an idea of annexing the smallest portion of German territory, with only 100,000 inhabitants of Teutonic blood, all Germany would not be united as one man to resist her? Is there not a strong national feeling in that Germanic race?— are they not nearly 40,000,000 in number?—are they not the most intelligent, the most instructed, and have they not proved themselves the most patriotic people in Europe? And if they are not dissatisfied, why should we stand out for better conditions, and why should we make greater efforts and greater sacrifices to obtain peace than they? I may be told, that the people and the Government of Germany are not quite in harmony on these points. [Cheers.] Hon. Gentlemen who cheer, ought to be cautious, I think, how they assume that

Governments do not represent their people. How would you like the United States to accept that doctrine with regard to this country? But I venture to question the grounds upon which that opinion is formed. I have taken some little pains to ascertain the feeling of the people in Germany on this war, and I believe that if you were to poll the population of Prussia —which is the brain of Germany—whilst nineteen-twentieths would say that in this quarrel England is right and Russia wrong; nay, whilst they would say they wished success to England as against Russia, yet, on the contrary, if you were to poll the same population as to whether they would join England with an army to fight against Russia, I believe, from all I have heard, that nineteen-twentieths would support their King in his present pacific policy.

But I want to know what is the advantage of having the vote of a people like that in your favour, if they are not inclined to join you in action? There is, indeed, a wide distinction between the existence of a certain opinion in the minds of a people and a determination to go to war in support of that opinion. I think we were rather too precipitate in transferring our opinion into acts; that we rushed to arms with too much rapidity; and that if we had abstained from war, continuing to occupy the same ground as Austria and Prussia, the result would have been, that Russia would have left the Principalities, and have crossed the Pruth; and that, without a single shot being fired, you would have accomplished the object for which you have gone to war. But what are the grounds on which we are to continue this war, when the Germans have acquiesced in the proposals of peace which have been made? Is it that war is a luxury? Is it that we are fighting—to use a cant phrase of Mr. Pitt's time—to secure indemnity for the past, and security for the future? Are we to be the Don Quixotes of Europe, to go about fighting for every cause where we find that some one has been wronged? In most quarrels there is generally a little wrong

on both sides; and, if we make up our minds always to
interfere when any one is being wronged, I do not see always
how we are to choose between the two sides.   It will not do
always to assume that the weaker party is in the right, for
little States, like little individuals, are often very quarrelsome,
presuming on their weakness, and not unfrequently abusing
the forbearance which their weakness procures them.   But the
question is, on what ground of honour or interest are we to
continue to carry on this war, when we may have peace upon
conditions which are satisfactory to the great countries of
Europe who are near neighbours of this formidable Power?
There is neither honour nor interest forfeited, I think, in
accepting these terms, because we have already accomplished
the object for which it was said this war was begun.

The questions which have since arisen, with regard to
Sebastopol, for instance, are mere points of detail, not to be
bound up with the original quarrel.   I hear many people say,
'We will take Sebastopol, and then we will treat for peace.'
I am not going to say that you cannot take Sebastopol—I am
not going to argue against the power of England and France.
I might admit, for the sake of argument, that you can take
Sebastopol.   You may occupy ten miles of territory in the
Crimea for any time; you may build there a town; you may
carry provisions and reinforcements there, for you have the
command of the sea; but while you do all this, you will have
no peace with Russia.   Nobody who knows the history of
Russia can think for a moment that you are going permanently to occupy any portion of her territory, and, at the
same time, to be at peace with that empire.   But admitting
your power to do all this, is the object which you seek to
accomplish worth the sacrifice which it will cost you?   Can
anybody doubt that the capture of Sebastopol will cost you a
prodigious sacrifice of valuable lives; and, I ask you, is the
object to be gained worth that sacrifice?   The loss of treasure
I will leave out of the question, for that may be replaced, but

we can never restore to this country those valuable men who may be sacrificed in fighting the battles of their country—perhaps the most energetic, the bravest, the most devoted body of men that ever left these islands. You may sacrifice them, if you like, but you are bound to consider whether the object will compensate you for that sacrifice.

I will assume that you take Sebastopol; but for what purpose is it that you will take it, for you cannot permanently occupy the Crimea without being in a perpetual state of war with Russia? It is, then, I presume, as a point of honour, that you insist upon taking it, because you have once commenced the siege. The noble Lord, speaking of this fortress, said:—
'If Sebastopol, that great stronghold of Russian power, were destroyed, its fall would go far to give that security to Turkey which was the object of the war.' But I utterly deny that Sebastopol is the stronghold of Russian power. It is simply an outward and visible sign of the power of Russia; but, by destroying Sebastopol, you do not by any means destroy that power. You do not destroy or touch Russian power, unless you can permanently occupy some portion of its territory, disorder its industry, or disturb its Government. If you can strike at its capital, if you can deprive it of some of its immense fertile plains, or take possession of those vast rivers which empty themselves into the Black Sea, then, indeed, you strike at Russian power; but, suppose you take Sebastopol, and make peace to-morrow; in ten years, I tell you, the Russian Government will come to London for a loan to build it up again stronger than before. And as for destroying those old green fir-ships, you only do the Emperor a service, by giving him an opportunity for building fresh ones.

Is not the celebrated case of Dunkirk exactly in point? In 1713, at the treaty of Utrecht, the French King, under sore necessity, consented to destroy Dunkirk. It had been built under the direction of Vauban, who had exhausted his genius and the coffers of the State, in making it as strong as science and money could make it. The French King bound himself to demolish it, and the English sent over two Commissioners to see the fortress thrown to the ground, the jetties demolished and cast into the harbour, and a mole or bank built across the channel leading into the port ; and you would have thought Dunkirk was destroyed once and for ever. There was a treaty binding the King not to rebuild it, and which on two successive occasions was renewed. Some few years afterwards a storm came and swept away the mole or bank which blocked up the channel, by which accident ingress and egress were restored ; and shortly afterwards, a war breaking out between England and Spain, the French Government took advantage of our being engaged elsewhere, and rebuilt the fortifications on the seaside, as the historian tells us, much stronger than before. The fact is recorded, that in the Seven Years' War, about forty years afterwards, Dunkirk, for all purposes of aggression by sea, was more formidable than ever. We had in that case a much stronger motive for destroying Dunkirk than we can ever have in the case of Sebastopol ; for in the war which ended in the peace of Utrecht, there were 1600 English merchant-vessels, valued at 1,250,000*l.*, taken by privateers which came out of Dunkirk.

Then, again, in the middle of the last century, we destroyed Cherbourg, and during the last war we held possession of Toulon ; but did we thereby destroy the power of France ? If we could have got hold of some of her fertile provinces — if we could have taken possession of her capital, or struck at her vitals, we might have permanently impoverished and diminished her power and resources ; but we could not do it by the simple demolition of this or that fortress. So it would be in this case—we might take Sebastopol, and then make peace ; but there would be the rankling wound—there would be a venom in the treaty which would determine Russia to take the first opportunity of reconstructing this fortress. There would be storms, too, there,

which would destroy whatever mole we might build across
the harbour of Sebastopol, for storms in the Black Sea are
more frequent, as we know, than in the Channel; but even
if Sebastopol were utterly destroyed, there are many places
on the coast of the Crimea which might be occupied for a
similar purpose.

But then comes the question, Will the destruction of
Sebastopol give security to the Turks? The Turkish Empire will only be safe when its internal condition is secure,
and you are not securing the internal condition of Turkey
while you are at war; on the contrary, I believe you are
now doing more to demoralise the Turks and destroy their
Government than you could possibly have done in time of
peace. If you wish to secure Turkey, you must reform its
Government, purify its administration, unite its people, and
draw out its resources; and then it will not present the spectacle of misery and poverty that it does now. Why, you
yourselves have recognised the existing state of Turkey to be
so bad, that you intend to make a treaty which shall bind the
Five Powers to a guarantee for the better treatment of the
Christians. But have you considered well the extent of the
principle in which you are embarking? You contemplate
making a treaty, by which the Five Powers are to do that
together which Russia has hitherto claimed to do herself.
What sort of conclusion do you think disinterested and impartial critics—people in the United States, for instance—will
draw from such a policy? They must come to the conclusion
that we have been rather wrong in our dealings with Russia,
if we have gone to war with her to prevent her doing that
very thing which we ourselves propose to do, in conjunction
with the other Powers. If so much mischief has sprung from
the protectorate of one Power, Heaven help the Turks when
the protectorate of the Five Powers is inaugurated! But, at
this very moment, I understand that a mixed Commission
is sitting at Vienna, to serve as a court of appeal for the

Danubian Principalities; in fact, that Moldavia and Wallachia are virtually governed by a Commission representing Austria, England, France, and Turkey.

Now, this is the very principle of interference against which I wish to protest. From this I derive a recognition of the exceptional internal condition of Turkey, which, I say, will be your great difficulty upon the restoration of peace. Well, then, would it not be more statesmanlike in the Government, instead of appealing, with clap-trap arguments, to heedless passions out of doors, and telling the people that Turkey has made more progress in the career of regeneration during the last twenty years than any other country under the sun, at once to address themselves to the task before them—the reconstruction of the internal system of that empire? Be sure this is what you will have to do, make peace when you may; for everybody knows that, once you withdraw your support and your agency from her, Turkey must immediately collapse, and sink into a state of anarchy. The fall of Sebastopol would only make the condition of Turkey the worse; and, I repeat, that your real and most serious difficulty will begin when you have to undertake the management of that country's affairs, after you withdraw from it, and when you will have to re-establish her as an independent State. I would not have said a word about the condition of Turkey, but for the statement twice so jauntily made about her social progress by the noble Lord the Member for Tiverton. Why, what says the latest traveller in that country on this head? Lord Carlisle, in his recent work, makes the following remarks on the state of the Mahometan population, after describing the improving condition of the Porte's Christian subjects :—

'But when you leave the partial splendours of the capital and the great State establishments, what is it you find over the broad surface of a land which nature and climate have favoured beyond all others, once the home of all art and all civilisation? Look yourself—ask those who live there—deserted villages, uncultivated plains, banditti-haunted mountains, torpid laws, a corrupt administration, a disappearing people.'

Why, the testimony borne by every traveller, from Lamartine downwards, is, that the Mahometan population is perishing— is dying out from its vices, and those vices of a nameless character.   In fact, we do not know the true social state of Turkey, because it is indescribable; and Lord Carlisle, in his work, says that he is constrained to avoid referring to it.   The other day, Dr. Hadly, who had lately returned from Turkey, where he had a near relation, who had been physician to the Embassy for about thirty-five years, stated in Manchester that his relative told him that the population of Constantinople, into which there is a large influx from the provinces, has considerably diminished during the last twenty years, — a circumstance which he attributes to the indescribable social vices of the Turks.   Now, I ask, are you doing anything to promote habits of self-reliance or self-respect among this people by going to war in their behalf?   On the contrary, the moment your troops landed at Gallipoli, the activity and energy of the French killed a poor pacha there, who took to his bed, and died from pure distraction of mind; and from that time to this you have done nothing but humiliate and demoralise the Turkish character more than ever.   I have here a letter from a friend, describing the conflagration which took place at Varna, in which he says, it was curious to see how our sailors, when they landed to extinguish the fire in the Turkish houses, thrust the poor Turks aside, exactly as if they had been so many infant-school children in England.   Another private letter, which I recently received from an officer of high rank in the Crimea, states :—

'We are degrading the Turk as fast as we can; he is now the scavenger of the two armies as far as he can be made so.   He won't fight, and his will to work is little better; he won't be trusted again to try the former, and now the latter is all he is allowed to do.   When there are entrenchments to be made, or dead to be buried, the Turks do it.   They do it as slowly and lazily as they can, but do it they must.   This is one way of raising the Turk; it is propping him up on one side, to send him headlong down a deeper precipice on the other.'

That is what you are doing by the process that is now going on in Turkey. I dare say you are obliged to take the whole command into your own hands, because you find no native power—no administrative authority in that country; and you cannot rely on the Turks for anything. If they send an army to the Crimea, the sick are abandoned to the plague or the cholera, and having no commissariat, their soldiers are obliged to beg a crust at the tents of our men. Why, Sir, what an illustration you have in the facts relating to our sick and wounded at Constantinople of the helpless supineness of the Turks! I mention these things, as the whole gist of the Eastern Question lies in the difficulty arising from the prostrate condition of this race. Your troops would not be in this quarter at all, but for the anarchy and barbarism that reign in Turkey.

Well, you have a hospital at Scutari, where there are some thousands of your wounded. They are wounded Englishmen, brought there from the Crimea, where they have gone 3000 miles from their own home, to fight the battles of the Turks. Would you not naturally expect, that when these miserable and helpless sufferers were brought to the Turkish capital, containing 700,000 souls, those in whose cause they have shed their blood would at once have a friendly and generous care taken of them? Supposing the case had been that these wounded men had been fighting for the cause of Prussia, and that they had been sent from the frontiers of that country to Berlin, which has only half the population of Constantinople, would the ladies of the former capital, do you think, have allowed these poor creatures to have suffered from the want of lint or of nurses? Does not the very fact that you have to send out everything for your wounded, prove either that the Turks despise and detest, and would spit upon you, or that they are so feeble and incompetent as not to have the power of helping you in the hour of your greatest necessity? The people of England have been grossly misled regarding the state of Turkey. I am bound to consider that the noble Lord the Member for Tiverton expressed his honest convictions on this point; but certainly the unfortunate ignorance of one in his high position has had a most mischievous effect on the public opinion of this country, for it undoubtedly has been the prevalent impression out of doors, that the Turks are thoroughly capable of regeneration and self-government—that the Mahometan population are fit to be restored to independence, and that we have only to fight their battle against their external enemies, in order to enable them to exercise the functions of a great Power. A greater delusion than this, however, I believe, never existed in any civilised State.

Well, if, as I say is the case, the unanimous testimony of every traveller, German, French, English, and American, for the last twenty years, attests the decay and helplessness of the Turks, are you not wasting your treasure and your men's precious lives before Sebastopol, in an enterprise that cannot in the least aid the solution of your real difficulty? If you mean to take the Emperor of Russia eventually into your counsels—for this is the drift of my argument—if you contemplate entering into a quintuple alliance, to which he will be one of the parties, in order to manipulate the shattered remains of Turkey, to reconstitute or revise her internal polity, and maintain her independence, what folly it is to continue fighting against the Power that you are going into partnership with; and how absurd in the extreme it is to continue the siege of Sebastopol, which will never solve the difficulty, but must envenom the State with which you are to share the protectorate, and which is also the nearest neighbour of the Power for which you interpose, and your efforts to reorganise which, even if there be a chance of your accomplishing that object, she has the greatest means of thwarting! Would it not be far better for you to allow this question to be settled by peace, than leave it to the arbitrement of war, which cannot advance its adjustment one inch?

I have already adduced an illustration from the history of this country, as an inducement for your returning to peace. I will mention another. We all remember the war with America, into which we entered in 1812, on the question of the right of search, and other cognate questions relating to the rights of neutrals. Seven years before that war was declared, public opinion and the statesmen of the two countries had been incessantly disputing upon the questions at issue, but nothing could be amicably settled respecting them, and war broke out. After two years of hostilities, however, the negotiators on both sides met again, and fairly arranged the terms of peace. But how did they do this? Why, they agreed in their treaty of peace not to allude to what had been the subject-matter of the dispute which gave rise to the war, and the question of the right of search was never once touched on in that treaty. The peace then made between England and America has now lasted for forty years; and what has been the result? In the meantime, America has grown stronger, and we, perhaps, have grown wiser, though I am not quite so sure of that. We have now gone to war again with a European Power, but we have abandoned those belligerent rights about which we took up the sword in 1812. Peace solved that difficulty, and did more for you than war ever could have done; for, had you insisted at Ghent on the American people recognising your right to search their ships, take their seamen, and seize their goods, they would have been at war with you till this hour, before they would have surrendered these points, and the most frightful calamities might have been entailed on both countries by a protracted struggle.

Now, apply this lesson to the Eastern question. Supposing you agree to terms of peace with Russia, you will have your hands full in attempting to ameliorate the social and political system of Turkey. But who knows what may happen with regard to Russia herself in the way of extricating you from your difficulty? That difficulty, as respects Russia, is no doubt very much of a personal nature. You have to deal with a man of great, but, as I think, misguided energy, whose strong will and indomitable resolution cannot easily be controlled. But the life of a man has its limits; and, certainly, the Emperor of Russia, if he survive as many years from this time as the duration of the peace between England and America, will be a most extraordinary phenomenon. You can hardly suppose that you will have a great many years to wait before, in the course of nature, that which constitutes your chief difficulty in the present war may have passed away. It is because you do not sufficiently trust to the influence of the course of events in smoothing down difficulties, but will rush headlong to a resort to arms, which never can solve them, that you involve yourselves in long and ruinous wars. I never was of opinion that you had any reason to dread the aggressions of Russia upon any other State. If you have a weak and disordered empire like Turkey, as it were, next door to another that is more powerful, no doubt that tends to invite encroachments; but you have two chances in your favour—you may either have a feeble or differently-disposed successor acceding to the throne of the present Czar of Russia, or you may be able to establish some kind of authority in Turkey that will be more stable than its present rule. At all events, if you effect a quintuple alliance between yourselves and the other great Powers, you will certainly bind Austria, Prussia, and France to support you in holding Russia to the faithful fulfilment of the proposed treaty relating to the internal condition of Turkey. Why not, then, embrace that alternative, instead of continuing the present war? because, recollect that you have accomplished the object which Her Majesty in her gracious Speech last session stated that she had in view in engaging in this contest. Russia is no longer invading the Turkish territory; you are now rather invading Russia's own dominions, and attacking one of her strongholds at the extremity of her empire, but, as I contend, not assailing the real source of her power.  Now, I say you may withdraw from Sebastopol without at all compromising your honour.

By-the-by, I do not understand what is meant, when you say that your honour is staked on your success in any enterprise of this kind.  Your honour may be involved in your successfully rescuing Turkey from Russian aggression; but, if you have accomplished that task, you may withdraw your forces from before Sebastopol without being liable to reproach for the sacrifice of your national honour.

I have another ground for trusting that peace would not be again broken, if you terminate hostilities now.  I believe that all parties concerned have received such a lesson, that they are not likely soon to rush into war again.  I believe that the Emperor of Rusisa has learnt, from the courage and self-relying force displayed by our troops, that an enlightened, free, and self-governed people is a far more formidable antagonist than he had reckoned upon, and that he will not so confidently advance his semi-barbarous hordes to cope with the active energy and inexhaustible resources of the representatives of Western civilisation.  England also has been taught that it is not so easy as she imagined to carry on war upon land against a State like Russia, and will weigh the matter well in future before she embarks in any such conflict.

I verily believe that all parties want to get out of this war—I believe that this is the feeling of all the Governments concerned; and I consider that you have now the means, if you please, of escaping from your embarrassment, notwithstanding that some Members of our Cabinet, by a most unstatesmanlike proceeding, have succeeded in evoking a spirit of excitement in the country which it will not be very easy to allay.  The noble Lord the Member for London, and the noble Lord the Member for Tiverton, have, in my opinion, ministered to this excited feeling, and held out expectations which it will be extremely difficult to satisfy.

Now, what do you intend to do if your operations before Sebastopol should fail? The Secretary-at-War tells us that 'Sebastopol must be taken this campaign, or it will not be taken at all.' If you are going to stake all upon this one throw of the dice, I say that it is more than the people of England themselves had calculated upon. But if you have made up your minds that you will have only one campaign against Sebastopol, and that, if it is not taken then, you will abandon it, in that case, surely, there is little that stands between you and the proposals for peace on the terms I have indicated.

I think you will do well to take counsel from the hon. Member for Aylesbury (Mr. Layard), than whom—although I do not always agree with him in opinion—I know nobody on whose authority I would more readily rely in matters of fact relating to the East. That hon. Gentleman tells you that Russia will soon have 200,000 men in the Crimea; and if this be so, and this number is only to be ' the beginning,' I should say, now is the time, of all others, to accept moderate proposals for peace.

Now, mark, I do not say that France and England cannot succeed in what they have undertaken in the Crimea. I do not set any limits to what these two great countries may do, if they persist in fighting this duel with Russia's force of 200,000 men in the Crimea; and, therefore, do not let it be said that I offer any discouragement to my fellow-countrymen; but what I come back to is the question—what are you likely to get that will compensate you for your sacrifice? The hon. Member for Aylesbury also says, that ' the Russians will, next year, overrun Asiatic Turkey, and seize Turkey's richest provinces'—they will probably extend their dominion over Asia Minor down to the sea-coast. The acquisition of these provinces would far more than compensate her for the loss of Sebastopol. I suppose you do not contemplate making war upon the plains in the interior of Russia, but wish to destroy

Sebastopol; your success in which I have told you, I believe, will only end in that stronghold being rebuilt, ten years hence or so, from the resources of London capitalists. How, then, will you benefit Turkey—and especially if the prediction is fulfilled regarding Russia's overrunning the greater portion of Asiatic Turkey? I am told, also, that the Turkish army will melt away like snow before another year; and where, then, under all these circumstances, will be the wisdom or advantage in carrying on the war?

I have now, Sir, only one word to add, and that relates to the condition of our army in the Crimea. We are all, I dare say, constantly hearing accounts, from friends out there, of the condition, not only of our own soldiers, but also of the Turks, as well as of the state of the enemy. What I have said about the condition of the Turks will, I am sure, be made as clear as daylight, when the army's letters are published and our officers return home. But as to the state of our own troops, I have in my hand a private letter from a friend in the Crimea, dated the 2nd of December last, in which the writer says,—

'The people of England will shudder when they read of what this army is suffering—and yet they will hardly know one-half of it. I cannot imagine that either pen or pencil can ever depict it in its fearful reality. The line, from the nature of their duties, are greater sufferers than the artillery, although there is not much to choose between them. I am told, by an officer of the former, not likely to exaggerate, that one stormy, wet night, when the tents wore blown down, the sick, the wounded, and the dying of his regiment, were struggling in one fearful mass for warmth and shelter.'

Now, if you consult these brave men, and ask them what their wishes are, their first and paramount desire would be to fulfil their duty. They are sent to capture Sebastopol, and their first object would be to take that strong fortress, or perish in the attempt. But, if you were able to look into the hearts of these men, to ascertain what their longing, anxious hope has been, even in the midst of the bloody struggle at Alma or at Inkerman, I believe you would find it has been, that the conflict in which they were engaged might have the effect of sooner restoring them again to their own hearths and homes. Now, I say that the men who have acted so nobly at the bidding of their country are entitled to that country's sympathy and consideration; and if there be no imperative necessity for further prosecuting the operations of the siege, which must— it will, I am sure, be admitted by all, whatever may be the result—be necessarily attended with an immense sacrifice of precious lives—unless, I say, you can show that some paramount object will be gained by contending for the mastery over those forts and ships, you ought to encourage Her Majesty's Government to look with favour upon the propositions which now proceed from the enemy; and then, if we do make mistakes in accepting moderate terms of peace, we shall, at all events, have this consolation, that we are erring on the side of humanity.

# RUSSIAN WAR.

## II.

### HOUSE OF COMMONS, JUNE 5, 1855.

[On March 15, 1855, an attempt was made to restore peace, by assembling the representatives of the principal European Powers in Vienna, with a view to finding a basis for negotiations. It was believed that the prospects of peace were brighter since the death of the Emperor Nicholas (March 2). The chief object of the Conference was to limit the naval force of Russia in the Black Sea. But to this Prince Gortschakoff, who represented Russia, would not agree, and the negotiations broke down. The Conference sat till April 26, and the dissolution of the Conference was announced on June 5. The House was engaged in debating two resolutions: one of Sir Thomas Baring, which merely regretted the failure of the Vienna negotiations; and another, of Mr. Lowe, which averred that the refusal of Russia to restrict her naval force in the Black Sea, had exhausted the means of suspending hostilities by negotiation. The former motion was agreed to.]

I CONSIDER that the announcement which the noble Lord at the head of the Government has just made, ought not to prevent this House from discussing the important subject now before it; for, whatever may be the result of the division here, certainly there is no other topic which now so much engrosses public attention out of doors. The minority of Members of this House who wish to raise this question, and who belong to what is called the Peace party, have been stigmatised as enemies of their country, and traitors to the cause in which it is engaged. Why, my impulsive friend the Member for Lambeth (Mr. Wilkinson), and others who followed him, if they had at all read the recent history of this country, would have been ashamed of the charges they have made, because of their very triteness, and because they have at former periods been levelled at men of undoubted patriotism, who were totally undeserving of these reproaches. We know, for example, that it was attributed to Burke, that he had caused the American War, and that distinguished man complained feelingly of having been denounced as an American. We know also that the great Chatham himself did not escape that imputation; and I need not tell the occupants of the Treasury-bench that their illustrious chief in former days, Charles Fox, was ridiculed and denounced in every way as having been the hireling tool of France. In one of Gilray's inimitable caricatures, Fox is represented as standing on the edge of Dover cliffs, with a lantern in his hand, signalling to the French to come over and invade us; and, indeed, we read in Horner's ' Memoirs,' that it was seriously discussed whether Fox was not actually in the pay of France. Therefore I say that hon. Gentlemen who have no facts or imagination of their own on which to base their arguments, ought really to be ashamed to reproduce absurd and calumnious partisan accusations of this kind in such a debate.

I claim the same standing-ground, in discussing this question of peace or war, as any other hon. Gentleman. I will deal with it as a politician, strictly on the principles of policy and expediency; and I am prepared to assume that wars may be inevitable and necessary, although I do not admit that all wars are so. We, therefore, who took exception to the commencement of this war on grounds of policy, are not to be classed by individual Members of this House with those who are necessarily opposed to all wars whatever. That is but

a device to represent a section of this House as advocates of
notions so utopian that they must be entirely shut out of the
arena of modern politics, and their arguments systematically
denied that fair hearing to which all shades of opinion are
fairly entitled, no matter from what quarter they may
emanate.  I say, that we have all one common object in
view—we all seek the interest of our country; and the only
basis on which this debate should be conducted is that of the
honest and just interests of England.

Now, the House of Commons is a body that has to deal
with nothing but the honest interests of England; and I
likewise assert that the honest and just interests of this
country, and of her inhabitants, are the just and honest
interests of the whole world.  As individuals, we may act
philanthropically to all the world, and as Christians we may
wish well to all, and only desire to have power in order to
inflict chastisement on the wrong-doer, and to raise up the
down-trodden wherever they may be placed; but I maintain
that we do not come here to lay taxes on the people for the
purpose of carrying out schemes of universal benevolence, or
to enforce the behests of the Almighty in every part of the
globe.  We are a body with limited powers and duties, and
we must confine ourselves to guarding the just interests of
this empire.  We ought, therefore, to cast to the winds all
the declamatory balderdash and verbiage that we have heard
from the Treasury-bench as to our fighting for the liberty and
independence of the entire world.  You do not seriously mean
to fight for anything of the kind; and, when you come to
examine the grave political discussions of the Vienna Conferences, you find that the statesmen and noble Lords who
worked us into this war, and whipped and lashed the country
into a warlike temper by exciting appeals to its enthusiasm,
have no real intention to satisfy the expectations which their
own public declarations have created.  I say, we are dealing
with a question affecting the interests of the realm, and one

which may be discussed without any declamatory appeals to passion from any part of the House.

I now wish to refer to the speech of the right hon. Gentleman the Member for Southwark (Sir W. Molesworth). If there be a right honourable or honourable Gentleman in this House whose opinions I have a right to say I understand, it is the right hon. Baronet. I say most deliberately—and he cannot contradict me—that never in this world was there a speech delivered by any honourable Gentleman so utterly at variance with all previous declarations of opinion as that delivered by the right honourable Gentleman last night. Does the right hon. Gentleman remember a *jeu-d'esprit* of the poet Moore, when dealing, in 1833, with the Whig occupants of those (the Treasury) benches, shortly after they had emerged from a long penance in the dreary wilderness of Opposition, and when the Whigs showed themselves to be Tories when in office? Does he remember the *jeu-d'esprit?*— why, I think he and I have laughed over it, when we have been talking over the sudden conversions of right honourable Gentlemen. The poet illustrated the matter by a story of an Irishman who went over to the West Indies, and, before landing, heard some of the blacks speaking tolerably bad English, whereupon, mistaking them for his own countrymen, he exclaimed, ' What! black and curly already?' Now, we have all seen metamorphoses upon those benches—how colours have changed, and features become deformed, when men came under the influence of the Treasury atmosphere; but I must say that never, to my knowledge, have I seen a change in which there has been so deep a black and so stiff a curl. I confess I should very much like to make the right hon. Gentleman read that admirable speech which he delivered, not merely on the great Pacifico debate, when he denounced an intermeddling policy on the part of the noble Lord at the head of the Government, but also the speech which he made in Yorkshire at the time of the threatened

rupture with France upon the Syrian question. I wish the
right hon. Gentleman could be forced to read to the House
the speech he made in the open air to the people of Leeds
about going to war for the Mahomedan race, and for the
maintenance of its ascendancy in European Turkey. I should
like to see the right hon. Gentleman just stand at the table,
and to hear him read aloud that speech.

I will now come to the right hon. Gentleman's arguments.
The right hon. Gentleman says, the question is now, whether
the Government did right in refusing to make peace on the
terms proposed by Russia? Now, that, I assert, is not the
whole question. The real question which is involved in
the debate, and which the House has to decide, is, whether
the plan proposed by the Government was the best and only
one that could be devised, and whether the difference between
the plan submitted by Russia and that proposed by our
Government was such as warranted a recommencement of the
war. What is the difference between those propositions?
It is the Government of this country that we have to deal
with, and shall have to deal with in future. They must be
held responsible for the war; they will reap all the glory, if it
be successful, and on them must rest the responsibility should
it be, unhappily, unsuccessful. What, then, I ask, is the
difference between the propositions of the Government and
those of Russia? The difference is this—whether Russia
shall keep four ships of the line, four frigates, and a proportional number of smaller vessels in the Black Sea; or whether
all navies of the world shall have free access to the Black
Sea, and Russia be left, like any other country, to have as
many ships as she pleases. I will not go over the ground so
ably traversed by my right hon. Friend (Mr. M. Gibson), but
upon the question of the limitation of force I wish to make
one remark. You offer to allow Russia to have four ships of
the line, four frigates, and a proportion of smaller vessels.
Now, I have been told by a nautical man, fully competent to

give an opinion upon such a subject, that if Russia had
accepted your terms, had burnt or sunk all her old 74's, and
green timber-built ships, and had sent to the United States
for four line-of-battle ships of the largest size, fitted with
screws, mounting 130 guns of the largest calibre, and for four
frigates of that elastic character which the Americans give to
their frigates, carrying some 70 or 80 guns of the heaviest
calibre, and all those vessels fitted with screws, she would
then have possessed a far better and much more powerful
navy than ever she had before in the Black Sea. Such a
navy would have been more than a match for double the
number of ships such as Russia now has in that sea. If that
be the case, what injury will you inflict upon Russia—what
diminution of naval power will you enforce — what great
reduction of force are you going to demand for the protection
of Turkey ?

I know I may be told, ' Then why did not Russia accede to
those terms ?' Russia resisted that plan as a point of honour,
and not as a question of force; she rejected it on principle.
The right hon. Gentleman says, ' If you allow Russia to have
free action in the Black Sea, and you are to have free access
yourself, then you will be obliged to keep up a large navy
and a large peace establishment always to watch Russia.'
But suppose Russia had signed her name to a piece of parch-
ment, would you have such implicit faith in her as to reduce
your forces to a peace establishment? I would ask the right
hon. Gentleman, who, in his inflammatory harangue last
night, told us we were to have a six years' war, whether, if
the large sums expended in a six years' war were put out at
interest, the yearly return would not be more than sufficient
to provide a sufficient force to watch Russia in time of peace?
No one supposes for a moment that, if you had come to terms
with Russia, you were going at once to reduce your war
establishment. You will not believe anything which Russia
promises. You say, ' It is of no use taking the guarantee of

Russia; we must insist on her diminishing the number of her ships in the Black Sea.' And if she did promise to diminish the number, you would not trust her—and, with your present views, properly so.

But when you undertake to maintain the independence of Turkey, you have a task upon your hands which is not to be performed without great expense. It cannot be done without great armaments constantly on the watch over Turkey. You have bound yourselves to the task of maintaining a tottering empire which cannot support itself, and such a task cannot be accomplished without a vast expenditure. You likewise ask for securities. Now I ask the noble Lord the Member for the City of London (Lord John Russell), to hear what the great model of the Whigs in Opposition said upon that subject. Mr. Fox, when the Tories of his day were urging, as the noble Lord is now urging against Russia, that we must have security against future aggressions of France, said:—

'Security ! You have security; the only security that you can ever expect to get. It is the present interest of France to make peace. She will keep it, if it be her interest. Such is the state of nations ; and you have nothing but your own vigilance for your security.'

That rule still holds good, and will hold good so long as the world lasts in its present character. I maintain that, whatever parties there be in this House, whether for peace or war, if the majority of this House acknowledges as a duty or a matter of interest or policy, to maintain Turkey against the encroachments of Russia, they can never expect to have a small peace establishment; and, I will say honestly, if we recognise as parts of our policy the sending of armed bodies of land forces to the Continent, into the midst of great standing armies, and into countries where the conscription prevails, I should be a hypocrite if I ever said we could expect to continue what has been the maxim of this country—the maintenance of a moderate peace establishment. If that is to be our recognised policy, we must keep up a large standing army,

and place ourselves to some extent on a par with Austria,
France, and Russia ; and, if we attempt to interfere in Continental politics without such preparations, then, I say, the
country is only preparing a most ignominious and ridiculous
exposure of weakness.

Is the right hon. Gentleman—who has been equalled by no
one in his vituperation of the Emperor of Russia and the
Russian Government—aware, as a Cabinet Minister, that the
Government has made this country a party to a binding engagement with Russia, to a treaty binding oursleves, in conjunction
with Russia, to interfere in the affairs of Wallachia and Moldavia ?   You, who said last night Russia was without shame,
and attributed to her every vile principle, I ask, as a Member
of the Cabinet, are you aware that a treaty has already been
signed and concluded, so far as can be at present, in which
this country binds itself, in conjunction with Russia, Austria,
France, and Turkey, to be the guardian of Wallachia and
Moldavia ; to act with Russia in interfering by force of arms,
and, in fact, forming a tribunal which virtually will constitute
the Government of Wallachia and Moldavia ?   I repeat, that
by the first protocol, you have bound yourself, in partnership
with Russia, to be virtually the governors of Wallachia and
Moldavia.   I will show you what engagements you entered
into with that Government which it suits you for the moment
to denounce, because, within forty-eight hours, the newspapers
had brought you the news of some imaginary triumph, but
which you would slaver with your praise to-morrow, if it
suited your purpose.   The 7th Article of the first protocol
says :—

‘ In the event of the internal tranquillity of the said Principalities being
compromised, no armed intervention shall take place in their territories without being or becoming the subject of agreement between the high contracting
parties.

‘ The Courts engage not to afford protection in the Principalities to
foreigners, whose proceedings might be prejudicial either to the tranquillity
of those countries, or to the interests of neighbouring States.  Disapproving

such proceedings, they engage reciprocally to take into serious consideration the representations which may be made on this subject by the Powers, or even by the local authorities.'

So that if the Governor of Bucharest makes a report of some local émeute, you are bound, in conjunction with Russia, to interfere. But what is the conclusion of the protocol? I blushed when I read it, and I believe there are other hon. Gentlemen who share my feelings :—

'On its side, the Sublime Porte will enjoin on the Principalities not to tolerate in their territory foreigners such as above described, nor'— and this is the gist of the article —' to allow the local inhabitants to meddle with matters dangerous to the tranquillity of their own country, or of neighbouring States.'

And the name of ' John Russell' is put at the foot of this protocol, the object of which is to prevent the inhabitants from interfering in matters which may be dangerous to the tranquillity of their own country. Mark the child and champion of revolution when he breathes the air of Vienna. My hon. Friend the Member for Aylesbury (Mr. Layard) cheers these sentiments; he cheers my denunciations of these arrangements; but has my hon. Friend pursued that bold, consistent, and manly course upon this question, which I think, with his declared opinions, he ought to have taken? It is well known that the sympathies of my hon. Friend were in favour of this war, because he believed it would be advantageous to the independence or the good government of such States as Wallachia, Moldavia, and Servia. But has my hon. Friend so little sagacity as not to see that all this waste of blood and treasure has had very different objects? And why has my hon. Friend, seeing what is the tendency of the war—seeing, from these protocols, what is to be its conclusion — not denounced it, since he has declared that a war with such objects as the Government had in view would be a wicked war?

Before the outbreak of the war, I was applied to by some

illustrious men, and requested not to oppose it, because, as I was hopefully told, it was likely to tend to the emancipation of the down-trodden communities on the Continent. I gave my opinion upon the subject in writing, more than eighteen months ago, and I would not now change a word of it. I warned those distinguished persons, that if they expected that a war originating in diplomacy, as this war has originated, carried on by enormous regular armies, as this war has been carried on, and having a direction and a purpose given to it by the men who are now at the head of our Government and of the Continental Governments, could by any possibility satisfy their aspirations, they would deceive themselves. I said, my only fear was, that the war would have just the opposite result; that it would strengthen the despotisms they wished to check, and depress still lower the communities they wished to serve. That is the tendency, that is the inevitable destiny of this war. But to revert to my right hon. Friend (Sir W. Molesworth), and his charges against Russia and the Russian Government. I am not here to defend the Russian Government; no one can be more opposed than I am to the policy of Russian despotism; but I must say, I think it is unjustifiable, I had almost said scandalous, for a Member of a Cabinet which has been a party to these confidential, and, as I think, most unworthy engagements, in conjunction with the Russian Government, to get up in this House, and speak of the Russian Government and people as my right hon. Friend spoke of them last night. But this game of see-saw in argument has not been confined to him alone; it has been the characteristic of every Member of the Government. There has been a constant change of tone and argument to suit the momentary impulses of passion out of doors, and of the press. At times, so obvious is the effect produced by a few leading articles, that I could almost imagine, if I were living in another country where constitutional government was carried on with less decorum than in this country, that some secrets

had oozed out from some Member of the Cabinet, or from the
wife of some Member of the Cabinet, to the editor of a newspaper, to the effect that there were disagreements in the
Cabinet; that there was a peace party and a war party; that
the war party was less numerous but more active than the
peace party, and that the peace party required sometimes to
be whipped into capitulation; and I could imagine the newspaper then dealing out a few blows in the shape of leading
articles, from day to day, until the peace party had changed
its tone, and given way to the war party.  So complete a
change of language have we seen, that I can almost imagine
the case to have happened even here, which I have supposed
possible in another country.

What has been the language of the noble Lord the Member
for London (Lord John Russell)?  At the Conferences he was
as amiable, polite, and agreeable as it is his natural wont to
be to those with whom he associates in private.  But immediately upon his return to England and to the House of Commons, he falls back into his old strain, just as if he had never
been to Vienna, and talks of Russia having established great
fortifications upon the German frontier and in the Baltic, and
of the system of corruption, intimidation, and intrigue carried
on by her in the German Courts.  Have the noble Lord's
logical faculties been so impaired at Vienna, that he does not
see that the obvious reply to him is: which of the Four Points
was to rectify these evils—which of them was to put a stop
to the erection of fortifications in the Baltic, or to prevent
Russia from interfering with the German Courts?  There is
surely no guarantee against the rebuilding of Bomarsund, or
for the security of the Circassians.  The independence, freedom, and civilisation of the world, seem to be entirely forgotten by the noble Lord when he goes to Vienna, for he
then drops down to the sole miserable expedient of limiting
the Russian fleet.  If we go into another place, what is the
language held by Lord Clarendon?  I felt great astonishment

at the speech that noble Lord made the other night; I suppose it was calculated to attain some object for the moment, but I doubt whether it will attain any permanent object which will be satisfactory to the noble Lord. He talks in the same strain, and denounces Russia as if he had never been a party to these arrangements with regard to Wallachia and Moldavia. Some of the noble Lord's observations with respect to the strength of Sebastopol were, I think, disingenuous; for he asked, why should the Russians have such an immense collection of materials, if it was not intended for some great aggression? But the noble Lord could not be ignorant that the great strength of Sebastopol had been created since our army appeared before it, and that ammunition and provisions have been arriving in convoys of from 500 to, as Lord Raglan has himself stated, 2000 carts at a time. To talk in such a strain immediately after the Conferences, was not worthy of the audience the noble Lord addressed, and hardly complimentary to the English public. The noble Lord the Member for London also alluded to Germany in a way which will hardly be looked upon in that country as a proof of his good sense or wisdom. He talked of the corruption of the German Courts, and of the manner in which they were interfered with and controlled by the Russian Government; but, from what we are informed by the newspapers is going on in Germany, I fancy we are much mistaken as to the tendency of public opinion, if we suppose there is any difference of views between the people and the Governments of Germany with regard to the war. I am told, and I have taken some pains to inquire — it is our duty to take pains in such a matter—that there is no party in Germany which wants to join in this war. There may be many who are well-wishers to our cause, and others whose sympathies are with Russia; but I am informed, and I believe correctly, that there is no party in Germany who wishes to break the peace, and enter into hostilities with Russia in the present quarrel. And if you reflect for a moment

upon the past history of Germany, in relation to France and
Russia, you will see reason why in their traditions there
should be no feelings of dread and hostility to Russia. The
past recollections of Germany are indeed favourable rather
than otherwise to Russia, and hostile to France. It may be
thought the wrong moment to say it, but I hold that upon
this question, and upon all other questions, we should speak
in this House without reserve, as if our debates were not
published; and I say it is very well known that the feeling
in Prussia and the north of Germany is one of dread of
France. This feeling may have arisen in part from the long
sufferings and dreadful sacrifices made by the people of
Prussia and Northern Germany in the great revolutionary
war with France, but it also arises in part from the circumstance that France is contiguous to the Rhenish provinces of Prussia, and it has been thought that she entertains
rather envious feelings towards them. But, whatever may
be the cause, there is in every cottage of Prussia a recollection rather favourable to Russia than hostile, as compared with France. There is, indeed, hanging in almost
every cottage in Prussia some memorial of the atrocities
and sufferings caused by the French in the last war, while
the traditions with regard to Russia are, that she helped
to emancipate them from the rule of Napoleon. This may
show why Germany is not so anxious to enter into hostilities with Russia. There is another reason. You forget
that in this war you have never committed yourselves to
any principle which shall be a permanent safeguard against
Russia. You have invited Germany to enter into war with
Russia, her next-door neighbour, and a powerful neighbour,
for your purposes; but you have given Germany no security
that Russia, at the close of the war, will not retaliate upon
that Power. And now it may be said, since the result of the
Conferences is known, that you have gone to Vienna, and, after
talking so boldly about fighting the battle of Germany, of

Europe, and of the whole civilised world, you have dropped your pretensions, and do not say a word about giving security to any part of the Continent of Europe.

I was talking, the other day, to a gentleman in this country, a Prussian, who has more right to speak in the name of his countrymen than any man here. He said, 'I confess I think you Englishmen are unreasonable and a little arrogant. You expect us to go to war with Russia—we, a nation of 16,000,000 or 17,000,000, against a nation of 60,000,000. But you do not take into account, that when you are tired of the war you can withdraw and occupy an impregnable position, while we are always at the door of this vast empire; and yet you try to hound us into this war, and to force us into it, without allowing us a voice in the matter. Your conduct is that of a man who tries to drive a dog to make an attack upon a bull.' Well, if we look back upon the course we have pursued, is there not something that warrants this · opinion?

I warn the noble Lord the Member for the City of London, that, in dealing with Germany, he has to do with an educated people, every man of whom reads his newspaper, and where the middle classes are so educated that you may buy bread in the Latin language, if you do not know German. Is it not, then, rather arrogant and unreasonable, when the noble Lord in this House denounces the whole German people as having been corrupted by Russia? I say that, if the English people had the conscription, as they have in Prussia, so that when war was declared every man in the country would be liable to be called out, and every horse and cart might be taken for the purposes of the army, we should be more chary how we called out for war. Our pot-house politicians would not then be calling out for war with Russia, but we should have a Government who would take a more moderate tone than this does, for it would require those sacrifices that bring home the miseries of war to the people.

I have said from the first, and I said it long before you sent a man from these shores, 'If you make war upon Russia, vindicate your rights or avenge your wrongs with your own strong arm, the navy; but do not send a man to the Continent or Turkey in the capacity of a land force. Do not send an army over the backs of the whole population of central Europe, where you have 1,000,000 men with bayonets in their hands, who stand between you and the gigantic Power that you are opposed to, and affect to dread.' I say that you ought to have occupied the same ground that Austria and Prussia took; and if you had done so, instead of rushing into war—driven into it, I admit, by the populace and the press—you would have been right, for you have it proved now that Austria and Germany would have averted these evils that you dread, for Austria and Prussia would have made it a *casus belli*, if Russia had crossed the Balkan. And why, I want to know, were you not content to remain in England, in your island home, your inaccessible fortress, sending your fleet into the Black Sea, if you chose, and telling Austria and Germany, 'Here is a great danger; here is a mighty Power that threatens to engulph this fair Europe; if you take your part for its protection, our fleets shall help you, and we will take care that no harm shall come to Turkey by sea, but not a soldier shall move from England until you put yourself in motion for the defence of Turkey?'

Why, Sir, will any one now say that this would not have been a wise policy? But then it is said, that if we had done this, the Russians would have been in Constantinople. No, they would not; for this is my whole argument—and I am coming to it—that Austria and Southern Germany have more interest in keeping the Russians from Constantinople than we have. I have heard and read in *Hansard*, that every leading statesman in this or the other House of Parliament, within the last eighteen months, has declared that Austria and Germany are more interested in this question than we are.

It has been stated by the noble Lord the Member for Tiverton (Viscount Palmerston); it has been asserted by the noble Lord the Member for London (Lord John Russell); it has been stated by Lord Clarendon; it has been asserted by Earl Derby; it has been alleged by Lord Lyndhurst. In fact, there is not a leading mind in either House of Parliament who has not told us that Austria and Germany have a greater interest in this war than we have. Well, then, in the name of common sense, why did not we, who were infinitely safer from this alleged great danger, wait until those, who had a greater interest than we had, chose to move with us? Why should we go from our position of security, if these pusillanimous empires would not step in? I know it has been said, that we are fighting the battle of civilisation. Yes, we are fighting the battle of civilisation with 30,000 or 40,000 men; and I believe we have never had more than 30,000 men in the Crimea at any one time.

I see it stated by the *Times* correspondent, who re-states what he has before asserted, that we have lost half our army because we had not sufficient men to do duty in the trenches. But is that the proper function and duty of Englishmen, to fight for Germany, because the Germans are corrupt and will not fight for themselves? Give me rather the doctrine propounded by Prince Gortschakoff at Vienna, and let the blood of Englishmen be for England and the English. Now, I do not say this in disparagement of Austria and Germany. I maintain, on the contrary, that they have taken a more enlightened and calmer view of this question than we have. But the English people, partly stimulated by the noble Lord the Member for the City of London—for he has been the great offender—the English people have clamoured for war, and they would not give time for those combinations to be formed that would have averted the danger, and would have enabled us to take common ground with Austria and Germany.

But now, I say, that we know Austria and Germany will not act with us, are we to go on pursuing the same course? It would most certainly be a curiosity to go through *Hansard*, during the last eighteen months, and take out the passages in which statesmen have expressed the opinion that Austria was going to join us. The Government put it into the Speech of Her Majesty from the Throne; and, as if that was not sufficient, they have been repeating it in every speech they have made ever since. I cannot even except the right hon. Gentleman the Member for Carlisle (Sir J. Graham). The right hon. Member for the University of Oxford (Mr. Gladstone), in his celebrated Budget speech, mentioned it as some compensation for the income-tax, and said that while he was speaking it was probable that Austria had actually joined us. It is impossible to read all these extracts to the House; but here is a specimen from the speech of the noble Lord the Member for London, delivered no later than December 22, 1854. The noble Lord said:—

'If, however, Russia should not consent to such very moderate terms as it will be our duty to propose, . . . . I feel convinced that we shall, before the opening of the next campaign, have the alliance of Austria, both in offensive and defensive operations.'

Now, I ask, are you going to carry on the war upon land? I mean, are you going to commit yourselves to take Sebastopol? Are you about to re-commence the war for an object which you have repudiated? because, although the noble Lord and the right hon. Gentlemen who sit on the Treasury-benches, come here one day and tell us one story, and another day tell us another story (I admit, we, on this bench, have been beguiled by them, but I promise them we will behave better, and be more cautious for the future)—although, I say, we allow this to go on, foreign Governments are not deceived by such double dealing, and it is seen by these protocols, which are published all over the world, that our Government proposed, in the late Conferences, to withdraw from the Crimea, leaving Sebastopol a 'standing menace' as before. That is the proposal made by our own Government. The only difference between us and Russia is the infinitesimal question of the armed ships; and I agree with my right hon. Friend the Member for Manchester (Mr. M. Gibson), that for the safety of Turkey, the Russian proposal is better than that of the Allies.

Now, everybody knows that we are re-commencing the war with the determination—at least, if we can gather from the language of the noble Lord and the right hon. Gentleman what they mean—with the determination to take Sebastopol. But I would ask those upon whom the responsibility for the future rests, whether it is worth the blood and treasure which we must pour out like water in order that we may take Sebastopol (if we take it at all),—if, on the other hand, the capture of the place is to be accompanied by that policy of the Government which, I think, will prevent as much as anything their obtaining any popular support on the Continent, namely, that under no circumstances will they make any change in the existing territorial arrangements of Europe? If that policy is adhered to, there seems to be no other object in taking Sebastopol than knocking about the ears of brave men a certain amount of bricks, mortar, and rubbish—sacrificing an immense amount of human life, in order that we may point to those mounds and say, 'We did it;' although Russia may, after the peace, borrow the money of any banking-house in London, and in three years build it up again stronger than ever.

Now, what is the plan, what the object, of this re-commencement of the war? Is it to reduce the preponderance of Russia in the Black Sea? Let us discard passion, and bring this question to the test of our own homely common sense. Let us take, for example, some other country. Suppose it was proposed to reduce the preponderance of the United States of America in the Gulf of Mexico; what would be the train of reasoning, in the absence of all passion, and with the benefits of unclouded intellects? Should we not naturally say, the preponderance of America in the Gulf of Mexico springs from her possessing New Orleans, the great outlet of the commerce of the Southern States, and from her having vast and fertile territories on the banks of the Mississippi, the Missouri, and the Ohio, where many millions of industrious men are cultivating the soil, and adding to the internal wealth of that great empire? and would not the conclusion be: this is a natural preponderance, inherent in the very nature of her territory, and her occupation? Now, then, turn your eyes to the Black Sea, and you have precisely the same causes, leading to the same consequences. Why has Russia preponderance in the Black Sea? Because she has fertile provinces, which are cultivated and made productive, and rich and prosperous ports and harbours, where her commerce is carried on. I was speaking lately to a gentleman who knows that country well, and has the largest commercial relations with it of any man in England, and he tells me that he does not believe there is any part of the United States of America which has made such rapid progress in wealth and internal production, since the repeal of our Corn-laws, as those southern provinces of Russia. It was estimated that Russia exported the year before last, from ports in the Black Sea, 5,000,000 quarters of grain of all kinds; and the calculation has been made, that if for the next twenty years those exports went on increasing as they have increased during the last five years, Russia would then be exporting from 15,000,000 to 20,000,000 quarters of grain annually. Believe me, that is the source of Russian preponderance. The country is developing itself. I admit, if you please, it is a youthful barbarism, but it will, doubtless, grow into something better; and, so long as a vast amount of produce is brought into the Black Sea for shipment to the rest of the world—so long as the territory of Russia borders on that sea, with no other neighbour than Turkey—a country wholly unproductive and unimproving, in comparison—all the Powers on earth cannot take away the preponderance of Russia, because it is founded in the inherent nature of things.

What, I again ask, are we fighting for? It has been whispered that we are fighting because it is more the wish of France that we should fight than our own. But are we quite sure that the war now carrying on is not against the wishes of the French people? Gentlemen who have communications with France, and sources of private information, tell me they hear that the war, never looked upon enthusiastically, is regarded with more and more dislike by the French people. What is the wish of the French Government? I know I am about to tread on delicate ground, but I hold it is our duty to speak out in the face of such mighty events, and, as I believe, possible calamities, as are impending over this country. I come, then, to this point: Is it the wish of the French Government that this war should be carried on, or is it ours? It is industriously whispered, that the French dynasty has so much at stake, that it dare not withdraw the army from Sebastopol, on account of the moral effect it would produce on the French people and on the army. My hon. Friend (Mr. Bright) and myself received a communication of some authenticity, as we believed, that the French Government had given an intimation to our Government, that they were willing, if we were, to accept an alternative upon the terms which are the last published proposals in the protocols which have been presented to us. We all know a meeting of what was called the 'party supporting the Government' was summoned not long since at the noble Lord's office in Downing-street. There and then, after the noble Lord had said it was for the purpose of private and confidential communication, and that the newspaper press were not present, he was asked by the hon. Member for Manchester (Mr. Bright) whether what we had heard and believed to be true was founded upon fact—that intimation had come from the French Government to lead our Government to understand that terms similar to those offered at Vienna by M. Drouyn de Lhuys would be accepted, and that a refusal had been given by our Government? The noble Lord refused to answer that inquiry, though he was pressed to do so. I myself pressed him to answer, and, that it may not be supposed I am committing any breach of confidence, I said, if he would answer the question—merely say, No—I should treat it confidentially; but if he allowed me to go out of the room with a confirmed impression of that which I had received from very good sources, I should make no secret of what had passed there.

Now, I say, this is a most serious thing for this country, for this reason: You have now contrived to detach all Germany from you—that is to say, you have no hope of Germany or Austria joining you. It is a matter now decided. You cannot delude yourselves now with the hope that Austria or Germany will take part in this contest. But what will be your fate if, by-and-by, it can be proved that England has been the cause of recommencing this war, contrary to the inclinations of the French Government and the French people? May it not by possibility lead to the very opposite of what we are all hoping from this union between the two countries? May it not lead to further estrangement? and then see in what a responsibility it lands you. If you are more opposed to coming to terms of peace than France is, does it not throw on you the responsibility of doing something very different from what you are now doing towards carrying on the war? Will it not, by-and-by, be found that your force is small, and the French force is great? I do not think this is the proper time to bring up the whole particulars, but I marked two observations on two particular occasions. The hon. Member for Inverness-shire (Mr. H. Baillie) stated that our forces are 40,000 short of the

number voted in this House. The noble Lord (Lord J. Russell)
stated last December that our forces were then 20,000 short
of the number voted in this House. The hon. Member for
Inverness-shire stated that our militia regiments are reduced
to mere skeletons, and in Ireland and Scotland are almost
disbanded, except the officers. But if this be true—if it be
true that you still want 40,000 men to make up the number
—may it not be fonnd, by-and-by, that you are urging on
this war in blind heedlessness, in the same way as everything
has been done by this Government from the beginning, and
that you have not looked three months before you to see what
may be the consequences of the want of that foresight which
the Government ought to have shown? I am speaking of the
present moment, when the country is under a state of excitement. But those who have intelligence, and those who have
studied the maps of the country, may readily understand and
see how much has been made out of a little; and that there
has been much said, within the last few days, which it will
be found the results do not justify.

I have said that I set no limits to the power of France and
England, provided they would pnt out that power, and exhibit their strength; but I am not qnite sure that you are in
a better condition in the Crimea now than you were before
this recent achievemeut at Kertch. I once asked a Russian
merchant what were the actual means of supply of food derived by Russia, and I did not learn that Kertch was at all
relied upon for any great supply to the army in Sebastopol.
I was assured that this was the fact; and if so, it may be
accepted as a qualification of the great excitement that has
been raised in consequence of our late achievements in the Sea
of Azoff. A large holder of corn, deposited at Kertch, told
me that the Russian Government had informed him that they
could not be responsible for the safety of his corn. This was
five months ago. Long before the Conferences at Vienna, he
gave notice of this to his agents at Kertch, and also at other

parts on the coast of the Sea of Azoff. I believe there has been a great deal of exaggeration about this little expedition to the Sea of Azoff; but if there has not been, then greater is the disgrace that attaches to those who had not executed it sooner. I am not sure that this expedition had any higher motive than that of a desire to do something which should gratify the people of this country: for the cry of the people always is, ' Do something.' But my opinion is, that, whenever any individual, whether he be a Minister of State, or a Commander-in-Chief, does something, merely because he is told by somebody else to do it, that that something, in nine cases out of ten, is wrong. I am not sure that even the expedition to Sebastopol itself had any higher motive than that of a wish to do something that should gratify the wishes of the people. But, at all events, I give it as my opinion, that, while your expedition in the Sea of Azoff has led to the destruction of a vast amount of private property, and while it will add no renown to your name, I believe it will have no better effect on the result of the war than your marauding expedition in the Gulf of Finland last year. I believe that the great sources of relief to the army in Sebastopol are Perekop and Simpheropol. Both those places are fortified as well as Sebastopol, and it is through them that supplies of food are obtained for the Russian army.

Well, then, about the difficulty of transporting food to the Russian army across the steppes to the Crimea, I was talking to a merchant of Odessa on that subject; and he said, that in time of peace thousands of carts and waggons, drawn by bullocks, were employed for conveying articles of commerce over these vast steppes to Odessa, Taganrog, and other ports on the Sea of Azoff; but that the war having suspended all that, the Russian Government would now avail itself of those same means of transportation for conveying supplies from Perekop and Simpheropol to Sebastopol. This has, in fact, been already done.

Now, I ask, is it not better for us that we should view these things in this light, than give ourselves up to the effervescence prevailing out of doors? Is it not better to look calmly at these things, and consider what it is that Russia can really do, than to yield up our feelings to a momentary, and, it may be, a doubtful triumph? But when I said that the power of England and of France united could hardly be resisted by any single Power in Europe, or the world, I did not forget that there was one power, a single and a hidden power, by which the mightiest armies may be vanquished— pestilence and disease. I have read an extract from a report of Mr. Spencer, giving an account of a tour in the Crimea, and of the influence of the climate, which had sole reference to the summer season. I never heard of any one necessarily suffering in the winter season. On the contrary, my belief is, that, let a man be well fed, well clothed, and well sheltered, he may live anywhere; and there is no necessity that the constitutions of Englishmen should suffer more in winter in the Crimea than in England. But that is not the case in summer. The best authorities tell you that it is hardly possible for an Englishman in the Crimea, or a foreigner, unless he take every possible precaution, to escape infection in the summer months of July, August, and September. You sin against the law of nature if you go out in the sun in the day, and you equally sin if you go out in the night dews. Such, again, is the effect of the climate, that if you partake of new corn, or of fruit in undue measure, these things will bring on intermittent fever. Now, these precautions our soldiers disregard, as they ever have disregarded, and therefore is it that I dread the months of July, August, and September, for our troops in the Crimea. Has all this been thought of by the Government? Does it not devolve on them to consider these things? Whatever may be the fate of our army in the Crimea this summer, upon them, I say, and upon their shoulders, will rest the responsibility. If they should be fortunate—if pestilence and disease should happily not approach; but a deviation, as it were, in the succession of the climate should take place—then the honour and the glory, such as it may be, will undoubtedly be shared by them, and any successful enterprise of our army will redound to their repute. But if, on the other hand, your army should be destroyed by pestilence and disease, if there should be a repetition of the disasters of the last winter, then your power will be at an end; and be assured that, to effect the destruction of your power, there is nothing short of physical violence that may not happen to you. Nothing can happen but disgrace from the miserable pretences advanced in support of this war. When the Government was showing forth in magniloquent phrases the great objects of the war, well might the people be deluded; but now they know the state of things better, now they know that the war wholly depends upon so trifling a matter as that of allowing ingress and egress of foreign ships into and from the Black Sea. It is on such an infinitesimal point of difference that this war, involving so vast a sacrifice of life, and wealth, and human happiness, depends. Is there not, then, I would ask, something resting upon us as the House of Commons in this matter? Have not hon. Gentlemen noticed the state to which the argument has been brought? Have they not observed to what public opinion has been brought on this subject out of doors? No man seems to know his friend; no man seems to have confidence in public men. One serious difficulty in carrying on this war is the want of an open and frank declaration of opinion on the part of public reputations.

But there are other circumstances that ought to make us reflect. I allude not to the possibility of a bad harvest; but there are possible contingencies which may place this country in a most perilous condition, and that chiefly arising, as I have said, from the utter want of confidence in public men. But how has that want of confidence arisen? My belief is, that it is because public men have been wanting in self-respect. It is because they have too readily yielded up their better judgment to the momentary inspiration or dictation of others. What are we, the Members of this House, set apart for, but to study these high matters—to devote our thoughts to the consideration of questions involving the well-being of our countrymen, and to promote to the utmost of our capacity the prosperity of those whose interests are confided to us? It is true, the public out of doors have gone heartily with the Government in this war; but we all know that the public have entertained very erroneous notions as to what was the object of the war, and as to what would be its ultimate effect.

What was the tone of public opinion when the war broke out? Did it not exhibit the grossest arrogance and ignorance of the enemy we had to contend with? Did we—did the country—did the press, speak as if we were going 3000 miles to invade an empire of 60,000,000 people? I rest my case entirely upon your infatuation in invading Russia with a land force. If you had confined yourselves to naval operations—if you had done that which I believe the House of Commons would have done, if it had acted upon its own judgment—in what a different position you now would have been! There would have been none of this discontent; you would have sent out your ships, the greatest spectacle of a naval armament that ever left your shores; there would have been no misery, no disease, no want of discipline, no disasters there. Your ships rode triumphant upon every sea, and if they had not come back victorious, owing to the enemy keeping behind his fortifications, they would, at least, have presented no spectacle of abject misery and signal distress. It is your attempt to do too much, without knowing what you were about, which has brought this calamity upon you.

Much as I blame Lord Raglan for not making a road, and for mismanagement in carrying on the war, yet I contend that, if you send an army to invade Russia, you must prepare yourselves for inevitable disaster. You may repair that disaster, possibly. It may be so; but when you determine to invade an empire consisting of 60,000,000 of people 3000 miles off, I say that the thing was undertaken in blind obedience to a cry out of doors, against and over which the statesmen of this country ought to have exercised a counteracting influence and control.

You sent a land force 3000 miles away to subdue your colonists in America. That force had a population of from 2,500,000 to 3,000,000 to contend with. It was miserably worsted. Mismanagement, no doubt, existed there; but, if there had been no mismanagement, how long, I ask, could that war have endured? We know the history of the invasion of Russia by Napoleon I. He invaded that empire supported by half a million of bayonets, and there was, at all events, this much logic and argument in his proposition, that he said, 'I will strike at the heart of the empire, and will take security for peace in the capital of Russia.' But you are not going to the heart of Russia, with all Europe at your back, as he had; for, with the exception of Spain, he had all Europe at his feet, and all her legions at his side. You know the result. You know the spirit of Russia then. Have you any reason to suppose that Russia now, with the stimulus of that example before her, will show a less stubborn resistance to you than she did to Napoleon I? My firm belief is, that she will not. My belief is, that you have entered upon a task the most arduous and difficult which this nation ever undertook, and that you will have to put forth more than twice the energy, you will have to send more than twice the men, and to spend more than twice the money in one year, than you have yet done, before you will succeed in accomplishing the object you have in view.

Ought we not, then, fairly to tell the people of this country that? Ought we not to check them, rather than to

encourage their exaggerations? Suppose you receive unexpected accounts of disasters from the Crimea, of prostrations
from cholera, from intermittent fever, or from the plague—for
who can tell what may happen? Is it not wise, instead of
cheering the Minister, when he tells us that the Conferences
are at an end, to endeavour to subdue the spirit of the
country—I do not say to subdue its spirit in any righteous
cause—but to let the people know fully and frankly what they
have before them?

I blame the Government for having behaved falsely and
treacherously to the people, and I tell them that there will be
a day of reckoning for them in this matter. What said the
noble Lord the Member for Tiverton, in one of those declamatory harangues with which he occasionally favours the House?
He said, 'The people of this country are our reserve force,
and we will equip our army from that reserve.' I ask him
what he is now doing with that reserve? The noble Lord
the Member for London said, at the end of last year, 'We
shall have 180,000 or 200,000 Englishmen under arms, and
foreign levies to aid them.' Where are the 180,000 or
200,000 Englishmen? I say that there has been the same
child's play now, up to the last minute, that there has been
from the commencement. All I ask of you is, that you will
deal candidly with the public. I have noticed in history,
that if ever the mass of the people have become cruel, and
revengeful, and unreasoning in their violence to Governments, it is invariably because they have been betrayed and
deceived by them. There is nothing by which you will
so surely risk the loss of public favour, and entail a great
public calamity when your influence is gone, as by attempting to conceal from the people of this country the whole
amount of difficulties and dangers which are now impending
over you.

It is in this spirit, and because I will not be responsible in
the slightest degree for what may happen in this matter, that

I wish to speak out on this occasion; and I warn the House of Commons, that there are no institutions of the land which may not be endangered from the reaction which may result from your over-sanguine confidence in what you are undertaking. I have seen a spirit out of doors which is preparing for sudden and strange freaks of revenge, under a sense of bitter mortification and disappointment; I have seen those who have been the first to clamour for war, after the earliest disasters of the campaign, meeting together to denounce those who are the highest in the land as the most responsible; and when I see what has been the line pursued, in the face of what I must believe to be superior knowledge—when I see the way in which, in high places, the passions of the people have been pandered to, and momentary triumph sought at the risk of great future disaster—I must say that I think those who adopt such conduct deserve the retribution which I have spoken of.

There was a meeting recently held in Derby, which was reported in the London papers, and it was one of those meetings which were described as the beginning of an agitation which was to cover the land. My hon. Friend the Member for Derby was present; and what was the tone of that meeting? It was called, mind you, by the inhabitants of Derby, for the purpose of instructing their Members, and the meeting was held up as one which should be imitated throughout the country. It is good and wholesome for us, therefore, to hear what was said upon that occasion. I find the Rev. W. Griffiths speaking there after this fashion :—

'For myself, I say, that whatever measures are proposed, if they are meant for the benefit of the few, and not to promote the interests of the many, I would say, Down with the coronets, if they are to ruin the nation! I have no objection to coronets, ribands, nor to the gewgaws which illumine certain illustrious houses—illustrious by courtesy—provided they will keep all the pleasure and injury of them to themselves ; but if we are to be robbed, over-taxed, and have unjust and unequal laws, just because a few coroneted heads choose to have it so, then the time is come when the working men of Great

Britain must look the aristocracy in the face, demand the why and the where-fore, and not be content with a shilly-shally answer.  One word more.  There will be more money wanted ere long—the young Prince will want a wife, and then he will want a marriage settlement.  I say, let him get it from his father and mother, who have enough to keep them all.  You must begin there.  It is no use cutting off twigs, and letting huge branches remain.  I, for one, think that one palace is enough for one Sovereign.'

A Mr. Parkinson seconded the resolution, saying that—

'It had been proved, to the satisfaction of the meeting, that they were governed by an aristocratic Government who were incompetent for their work ; therefore it was the duty of every man to endeavour to destroy the system under which they had been so misruled.' .

Now, I have been considered not to have dealt always very gently with the aristocracy of this country ; but I should say to that rev. gentleman, from what I have noticed of these proceedings, that for whatever disasters may happen in this country, there is not one member of the aristocracy, out of the Cabinet, whom I should consider responsible as an individual for these disasters.  So far as I am concerned, I will never truckle so low to the popular spirit of the moment as to join in any cry which shall divert the mass of the people from what I believe should be their first thought and consideration, namely, how far they themselves are responsible for the evils which may fall upon the land, and how far they should begin at home before they commence to find fault with others.  The first thing that multitudes of men do, when they fall into errors, is to seek for victims, and this ought to be a warning to those who have influence in the land not to stimulate the passions which we have lately seen prevailing in the country, unless they can see some tangible and satisfactory result to arise from the passions they rouse.

That is all my case.  If the Russians were besieging Ports-mouth, I should not talk about what was to be done ; and if I could not work in the field, I would do so in the hospital.  I should not then ask for any one to allay the excitement of the people ; but I now repeat—and I have repeated it again

and again—you have undertaken a war with an empire of
60,000,000 of people 3000 miles away, and the people of
this country, and those who guide them, do not fully appreciate the importance, the magnitude, and the danger
of this undertaking; and that is why I have counselled
moderation and caution, and why I have made the present
long—and, I am afraid, somewhat tedious—appeal to the
House.

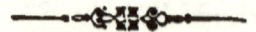

# RUSSIAN WAR.

## III.

### MANCHESTER, MARCH 18, 1857.

[On March 3, 1857, the House of Commons affirmed, by a majority of 14 (263 to 249), Mr. Cobden's resolution on the conduct of the China war. This was treated by Lord Palmerston as a vote of want of confidence, and an appeal was made to the country. No time was lost in summoning a new Parliament, and no pains spared to inflame the public mind against those who had challenged Lord Palmerston's policy. The sitting Members in Manchester had been Mr. Bright and Mr. Milner Gibson. Their re-election was opposed by Sir John Potter and Mr. Turner, and was opposed successfully. As Mr. Bright was suffering from illness, Mr. Cobden advocated his cause before the Manchester electors, in the following Speech, which deals chiefly with the policy of Lord Palmerston in the Russian war.]

I APPEAR before you on this occasion as the humble representative of my friend, Mr. Bright, and in his name I thank you in the outset for the kind reception with which you have greeted the mention of his name, and I thank you also for the all but unanimous vote with which you have announced his candidature at this election.

Now, I appear before you on the present occasion under circumstances which I certainly never expected to encounter again. I have, on former occasions, found my name prominently associated with measures in the House of Commons and in the country, that have led to dissolutions of Parliament, and to the fall of Ministries. That was when I was connected with those movements in which our object was

to cause dissolutions of Parliament and destructions of Ministries. For three times, I believe, Parliament has been dissolved,
the fact arising out of questions with which my name was
prominently associated. But I certainly never did expect to
see again a dissolution with which I should be associated.
Now, what are the circumstances under which this has arisen?
You have heard something about the China war. I am not
going into the details of that war again. I only want just to
lay before you, in the briefest possible form, the circumstances
in which the country has been placed with reference to that
question. On the assembling of Parliament, we found ourselves engaged in two wars,—the one with an empire of
350,000,000 of people, with a territory about eight times as
great as that of France, and about ten times the population;
the other was with Persia, one of the most ancient empires of
the world. Parliament and the people had had no voice in
declaring these wars; troops were moving from India to
Bushire, troops were moving from Ceylon to Hongkong, and
war was going on at our expense, and you had no voice in
declaring that war. On the assembling of Parliament, a
demand was made from the Ministry for information respecting the Persian war. The answer we got was, that it would
be contrary (it is the stereotyped answer), that it would be
prejudicial to the interests of the country that any papers
should be given referring to the origin of the Persian war.
But I found on the table of the House of Commons all the
papers having reference to the Chinese war. Now, it is a
very rare thing indeed that we are so fortunate as to find such
a record of what is going on in our name and behalf. But I
found the papers all in order, and everything that could be
had to give an account of the origin of the Chinese war. I
read those papers, as I was in duty bound to do. The conclusion I came to I stated in my place in the House of
Commons, and I am not going to repeat the arguments
now. But what I want to ask here is, what I asked in

London the other day, was it anything contrary to my duty
as a Member of Parliament, and as a representative of the
people, that I should read those papers, and express an
opinion, and call for an opinion of the House with reference
to proceedings which were involving this country in daily
expense, and which might undoubtedly incur a vast expense,
both of blood and treasure?

Well, I read the papers; and, coming to the conviction
that the origin of this war was a blunder and a crime, I
framed a resolution, which I showed to my right hon. Friend
here, and asked him if he would like to second it; and,
without consulting any other human being, I put that motion
on the table of the House of Commons, and it lay there for a
fortnight before my turn came for bringing on the motion.
Singular to say—for it is an unusual thing—not one word of
that resolution, nor one syllable, was altered to accommodate
the mind of any Member of the House of Commons.

Well, I am told—and we hear it daily repeated in the
columns of some of the London papers, whose audacity of
assertions certainly sometimes astounds me even, though I am
habituated to the perusal of the *Times* newspaper; but there
is still every day the reiterated falsehood, as if the people had
not yet had enough of it, that this was a motion brought
forward in a factious spirit, and with a coalition of parties, in
order, forsooth, that we might overturn the Government, and
get possession of their places.

Well, now, there is a great question involved in this, which
I think the people of this country ought to take very much to
heart. Do you want the Members of the House of Commons
to look after your rights, and watch the expenditure, and to
guard you from getting into needless and expensive wars?
['Yes.'] Well, but you are not going the right way to work
about it, if what I hear in your newspapers is going to be
verified in the course of a fortnight in the election; for I am
told that those Members who joined in that vigilant care of

your interests, and voted according to the evidence before us
on the question of that war, are all to be ostracised,—sent into
private life,—and that you are going to send up there men—
to do what? to look after your interests? No; to go and do
the humble, dirty work of the Minister of the hour. In fact,
that you are going to constitute Lord Palmerston the despotic
ruler of this country. ['No, no.'] Well, but if he is not
checked by Parliament, — if, the moment Parliament does
check him, he dissolves Parliament, and, instead of sending
up men who are independent enough to assert their and your
rights, you send up mere creatures of his will, what is that
but investing him with the powers of a despot? Ay, and let
me tell you that it is a despotism of the clumsiest, most expensive, and at the same time most irresponsible kind on the
face of the earth; because you surround the Minister with the
sham appearance of a representative form of Government;
you cannot get at him while he has got a Parliament beneath
whose shield he can shelter himself; and if you do not do
your duties in your elections in sending men up to the House
of Commons who will vigilantly watch the Minister of the
day, then, I say, you are in a worse plight, because governed
in a more irresponsible way, than if you were under the King
of Prussia or the Emperor of the French.

But who is Lord Palmerston, that we are to invest him
with this power? Who is he? ['A traitor.'] No, I will
say nothing worse of him here than I have said to his face in
Parliament; but, when I want to know what a man is, I ask,
What has he done? There is no other test like that. That
was Napoleon's question always, if anybody talked to him
about somebody being a great man,—What has he done?
Well, now, Lord Palmerston has been fifty years in Parliament—['Fifty-two']; fifty-two years in Parliament. Well,
he has belonged, I believe, to every Government excepting
one during those fifty years. I remember the *Times* newspaper, which spent about fifteen years in trying to blacken his

reputation, and is now polishing him up every day, once said, when it had said everything else that was gross, vile, and vituperative about him, that he had been 'boots' to every Administration for thirty years. Now, I beg you to understand that this is the language of the *Times*, and not mine. But with what has his name been associated? ['Peterloo.'] Yes, Peterloo. I remember, that on this very spot of ground, when the people were cut down and trampled upon by the yeomanry cavalry, Lord Palmerston was one of the Government, and voted in favour of that outrage.

Well, but what has he done since?—because men may have been, in the early part of their career, by circumstances, like Sir Robert Peel, put into a certain groove, and hardly answerable for the course they were obliged to run. But what has he done since that he had been able to take his own choice? What does he propose now to do? He was a member of the Reform Ministry in 1831; he left his old party, and joined the Whigs as a Reformer. But was he one of those who put forward the cause of Reform, or was he there as a drag-chain? I have seen to-day a speech, which has been sent to me, delivered by Sir James Graham, at Carlisle. He says:—'I and Lord John Russell are the only two Cabinet Ministers remaining alive who formed the Government which brought in the Reform Bill of 1831;' and he says, 'We had Lord Palmerston amongst us; but I very soon found out that he was not very much disposed for the work that we were engaged in.' In December, 1853,—that is, little more than three years ago,—he belonged to the Ministry of Lord Aberdeen. Now, Lord Aberdeen was, I considered, a very liberal man; but we were all deluded with the idea that Lord Palmerston was the great champion of democracy, and Lord Aberdeen was always the friend of despotism;—I was not taken in by that, but a good many people were.

Well, but what did Lord Palmerston do in December, 1853, when Lord Aberdeen's Government was preparing a new

Reform Bill, to be brought in in the session of 1854? Lord
Palmerston left Lord Aberdeen's Government because he objected to that modicum of Reform that was then proposed;
that bill, bearing on its back the names of Lord John Russell
and Sir James Graham—certainly not two very rash or democratic Reformers—that bill, which proposed to give a 10*l.*
franchise to the counties, and a slightly reduced franchise to
the boroughs,—so slightly reduced that some of my friends
thought it would rather operate as a restriction in some
boroughs than an extension; that bill was too much for Lord
Palmerston to swallow; and he left Lord Aberdeen's Cabinet
avowedly because he objected to that bill. Well, what has he
done since? What has he done this very session? Why, he
has opposed everything that can bear the mere semblance of
Reform. He voted against Locke King's motion for a 10*l.*
county franchise, which formed part of the bill of 1854; he
has opposed even the 40*s.* freehold franchise for Scotland, if
you may believe the Lord-Advocate of Scotland (Mr. Mon-
creiff), who is in the Ministry, for he has gone down there
and announced that.

Now, will you tell me on what ground I am to be called
upon to surrender my independence and freedom of thought
and action to the will of a Ministry such as this? Why,
what do you propose to get by such a process? It appears
to me it is about the most audacious attempt upon your
credulity that ever was practised in this country, to think of
raising the cry at an election in favour of one man,—for there
is no other cry attempted on the hustings,—and for that man
to be the leader of the Liberal party, without having one
Liberal tenet in his profession of faith.

When I read of men that I have hitherto considered to be
earnest Reformers, — when I have read their speeches and
addresses, in which they have said, 'I am for the ballot; I
am for the extension of the suffrage; I am for shortening
Parliaments; I am against church-rates; and I will give my

hearty support to Lord Palmerston's Government,'—my natural question is, 'Are these men idiots, or are they dishonest?' because, if you attempt to carry out a business in private life, you do not go to a man that you know is directly opposed, in his view, to what you wish to accomplish, and put yourself under his guidance. Lord Palmerston is not content with a mere passive resistance to what you desire as Reformers. He lends an active opposition,—he votes and speaks against every measure of Reform that is brought into the House of Commons. [Cheers.] Well, and what is it for? Because we are told that Lord Palmerston is a great friend of freedom abroad.

Well now, go and ask those men in this country who represent freedom abroad ;—ask Kossuth. I will tell you what happened within my knowledge ; it is no breach of confidence to say it. When that illustrious Hungarian was expected in England, after his imprisonment in Turkey, my lamented friend Lord Dudley Stuart—whose devotion to the cause of these foreign refugees was as unbounded as it was sincere—went down to Southampton to meet Kossuth, and receive him on his arrival. Having to wait a day or two there, and being in the neighbourhood of Broadlands, where Lord Palmerston lives, he went and saw the noble Lord, and received from him a request to bring Kossuth over (on his arrival at Southampton) to Broadlands, to see him. I remember receiving a letter from Lord Dudley Stuart, announcing to me this piece of intelligence with the greatest glee. He was delighted at the opportunity of taking Kossuth over to see Lord Palmerston ; and, as soon as he arrived, he announced to him the pleasing invitation. To his astonishment, he found Kossuth would not accept it. He would not go near Lord Palmerston ; and I have got a letter from Lord Dudley Stuart, asking me to use all my influence with Kossuth to induce him to go and call upon Lord Palmerston. He would not do it ; and my answer to Lord Dudley Stuart was this :—' You may depend upon it, Kossuth knows a great deal more about Lord Palmerston than you do.' I could not go into the particulars now, but they are all familiar to me.

Every transaction of Lord Palmerston's foreign policy is known to me; I defy any human being to show an instance where anybody on the face of the earth has been happier or freer in consequence of Lord Palmerston's foreign policy. He endorsed the invasion of Rome by the French. We have it in the blue-books. He was the first, in red-hot haste, to congratulate the present Emperor of the French after his usurpation, when the blood was still flowing in the streets of Paris. He refused to see an envoy sent from the Hungarians, because, he said, he could treat with nobody but the Austrian Government. He treated the Italians in the same way. Are these facts, or are they not? ['Yes, yes.'] Nobody denies them. Do you think, then, it is consistent with common sense that the man who has no love for liberty or progress at home should have any love of the kind to export to foreign countries? Do you not think that liberalism, like liberality, like progress, like charity, should begin at home?

Well, which other title does he present to our confidence, that the people of this country should be called upon by the impudence of three or four metropolitan journals, who have reasons best known to themselves, which I hope will be exposed some day, to lie down upon their bellies in the dust before this man? What has he done? We are told that he carried the Russian war to a triumphant conclusion.

Now, I will tell you what he did in that war. Lord Palmerston was a member of the Government which declared the war. If he be the man of talent, with the powers of administration which we are told he has,—if he be a man of this towering genius, that we are all suddenly called upon to discover at the age of seventy-three,—was he not likely, at least, three or four years ago, to have had a share of that energy, so that he might have imprinted a portion of his policy upon the Government during the time he was one of them? He was responsible for every blunder, just as much as any member of the Government. And what is the Cabinet now? Why, a majority of the Cabinet now was the majority of the Cabinet then. Lord Palmerston was not called upon to make a new Cabinet in order to carry on the war; certain members of the Cabinet—a minority—seceded from it, and left the majority, of whom Lord Palmerston was at the head. That majority is quite as responsible for everything that occurred during the early progress of the war, as they can claim to be entitled to any merit for any improvement in the conduct of the war when that minority seceded. But did Lord Palmerston ever himself lend his word to this imposture that is practised in his name? No; to do him justice, his toadies practise the imposture, but he has told us, manfully and in a straightforward way, that he did not share in the delusion himself. For what has he done? When Lord Aberdeen seceded from the Government, Lord Palmerston told Sir James Graham and the rest of the friends of Lord Aberdeen who remained in the Government, that he would carry on the Government and the war upon precisely the same principles that they had been carried on by Lord Aberdeen; that there should be no change in his foreign policy; and that he would only ask the same terms of peace as Lord Aberdeen would have been content with. That was not only mentioned privately in the course of their discussions with themselves, but it came out in the House of Commons. Did Lord Palmerston himself ever come before us to complain of anything that had been done in the early conduct of the war whilst he was a member of the Cabinet? No; on the contrary, he defended everything.

When Mr. Roebuck brought forward his motion for inquiring into the scenes going on before Sebastopol, to try and hunt out, if he could, the cause of the ruin and disaster that had befallen our army, did Lord Palmerston get up in his place

in the House, and say, ' Here are admitted evils, I grant
to the honourable and learned Gentleman, fair subjects for
inquiry?' No; he stood by things as they were,—defended
everything, and resisted an inquiry by the Committee.  But,
what is more, after the Committee was appointed, and had
sat and inquired into the proceedings at Sebastopol, when
Mr. Roebuck brought forward a motion in the House of
Commons, consequent on the inquiry, did Lord Palmerston
assist him? No; he voted against him again.

What has he done besides?  After sending out a couple of
men,—able and competent men, Sir John M'Neill and Colonel
Tulloch,—and after they had brought home a report, certainly
as able and, I believe, as conscientious as was ever made
by public men,—what did Lord Palmerston do?  Did he
back up his own commissioners?  No.  He would have done,
if it had been Smith, Jones, or Robinson that had been concerned; but they were Lords and Earls who were in question;
and what did he do?  He appointed a commission of military
men to inquire into the conduct of the commissioners!  And
then, when public opinion rises to demand some improvement
upon this state of things, what does he do?  He insults these
distinguished men by sending them a present each of a thousand pounds, which they sent back again—just the amount
that was paid some time ago to a policeman for having
captured a celebrated political criminal.

Now, this is the sort of man that we are called upon all at
once to fall down and worship!  Why, I say the brazen image
shall have no worship from me.  But I want to ask these
people that are here in Manchester, and I want you to put
the question to them—I will first take Mr. Aspinall Turner.
[Groans.]  No, no, no; we will deal with him with reason,
and not with clamour.  I want to put something before
you that you may probably have the opportunity of asking
them.  The great complaint against us, on the part of these
gentlemen is, that we are too independent of this Minister.

Now, ask them this question : What would they have had us
do in the case of that vote the other night, that was designed
to do justice to Colonel Tulloch and Sir John M'Neill?  I
was in the House of Commons, waiting for the division, and
certainly should have voted against the Government; but
Lord Palmerston, seeing which way the wind blew, after
having spoken against the motion, got up and said, 'I won't
divide the House upon it.'  Now, I want to know how
Mr. Aspinall Turner would have voted on that occasion?
Would he have considered it very factious if he had joined
the Member for Devonshire, who sits on the other side of the
House, in voting against the Government?  Why, I see this
Mr. Turner's name, as President of the Commercial Association, signed to a memorial, in which he states the whole of
the facts I am stating, and says that Lord Palmerston has not
only failed to do justice to these eminent officers who went out
to make the inquiry, but has also given encouragement and
promotion to the very men who are proved to have been culpable and neglectful.  Now, I must say I think Mr. Aspinall
Turner is looking very much like a 'conspirator' in this
matter,—he is guilty of a 'coalition' with somebody to turn
out a Minister.  Well, what are we to do under these circumstances?  Are we to follow this Minister, or to follow the
dictates of our own judgments and consciences?

Now, I hear it said that we have been a thorn in the side of
three Governments.  We are told that three or four of us
have been a thorn in the side of Lord Aberdeen, Lord John
Russell, and now of Lord Palmerston.  I can only say this,—
if Manchester should send up the two gentlemen that are
now candidates in opposition to my honourable and right
honourable Friends, *they* won't be thorns in the side of any
Government.

Well, but what do you want done in Parliament?  Do you
send up men to Parliament just to be told off into one lobby
or the other, according as the whipper-in of the Treasury

decides? I suppose you want your Members to do something
better than follow the bidding of the Treasury whip. Do you
think there is much danger now of your catching Members of
Parliament likely to be too independent? I can assure you,
you will find it just the contrary. And if the threats now
held out should be carried into effect,—if you should, unhappily for yourselves, lose those two Members you have got,
I will venture to say it will be long before you will have to
complain that the new ones will be too independent when they
get into Parliament. Why, it is the very thing of all others
most difficult to find in London—independence. Only cast
your memories back; how few men have we got permanently
to join us in our attempt, even, to stand against a Government! Four or five, or six or eight, or ten. I could count
them all on my ten fingers, who remained resolute and determined to maintain an independent course. And why? Because the temptations, blandishments, and seductions practised on Members of Parliament are very well known to those
engaged in that House. Do you think I was not tempted,
like everybody else? I have had my cards, my dinner cards,
as large as that (exhibiting a half sheet of paper), and from
Lord Palmerston, too.

When I went up to Parliament in 1841, it would have
been much easier and more pleasant to many minds, and
a much more agreeable life, if I had at once fallen into
the track, and, instead of instituting an independent resistance to Government when I chose, I had joined the
governing class, and become one of their humble servants.
But the very first day I went into Parliament, in 1841, when
the lines of party were still visible, when there was a great
gulf between the two great parties on the two sides of the
House—when Sir Robert Peel had his 390 or 400 men, and
Lord John Russell his 270 or 280 men—the very first time I
got up and spoke as the Member for Stockport, I declared I
came there to do something—to repeal the Corn-laws, and

I would know neither Whig nor Tory until that work was done.

Well, now, suppose I had pursued another course—suppose I had allied myself to the Whig party, which was then the most Liberal, and which had then adopted what was considered to be an advanced position at that time, an 8*s.* fixed duty,—suppose I had joined that party, as I might have done, and depended upon them, and not upon an abstract principle, for the success of our agitation, do you think we should ever have got the total and immediate repeal? No; it would not have been possible; because we should have told Sir Robert Peel and the party opposite, 'We are not going to take it from you at all; it is a party question—a Whig question, and we are going to take the repeal of the Corn-laws in no other way.' But when Sir Robert Peel and the party opposite saw we were in earnest, and did not make a party question of our principle, he did the work for us, which the Whigs never could have done. Are we not to pursue the same course again? Am I, because I find Mr. Disraeli and Sir John Pakington coming round to principles I have been advocating—am I, at the moment which offers a fair chance of success to my opinion, to say, 'No, I will not join you; that would be conspiracy—that would be a coalition?'

Well, now, what is it, after all, that the so much-abused Manchester School wants? Why, they say we want to abolish all our standing armies and navies, and leave you, like so many Quakers, at the mercy of the whole world. Any man who has lived in public life, as I have, must know that it is quite useless to contradict any falsehood or calumny, because it comes up again next day just as rife as ever. There is the *Times* newspaper always ready to repeat it, and the grosser the better. Have I not, in the House of Commons, advocated the expenditure of 10,000,000*l.* on our protection? and that is pretty nearly as much as the Americans spend for civil and military purposes and everything put together. It may be a question whether it will be 10,000,000*l*. or 15,000,000*l*. The Duke of Wellington managed to make a sum under 12,000,000*l*. do. But they tell us that I want to deprive you of your defences against your enemies. Why, what has been my argument for the last seven years on this question? You cannot have a reduction of taxation unless you have a reduction of your military and naval establishments; and you cannot have a reduction of your military and naval establishments if you allow a Minister to be constantly involving you in wars or in dangers of wars.

Well, now, what do I hear every night in the House of Commons and in the House of Lords? Lord Derby, Mr. Gladstone, and Mr. Disraeli have used almost the identical language which I have used seven or eight years ago. Here is my programme, ' Non-intervention ; ' here is my programme, ' Diminished expenditure in your armaments, and diminished taxation if you follow that policy.' But am I, when I see this policy, which seems to be advocated and very rapidly adopted by the whole Conservative party in the House of Commons, am I then immediately to turn from the course I took seven years ago and say, 'If you offer to reduce the establishments 2,000,000*l*. a year, you only want to make a factious opposition to the Government?' I want such factious opposition.

Now, I want you to bear in mind, though you have got Free Trade, you are interested in getting something else, and you will find something else. I speak to young men, to young men in shops and warehouses, foremen in places of business, who want some day to have the chance of being masters. I want the operative who is qualifying himself to be a freeman, and who hopes some day to be a capitalist, to have the chance that he may carry out his views and see the career before him. This was the feeling I had seven or eight years ago, when we launched our assault upon the protective system. But there is a great deal more to do, if you will make this country a place to live in, and for your children to thrive in, and give a chance to every man, as I should like to see, of rising in the world, becoming the head of a family, and finding employment for his labour, and supply him with all the advantages of capital if he sets up to be a master. How is this to be done, but by widening the circle of business operations, and by diminishing the pressure of your taxation?

Now, what do we see in London? Twenty or thirty thousand unemployed workmen. Why are they unemployed? You don't find that the newspapers connect cause and effect. They are unemployed because capital is scarce; they are unemployed because money is worth 6 or 7 per cent. at the banks. Who will lay out his money in building houses, to pay him at the rate of 6, or 7, or 8 per cent., if he can get that percentage for the money he puts into the banks? Consequently there is no money being invested in buildings, because you have now such a high rate of interest. And why is there such a high rate of interest? Because the floating capital of this country has, during the last two or three years, been wasted in sudden and extraordinary expenses. But you don't see your newspapers, that were bawling for the war, honestly tell the people in London that the reason they are suffering want of employment is, that this floating capital, which is always a limited quantity in the country—the floating capital which sets all your fixed capital in motion—has been exhausted, wasted, by the course that has been pursued. It may have been necessary or not, I am not now going into that question; but, I say, let cause and effect be connected, don't let the people be deluded.

They tell these poor people in London they may emigrate; but I say it is downright quackery to talk of relieving the country of 20,000 or 30,000 people by means of emigration. Moreover, if we remain at peace, and keep our Ministry in

order, during the next two or three years, there will not be
enough builders and joiners for the work that will have to be
done. It is downright quackery, and insulting your understanding, to say you must make people emigrate, as a means
of relieving you of such a large surplus population. It is all
moonshine.

Now, I say, if you are to have a progressive development of
your trade, you must pursue a policy favourable to it. You
must enable your Government to reduce taxation, and especially that taxation which presses on the labouring and on the
middle classes—I mean the taxation that is laid in an indirect
form upon your articles of consumption. The more you remove these taxes, the more your trade will expand, the more
your population may increase and flourish, and the happier
will be the condition of the country.

But you have come now to a dead stand-still; and this is
one of my great complaints against this Government. It is
the most incompetent Government in matters of finance that
we have had since that of Sir Robert Peel. Here you are,
laying on increased taxes on your tea and sugar—here you are,
at this moment, to gratify the people who have cried out
against a 16*d.* income-tax, taking off 9*d.* from the tax. And
it is perfectly certain, as Mr. Gladstone says, that the Government have not the means before them to do it honestly; and
next year, unless you have a reduction of expenditure, there
must be an increase of taxation. I appeal to my right hon.
Friend here (Mr. Gibson), who has looked into the matter as
well as myself, whether it is not inevitable. And, in two
years from that time, if you do not reduce your expenditure,
you will have a deficit of something like 10,000,000*l.* But
how to make it up? Your present Prime Minister, who lives
from hand to mouth in his political career—who has never
cared for the morrow so that he can keep on for to-day—he
is pursuing a most ruinous course of finance; and, if you had
called out for the whole 16*d.* being taken off, instead of the

9*d.*, he would still have let it go, and left it to somebody else
to find out how to make up the deficiency next year.

And not only that, but look at your Indian finances.—
Nobody looks at them ; you have put his screen before your
faces, so that you are hidden from India, and India is hidden
from you.   And so your Government sits down in London,
and writes out to that country, in order to send one army to
the Persian Gulf, and another to Hongkong ; and that the
Indian Treasury must pay for it, or the half of it.   They have
no voice in the matter out there.   And how stand your Indian
finances ?   Deficit on deficit every year—deficit last year, and
the year before that—a constantly accumulating deficit.   And
what has been done to meet it ?   They tried for a loan some
time ago, at 4½ per cent., but could not get the money.   Then
they have tried to realise it in India, at 5 per cent. ; but could
not get the money.   And the last advices are, that you *cannot*
get the money.   But, as Sir Robert Peel told us in the House
of Commons, on some occasion, you are as much responsible
for the finances of India as you are for the finances in
Downing Street ; and, if you allow things to go on in this
reckless way, by which you become embarrassed at home and
embarrassed abroad, the time of reckoning will overtake you,
as it does overtake all spendthrifts, and there will be an evil
day for you and your children, sooner or later.

Now, is it to be considered unreasonable that we have
joined Mr. Gladstone in his motions ?   I voted for his motion
that there should be a reduction of the expenditure, and
Mr. Disraeli also voted with him.   Were we, then, to go into
the other lobby, because we found Mr. Gladstone and Mr.
Disraeli voting with us on that occasion ?   I believe they were
right.   I believe that they both took a most philosophical
and able view of our finances ; and what I want you to
consider is, whether you think the men who take the independent course which I have suggested, whether you think
they are men who ought to be denounced here, by interested

and jealous individuals, because they have had the manliness to do their duty?

I come now, for a moment, to the conduct of my right hon. Friend here, and to the conduct of my honourable Friend whom I represent here on this occasion. I have lived with Mr. Bright in the most transparent intimacy of mind that two human beings ever enjoyed together. I don't believe there is a view, I don't believe there is a thought, I don't believe there is one aspiration in the minds of either of us that the other is not acquainted with. I don't know that there is anything that I have sought to do which Mr. Bright would not do in my place, or anything that he aims at which I would not accomplish if I had the power. Knowing him, then, I stand here, in all humility, as his representative; for what I have long cherished in my friend Mr. Bright is this, that I have seen in him an ability and an eloquence to which I have had no pretensions, because I am not gifted with the natural eloquence with which he is endowed; and that I have had the fond consolation of hoping that Mr. Bright, being seven or eight years younger than myself, will be advocating principles—and advocating them successfully—when I shall no longer be on the scene of duty. With those feelings, I naturally take the deepest interest in the decision of this election. I feel humiliated—I feel disgusted to 'see the daily personal attacks — the diatribes that are made against this man—with his health impaired for the moment,—his health impaired, too, in that organ which excites feelings of awe, and of the utmost commiseration for him on the part of all right-minded men. Yes; whilst this man is not able to use those great intellectual powers with which God has gifted him—whilst their full activity is suspended for the day—the vermin of your Manchester press, the ghouls of the *Guardian*, are preying upon this splendid being, and trying to make a martyr of him in the midst of his sufferings!

Well, now, what are the motives with which these men

are actuated? Are they public motives? Why don't they allege one public ground for their hostility? Where is the public ground—where is the one fact—what have they to allege against this man? No; it is vile, dirty, nasty, fireside jealousy.

I will deal very candidly with you, men of Manchester, in this respect. I say you have not the character, or the fame, or the destinies of John Bright in your hands; but I will tell you this, that your own character and reputation are at stake. Your character and reputation with the country, and with the world at large, are at stake in the conduct which you pursue on this occasion. One who has served you so faithfully and so assiduously—even to the partial destruction of his own health—who is no longer able to appear before you,—why, the manhood that is in you must all rebel against the cowardly assaults that are made upon him. But I believe the hostility is a personal one. I believe it is confined to a select few. They may, perhaps, make dupes of others; and, unless you be watchful, they may make dupes of some of you.

But what are the alleged faults of this man—what have you to say against him? I told you before that you must go to the House of Commons for his character—to either side of the House of Commons—and I will venture to say you will hear but one opinion of him from Whig, Tory, or Radical. I will tell you what I heard one of the oldest and most sagacious men in the House of Commons say: that he did not believe there was any man in the House, with the exception of Mr. Bright and Mr. Gladstone, who ever changed votes by their eloquence. Now, that is a great tribute to pay to men; because although we, many of us, may probably convince people by our arguments, we do not convert them and make them change their votes,—it requires logic and reasoning power; but it requires something else — it requires those transcendent powers of eloquence which your representatives possess.

Now, as to my friend here, who sits beside me (Mr. Gibson), he was not of my selection; he was selected in the parlour of my late revered friend, Sir Thomas Potter, and I was at the time not a very enthusiastic supporter of the right hon. Gentleman. He was brought here, and, as I always went with those good men who at that time took the lead—Sir Thomas Potter, Mr. Kershaw, Mr. Callender, and others—I joined them, and fought the battle, and we won it for them. But this I will say of him, that though he sometimes has an arch look, and sometimes seems as if he were almost quizzing you, and you fancy that there is a little twist of sarcasm about him in all he says and all he looks, yet this I will say of him, that there is an earnestness in his character which I every day more and more appreciate, and which I did not when I first saw him—as many others may not, when they first see him—give him credit for.

Well, now, how has my right hon. Friend employed himself? He might have gone into office, and *was* in office. He is a man bred in fashionable life—he has not the same excuse that I have for keeping out of that sort of company. If he had allowed himself to be absorbed in the aristocratic circles of London—nobody can doubt, who sees him, that he would have been an ornament to those circles. He might have led a very happy life there; and, being Member for Manchester, they would have been, I dare say, very proud of him. And then there would have been none of this opposition now set up against him. But he has taken an independent course. He has worked in favour of great questions—great questions affecting the interests of the people. There is one question which he carried—I will almost give him credit for carrying it single-handed—and that is the question of the newspaper stamp. He carried that, and the repeal of the advertisement duty; he carried them by his dexterity and ability in debate; by his exquisite tactics, by his knowledge of the forms of the House, and by accepting the assistance of hon. Gentlemen on

the other side of the House.  Now he has incurred the
hostility—[cries of 'The *Guardian*']—ay, and not only of
the *Guardian;* we have had black marks put opposite our
names from more papers than the *Guardian.*

I remember the first time I spoke in public after returning
home from a temporary absence on the Continent, in 1847.
It was at a dinner party in London, at which I took the
chair; and I took the opportunity of launching this question
of the press, and saying that the newspaper press of England
was not free, and that this was a thing which the Reformers
of the country ought to set about—to emancipate it.  Well,
I got a most vicious article next day from the *Times* newspaper for that, and the *Times* has followed us both with a
very ample store of venom ever since.  But now, these are the
very men, men like my right hon. Friend, who undertook these
great questions, and braved the hostility of interested parties,
that the rank and file of their constituents ought to support,
and protect from the vengeance threatened against them.

I am told there is a complaint made of these gentlemen by
my friend Mr. Alderman Neild, of whom I always wish to
speak with respect, as an old friend of mine, and who thinks
they do not pay sufficient attention to private bills in London.
My opinion is that there is a good deal too much made of
that.  The fact is, the less you have to go to London for
private bills the better.  You want the bill carried in Parliament,
the thing is done by the House of Commons; and, let me tell
you, when you want a man who has influence in that House,
to assist you in obtaining a bill, you must go to just such a
man as my right hon. Friend, or Mr. Bright—men who have
force in the House, who have the ability to make themselves
felt when they speak in that House.  I tell you that those
men who are independent in that House, who have the power
of speaking so as to command the attention of the House, will
do more for you by what they say in half-a-dozen words,
than an hour's talk will do for you from one of those toadies

who are always known to be at the beck and call of the
Government.

But I am told that this Manchester School, as it is called,
do not pay sufficient attention to the interests of Manchester.
Now, I think we have done as much for Manchester as anybody.  Have you not got your daily newspapers now?  But
for my right hon. Friend you might have had to be content
with news three days old.  Have you not got an addition to your
register of 4000 names now?  Who was it that got those 4000
names added to your register, by having the clause inserted in
favour of the compound householders?  It was Mr. Bright.
No man of less energy or influence than he could have done
it, because it is a thing repugnant to the governing class in
the House of Commons to have any addition to the register
at all.  I ask those 4000 men how they are going to vote?
I don't say to those men, ' You are not to exercise your vote,
or your power, independent of Mr. Bright or anybody else ;'
but this I say, ' Shame upon you if, having got the franchise
for yourselves by a man who advocates the extension of the
franchise to others, you give the power vested in you to the
hands of somebody else, who will refuse the franchise to those
who have not got it.'

Well, but now, this Manchester School, and their getting
the Corn-laws repealed, and Free Trade established, by which
the trade of this country has pretty nearly doubled during the
last twelve years—I say, who has benefited so much as Manchester by that?  But if you come to your own local affairs—
I tell these gentlemen who are setting themselves up, and
swelling about as aldermen, and say we are people who have
not attended to the interests of Manchester—I tell them they
owe everything to us, even their dignity.  If I were to take
the watch out of the pocket of my friend in the chair there,
and read the inscription upon it, it would show that it was
given to him by a number of us, who associated together to
get a charter of incorporation for Manchester.

And our friend here (Mr. G. Wilson), who, from the time
he was a boy of eighteen years of age, and was working day
and night as a secretary on Poulett Thompson's committee—
who has worked on all the questions carried through the town
of Manchester ever since, and gone through all the drudgery
for it in getting the charter of incorporation; and during the
constant labour of seven years, for the repeal of the Corn-
laws; and who is working now—and, it seems, working too
much, for these gentlemen;—this is the man, they say, who
does nothing for Manchester—who does not look after the
local affairs of Manchester.

Let me speak of my friend Mr. Alderman Neild—I shall
not do so in any spirit of egotism now, because I may, without
vanity, say that it does not at all add to my fame with regard
to this transaction in Manchester; but it so happened that,
on one unlucky day for the lord of the manor of this place,
his steward summoned me, along with ten or twelve other
gentlemen, to elect a boroughreeve and constables for Manchester. I was taken into some dingy, cobwebbed, murky
hole, and sat down with those gentlemen to elect a boroughreeve and constables for Manchester. After we had finished
our business we were entitled, I think, to a leaden ticket, for
some soup or a dinner. I said immediately, ' Well, what in
the world does all this mean? Can it be that Manchester '—
for I was not an old inhabitant of the town—' is it that in
this great town of Manchester we are still living under the
feudal system? Does Sir Oswald Moseley, living up in
Derbyshire, send his mandate down here, for us to come into
this dingy hole to elect a government for Manchester, and
then go and get a ticket for soup at his expense? Why, now,'
I said, ' I will put an end to this thing.' And it so happened
that just at that moment my friend, Mr. Neild, was trying to
get some amendment to the Act of Parliament by which the
affairs of the police were carried on in this borough. But my
friend Mr. Neild went to work in that, as he went to work in

everything—it was by a little bit of compromise and concession.  He went to the party who were already in possession
of the power of the town, and asked them to co-operate; and
they got some unworthy people to come to their meeting and
upset the benches, and make a great confusion, and the whole
meeting was destroyed; and, in fact, Mr. Neild was very
much discomfited.  Well, I wrote to Mr. Neild, and, if he
does me the honour to preserve anything that I write to him,
he has the note now.  I said, 'If you will do this thing in
the way that I intend to do it, and you will join with me, I
will undertake to say that we will get a charter of incorporation for Manchester.'  Mr. Neild—who had tried, what is a
common thing with these gentlemen, something that will
please everybody, but pleases nobody—came to me, like an
honest, excellent, true-hearted man, as he is, and he says, 'I
have tried my way, and it does not answer; I will go with
you; all I stipulate is, that you will not take any course but
what is consistent with morality and honour, and I will join
you in any way you choose in order to put an end to this
state of things.'  We were three years at that work; and
at one time he was 1200*l.* out of pocket, and I was between
700*l.* and 800*l.* deficient, but we got the charter.

I ask these new-fledged aldermen—not the worthy and true-
hearted men we see on this platform—I ask these men who
are running about and saying that we will attend to nothing
but the great national questions—I ask them, Are there in
Manchester any men who have left their impress upon the
town of Manchester more than the four men who are stigmatised by these people as never paying any attention to local
matters?

I am going to Huddersfield to-morrow.  If my voice does
not fail me, I should like to come back and have one more
great meeting in this hall—but it must be on one condition,
and that is, that the gentlemen here set to work.  Our late
friend, Sir Thomas Potter, if he had been living, would have

been amongst us ; and he never allowed a meeting to go off without his famous and memorable words, 'Work, work, work.' With these words, I wish to dismiss you.

I tell you, here is a combination, I call it a conspiracy—a foul conspiracy,—to upset two of the ablest men in the House of Commons. One of them is absent, and therefore it is no flattery to say it of him, that, if the House of Commons had the power of returning three men to be Members of their body, I have not the least hesitation in saying that one of these men, if he was not in Parliament, would be John Bright. Now, he is well known to you, and my friend Mr. Gibson is known to you as a great worker in the good cause.

You are asked to dismiss these men without a cause. I tell you that it is you, and not they, who are upon your trials. You may dismiss them, but if you do you will never have them back again, for they will not be out of Parliament a month. And what will you have in the place of them? I will avoid personalities. I have only dealt with Lord Palmerston as a person because he has been put forward as a policy. He is the only policy put forward on which the elections are to turn. I am obliged to deal with the man as a policy.

But now, as to your two candidates. There is Mr. Lowe. See him, and hear him, before you choose him. You have had one specimen of ministerial oratory on this platform, and I want you to hear more of these 'right honourable' and 'honourable' members of the aristocracy. Let them come and talk to you, and you will then know better how to appreciate the men you have got. Hear Mr. Lowe. I have heard him, and I will say this—and in saying it I shall be borne out by any impartial man in the House of Commons—that, considering that he had some reputation for ability when he was at Oxford, and as a writer in the *Times*, he is the most conspicuous failure in the House of Commons. Then there is my friend Sir John Potter. I will say nothing upon this subject except this : I am sorry to see him in opposition to his old friends.

But this I say of the two candidates who are rivals for the representation of your city, that if you want to exchange your present talented Members—if you want to lose the proud distinction you have attained—send them ; but if you want still to show yourself to the world as having two Members able to grapple with other men in that great arena of intellectual gladiatorship, the House of Commons,—if you want still to show to the world, as you have done already, that Manchester, at all events, is something, then keep your present Members. But, on the other hand, if you think you have had fame and distinction enough, and want to fall into utter insignificance, and to hear a shout of scorn and indignation at the result of your election, then return the two men you are asked to send in the place of your present representatives.

# AMERICAN WAR.

## I.

### HOUSE OF COMMONS, APRIL 24, 1863.

[The *Alexandra* was a three-masted wooden vessel, which was seized by the Commissioners of Customs at Liverpool, on the ground that it was being equipped contrary to the provisions of the Foreign Enlistment Act. The case which arose out of the seizure formed the subject of a trial in the Exchequer before Chief Baron Pollock, on June 22, and ended in a verdict for the defendants.]

THE legal points that have been discussed in connection with this question are, undoubtedly, of the greatest importance; but I apprehend that no one will expect that any conclusive result will arise from this passage of arms between Gentlemen learned in the law in this House upon a question which is, I believe, now pending before the Law Courts. When the hon. Member for Liverpool (Mr. Horsfall) gave notice of his motion, I had no idea he could have contemplated any such result, or that he could have wished this question to be confined to the mere technical aspect which has been sought to be given to it. I think a larger and more important question is before us. It is not merely the vessel (the *Alexandra*) now under consideration, that public report charges with being intended to commit a breach of the Statute Law. It is said there are many vessels now building with the same object in view, and I apprehend that this is a proper time in the interests of this country—in the interests of this country, and no other country—to offer a few remarks upon this subject. I expressly speak of the interests of this country, because we are constantly met by phrases such as, 'You are consulting American interests ;'—' You are neglecting the honour of this country.' I wish to consider British interests in my observations on the Foreign Enlistment Act, and I will consider no other interest; and I maintain, at the outset, there is no other country in the world that has a quarter—I say deliberately a quarter—of the interest in upholding the system of international law, of which the Foreign Enlistment Act is the basis.

Now, the hon. Member for Liverpool (Mr. Horsfall) has to-night—as was done by the hon. and learned Solicitor-General (Sir W. Atherton) on a former occasion—mixed up another question which has tended to bewilder and confuse the public mind here and out of doors, and the world over, as to two questions which are totally distinct. The hon. Member opposite has referred—and the greater part of his speech was made up of that subject—to the practice of buying and selling and exporting arms and munitions of war. I am sorry that topic was touched upon, both now and on a former occasion, when I was not present, though I have read the proceedings. There is no law in this country that prohibits the buying and selling or manufacturing or exporting arms and munitions of war. It has been truly said by the hon. and learned Member for Plymouth (Mr. Collier), and by the hon. and learned Gentleman the Solicitor-General (Sir W. Atherton), that there is no country that has furnished such high authorities upon that subject as America itself. From the time of Jefferson, who, in that admirable passage read by the hon. Member for Plymouth, exhausted the whole argument in a few lines, down to the present time, every great authority in that country has clearly and distinctly laid down, that a Government is not

responsible for the dealings of its subjects in the munitions of
war. They carry on such a traffic at their own risk, and, if
they attempt to run a blockade, the Government is not responsible, and their act never ought to be made the subject of
diplomatic communication or complaint. I am astonished that
Mr. Adams and Mr. Seward should have mixed that question
up in their correspondence with that of equipments for war.
I will not say I was astonished at Mr. Seward, because he
writes so much, that he is in danger of writing on every subject, and on every side of a subject; but I am astonished that
Mr. Adams should have mixed this question up with what
is really a vital question—that of furnishing and equipping
ships of war. There is only one reason why I am not sorry
Mr. Adams has touched upon that subject. He has alluded
to large and systematic operations being carried on in this
country for sending munitions of war to blockaded ports.
That involves the risk of being seized by the cruisers of the
Federal States; and, as the only mode of punishing those who
violate the blockade is in the hands of those who are maintaining the blockade (and we know the blockade is violated
systematically—we know there are joint-stock companies to
do it)—as the only authority that can punish the guilty
parties, by the confiscation of their property, is the Federal
Government, through the Prize Courts; and as the only police
that can seize them are the Federal cruisers, it is well the
country should know what is going on; because, if in the
crowd of steamers sent out now, for the first time, to carry on
our commerce with the West Indies—though a few years ago
we were obliged to pay 250,000*l.* a year for a line of steamers
to carry our letters there—if, I say, in that crowd of steamers,
one or two innocent vessels should be detained by the blockading squadron, I think Mr. Adams has so far done good in
showing that their Government is entitled to some forbearance from us if those one or two innocent vessels should suffer
with the guilty. I am not going into the question of the

blockade now. I promise that I will deal with that question separately another time, and I shall be just as ready to meet your arguments on English grounds then as I am on the question now before us.

Now, coming to the real and only question before us—the infringement of our own Foreign Enlistment Act—what are the grounds upon which I desire to see the Government exercise the greatest vigilance in preventing the violation of that law? I say, first, it is because we, of all other countries, have the most at stake in seeing that law observed. How do I hope ever to see the Government supported—how do I hope to see public opinion sanction the vigilant observance of that law, but by making it clear to this House and to the country, that the Americans have a claim upon us for the due observance of that law, inasmuch as they have themselves at all times exercised a fair reciprocity towards us when we have had occasion to appeal to them, when we have been in their present position? I am glad to hear hon. Gentlemen who sit opposite say, ' No, no.' I like to hear an opponent say ' No,' if he will listen to me. And when he has listened, I challenge him, in all the records of our State papers, to show an instance, in our diplomatic correspondence, of a despatch having been written complaining of any unredressed grievance under the Foreign Enlistment Act of the United States. Now, what has been the conduct of the American Government with reference to this system of legislation? My hon. and learned Friend the Member for Plymouth stated truly, that all the legislation that has taken place in America upon the question of foreign enlistment has been at the instance, and in behalf, I may say, of European Governments; and I will add, that in a majority of cases, it has been at the instance and for the benefit of England. I will take the first Act, passed in 1794. I am not going to dwell on historical subjects, or to repeat the familiar history of Mr. Genet, and his proceedings in 1793; but the passing of that Act so remarkably illustrates the good

faith of the American people, that it cannot be passed over
without notice.   The United States had then been ten years
an independent nation, owing its independence mainly to the
assistance given by France.   In the course of these ten years
France had gone through a revolution; it had become a sister
Republic; and it sent out an envoy to America, claiming
assistance, and for the right of fitting out cruisers in American
ports.   It was against England, the old enemy of both, that
it sought this advantage.   What was the conduct of America
under these circumstances, the most trying that could be
imagined?   Why, we know that it required all the moral
power of Washington to enforce this law.   Not the law of
America, for in 1793 the United States had no enlistment
law; but they put themselves under the common law of
England, or what may be called international law, and they
gave us all the protection which they now ask us to give
them.   In 1794, they passed a Foreign Enlistment Act, and
at whose instance?   I will not weary you with long extracts,
or historical references of my own; I will give you what was
said by an English statesman, whose views will probably be
heard with some respect on the other side.   Mr. Canning,
speaking of the passing of our Foreign Enlistment Bill, in
1819, said : —

'In 1794, this country complained of various breaches of neutrality committed on the part of citizens of the United States of America.  What was the
conduct of that nation in consequence?  Did it resent the complaint as an
infringement of its independence?  Did it refuse to take such steps as would
insure the immediate observance of neutrality?  Neither.  In 1794, immediately after the application from the British Government, the Legislature
of the United States passed an Act, prohibiting, under heavy penalties, the
engagement of American citizens in the armies of any belligerent Power.'

That was not merely an Act to prevent enlistment, it was
a Foreign Enlistment Act, embracing our own provisions
with reference to ships of war.   That was the opinion of
Mr. Canning.

I come now to the next case, in which the Americans

carried out and enforced, in its entirety, the principle of
neutrality, under the provisions of the Foreign Enlistment
Act, in the year 1818.  At that time, the Spanish American
Republics were in revolt against the mother country.  We
generally sympathise with everybody's rebels but our own.
Mr. Canning and Lord Castlereagh brought into this House, in
1819, a Foreign Enlistment Bill, which was intended to make
provision for the more faithful observance of our neutrality
towards the Spanish colonies.  This Bill met with great resistance from the Whig party ; and, among others, it was
opposed by Sir James Macintosh.  I will read an extract
from the speech of Lord Castlereagh, whom hon. Gentlemen
opposite—even those below the gangway—will probably deem
an authority.  Lord Castlereagh, speaking on that Bill on the
13th of May, and using the mode of argument that would tell
effectually with his Whig opponents, said :—

' It was a little too much in the hon. and learned Gentleman (Sir James
Macintosh) to censure the Government of this country, as being hostile to
the South Americans and partial to Spain, while we had delayed doing what
another Government, which he would allow to be free and popular, had done
long ago.  He would ask him, had the United States done nothing to prevent
their citizens from assisting the South Americans ?  They had enacted two
laws on the subject, nearly of the same tendency as that now proposed.'

Now, I beg to remind the House, that not only is it true, as
my hon. and learned Friend the Member for Plymouth says,
that the American Government has passed its Foreign Enlistment Acts at the instance of European countries, but there
is this remarkable fact also to be borne in mind, as proving
the good faith of that Government and people, that they have
passed those Acts in direct opposition to the sympathies, and
even to the supposed interests, of the country.  In every one of
the three cases to which I have to refer, they went against the
national sympathies, and it required all the influence of the
leading and authoritative politicians of the United States to
carry the law against the popular feelings of the country.  But
now I come to the strongest case of all.  I am going to bring as a

witness a person who is present—the noble Lord (Palmerston) at the head of the Government. In 1837, as most of us are old enough to remember, a rebellion broke out in Canada, and when this House met in January, 1838, we were in a state of great apprehension with reference to the state of affairs on the North American Continent. Our apprehensions arose, not so much with respect to the rebellion in our own colonies, as on account of what was passing on the frontier of the United States. Great excitement prevailed among the border population, which sympathised strongly with the rebels; and the danger we felt was, that that state of things might lead to a collision with the United States. Soon after the meeting of the House, Sir Robert Inglis, interpreting the general anxiety of the country, rose and asked the noble Lord, who is now at the head of the Government, but who was then Foreign Minister, if he had any objection to state what were at that moment the relations between Mr. Fox, our representative at Washington, and the Government of the United States. Lord Palmerston replied, that fortunately he was able to give exact information, as he had received a despatch from Mr. Fox the day before; from which I infer, that the noble Lord and Sir Robert Inglis had agreed beforehand that this important question was to be put. The noble Lord went on to describe the state of excitement and dangerous agitation prevailing on the frontiers of Canada; how the rebels had taken possession of a place called Navy Island; how they had flocked there, and been joined by citizens of the United States, and how arms had been furnished to them; and how there existed, in fact, a most dangerous state of excitement. The noble Lord further said, that the Governor of Canada, Sir Francis Head, had sent a despatch to Mr. Fox, at Washington, complaining of this most unfortunate and menacing state of affairs; and now I will read the continuance of the noble Lord's speech with reference to the conduct of the American Government on that occasion :—

'Mr. Fox immediately communicated these facts to the President of the United States, and received in reply a most friendly communication. In the first instance, he had a verbal communication from Mr. Forsyth, the United States' Foreign Secretary, containing an expression of sentiments such as might be expected from the friendly spirit of the United States' Government, and the high sense of honour by which that country has been actuated in its dealings with foreign countries. On the 5th ult. Mr. Fox received a note from Mr. Forsyth, in which was a passage to this effect :—" That all the constitutional Powers vested in the Executive would be exercised to maintain the supremacy of those laws which had been passed to fulfil the obligations of the United States towards all nations which should unfortunately be engaged in foreign or domestic warfare." In addition to this assurance, that all the powers now vested in the central Government should be used to preserve neutrality, the President, on the 5th, sent down a special Message to Congress, stating, that though the laws as they stood were quite sufficient to punish an infraction of the neutrality, they were not sufficient to prevent it, and asking Congress to give the Executive further power for that purpose. Upon the receipt of this communication, a short discussion, in which many of the leading men, including Mr. Clay, Mr. Calhoun, and others of high character, participated, took place in Congress, and, without exception, all who spoke expressed sentiments of a most friendly disposition towards this country ; stating a strong opinion that the laws should be enforced, and that if, as they stood, they were insufficient, stronger powers should be given to the Executive.'

Now, let us pause to do justice to those great men, Mr. Clay, Mr. Calhoun, and others, who brought their great influence to bear at a time of immense excitement and dangerous animosity, and who threw their temporary popularity to the wind, in order that they might—as every man of public influence ought to do—make themselves the depository of the influence which they possessed for their country's advantage. I am going to put an hypothetical case. Let us suppose, that instead of the friendly answer which the American Government returned, the President had replied to Mr. Fox in these terms : 'I hope the people and Government of the United States will believe that we are doing our best in every case to execute the law, but they must not imagine that any cry which may be raised will induce us to come down to Congress with a proposal to alter the law. If this cry is raised for the purpose of driving the President's Government to do something which may be contrary to the dignity of the country, in the way of altering our laws, for the purpose of pleasing another Government, then all I can say is, that such a course is not likely to accomplish its purpose.' Now, with the simple alteration of the words ' United Kingdom' for ' the United States,' ' this House' for ' Congress,' and ' Her Majesty's Government' for ' the President's Government,' we have exactly the language which was used by the noble Lord three weeks ago.

I wish now to draw your attention to what was done in consequence of that promise of the American Government. Why, notwithstanding that the Foreign Enlistment Act, as it stood, was much more stringent than ours, and gave greater powers than ours now does, they passed a supplementary Act for the year, which gave such powers to the Government that one would hardly believe that such arbitrary powers would have been given to the Government of the United States. I hear cries of ' Hear, hear!' of a rather doubtful tone from the other side; but let hon. Gentlemen remember that that Act was passed twenty-five years ago, and nobody then said that the Americans were fond of submitting to tyranny. By this temporary Act, which received the assent of the President on the 10th of March, 1838, it was enacted—

' That the several collectors, naval officers, surveyors, inspectors of customs, marshals and deputy-marshals of the United States, and every other officer who may be empowered for the purpose by the President of the United States, are hereby respectively authorised and required to seize and detain any vessel which may be provided or prepared for any military expedition or enterprise against the territories or dominions of any foreign Prince or Power,' &o.

It gives them power to seize a vessel without any proof—an absolute power to seize on suspicion, and detain any vessel for ten days, during which time they may gather evidence on the matter. If there was no proof, the vessel was then to be released; but she was liable to be seized again if any new case should arise. To carry out this arbitrary and temporary Act, the whole powers of the militia and the volunteers of the

country were placed at the disposal of these officers. That
affords the third instance of the mode in which the American
Government has legislated for the benefit of European States.
But there is a fourth case, which affords another example,
which occurred on the occasion of the Crimean war. On the
breaking out of the war with Russia, in 1854, we sent a
communication to the American Government, and a duplicate
of it was sent from the French Government. We asked the
American Government—

'In the spirit of just reciprocity to give orders that no privateer under
Russian colours shall be equipped, or victualled, or admitted with its prizes in
the ports of the United States, and also that the citizens of the United States
shall rigorously abstain from taking part in armaments of this nature, or in
any other measure opposed to the duties of a strict neutrality.'

I will not now refer to the conduct pursued by the American
Government in reference to the ship that was about half built
for the Russian Government in America, and the building of
which was suspended. I heard some person whisper, that the
building of that vessel was suspended because the Russian
Government could not find the money to finish it; but will
any one believe that, when it is known that the Russian
Government were at the time spending millions a week at
Sebastopol? The vessel was not finished until three years
after the war with Russia. There was another vessel, called
the *Maury*, which was suspected of being intended for the
Russian Government, and was stopped under circumstances
which showed a great deal more activity and vigilance than
we have exhibited in the case of the *Alabama*. What I want
to deduce from all these facts is this:—First, that the American Government have, from the very formation of their
Union, shown a willingness to observe, maintain, and enforce
a strict neutrality in reference to the wars which have frequently taken place amongst European States. Next, that
they have done it under circumstances of the utmost difficulty.
It is easy enough to maintain neutrality when you have no
feeling the other way to contend with. They did it in spite

of their sympathies, and in opposition to their wishes. There can be no doubt, that in the case of the Canadian rebellion, there was a strong feeling amongst the mass of the American people that a successful rebellion in Canada would have led to the annexation of Canada to the United States. There is no doubt that the strongest national yearnings were enlisted on the side of the Canadians; and I want to call the attention of the House to the fact, that, in spite of these temptations to go wrong, the United States have uniformly gone right on this question. We may have had other grounds of complaint—I think, for instance, that in regard to our enlistments in America, they persisted in their resentment against us in a manner that partook of unfriendly severity, if not of direct hostility; but in the matter of their Foreign Enlistment Acts, I repeat again, and let no one answer me with a vague statement of what he has heard somewhere or other—I challenge any one to show me in all our diplomatic correspondence a despatch which complains of an unredressed grievance under those Acts.

I have mentioned these circumstances in the hope that they may become generally known, and in order that they may bring the sentiments of this House, and the public opinion of this country, to a temper which shall incline us to act by the United States as they have acted by us. If the motives which I have appealed to in this statement of facts will not have that effect, then I do not know that I ought to spend another minute in trying to bring any other motives to bear upon the minds of my countrymen. I do not intend to appeal to your fears, that would be out of the question; but I will not sit down without saying a word or two with reference to the interest we have in the question. If gratitude for the past observance of an honourable neutrality is not sufficient, let us look at what will be the consequence of pursuing another course. The hon. and learned Gentleman the Solicitor-General, in a speech from which I may not quote, as it was delivered

in a previous debate this session, and which he has published
as a pamphlet, laid it down, that we have only to deal with
municipal law, and that the Foreign Enlistment Act was
passed at our own will and pleasure, and that we may repeal
it in like manner at our own pleasure. The Solicitor-General
laid it down broadly, that the Foreign Enlistment Act was
simply a measure of municipal law, which we might repeal at
our own will and pleasure. Now, I join issue with the hon.
and learned Gentleman, and I say we are bound as distinctly
to the United States by the rules of honourable reciprocity in
this case as if treaty engagements existed. We have gone to
the Americans, begging them not to allow their citizens to
molest us; begging them not to allow privateers to be fitted
out; and when it is clear that there has been no violation
of their law, we are, I contend, bound to observe the same
honourable neutrality. The hon. and learned Gentleman says,
that if we choose to allow both parties to come and buy ships
of war here, no infringement of our neutral position would,
as a consequence, take place. That may be an abstract legal
truth; but what must we say of a statesman who stands up in
the House of Commons and gives expression to such a dictum
as that, to be quoted hereafter in Washington? I am not
going to discuss points of law with the hon. and learned Gentleman; that would be an act of presumption on my part;
and we may possibly observe neutrality either by abstaining
from assisting either party in the contest, or by rendering
assistance to both. Is that, however, let me ask, a state of
things which we ought to covet?

I should like to know from hon. Gentlemen opposite what
would be our fate if any of those numerous wars in which
we have been engaged, and to the recurrence of which we
are liable, if this doctrine were carried fully into effect?
If, for instance, the little dark cloud which threatened a
rupture with Brazil, had burst upon our heads, America
would, according to the theory of the hon. and learned

Gentleman, be entitled not only to build ships for us, but might fit out vessels for the Brazilian Government, to cruise in the name of that Government and with the commission of the Brazilian Emperor, against our commerce. But I will not rest my argument merely on the ground that this is a thing which might possibly happen, if we were to adopt the line of policy to which the hon. and learned Gentleman has, as I think, so unwisely referred. Can we, I would ask, look for the maintenance of the law relative to foreign enlistment in America or elsewhere, unless we ourselves set the example of good faith ? You have not only in America, but in France, a most stringent law on this subject. I wrote to a friend in France to ascertain what was the mode of proceeding there, in order to prevent vessels slipping from their ports, as the *Alabama* had done from ours; and I was told, that they required no Foreign Enlistment Act for the purpose. By a penal code, which I believe all the nations of the Continent imitate more or less, any citizen of France, who, without the consent of the Government, commits an act of hostility against a Foreign Power, by which the country incurs the risk of war, is liable to transportation. The law further provides, that anybody who fits out a ship of war, or does any hostile act, owing to which an enemy inflicts reprisals on a French citizen, will likewise be held subject to the same penalty. This, you may say, is very severe ; but then you want reciprocity with that country. The French do not ask you to pass a law in accordance with their model ; but what both France and America will require is this—that you will, in the event of war, as far as lies in your power, prevent privateers from going out and preying upon their commerce. You may choose any way you please to do it ; but surely you have too much common sense to imagine that you can induce America to abstain from such a system in the future, unless you observe the laws of a fair reciprocity in her regard.

Now, is there, let me ask, no way in which you can prevent

ships of war from sailing from your ports, threatening, as
they do, the commerce of a friendly country, all of them built
in England, manned from England, armed and equipped from
England, that were never intended for any destination, but
are roaming the seas without any fixed goal, and marking
their track by fire and devastation ? That is the question to
which you have to address yourselves; and, unless you are
prepared to set your face against this system, the Foreign
Enlistment Act will be, as the hon. and learned Member for
Plymouth said, a dead letter; and if it be made a dead letter
here, most assuredly the same state of things will result
elsewhere.

Who, then, I should like to know, has the most to lose
by the adoption of this system? I will show, by giving
some figures, which tell us how large a proportion of the property afloat on salt water belongs to British capitalists. The
lowest estimate I have heard formed of the value of this
property, as entered through the insurance offices in the City
and other quarters, shows that we have upon an average
100,000,000l. to 120,000,000l. sterling worth of the property
of British capitalists on the seas. Rest assured, no other
country has 30,000,000l. worth, and that you have as much
property at stake upon the ocean as all the rest of the world
put together. You have, moreover, 10,000,000 people in
these islands to feed upon food brought from foreign countries.
You get three-fourths of the tea and four-fifths of the silk
from China; more than one-half of the tallow and hemp from
Russia; there is more cotton, more wheat, more Indian corn,
brought to us than to any other country. You, who are so
powerful here, and can set the world at defiance in your island
home, are, the moment a war of reprisals is made on your
commerce, the most vulnerable. The hon. Gentleman who
says ' No,' does not understand the position of the commerce
of England. But be that as it may, is there, I would ask,
nothing we can do to show our good faith in this matter? Is

it not derogatory that we should have any one in this country,
and especially in this House, claiming to be educated and
reflective, who would for a moment consent to put himself on
the side of those who are committing those acts against the
law of the country and its future welfare? I want public
opinion to be ranged on the side of law in this as well as in
every other matter. Is there any person who wishes to give
his sanction to an offence against the law of the country?
Every person engaged in the building of ships of war, under
the circumstances to which I have referred, subjects himself
to penal consequences—to fine and imprisonment. Is there
any person who will encourage such a practice as that? Is
there nothing we can do to show that we wish to put it
down? The case of the *Alabama* is one that is, perhaps,
clearer than the case of the *Florida*, or the *Japan*. The last-
mentioned vessel was, however, one not only built here for
the Confederate Government, but manned by Englishmen
surreptitiously conveyed on board the ship. The *Alabama*,
it was said, escaped from our port under the pretence of
going on a trip of pleasure, and it was stated in one of the
despatches that orders were issued to have the vessel stopped
at Nassau. If she was to be stopped at Nassau, why was she
not stopped elsewhere? That vessel has been paying visits
to our ports in other islands, and has been received with
something like favour and consideration. There is a legal
difficulty, I know, raised—that you cannot stop a vessel after
her first voyage; but my answer is, that the *Alabama* has
never made a voyage at all; she has been cruising about, and
has no home. Why do you not forbid the re-entry of those
vessels into your ports, that left them, manned by a majority
of English sailors, in violation of the Foreign Enlistment
Act? Would any person have a right to complain of that?
Proclaim the vessels that thus steal away from your ports
outlaws, so far as your ports are concerned. If you were to do
what I suggest, other countries would follow your example,

and put an end to those clandestine proceedings by making them unprofitable.

It is our duty, in reference to the obligations of the past —it is our duty, in reference to the stake we have in future, to put an end to the present state of things. The whole system of the Foreign Enlistment Act is, I may add, only two hundred years old. The ancients did not know the meaning of the word 'neutrality,' as we know it at the present day. In the middle ages, people were hardly aware of such a thing as neutrality ; the first Foreign Enlistment Act is hardly two hundred years old, and since that time that system of legislation has grown up. It has been a code of legislation that has gradually grown up, and is now looked to by the nations to assist in keeping the peace, and preventing the catastrophe of a general war. Shall we be the first to roll back the tide of civilisation, and thus practically go back to barbarism and the middle ages, by virtually repealing this international code, by which we preserve the rights and interests of neutrality ?   I cannot but think that this House and the country, when they reflect on the facts of the case, will consider, that if they in any way lend their sanction to such a retrograde policy, they would be unworthy of themselves, and would be guilty of a great crime against humanity.

# AMERICAN WAR.

## II.

### ROCHDALE, NOVEMBER 24, 1863.

[At the general election of 1859, Mr. Cobden was returned for the borough of Rochdale, and sat for this town during the rest of his life. The following was one of his annual addresses to his constituents.]

It is to me, as your representative, a very happy and pleasant omen to find my arrival here greeted by so large an assemblage of my friends. It is not an unreasonable thing,— I think it is the least that can be expected from a Member of Parliament, that he should, once a year at least, meet his constituents face to face, to state to them his views upon the passing events of the day, and to hear from them in a public assembly like this what are their wishes and opinions with reference to his future conduct. Generally, when a Member makes his annual appearance, it is expected that he should have something to relate about the proceedings of the immediately preceding session of Parliament. Well, I should be very much at a loss for a text, if you confined me to the topics furnished by our proceedings during the last session. The best I can say of the present Parliament is, that it is drawing near to its end. It failed to perform any service for the country when it was in its prime, and therefore you will not expect any good from it in its decrepitude. The sooner it is returned to the country to undergo the renewal of the representative system, I think the better for the country, and the better for Parliament. Now, I think, when a new Parliament meets, it will have to be furnished with principles from the country. The great lack of the present Parliament is, that it is destitute of principle or purpose. Probably we, whom we will call the Free-traders of this country—we have a right to call ourselves Free-traders here, if we have anywhere—probably we are largely responsible for that state of things in Parliament. We have been, contrary to our professed principles, a kind of monopolists of the public arena for nearly the last quarter of a century. It will be twenty-five years next month since my friend here to my left (Mr. Bright), and so many around me, first joined together to commence that effort which has been alluded to by your Mayor, and which has ended now in the complete recognition of Free-trade principles. Now, during all that time, we may be said to have occupied pretty exclusively the attention of political parties and of statesmen. I found the field occupied by labourers who were advocating other principles. For instance, there were the advocates of parliamentary reform; there were the advocates of religious equality,—and by religious equality, I mean to deal, for instance, with that great and glaring abuse of the system of religious equality—the Irish Church,—which Lord Brougham has denounced as the foulest abuse in any civilised country. Well, we elbowed out of the way these questions; we had a question in hand that would not bear delay—we were advocating a question of bread, and employment for the people. After having accomplished our object,—and this last session of Parliament has finished the work, — it had just languid force enough to carry the last remaining measures to complete the Free-trade system—helped a little by the extraneous and rather exceptional proceeding of a foreign treaty—but at last, this present Parliament has completed the work of Free Trade. By Free Trade, I mean that it has settled that great controversy as between Protection and Free Trade. At least, there protection ends to-day; but our children must carry on the work. There is still the question of direct and indirect taxation; there is still the question of a large reduction of expenditure in the Government. But the great controversy as between Protection and Free Trade is now settled, and I say the next Parliament will require to be endowed with new principles by the country when we have another general election.

Now, some people say that there is great apathy and indifference in the country. I don't think there is a want of interest in the country upon public affairs. I think there is a lively interest in the public proceedings of the whole world, and the public mind is very demonstrative. But what I observe is this, that the attention of the country seems to be rather given to the affairs of other nations than to our own. We are something as a nation as you would be in Rochdale as a borough, if your Town Council were pretty generally employed in discussing the affairs of Preston, Blackburn, or Manchester, instead of its own. And it is curious enough, that whilst we are devoting more than ever of our attention to foreign politics, we are still constantly professing the principle of non-intervention. We have non-intervention on our lips, but there is always a desire for a little intervention in the corner of our heart for some special object or other abroad. I don't charge this against any particular party or any Government. We have all our little pet projects of non-intervention. For instance, some would manage the affairs of the Americans; others would take in charge to regulate the affairs of Poland; others are interested in Italy; and so it is that, in spite of our professions of non-intervention, we are, in fact, I think, as far as my observation goes, interfering more than ever with the affairs of foreign countries. Some people say it is the telegram; they say that Reuter's telegram is the daily morning dram, and that it so stimulates the palate, and comes in contact with the brain—America with a great battle, or Poland, or somewhere else—that we have no taste for the simple element of which our domestic affairs are made up. Now, for instance, we have at the present moment a party in this country advocating an interference in the affairs of America; for when I say interference, I mean that party here who advocate either recognition, or something which means interference, if it means anything.

I have seen lately the report of two meetings of constituents in the west of England, one at Bristol and the other at Plymouth, in which Members, Liberal Members, representing popular constituencies, have been recommending that the Government should enter into arrangements with some foreign country of Europe, in order to recognise the Southern States of America, and put an end to that war. [A Voice: 'Very proper.'] And you will observe, that the idea which pervaded the public mind, at least which pervaded it in the two cases I allude to—the speakers and the audience—the idea was, that this affair in America was to be settled in a peculiar way, according to the dictates of these particular parties. Well, now, I think, from the beginning, that during this American war, this lamentable convulsion, from which you have suffered so much, I think that one of the great fundamental errors in the conduct of statesmen, in the conduct of Governments, and in the conduct of a large portion of the influential classes in this country, has been, that they have made up their minds that union cannot be the issue of this civil war in America, and that there will be a separation between North and South. I told you when I was here last, when that spirit, if possible, was more rife than now, I told you that I did not myself believe that the war would issue in that way. I have stated that opinion since in the House of

Commons; and I declare to you, that, looking at what is called in a cant phrase in London, ' society ;' looking at society—and society, I must tell you, means the upper ten thousand, with whom Members of Parliament are liable to come in contact at the clubs and elsewhere in London; looking at what is called ' society'—looking at the ruling class, if we may use the phrase, that meet in the purlieus of London, nineteen-twentieths of them were firmly convinced from the first that the civil war in America could only end in separation. Now, how far that conviction—how far the wish was father to the thought, I will not pretend to say. I believe that the feeling has been a sincere one; and I believe it has also been founded on the belief that, looking at the vast extent of territory occupied by the insurgents in the civil war, it was impossible to subjugate it by any force that could be brought against them by the North.

But there has been, I must say, a most lamentable display of ignorance amongst those classes to which I refer, if you may judge by the conduct of the organs of the press, which may be considered the exponents of their views;—errors, for example, in the course of mighty rivers, which those in England can bear no comparison to, but described in your leading organs in London as running one into the other, utterly regardless of the rights of geography. There are States in America of 1,500,000 inhabitants, where there are vast shipping ports for raw produce to be shipped into various parts of the world. In the interior of that country, in one city, I have seen a mile of steam-boats moored side by side, not lengthways; and those great cities and the great commerce they possess form part of the strength and resource of North America. Your ruling classes in this country know nothing of this; you don't find it in the books of Oxford and Cambridge, which the under-graduates are obliged to learn before they can pass their examination. It is in utter ignorance of these resources that this opinion has grown up. Accident, perhaps, more than anything else, has made me acquainted as well with the statistics and geography of that country as my own. I think no one in this vast assembly will ever live to see two separate nations within the confines of the present United States of America. I have never believed we should, and I believe it less than ever now. But I will tell you candidly, that if it was not for one cause, I should consider as hopeless and useless the attempt to subjugate the Southern States; and I will tell the parties upon whose views I have been commenting, that it is the object and purpose which they have that has rendered success by the Secessionists absolutely impossible. Indeed, if the moral and intellectual faculties of this country had not been misled upon that question, systematically misled, they would have been unanimous and of one opinion. We were told in the House of Commons by one, whom it was almost incredible to behold and think of saying so—who was once the great champion of democracy and of the rights and privileges of the unsophisticated millions,—we heard him say—I heard him say myself—that this civil war was originated because the South wished to establish Free-trade principles, and the North would not allow it. I have travelled—and it is for this that I am now going to mention, that I touch upon the subject at all—I travelled in the United States in 1859, the year before the fatal shot was fired at Fort Sumter, which has made such terrible reverberations since. I travelled in the United States —I visited Washington during the session of the Congress, and wherever I go, and whenever I travel abroad, whether it be in France, America, Austria, or Russia, I at once become the centre of all those who form and who avow strong convictions and purposes in reference to Free-trade principles. Well, I confess to you what I confessed to my friends when I returned, that I felt disappointed, when I was at Washington in the spring of 1859, that there was so little interest felt on the Free-trade question. There was no party formed, no public agitation; there was no discussion whatever upon the subject of Free Trade and Protection. The political field was wholly occupied by one question, and that question was Slavery.

Now, I will mention an illustrative fact, which I have not seen referred to. To my mind, it is conclusive on this subject. In December, 1860, whilst Congress was sitting, and when the country was in the agony of suspense, fearing the impending rupture amongst them, a committee of their body, comprising thirty-three members, being one representative from every State then in the Union,—that committee, called the Committee of Thirty-three, sat from December 11th, 1860, to January 14th, 1861. They were instructed by Congress to inquire into the perilous state of the Union, and try to devise some means by which the catastrophe of a secession could be averted. Here is the report of the proceedings in that committee [holding up a book in his hand]. I am afraid there is not another report in this country. I have reason to know so. There are forty pages. I have read every line. The members from the Southern States, the representatives of the Slave States, were invited by the representatives of the Free States to state candidly and frankly what were the terms they required, in order that they might continue peaceable in the Union; but in every page you see their propositions brought forward, and from beginning to end there is not one syllable said about tariff or taxation. From the beginning to end there is not a grievance alleged but that which was connected with the maintenance of slavery. There were propositions calling on the North to give increased security for the maintenance of that institution; they are invited to extend the area of slavery; to make laws, by which fugitive slaves might be given up; they are pressed to make treaties with foreign Powers, by which foreign Powers might give up fugitive slaves; but, from beginning to end, no grievance is mentioned except connected with slavery,—it is slavery, slavery, slavery, from the beginning to the end. Is it not astonishing, in the face of facts like these, that any one should have the temerity, so little regard to decency and self-respect, as to get up in the House of Commons, and say that secession has been upon a question of Free Trade and Protection?

Well, this is a war to perpetuate and extend human slavery. It is a war not to defend slavery as it was left by their ancestors—I mean, a thing to be retained and to be apologised for,—it is a war to establish a slave empire,—a war in which slavery shall be made the corner-stone of the social system,—a war which shall be defended and justified on scriptural and on ethnological grounds. Well, I say, God pardon the men, who, in this year of grace 1863, should think that such a project as that could be crowned with success. Now, you know that I have, from the first, never believed it possible that the South should succeed; and I have founded that faith mainly upon moral instincts, which teach us to repudiate the very idea that anything so infamous should succeed. No; it is certain that in this world the virtues and the forces go together, and the vices and the weaknesses are inseparable. It is, therefore, that I felt certain that this project never could succeed. For how is it? There is a community with nearly half of its population slaves, and they were attempting to fight another community where every working man is a free man. It is as though Yorkshire and Lancashire were to enter into conflict, and it was understood that in the case of one, all the labourers who did the muscular work of the country, whether in the field or in the factory, whether in the roads or in the domestic establishments—in the one case, you would have that bone and muscle, the sinew of the country, eliminated from the fighting population, and not only eliminated from the fighting population, but ready to take advantage of this war, either to run away or fight against you. How could we, so circumstanced, fighting against a neighbouring country, where every working man was fighting for his own—how could we have a chance, if our physical force was crippled, and we were devoid of all moral influences? That is the condition in which these two sections of the United States are now placed. In the one case, you have a condition in which labour is held honourable. Have we not heard it used as a reproach by some people, who fancy themselves in alliance with the aristocracy—some of our Ministers, who would lead us to suppose they are of the aristocratic order?

Now, we hear it used as an argument against the North, that their President, Mr. Lincoln, was a 'rail-splitter.' But what does that prove with regard to the United States, but that labour is held in honour in that country? And with such a conflict going on, and with such an example as I feel no doubt will follow, I cannot, if I speak of such a contest as that, say that it is a struggle for empire on the one side, and for independence on the other. I say it is an aristocratic rebellion against a democratic Government. That is the title I would give to it; and in all history, when you have had the aristocracy pitted against the people, in a hand-to-hand contest, the aristocracy have always gone down under the heavy blows of the democracy. When I speak this, let no one say I am indifferent to the process of misery and destitution, and ruin and bloodshed, now going on in that country. No. My indignation against the South is, that they fired the first shot, and made themselves responsible for this result. I take, probably, a stronger view than most people in this country, and certainly a stronger view than anybody in America, of the vast sacrifices of life, and of economical comfort and resources, which must follow to the North from this struggle. They are mistaken if they think they can carry on a civil war like this, drawing a million men from their productive industry, to engage merely in a process of destruction, and spending their two or three hundred millions sterling—I say they are mistaken and deluded if they think they can carry on a war like that without a terrible collapse, sooner or later, and I am sure that there will be a great prostration in every part of the

community. But that being so, makes me still more indignant and intolerant of the cause; but of the result, I have no
more doubt than I have on any subject that lies in the future.

And now I would ask you—why do some people wish that
the United States should be cut up in two? They think it
desirable that it should be weakened. Will that view bear
discussion for a moment? I hold not. I am of the opinion
which our statesmen held in the time of Canning, who
thought it desirable for Europe that America should be
strong; desirable that she should be strong, because it would
thereby prevent European Powers from interfering in American affairs. That has been the case hitherto. That country
has prospered. It has never come to interfere with European
politics, and it has kept European Governments from interfering in other American States which have not been so
prosperous or so orderly as the United States. And now see
what has followed. See what has happened already from this
disruption of the United States. You have France gone to
Mexico; you have Spain gone to San Domingo. Why, there
are horrors unutterable now going on in San Domingo, because Spain has gone and invaded that country with the view
to re-conquest; and the French Government has embarked in
a career in Mexico which I will only characterise as the
greatest mistake committed by the monarch of that country.
This enterprise would never have been undertaken if the
United States had not been in the difficulties of this civil
war; and it is the least creditable part of these two enterprises
that they have been undertaken because America was weak.
But it only required that the North should have been a little
weaker, and then these silly people would have been going
about for an interference in America, and then they would have
carried out their project, and you would have had France and
other Powers going over to America to meddle in that quarrel.

Now, is that desirable? Don't you think we have enough
to do at home? Do you think, now, that Europe has so much

wisdom to spare in the management of her affairs, that she can afford to cross the Atlantic to set the new world in order? If so, what is the meaning of the utterances which we have lately heard from Imperial lips, calling for a Congress of the Powers of Europe? And what for? To form a new pact for the European States, because the arrangement entered into at the Treaty of Vienna is, to use the Emperor's own words, torn all to tatters. Well, but that is not very consolatory for us. We fought for more than twenty years, we spent a thousand millions of treasure in that great war, and the only result we have to show is the settlement at the Treaty of Vienna;— and now we are told that it is all torn to tatters! Well, I say, that does not encourage us to enter upon a similar career again—at all events, it means this, that Europe has quite enough to do at home, without going, at the instigation of silly people, to interfere with the affairs of America. I would not be thought to say one word against the project of the Emperor of the French to hold a Congress. There is one passage in his address which prevents my treating it with unqualified opposition or indifference. For the first time, a great potentate — the head of the most powerful military nation of Europe—has called a Congress, to devise, amongst other measures, the means of reducing those enormous standing armaments, which are the curse and the peril of Europe at this time. But this I would say, that if there should be a Congress, and this part of the programme—a diminution of armaments—is made the primary and fundamental object of that Congress, I am afraid from past experience that it would probably only lead to an increase of the evil. For I remember the Congress in 1856, after the Crimean war, which war was to establish peace, and enable us to reduce our armaments. After that war, we had a Congress in Paris in 1856, and they arranged the peace of Europe.

Well, what has happened since? There are nearly a million more men trained to arms in the two services in Europe now

than there were before the Crimean war, and England itself
has 200,000 of these men, besides a gigantic scheme of fortifications such as the world never saw before in one project.
One of the objects for which the Congress is to be called is
to arrange the difficulties and troubles in certain European
States. There is the case of Poland particularly referred to.
I am not unmindful of the claims of Poland, or of other
countries struggling for what they consider their rights; that
is, where they can show a programme of grievances such as I
believe the Poles can do; but I have not much faith in the
power of any one country to go and settle the affairs of
another country upon anything like a permanent basis; and
there is the ground on which I am such a strong advocate of
the principle of non-intervention; it is because intervention
must almost, by its very nature, fail in its object. There are
two things we confound when we talk of intervention in
foreign affairs. The intervention is easy enough, but the
power to accomplish the object is another thing. You must
take possession of a country, in order to impress your policy
upon it; and that becomes a tyranny of another sort. But
if you go to intervene in the affairs of Poland, with a view to
rescue them from the attacks of Russia, I maintain that so
far as England is concerned, you are attempting an impossibility; and if you cannot do it by physical force, if you cannot
do it by war, then I humbly submit that you are certain to
do it more harm than good if you attempt to do it by diplomacy. Mark what has been done in Poland on this occasion.
We have had three Powers, every one writing despatches
stating that, unless certain measures are acceded to, Russia is
threatened with the force of these united Powers. What has
been the effect of that? You have made the whole Russian
people united as against these foreign Powers. They might
not have been so exasperated against their own people, but
immediately foreigners step in, you have had the whole Russian people roused to a patriotic frenzy—not to oppose the

Poles, but to oppose some outside Powers that are attempting to interfere with them. The consequence is, that the Poles, who have been encouraged to go on by the hope of foreign interference, have been placed in a position far more perilous to them than if you had never interfered at all. Some people will say, do you intend to leave these evils without a remedy? Well, I have faith in God, and I think there is a Divine Providence which will obviate this difficulty; and I don't think that Providence has given it into our hands to execute His behests in this world. I think, when injustice is done, whether in Poland or elsewhere, the very process of injustice is calculated, if left to itself, to promote its own cure; because injustice produces weakness—injustice produces injury to the parties who commit it.

But do you suppose that the Almighty has given to this country, or any other country, the power and the responsibility of regulating the affairs and remedying the evils of other countries? No. We have not set a sufficiently pure example to be entitled to claim that power. When I see that Russia is burning Polish villages, I am restrained from even reproaching them, because I am afraid they will point Japanwards, and scream in our ears the word 'Kagosima!' Now, that word Kagosima brings me to a subject upon which I wish to say one or two words. I see that my noble Friend, the Secretary of the Admiralty (Lord Clarence Paget), who always enters upon the defence of any naval abomination with so much cheerfulness, that he really seems to me to like the task; he has been speaking at a meeting of his constituents, and he alluded to the horrible massacre which took place in Japan, to which, amongst others, I called your attention; and he says it is quite wrong to suppose that our gallant officers ever contemplated to destroy that town of Kagosima, with its 150,000 of rich, prosperous, commercial people—they never intended it—it was quite an accident. Well, unfortunately, he cannot have read the despatch which appeared in the *Gazette*, addressed to his own department, the

Admiralty, for it is stated in that despatch that the admiral had himself threatened the Japanese envoys who came on board his vessel the day before the bombardment of that city, that if they did not accede to the demands made upon them, he would next day burn their city. The threat was actually made, and the conflagration was only the carrying out of the threat. But there was another fact in connection with that affair for which I feel greatly ashamed and indignant. It is for the way in which it was managed—the stealthy, shabby, mean way in which it was managed — to make it appear that the Japanese were the aggressors in that affair. Lord Russell's instructions to Admiral Kuper were, that he might go and take this Japanese prince's ships of war, or he might shell his palace, or he might shell his forts. He does not tell him to do all these things; he was to go to demand satisfaction, and, in case that satisfaction were not given, he suggested to do certain things by way of reprisals, and one of the things he was ordered to do was to take these ships belonging to this prince. Well, the ships were moored—hid, as it were, concealed away—at some distance from the city, and steamers were sent by our admiral to seize these vessels, and they were not within miles of the fort which was firing on our ships. If the admiral had contented himself with trying to seize these ships, which were three steamers of great value, which had been bought from Europeans—had he contented himself, according to his instructions, with trying to seize these steamers, and waited to see if this brought the prince to his senses, there would have been no conflagration. But how did he act? He lashes these steamers alongside his own steamers, and then with his whole fleet goes under the batteries of the Japanese, and waits for several hours; and when the Japanese fire on him, he says that the honour of the British flag required that he should at once commence to bombard the palace, because he had been attacked first.

Now I remember—I remember quite well, in the case of a very analogous proceeding—in the case of our last war with the Burmese, I wrote a digest of the Blue Book giving an account of that terrible war, and to which I gave the title of ' How wars are got up in India'—I remember precisely the same manœuvres were resorted to. Some of the ships of war belonging to the Burmese Government were seized by our naval officers from under their forts, and because they fired on these vessels in the act of carrying off their whole navy, it was said that they commenced the war, and the honour of the British flag required immediately the bombardment of the place. Let us suppose that a French fleet came off Portsmouth, and took three of our ships of war at Spithead, and lashed them alongside their steamers, and then came within range of our forts at Portsmouth ; if the commander of these forts had not fired on these ships with all the available resources he had, he would assuredly have been hung up to his own flag-staff on the first occasion. Well, now, is it not deplorable that we English, directly we get east the Cape of Good Hope, lose our morality and our Christianity?—that we resort to all the meanness, and chicanery, and treachery with which we accuse those oriental people of practising upon us ? But we forget what De Tocqueville says in speaking of similar proceedings of ours in India. He says, ' You ought not, as Englishmen and Christians, to lower yourselves to the level of that people. Remember, your sole title to be there at all is because you are supposed to be superior to them.' Do you suppose these things can be done by us Englishmen with impunity —do you think there is no retributive justice that will mete out vengeance to us as a people if we continue to do this ; and if there is no compunction on the part of this community ?

There is a writer at Oxford University, one who writes bold truths in the most effective manner, who is doing it for the instruction of the next generation of statesmen—that is the Professor of History at Oxford. Mr. Goldwin Smith, treating of this very subject, says: ' There is no example, I believe, in history, from that of imperial Rome down to that of imperial France, of a nation which has trampled out the rights of others, but that ultimately forfeited its own.' Do you think those maxims, which we tolerate in the treatment of three, four, or five millions of people in the East—do you think that they will not turn back to curse us in our own daily lives, and in our own political organisation? You have India; you have acquired India by conquest, and by means which no Englishman can look back upon with satisfaction. You hold India; your white faces are predominating and ruling in that country; and has it ever occurred to you at what cost you rule? We have lately had a report of the sanitary state of the army in India; why, if you take into account the losses we sustain in that country by fever, by debauchery, by ennui, and by climate; if you take into account the extra number of deaths and invalids in the army and civil service, in consequence of the climate, you are holding India at a cost—if I may be permitted to use the term—of a couple of battles of Waterloo every year. Is there not a tremendous responsibility accompanied with this, that you are to tolerate your lawless adventurers to penetrate not only into China, but in Japan, in your name? The history of all the proceedings in China at this time is as dishonourable to us as a nation as were the proceedings in Spain in the times of Cortes and Pizarro. When they fought, they did not commit greater atrocities than Englishmen have done in China. They have them mixing up themselves in this civil war and rebellion for the sake of loot, for the sake of plunder, entering towns, and undertaking to head these Chinese—aiding the Chinese Government—in storming these defenceless towns. They are so far off; their proceedings are done at so great a distance, that you don't feel them or see them, or know your responsibility; but they will find you out, and find out your children. I remember when in the House of Commons, I brought the conduct of our agents at Canton, who

were opposing the Chinese authority—that is, the authority
of the Chinese Government—I was met by the present Prime
Minister with this argument: Why do you have such sympathy with this Chinese Government? Why, it is so detest-
able to government of life and property, and the people are
so insecure, that you can buy a substitute for a few hundred
dollars if you are ordered to be executed,—another Chinaman,
who will go and be executed for you. So terrible is the
Government, that they don't value life as they do in other
countries. Now, what are they doing? I get up and oppose
our assistance to the present Tartar Government, and am
answered by the same Prime Minister, why, you are defending
the Taepings; they are such monsters of humanity, and so
odious, and all the rest of the epithets are applied to them
which were applied to the Chinese Government. Yet now you
are supporting the Government against the rebels, when five
or six years ago Lord Palmerston told you the Government
was so odious, that life was not valued under it. How is it
that our Government is found in alliance with the most odious
Governments of the world? There is the Government of
Turkey, which is our especial pet and protégé. There is the
Government of China ; we have lately been interfering to help
the Emperor of Morocco ; and the Government of Austria,
which is only a Government and an army, and not a nation,
is also our pet and ally.

I will only say one word before I sit down, upon a subject
which I hope to see the order of the day again. I am talking
very much against my own principles upon these distant questions, but it is because they are made home questions and
vital questions by the course pursued by other parties; but I
want to see us called back to our own domestic affairs, and
first and foremost amongst those affairs, I consider—notwithstanding the attempt to shelve—first and foremost, and that
which lies at the bottom of all others, is a reform in the
representation of the country. It has been a fashion of late

to talk of an extension of the franchise as something not to be tolerated, because it is assumed that the manners of the people were not fitted to take a part in the Government; and they point to America and France, and other places, and they draw comparisons between this country and other countries. Now, I hope I shall not be considered revolutionary—because at my age I don't want any revolutions—they won't serve me, I am sure, or anybody that belongs to me. England may perhaps compare very favourably with most other countries, if you draw the line in society tolerably high—if you compare the condition of the rich and the upper classes of this country, or a considerable portion of the middle classes, with the same classes abroad. Well, I admit the comparison is very favourable indeed. I don't think a rich man—barring the climate, which is not very good—could be very much happier anywhere else than in England; but I have to say as follows to my opponents, who treat this question of the franchise as one that is likely to bring the masses of the people down from their present state to the level of other countries.

I have been a great traveller,—I have travelled in most civilised countries, and I assert that the masses of the people of this country do not compare so favourably with the masses of other countries as I could wish. I find in other countries a greater number of people with property than there are in England. I don't know, perhaps, any country in the world where the masses of the people are so illiterate as in England. It is no use your talking of your army and navy, your exports and your imports; it is no use telling me you have a small portion of your people exceedingly well off. I want to make the test in a comparison of the majority of the people against a majority in any other country. I say that with regard to some things in foreign countries we don't compare so favourably. The English peasantry has no parallel on the face of the earth. You have no other peasantry like that of England—you have no other country in which it is entirely divorced from the land. There is no other country of the world where you will not find men turning up the furrow in their own freehold. You won't find that in England. I don't want any revolution or agrarian outrages by which we should change all this. But this I find to be quite consistent with human nature, that wherever I go the condition of the people is very generally found to be pretty good in comparison to the power they have to take care of themselves. And if you have a class entirely divorced from political power, and there is another country where they possess it, the latter will be treated with more consideration, they will have greater advantages, they will be better educated, and have a better chance of having property than in a country where they are deprived of the advantage of political power. But we must remember this : we have been thirty years—it is more than thirty years since our Reform Bill was passed ; and during that time great changes have taken place in other countries. Nearly all your colonies since that time have received representative institutions. They are much freer in Australia and New Zealand, and much freer in their representative system than we are in England ; and thirty years ago they were entirely under the domination of our Colonial Office. Well, go on the Continent, you find there wide extension of political franchises all over the country. Italy, and Austria even, is stirring its dry bones ; you have all Germany now more or less invested with popular sovereignty ; and I say, that, with all our boasted maxims of superiority as a self-governing people, we don't maintain our relative rank in the world, for we are all obliged to acknowledge that we dare not entrust a considerable part of the population of this country with political power, for fear they should make a revolutionary and dangerous use of it. Besides, bear in mind, that both our political parties — both our aristocratic parties, have already pledged themselves to an extension of the franchise. The Queen has been made to recommend from her throne the extension of the franchise; and you have placed the governing classes in this country in the wrong for all future time, if they do not fulfil those promises, and adopt those recommendations. They are placed in the wrong, and some day or other they may be obliged to yield to violence and clamour what I think they ought in sound statesmanship to do tranquilly and voluntarily, and in proper season. If you exclude to the present extent the masses of the people from the franchise, you are always running the risk of that which a very sagacious old Conservative statesman once said in the House of Commons. He said, ' I am afraid we shall have an ugly rush some day.' Well, I want to avoid that ' ugly rush.' I would rather do the work tranquilly, and do it gradually.

Now, Gentlemen, all this will be done by people out of doors, and not by Parliament; and it would be folly for you to expect anybody in the House of Commons to take a single step in the direction of any reform until there is a great desire and disposition manifested for it out of doors. When that day comes, you will not want your champions in the House of Commons. You have one of them (Mr. Bright) here; you could not have a better. He and I began work at the same time, but I had the misfortune to be seven or eight years older. Now, he has a good Reform Bill in him yet. But I am not sure that I shall live to be able to afford you much help in the matter.

Now, before I sit down, I will merely say, I congratulate you that the prospects and condition of this community are not so bad as they were last year, and I hope they may not be worse than they are now. The ordeal through which you have passed has been creditable to the employers and employed. Some men rise in the world by adversity: I think you have done so. You have shown you are able to bear yourselves manfully against a very cruel and sudden disaster. I do not think that what has occurred will be without its significance, even in a political point of view. I have heard in all directions that it is an unanswerable argument, so far as you are concerned in Lancashire, that the conduct, the bearing, the manliness, the fortitude, the self-respect with which you have borne the ordeal through which you have passed, commend you to the favourable consideration of those who have the power to enlarge the political franchise of this country. I think that what you are going through will have another salutary consequence. It is a cruel suspense to which you are subjected, with cotton at 20*d.* or 2*s.* a pound instead of at 5*d.* or 6*d.* But be assured that it is working its own cure, and in a way to place the great industry of this country upon a much more secure foundation hereafter than it has been on before. The Cotton Supply Association in Manchester—I am not at all connected with it, and therefore I speak as an outsider, but one that has been looking on— has, I think, rendered a service to this district and to humanity, which probably it will be hardly possible to trace through future ages, in the diffusion of cotton-seed throughout that portion of the world where cotton can be grown, and by making the natives acquainted with the use of the machinery necessary to clean it; and by that means, I have no doubt that, in addition to a supply of cotton that will sooner or later come from the valley of the Mississippi from African free labour — for I sincerely hope there will never be another cotton-seed planted in the ground, with a view to your future supply, by a slave in America—that from all those sources you are sure—morally certain—hereafter to be supplied with that essential article for your comfort and prosperity, to a larger extent, and on better terms, and on a more secure basis than ever you have enjoyed before.

# CHINA WAR.

## HOUSE OF COMMONS, FEBRUARY 26, 1857.

[The words of the celebrated motion, whose introduction forms the subject of
the following Speech, were :—'That this House has heard with concern of
the conflicts which have occurred between the British and Chinese authorities on the Canton River ; and, without expressing an opinion as to the
extent to which the Government of China may have afforded this country
cause of complaint respecting the non-fulfilment of the Treaty of 1842, this
House considers that the papers which have been laid on the table fail to
establish satisfactory grounds for the violent measures resorted to at Canton
in the late affair of the *Arrow*, and that a Select Committee be appointed
to inquire into the state of our commercial relations with China.' The
motion was carried, on March 3, by fourteen votes (263 to 249). Lord
Palmerston dissolved Parliament, and gained a considerable accession to his
followers by the expedient.]

WHEN I see to how large an extent the national conscience
has been moved upon the question to which I am about to
invite the attention of the House, judging from the manifestations of opinion given by those organs of opinion by which we
learn what is passing in the minds of the people of this great
nation, and believing, from all the indications which we can
have, that there is a large amount of sympathy felt for the
subject of my Resolution, I can only regret that the task
which I have to perform has not fallen into abler hands.

But let me, therefore, stipulate at the outset that, whatever
may be the decision of the House, it may be taken on the
merits of the case, and that it shall not be allowed to suffer,
to any degree, on account of its advocate. I beg distinctly to

state that I have no personal or party object in view, and that
I have no motive whatever but to arrive at a just decision on
the important question which I am about to submit.  Personally, I have every motive for avoiding to give pain to any
one, and still more to visit with retribution the gentleman
who now fills the situation of Plenipotentiary at Hongkong,
who, except his conduct is endorsed and adopted by the
Government, I hold to be entirely responsible for the proceedings which I am about to bring under your notice.  Sir
John Bowring is an acquaintance of mine, of twenty years'
standing.  I can have no vindictive feeling against him, and
I have no desire for vengeance upon any person.  I wish the
Government had not adopted a hasty decision upon this
subject, as we might then, without embarrassment, have come
to a consideration of the case before us solely with the object
of dealing with it on the principles of justice.

Now, to begin at the beginning, it appears that on the
8th of October last, a vessel called a lorcha—which is a name
derived from the Portuguese settlement at Macao, on the
mouth of the Canton River, opposite to that where Hongkong
lies, and which merely means that it is built after the European model, not that it is built in Europe—was boarded in
the Canton River by Chinese officers.  Twelve men were
taken from it, on a charge which appears to be substantiated
by the depositions of witnesses, that some of them had been
concerned in an act of piracy.  Twelve men were removed
from, and two were left in charge of, the ship.  Immediately
upon the matter coming to the knowledge of Mr. Parkes, our
Consul at Canton, he made a demand upon the Governor of
Canton, claiming the return of these men, on the ground that,
by the treaty between this country and China, any malfeasants
found on board of a British vessel, and claimed by the Chinese
authorities, should be demanded from the Consul, and not
taken by the Chinese officers out of a British ship.  The
answer given to Mr. Parkes—and the whole of the question

turns upon this point—was, that the ship was not a British but a Chinese ship. The matter was referred to Sir John Bowring at Hongkong, which is about six hours' steam passage from Canton. On the 10th, that is, two days after, nine of these men were returned to Mr. Parkes. Three others, against whom grave suspicion existed, were retained, in order that their case might be further inquired into. And thus the matter remained, when Sir John Bowring determined that unless, within forty-eight hours, the whole of the men were returned in a formal and specified manner, and an apology offered for the act of the Chinese officers, and a pledge given that no such act should be committed in future, naval operations should be commenced against the Chinese. On the 22nd of October the whole of the men were returned ; and a letter was sent, in which Yeh, the Chinese Governor of the province, stated that the ship was not a British ship, that the English had really no concern in it, but that he returned the men at the instance of the Consul. That letter was accompanied by a promise that, in future, great care should be taken that British ships should never be visited improperly by Chinese officers. On the 23rd—that is to say, the day after—operations were commenced against the Barrier Forts on the Canton River. From the 23rd of October to the 13th of November, these naval and military operations were continuous. The Barrier Forts, the Bogue Forts, the Blenheim Forts, and the Dutch Folly Forts, and twenty-three Chinese junks, were all taken or destroyed. The suburbs of Canton were pulled, burnt, or battered down, that the ships might fire upon the walls of the town ; and bear in mind that these suburbs contained a population entirely dependent upon the foreign trade, and were our only friends in the neighbourhood of that city. These operations continued until the 13th of November ; the Governor's house in the city was shelled, and shells were thrown at a range of 2000 yards that they might reach the quarter in which the various Government officers

resided at the other side of the town. These things are set
forth in the pathetic appeals made by the inhabitants, by
repeated communications from the Governor, and by the
statements of deputations, including some men of world-wide
reputation, such as the Howquas and others engaged in
trade. This was the state of things up to the date of the last
advices.

I lay these things before the House as the basis for our
investigation, not with the view of appealing to your humanity, not with the view of exciting your feelings, but that
we may know that we are at war with China, and that great
devastation and destruction of property have occurred. What
I ask is, that we shall inquire who were the authors of this
war, and why it was commenced? and that I ask, not in the
interest of the Chinese, but for the defence of our own honour.
I ask you to consider this case precisely as if you were dealing
with a strong Power, instead of a weak one. I confess I have
seen with humiliation the tendency in this country to pursue
two courses of policy—one towards the strong, and the other
towards the weak. Now, if I know anything of my countrymen, or anything of this House of Commons, that is not the
natural quality of Englishmen. It never was our ancient
reputation. We have had the character of being sometimes a
little arrogant, a little overbearing, and of having a tendency
to pick a quarrel; but we never yet acquired the character of
being bullies to the weak and cowards to the strong. Let us
consider this case precisely as if we were dealing with America
instead of China. We have a treaty with China, which, in
our international relations with that country, puts us on a
footing of perfect equality. It is not one of the old conven-
tions, such as existed between Turkey and the other European
States, in which certain concessions were made without binding clauses on both sides. Our treaty with China binds us to
a reciprocal policy, just as our treaty with America does; and
what I say is, let us, in our dealings with that country,

observe towards them that justice which we observe towards the United States, or France, or Russia.

I ask, what are the grounds of this devastation and warfare which are now being carried on in the Canton River? Our Plenipotentiary in China alleges that a violation of our treaty rights has taken place in regard to this vessel, the *Arrow*. In the first place, I think that is a question which might have been referred home, before resorting to extreme measures. In the next place, I ask, what is the case, as a question of international law? I will take the opinion of one of the highest legal authorities of the country; for I should, after the statement which I heard made by Lord Lyndhurst in another place on Tuesday evening, think myself very presumptuous if I were to detain you by any statement of my opinions. I heard Lord Lyndhurst declare that, with reference to this case of the *Arrow*, the Chinese Governor is right; and I heard him say that, in giving his opinion, he could not do better than use the very words used by the Chinese Governor—that this vessel, the *Arrow*, is not in any respect a British vessel.

But we have other grounds of testing the legality of this matter. When Mr. Parkes communicated the fact of this visit to the lorcha to Sir John Bowring, he received an answer; and what was that answer? Sir John Bowring, being then within six hours' steam from Canton, receives the letter written by Mr. Parkes on the 10th, and on the 11th he writes a letter, in which he says:—

'It appears, on examination, that the *Arrow* had no right to hoist the British flag; the licence to do so expired on the 27th of September, from which period she has not been entitled to protection. You will send back the register, to be delivered to the Colonial-office.'

And on the following day, when not called upon to refer to the subject, he says:—

'I will consider the re-granting the register of the *Arrow*, if applied for; but there can be no doubt that, after the expiry of the licence, protection could not be legally granted.'

Now, I might stop here. Here is the whole case. But what course did Sir John Bowring recommend Mr. Parkes to take under these circumstances? I ask you to consider the matter as though you were dealing with another Power. If you please, we will suppose that, instead of being at Hongkong dealing with Canton, we are at Washington dealing with Charleston. Not long ago, a law was passed in South Carolina which went very much against the most cherished predilections of this country, by requiring that when a coloured citizen of this country—as much an Englishman as you or I— arrived at Charleston, he should be taken out of the English ship, put into gaol, and kept in custody there until the ship was ready to sail. Now, if there could be one measure more calculated than another to wound our susceptibilities as a nation, it was that. What did our Consul at Charleston do? Did he send for Her Majesty's ships of war, and bombard the Governor's residence? No; he sent to Washington, and informed our Minister of the matter. The Minister went to the Secretary for Foreign Affairs, and received an explanation, which amounted to nothing else than this,—' We are in a difficulty, and you must have patience with us.' And we had patience, and did not resort to force.

Now, had this case which we are considering occurred in America, what would have been the course of our Ambassador at Washington when he received the letter of our Consul at Charleston, saying that he had demanded reparation from the American authorities there? When he referred to the documents which he had in his archives, and found that, owing to the lapse of time, the instrument upon which the Consul had proceeded had become void, and therefore he had no legal standing-ground as against the American Government—which was precisely the case, as admitted in this instance, the licence having expired fourteen days before—he would have written back to the Consul, saying, ' You have been too precipitate. The captain of the ship, by neglecting to renew his licence, has placed himself in an illegal position. You have been very rash in demanding redress from the Governor of South Carolina. Make your apology as soon as you can, and get out of this business.' What was the conduct of Sir John Bowring? After telling Mr. Parkes that the licence had expired, and that the *Arrow* had no right to hoist the British flag, he added, 'But the Chinese have no knowledge of its expiration.'·

When I read that letter in the country, it was in the *Times* newspaper, I would not believe its fidelity, but sent to London for a copy of the *Gazette*, in order that I might read the document in the original. Always wishing to save the character of an absent man, and believing that that must have been penned in a moment of hallucination, I say that it is the most flagitious public document that I ever saw. The statement itself being published, reveals a state of mind which warrants one in saying, and compels one to say, that the statement is false; because there is an avowal of falsehood, and a disposition to profit by it. I have frequently complained of the number of public documents which are laid before us in a mutilated shape; I always regard with suspicion any letters which are headed 'Extract;' but what was the right hon. Gentleman about who had the revising of these documents? Why did he not leave out that part of the letter? For the credit of the country, and his own credit, I wish he had. At all events, let it be understood that, if we follow out the policy adopted by Sir John Bowring upon no better foundation than this, we take upon ourselves the responsibilities of his acts, and share the guilt of that statement.

Now, connected with this transaction there are questions as to whether, when the *Arrow* was boarded, she had her colours flying, and that her English master was on board. After what we have heard, I think all these questions secondary; but I am by no means satisfied that we stand any better in

regard to them than in regard to that to which I have just
referred. Hon. Gentlemen who have read the correspondence
will have observed that in the first letter written on this subject by Consul Parkes, he says he has proof in his possession
showing, beyond the possibility of doubt, that when the
vessel was boarded there was a British captain on board, that
he remonstrated against the acts of the Chinese, and that the
British flag was also flying at the time. Now, the fact turns out
afterwards that the captain, in his own declaration, states that
he was not on board the vessel; that he was taking his break-
fast with another captain in another vessel. That, however,
I regard as altogether of secondary importance.

But there is another illegality in this matter. Here are
two illegalities which you have to contend with. First, the
clear doctrine of constitutional law, laid down by Lord Lyndhurst, that you cannot give rights to a Chinese shipowner, as
against his own Government. An unlearned man like myself,
and the Chinese Governor Yeh, seem instinctively to have
come to the same conclusion. I cannot, for the life of me, see
how it is possible that we can invest ourselves with the power,
at Hongkong, of annexing the whole Chinese mercantile
marine,—of protecting it against its own Government, and
absolving Chinese subjects from their natural allegiance.
But, besides the illegality admitted by Sir John Bowring,
there is another: Even admitting that the lorcha's register
was all in order, and that the licence had been paid up, still
it is declared authoritatively, and is beyond a doubt, that the
Hongkong Government had no power to violate the statute
laws of this country by giving any such licence. The Hongkong Legislature cannot act in contravention of the fundamental principle of our Navigation Act; and therefore the
whole register and licence were mere waste paper, even if
they were in order.

Thus you have a threefold illegality to struggle against.
The noble Lord (Palmerston), I see, is taking a note. I wish

him to answer one thing that was said by his colleague in another place. Lord Clarendon, alluding to this point, used a very fallacious argument. He said, a Hongkong register could not give imperial rights to a ship, but could give only British protection to a ship in China. That is the very place where we say it cannot give protection. It can give protection anywhere else but there. How can the proceedings of the Hongkong Government, irrespective of the Legislature of this country, have any force in China? It is only through the instrumentality of an Act of Parliament here that the Hongkong Legislature exists at all; and none of its acts are binding in China, or anywhere, in fact, without the confirmation of this country.

I do not wish to convert this into a legal debate, and it would be presumption in me to say another word on this part of the question. The Duke of Argyle, indeed, finding himself beaten on the law of the case, says, 'Do not argue this case on low, legal, and technical grounds. You must try it on broad, general grounds.' I leave it to other Members of this House to vindicate the legal profession, which lies at the foundation of all civilisation, from the unworthy aspersions thus inferentially cast upon it.

Assuming, then, that the whole thing was illegal on our part—and this cannot be denied, for no lawyer with a reputation at stake, and who is not on the Treasury-bench, will venture to assert a doctrine contrary to that laid down by Lord Lyndhurst—I pass to another branch of the question, with which I can more appropriately deal. It may be true, that although the Chinese did not violate the law, still they might have had the intention to insult us. It is alleged, that in boarding the *Arrow*, the Chinese authorities did it premeditatedly, in order to insult us. Having the law on their side, they yet might have enforced it with that view. I say that is quite a distinct issue;—but let us see what grounds there are for

this assertion. In the first place, without travelling out of the
question, I may remind you of the exceptional character of
the trade carried on by European vessels on the coast of
China. We all know that a great deal of irregular trade
exists on that coast. Do you suppose it a very extraordinary
thing that the Chinese authorities should board a vessel of
European build, and carrying the British flag? In the correspondence relating to the registration of colonial vessels at
Hongkong, Sir John Bowring gives a case in which two
vessels entitled to bear our flag were seized by the Chinese
authorities because they had cargoes of salt. Being seized
under the Treaty, their contents were liable to confiscation;
but the Chinese Government had no right to retain the vessels
themselves. The Chinese having taken the vessels to empty
them, having dismantled them, and having kept them too long,
our agents made a demand for their return, and sent a ship-of-
war's cutter to bring them away. This might have been all
very regular; but it only leads to the inference that the
Chinese have occasion to visit our vessels without necessarily
intending to insult us.

I hold in my hand a communication from an American
gentleman, who left Canton on the 16th of last November,
and was one of those who entered within the walls of that
town in the rear of our forces. His name, which I am at
liberty to mention, is Cook; he lives at Whampoa, where he
has been for four years, holding the position of United States
Marshal, and therefore having jurisdiction over the flag of his
own country. In course of conversation, Mr. Cook, in answer
to my inquiries, stated many cases in which British ships,
with the British flag, were engaged in smuggling transactions; and he mentioned one in particular, of so very
glaring a nature, that I asked him to put it on paper, in
order that I might read it publicly. I give this as an
example of what has been going on in the neighbourhood of
Canton, because it affords a valid plea for what the Chinese

authorities have done in this case of the lorcha.  Mr. Cook,
in his letter, written to-day, says :—

'In answer to your query, whether I have any objections to the use of my
name regarding our conversation on China matters, I say, most certainly
not ; and I will give you the facts in regard to the seizure of the lorchas as
nearly as possible, from memory, having no data to refer to.  During the
summer of 1855, in June or July, there lay near our chop, which is close to
Her Britannic Majesty's Vice-Consulate at Whampoa, from ten to fifteen
lorchas, engaged in smuggling salt, and eight or ten of this number hoisted
British flags during the day, the salt being discharged at night.  The number
of vessels was so large at that time, in consequence of the Mandarin
boats having been sent above Canton to repulse the rebels.  But the Government could not keep ignorant of so bold a matter long, and twelve or fifteen
Mandarin boats, each containing upwards of sixty men, made their appearance
early in the morning, and captured the whole fleet, five or six of which had
British flags flying at the time, the Europeans (generally a captain) as well as
the Chinese jumping overboard and swimming to the different vessels for
safety, several of whom came on board of our vessel.  The Mandarin force
took the captured fleet to Canton, and the parties having the right to fly the
flag subsequently claimed their vessels, which were eventually returned, and
the remainder retained by the Government.  This is by no means an isolated
case as regards the illegal use of the flag, and you have only to refer to the
Hongkong papers to find plenty of cases where the right was questioned to
grant the flag, as it had been done by the Hongkong authorities.'

In justice to Mr. Cook, I must say—and without this proviso he would, I am sure, feel that I had been guilty of a
breach of faith — that he is as completely anti-Chinese as
anybody I ever met.  He wishes every success to every one
who will go and attack the Chinese for the purpose of making
them more American and more European in their notions,
and he would not be supposed to say a word to save them
from any horrors that you may inflict upon them.  Yet he
candidly tells me, ' You have chosen a quarrel which is the
most unlucky that you could possibly have stumbled into,
for ' (he adds) ' you have not a leg to stand upon in the affair
of the *Arrow.*'  I confess I listened with some humiliation to
what he said of the doings of ships carrying our flags ; and
when so much is asserted about our flag being insulted, I
cannot help feeling that it is such transactions as these which

dishonour and insult our flag. Mr. Cook, who, as the American Marshal, has control over the American flag, also said to
me, in a very significant tone, ' I don't allow any such doings
as these under our stars and stripes.'

In what position do we place the Chinese authorities by our
licences? I will tell you, on the same authority. A Chinese
goes to Hongkong, and by means of some mystification which
they have adopted there — such as becoming the tenant of
Crown lands, or becoming a partner with somebody else who
is—for, you will observe, the Chinese are infinitely clever in
matters of partnership, and are exceedingly prone to limited
liability—a Chinese subject, I say, goes to Hongkong, obtains
an English ship, and then gets an Englishman for a captain.
What sort of man is this captain? Why, any man with a
round hat and a European coat on will do. He is put on
board, and called the nominal captain. The ship is owned by
a Chinese; but they keep this man on board, who is generally
some loose fish—some stray person, or runaway apprentice;
for in this case you have Mr. Kennedy and another witness
both stating their ages at not above twenty-one. When we
hear of young men of twenty-one being placed in positions of
this sort, I think we may draw a very natural inference. In
fact, they are, I am told, nearly always runaway apprentices
of idle young seamen. They have plenty of grog to drink,
and nothing else to do but to drink it, for they are not expected
to take any share whatever in the working of the ship.

That is the process which is going on in the Chinese waters,
and it is most dishonourable, I contend, to us as a nation, to
permit it. One of the consequences which I should expect
from the appointment of a Committee would be a strict
inquiry into the trade carried on with China, and an endeavour to devise some scheme to put a stop to this disgraceful system of obtaining licences. Hon. Gentlemen will
be able now to see, from the letter which I have read, the
advantages of having one of these licences. A dozen smug-

gling vessels are seized; half of them, having a colonial register, are entitled to carry the British flag, because they have paid the licences and are registered. The Chinese authorities take out their cargoes, but are obliged to return the vessels. As to the other half of the vessels, they are seized and confiscated with their cargoes, and the smugglers also are kept. So that a smuggler who has a register can carry on his trade with nothing to fear, except the occasional loss of his cargo. This, then, is a reason why we ought to be tolerant to the Chinese, and not assume, as a matter of course, that they intended to insult us because they boarded this lorcha, even though the British flag might be flying at the time.

I must beg the House to remember who the correspondents were. On the one side, you have Consul Parkes, a gentleman of considerable ability, no doubt, and a good linguist (I believe some of us saw him not long ago, when he came over with the Siamese Treaty), but still a young man, without experience, and without having gone through the gradations of civil employment calculated to give him that moderation, prudence, and discretion which he may one day possess; and, on the other side, the Governor of a province which, according to Mr. Montgomery Martin's book, contains 20,000,000 inhabitants,—a Cabinet Minister, and one who has no doubt gone through all the grades of civil employment. Now, bear these facts in mind, and I ask any man who has read this correspondence, does it bear on the face of it the slightest intimation that the Chinese Governor wished to insult the British authority? Must it not be admitted—as was said by Lord Derby, in that brilliant and admirable speech of his—that, 'on the one side, there were courtesy, forbearance, and temper, while on the other there were arrogance and presumption?'

The correspondence loses half its effect, if we do not bear in mind the dates and the circumstances under which it was written. While it was being carried on, every day witnessed the demolition of some fort, or the burning of some buildings; and yet here, on the 12th of November, a fortnight after his own house had been shelled and entered by a hostile force—(I have no doubt that the officers and men who performed their duty conducted themselves with all moderation, but I am informed that they were followed by a rabble, who destroyed a great deal of valuable property)—Commissioner Yeh writes to Sir John Bowring in this mild and conciliatory tone:—

'Again, the twelve men seized were all taken back by Hew, assistant magistrate of Nanhae, on the 22nd ult.; but Consul Parkes declined to receive either them or a despatch sent with them from me. The letter under acknowledgment says that, had the authorities been accessible to the Consul, the affair might have been disposed of in a single interview. The assistant magistrate, Hew, was sent twice with the men to be surrendered; it is through him that (foreign) correspondence with me is always transmitted. Now, the assistant magistrate is a commissioned officer of the Chinese Empire. Heretofore any foreign business that has had to be transacted by deputy has been transacted by officers similarly deputed, and the present was a case of all others requiring common conference; but Consul Parkes had made up his mind not to consent to what was proposed. On a subsequent occasion, I sent Tseang, Prefect of Lay-chow-foo, to the foreign factories, to consider what steps should be taken; but the Consul now insisted on something more than (the rendition of) the men captured on board the lorcha. There being in all this no inaccessibility on the part of Chinese officials, what was there to make an immediate adjustment impracticable? Yet on the 23rd, 24th, and 25th nlt., the different forts of the city were occupied or destroyed; and from the 27th ult. to the 5th inst. a cannonade was kept up, by which numberless dwelling-houses in the new and old city were consumed with considerable loss of life. I still forbore, remembering how many years you had been at peace with us; but the people were now gnashing their teeth with rage at the terrible suffering to which they had been subjected. Imagine it, that the simple fact being that a seizure was made by the Chinese Government of Chinese offenders, whom it was a duty to seize, it is pretended that the British ensign was hauled down; and this is followed up by a movement of troops and a cannonade to the infliction of terrible suffering on the people. I must beg your Excellency to pass an opinion on such a state of things.'

Does not this letter prove that the man who wrote it under such harrowing circumstances had, above all things, a desire to conciliate and smooth down the differences which existed?

Nothing is more striking in this correspondence than the manner in which Commissioner Yeh constantly harps upon the same string—that the *Arrow* was not a British vessel. I have counted in the papers no less than eight letters in which that declaration is reiterated in different forms to Consul Parkes, to Sir John Bowring, to Admiral Seymour, and, I believe, even to the American representative. There are in-stances in which his language is as terse, logical, and argu-mentative as if it had been Lord Lyndhurst himself who spoke. Here is an example—and I read this extract, because it is the very dictum laid down by Lord Lyndhurst the other night. Writing to Sir John Bowring on the 21st of October, Yeh says,—' The whole question amounts to this—a lorcha built by a Chinese purchased a British flag ; that did not make her a British vessel.' I venture to say that West-minster Hall, with the Court of Chancery to boot, could not frame a decision more terse and more comprehensive than that. It is the whole law of the case. A Chinese, by buying a British flag, cannot make a Chinese vessel a British vessel. And it is a most remarkable thing, that during the whole of this discussion our authorities never once attempted to answer this argument. What is still more remarkable, Lord Cranworth talked a good deal about something else the other night, but he never attempted to answer it. I have no doubt we shall hear the Attorney-General talk a good deal about something else to-night. But I venture to say that we shall not hear any man, with a character to lose as a lawyer, much less a man who aspires one day to sit on the woolsack, declare in express language that the dictum of Commissioner Yeh is unsound in law. Here is another instance. Yeh writes to our Plenipotentiary on the 17th of November :—

' I have always understood foreign flags to be each one peculiar to a nation, they are never made so little of as even to be lent ; how, then, could a foreign nation do anything so irregular as to sell its flag to China ? '

Observe the acute reasoning of this man. He puts the question at once upon its real footing—'You have not made a Chinese vessel a British vessel; you have only sold your flag to a Chinese vessel.' He then goes on :—

'This appears to your Excellency a proceeding in accordance with law ; all I can say is, that I am not aware that foreign nations have any such law. As I have said before, therefore, had the flag belonged *bonâ fide* to a British merchant-vessel, it would have been proper to follow some other course than the one pursued ; but the fact being, that a Chinese had fraudulently assumed the flag, why should Mr. Consul Parkes have put himself forward as his advocate ? Simply because he wanted a pretext for making trouble.'

Upon my honour, I believe the whole matter is contained in these last words. I believe there was a preconceived design to pick a quarrel, and I very much suspect that there has been more or less encouragement forwarded from head quarters.

I might read numberless passages from the correspondence, but as the attention of hon. Gentlemen has already been called to them by the discussion which has occurred in another place, it is unnecessary for me to trouble the House with any lengthy quotations. I may say, however, that all the communications on the part of the Chinese authorities manifest a forbearance, a temper, and a desire to conciliate, which should put to the blush any man who asserts that they intended to insult the British representatives. I observe that in another place Lord Clarendon did not content himself with referring to recent transactions, but he said that for a long time past the Chinese Government and authorities have been encroaching upon the rights of foreigners, and have shown a disposition to infringe the Articles of the Treaty. I can only say, that if such conduct has been pursued by the Chinese authorities, it was the duty of Her Majesty's Government to take earlier steps to check their proceedings. Why did the Government allow us to drift into a quarrel, in which our cause is bad, if for years sufficient grounds have existed for their interference ? If, as

Lord Clarendon tells us, these wrongs have been inflicted upon English, French, and Americans, why, in the name of common sense, did not that noble Lord, or the Prime Minister, or some one in authority, say to France and to the United States, ' We are joint parties to the Treaty with China; our rights are invaded; the terms of the Treaty are not fairly fulfilled; let us make joint representations on the subject at Pekin?' That would have been a statesmanlike mode of proceeding; but why did the Government allow these infractions of the Treaty to go on until your representatives have stumbled into a quarrel, and commenced a war, for which, in the opinion of your best lawyers, there is no legal grounds? I deny that the assumption of Lord Clarendon is true. I say, that if you refer to the blue-books that have been laid upon the table since 1842, you will find most striking proofs that the Chinese authorities, in every part of the empire to which we have access, have manifested the most consistent and earnest desire to carry out the provisions of the Treaty.

I will make one remark with reference to the correspondence recently laid before us. Why was this blue-book laid upon the table on the very morning of the day on which Lord Derby was to call attention to the subject, and why was a paper presented in the name of the Sovereign caricatured by being termed ' Correspondence respecting Insults in China?' My experience in these matters almost tempts me to say that this blue-book was laid upon the table on that morning for the very purpose of mystifying us. Many hon. Members—plain, simple-minded country gentlemen—who have not so voracious an appetite for blue-books as I have, would say, ' Mercy on us! Here is a book of 225 pages, all about the insults we have suffered in China. It's high time that Lord Clarendon should interfere for the protection of British interests, and it's quite right to go to war on the subject, if necessary.' I have read the blue-book through;

and what is it? It consists of garbled extracts from correspondence extending from the year 1842 to the year 1856. What do these extracts relate to? A few street riots, a few village rows. An Englishman straying out of bounds to shoot, is hooted back by the peasants. An Englishman goes out shooting, shoots a boy, and blinds him. The Consul awards the boy 200 dollars to buy a piece of land. That is put down as an 'insult in China.' When I commenced reading the book, I thought—'Here is the record (garbled, as I will afterwards show you) of all the disputes and misunderstandings we have had with China since we concluded the Treaty which gave us access to the five ports of that empire.'

Now, I will ask the House to turn their attention to the position occupied by this country during the same time with regard to the other great Powers of the civilised world. What have been your relations with the United States during that period? Three times you have been on the verge of war on the subjects of boundary disputes, enlistment disputes, and fishery disputes. I have seen a large fleet at Spithead reviewed by the Queen, well knowing at the time its significance—that it was meant to back the representations we were making to those who are our co-religionists, and, I may almost say, our countrymen. Then what has been our position with regard to France? Twice we have debated the measures to be adopted in order to guard against the possible descent of the French upon our shores. We have called out our militia, and we have increased our fleet, for fear of violent proceedings on the part of France. What have been the relations existing between England and Russia? Those Powers have engaged in the most gigantic duel ever fought; they have waged the most bloody and costly war—for the time of its duration—that ever occurred—a war in which four or five empires were involved. I may be told that China is now plunged into revolution; but, within the last sixteen

years, has not all Europe been plunged into revolution?
Talk of insults to England! Were not all the English workmen in France driven from the railroads in that country?
If such a thing happened in a country whose manners, habits,
and religion are similar to our own, ought we not, in dealing
with an empire to which we have so recently gained admission, and which has had so little contact with the Western
world, to have exhibited more tolerance and moderation? Is
it not an insult to this House to bring down such a blue-
book as that upon the table, in order to make up a case
for Lord Clarendon, on the ground that we have had constant
reasons to complain of the breach of our Treaty with China?
I have said I would show the House that the extracts contained in this book are not fairly given. Many of these
extracts are collected from returns which were laid before the
House long ago, and I will trouble the House with some
extracts from the original papers.

Now, here is a letter from Sir John Davis, the British
Plenipotentiary, addressed to Lord Palmerston, and dated
' Hongkong, Feb. 15, 1847,' which, if it be in the blue-book
before us, I have not been able to find :—

' My Lord,—I deemed it right, on the approach of the Chinese year, when
Canton is crowded with idle persons, to address the enclosed official despatch,
on the 2nd instant, to Captain Talbot, not that I have any expectation of the
occurrence of acts of violence and disorder, if our own people will only behave
with common abstinence.

' The following extract of a letter from Major-General D'Aguilar, now at
Canton, will tend to corroborate all that Rear-Admiral Sir Thomas Cochrane,
myself, and the Consul, have had occasion to report upon this subject ; and we
have none of us any motives for seeking popularity by appealing to passion
rather than reason :—

' " I have been a great deal on the river, and constantly in the streets
about the factories, and extended some of my walks close to the city gates,
and have never met with anything but courtesy and civility. I believe a great
deal—I may say everything—depends upon ourselves, and that a kind manner
and a bearing free from offence is the best security against all approach to
violence and insult." '

Before I read a letter in a kindred spirit from Admiral

Cochrane, I may observe, that I have sometimes been accused of entertaining feelings hostile to the military and naval services. I have many excellent and brave friends in both services, and, although I am a friend to peace, yet in a case of veracity I would take the word of a soldier or a sailor rather than that of any one else. This letter is dated ' Her Majesty's ship *Agincourt*, Hongkong, Nov. 20, 1846 :'—

' My dear Governor,—In pursuance of the intention I communicated to you, of visiting Canton for the purpose of seeing, before my departure for England, the changes that may have occurred in the four years that have elapsed since I was last there, as well as to ascertain how far any just cause existed for the apprehensions of the British merchants residing at Canton, or for a ship of war being constantly stationed off the factory gardens, to her imminent peril, were any real hostilities to take place, I went there from hence on Sunday and on Monday, landing in plain clothes, accompanied by my flag-lieutenant and Captain M'Dougal. I walked for full six hours in every part of the town where I thought it likely to meet a crowd, finding myself, without intending it, close to the dreaded city gate, within seven or eight doors of which I passed some time in a shop, making purchases, the doors surrounded as usual by lookers-on from the crowded street that leads to the gate, of whom not a single individual showed the slightest incivility. On the contrary, some in the most friendly and respectful manner examined the texture of my coat as well as my gloves, the latter being, as you know, a curiosity to them. In short, I sought every position where public feeling was likely to be exhibited, and blinked none ; and I can positively declare that I, and those with me, passed through the streets with as much freedom and as little inconvenience as in any street in London, and met with precisely the same reception I have done at Shanghai or Ningpo, and if any circumstance had been required to confirm the opinion I have more than once expressed— namely, that the Chinese will never be the aggressors—the visit of Monday would fully do so ; and if I required further proof of the bullying disposition of my own countrymen among foreigners in the first instance, and their unreasonable expectations as to anticipated protection afterwards, it will be found in what has already passed, and in the statements made to you by the Consul on the first recall of the *Nemesis*, and another by her commander on her arrival here, that, on being ordered down the river after lying three months without moving from the factory gardens, the merchants made loud complaints, and I expected to have heard that she had been followed by a petition for her return. If the merchants would believe that their best, and by far most efficient, protection is to be found in their own circumspect conduct in treating the people with urbanity and goodwill, and avoiding rather than seeking sources of conflict, I feel persuaded that they will soon practically discover in these measures more persuasive advocates with the Chinese than in all the force I could bring against them.'

I do not know whether my right hon. Friend (Mr. Labouchere) can find that letter in the blue-book, but I have not been able to find it. The correspondence appears to me to have been culled to find some letters of a very different character.

I will only trouble the House with one other letter. It is a letter by Sir John Davis, written in 1846. You had riots at Canton afterwards, and great destruction of property. The letter is dated the 12th of November, 1846, and Sir John Davis, writing to Lord Palmerston, says:—

'I am not the first who has been compelled to remark, that it is more difficult to deal with our own countrymen at Canton than with the Chinese Government; and I offer the last proof of this in the fact, that it has cost me infinitely more trouble to make Mr. Compton pay a fine of 200 dollars, than to obtain compensation to our merchants of 46,000 dollars for losses which occurred partly from their own misconduct.'

I did not find that letter in the blue-book. Sir John Davis, also writing to Lord Palmerston, on the 26th of January, 1847, says:—

'I may add, that the subjects of every other civilised Government get on more quietly with the Chinese, and clamour less for protection than our own.'

Lord Clarendon gave great prominence to the case of the merchants.

Now, it is probable that I am the only man who would say on this subject what I am about to say, without being misunderstood. No one will doubt my mercantile tendencies. All my sympathies are with the mercantile classes, and my public life has been passed in enlarging the sphere of their honourable and beneficial employment. Lord Clarendon called attention to the English merchants in China, and said, they were all in favour of the violent proceedings which have been carried on in Canton. In one of these papers—which I need not read to you—I find a communication on that subject, written in 1847, by Sir George Bonham, who says, there are a great many young

men there, some of them engaged as junior partners and
clerks at Canton, who have not a large stake at issue, and
who are naturally eager to have access to the country, and
to compel the Chinese to break down the barriers to their
excursions; but that, on consulting the older and more experienced men, he did not find that they were in favour of
hostile proceedings, although he admitted they were in a
minority.    I sympathise with the position of the English
merchants at Canton.    It is not a pleasant thing to live on
the borders of a river, and not to have a distance of two miles
for exercise.    At all events it would not suit me, who am
fond of exercise, and I should be most glad to see them in
the course of being emancipated from that state of duress in
which they are placed at Canton.    One of my reasons for
regretting that which is being done is, that it tends to retard
indefinitely any such extension of the liberty of my countrymen.    But while I say this, I cannot lose sight of the fact
that there are a great many merchants in China who are
engaged in a traffic of a very exceptional character, which
is detrimental not merely to the health but to the morals,
to the souls and bodies of the Chinese.    That trade is founded
on a certain degree of licence and lawlessness; it flourishes in
times of disorders and commotion, and, anything which
plunges the East into anarchy and confusion, is promoting
the interests of these merchants and serving their unholy
gains.    With those merchants I have no sympathy; but I
am afraid that English merchants abroad do to some extent
merit the reflections made by the gallant men whose letters
I have read.    And I doubt whether it is always for their
benefit, as merchants, that they are placed in a position which
enables them to summon to their aid an overwhelming force,
to compel the authorities to yield to their demands.    If hon.
Gentlemen opposite will not take offence at a reference to a
bygone question, I should say, that there may be too much
protection for British merchants as well as for British agri-

culture. It is a fact, that while our exports are going on increasing, they are passing more and more through the hands of foreigners, and not through the hands of Englishmen. I speak from ocular observation and personal experience when I say, that if you go to the Mediterranean, or the Levant, or to any of the ancient seats of commercial activity, you will find the English merchants, with all their probity and honour, which I maintain is on an equality with that of any other people, have been for some time in foreign countries declining in numbers. At Genoa, Venice, Leghorn, Trieste, Smyrna, Constantinople, you will find that the trade has passed out of the hands of British merchants, and into the hands of the Greeks, Swiss, or Germans, all belonging to countries that have no navy to protect them at all. This is the fact; and what is the inference? It may be that English merchants are not educated sufficiently in foreign languages; but it may be also that Englishmen carry with them their haughty and inflexible demeanour into their intercourse with the natives of other countries. The noble Lord inscribes ' *Civis Romanus sum* ' on our passports, which may be a very good thing to guard us in our footsteps. But ' *Civis Romanus sum* ' is not a very attractive motto to put over the door of our counting-houses abroad.

Now, without wishing to do more than convey a friendly warning to a class with whom I have so great a sympathy, I may remark, that our merchants have at present a very large trade in China, in South America, and in India; and the same failings which have lost the footing of our merchants in the Mediterranean, may be also a disadvantage to us in China and elsewhere.

I come now to the consideration of the case of the Chinese merchants, as it is put forward by Lord Clarendon, and I will take the memorial of the East India and China Association of Liverpool. These gentlemen are telling our Foreign Minister what they wish him to do in China; and let hon.

Gentlemen hear what these moderate gentlemen wish to see effected :—

> 'That a revision of the tariff of Customs duties should be made consistent with the spirit of the Treaty concluded by Sir Henry Pottinger—namely, an *ad valorem* duty of five per cent. on imports and exports.'

That is certainly a tariff which I should like to see applied to Liverpool. Let my Liverpool friends begin at home, and put themselves on the same platform with the Chinese. They then go on to say :—

> 'The British Government should insist on the right of opening to foreign trade any port on the coast of China, or on the banks of any navigable river, at any time they may think fit, and of placing Consuls at such ports ; that our ships of war should have the free navigation of and access to all the rivers and ports of China.'

Let us by way of illustration, and bringing the matter nearer home, suppose that this is a document which has come to us from Moscow, and that it is addressed not to China but to Turkey. Let us read it thus :—'The Russian Government should insist on the right of opening to foreign trade any port on the coast of Turkey, or on the banks of any navigable river, at any time they may think fit, and of placing Consuls at such ports ; that Russian ships of war should have the free navigation of and access to all the ports and rivers of Turkey.' Can you imagine anything more stunning than the explosion that would take place at Liverpool if such a ukase as that was to come to us from Russia? As a friend, not an enemy, of these gentlemen, I must say that such language as that is to be reprobated. I say it is to be reprobated, because it tends to place us who sympathise with mercantile men at a great disadvantage as regards even the naval and military classes. Contrast the kind and conciliatory language used by General D'Aguilar and Admiral Cochrane with the downright selfish violence and unreasoning injustice with which the Liverpool Association would treat an empire containing 300,000,000 people. I think I know more about the trade of China than these gentlemen, and I will venture to say, that there is not

a great empire in the world where trade is so free. I only
wish that we had, not five ports but, one port in France,
Austria, or Russia, where we should have the same low tariff
as we now have in China. There is not a country on the
face of the earth where trade is carried on with greater facility
than in China. There is no place where if you send a ship
you can get her unloaded and loaded with greater despatch,
where the port charges and other expenses are so moderate,
or where you are more certain to find a cargo of the produce
of the country. You will find that statement corroborated by
the evidence of captains who have sailed to every quarter of
the globe, and who have stated before a Committee of this
House that there is no country in the world where trade can
be carried on with greater facility than in China. Mr. Cook,
the gentleman to whom I have already referred, confirmed it
to me to-day. He said, ' I have known a ship of 1500 tons
coming into Whampoa, discharging her ballast, taking in
her cargo, and sailing in five days.' He added, ' Can you
beat that in Liverpool?' I am afraid not.

But what is it the Liverpool Association want? Do they
think that by opening a dozen other ports they will necessarily, by sheer violence, increase their trade? That was
tried in the last war. We all remember the gloom which
hung over this country in the summer of 1842. It was once
remarked by Sir R. Peel, that the fine harvest of that year
and the news of the Chinese Treaty saved England from the
most fearful state of panic and distress. We all know that
the report of the Treaty with China, when received here,
raised the most extravagant expectations. Our friends in
Lancashire threw up their caps, and said, ' In an empire of
300,000,000 people, and with free access to the northern
ports, if every Chinaman buys a cotton nightcap, all our mills
will be kept going.' What, then, have been the results to our
exports? During the last three years, our exports to China
have not averaged more than 1,250,000*l.* Before the war

broke out, we had frequently years in which our manufactured exports amounted to as much as that. In fact, since 1842 we have not added to our exports in China at all, at least as far as our manufactures are concerned. We have increased our consumption of tea; but that is all.

I have here a letter, from the East India and China Association of London, signed by my hon. Friend the Member for Lancaster (Mr. Gregson), and written in so different a spirit from that of the Liverpool Association, that I have not one word to say against it, except that my hon. Friend has too great dependence upon what can be done for him by force of arms in China. You will find it stated in that letter that—

'Our trade with China has become one of the greatest importance. The import at the time of the Treaty was, in 1842, 42,000,000lbs. of tea; in 1856, 87,000,000lbs.'

It is hardly fair to compare these years, because 1842 was a year of war, while 1856 was a year of large consumption. The statement in the letter with respect to silk is still more fallacious. It is this:—

'In 1842 (yearly average), 3000 bales; in 1856, 56,000 bales.'

Well, that may be accounted for by the failure of the silk crops in France and other parts of Europe; and it is an illustration of the immense resources of China, that when you have a sudden demand for silk, owing to the failure of the crops in Europe, by sending silver you can get any supply you want from China, no matter how unexpected may be the demand. But it is not fair to put that as the normal state of our trade.

I have said that our imports have increased. Those imports have been paid largely by opium. It is said that our exports to India have also increased. True, our merchants may send their longcloths to India, and there exchange them for opium; that opium may go to China, and in return for it we may get silver back to India or to England. But I apprehend that if the land in India were not employed in growing poppies, it would be employed in growing something else, enabling the natives to buy the longcloths of England, and that if the Chinese were not spending large sums upon opium, they, too, would buy something else. That question, however, I shall not go into; it is a very large one, and would be apt to excite angry passions. What I wish to say is, when the Liverpool merchants ask you to compel China to admit them to all her rivers, accompanied by ships of war, and to allow them to set up their shops wherever they please, do not, upon their authority, be deluded into the belief that the war in 1842 has increased our trade with China, and that a new war is likely to be followed by similar results. I venture to predict that the hostilities in which we are now engaged with China will diminish, not increase, our exports.

Having trespassed so long upon the attention of the House, I shall allude to only one other point—the claim of foreigners for admission to Canton. I have been careful to word my motion with a salvo upon that question. I am of opinion, whatever doubts may be entertained by others, that when the Treaty was signed in 1842, it was contemplated that foreigners should have as free access to Canton as to Shanghai or any other of the open ports. But a controversy has been carried on on that subject between our officials at Hongkong and the authorities at Canton. In the papers will be found despatches, not only from Mr. Bonham, but from the noble Lord now at the head of the Government, in which the very best possible grounds are urged why our authorities at Hongkong should not persist in trying to gain admission for English merchants to Canton. It is stated, and I think in good faith, that the population of Canton, and, in fact, the population of that province of which Canton is the capital, is fierce and ungovernable; that they have hostile feelings towards the English; and that, if our merchants were admitted into Canton, the greater contact would only lead to greater ill-will. I believe that apprehension is well founded. Whether it arises from the fierce and lawless disposition of the Chinese, or from their past intercourse with the East India Company—which, we all know, yielded much for a little temporary peace—or whether it appertains to their southern clime, for in all countries the southern region is inhabited by the more fierce and turbulent part of the population—I know not; but certain it is that these Cantonese entertain feelings of the most hostile kind towards the foreigners, and I believe it was in good faith that it was urged by the Chinese Commissioner, by our own Plenipotentiary, and by Lord Palmerston himself, that it was not desirable to press further the question of admission into Canton.

But let our merchants bear in mind, that what we are now fighting for is not the admission of foreigners into Canton. The *sine quâ non* of Sir John Bowring, who certainly, I believe with Lord Derby, has a monomania about getting into Canton, is that the foreign authorities, not the foreign merchants, should be allowed to enter that city. I will ask the House, is it worth while fighting for this, that Sir John Bowring should have the right to go into Canton in one costume or another, especially when the Governor was ready to meet him half way out of the town? I have always thought, that if a person of state and dignity left his own palace to meet another half way, it was a greater compliment than staying and making the reception at home. I cannot understand what we are fighting for, and why Sir John Bowring should think himself degraded by an interview with Governor Yeh at Howqua's packing-house. This is a topic worth nothing but a laugh.

But is this admission to Canton, for which we are fighting, of any use? Canton is a walled city, occupied by a native population, with streets eight feet wide. Would any Englishman ever dream of living in such a place? Does an Englishman live in the Turkish quarters of Constantinople? No; the habits and religion of the two races separate them. What would be the advantage to English residents in that part of China to admission into Canton? If they had free access into the country, and could take a ride or a walk for exercise, that would be a benefit to them; but the population in the neighbourhood is turbulent and insubordinate, and our countrymen are not likely to receive good treatment there; and if the privilege were conceded, nobody would ever go into the city except to stare about him, or to make an observation for his note-book. I apprehend that what the Cantonese authorities say is true—that the population is so turbulent, that Englishmen could not expect very good treatment.

But if admission to Canton were desirable, is this the time for pressing it? The blue-book teems with reasons against such an idea. What do the inhabitants of Canton say in their address? They say :—

' The late affair of the lorcha was a trifle; it was no case for deep-seated animosity, as a great offence that could not be forgotten; yet you have suddenly taken up arms, and for several days you have been firing shell, until you have burned dwellings and destroyed people in untold numbers. It cannot be either told how many old people, infants, and females have left their homes in affliction. If your countrymen have not seen this, they have surely heard, have they not, that such is the case? What offence has been committed by the people of Canton that such a calamity should befall them? Again, it is come to our knowledge that you are insisting on official receptions within the city. This is doubtless with a view to amicable relations; but, when your only proceeding is to open a fire upon us which destroys the people, supposing that you were to obtain admission into the city, still the sons, brothers, and kindred of the people, whom you have burned out and killed, will be ready to lay down their lives to be avenged on your countrymen, nor will the authorities be able to prevent them '

There is great good sense in that; and one of Governor Yeh's letters might have been penned by the Duke of Wellington—it is so sententious. I allude to that in which Governor Yeh, in answer to Sir John Bowring, who asked for admission to Canton, stated that he could not go out of his palace on account of the people, who were complaining of the proceedings of the English. He says, 'If I went into the town, I do not know how I should ever get out again;' meaning that the people would so crowd upon him with their complaints. On the same subject, Governor Yeh wrote to Sir John Bowring :—

'In a letter from his Excellency Admiral Seymour, received some days ago, he says, that the present proposition is in no way connected with those of former years; that his demand is simply for the admission of the foreign representatives. The proposition made before was objected to by the entire population of Canton; the people affected by the present proposition are the same Canton people; the city is the same Canton city; it is not another and separate Canton city. How can it be said that there is no connection whatever between the two propositions? But more than this, the Canton people are very fierce and violent, differing in temper from the inhabitants of other provinces; admission into the city was refused you in 1849 by the people of Canton; and the people of Canton of the present day are the people of Canton of the year 1849; and there is this additional difficulty in mooting the question of admitting British subjects into the city now, namely, that the strong feeling against your Excellency's countrymen having been aggravated by the terrible suffering to which the people have been subjected without a cause, they are even more averse to the concession than they were before.'

That is perfectly natural, and should have put an end to the mooting of the question at the time. It is important that hon. Gentlemen should address themselves to this point, on which there is much misconception out of doors—namely, do the Chinese authorities act in good faith when they tell you that they cannot with convenience or safety carry out that clause of the Treaty which provides for the admission of the English into Canton? I believe that they act in good faith, and the facts, I think, prove it. A previous Governor of Canton wrote to his Emperor with quaintness, but much truth,—'The inhabitants of Canton who are anxious to fight are many, but those who are conversant with justice are few.' I think that this may also be said of the merchants of Liverpool, whose memorial I have read. The papers already before Parliament are full of proofs of the kind. There is a communication from Sir George Bonham, stating that when a number of our merchants removed to Foo-Chow-foo they took with them their native servants from Canton ; but these were found to be so pugnacious that the inhabitants of the province of Fokien, in which Foo-Chow-foo is situated, begged that they (the Cantonese) might all be sent away.  But, under any circumstances, I do not think that our admission to the city of Canton would be of a farthing's use.  There are thousands of inhabitants outside the walls, in the suburbs which have been destroyed, and these are the shopkeepers and brokers.  It is with them that we do business, and, if we had free access into the city, we should still have to do our business outside.  Therefore, we have no grievance against the Chinese for not opening Canton.

But, supposing everything I have said on this subject could be contradicted and invalidated, I have only to ask, whether it is right that, with respect to a country with which we have Treaty alliances, our representative should be allowed to declare war, and carry on war, without sanction from this country?  That is a question which I intend scarcely to touch upon, because others will be able to deal with it better ; but it is apparent, on the face of these papers, that the very difficulty into which we have fallen was foreseen, and that our authorities on the spot have been warned against the very acts they have committed.  It is not merely that they have acted against general principles, which it is the interest of all nations to regard ; but Sir John Bowring has acted positively contrary to his instructions in regard to the employment of troops.  There are letters from Lords Malmesbury and Granville, and particularly one from Earl Grey, which one can read and understand ; and these letters gave peremptory directions, that on no account aggressive measures should be resorted to without recourse to England.  You have, therefore, to deal with your representative abroad, who not only has violated a sound principle of international law, but has gone against express injunctions.  I perceive a great change in the tone of the correspondence between Sir John

Bowring and Lord Clarendon, and that which passed between him and other Ministers with whom he had to deal. When Lord Clarendon came into office, there seemed to be some slackening of the rein, leading to the inference that the check previously held over our representative was withdrawn, and that we were 'drifting' into a war with China, as we had into the late war, from the want of a firm hand on the part of persons in authority. Recollecting the instructions of Earl Grey, and looking into the correspondence that has taken place, I cannot help surmising that something must have occurred to lead our Plenipotentiary to suppose, that if we got into a conflict with the Chinese on the question of entering Canton, it would not be unfavourably regarded at home. The manner, then, in which we have been dragged into war, and the position of difficulty in which we have been placed, are much to be deplored. But, looking to the future, I think that you must confess that you find yourselves in a very difficult position. What are you going to do? You have destroyed the whole of the suburbs of the town of Canton; you have destroyed the modern residences of the merchants down to the river's edge; you have destroyed several hundred yards of streets in the old town; that is to say, the busy places of commerce. Right and left, houses have perished, or been burnt up by incendiaries, pillaged by rebels, or bombarded in order that freer range may be given to our guns. I have spoken to some of those who have come from China since this affair began, and they assure me that capitalists will desert Canton, and that the town will never be able to recover its business. They have deserted Canton because they felt too insecure to carry on their business, and it is supposed that that feeling will be lasting. The general impression is, that capital will depart from Canton, and receive employment in other ports. You have, therefore, destroyed that very port on which your commerce depended. It is surely not that for which you are carrying on war.

And what is to be your position for the future? You have
entered into a war which cannot be defended.  Sir John Bowring did not tell Commissioner Yeh that this was not a legal
ship; but our debates are published to the world.  Lord Lyndhurst is an authority in America and France as well as here
What will they think of us when they read that the noble
and learned Lord has declared the quarrel to be founded, on
our part, on a triple illegality, and that we cannot really
urge a single fact in defence of our conduct?  We had a very
good case before, if we had chosen to insist upon it; but the
noble Lord at the head of the Government has given up the
claim for admission into Canton.  You might have gone to
Pekin and said, ' Fulfil the Treaty of 1842, open the gates of
Canton as you promised to do.'  But Lord Clarendon says
that this quarrel has nothing whatever to do with that.  No;
it was necessary that that ground should be abandoned,
because, bad as this case is, the present Government could
rely upon no other defence than this about the *Arrow*, inasmuch as the question about entering would get up an old
controversy, to which other nations were not parties.  They
were, therefore, obliged to raise a quarrel in which they
expected other nations would join.  But do you suppose that
France and America will join with you now, and join in
making common cause with you on the ground of this *Arrow?*
I speak advisedly when I say, that I believe the American
Government will not approve the course that has been taken.
I believe they will not join in these violent proceedings.
There are some people who know the French Government
better than I do; but is it likely, when you have so bad,
so wretched, and so dirty a case as this of the *Arrow*, that
any one will take share in it on your side?  You must give up
your case some time or other; and when so proper a time
as this to declare that you do not approve these miserable
proceedings, which have been carried on in your name un-
warrantably by your subordinate representatives?

But may not this war, if it should go on, lead to complications with other Powers? May it not lead to complications with America? I see in these papers that the American merchants immediately protested against it. An American house at Canton has publicly protested against this war, as having been commenced without notice, and have declared that they will therefore hold England responsible for any damage that may be done to their property. Well, what do you propose for the future? Part of the wall of Canton was battered down in the expectation that the Governor would yield. But he has not yielded, although you have bombarded the city itself, and thrown shells into it. What, then, do you propose to do? You have done everything short of burning the town—if, indeed, that has not been commenced. If you do that, you will raise a cry of horror from every civilised people. I see by the Indian papers that the *Friend of India*, which is always a great advocate of annexation, tells Sir John Bowring to play the part of another Clive, and to enter upon a career of conquest, and to annex China as we have annexed India. Are you sure that extensive territorial acquisitions in China would be acquiesced in by other Powers? The United States of America are only half the distance from China that you are. They have a great Pacific as well as an Atlantic empire. I am not sure that America would acquiesce in your making an India of China. Does anybody who knows anything about China believe that you could annex it? It is an empire of 300,000,000 people. How are you to govern them? Nobody that has ever thought upon the subject would dream of your being able to do so.

Then what do you propose to do? I say, undo what you have done. The wisest course which you could adopt would be to repudiate the acts of your representative, who has acted without authority and without instructions. That would be a statesmanlike and prudent course. Disavow the acts of your representatives in this miserable affair of the *Arrow*; but try,

at the same time, to get those facilities of international intercourse in that great country which your merchants so much
desire, and which your representations will, in all probability,
enable you to obtain. America and France would lend you
a joint influence in making such representations, which you
never can hope to have while you are fighting on behalf of
this affair of the *Arrow.*

But I have said enough with regard to my view upon the
subject; I leave the matter in the hands of the House. I
hope we shall not hear it said in this House—as it has been
in another place—that these are barbarous people, and that
you must deal with them by force. I tell you, that if you
attempt to deal thus with them, it will be a difficult matter,
and one, too, that will be costly to the people of this country.
You will be disappointed, and deservedly so, if relying upon
the supposition that you will be able to coerce the Chinese
Government by force—you will be disappointed if you think
that you will be repaid by increased commerce for the employment of violence. If you make the attempt, you will be
disappointed again, as you have been disappointed before.
And are these people so barbarous that we should attempt
to coerce them by force into granting what we wish? Here
is an empire in which is the only relic of the oldest civilisation
of the world—one which 2700 years ago, according to some
authorities, had a system of primary education—which had
its system of logic before the time of Aristotle, and its code
of morals before that of Socrates. Here is a country which
has had its uninterrupted traditions and histories for so long
a period—that supplied silks and other articles of luxury to
the Romans 2000 years ago! They are the very soul of commerce in the East. You find them carrying on their industry
in foreign countries with that assiduity and laboriousness
which characterise the Scotch and the Swiss. You find them,
not as barbarians at home, where they cultivate all the arts
and sciences, and where they have carried all, except one, to a

point of perfection but little below our own—but that one is war. You have there a people who have carried agriculture to such a state as to become horticulture, and whose great cities rival in population those of the Western world. There must be something in such a people deserving of respect. If, in speaking of them, we stigmatize them as barbarians, and threaten them with force because we say they are inaccessible to reason, it must be because we do not understand them; because their ways are not our ways, nor our ways theirs. Is not so venerable an empire as that deserving of some sympathy—at least of some justice — at the hands of conservative England? To the representatives of the people in this House I commend this question, with full confidence that they will do justice to that people.

# FOREIGN POLICY.

# FOREIGN POLICY.

## I.

### HOUSE OF COMMONS, JUNE 12, 1849.

[In the year 1849, the revolutionary or reforming spirit, which had agitated Europe for a year before, was either repressed by violence, or had grown languid by reaction. Among the events, however, which excited the feelings of the English people strongly, was the armed intervention of Russia in the affairs of Hungary, and in support of the despotism of Austria. There is little doubt that the indignation which was roused in England at this act of the Emperor Nicholas, gave strength, a few years subsequently, to the feeling which prompted the Crimean War. Mr. Cobden on both occasions pleaded for the adoption of a principle of non-intervention. On the present, his motion, which ran, ' That an humble address be presented to Her Majesty, praying that she will be graciously pleased to direct her Principal Secretary of State for Foreign Affairs to enter into communications with Foreign Powers, inviting them to concur in Treaties, binding the respective parties, in the event of any future misunderstanding, which cannot be arranged by amicable negotiation, to refer the matter in dispute to the decision of arbitrators,' was rejected by moving the previous question. Majority, 97 (176-79).

I DO not remember rising to address the House on any occasion when I felt more desirous to be indulged with its attention ; because, representing as I do a very numerous body out of this House, who take a deep interest in the question, I feel regret on their account, as well as for the cause I have in hand, that there should be so much misapprehension in the House in reference to the motion I am about to make. What has just fallen from the hon. Member for Bucks (Mr. Disraeli) is a proof of this misconception ; for he would not have presumed to sneer at a motion before it was made, unless he had conceived that there was something so unreasonable and preposterous about it, that it ought to be condemned before it was heard. I have heard that hon. Gentleman indulge in a sneer before, on many occasions; but they have been *ex post facto* sneers. I have never until now heard him sneer at a matter by anticipation. He has grounded that sneer on an observation drawn forth by a subject which was calculated above all others to move the milk of human kindness in our bosoms. How it was possible for an hon. Member, in reference to the answer returned by the American President to Lady Franklin's letter, to indulge in a sneer of that kind, I cannot understand; unless it be that the hon. Gentleman is incapable of anything but sneering. I accept those acts of the American and Russian Governments as proofs that we live in altered times. As the right hon. Member for the University of Oxford (Mr. W. E. Gladstone) has well observed; at no former period of the world's history has there been an instance of foreign Governments sending out, at their expense, to seek for scientific adventurers, unconnected with their own community. Accepting this as a proof that we live in different times from those that are past, I think there is nothing unreasonable in our seeking to take another step towards consolidating the peace of nations, and securing us against the recurrence of the greatest calamity that can afflict mankind.

I stand here the humble representative of two distinct bodies, both of some importance in the community. In the first place, I represent on this occasion, and for this specific motion alone, that influential body of Christians who repudiate war in any case, whether offensive or defensive; I also represent that numerous portion of the middle classes of this country, with the great bulk of the working classes, who have an abhorrence of war, greater than at any former period of our history, and who desire that we should take some new precautions, and, if possible, obtain some guarantees, against the recurrence of war in future. Those two classes have found in the motion which I am about to submit a common ground—and I rejoice at it—on which they can unite without

compromising their principles, on one side or the other. It is
not necessary that any one in this House, or out of it, who
accedes to this motion, should be of opinion that we are not
justified, under any circumstances, in resorting to war, even
in self-defence. It is only necessary that you should be
agreed that war is a great calamity, which it is desirable we
should avoid, if possible. If you feel that the plan proposed
is calculated to attain the object sought, you may vote for it
without compromising yourselves on the extreme principle of
defensive war. I assume that every one in this House would
only sanction war, in case it was imperatively demanded on
our part, in defence of our honour, or our just interests. I
take it that every one here would repudiate war, unless it
were called for by such motives. I assume, moreover, that
there is not a man in this House who would not repudiate
war, if those objects—the just interests and honour of the
country—could be preserved by any other means. My object
is to see if we cannot devise some better method than war for
attaining those ends ; and my plan is, simply and solely, that
we should resort to that mode of settling disputes in communities, which individuals resort to in private life. I only
want you to go one step farther, to carry out in another
instance the principle which you recognise in other cases—
that the intercourse between communities is nothing more
than the intercourse of individuals in the aggregate. I want
to know why there may not be an agreement between this
country and France, or between this country and America, by
which the nations should respectively bind themselves, in case
of any misunderstanding arising which could not be settled
by mutual representation or diplomacy, to refer the dispute to
the decision of arbitrators. By arbitrators I do not mean
necessarily crowned heads, or neutral states ; though we have
examples where disputes have been referred to crowned heads,
and where their arbitrament has been eminently successful.
There is a case where the United States and France referred

a dispute to England ; a case in which England and the
United States referred a dispute to Russia—one in which the
United States and Mexico referred a question to Prussia, and
one in which the United States and England referred a case
to the King of the Netherlands. These cases were all eminently successful. If one failed in its immediate object, there
is no instance in which a war has followed after such a reference. But I do not confine myself to the plan of referring
disputes to neutral Powers. I see the difficulty of two independent states, like England and France, doing so, as one
might prefer a republic for the arbitrator, and the other a
monarchy. I should prefer to see these disputes referred to
individuals, whether designated commissioners, or plenipotentiaries, or arbitrators, appointed from one country to meet
men appointed from another country, to inquire into the
matter and decide upon it ; or, if they cannot do so, to have
the power of calling in an umpire, as is done in all arbitra-
tions. I propose that these individuals should have absolute
power to dispose of the question submitted to them.

I want to show that I am practical on this occasion, and,
therefore, I will cite some cases in which this method of
arranging difficulties has already been resorted to. In 1794
we had a Treaty with America, for the settlement of certain
British claims on the American Government. Those claims
were referred to four commissioners, two appointed on each
side, with the proviso that they should elect unanimously, an
arbitrator; in case they should not agree in the choice of an
arbitrator, it was provided that the representatives of each
country should put the names of certain arbitrators into an
urn, one to be drawn out by lot ; and this arbitrator and the
four commissioners decided by a majority all the cases brought
before them. Again, in the Treaty of 1814 with the United
States, provision was made for settling most important matters, precisely in the way I now propose. Provision was
made for settling the boundary between the United States

and Canada, for some thousands of miles; also for defining the right to certain islands lying on the coast; and for settling the boundary between Maine and New Brunswick. The plan was this: each country named a commissioner; the commissioners were to endeavour to agree on these disputed points; and the matters on which they could not agree were referred to some neutral state. All the matters referred to them—and most important they were—were arranged by mutual conference and mutual concessions, except the question of the Maine boundary, which was accordingly referred to the King of the Netherlands. Afterwards, exception was taken to his decision by the United States; the matter remained open till the time of Lord Ashburton's mission; and it was finally settled by him. But in no case has any such reference ever been followed by war. In 1818 there was a Convention with America, for settling the claims made by that country for captured negroes during the war. It was agreed to refer that matter to the Emperor of Russia; and he decided in favour of the principle of compensation. He was then appealed to by both the Governments to define a mode by which this compensation should be adjudged; and his plan was this: he said, ' Let each party name a commissioner and an arbitrator; let the commissioners meet, and, if they can agree, well and good; if not, let the names of the arbitrators be put into an urn, and one drawn out by lot; and that arbitrator and the two commissioners shall decide the question by a majority.' This method was adopted, and compensation to the extent of 1,200,000 dollars was given, without any difficulty. Hence, it appears that what I propose is no novelty, no innovation; it has been practised, and practised with success; I only want you to carry the principle a little farther, and resort to it, in anticipation, as a mode of arranging all quarrels.

For this reason, I propose an address to the Crown, praying that Her Majesty will instruct her Foreign Secretary to propose to foreign Powers to enter into treaties, providing that,

in case of any future misunderstanding, which cannot be
settled by amicable negotiation, an arbitration, such as I have
described, shall be resorted to.   There is no difficulty in
fixing the means of arbitration, and providing the details;
for arbitration is so much used in private life, and is, indeed,
made parts of so many statutes and Acts of Parliament, that
there is no difficulty whatever in carrying out the plan, provided you are agreed as to the policy of doing so.   Now, I
shall be met with this objection—I have heard it already—
and I know there are Members of this House who purpose
to vote against the motion on this ground: they say, ' What
is the use of a treaty of this sort, between France and England, for instance; the parties would not observe the treaty;
it would be a piece of waste paper; they would go to war, as
before, in spite of any treaty.'   It would be a sufficient
answer to this objection to say, ' What is the use of any
treaty ?  What is the use of the Foreign Office ?  What is the
use of your diplomacy ?'  You might shut up the one and
cashier the other.   I maintain, that a treaty binding two
countries to refer their disputes to arbitration, is just as likely
to be observed as any other treaty.   Nay, I question very
much whether it is not more likely to be observed; because,
I think there is no object which other countries will be less
likely to seek than that of having a war with a country so
powerful as England.   Therefore, if any provision were made
by which you might honourably avoid a war, that provision
would be as gladly sought by your opponents as by yourselves.   But I deny that, as a rule, treaties are violated; as
a rule, they are respected and observed.   I do not find that
wars, generally, arise out of the violation of any specific treaty
—they more commonly arise out of accidental collisions; and,
as a rule, treaties are observed by powerful States against the
weak, just as well as by weak States against the powerful.
I, therefore, see no difficulty specially applying to a treaty of
this kind, greater than exists with other treaties.   There

would be this advantage, at all events, in having a treaty
binding another country to refer all disputes to arbitration.
If that country did not fulfil its engagement, it would enter
into war with the brand of infamy stamped upon its banners.
It could not proclaim to the world that it was engaged in a
just and necessary war. On the contrary, all the world
would point to that nation as violating a treaty, by going to
war with a country with whom they had engaged to enter
into arbitration. I anticipate another objection which I have
heard made: they say, ' You cannot entrust the great interests of England to individuals or commissioners.' That
difficulty springs out of the assumption, that the quarrels
with foreign countries are about questions involving the
whole existence of the empire. On the contrary, whenever
these quarrels take place, it is generally upon the most minute
and absurd pretexts—so trivial that it is almost impossible,
on looking back for the last hundred years, to tell precisely
what any war was about. I heard the other day of a boy
going to see a model of the battle of Waterloo, and when he
asked what the battle was about, neither the old soldier who
had charge of the exhibition, nor any one in the room, could
answer the question. I may quote the remark made the
other night by the noble Lord (J. Russell) at the head of the
Government—that the last two wars were unnecessary—in
which I quite agree with him.

But, to return to the point whether or not commissioners
might be entrusted with the grave matters which form the
subjects of dispute between nations, I would draw the attention of the House to the fact, that already you do virtually
entrust these matters to individuals. Treaties of peace, made
after war, are entrusted to individuals to negotiate and carry
out. Take the case of Lord Castlereagh, representing the
British power at the Congress of Vienna. He had full power
to bind this country to the Treaty of Vienna. When, on the
20th of March, 1815, Mr. Whitbread brought on the subject

of the Treaty, with the view of censuring his conduct and that of the Government, Lord Castlereagh distinctly told the House, 'I did not wait for instructions at Vienna; I never allowed the machine of the Congress to stand still for want of my concurrence on important matters; I took upon myself the responsibility of acting; and if the interests and honour of England have been sacrificed, I stand here alone responsible.' I want to know, whether as good men as Lord Castlereagh could not be found to settle these matters before, as after, a twenty years' war? Why not depute to a plenipotentiary the same powers before a conflict as you give him after? For these matters can only be settled by empowering individuals to act for you; and let the Government instruct them as they will, a discretionary power, after all, must be left, when they are to bind the country towards other States. Take the case of Lord Ashburton, settling the Maine boundary question in America. He had the power to bind this country to anything he set his hand to. No doubt he had his instructions from the Government, but he presents his credentials to the American Government, and is received by them as authorised to bind this country to anything he agrees to do. All I want is, that this should be done before, and not after, engaging in a war—done to avert the war, rather than to make up the difference after the parties are exhausted by the conflict.

Probably I shall be told that there are signs of a pacific tendency on the part of the Government and the country; it will be said that we are carrying out a pacific policy, and that there is no necessity for passing any resolution to impose on the Government the obligation of giving us this guarantee. But I do not see that this is in process of being done. I do not see any proof, in the last five or six years, that the Government has been increasing in its confidence of peace being preserved, or gaining security for its preservation. In the last ten years we have increased our armed forces by

60,000 ; in the army, navy, and ordnance, the expenditure has been augmented sixty to seventy per cent. From 1836, down to last year, there is no proof of the Government having any confidence in the duration of peace, or possessing increased security against war. I think the inference is quite the contrary. In the committees on which I have been sitting, I have seen an amount of preparation for war which has astounded me ; and I dare say other honourable Gentlemen would share my alarm at the state of things. But I confess, when I have looked into what we are doing in the way of provision of warlike stores, means of aggression, and preparations for defence against some foreign enemy, I have been astonished at the warlike expenditure that is going on. What will honourable Gentlemen think when they know that we have 170,000 barrels of gunpowder in store ? Besides that, we have sixty-five millions of ball-cartridges made up ready for use. (Hear, hear, and a laugh, from the Protectionist benches.) The public will not laugh when they read what I say. They will not join the honourable Members for counties opposite in laughing at this statement. We have 50,000 pieces of cannon in store, besides those afloat, and in arsenals, and garrisons, and batteries. There are 5,000,000 of cannon-balls and shells in the stores, and 1,200,000 sand-bags, ready for use whenever they are needed. There is a provision equal to three or four years' consumption of these articles in the height of the French war. You have, in barrelled gunpowder alone, a supply equal to nearly three years' consumption of that article in the height of the French war, and equal to fifteen years' consumption at the present rate, to say nothing of the sixty-five millions of ball-cartridges. Does this look as if the Government thought we had made any great way in the preservation of peace ? Is it the part of a country, assured of peace, to make all this provision against war ? You have spent, in the last five or six years, on an average, twice as much in fortifications, in steam-basins, in docks, in barracks, in means of aggressive and defensive warfare, as at any period since the peace; and my hon. Friend the Member for Montrose (Mr. Hume), who has looked much longer and deeper into those subjects than I have, believes it is more than was spent in the same time for those objects during the war. Since 1836 you have doubled the expenditure of the ordnance department. It is in that department that the great increase takes place; because, in the progress of mechanical invention, and the improvements made in the science of projectiles, it is found that the artillery and engineer corps are the arms of the service on which the fate of battles mainly depends.

So, again, in the case of steam-basins. A great discovery came to the aid of civilisation — the discovery of Fulton — which he and others probably hoped would be made contributory to the unalloyed improvement and happiness of mankind. What has been the effect in our case? We commenced the construction of a steam-navy. I do not say whether it was necessary or not, but I want you to try and make it in some degree unnecessary in future. The Government continued to increase the steam-navy, until we had as much money spent in steam-vessels of war as we had invested in our merchant-steamers. I made this statement last year; I repeat it advisedly, as capable of the strictest proof. It was then received with incredulity and surprise by the right hon. the Chancellor of the Exchequer (Sir C. Wood); some facts which I showed him afterwards rather staggered him, and I am now prepared to prove that when I stated the fact last year, it was strictly true that we had invested in steam-vessels of war a larger amount than the whole cost of our mercantile steam marine; that we had expended far more in steam-basins and docks for repair of those vessels than was invested in the private docks and yards, for building and repairing private steamers.

What are we to deduce from these facts? That instead of making the progress of civilisation subservient to the welfare of mankind—instead of making the arts of civilisation available for increasing the enjoyments of life—you are constantly bringing these improvements in science to bear upon the deadly contrivances of war, and thus are making the arts of peace and the discoveries of science contribute to the barbarism of the age. But will anybody presume to answer me by the declaration that we want no further guarantee for the preservation of peace? Will any one tell me that I am not strictly justified and warranted in trying, at all events, to bring to bear the opinion of this House, of the country, and of the civilised world, upon some better mode of preserving peace than that which imposes upon us almost all the burdens which war formerly used to entail? We are now spending every year on our armaments more than we spent annually, in the seven years' war, in the middle of the last century. Therefore, far from being deterred by sneers, I join most heartily and contentedly with those worthy men out of the House, who are inspired by higher motives than I can hope to bring to bear on this occasion, and which I could not probably so rightly urge as I do those which come within your province; I join most heartily in sharing the odium, the ridicule, the calumny, and the derision, which some are attempting to cast upon those advocates of peace and of reduced armaments.

But I wish to know where this system is to end. I have sat on the army, navy, and ordnance committees, and I see no limit to the increase of our armaments under the existing system. Unless you can adopt some such plan as I propose, unless you can approach foreign countries in a conciliatory spirit, and offer to them some kind of assurance that you do not wish to attack them, and receive the assurance that you are not going to be assailed by them, I see no necessary or logical end to the increase of our establishments. For the progress of scientific knowledge will lead to a constant increase of expenditure. There is no limit but the limit of taxation, and that, I believe, you have nearly reached. I shall probably be told that my plan would not suit all cases.

I think it would suit all cases a great deal better than the plan which is now resorted to. At all events, arbitration is more rational, just, and humane than the resort to the sword. In the one case, you make men what they are never allowed to be in private life—the judge in their own case; you make them judge, jury, and executioner. In the other case, you refer the dispute to impartial individuals, selected for their intelligence and general capabilities. In any case, and under any circumstances, I do not see why my plan should not have the advantage over that now adopted. If I am opposed by supposititious cases, and told that my plan would not apply to such, I take my stand upon past experience, and will show you numerous instances where it would have applied. Nay, I am prepared to show that all the unavoidable quarrels we have had during the last twenty years—I mean those which could not have been avoided by any conduct on the part of our Government—all these might have been more fitly settled by arbitration than in any other way; and I will appeal to the right hon. Gentlemen on both sides of this House, who have filled the highest offices of Government, when such disputes have arisen, whether they would not have felt relieved from harassing responsibilities, had they had this principle of arbitration to rely on, in these cases.

Take the case of 1837, when a dispute arose with Russia, about the confiscation of a ship in the Black Sea, called the *Vixen*. The noble Lord, the Member for Tiverton, was then Foreign Secretary. He knows very well that this vessel was sent to the Black Sea by a certain party, with a particular object; the thing was entirely got up. I was in Constantinople at the time, and knew the whole history of it. That vessel was freighted and sent to the coast of Circassia, for the very purpose of embroiling us with Russia; and immediately she was seized, there was a party in this country ready to raise an excitement against the noble Lord, for submitting to the arrogant spoliation of the Russian Government. Had we

then had an arbitration treaty with Russia, would not that
have been the best possible resource for the noble Lord in that
case, and have enabled him to escape the party attacks made
upon him in this country? That question, which, after all,
did not involve an amount of property exceeding 2000*l.* or
3000*l.*, might have been settled by a petty jury of twelve
honest tradesmen, quite as well as by the noble Lord at the
Foreign Office.

Will any one, for a moment, tell me that the disputes about
the boundary between Maine and New Brunswick, and the
misunderstanding respecting Oregon, might not have been
settled by arbitration? I prefer the appointment of commissioners to that of crowned heads—because I would have
men who are most competent to judge of the subject in dispute. For instance, this was a geographical question : why
should not the two ablest geographers of this country have
met those of the United States, assuming them otherwise qualified by moral character and general attainments, and have been
authorised to call in an umpire, if necessary? Supposing the
case to have been left to the decision of such an umpire as
Baron Humboldt, for example; would he not have decided far
more correctly than any war would be likely to do? I know
that the Oregon question caused the liveliest apprehensions
to those who were engaged on both sides, in this dispute, in
1846. I am aware that Mr. M'Lane, the American Minister,
felt the greatest solicitude, and manifested the deepest anxiety
on the arrival of every packet, and I know how anxious he
was that the right hon. Gentleman (Sir R. Peel) should
remain in office till the question was settled. I know what
he felt, and what every Minister in a similar position must
feel, on such occasions. The great difficulty was lest party
spirit and popular excitement should arise on either side of the
water, to hinder and perplex the efforts of those who were
interested in its settlement. It is to remove that difficulty
in future—to prevent the interposition of bad passions and

popular prejudices in these disputes—that I desire to have provision made, beforehand, for the settlement of any quarrel that may arise by arbitration.

There was another case, in 1841, the danger from which was, in my mind, the most imminent of all—I mean the case of Mr. M'Leod, who had been taken and imprisoned by the State of New York. and tried for his life, for having, as he himself avowed, taken part in the burning of the *Caroline*, in which an American citizen lost his life. Our Government claimed to have this question decided between the general Government of the United States and themselves. But the Government of the United States said that they had not the power to remove the case out of the New York Court, and that they could not prevent the State of New York proceeding in the matter. We all know the excitement which took place on that occasion. There was great irritation in America, and great excitement in this country. Now, if Mr. M'Leod had been executed, what would the consequence have been in this country? Why, the old cry of our honour being involved would have been raised. [An hon. Member: 'Certainly.'] An hon. Member says, 'Certainly.' But what means would you take to vindicate your honour? You would go to war, and, for the one life that had been taken away, you would sacrifice the lives of thousands, nay, perhaps, tens of thousands. But would all this sacrifice of human life restore the life of the man on whose account you were fighting? Would it not be much wiser if, instead of resorting to war,—which is nothing but wholesale murder, if war can be avoided,—you had recourse to arbitration, by which, indeed, you could as little restore the individual to life, as by the employment of all your military forces, but by which you might obtain a provision for his widow and family, and which, be it re-marked, is no part of the object of those who engage in wars?

Now, there is another case, upon which I call the right

hon. Gentleman opposite (Sir R. Peel) as a witness into court —the case of Mr. Pritchard, a missionary, and the consul of this country at Tahiti, who had been put under arrest by the French admiral. When this news first arrived in this country, from a distance of 12,000 or 14,000 miles, the press, both here and in France, sounded the tocsin, and national prejudices and hatreds were invoked on both sides. The French Minister, M. Guizot, was told that he was going to succumb to the dictation of England; and in this country, it was said that the honour of England was sacrificed to the insolence of France. The right hon. Gentleman (Sir R. Peel), then at the head of affairs, rose in his place in this House, and declared that the insult offered was one of the grossest outrages ever committed, and was inflicted in the grossest manner. That added to the difficulty of dealing with the question in the proper manner. M. Guizot and Lord Aberdeen also complained of the conduct of the press of both countries, which exasperated the national animosity on that occasion, and rendered it more difficult to settle the question amicably. I now ask the right hon. Gentleman, if he would not have felt consoled and happy, in 1844, if a treaty of arbitration had existed between this country and France, by which this miserable and trumpery question might have been at once withdrawn from the arena of national controversy, and placed under the adjudication of a commission set apart for that purpose?

I may be told that none of these instances had led to or terminated in war. That is true. But they led to an enormous amount of expenditure; and, what is worse, to lasting hate between nations. I have no hesitation in saying that these disputes have cost this country 30,000,000*l.* sterling. They not only led to expenditure in preparation for war at the time, but they occasioned a permanent increase in your establishments, as I have shown you on a former occasion, and you are now paying every year for the increase of these establishments which was then made.

Now, I would ask, in the face of these facts, where is the argument you can use against the reasonable proposition which I now put forward? I may be told that, even if you make treaties of this kind, you cannot enforce the award. I admit it. I am no party to the plan which some advocate—no doubt with the best intentions—of having a Congress of nations, with a code of laws—a supreme court of appeal, with an army to support its decisions. I am no party to any such plan. I believe it might lead to more armed interference than takes place at present. The hon. Gentleman opposite, who is to move an amendment to my motion (Mr. Urquhart), has evidently mistaken my object. The hon. Gentleman is exceedingly attentive in tacking on amendments to other persons' motions. My justification for alluding to him, on the present occasion, is, that he has founded his amendment on a misapprehension of what my motion is. He has evidently conceived the idea that I have a grand project for putting the whole world under some court of justice. I have no such plan in view at all; and, therefore, neither the hon. Gentleman, nor any other person, will answer my arguments, if he has prepared a speech assuming that I contemplate anything of the kind. I have no plan for compelling the fulfilment of treaties of arbitration. I have no idea of enforcing treaties in any other way than that now resorted to. I do not, myself, advocate an appeal to arms; but that which follows the violation of a treaty, under the present system, may follow the violation of a treaty of arbitration, if adopted. What I say, however, is, if you make a treaty with another country, binding it to refer any dispute to arbitration, and if that country violates that treaty, when the dispute arises, then you will place it in a worse position before the world—you will place it in so infamous a position, that I doubt if any country would enter into war on such bad grounds as that country must occupy.

I may be told that this is not the time to bring forward

such a motion. I never knew a good motion brought forward
in a bad season. But it may be said, that the time is badly
chosen, because there are wars on the Continent now. I quite
disagree to that. Is there anything in those wars so inviting,
that we should hesitate before we take precautions against
their recurrence? I should have thought, on the contrary,
that what is taking place on the Continent is the very reason
why we should take every precaution now. There were none
of these wars, with the exception of that between Schleswig
and Denmark, to which international treaties would apply;
because they are all either civil wars, or wars of insurrection,
and rebellion. This war between Schleswig and Denmark
was an instance of the very insignificant means by which
you could produce widespread mischief in this commercial
age. Is there a case where the principle of arbitration, in
the persons of first-rate historians or jurists, could be adopted
with more advantage than in the case of Schleswig and
Denmark? It is difficult to see how the dispute is ever
to be settled by going to war, for one party being stronger
by land, and the other by sea, there may be no end of the
conflict. But see what mischief this dispute has occasioned
to others. The blockade of the Elbe, the great artery of the
north of Europe, has shut out their supplies, not from
Schleswig, but from Germany. It has interrupted the commerce of not merely a small Danish province, but the whole
world. The people of Schleswig, who have comparatively no
manufactures, are not punished, but your fellow-citizens in
Manchester, your miners in Northumberland, and the wine-
growers of the Gironde are punished. Mischief is done all
over the world by this petty quarrel, which could be more
properly settled by arbitration than by any other means. Let
not people turn this matter into ridicule by saying that I
want to make arbitration treaties with everybody — even
Bornean pirates. Hon. Gentlemen may create a laugh by
coupling together a Bornean pirate and a member of the

Society of Friends. But I do not want to make treaties
with Bornean pirates or the inhabitants of Timbnctoo. I
shall be quite satisfied, as a beginning, if I see the noble
Lord, or any one filling his place, trying to negotiate an
arbitration treaty with the United States, or with France.
But I should like to bind ourselves to the same principle
with the weakest and smallest States. I should be as willing
to see it done with Tuscany, Belgium, or Holland, as with
France or America, because I am anxious to prove to the
world that we are prepared to submit our misunderstandings,
in all cases, to a purer and more just arbitrament than that
of brute force. Whilst I do not agree with those who are
in favour of a Congress of nations, I do think that if the
larger and more civilised Powers were to enter into treaties of
this kind, their decisions would become precedents, and you
would in this way, in the course of time, establish a kind
of common law amongst nations, which would save the time
and trouble of arbitration in each individual case.

I do not anticipate any sudden or great change in the
character of mankind, nor do I expect a complete extinction
of those passions which form part of our nature. · But I do
not think there is anything very irrational in expecting that
nations may see that the present system of settling disputes
is barbarous, demoralising, and unjust; that it wars against
the best interests of society, and that it ought to give place
to a mode more consonant with the dictates of reason and
humanity. I do not see anything in the present state of
European society to prevent us from discussing this matter,
and hoping that it may be brought to a satisfactory conclusion. I have abstained from dwelling on those topics,
which may excite the feelings of hon. Gentlemen opposite.
I have not entered into the horrors of war, or the manifold
evils to which it gives rise. I will, on the present occasion,
content myself with the description of it by Jeremy Bentham,
who calls it ' mischief on the largest scale.' I will leave these

topics, and that mode of handling the question, to others who may discuss the matter, either here or elsewhere. I have stated clearly, explicitly, and in a matter-of-fact manner, what my object is, in order that it may not be misunderstood. I have shown examples in which this plan has been adopted. All I want is, that we should enter into mutual engagements with other countries, binding ourselves and them, in all future cases of dispute which cannot be otherwise arranged, to refer the matter to arbitration. No possible harm can arise from the failure of my plan. The worst that can be said of it is, that it will not effect its object—that of averting war. We shall then remain in that unsatisfactory state in which we now find ourselves. I put it to any person having a desire to avert war, whether, when he sees that the adoption of this plan can do no harm, it is not just and wise to try whether it may not effect good. As it is likely to have that effect in the opinion of nearly 200,000 petitioners to this House—as that is the opinion declared by 150 public meetings in this country—as it is the opinion expressed by members of several town councils who calmly discussed this matter in their large boroughs—as it is the opinion of so many of your reflecting and intelligent fellow-citizens—will you refuse to them, under the circumstances I have stated, this, the only mode that has been propounded, of affording a guarantee against war, which we all equally deprecate?

# FOREIGN POLICY.

## IL.

### LONDON, OCTOBER 8, 1849.

[The Austrian Government had in the autumn of 1849 advertised in the London papers for subscriptions to a loan of 71,000,000 florins (7,100,000*l.*) The loan was rendered necessary in consequence of the condition in which the Austrian finances had been placed by the Hungarian revolt, and the measures adopted to put it down. Mr. Cobden called public attention to the facts, and at a meeting at the London Tavern made the following Speech on this resolution :—' That the Government of Austria, having proposed to raise a loan in foreign countries, capitalists and men of business are thereby invited to investigate the financial position of the said Government, and the probability of its repaying the loan thus proposed to be contracted ; and that it is the opinion of this meeting that no valid security is tendered, or can be offered, in the present state of the Austrian Government, which would justify prudent men in taking any part of the said loan.']

It has been my privilege to address my fellow-country-men probably as often, and in as great a variety of places, as any man now living; but I will say, with unfeigned confidence, that there never was an occasion when I stood before my countrymen on more solid and firm grounds of justice, of humanity, and of sound political economy, than I do at this moment.  Objections have been taken to the course I have pursued in this matter, on the ground that

I am not adhering to sound principles of political economy. I suppose it was thought that this was the most vulnerable point on which one who had said so much on the subject of Free Trade could be assailed. I will begin, then, with that which the enemy considers his strong ground of attack; and I say, that, as I have gone through the length and breadth of this country, with Adam Smith in my hand, to advocate the principles of Free Trade, so I can stand here, supported by the same great authority, to denounce—not merely for its inherent waste of national wealth, not only because it anticipates income and consumes capital, but also on the ground of injustice to posterity, in entailing upon the heirs of this generation a debt which it has no right to call upon them to pay—the loans we have this day met to consider. But, whilst I come here to denounce as unjust, to expose as wasteful, and to demonstrate to be impolitic, the system of lending money for the purposes for which Austria comes to borrow, I confine myself to this. I do not purpose to recommend that we should go to Parliament for a law to prohibit men from lending money, if it be their wish to do so. All I say is, that I come here to try, in a humble way, to do that which I have done for Free Trade—to popularize to the people of this country, and of the Continent, those arguments with which Adam Smith, David Hume, Ricardo, and every man who has written on this subject, have demonstrated the funding system to be injurious to mankind, and unjust in principle. I come here to try to show to our fellow-countrymen, that they will act upon a wrong principle, and do injury to society, by lending the proceeds of their hard and industrious labour to the Austrian Government, to be expended in that bottomless gulf of waste—armies and standing armaments. I come here to show the impolicy, on general principles, of taking such a course. But in this particular instance I am not going to confine myself to the general principle. I appeal to every individual who thinks of lending money to the Austrian

Government, to pause before he does so; because he is going to intrust his money to a Power that has thrice committed an act of bankruptcy. [An observation was here made by an individual which led to cries of 'Turn him out,' and some confusion ensued.] Mr. Cobden proceeded:—Turn nobody out. If he be a man who has subscribed to this loan, he can only have paid. ten per cent. as a deposit, and, if you will only keep him here, before I have done I will satisfy him that it will be for his interest to forfeit the deposit. I will satisfy him that it will be to his interest to forfeit his ten per cent., and to pay no more.

But to resume. I say that the Austrian Government has three times committed acts of bankruptcy, under circumstances of great and scandalous injustice, for, while personal interests—Imperial interests—have been well taken care of, the general public—the subscribers to the loans—have been basely sacrificed. Now, what has been the progress of Austrian finance since the great war? When the Austrian Government come to us to borrow money, the least they can do is, through their agents, Messrs. Hope and Co., to give us a *bond fide*, detailed, and candid debtor and creditor statement of their accounts; but we have no such statement from that Government. In the absence of such a detailed and official statement, then, we are bound to have recourse to the best private authorities we can find. I will take a work of standard reputation, which was published in 1840, under the title of 'Austria and its Future,' a work well known to be from the pen of Baron Andrian, who, last year, ably filled the office of Ambassador from the Central German Power to the British Court, and a work of standard authority on such matters. After a precisely detailed statement of all the various shuffling manœuvres—borrowing, loaning, lotteries, and every possible device—with which the Austrian Government had been mystifying its finance for twenty-five years—from 1815 to 1840—the author sums up by saying that, from

1815 down to 1840, a period of profound peace, the Austrian
Government has doubled its debt in nominal value, but
quadrupled its debt in real amount, and has increased the
interest for which it is liable tenfold. The same work was
republished, in 1846, by the same author, with an additional
volume; and the author tells us that, at that time, not one
word had been said to disprove his statements respecting Austrian finance. He adds, that since the period when his book
was first published, 8,000,000*l.* more have been added to the
national debt of Austria; and it therefore comes to this—that
from 1815 to 1847 the Austrian Government, during a period
of profound peace, without a foreign war on its hands during
the whole of that time, has gone on, every year, spending
more than its income, and constantly adding to the amount
of its national debt. Then, in 1848, whilst Austria had from
300,000 to 400,000 men under arms—the produce of all this
wasteful expenditure—came that revolutionary epidemic,
which passed over the Continent, and the Government of
Austria fell like a house of cards, notwithstanding the
bayonets by which it was supported, and, from that time
to this, the Austrian empire has been in a state of complete
anarchy and disorder. Vienna, Pesth, Venice, Milan, Prague
—every capital of the empire but Inspruck—have been bombarded by the forces of the Austrian Government, or have been
in a state of siege; we have seen the Bank suspending specie
payments, the Government prohibiting the exportation of the
precious metals, to prevent the foreign creditor from being
honestly paid his due; and during all this anarchy and confusion, both political and financial, the Austrian Government
has expended, at least, double the amount of its annual income. I should be afraid to state what I have heard persons of good authority say is the amount of the floating
debt, now standing over, in the Austrian empire; but I am
within the mark when I say, that there is at least 20,000,000*l.*
sterling held over in Austria as the result of the last eighteen

months' social, political, and financial anarchy. And it is to enable the Austrian Government to redeem a part of that enormous floating debt that they now have the audacity—for I cannot call it by any other name—to come before the people of Western Europe, and ask the honest Dutchman, the industrious Englishman, the painstaking, saving Swiss or Frenchman—they do not care who it is—out of their hard earnings, to lend them money—that is, to throw it into a bottomless pit of waste and extravagance.

Now, I ask you, if an individual has committed acts of bankruptcy three times, is he not very likely to commit such an act again, if it answers his purpose? Well, the Austrian Government has every motive to declare itself bankrupt again, because it is utterly impossible that, in any other way, they can recover from their financial embarrassment. They never can pay their debt. They may now borrow 7,000,000*l.* sterling, as a means of paying off a fraction of the debt they have already incurred, and that 7,000,000*l.* they are asking for on rather humiliating terms; but I warn all men, whether in this country or abroad, that this is only the beginning of borrowing, on the part of the Austrian Government. If their finances are to be retrieved by borrowing, this is but a drop in the ocean to what they must borrow afterwards; and you must bear in mind, that they who lend their money first will be swamped and sacrificed to those who lend afterwards, and with whom the Government will have to submit to harder bargains. When I state these facts, I do not mention them for the information of Messrs. Hope and Co., or any other large banking company, in London, Amsterdam, Antwerp, or Vienna. I perfectly understand, though not a farthing of this Austrian loan should be repaid—though the Government shall never redeem a farthing of it—that it may still be a very profitable thing to those agents and bankers, who raise the money through their connections and customers. I hold in my hand the advertisement put forth by the

Austrian Government in our papers, and this is my justification for coming here to-day. We have not met to talk
over Austrian finances and affairs, to uncover their sore places,
and to tell all these hard truths, without having been invited
to it. Here is an advertisement, put into our papers, at the
expense, I suppose, of the Austrian Government, inviting
everybody to subscribe to the loan. The advertisers are so
accommodating, that, in order that nobody may be excluded,
they say that bonds will be issued for sums as low as 100
florins, or 10*l.* It is said that the pith of a lady's letter
is to be found in the postscript, and I entreat the attention
of all persons, whether here, in Holland, or in Germany—
(for I am not merely speaking to a few of my countrymen
in this room, but what I say will be read in Holland, in
Germany, and in France)—to the last line of this advertisement. It runs thus:—'Any subscriber to a higher amount
than 25,000 florins, that is, 2500*l.*, or any person who collects
subscriptions to an amount surpassing that sum, will receive
a commission of ¼ per cent. on the amount of the payments
made.' Now, I ask you, if any shopkeeper or huckster in
London put an advertisement outside his window,—'Anybody who brings a customer to my shop, who may purchase
5*s.* worth of potatoes or vegetables, shall have a commission
of 2*d.* on that amount,' would you not pass by on the other
side, and take especial care to have no dealings at his shop?
Would you not naturally say to yourselves, 'If that man sold
a good article, if he was true to his word in his dealings, if he
never cheated anybody, if he had not committed foul acts
of bankruptcy, or, probably, of robbery, he would not be under
the necessity of offering bribes to obtain customers?'

I wish you, and those small capitalists who are invited to
put their 10*l.* into this raffle, where there are no prizes, to
bear in mind, that we do not think that our meeting will
convert any of those bankers, or agents, or brokers, whether
in Amsterdam or Vienna, who have been called on to find

out unwary people, and get them to subscribe their 25,000 florins. We never expected to convert them, or to meet them on this platform. We expect that all those organs of the press, which are under the influence of these parties,—and they are not a few,—we expect that they will not meet what I now say by argument, but they will do what they are bid to do and to say, and will abuse me well. [Here a person exclaimed that ' there were 10,000 people outside, who wanted to get in.'] Mr. Cobden continued :—I am glad to hear that there are so many assembled outside, but they must be content with reading in the newspapers to-morrow what we are now saying. It is to those small capitalists, of whom I was speaking,—the unwary, the incautious, and the uninformed class,—that I wish to speak the voice of warning; and, if they will listen to me, I will give them the opportunity of testing the opinion of the great capitalists, with respect to this loan. Messrs. Hope and Co., of Amsterdam, the agents for the loan, have offered it on such terms as, if carried out, would pay 5*l.* 14*s.* per cent. interest. Now, I would advise some canny Dutchman to go to the counting-house of Messrs. Hope and Co., and say this to them,—' You have offered to me to take part in a loan, by which I shall get 5*l.* 14*s.* interest per cent.; that is, nearly twice as much interest as we get in Amsterdam, in an ordinary way ; I should be content with 4 per cent. interest, if it were secure ; I propose to take 1000*l.* of your loan ; and I will be content to receive 4 per cent. interest, and give you the remaining 1*l.* 14*s.*, if you will endorse my bond, as a guarantee for the payment.' No, no ; the firm are not likely to be caught in that way, you may depend upon it. I was talking the other day to a gentleman in Lombard-street—one of the most experienced, sagacious, and able men in that quarter, which is not renowned for gullible people—and I asked him for his opinion upon this loan. Bear in mind, he is a man more consulted by the Government, and Committees of the House of Commons, on

such matters, than any one else on the east of Temple-bar.
He replied, ' I do not believe that 2co,000*l.* will be raised in
all Lombard-street, and certainly not one shilling's worth will
be taken to hold.' No, the capitalists will not take it to hold.
If they subscribe, they will take the scrip at 10 per cent.
deposit, in the hope of transferring it, at a premium, to some
one, who will lose his money, not being so well informed
of the valueless character of the security.   It is on that class
that the loss will fall.   I knew myself, many years ago, when
resident in the City, a man who worked as a porter, on
weekly wages—his family and himself being reduced to that
state that they had no other earthly dependence—and yet,
that man had Spanish bonds, to the nominal amount of more
than 2000*l.* in his pocket, which he had purchased when in
better circumstances.   They were not worth more than waste
paper; but I never heard that the great houses that contracted that loan were ruined by it.   No, it passed through
their hands, and came into the hands of poor men, like this
porter, who had no experience and knowledge in such matters;
and it is to protect such poor men that I now utter the voice
of warning.

Now, I ask, when it is known that every word I say is
strictly within moderation, and the bounds of truth,—when
there is not a man in Lombard-street but would endorse every
word I utter as to the valueless character of this loan,—is it
not something hateful, humiliating, and disgusting, that we
have leading organs of the press which lend their influence,
not to throw a shield over the unwary and innocent, but to
serve the purpose of those who have cunning and ability to
protect themselves?   They do not come out—that is why I
blame them — in their leading articles, and tell the people,
with the authority of their own pen, that Austria is trustworthy—that this loan is a good investment.   No; they do
not do anything of the kind; but they do their work in the
best way they can,—by inuendo, by indirect influence, and by

trying all they can to traduce the men who come forward, and tell the truth in this matter. When I take up a public question of this sort, and find, instead of my arguments being refuted, that I am personally attacked, I consider it the triumph of my cause. But the fact is, that these are not the only parties that look with disfavour on this meeting to-day. I have no hesitation in saying that there is not a Government in Europe that is not frowning upon this meeting. It is not merely Austria that disapproves of the meeting. I do not believe that our Government likes it. I say so much, because I see that the organs of the press, especially under the influence of the Government, and one, in particular, established as the advocate, *par excellence*, of the sound principles of political economy, enounced by Adam Smith, are forward in condemning this meeting. I consider this as the germ of a great movement, which will lay bare the pretensions of every Government that comes before the world for a loan; and will show the bankrupt state—if it be bankrupt—of the exchequer of their country; and will hold up to execration the objects for which men attempt to obtain such loans.

I consider this almost as much a Russian as an Austrian loan. I do not separate the two countries. You remember when I spoke before, in this place, strongly on the subject of the Russian finances. I come here now to repeat every word I then uttered. I claim no great merit for myself in presuming to understand more properly the state of Russian finances than many others. It is from accident that I have had opportunities — and few men, probably not six men in England, have had my opportunities — of investigating and ascertaining, upon the best and safest authority, on the spot, where alone you can properly understand the matter, what actually is the state of the resources of Russia; and I say, again, that the Russian Government, in the matter of finance, is nothing more nor less than a gigantic imposture. There are men in Western Europe who know what I say to be true, and yet lend themselves to spread an opposite delusion. You have seen in the newspapers, that the Government of Russia have taken 2,000,000*l.* of this Austrian loan, and that the Russian Government was going to subscribe to the Pope's loan, and going to lend the Archduke of Tuscany a round sum. This is systematically done. These paragraphs are put into the papers by men employed by that cunning Government, to throw dust in the eyes of people. That Government last year spent more than its income, and this year its deficit is enormous. Russia has not paid the expenses of the Hungarian campaign; it has made forced contributions, taking the taxes in advance, in the territories through which the troops moved, and has given Treasury receipts; and at this moment the Russian Government has no alternative but to increase its paper money, and begin an act of bankruptcy again, or to come to Western Europe for a loan. When she comes here, let her well understand that we will be here also.

It is not on mere economical grounds, or on grounds of self-interest alone, that I oppose these loans; I come here to oppose the very principle on which they are founded. What is this money wanted for? Austria, with her barbarous consort, has been engaged in a cruel and remorseless war; and the Austrian Government comes now, and stretches forth its bloodstained hand to honest Dutchmen and Englishmen, and asks them to furnish the price of the devastation which has been committed. For there is little difference whether the money subscribed to this loan be furnished a little before or after. The money has been raised for the war by forced contributions and compulsory loans, for which Treasury receipts have been given, in the confident expectation that this loan would be raised to pay them off. I consider that this is on principle most unjust and indefensible. Happily, by the ordinance of Divine Providence, war is in its nature self-destroying; and if a country engaged in hostilities were left

to itself, war must have a speedy termination.  But this
system of foreign loans for warlike purposes, by which
England, Holland, Germany, and France are invited to pay
for the arms, clothing, and food of the belligerents, is a
system calculated almost to perpetuate the horrors of war;
and they who lend money for these purposes are destitute
of any one excuse, by which men try to justify to their own
consciences the resort to the sword.  They cannot plead
patriotism, self-defence, or even anger, or the lust of military
glory.  No; but they sit down coolly to calculate the chances
to themselves of profit or loss, in a game in which the lives
of human beings are at stake.  They have not even the pleasure—the savage and brutal gratification, which ancient and
pagan people had, when they paid for a seat in the amphi-
theatre, to witness the bloody combats of gladiators in the
arena.

I wish, in conclusion, that it should be borne in mind by
capitalists everywhere, that these are times when it behoves
them to remember that property has its duties as well as its
rights: I exhort the friends of peace, and advocates of disarmament, throughout the civilised world, to exert themselves
to spread a sounder morality on this question of war loans,
and to impress upon the capitalists of the world, that they
who forget their duties are running the risk of endangering
their rights.

# FOREIGN POLICY.

## III.

LONDON, JANUARY 18, 1850.

[The Russian Government was attempting, at the beginning of the year 1850, to negotiate a loan, ostensibly for the construction of a railway from St. Petersburg to Moscow. There was reason to believe that the true object of this financial operation was to cover the deficit occasioned in the Russian finances by its armed intervention in Hungary. A meeting was called at the London Tavern to protest against this loan, and Mr. Cobden moved the first resolution at the meeting in the following words :—' That the Government of Russia having proposed to raise in this country a loan of five millions and a half, professedly for the purpose of completing a rail-road from St. Petersburg to Moscow, but really to replenish the Imperial exchequer, exhausted by the expenses of the war in Hungary, this meeting is of opinion that to lend money to the Emperor of Russia for such an object would virtually be to sanction the deeds of violence and blood committed by him in Hungary, and to furnish him with the temptation and the means for carrying on future schemes of aggression and conquest.']

I CONGRATULATE the Peace Society and the friends of peace in this country, that the Emperor of Russia has been obliged — unconsciously been obliged, as we must as a matter of courtesy suppose—to affix his name to a document which is not true, in order to obtain a loan of five and a half millions in this country. I say that that document which has been signed by the Emperor of Russia contains an untruth. I know it to be untrue, and it is known to everybody in

St. Petersburg to be untrue. But I accept the untruth as the highest tribute that could possibly be paid to the moral power of the Peace party in this country.

I was saying that the pretence put forth by the Emperor of Russia, that he requires this money to complete the railroad from Moscow to St. Petersburg, is unfounded in truth. I was at St. Petersburg about two years ago, and at that time the rolling stock of that railway was furnished. They had then one hundred locomotives; and I travelled on a portion of the line by means of one of them. They had one thousand wag- gons and carriages; and I was told all the iron was upon the ground and paid for, but that some part of the embankments remained unfinished; and looking at the martial tendencies of the Emperor of Russia, I do not think it likely that those embankments will be completed for ten years to come, at least; for, judging from his conduct hitherto, we must expect that he will continue to spend his money as fast as he gets it, like a great overgrown colossal baby, on his soldiers rather than on those substantial improvements which alone can add to the civilisation, the power, and the happiness of his country.

But why do I argue this point? Nobody believes that the money is wanted by Russia for the railroads. I take it that everybody assumes to the contrary. But I will con- vict the Russian Government of falsehood in this respect from their own ukase. They say they want the money within six months. Whoever heard of five and a half millions being required for making a railroad in six months? Some of you here, unhappily, no doubt, have had some experience in rail- way calls, but did you ever know them come from any one board of directors so thick and fast as they are to come from the Emperor of Russia? 20*l.* two days after allotment, 10*l.* on the 15th of February, 10*l.* on the 15th of March, 10*l.* on the 15th of April, 10*l.* on the 15th of May, and 10*l.* on the 15th of June, and the remainder on the 15th of July next!

Why, here are railway calls for one railway alone at the rate of nearly one million a month, and that in a country where, up to the month of March, no work can be done in the way of forming embankments, and consequently this money is wanted for the purpose of being expended in excavating and embanking in the months of April, May, June, and July. I really pity the mendicant Czar who is obliged to come to us with such a story. Is it not humiliating? And then, after putting forward this pretence that the money is wanted for a railroad, after beginning his imperial ukase by saying what was not the truth—I must in courtesy presume that he did not know that it was not the truth—he winds up at last (as though doubting whether or not he would be believed) in the fifth paragraph by promising that the account of the sums derived from this loan shall be kept as the former loans raised for this same railroad were kept—distinct from all other items of the State revenue and expenditure. He wants here to open the door if possible even wide enough for the most scrupulous Quaker to subscribe to his loan. He tells you not only that the money is not wanted for war or for paying soldiers, but that it is entirely for the construction of the railroad, and as a proof that it is so, he says he will give separate accounts of the manner in which it is expended. If he does so, all I can say is, that it is what he never did before.

I have been subjected to the reiterated charge that I am not consistent with my own principles, the principles of Free Trade, when I come here to denounce this loan, and people have asked—'Why won't you let us lend our money in the dearest market, and borrow in the cheapest? Why not have free trade in money as well as in everything else?' I have no objection to people investing their money, if they like to do so, but I claim the right, as a free man in a free country, to meet my fellow-citizens in public assembly like the present, to try and warn the unwary against being deceived by those agents and moneymongers in the city of

London who will endeavour to palm off their bad securities
on us if they can.  If they can succeed in spite of our warning, and I am not going to coerce them or to dictate to
them, we shall have done our duty in giving this warning in
time ; and those who do not follow our advice now will, perhaps, by-and-by, wish they had done so.  That, however, is
their business, not mine.

It is asked of me this morning by a leading journal, whether I oppose this loan on the ground of its immorality or on
the ground of its being unsafe?  I say I oppose it on both
grounds ; for, in my opinion, whatever is immoral is unsafe.
But, apart altogether from these grounds of its inherent immorality and insecurity, I stand here as a citizen of this
country and as a citizen of the world, to denounce the whole
character of this transaction as injurious to the best interests
of society.  I will take first the politico-economical view of
the question, because it is supposed that on this question I
am particularly weak in that direction.  Now, I take my
stand on one of the strongest grounds in stating that Adam
Smith and other great authorities on political economy are
opposed to the very principle of such loans.  What is this money
wanted for?  It is to be wasted.  It is to go to defray the expense of maintaining standing armies, or to pay the expenses of
the atrocious war in Hungary.  Then what does it amount to?
It is so much capital abstracted from England and handed
over to another country to be wasted; it alienates from the
labouring population of this country a part of the means by
which it is employed, and by which it is to live.  I say that
every loan advanced to a foreign Power to be expended in
armaments, or for carrying on war with other countries, is as
much money wasted and destroyed for all the purposes of
reproduction as if it were carried out into the middle of the
Atlantic and there sunk in the sea.  And I make no distinction whether the interest be paid or not—for if it be paid by
the Emperor of Russia, it is not paid out of the proceeds of the

capital lent—it is not paid by the capital itself being invested
in reproductive employment—but it is extorted from the labour,
the industry, and the wretchedness of his people, who have
to pay the interest of that capital which has not only not
been employed in reproductive labour, or even thrown into the
ocean, but far worse, in obstructing industry, in devastating
fair and fruitful lands, and in suppressing freedom.  I say,
then, I stand here as a political economist to denounce every
transaction such as this as injurious to every class of the community, from the highest to the lowest, because it stops employment, impedes industry, and withdraws from us the very
sources of profitable labour.  Therefore, I say, it must injure
every one more or less, from the Government itself down to
the humblest mechanic or farm labourer who depends on his
weekly wages for his subsistence.  But I stand here also to
denounce this loan as a politician, as a member of society, and
as a taxpayer.  For what is the object of this loan?  It is to
enable the Emperor of Russia to maintain an enormous standing army; and what is the consequence?  Why, that every
other country in Europe is obliged to keep up an enormous
armament also.  What say the statesmen of France?  They
say, ' We are obliged to keep 500,000 armed men because
Russia keeps 800,000;' and we are here in England accustomed to cite the hostile position of Russia, as a reason why
we keep our enormous fleet.  I should not be surprised if, in
the very next session, when I bring forward a motion asking
to reduce our armaments, you find, what I have before found,
this very example of the Russian fleet cited as a reason why
we cannot reduce our navy.

What has been very recently the attitude and position of
Russia as regards this country?  Have we not had our fleet
—a fleet maintained in the Mediterranean at an enormous
expense, by you the taxpayers of this country—have we not
had it sailing to the Dardanelles; and have we not had constant talk of a collision between Russia and this country on

the subject of Turkey? Why, it is the acknowledged and traditional policy of this country—I do not say a word as to the wisdom of that policy—that we are to defend Turkey against all comers, and to maintain, at all hazards, the integrity of that empire against the aggressions of foreign Powers. When we speak of foreign Powers, we mean only Russia; and it is the common talk with every one who knows anything of Continental affairs, that in the spring Russia means to attack Turkey in her Danubian provinces, in which case the taxpayers of this country may be called upon to equip fleets, which Russia will combat with the means borrowed from yourselves.

We read in the history of Holland, that on one occasion when a Dutch town was besieged, its merchants sold sulphur to the enemy with which to make gunpowder to fire on themselves. When we read this we look on the Dutch as a mercenary people, who had no idea of patriotism or national dignity; yet what shall we say of England, if we have to record that, in the year 1850, there were found men in London ready to endorse the desperate wickedness of Russia by lending her money to continue the career of violence she has hitherto maintained? I oppose this loan then on grounds totally apart from the abstract principles of morality or any consideration as to the nature of the security offered. I, as a politician, a citizen, and a taxpayer, have, in common with you all, a right to protest against transactions of this kind, whencesoever they come, or by whomsoever contracted. But I denounce also the morality of this loan. We have latterly had a strange doctrine, half hinted, half expressed, but not very confidently broached, that you must not question what a man does with his money; that you must only inquire how much per cent. is to be obtained, and that if the interest be five instead of four per cent. that is quite sufficient to sanctify the transaction. That is the doctrine I hear put forth in the name of my fellow-citizens. If it be really their doctrine, I can only say that the Emperor of Russia has given them credit for a much higher standard of morality than they possess. He was afraid to avow his real objects. He was obliged by his council to tell a fib, by asking the citizens of London to lend him money for railway purposes, instead of war. He did not know his men, he took too high an estimate of their morality, for they now propose unblushingly to lend him money, simply because he proposes to give them five per cent. interest instead of four.

Now, what is this money wanted for? Simply and solely to make up the arrears caused by the exhaustion of the Hungarian war. I am not in the habit of boasting at public meetings of what I may have done on former occasions, but if I were a boaster I should exult that the assertions I made on this spot in June last, and which have been subjected to so much sarcasm from foes and friends—I should, I say, feel some exultation that this poverty-stricken Czar has been obliged to come forward and verify every word I then said. What has become of the two millions we are told the Emperor had subscribed to the Austrian loan? What has become of the 500,000*l.* he was going to advance to the Pope, or the half million he was going to bestow in his generosity on the Grand Duke of Tuscany? Oh, he ought to pay his scribes well in Western Europe, who have told so many lies for him. He ought to pay them well, seeing that they have been subjected to this full refutation of all they have said on his behalf at the hands of the Czar himself. If I had been employed to write up the wealth, power, and riches of a man who six months after was obliged to come before the citizens of London and sign his name to such a humiliating document as this imperial ukase, I should expect to be exceedingly well paid for the loss of character I had sustained.

Well, I stand here to repeat the very words I uttered twice on this platform at times when few would believe me. I say that the Russian Government in matters of finance has been for years—successfully, until now the bubble has burst—the most gigantic imposture in Europe. I use the words, as I do every word I say at a public meeting, advisedly. I have used them before, and, after due investigation, I come here to repeat them. I say that this money is wanted for the purpose of sustaining the ambition, the sanguinary brutality of a despot, who has all the tastes of Peter the Great, and all the lust of conquest of Louis XIV, without the genius of the one or the wealth of the other; and who would apply these principles to a great part of Europe, forgetting that this is the nineteenth instead of the seventeenth century; while utterly wanting, not merely the ability which would enable him to play such a part in history, but even the pecuniary means of enjoying the taste he possesses.

What are the real objects of the loan? To make up deficiencies, to pay debts incurred by the Emperor of Russia while inflicting the most wanton injuries on Hungary. I said before that the expenses of that war were not paid, and now I will tell you how it was carried on. The army was moved from the interior, not at the expense of the military chest, for, as I told you, that chest was empty, and could not afford the means for transporting the Russian guards from St. Petersburg to the confines of Hungary. The way the Emperor managed it was this:—He sent out orders to all the landowners and farmers on the line of march, commanding them to deposit at certain points indicated supplies of provisions and forage for the army. When the troops arrived, these provisions were taken possession of by the commissariat, and receipts were given, which receipts were to be received as cash in payment of taxes. So that when the taxes became due, and these receipts were handed in instead of money, it was found that the resources of the country had been all anticipated. The Government, then, has not the necessary means of carrying on its affairs. It is said that three millions sterling of these Treasury notes have been issued, accompanied by a ukase avowing that they had been issued on account of the expenses of the Hungarian war. You will thus see that these supplies have been just so much provisions borrowed from the agriculturists of the country through which the army passed, and that the Government hopes to raise the money to pay for them by coming to England for a loan. And I say that this money, now about to be raised by way of loan, is just as much issued for cutting the throats of unoffending men in Hungary, devastating their villages, and outraging their women, as if it had been lent before a single soldier had begun his march. I say in this case, as I said in the case of Austria, that it makes no difference whether the money be lent a little before or a little after. The operations were based on the expectation of a loan from England, temporary expedients were used pending the realisation of that loan, and therefore, the English capitalists who advance their money will really be the abettors of the crimes and the cruelty of these Continental despots.

Such are the purposes, and not railways, for which this money is wanted ; and are we to be told that because the loan will pay five per cent. we are not to inquire into the purposes for which it is raised? I can only say, that if a man has a right to make the most he can of his money without any inquiry as to the means, there was a very worthy man used harshly the other day at the Old Bailey, by being sentenced to twelve months' imprisonment and hard labour for only being the landlord of some infamous house out of which he realised a profit of twenty per cent. It is quite certain that this man may console himself in his confinement by thinking that his conduct was quite consistent with the new code of morality lately introduced into the City. But I do not reckon much on moral restraints. I think more may be done by appealing to motives of self-interest, and showing the risk there is in subscribing to these loans. Who would go and lend money to an irresponsible despot who never publishes any account

of his income or expenditure? I was looking through the
*Almanach de Gotha*, thinking I might find in it some traces
of the income and expenditure of Russia. There was something more or less on that subject respecting every other
state, but when I came to Russia I found these expressions:
' We are sorry to be altogether without information as to the
revenue or expenditure of Russia.' Now, that is the investment which is considered good in the city of London, simply
because the borrower is a thousand miles off. How would
a man, whose affairs were in such a state, but living in England, be received if he attempted to borrow money? How
would you like it in the case of railways? At present,
although you have six-monthly meetings, auditors, secreta-
ries, and the most complete surveillance, yet, by a strange
inconsistency, one of the parties most diligent in abetting the
Emperor of Russia is as anxiously abetting a Government
audit to look after the affairs of the railways. That is my
first objection. We do not know what security we are to
have for this money, which we know is wasted in unproductive employment. The next objection I make to this investment is, that you are lending money to a sovereign who
founds his throne on the most combustible elements in all
Europe. It is not irrelevant to the subject, if a sovereign
comes here publicly to solicit money from the citizens of
London, to say a word as to the prospects of his empire. The
Emperor of Russia is the only sovereign in the world who
rules over white slaves—twenty millions of serfs, who are
bought and sold with the land. Do you think that a safe
state of society in the present age? The ideas and principles
of freedom have been marching from west to east for centuries,
and slavery and serfdom have disappeared before the spirit of
the age, until progress was arrested on the confines of Russia.
Do you think it will long stop there in these days of the
steam-boat, the railway, and the telegraph? On the contrary,
you must expect that the serfs of Russia, being men, will

prefer freedom to slavery ; and that, being ten to one of their masters, they will do in Russia as they have done in every other country in Europe, sooner or later assert their freedom.

What security do you think you will have when the conflagration takes place in Russia, as it most probably will before many years have passed away?—because there never has been a case in which the emancipation of the serfs on a large scale was effected except through the agency of a revolution. What do you expect for your loan in the event of a revolution in Russia ? What will the people of Russia say of the men who lent their money to enable the Emperor to maintain his tyranny over his serfs ? I say they will repudiate the debt. And, mind you, this custom of lending money by more refined states to barbarous Governments is a great means of perpetuating their tyranny. It gives them the power of governing in a way which they could not attempt if depending on their own people for the supplies. Go back to your own history—to the time of the Plantagenets, when England obtained her liberties step by step. How? Through the necessities and embarrassments of her kings. One got a loan for one franchise, another redeemed his jewels with another. That was the way in which the people of this country wrung liberty from their sovereigns, time after time, through their necessities; but if our ancient kings could have gone to the more solvent states of Italy, or the merchants of Venice, who stood towards England then pretty much as England stands towards Russia now, and could have borrowed five millions independently of their people, when, think you, would the liberties of the people of England have been secured ? Where would have been the liberties of England under such circumstances? And do you not think these things will pervade the minds of the masses in the east of Europe ? Will they not ask you by what right you lend your money to any irresponsible despot, to enable him to perpetuate their slavery? What answer can you give them? Why, we got five per cent. for our money!

But there is another difficulty which I wish those who lend money to the Russian Government to bear in mind. We may not be strong enough in this room, although we represent pretty much public opinion out of it; we may not be strong enough, by this expression of opinion, to prevent people lending their money to Russia; but let them well understand that we, the taxpayers of England, who are no parties to the loan, will be no parties to the collection of their debts. Hitherto, there has been a sort of vague notion that if Governments fail in paying their debts to the English creditors, the powers of our Government may be brought to bear to enforce payment. There has been some correspondence between parties so interested and Lord Palmerston, and the noble Lord, although declining to interfere, yet reserved to himself the power of interfering if he thought proper. Now, I tell those who lend their money to the Russian Government, with an idea that they can make our Government the collector of their debts, that we have sufficient power to prevent them making our foreign Minister a bumbailiff. I warn those who lend their money to these bankrupt Governments, whether in Europe or elsewhere, that we have the power—we, the taxpayers of this country—to prevent our Government sending, at the instance of these loanmongers, ships of war or even diplomatists to demand their money. On the contrary, I believe from my heart, that if the time should come—and most assuredly many in this room will live to see it, when not one farthing of this Russian loan will be paid—I believe that the enlightened opinion of this country will exult in the loss of the money, not from ill-will to the unfortunate people who hold the bonds, but from a belief that it is a righteous retribution, and that it will operate as a warning to prevent similar transactions in future. Are not these important points for consideration? Will any one deny that we have the power of preventing the Government putting the taxpayers to expense in collecting these loans? Will it not make an important change in the prospects of these loan-mongers, when it is known to the world that the taxpayers of England separate themselves altogether from the speculators in such matters?

There is another uncertainty which I wish to point out to the holders of these loans. Nobody can deny that there is a change of opinion on the whole subject of these foreign loans; nobody can deny that we have put their promoters on the defensive, and that on the grounds of political economy, expediency, and justice, they are gradually losing ground in public opinion. That is the work of six months. We have only begun our work. But is it not very clear, that as this opinion goes on gathering strength, and as the raising of loans becomes more difficult in this country, it will diminish the chances of the payment of the interest of loans already effected? Let it be once known that there will be no more loans, and we shall soon have repudiation all over the world. Since the peace of 1815, the Governments of Europe have borrowed more money than they have paid interest to their creditors. That is to say, the kind and agreeable British public have been lending money out of one pocket, and receiving it back in interest in the other. But let them once see that there is no more chance of getting your cash, and you will see that a very slight chance remains of your dividends. But I do not come here with the idea of warning any of those capitalists who take this loan as agents, or the speculators who write for it. We all understand how that is done now. A certain house engages—I'll let you behind the scenes a little. A certain house undertakes to be the contractor. As soon as the contractor has settled his terms—and they do not always tell you the whole of the terms—he sends out circulars to his friends; that is, those speculators whose names he has in his books, and who are accustomed to put down their names for a certain amount of these loans. These brokers, bankers, and speculators are all invited to put down their names as subscribers to the loan. They send in their names for 50,000*l.*, 30,000*l.*, or 20,000*l.* And why? Because they expect to be able to redistribute these sums to their customers, their clients, and their acquaintances, at a profit—not with the view of holding the stock themselves. I venture to say, that not five per cent. of the loan which will be subscribed for up to Monday next will be taken by parties who really intend to hold it as a permanent investment.

I came down this morning from the west end of the town in an omnibus, sitting opposite to a gentleman. As we were riding along he looked out of the window and saw a placard with the words, 'Great meeting on the Russian loan.' He said to me, 'Mr. Cobden is going to have a meeting, I believe.' 'Yes,' I said, 'I believe he is.' 'It's very odd,' he observed, 'that he should presume to dictate to capitalists as to how they should lay out their money.' 'Well,' I said, 'if he attempts to dictate, it is rather hard. But I suppose he allows you to do as you like.' 'But,' said he, 'he holds public meetings to denounce this loan; yet I should not wonder if he would be very glad himself to have 20,000*l.* of it.' I said, 'Have you taken any yourself?' He replied, 'I have—50,000*l.*, and I intend to pay it all up.' I then said to him, 'Would you like to leave that property to your children?' 'No,' he said, 'I don't intend to keep it more than two years at the outside, and I hope to get a couple per cent. profit upon it.'

Now it is with that view that that gentleman is going to pay up his calls—that is, if he thinks of doing so. That is not the ordinary case; they generally pay up one call, and then sell the stock at any profit which they can get upon it; and the loss of holding these securities—I said it before, and I repeat it now—the loss falls upon individuals who were totally unconnected with the taking of the loan—tradesmen retired from business, widows and orphans, trustees and others who invest money in what they regard as a permanent security, in order to obtain the interest upon it. Well, now, I declare most solemnly, after looking into this subject of Russia, as I have done for the last eighteen years, that I would not give 25*l*. per cent. for the Russian Five per Cent. Stock, which is being dealt in to-day by the bulls and bears at 107—I would not take 100*l*. worth of it at that price for permanent investment, and with the view of leaving it as a part of the dependence of my children. We do not profess to come here to advise those brokers and capitalists who originally take these loans ; we know that they always make money, even when other people lose. I ask you to go back to the loans which have been contracted—for instance, by the house of Messrs. Baring and Co. I ask you to inquire for yourselves how some of the loans which have been taken by that house have turned out in relation to the interests of those who have ultimately become the depositories of the bonds. The contractors did not perhaps lose by them ; but I get letters daily from persons who have had Spanish bonds, Guatemala bonds, Portuguese bonds, and the rest, describing the sorrows and sufferings which they have experienced as the result of having been entrapped into purchasing such bonds.

I say, then, that in coming here to denounce this transaction, we do so in the interest of the unwary ; we do so to guard against these transactions, men who have not had the same opportunity as some of us have had of investigating this matter. And if we can by this means place an obstacle in the way of these warlike and despotic sovereigns, when they are coming to raise money from the civilised industry of this country, in order that it may be expended in barbarous waste in Russia and other countries, I say that we shall have done society good service. I ask only for just so much confidence in what I say as I am entitled to in consequence of what I asserted before with regard to the state of the Russian finances. Take nothing for granted in reference to Russia. Systematic fraud and deception, and lying and misrepresentation, are the policy of the Government of that country. A great part of the very money which is now about to be loaned in this country will, I have no doubt, be spent in espionage in Constantinople—in bribing employés and functionaries there, and in bribing a portion of the press in Germany and in France. [Cheers, and loud cries of the ' *Times*,' followed by hissing.] We cannot believe that any of the press of England would be bribed. [Laughter, and renewed cries of the ' *Times*,' amidst which were heard the words ' *Morning Post*.'] To be sure, some of our newspapers have been doing the work of despotism rather heartily. And now they seem disposed to play the part of vampires or ghouls. They are worse than vampires and ghouls. How shall we describe those indescribable monsters who, when their foes have fallen, when they are gone into exile, when they are separated from their wives and children, when they are starving in the streets,— brought down to the begging of their bread in the midst of winter,—how, I ask, shall we describe the wretches who are then base enough to traduce the character of such men? I spoke of ghouls and vampires. They prey upon the corpse of the material body : we have had no monster as yet which lived by destroying the character of a fallen foe.

Now, Gentlemen, this money will be spent, I say, in bribing the Continental press—in paying for an insurrection in Paris, no matter whether it be a red republican or a legitimist insurrection, so that it causes confusion and violence —ay, in paying somebody to create confusion in this room, if they durst. Talk of red republicanism being anarchical ! There is nothing in the world so anarchical as the despotism of St. Petersburg. Let it not be concluded, from what I say of the Russian Government, that we have here fallen into the great delusion which prevails in this country on the subject of the character of the Russian people. I have had before to

correct some misapprehensions with regard to the finances
and resources of Russia. There is nothing in reference to
which there is so almost universal a misapprehension as
exists with regard to the character of the great mass of the
Russian people. In the first place, we have them represented
to us as a collection of barbarous and discontented hordes,
who are anxious to quit their country, and to pour, like an
avalanche, on Western Europe. There is no greater delusion
in the world than the supposition that the population of
Russia have any desire to leave their native land. There is
not a people in the world who are prouder of their country
than are the Russians of theirs. There is not a people in the
world who are less disposed to cross their frontiers to commit
an act of depredation or spoliation, much less who would
leave their country to become permanent settlers in another
land. I speak now of the national character. Nor are the
Russians a warlike people. There is no greater delusion than
the supposition that we have to deal with the Russians as a
warlike people. Why, the army is so unpopular, that when
the Russian peasant is torn from his village by the conscription, there is a procession in the village, of which the priest is
the leader, which resembles a funeral ceremony. When I
was at St. Petersburg, an English merchant described to me
a striking scene, in order to illustrate the repugnance of the
Russian people to enter the army. He said that he entered a
street in St. Petersburg where a surgeon was examining the
conscripts, in order to ascertain whether or not they were fit
for the service. Some conscripts had entered a house. They
were there denuded and examined, in order that it might be
seen whether they were fit to be admitted into the army.
One of the men was declared to be unfit for the service; and
so great was his excitement, that in the frenzy of his delirium
and joy, he actually rushed from the house into the street in
the state of nudity in which he had been examined. Well,
now, I say the character of the Russian people is a gentle

character. They have a great regard for human life. They are, indeed, as slaves, addicted to slavish vices; they lie, they pilfer, and they are too apt to get drunk, or at least to indulge in the use of intoxicating liquors. But great crimes— the crimes of murder and violence—are rare in Russia; and I wish it to be distinctly understood, that in dealing with the Emperor Nicholas we will not allow it to be said that we stand here to menace or affront a population of sixty millions of people.

But what will be the grievance of this people as against you? It is you who enable the Government to maintain its enormous army; it is you who enable the Emperor to keep up a navy for which he drags twenty or thirty thousand of his vassals from their villages, placing them for six months in the year in barracks in order that they may, for three summer months, sail on board his ships in the Baltic and the Black Sea, to the great amusement of British and American sailors. The Russians have even a greater horror of the sea service than they have of the land service. They are dragged from their villages to be put into ships of war, and imprisoned in barracks at Cronstadt, and all because you lend the Emperor of Russia money to enable him to do this. Once withdraw these loans, and from that moment the whole policy of the Emperor of Russia, as well as of the Emperor of Austria, will be changed. Russia would no longer be able to menace Turkey—Russia would no longer be able to send its army into Hungary—Russia would no longer be able to hire these spies and journals in Western Europe; and the Emperor, not having the means of coercion placed in his hands by foreign aid, would be obliged to conciliate his people, in order to govern them securely.

I would, in conclusion, exhort those who may read what I am saying, to consider well before they invest one farthing of their money in a security based upon the life of an individual like this, one who does not belong to a long-lived family, and whose son may be utterly unfitted to cope with the difficulties which await him, when the present Czar dies. In thus lending your money, you place it upon a volcano. You may rise any morning and find that the vast empire has been torn asunder, that a spirit of violence and insubordination is spreading throughout its serf population. Come it will—it may come on any day. This boasted Emperor of Russia, of whose energy and talents we hear so much, is doing the most likely thing which a man could do to precipitate and render inevitable such a convulsion as I speak of. Instead of conciliating the nobles, he is holding them with the tight hand of despotism—he is pretending to give emancipation to the serfs only to disappoint their hopes; and, instead of employing the energies and resources of the empire in preparing for the greatest evil which could hang over any country, namely, that which arises from the possession of twenty millions of serfs, he is increasing his expenditure, embarrassing his finances, enlarging his army and navy, trying to keep the whole of Europe in a state of perturbation, and making enemies to himself of every civilised people on the face of the earth.

I ask all who may read what I say not to be daunted by what they are told is said in the City, by the statement that everybody is laughing at them—that everybody is laughing at Mr. Cobden's letter. They said that everybody was laughing at my letter about the Austrian loan. We were told then, in reference to the Austrian loan, as we are told now with regard to the Russian, that it was all taken before we met. Well, now, I was calculating this morning, before I came here, what is the present state of the account of those who took the Austrian loan. I am very happy to say that that loan has remained principally in the hands of the first subscribers; that it is the great bankers, the great brokers, the great speculators who had been really caught in this case; and for that very reason, and no other, you will never hear of another Austrian loan.    Now, what is the present state of the account of those speculators?    I find, by a very short calculation which I made this morning, that at the present rate on the Exchange, they have had a loss on that loan up to this day of 145,000*l.*    So I think the laugh is on the other side of the face—and it is only the beginning of the laugh. We ask, therefore, everybody who has a conscience which is proof against one per cent.—on the ground of morality, on the ground of political economy, on political grounds, and on the ground of personal safety and security, we ask every one to ponder when he reads what has been said to-day – we ask all to do their utmost to discredit this most nefarious attempt on their credulity and their pockets.

# FOREIGN POLICY.

## IV.

### HOUSE OF COMMONS, JUNE 28, 1850.

[On June 24, Mr. Roebuck made the following motion :—'That the principles which have hitherto regulated the Foreign Policy of Her Majesty's Government are such as were required to preserve untarnished the honour and dignity of this country, and at all times best calculated to maintain peace between this country and the various nations of the world.' The motion was carried by 46. (310 to 246.) The motion was in answer to a censure on Lord Palmerston's Administration carried on Lord Stanley's (the late Lord Derby's) motion in the House of Lords. The occasion of the censure was the support given by Lord Palmerston to one Pacifico, a Jew, who claimed to be a British subject, and pretended to have suffered great losses in a riot at Athens.]

IT was my wish to have done to-night, what I have frequently done before—to have given a silent vote ; finding, as I do, that nearly all the arguments on both sides have been stated by other Members much better than I could state them ; but I have been referred to, in common with several other Gentlemen on this side of the House, as likely to take a course different from our neighbours on this occasion, and I therefore think it necessary to say a few words.

First, I am anxious that, so far as I am concerned, the question should be put on its legitimate issue, and that it may not be still ·suggested that I am here for the purpose of indulging in a personal opposition; I trust that, at all events, I may be exempted from any such charge. In the next place,

I wish it to be understood, so far as I am concerned, that there is nothing in this case which involves any plot, conspiracy, or cabal of any kind whatever. The hon. Member for Sheffield (Mr. Roebuck) is the author of this motion; do you accuse him of being in any plot, conspiracy, or cabal? He has taken the initiative in the matter, and those who participate in the discussion merely comment upon the resolution so submitted to them by the hon. and learned Member. Lastly, I hope I may be exempted, at all events, from the sweeping charge made against Members who do not support this motion—that they are in the interest of despotism all over the world.

I have heard from several Gentlemen around me, some of whom I do not think extremely democratic, whom I have by no means found always supporting extreme Liberalism, very considerable intolerance towards those who do not take the same view with themselves in relation to the Government on this occasion. I will ask those Gentlemen, do they think me an ally of Russia or of Austria? Do they think I have shown less sympathy for the Hungarians or Italians than they have,—that I have less cosmopolitan sympathies than they? If, then, they admit me to be as liberal as themselves, surely they may allow me the freedom of taking the view my conscience dictates in a matter which has nothing on earth to do with constitutionalism or despotism.

As I understand it, the first thing before us is the conduct of our Government in Greece, though the hon. Member for Sheffield has widened that question, by the wording of his resolution, so as to cover the whole foreign policy of our Government. But as to the conduct of our Government in Greece, why, if this subject had been set before us in February, or even in March, within a few weeks after we had heard that fifteen British vessels of war had assembled in the Bay of Salamis to blockade the coast of a friendly Power, there would scarcely have been any difficulty in approaching

the subject in a calm and dispassionate way, apart from all
the extraneous matter with which it has been now encum-
bered. Really, when those who oppose this motion are off-
hand charged with plot, conspiracy, and cabal, I am tempted
to ask whether there has not been some little plot, conspiracy,
and cabal to get up an artificial excitement in the country on
the subject. Yes, I have seen placards and circulars; I am
not speaking without knowledge. However, the question is,
what was the conduct of our Government in relation to the
affairs of Greece? I have not brought my blue-books down
with me, and I shall not read a single line to you; but, as
there is much mystification on the subject, and as I wish to
deal fairly with all, I will state the case in a few words, so
that no one may take exception to it.

In the first place, Mr. Finlay, a Scotch gentleman, settles in
Greece twenty years ago, taking up his residence at Athens,
not as a merchant, not to promote British commerce in that
quarter of the world, but as a denizen of Greece. He purchases land in Athens and the neighbourhood; I have seen the
land, and I saw the much-discussed palace, just as it was
rising from this land. Land was bought on speculation, not
only in Athens but in the neighbourhood. Mr. Finlay thus
became interested in the prosperity of Athens. The Court of
Greece and its Government were at this time established at
Nauplia; it was desired by the proprietors and inhabitants of
Athens that the Government should resume its ancient and
classic seat, by removing to Athens. The landed proprietors
of Athens, deeply interested in again making it the metropolis
of Greece, instead of allowing it to remain what it was, little
better than a village of huts, all signed an engagement with
the commune or municipality of Athens to furnish land for
erecting public buildings upon, the price fixed being equiva-
lent to about 3¼*d.* to 3½*d.* per square yard. I do not intend
to go through all the correspondence on the subject of Mr.
Finlay's claim; I merely want to bring the matter to the

point on which you must all agree. Mr. Finlay was one of
more than one hundred persons who thus sold land to the
Greek Government; that is admitted by all parties in the
correspondence.   Among these proprietors who sold their
land for palaces and public buildings were several foreigners,
and among these foreigners were two whom Sir E. Lyons,
in his first letter to Lord Aberdeen, speaks of as fellow-
sufferers with Mr. Finlay—Mr. Hill, the agent of the Episco-
palian Society of America, and the Russian Consul-General.

These are facts that nobody denies.   I do not desire to
go into any controversy, but simply to draw the attention
of the House and of the country to the fact, that all the
other proprietors of these lands, without exception, agreed
to the terms, and accepted the terms, that were offered by the
commissioners appointed by the municipality for that purpose.
['No.'] Does the hon. and learned Member for Southampton,
with his blue-book before him, mean to say that the fact
is not stated in that blue-book as I have given it?   ['No,'
from Mr. Cockburn.]   Why, it is stated there expressly.
['No.']   Will the hon. and learned Member tell me that
Mr. Hill and the Russian Consul-General accepted the
money, or that they did not stand in the same position with
Mr. Finlay?   I know Mr. Hill; it is an honour to any one
to be acquainted with him; for, as it is well stated by Sir
E. Lyons, in that first letter of his to which I have referred,
there is no one to whom the rising generation of Greeks is
more indebted than to Mr. Hill and his family.   Mr. Finlay
refused to take the money which the bulk of the other proprietors accepted; a long controversy ensued, and the result
was the approach of our ships of war to the Bay of Salamis.
I have not stated anything so far that any one can deny.

Now we come to M. Pacifico.   M. Pacifico had his house
outrageously attacked; that no one can deny; he sends in
his bill to the Government, and, with that bill in our hands,
our ships of war enter the Piræus.   I blushed with indig-

nation when I read the inventory of M. Pacifico. It is no matter of surprise that hon. Members have deprecated any allusion to the details of that bill, as if the whole of this question was not a question of details. ['No, no.'] Why, with the exception of the apology required for the insult to Fantome, all the rest is a matter of money. ['No, no.'] I beg pardon; I say all the rest is a matter of money, and your exclamations only show how you are acting in this case upon blind passion and party spirit. M. Pacifico sends in his bill to the Government; he charges for a bedstead 150*l.*, he charges for the sheets 30*l.*, he charges for the pillow-case 10*l.*, for two coverlids 25*l.* This inventory is so deeply disgraceful to all concerned in it, that, first, you tried to evade the question, by saying the case was not one for *nisi prius* details, and then you turned round, and said that Pacifico brought all this furniture to Athens, to sell it to the King of Greece. But if we go into the bill for the personal apparel, the every-day working apparel of M. Pacifico and his family, we find there just the same sort of thing; it is all in unison with the 150*l.* bedstead. Why, there is a gold watch with appendages put down at 50*l.* for one of the items. When I first read the account, I thought the whole thing was a mistake, and that in writing out the bill, pounds sterling had been put down instead of drachmas, for I am pretty sure that in every case drachmas instead of pounds would have much more nearly represented the real value of the articles.

Next comes the case of the six Ionian boats at Salcina, and their demand for 235*l.*—for I will not enter into details; then the case of the four Ionians, who charged the Greek authorities with having outraged them, and thumb-screwed them, and taken their boats, two to Patras, and two to Pyrgos. The Greek authorities controvert the statement of our Consul upon this subject, and the correspondence altogether puzzles us as to who is right and who wrong; but the noble Lord, nothing doubting, settles the matter in a few

lines, by ordering that the four complainants shall be paid
20*l.* each by the Greek Government.

Then comes the Fantome case. A British ship of war is
lying off Patras; a boat goes on shore at nine o'clock at
night, when it is dark; the coxswain lands a midshipman,
not at the usual place of disembarkation, but on the beach;
the midshipman goes to see his father, a boy preceding him
with a lantern; on his return he is taken into custody by
two officials and conveyed to the station, in default of giving
a satisfactory account of himself; the Greeks, bear you in
mind, not speaking one word of English, nor the Englishman
one word of Greek. Now, suppose a Frenchman landing in
the same way from abroad, by night, near Brighton, not
at the ordinary landing-place but on the beach, and observed
by preventive officers, neither party understanding one word
of the other's language, and mutual explanation being consequently impossible. Why, the blockademen would at once
put the landing party down for a French smuggler, and would
take him into custody and convey him to the station, where,
an interpreter being procured, the explanation deficient would
be supplied, and the arrested person be dismissed with all
proper apology. This was precisely what was done to the
midshipman. As soon as an interpreter was found, and it
was ascertained who the Englishman was, he was at once
liberated, and respectfully conveyed to his ship.

There you have the statement of all our grievances against
Greece. ['No, no.'] I will not go into the merits of them;
say the Greeks were wrong, or we were wrong, just as you
please; but admit they were wrong, and what I want to know
is, whether the wrong was not one that might have been
readily settled by other means than by sending fifteen ships
of war into the Bay of Salamis? I know I take a very
vulgar, mercenary view of the matter, but I repeat my
question,—Was there no other way to settle the question
than by this immense array of force? It is quite evident

that the only reason why this entire matter was not settled before, was the bad spirit that existed between our representative and the Government of Greece. I do not speak disparagingly of Sir Edmund Lyons; any other functionary under the same circumstances could scarcely have been so long there, any more than at Madrid or elsewhere, without getting mixed up with the local politics in the same way that Sir E. Lyons was. That was the origin and reason why it was found that for six or nine months there were no letters addressed by the noble Lord to Sir E. Lyons, and why there had been no adjustment of these petty differences until it was necessary to send fifteen ships of war to Athens.

Now, is there not something wrong at the bottom of this? Is there not something that requires to be mended? Is it worth while to have an Ambassador there with 5000*l.* a year embroiling you with the Government, and begetting bad blood and animosity? Why, I would rather have no one but a Consul there, whose duty it should be to look after your commerce, and who should be told, ' Never go to Athens at all, for, if you mix yourself up with political matters, somebody else shall be appointed in your place.' If you would do this, you would avoid the absurdity of having to employ fifteen vessels of war to collect a debt of 6000*l.* But everybody said that something else was meant besides obtaining redress for injuries to British subjects in Greece. I believe there was something in the background that I have not heard. It is said that the noble Viscount intended this demonstration at Athens as a menace to Russia. But I say, how does this answer its purpose as a demonstration against Russia? The moment the Court of Russia hear of the demonstration, I find that they send a remonstrance against the Government of this country—a remonstrance couched in language I never expected to hear from a semi-barbarous country like Russia to this: read, I ask you, the extraordinary language used by Count Nesselrode to Lord Palmerston, and then read the

answer of the latter, and see how different is the tone adopted
by him to a country which is powerful compared with what
he makes use of to one that is weak.

Well, then, I ask again, what was the advantage of this
demonstration, when the only result of it is a hectoring epistle
from Count Nesselrode, to which the noble Viscount sent a
very meek and lamb-like reply? The reason why I abhor the
policy of injustice and aggression—for I call it injustice and
aggression to send ships of war against a weak country to
enforce demands which might have been amicably settled—
is, that you place yourselves in such a position that you are
obliged to submit to language like this from the Russian
Court. And why are you obliged to submit to it? Because
you are weak, and weak only on account of committing an
injustice, and of being conscious of having done so; for otherwise, so far from this country being in a condition to be bullied
by Russia, such are the advantages you possess in the knowledge and use of mechanical science and in the advanced state
of the arts over Russia, that if you behaved with dignity to
small states, she would not venture even to look at you,
far less to use such language towards you.

I have asked, why was not this affair settled by other means
than by ships of war? I now come to a part of the policy
and conduct of the Foreign Office altogether irreconcilable with
the notions of those hon. Gentlemen who did me the honour,
to the number of eighty, of voting for my motion in favour of
international arbitration. It is quite clear, it is said, that
the noble Viscount did not resort to arbitration. My charge
against him is, that he did resort to arbitration after having
made use, in the first place, of fifteen ships of war. No sooner
was the demonstration known, than an envoy arrives from
France with tenders of mediation. And now, I must say, I
have read with feelings nearly akin to contempt for diplomacy,
the accounts of what took place between the noble Lord at the
head of the Foreign Office and M. Drouyn de Lhuys—I have

read the French accounts and the accounts in the blue-books, and must confess I have felt the most sovereign contempt for diplomacy. M. Drouyn de Lhuys came over in the most loyal spirit, as I believe, to offer to settle this beggarly affair of a few thousand pounds with Greece. He told the noble Lord frankly, as a proof of his sincerity, and he has repeated it in a letter to Lord Normanby, that it would be useful to the French Government to be allowed to settle it, or, to use a common American phrase, that it would give them 'political capital' in France. How did the noble Lord receive the approaches of M. Drouyn de Lhuys? Was it in the way any man of business, accustomed to the management of affairs, would have done? Did he say, 'We are much obliged to you; this affair of a few thousands has been a long time standing over,—take it and settle it, and we shall be very much obliged to the Government of France?' Would not that have been the rational and reasonable way of meeting him? Instead of this, what does the noble Viscount say? He higgles with M. Drouyn de Lhuys over the different words to be used,—over 'good offices,' 'mediation,' and 'arbitration.' I declare that both in French and English it fairly puzzles one to make anything out of it; but it appears, by the accounts, that the noble Lord insists he won't take 'arbitration'—it must be 'good offices.' M. Drouyn de Lhuys, in the French account of what took place, given by him to General Lahitte, describes himself to have entreated the noble Lord to extend a little the powers of the negotiators—to yield to an arbitration, and not to go determinedly on in the affair. But no; the noble Viscount was determined to have what he demanded; and all he would require of France was to persuade Greece to give what he asked. Baron Gros went out to Athens crippled by these conditions, but he set to work at once with Mr. Wyse. I think it is evident Baron Gros had the most earnest desire to settle the matter. Indeed, his character as a diplomatist was largely involved

in his success in arranging it, and he went to work evidently disposed to surmount every possible difficulty; but
when he came to the case of Pacifico, and heard from all
he conversed with in Athens the real facts of the case—when,
to use a vulgar phrase, he found it out, and discovered it was
an atrocious attempt at swindling, he could not swallow it.
What was going on at the very same time in London? At
this very same moment commence the ' good offices' between
the noble Lord and M. Drouyn de Lhuys. So he has two
negotiations going, one at Athens and the other at London,
and all to settle this paltry affair of a few thousand pounds.
It ended as might be expected—a little delay on the part
of a courier, some mistake or delay in not putting a letter
into the letter-bag in time for the night's post, and the
whole affair was broken off in London before they in Athens
could know what was doing. The negotiations were thrown
aside—our ships were ordered to do their worst—Greece
submitted—and you got your money. What follows? The
French Government, irritated by your conduct, withdraws
its Minister,—and now comes the quarrel I have with the
noble Lord—now comes my case against him for not accepting arbitration in the first instance. Actually, after your
ships of war had extorted the money from Greece, and a large
part of it was already placed in bank, the noble Viscount
consented, in the most humiliating way,—for I consider the
communications received from Lord Normanby most humiliating,—to accept what he had before refused, and you have
now returned to this state, that by France withdrawing its
ambassador you are obliged to do away all you have done
by means of your fifteen ships of war. And you have agreed
to substitute the Convention of London for the terms you
obtained by your fleet at Athens. Yes; have you not agreed
to give up the money lodged in the Bank for payment?
What do you call that? Your ships of war extort money
from Greece; the French Government tells you, ' Give that

money back ; you must take the terms of the Convention of London.' We yield, and so the matter ends. But it is not yet ended.

And here is my complaint against the noble Lord. It seems as if the system at the Foreign Office is calculated to breed and perpetuate quarrels. First, you submit to rebuke from Russia, and next you are humiliated before France—the two countries, some of our very knowing people say, we intended to terrify by our demonstration against Greece ; but the question is not yet settled. There are three arbitrators appointed to settle the question of Pacifico's claim against the Court of Athens. As my hon. Friends near me, who voted for my motion, will see, they have been obliged to resort to my plan of arbitration, and the matter, after all the display of force, is still left open, and requires three arbitrators to decide it. I cannot imagine a more complete triumph of the principle I advocated last year than the details of this proceeding. Why, here are hon. Gentlemen behind me groaning. I am not surprised at it, for they really must be groaning at the thought of their own inconsistency. For what are we called on to vote ?—that this matter has been most ably, justly, and dexterously managed. But I do not think it is finished at all ; for, independently of three arbitrators and of 'their good offices,' mind you, there is a very ominous little legacy left to us in the despatch of Lord Normanby in the probability of Greece quarrelling with us again. For my own part, seeing the unfortunate result of 'good offices,' I should not wonder if we had another quarrel with France for the exercise of her 'good offices' also. But it is said that there is, beside, some cause of quarrel with Russia, on account of vessels seized in the Levant and in the Greek ports, and M. Brunow has fairly given us notice he may have reclamations to make for the value of the property which fell into our hands, and for the loss we occasioned, and I should not be surprised if you had another blue-book

very soon, containing correspondence with respect to seizures
by the Russians; and all this has arisen because the Foreign
Office would not submit this pettifogging business to arbitration.    France would have been proud to be your arbitrator; you refused her.    Then came the Convention, and at
last comes an arbitration on the whole matter; only you
submit on the most humiliating terms to conditions you had
before refused.

Now, let us take in two sums what the actual result has
been, so far as we have gone, in obtaining what we demanded.
Our whole claim on the Greek Government was 33,000*l.*  The
whole amount we have actually received is 6400*l.*; so that,
as we stand at present, we appear before the nations of the
world as having made a demand for 33,000*l.*, and as having,
up to the present moment, received only 6400*l.*; and that
will show, in the face of the world, what the extent of your
injustice was in comparison with the justice of your claims.
And, looking to the claims of M. Pacifico, and to the opinions
of Baron Gros respecting them, I declare to you most solemnly
my firm belief is, that if the people of England understood the
merits of this question, and if they had read, as I have done,
the contents of the blue-books and of the inventory,—such is
the opinion I have of the generosity and justice of my countrymen, that, in spite of the galvanic effort to make this a
party question, they would be so disgusted, that they would
raise a subscription to pay back the Greek Government the
money it has given you.    In the next place, beside a vote
of approbation on account of this Greek affair, we are asked
to identify ourselves with the general foreign policy of the
Government since their accession to office.

Now, I say I should be the most inconsistent being on the
face of the earth if I gave such a vote.    Not many years ago, I
had to denounce, at a public meeting I called in Manchester,
the conduct of the noble Lord in the case of Syria; and I
remember afterwards denouncing his proceedings in Portugal

also. I moved in this House for a return of any vessels of
war belonging to us, which were at the time lying in the
Tagus, in reference to that business. I protested, too, at a
public meeting, and before a most enthusiastic audience, on
the noble Lord's conduct in the affairs of Sicily; and I am
now called on to vote my approbation of the proceedings
of the Foreign Office during the existence of the present
Administration. Why, I say if I did so, and gave that vote,
I think my mouth ought to be closed on any questions of
economy, retrenchment, or possibility of reducing our establishments for ever, because I am quite sure, if this system is
to continue, and if you are to send fifteen ships of war to
collect debts of 6,400*l.*, you not only cannot reduce your
establishments, but you have not establishments enough.
There has been a great deal said during the debate about
foreign intervention, but this is a principle which I thought
was acknowledged and admitted by all parties. Hon. Gentlemen on the other side of the House have never, since the
time of the Reform Bill, thought of anything so absurd as
obtaining popularity by the peculiar characteristic of being
the interferers in the affairs of other countries. I cannot
say there is as much wisdom on this side of the House, for
there seems to me a disposition here to take merit to the
party, because it has for its principle to interfere in the affairs
of other nations. That was not the doctrine of Lord Grey.
I remember the speech of the noble Lord in 1830. Nothing
electrified the country more than that exposition of his principles. He spoke of the wars of Mr. Pitt and of his successors
—of the 800,000,000*l.* of expenditure incurred in those wars;
and he pledged himself to the country that peace, non-intervention, and retrenchment, should be the watchwords of the
Whig party.

I ask the country fairly to decide whether the tone and
language of the speakers on this side of the House, on this
night, and in the course of this debate, have been in harmony

and unison with that sentiment of Lord Grey? Why, what has been the language of the hon. and learned Member for South-ampton (Mr. Cockburn), and for which he has been cheered to the echo? One-half of the Treasury benches were left empty, while hon. Members ran one after another, tumbling over each other in their haste to shake hands with the hon. and learned Member. Well, what did the hon. and learned Member say? I pass over his sneer against the men of peace and men of cotton, because we must allow gentlemen of the long robe some latitude, and allow them to forget the arena in which they are displaying their powers; but what would Lord Grey have said to the doctrine of the hon. and learned Gentleman, that we have no prospect of peace with the countries of Europe till they have adopted constitutional Governments? What sort of constitutional Governments? Is it our own? Why, even if they came so far as this, and suppose they adopt our form of Government, might not hon. Members in the Assembly at Washington get up and say, ' We will have no peace till we make the world republican?' The hon. and learned Gentleman seems to have set out with the doctrine, that we ought to interfere with the forms of Government of the na-tions of Europe, and, judging from the noble Lord's speech, I must say he appears to be no unwilling pupil in that school of policy. If the House of Commons votes its approbation of such sentiments, and the noble Lord acts on them, I think the Foreign Office will have undertaken the reform and con-stitutionalising of every country on the face of the earth. But do you think the people of this country, when they get cool, will see the wisdom of carrying out such a course? I claim for myself as much sympathy for foreigners struggling for liberty as any one in this House; but it is not true, as the hon. and learned Member for Sheffield (Mr. Roebuck) said, that I ever attended a public meeting, and said I was in favour of going to war, and that I made an exception from my general principles in favour of Hungary.

I am glad the hon. and learned Gentleman has stated this, and that I misunderstood him, as it may prevent my being misunderstood in future. I never in public advocated interference with the Government of foreign countries, even in cases where my feelings were most strongly interested in anything relating to their domestic affairs or concerns. When I see that principle violated by others, as in the case of the Russian invasion of Hungary, and when I see a portion of the press of this civilised nation hounding on that semi-barbarous empire, then, believing that this is almost the only country where there is a free platform, and where it cannot be corrupted, as a portion of the press may have been, I shall denounce it, as I denounced the Government of Russia, and, as I stated at the same time, I was ready to denounce our own Government also. But it is a matter of very small importance what my individual opinion may be, when you come to the question, whether the Government of this country shall become the propagandist of their opinions in foreign countries. I maintain this Government has no right to communicate except through the Government of other countries; and that, whether it be a republic, a despotism, or a monarchy, I hold it has no right to interfere with any other form of Government. Mark the effect of your own principle, if you take the opposite ground. If you recognise the principle of intervention in your Government, you must tolerate it in other nations also. With what face could you get up and denounce the Emperor of Russia for invading Hungary, after the doctrine advocated by the hon. and learned Member (Mr. Cockburn) tonight had been adopted by this country? I say, if you want to benefit nations who are struggling for their freedom, establish as one of the maxims of international law the principle of nonintervention. If you want to give a guarantee for peace, and, as I believe, the surest guarantee for progress and freedom, lay down this principle, and act on it, that no foreign State has a right by force to interfere with the domestic concerns of another State, even to confer a benefit on it, with its own consent. What will you say respecting the conduct of the noble Lord in the case of Switzerland? He joined there in an intervention, though the great majority of the Protestant cantons protested against it, and does the very thing he is seeking to prevent.

But I come back to my principle. Do you want to benefit the Hungarians and Italians? I think I know more of them·than most people in this country. I sympathised with them during their manly struggles for freedom, and I have admired and respected them, not less in their hour of adversity. I will tell you the sentiments of the leading men of the Hungarians. I have seen them all, and I must say that, much as I admired them during their noble struggle, what I have seen of them in adversity has entitled them, in my belief, to still greater respect, for I never saw men—except Englishmen, to whom they bear in many respects a close resemblance—bear adversity with such manly fortitude and dignified self-respect. They have avoided all expressions of sympathy from public meetings, and, loathing the idea of being dependent on the charity of others, have sought, by emigration to America and elsewhere, an opportunity of subsisting by the labour of their own hands. These men say,— 'We don't ask you to help us, or to come to our assistance. Establish such a principle as shall provide we shall not be interfered with by others.' And what do the Italians say? They don't want the English to interfere with them, or to help them. 'Leave us to ourselves,' they say. 'Establish the principle that we shall not be interfered with by foreigners.'

I will answer the hon. and learned Gentleman's cheer. He seems to ask, How will you keep out Austria from Italy, and Russia from Hungary? I will give him an illustration of what I mean. Does he remember when Kossuth took refuge in Turkey, and that Austria and the Emperor of Russia demanded him back? I beg him to understand that this

illustrious refugee was not saved by any intervention of the
Foreign Secretary.  Has it not been admitted that the Emperor of Russia gave up his claim before the courier arrived
from England?  What was it, then, that liberated them?
It was the universal outbreak of public opinion and public
indignation in Western Europe.  And why had public opinion
this power?   Because this demand for the extradition of
political offenders was a violation of the law of nations, which
declares that persons who have committed political offences in
one State shall find a sanctuary in another, and ought not to
be delivered up.  If our Government were always to act upon
this principle of non-intervention, we should see the law of
nations declaring itself as clearly against the invasion of a
foreign country as it has spoken out against the extradition
of political refugees.  Let us begin, and set the example to
other nations of this non-intervention.  I have no doubt that
our example and protest would exercise some influence upon
the Governments of Austria and Russia; but what possible
moral influence can this country have with those States when
the Government goes abroad to interfere with the domestic
affairs of other countries?

It is said, however, that the noble Lord (Palmerston) goes
abroad as the champion of liberalism and constitutionalism.
But I cannot fall into this delusion.  I cannot trace the
battle that we are taught to believe is going on under the
noble Viscount's policy between liberalism and despotism
abroad.   I do not think that the noble Lord is more democratic than his colleagues, or than the right hon. Gentleman opposite (Sir R. Peel).  I believe the noble Lord is of an
active turn of mind—that he likes these protocols and con-
ventions, and that the smaller the subject, the better it suits
his taste.  I do not find that the noble Lord has taken up any
great question of constitutional freedom abroad.  Did he ever
protest against the invasion of Hungary by Russia?  He
made a speech against Austria, I remember, on that occasion;

but he did not breathe a syllable against Russia. The only
allusion he made to Russia was in the nature of an apology,
uttered in a sense that seemed to justify the part taken by
Russia rather than otherwise. Then it is said, that in Italy
the noble Lord endeavours to establish constitutional government and representative institutions. The noble Lord told
Lord Minto to go to Italy, not, as he himself declared, to recommend Parliaments or representative assemblies, but merely
to advise the Government to adopt administrative reforms.
But that was not what the Italian people wanted. They
wanted security for their liberties by constitutional reforms,
and the adoption of a representative system; and that was
what the noble Lord did not recommend should be given to
them. I believe the progress of freedom depends more upon
the maintenance of peace, the spread of commerce, and the
diffusion of education, than upon the labours of Cabinets or
Foreign-offices. And if you can prevent those perturbations
which have recently taken place abroad in consequence of your
foreign policy, and if you will leave other nations in greater
tranquillity, those ideas of freedom will continue to progress,
and you need not trouble yourselves about them.

On this side of the House, some persons have been me-
naced with very terrible consequences, and with the adverse
opinion of the public, if they do not vote for this resolution.
I can only say, that I, like many other hon. Members, sit
commonly here and in committee-rooms of this House for
twelve hours in the course of the day. Allow two or three
hours a-day for the transaction of necessary business at home,
and that is not play, but hard work. But why should we
sit in this House and undergo this labour, unless to advocate those opinions and convictions which we believe to be
true and just? If I have one conviction stronger than another, it is one upon which I made a first public exhibition
of myself in print. The principle which I defend is assailed in this motion, and upon it, for fifteen years, my

opinion has been again and again recorded. I have never seen reason to change that opinion, but, on the contrary, everything confirms me in my conviction of its truth. If I remain in this seat, I will try to promote the progress of these opinions; and I hope to see the day when the intercourse of nations will exhibit the same changes as those which have taken place in the intercourse of individuals. In private life, we no longer find it necessary to carry arms about us for our protection, as did our forefathers. We have discontinued the practice of duelling, and something should be done to carry the same spirit into the intercourse of nations. In domestic life, physical correction is giving way to moral influence. In schools and in lunatic asylums this principle is successfully adopted, and even the training of the lower animals is found to be better done by means of suasion. Cannot you adopt something of this in the intercourse of nations? Whoever brings forward such measures shall have my support; and if it should happen, as the hon. Member (Mr. Bernal Osborne) has threatened me, that the consequences of my vote will be the loss of my seat in this House, then I say that, next to the satisfaction of having contributed to the advance of one's convictions, is, in my opinion, the satisfaction of having sacrificed something for them.

# FOREIGN POLICY.

## V.

### ROCHDALE, JUNE 26, 1861.

[The following Speech was made by Mr. Cobden before his constituents, after the French Commercial Treaty had been negotiated.]

I APPEAR here in conformity with a time-honoured practice in your borough, which has led your representative annually to come and give an account of his stewardship to you—to afford you an opportunity of conferring with him, and questioning him on any topic relating to his public duty and the interests of his constituency. That custom, I think, was justifiable in your case by the independent and honourable course which you have always followed in the election of your Liberal representatives to Parliament. But I appear here to-night under rather peculiar circumstances; for I have no account to give of my stewardship in Parliament, having been occupied for nearly eighteen months abroad, partly in prosecuting a public duty, and partly in quest of health. I have been, as your worthy Mayor (Mr. J. H. Moore) has stated, engaged in arranging a commercial treaty with France. I have been, as you are aware, honoured with the confidence of our Sovereign and, aided by colleagues whose services in the matter I would not for a moment appropriate to myself, I have been endeavouring to make such arrangements as shall lead two great countries, peculiarly designed by Providence to confer mutual benefits upon each other, but who, owing to the folly and perhaps wickedness of man, have been for centuries rather seeking to injure and destroy each other, to enter upon new relations. I have been seeking to form arrangements by which these two countries shall be united together in mutual bonds of dependence, and, I hope, of future peace.

It has been truly said by the Mayor, that France has been hitherto as a nation attached to those principles of commercial restriction which we in England have but lately released ourselves from, but which have cost us thirty years of pretty continuous labour, and the services of three or four most eminent statesmen, in order to bring us to our present state of comparative freedom of commerce. The French, on the contrary, have taken hardly a single step in this direction; and it was left for the present Emperor—and he alone had the power—to accomplish that object, and to his Minister of Commerce, who for the last eighteen months has scarcely given himself twenty-four hours of leisure—it was left for them to accomplish in France, in the course of a couple of years, what has taken us in England at least thirty years to effect. I mention this, because I wish—and I have a reason for it, which I will state in a moment—I wish it to be borne in mind what has been the magnitude of the task which the French Government has had to accomplish on this occasion. They had to confront powerful influences which were at the moment entirely unbroken, and they had to attack the whole body of monopoly in France; whereas, if you recollect, in this country our statesmen began by sapping and mining, and by throwing over the smaller interests, in order that they might form a coalition of them against the greater monopolies. Everything has had to be done in France during the last eighteen months. Much remains to be done, I hope much will be accomplished in a short time. I wish you to understand distinctly the magnitude of the task which the French Government has had to accomplish, because thereupon hangs a tale and an argument upon which I shall have a word to say in a moment. There is a peculiarity in the condition of French industry which gives the fair prospect of a reasonable anticipation of a mutual and beneficial intercourse between these two countries. It is a very singular fact that France, which, by its social organisations and by its political maxims, is perhaps one of the most democratic nations in the world—that this people are almost exclusively employed in the manufacture of articles of great luxury and taste, adapted almost exclusively for the consumption of the aristocratic and the rich, whereas England, on the contrary, the most aristocratic people in the world, is almost wholly employed in the manufacture of those articles which conduce to the comfort and the benefit of the great masses of the community. You have here, therefore, two peoples, who, by their distinct geniuses, are admirably suited for a mutual exchange of the products of their industry, and I argue very much, as your Mayor has intimated, in favour of the great advantages which the masses of the French people will derive from the Treaty which has been lately arranged with that country.

The French people—I am speaking of the working people —are, in comparison with the English people, a badly-clothed population. Any one who has travelled in the winter-time from Calais to Dover, cannot fail to have observed the contrast between those blue round frocks which the Frenchmen wear, and the more comfortable, because warmer, woollen and worsted garments which the English workmen at that season of the year possess. It reminds me—the condition of the French population in their clothing now—somewhat of the condition in which this population of England was placed, with regard to food, five-and-twenty years ago, before the Corn-laws were touched. At that time, our population was a badly-fed people,—living, too many of them, upon roots; there were some six or eight million quarters less of corn consumed than ought to have been consumed in this country, and which has been annually consumed since the people were permitted to obtain it. Just as Free Trade has enabled this people to be better fed, so will it enable the French population to buy better clothing, and by precisely the same process by which we have arrived at this result in England; partly because there will be a considerable importation into France of your plain and coarse manufactures, and partly because of the stimulus that will be given to the manufactures of the French themselves—just as your increased supply of corn in this country has come, partly from the importation of the produce of foreign countries, and partly by the important advantages which competition has afforded to your own agriculturists. And we, on one side, will obtain, and have obtained, great benefits from this change. The change on our side is our merit; the change on the other side is the merit of the French Government. What, I confess, as an Englishman, I have been led in this important duty most to consider, is how this matter has benefited you, not by what it will allow you to export, but by what it will allow you to import. This is the way by which I seek to benefit a population, by allowing more of the good things to come in from abroad.

Upon the imports are based the late measures of our Government; and I give the credit for the putting this great final coping-stone upon the edifice of Free Trade—I mean so far as the abolition of all protective duties goes—I give the merit to the present Government, and their great Chancellor of the Exchequer (Mr. Gladstone). They have abolished the last remaining protective duties in our Tariff. Now, mark what the advantage of this will be to us as a mercantile people —an advantage which has not been sufficiently appreciated, I venture to observe. By removing every duty upon all articles of foreign manufacture, we have made England a free port for manufactured goods, just as we had made it a free port for corn and for raw materials. The consequence is, that all articles of foreign manufacture may be brought to England without let or hindrance. We find a large consumption for them here ; and foreigners and colonists coming from Australia, and Canada, and America, may find in our warehouses, not merely all our produce which they want, but Swiss, and German, and French produce, which they may buy here without visiting the Continent to purchase there. This, I consider, is to us, as a mercantile people, an immense advantage, which will be by-and-by fully appreciated, the importance of which, I think, has not yet been altogether anticipated ; but, besides this, we are going to import commodities from France which have been hitherto prohibited, and which will not only be to their advantage, but to ours. Take, for instance, the article of wine. We all know that for a century or more, owing to an absurd Treaty which was made with Portugal, this country put a prohibitive duty upon French wines, and the consequence has been that the taste of this country has been perverted, and that which is the best article of its kind in the world has been almost a stranger in this land.

Well, besides the preferential duty which has included French wines, we have laid on such an enormous amount of duty that nothing but wines of the very strongest character, the effect of which could be suddenly felt in the head, were ever thought worth purchasing. When a man had to pay 6d. or 9d. for a glass of wine containing a few thimblefuls, he wanted something which would affect his head for his money ; he would not buy the fine, natural, and comparatively weak wines of France, though every other country in the world but

England has regarded French wines as the best wines in
the world. The English taste has been adulterated, and our
people, or those who could afford it, have preferred the nar-
cotic and inflammatory mixture which is called port, or even
sherry. A friend of mine lately had the curiosity to look
into our national ballads, with the view of finding out and
making a collection of drinking songs. He told me he
found that all the songs were in honour of French wines
— champagne, Burgundy, Bordeaux — and they were all
old songs, written at the time when our ancestors used
and preferred French wine; and that since they were not
allowed to obtain those wines, songs in favour of wine have
ceased. He drew this conclusion :—That when the people
drank French wines they became merry and sang; but
when they took to port and sherry it made them stupid,
and they went to sleep.

I don't know that I should like to go so far as a lamented
friend of mine, a former Mayor of Bordeaux, who happened to
be travelling in England, and paid us a visit in Manchester
to a dinner; and when his health had been drunk, he said—
‘Gentlemen, when I travel I have but one test of civilisation
everywhere. I ask, Do the people consume claret?’ That is,
the wine of Bordeaux. I don't go quite so far as that, but
I do say, in whatever point of view you regard it, whether
it is as a beneficial exchange with France, enabling you to
exchange the products of your industry with the greatest and
richest people on the Continent, whether it be in the interests
of temperance, or whether it be in the interests of health,
it is desirable that the taste of England should have at least
the opportunity of going back to that natural channel which
our forefathers followed when they had, as we now have,
access to French wines at a moderate duty, or at the same
duty as on other wines. I am not so sanguine as to expect
that a great trade is to grow up between France and England,
suddenly, to-morrow, or next year. It will require time;

but the door has been opened, and opened honestly, with all sincerity; and I have no doubt, after we have had a sufficient time to correct those errors into which our fore-fathers fell, that this work, like every other in which we have been engaged where restrictions have been removed, will be found favourable to the best interests of this country and of France.

Now, I confess that the work on which I have been en-gaged would have but small interest for me, if it had not conduced to something different and higher than the mere increase of the beverage of the people of this country. The object which I have sought, and which those who know me will know right well, has been not merely to promote the physical well-being of these two peoples—though that in itself is an object worthy of all care—but my aim and hope have been to promote such a change as shall lead to a better moral and political tone between the two nations. And this brings me to the point to which I said I would refer. Your worthy Mayor has alluded to the immense preparations now making by the Governments of these two countries for warlike operations. Those preparations, so far as the navies of the two countries are concerned, are undoubtedly—nay, avowedly—with the view to mutual attack or defence from those two countries alone. Well, now, we are not ignorant of the fact that the French Government and the French Emperor have been made responsible for this increase in our naval armaments. It is upon that point I want to say a word or two to you as my constituents, and I address myself to this subject with you, because it is one that is peculiarly germane to my first meeting with this constituency after a meeting which you held some eighteen months ago, in which you refused to establish a rifle corps in this town. At the time when that meeting was held I was in Paris, and read the proceedings with considerable interest. It was the only meeting I saw, during a peculiar fervour and violence of

agitation in this country, at which such a resolution was
arrived at ; and, without passing judgment upon the question
of volunteers in general—upon which I reserve myself, for
I don't know whether I shall have time to say anything on
the subject—all I wish to say is this, that, as far as my
experience goes, and it has not been small, as you may
suppose, in France, as far as the decision of this town was
come to on the ground that there was no danger from
France which warranted such a preparation, I come here
to tell you, in my judgment, you acted with perfect
propriety.

Now, I have spoken of the difficulties and the obstacles
which the French Government had to encounter in the work
in which they have been engaged for the last eighteen
months—the total subversion of their commercial system.  I
ask you, as I ask every reasonable man, is there no presump-
tive evidence calculated to make you pause before you believe
as probable or true what certain Admirals—one of them, I am
sorry to say, now no more—say as to the French Government
and the French meditating to attack or invade this country,
when you find that Government engaged in this most difficult
task, the subversion of their commercial system, by throwing
open the markets of that country to the manufactures of
England, and opening the markets of England to the productions of France?  I say, is there not something in this
fact to make you pause before you believe on the mere *ipse
dixit* of some not over-wise Admiral, who has never given
one fact to prove what he says, that it is the design of the
French Emperor to come and invade your shores without
cause of quarrel or without grievance assigned?  But I don't
ask you to rely upon probabilities of things in this matter.
I speak to you of facts—facts which have come within my
own knowledge — facts which I, perhaps, better than any
man in the world, have had the opportunity of knowing and
investigating.  It is alleged that the French have been

for some time making formidable preparations in their naval armaments.

Well, the first question I ask with regard to that is—What has been the proportion of money spent in France upon their naval armaments, and what has been the proportion spent in England for a similar purpose? There has been always between England and France, by a sort of tacit agreement, I may call it, a certain proportion or relation in the amounts expended in their respective armaments. If you take the navies of the two countries for the last century, you will find that, when in a normal state of peace, the French have had a navy little more than half the size of that of England. If you take the expenditure, you will find that the French naval armament has, during all that period, by a sort of tacit arrangement—as I have said—spent rather more than the half of what England has spent upon her navy. Well, then, I will take the ten years that preceded 1858 inclusive. I find that the expenditure of the French has been rather more than the half of what England has spent. I have taken the expenditure up to 1858 only for this reason —that if you take the French estimates you will not arrive at the actual expenditure. I admit that would not be a fair criterion of the amount of money spent in this manner; because they bring forward the estimates for the year, and afterwards there are supplementary votes, which increase the amount. But if you wait for two years, until the definitive balances and records of the French finances have passed through their audit offices, and have been published in what is called ' Les Règlements Définitifs du Budget,' then you have as reliable an account as any in the world. I have heard of no political party—and you know that in France party feeling is as bitter, or even more bitter, than in this country—I have never heard any foreigner even, but who would admit, without scruple or observation, that when these definitive budgets are published, they have a creditable and

reliable account of their expenditure. I have waited, and I
see that down to the last accounts, published up to the year
1858, the French, for ten years previously—during the whole
of the reign of this Emperor, and before his accession—have
expended little more than half of what has been expended in
England.

Well, but in England we have ships of war 20 per cent.
cheaper than in France; we have steam-engines 30 per cent.
cheaper; we have coals 40 per cent., and we have stores
20 or 30 per cent. cheaper. How is it, then, I ask, if France
has expended little more than half what we have in these ten
years — how is it, that in the year 1859 you suddenly hear,
as though it were an explosion, that France is coming to invade us, and has made undue preparations in her naval armaments; and that we must not be content with nearly doubling
our expenditure, and with a large expenditure on our standing forces, but must call upon the people of this country to
arm and enrol themselves as volunteers? There must be a
reason for this state of things. I speak always with too much
respect for the great masses of my countrymen, even when I
am confronting what I believe to be their delusions, to think
of passing over this subject without offering the best explanation I can to satisfy and assure the public mind upon this
question. I believe I can answer the question by stating that
there may be facts connected with our navy which will give
some colour to these outcries of alarm. The facts are these:—
The affairs of our Admiralty are most deplorably mismanaged.
That will not be denied by any one now that is acquainted
with what is going on at head-quarters. We had a Commission sitting last year, under the Queen's sign manual, to
inquire into the management of our dockyards. Men of
business placed upon that Commission made a tour of the
dockyards and arsenals. They examined them. And what
do you think was their report? The substance of it is in a
dozen lines, and I will read them to you:—

'The Royal Commission appointed last year reports that the control and management of the dockyards are inefficient from the following causes:—First, from the inefficiency of the constitution of the Board of Admiralty ; secondly, from the defective organisation of the subordinate departments ; thirdly, from the want of a well-defined responsibility ; fourthly, from the absence of any means, both now and in times past, of effectually checking expenditure from a want of accurate accounts.'

Now mark ; just endeavour as men of business to carry with the full meaning of this verdict by supposing it to apply to a private house of business. First, the constitution of the Board of Admiralty is defective, that is, of the body, the head of the governing body—that means, the masters don't know their business, and are not properly appointed. Then we have the defective organisation of the subordinate departments—that means, the foremen don't know their business. Then the want of clear and well-defined accounts — that means, that the masters, or those who call themselves masters, if you go and ask them why such a thing is not done, they will tell you that they are not responsible. And then, the fourth defect is that they don't keep reliable accounts, and therefore they don't know how the concern is carried on.

That is the judgment passed upon our Admiralty by a Commission under the Queen's sign-manual issued last year ; but at the present moment there is a Committee sitting in the House of Commons, inquiring again into the affairs of the Admiralty, examining the same witnesses and others, and trying to find out the evils of this mal-administration. Well, I have said that the French Government during the ten years ending with 1858, spent a little more than one-half what we spent upon their navy. Then comes the question, what has become of all this money? How have these people managed to waste the enormous sums they have taken and wrung from the pockets of the tax-oppressed people? I will give you one little item from my honourable Friend, who is now the Secretary of the Admiralty, Lord Clarence Paget. Speaking in the spring of 1859—I could give you the exact date—he attacked those

who were then in office; and he came into office a few
months afterwards in the same capacity. Now, he stated in
Parliament, that he had gone carefully over the accounts for
the eleven years previous to 1859, and he found five millions
sterling voted for the construction of ships of war which
could not be accounted for. Now don't let me be misunderstood. Neither Lord Clarence Paget nor myself mean to imply
that this money is stolen. The persons we criticise are honourable men as far as personal honour goes. I mean that they
are certainly not the men to put the money into their own
pockets. I will account for it in other ways, and I am here
to account for it to you. The money has been wasted by
making things which were useless. When the heads are
irresponsible, when the foremen are ignorant, and when there
are no accounts that can be relied upon, you may be satisfied
how the business must be carried on. I will give you an
instance of it, and it will explain this matter. It will explain
the whole mystery of what we have in hand. About the
year 1850 it was seen and admitted by the naval authorities
in both countries that, in consequence of the application of
steam for the propelling of ships, the old sailing vessels of
the line could no longer be relied upon in case of war. Both
France and England at that time came to the conclusion
that in future line-of-battle ships must have screw propellers
put in them. What was the course pursued by France?
France has one Minister of Marine—not a Board, like ours,
consisting of gentlemen upon whom it would puzzle even a
detective police officer to fix any responsibility. The Emperor and the Minister of Marine are in concert; and they
say, as wooden sailing line-of-battle ships will be useless in
future, we must cease building them; and they have ceased
building them. In England, we went on building line-of-
battle ships for sails, and have been building them ever
since. The French took their old vessels—their existing
vessels—and put screw steam-engines into them, and adapted

them for the purposes of war.  In England, we went on building and converting, and managing to build new vessels, as fast as we converted the old ones; and the consequence was that France, only having to buy steam-engines to put into their wooden vessels (whilst we were building vessels and buying steam-engines), had got her work done in less time, and at less expense than we have.  When it came in view almost immediately afterwards that, in consequence of this proceeding, the French appeared to have at one moment— according to the statement of one of our Admiralty—nearly as many line-of-battle ships with screws as we had, we heard a cry that the French wanted to steal a march upon us, because she had nearly as many steam line-of-battle vessels as we.  We never took stock of our line-of-battle steam and sailing vessels combined.  If we had, we should have found that we had at that time as many more line-of-battle ships as we had in 1850.  That is one of the ways in which this vast sum of money has been uselessly spent.

I will now come to five years later.  During the war in the Crimea, it was found that these iron-cased vessels for gunboats served the purpose admirably of protecting ships of war from those shells and combustible missiles which were the latest inventions for the purposes of war.  Immediately that was discovered, the Emperor orders two frigates to be built and covered with iron.  We knew what was going on, and the English Admiralty reported upon it.  They were in no great hurry in constructing the *Gloire*.  The keel of that vessel was laid down in the summer of 1858, and she was not completed with her armour on till the autumn of 1860.  What does our Admiralty do in the meantime?  We had one Admiralty after another; and as they succeed each other, you see them go down to Shoeburyness or Portsmouth for the purpose of trying experiments—first inviting Mr. Whitworth to see if he could manufacture a gun sufficiently powerful to send a rifled solid bullet through these iron plates; and at another time calling on Sir William Armstrong to do the same. In this way they continue to amuse themselves. In the meantime, the Minister of Marine and the Emperor said, 'What we want is something to protect us against the hollow shells which fall very much like hail on our wooden ships.' It is against these detonating shells that we wish to protect ourselves, and the French Government went on to complete these two vessels of war with iron armour. But there was no reason why these iron vessels should have been launched before ours. We voted the money; we have more iron, and more workmen capable of constructing such vessels, if the Admiralty had chosen to employ them. But there is no responsibility, no one who knows his business, and nothing was done. Then, because the French had their iron ship completed sooner than ours, a cry was raised that the Emperor was coming to invade us.

Now, I have examined this question, and, having taken the pains to inform myself upon it, I have no hesitation in saying that the idea of the French Government ever contemplating rivalling us in our naval force, still less of invading us—I say it from my conscience—I believe is as great a hoax and delusion upon this generation as anything we read of in history since the time of Titus Oates, and, indeed, as bad as anything as Titus Oates ever said. I have given you the judgment of this Royal Commission upon the Admiralty. Now I will read a few words uttered by Mr. Gladstone in the House of Commons, last year, upon the nature—upon the character—of our administration generally of public works :—

'He had no hesitation in saying that these and other circumstances of a like kind were entirely owing to the lamentable and deplorable state of our whole arrangements with regard to the management of our public works. Vacillation, uncertainty, costliness, extravagance, and all the conflicting vices that could be enumerated were united in our present system. There was a total want of authority to direct and guide when anything was to be done; they had to go from department to department, from the House of Commons to a Committee, from a Committee to a Commission, and from a Commission to a Committee again; so that years passed away, the public were disappointed, and the money of the country was wasted. He believed that such were the evils of the system, that nothing short of a revolutionary reform would ever be sufficient to rectify it.'

Mr. Gladstone was then speaking with reference to the administration of the Public Works in connection with the building of the British Museum. But the greatest of your national manufactures is the navy. Your dockyards are the great Government manufactories ; it is there, with their ships and machinery, that the largest amount of your money is spent, and the greatest waste takes place. And, bad as is the Board of Public Works, I believe it is the unanimous opinion of public men of all parties, except the half dozen who have been in the Admiralty, or the half dozen now in it, that of all the public departments, that which is the worst managed, the most irresponsible, and where the greatest waste prevails, is the Admiralty.

Now, I do not think it out of place or out of time to talk to you upon this subject—upon this fallacy, with reference to the designs and doings of the French Government and of the French Emperor in particular ; for upon that fallacy is based a claim upon the pockets which must be counted by millions sterling per annum. But I speak to you also in the character of your representative, who was placed in a responsible and delicate position with reference to this very question. I was in Paris at the time that all these meetings were convoked to form these rifle corps. I was there with the known object of endeavouring to promote a treaty of commerce between the two countries. I was first in the midst of the negotiations for the basis of the treaty, when there was the greatest excitement, and the greatest anxiety, and the greatest agitation in this country, for the purpose of getting up public demonstrations in favour of the rifle corps, avowedly to protect this country against France. The language held in this country— I can hardly trust myself to characterise it. I remember an account of a meeting in Somersetshire—I don't know that it could have taken place in a more appropriate county—there was a farmer speaking upon this subject, and somebody cried out to him — he was speaking of invasion by the French Emperor—'Suppose they come, what will you charge them for your corn?' And his answer was, 'They shall pay for it with their blood!' This was the language, and it is only a sample. It was going on through the country at a time when, I repeat it, not one act had ever been done by the French Government to warrant the supposition of any hostile feeling being meditated towards us, and at the very time when the French Government was about to enter upon a complete revolution in their commercial policy; which, if the French Emperor had such a design as to make an attack upon this country, would have convicted him of the most absolute folly—I was going to say madness—because at the same time that he was disturbing the commercial interests, and setting the ironmasters, the cotton-spinners, and all the great capitalists against him, he was said to be meditating just such an attack upon this country as would have required the support of those very interests to gain his ends. Nay, more, looking at him as an intelligent being—and that is his great characteristic, for he is a remarkably intelligent man— looking at him as an intelligent man, what must we say of his conduct in proposing at the same time to adopt a policy which would knit the two countries in the bonds of commercial dependence in such a way that it would have been difficult to have caused a rupture between them—for war tears asunder most of those sensitive fibres which constitute the body politic when it rends these mutual ties of commercial intercourse— what shall we say of a man who, though arming a few ships, was suspected of contemplating a piratical attack on this country? But supposing that might have been possible; I tell you candidly, that before I took a step in reference to this treaty, I satisfied myself upon these facts, which I am now narrating; and I tell you more, and I would tell to the French Government as I now tell to you, that if I found one fact to justify what had been stated here at that time in public meetings—if I found that the French Government had done anything to disturb that relation 'which has existed pretty nearly for a century in the proportions of the French and English navies—I should have suspected some sinister design on the part of the French Government, and should have considered myself a traitor to my country if I had allowed the Government of that country, on proof of any sinister intentions, to have made use of me to mislead or hoodwink England by leading me to suppose that my instrumentality was being used for the promotion of commercial intercourse, when I had grounds to believe they were entering upon a policy of war.

I have said that down to the year 1858 inclusive we have the finance accounts, showing what has been the expenditure of France compared with our own upon our navy. As we have not the audited accounts for 1859 and 1860—and I am not going to trust to estimates—I will not speak of the expenditure for these two years. But I can give you another proof that during last year, at the very time we were raising this cry of invasion, and charging the French Government with making undue and unprecedented preparations for an invasion of our shores—that we had last year, and during the whole of last year, a larger naval force, in proportion to that of France, than I have ever known in any normal natural time of peace within the last century. I will not speak of money, but of men. When you take the number of men voted and employed in the navy, you have the clue to all the other expenses of the navy; that is never attempted to be denied by any one who understands anything of these matters. During 1860, the French Government had voted 30,400 men and boys for their navy; and in the same year we had 84,000 men and boys voted for our navy. I will take what I know upon authority, and which will not be disputed by anybody. I will assume that the French navy possessed 34,000 men

and boys last year. I will throw in, also, a statement which
gives 3600 more than they actually had, and then taking
these 34,000 against our 84,000, it is as near as possible five
to two on our part; that instead of half, or a little more than
half, which has been the normal state of things, England last
year, at the time of all this hubbub, at the time when you
were invited to shoulder your muskets to protect your shores,
your proportion of armaments by sea was greater than it has
been in almost any time of peace that I can find in my re-
searches. I know they tell us that the French have got a
number of men in their mercantile marine who are all in-
scribed on the maritime inscription of France, and that such
inscription gives the Government the power to press those
men into their service; and you must consider that. Now, I
say, take all the able-bodied seamen the French have in their
mercantile marine, and add them to the men in the imperial
navy, and it will not bring them up to the number we have
in our royal navy. I am not one to advocate the reducing of
our navy in any degree below that proportion to the French
navy which the exigencies of our service require; and, mind
what I say, here is just what the French Government would
admit as freely as you would. England has four times,
at least, the amount of mercantile tonnage to protect at sea
that France has, and that surely gives us a legitimate pre-
tension to have a larger navy than France. Besides, this
country is an island; we cannot communicate with any part
of the world except by sea. France, on the other hand, has a
frontier upon land, by which she can communicate with the
whole world. We have, I think, unfortunately for ourselves,
about a hundred times the amount of territory beyond the
seas to protect, as colonies and dependencies, that France has.
France has also twice or three times as large an army as
England has. All these things give us a right to have a
navy somewhat in the proportion to the French navy which
we find to have existed if we look back over the past century.

Nobody has disputed it. I would be the last person who would ever advocate any undue change in this proportion. On the contrary—I have said it in the House of Commons, and I repeat it to you—if the French Government showed a sinister design to increase their navy to an equality with ours; then, after every explanation to prevent such an absurd waste, I should vote 100 millions sterling rather than allow that navy to be increased to a level with ours—because I should say that any attempt of that sort without any legitimate grounds, would argue some sinister designs upon this country.

I wish, therefore, not to be misinterpreted or misrepresented in what I say. What does the French Government say, in answer to these charges about their designs to invade us? It is curious to remark how they treat them. The French Government do not go and take stock of their navy, and insist that theirs is a small navy in proportion to ours; that would be an amount of forbearance and transparent modesty on the part of the Government towards their own people such as we do not expect in this country. The French Government pocket what we say as to their navy, and only answer, in their public speeches and their *Moniteur Officiel,* ' Gentlemen, we spend little more than half what you do upon our navy ; and if we have a navy so powerful that you are afraid of our invading you, we must make a great deal better use of our money than you.'

I have dwelt, perhaps, not needlessly long on this subject. It lies at the bottom of more than many simple-minded men understand. But now I leave that question, and I come to ask, how is this to be altered ? How is this peaceable reform, amounting to something almost revolutionary, of which Mr. Gladstone speaks—how is it to be accomplished ? Why, I tell you candidly it cannot be accomplished by Parliament. If it cannot be accomplished by people out of doors, it won't be accomplished at all. And this brings me to a subject on which I hope to deal when I meet you again expressly for its consideration; but it brings me to a question with regard to the present constitution of our Parliament and our parties. We are brought to a dead lock. I appeal to my friend Mr. Bright, and my friend Mr. Bazley, and to Sir Charles Douglas, and other Members of Parliament, who, I understand, are present, and I say we are brought to a dead lock in the House of Commons. We can do nothing. There is one party in this year, and the other party in the next year, and neither party is inclined to do anything, because they expect next year they may go out and the other party may come in, and so the 'outs' and 'ins' agree that nothing shall be done. Take the strongest party in the House of Commons, and the chief of that party, if he were to say that an orange shall be on the table in that position, and if the other party were to say that the orange should be there, no one would have power to prevent it. And so you see we are wasting our time and the public time in the House. I speak somewhat disinterestedly, for these reforms are not likely to lead to any very active occupation on my part; but I tell you, who are younger than myself, who wish to make your country worthy of her antecedents, you who are the pith and marrow of the rising generation — I tell you candidly that out of doors—I don't mean the non-electors merely, but I address the electors whose handiwork has brought about this dead lock—that unless they address themselves, by some decided and effective movement out of doors, to the remedying of these evils, your Parliamentary system, and the administration of your dockyards and public works, will be brought into a position which will be a scandal to the representative institutions which you have inherited from your fathers.

When I last had the honour of addressing you here, I spoke upon the subject of reform in Parliament. I had come back from America. I had been two years out of Parliament. I did not know much of what was going on there. I remember when coming to the meeting I spoke to my friend

Mr. Bright, who said that in the House of Commons they were about to propose a moderate extension of the franchise, and that he hoped the question would be settled. I thought so too. But if I read the debates in Parliament aright when I was far away, it appears that the question is anything but settled. It seemed to me that parties when in office made a profession of faith for reform in Parliament, and that when they got into Opposition they forgot their pledges; and it seemed to me that then the voting and speaking were directly in opposition to their former professions. We have a Government coming in on this very Reform question, and we have a Minister abandoning the question. I don't blame him so much for having actually postponed the question for a year, until he could get the census; I blame him more for the manner in which it was postponed than for the act itself. But now you have the census. You have the returns, at least a portion of them—the great outlines of the census for 1861 They present a battery, an arsenal of facts, which ought to be laid hold of by those who really wish to occupy themselves with the future destinies of their country, and ought to be made a ground of agitation—a movement for a complete and thorough reform of our representative system. I don't speak now of merely the extension of the franchise. If you do not get this redistribution of electoral power, you cannot get on. Observe the facts brought out by the census. You have certain counties where your great cities and manufacturing industries are carried on. You see, there, people are growing in wealth and population. You see others, as Lincoln, Cambridge, Suffolk, Buckingham, Dorsetshire, and Wiltshire, counties which are either retrograding in numbers or absolutely stagnant. But when you go into the House of Commons, you find these stagnant agricultural counties, and equally stagnant small agricultural boroughs, twenty or thirty of which have absolutely declined in population during the last ten years—you find the country governed,

if it is governed at all, by the representatives of those stagnant counties and decaying rural villages.  I cannot say it is
governed, because I tell you our Parliamentary system has
come to a negation.  But if you are to give a fresh impetus
to any measures of amelioration in the House of Commons, it
must be by giving a new basis to political parties, by making
that representation a reality which is now a fiction.  Until
you place the political parties and Government of this country
upon a basis of reality, instead of a fiction, you will continue
to have that scandalous waste of our time and resources which
you see going on.

I will assume that you have a redistribution of electoral
power, so that it is allotted in something like a fair measure
to the wealth and population of the country.  Well, the first
Parliament that was elected—if you had that reform—the
first Parliament elected would have a Government, in all
probability, which would see for its party, if not for its persons, the chance of a five, or seven, or ten years' lease of
power.  It would have an Opposition; but that Opposition
would not be expected to come in power the day, or week,
or year after.  Then that party would abandon all these questions of Parliamentary Reform.  You would have a Government there, and a party there known to be sent up to effect a
reformed state of things, and administer the state of things
better than in that fashion so eloquently described by Mr. ˙
Gladstone.  You would, on the other hand, have an Opposition which would not expect to come into office in the next
year, but which might hope, by good behaviour, and by
doing something to merit the confidence of the country, to
come in in the course of a few years, as was the case under
the late Sir R. Peel.  Thus, it might hope to grow up into
a majority of the House of Commons, and possess power.
These parties would then be obliged to fall back upon something tangible, solid, and useful to the country.  You would
place public men, like ourselves here on the platform, in the

House of Commons, who go there, I humbly conceive, rather to promote objects which we believe to be beneficial to the country, than with the hope of partaking in the emoluments and honours of official life. You would give us the consciousness of being there to fight some battle, and achieve some object worthy of the energies of men. Oh ! I look back with regret sometimes, and feel ashamed of the House of Commons, when I think of the years when I first entered that assembly, when there was a great line of demarcation between two great parties, when there was something at stake and worthy of the intellect, and worth growing older and greyer to accomplish ! What is there now to satisfy the ambition of any public man ? I have given an outline of the subject, and it will be for younger men in the country, if the country is to prosper, to carry out the details.

Before I sit down, I must say one word which affects our minds and spirits, and which meets us in our daily occupations—I refer to what is passing beyond the Atlantic. My friend, Mr. Bright, and myself, have been called ' the two Members for the United States.' We have admired their principles of non-intervention, and of economy in administration, and we have seen within the last two years the practical application of those principles in the affairs of Europe. I will not allude to the lamentable strife in America, further than to say, that I hope the principle of non-intervention will still be practised, notwithstanding the embarkation of two or three thousand soldiers for Canada. Let not our American friends consider this act done suspiciously, or to annoy : it is only in keeping with the system pursued at the Horse Guards, whenever a quarrel is going on.

I have been written to, and requested to allude to the principles of co-operation which are now being tried in this neighbourhood. I am always glad to see anything done—and I think our capitalists here will see their own interest in taking the same view of the question—that tends to bridge over and close up the great gulf which has hitherto separated the two classes of capitalists and labourers. I want both classes to understand the difficulties of their position. I want the labourers to see that capital is nothing but hoarded labour, and that labour is nothing but the seed of capital—that for either to thrive both must prosper; that they cannot do one without the other ; and if I said a word at this time, when there are dark clouds on the horizon, I would say it rather in a spirit of caution than in a spirit of incitement. I would advise the labouring men to remember for a moment, when they are seeking to invest their hard-earned earnings, and to consider whether there is a safe prospect of obtaining the raw material upon which to apply their machinery at a moderate price, or whether there may not be other circumstances calculated to throw the industry of this country into temporary disorder. For my own part, I confess I take for the future a sanguine view of the prospects of this region, and of Lancashire in general. I think it is possible the present difficulties in America may cause some temporary inconvenience to, and even derangement of, our industry, but I see good in the future coming out of the present state of things. I think it will draw attention in all parts of the world, where the raw material of our industry can be produced, to the production of that raw material, and that in future we shall be less dependent upon one region for its supply than we have been. I have long ago come to this conclusion, that humanly speaking, in an industrious and intelligent population like this, it is hardly possible that you can have, for a long time, any great obstacle to that prosperity which does, and which ought to, attend upon hard and persevering labour and ingenuity, such as is manifested in this district. I am, and always have been, very sorry that the most extensive, the most ingenious, and the most useful industry that ever existed on this earth, should have been dependent almost exclusively for the supply of the raw material upon an institution—the institution of slavery—which we must all regard as a very unsafe foundation, and, in fact, to the permanence of which we none of us can, as honest men, wish God-speed.

Gentlemen, I have finished what I had to say. You will hear, and I dare say have heard, a great deal about the re-action which is going on. You will hear it said that every-body is turning Conservative. I think we have been the most Conservative. I think that myself, and my friend Mr. Bright, and many I see about me, who have voted for twenty years for what have been considered very revolutionary measures, have been the great Conservatives of our own age. To those men who say we are losing ground, and the Con-servatives are gaining, I ask, What do you mean by Conser-vatives? What are they? Do they mean the men who would have prevented the repeal of the Corn-laws, or, if they could, would restore them? Do they mean the men who opposed the emancipation of the press, and who, if they could, would re-enact its shackles? If the Conservatives are men who seek for progress, I say we are those men. If they are the men who are stagnant and retrograde, we say experience has taught us that those are the greatest destructives the body politic can contain. I am, therefore, not afraid of the progress, the liberty, and the prosperity of our industry in this country. All I can say is—inform yourselves upon the relations this country bears towards France and other countries. Don't let yourselves be bamboozled and terrified into panic to the neglect of your own domestic duties. Look to the present state of all political parties. Deal with the representation in Parliament, with the view to accomplish such a change as will enable your representative institutions to work, and to continue for you that prosperity which has been growing for so long a time, since the enactment of the Reform Bill.

# FOREIGN POLICY.

## VI.

### HOUSE OF COMMONS, AUGUST 1, 1862.

In the very few remarks with which I shall trouble the House, it is not my intention to be the humble imitator of the able and eloquent men who, in this and the other House of Parliament, were formerly accustomed, at the close of our Parliamentary labours, to review the measures of the Session. No doubt there would be a good reason for my not following their example this evening, because I think there will be an absence of any measures to criticise. It is not my intention on this occasion to speak as a Member of any party, or as representing other Members in this House. But I may say, that I know in what I have to state, that I am the exponent of the opinions of many Members of this House, both present and absent; and, though I do not wish to assume the character of a political leader in any form, still, if I had yielded to some of the representations made to me, I should have made some such statement as I am about to make very much earlier in the Session. I repeat, that I do not profess here to be a party leader, and have never in this House cared much for party politics, for I have generally had something to do

outside of party; but I am of opinion, that in a free representative community the affairs of public life must be conducted by party. A party is a necessary organisation of
public opinion. If a party represents a large amount of
public opinion, then the party fills an honourable post, and
commands the confidence of its fellow-countrymen; but if a
party has no principles, it has been called a faction;—I would
call it a nuisance. If a party violates its professed principles, then I think that party should be called an imposture.
These are hard words, yet they are precisely the measures
which, sooner or later, will be meted out to parties by public
opinion; and, late as it now is, it may be well if we, who
represent both the majority and minority in this House,
should view our position, in order to see how we shall be
able to bear the inquest when the day comes, as it will
come, for our conduct and our character to be brought into
judgment.

Now, with regard to the majority, which I suppose we on
this side of the House may call ourselves, I shall take the
liberty of reminding the House what have in former times
been our professed principles. My hon. Friend evidently is
in a doleful key, and does not seem to anticipate much gratification or renown from this investigation. In his case, however, I would make an exception; for, if I were called upon
to make such a selection, he is the man I would fix upon as
having been at all times, in season and out of season, true and
faithful to his principles. What have been the professed principles of the so-called Liberal party? Economy, Non-intervention, Reform. Now, I ask my hon. Friend—and it is
almost a pity we cannot talk this matter over in private—if
we were to show ourselves on some great fête-day, as ancient
guilds and companies used to show themselves, with their
banners and insignia floating in the air, and if we were to
parade ourselves, with our chief at our head, with a flag
bearing the motto, 'Economy, Retrenchment, and Reform!'

whether we should not cause considerable hilarity? Of these three ancient mottoes of our party, I am inclined to attach the first consideration to the principle of Economy, because the other two may be said to have for their object to attain that end.

Now, how has our party fulfilled its pledges on the principle of Economy? Do my hon. Friends know to what extent they have sinned against the true faith in this respect? Are they aware that this so-called Liberal party, the representatives of Economy, are supporting by far the most extravagant Government which has ever been known in time of peace; that we have signalised ourselves as a party in power by a higher rate of expenditure than has ever been known, except in time of war? I don't mean merely that we have spent more money, because it might have happened that we had grown so much more numerous, and so much richer by lapse of years, that the proportionate amount of the burden on each individual was not greater; but not only have we as a party spent more money absolutely, but we have been more extravagant relatively to the means and numbers of the people. I have a short return here, which throws some light on the subject. I was so struck with it, that I took a copy. It is a return moved for by the hon. Baronet opposite, who has taken so much interest in financial questions (Sir H. Willoughby), and it is called a 'Return of the Taxation per Head,' and it gives you the amount paid by each individual of the population at four different periods extending over thirty years. In 1830, the taxation per head was 2*l.* 4*s.* 11*d.*; in 1840, it was 1*l.* 18*s.* 2*d.*;—you had just realised then the benefits of the Reform Bill;—in 1850, it was 2*l.* 1*s.* 5*d.*; and in 1860, it was 2*l.* 8*s.* 1*d.* ; so that in this year, during the existence of the present Government, and while this party was in power, the amount of taxation per head was larger than had been known for thirty years, or, indeed, in any year of peace. Not only have we spent more money per head, but our own Chancellor of the Exchequer, who has taken considerable pains to investigate the point, and bring it clearly to our full appreciation, told us, not long ago, that the taxation of the country had increased faster than its wealth, between 1843 and 1859. He told us that our expenditure had increased at a more than duplicate ratio to the increase of the wealth of the country. That is the statement of our own Chancellor of the Exchequer; so that this so-called party of Economy has been the most extravagant Government which has been known by the present generation.

Now, there is another illustration of this which I wish to bring home to my hon. Friends. How has this money been spent—on what has it been spent? I will give you an illustration of the increase that has taken place during the last four years. I will compare it—I am sorry to have to do it ; but we must have the whole truth out and make a clean breast of it — with the expenditure of the hon. Gentleman opposite. I find that in the Estimates for 1862-3, given by my right hon. Friend the Chancellor of the Exchequer in his Budget for this year—the army, militia, navy, fortifications, and packet service—(this last item was included in the Estimates of the right hon. Gentleman opposite, so I give it here to make the comparison fair)—were put down at 29,916,000*l.* In the Estimates for 1858-9, laid before the House by the right hon. Gentleman the Member for Buckinghamshire when he was in office, these same items amounted to 21,610,000*l.*, or 8,360,000*l.* less than our Estimates for this year. It is certainly wonderful how my hon. Friends can cry ' Hear, hear !' with so cheerful a voice. In these Estimates, I have included the 1,200,000*l.* which has been voted for fortifications this year. It is a convenient thing for noble Lords and right hon. Gentlemen to pass the money voted for these fortifications out of sight, because it does not appear in the regular Estimates ; but if we are spending 1,200,000*l.* this year for fortifications, it is clear that that is so much taken from the available resources of the country, and it must fairly come into the expenditure of the year in order to make a comparison.  In these four years we have increased the Estimates for these services above those of the party preceding us in office by 8,300,000*l.*—more than at the rate of 2,000,000*l.* a year.  How has that arisen?  On what ground can it be that we have increased these warlike Estimates by 8,000,000*l.* in these last four years—years of most profound, of most growing and increasing peace, so far as the tendency of affairs between this and neighbouring countries is concerned?

This brings me necessarily to refer to the noble Lord at the head of the Government.  One or two of my friends said to me before I began to speak, ' I hope you won't be personal,' and I have had a warning to keep my temper. I will promise to be exceedingly good-tempered, and not to be personal more than I am obliged.  But the noble Lord in this matter represents himself a policy.  I don't mean to absolve other parties who are with him from their responsibility in joining him.  I don't mean to say that the Chancellor of the Exchequer is not fairly responsible for the Estimates he brings forward.  He may have his motives.  He will give and take, probably, and agree to spend more money in one direction one year, if he can get some concessions next year. There must be compromises, no doubt, when fifteen men are working together.  But, so far as the *primum mobile* of this expenditure is concerned, I cannot leave the noble Lord out of the question.  He himself will not allow me to let him alone, because he is always first and foremost when anything of this sort is to be proposed or defended.  I have no hesitation in saying—and don't let my hon. Friends think I am going to be personal—that I put the whole of this increased expenditure down to the credit of the noble Lord.  I don't excuse those who allow him to spend and waste the money of the country, but he is the *primum mobile.*  I tell him now—

for it is the best thing to be plain and open, and I say it to
his face, for I don't want to go down into the country and
say it behind his back—that he has been first and foremost in
all the extravagant expenditure of the last twenty years.  I
have sometimes sat down and tried to settle in my own
mind what amount of money the noble Lord has cost this
country.

From 1840, dating from that Syrian business which first
occasioned a permanent rise in our Estimates—by the way in
which, in conjunction with the late Admiral Napier, he constantly stimulated and worried Sir Robert Peel to increased
expenditure — taking into account his Chinese wars, his
Affghan, his Persian war; his expeditions here, there, and
everywhere; his fortification scheme — which I suppose we
must now accept with all its consequences of increased military expenditure—the least I can put down the noble Lord
to have cost us is 100,000,000*l.* sterling.  Now, with all his
merits, I think he is very dear at the price.  But how has the
noble Lord managed to get this expenditure increased from
the Budget of the right hon. Gentleman opposite in 1858 to
the Budget of my right hon. Friend below by 8,300,000*l.*?
It has been by a constant and systematic agitation in this
country.  He has been the greatest agitator I know in favour
of expensive establishments.  It has always been, either in
this House, or at a Lord Mayor's feast, or at a school meeting, or a rifle corps meeting, or a mediæval ceremony, such as
the installation of a Lord Warden of the Cinque Ports at
Dover, a cry of danger and invasion from France.  It is a
very curious and extraordinary thing.  The noble Lord and
his friends came into office on two grounds—that they would
give us a better Reform Bill than hon. Gentlemen opposite,
and that they were the party which could always keep us on
friendly terms with France.  It has ended in their kicking
Reform out of existence altogether, and we have had nothing
but a cry of invasion from France ever since.  This policy of the

noble Lord has had two consequences. And when I speak of
the noble Lord's policy, I believe he is perfectly sincere, for
the longer I live the more I believe in men's sincerity. I
believe they often deceive themselves, and often go wrong
from culpable ignorance. The noble Lord shall not hear me
impute motives, and least of all will I charge him with wil-
fully and knowingly misrepresenting facts; but the noble
Lord's 'idea'—he talked of the ' monomania' of my hon.
friend the Member for Liskeard in opposing his scheme—of
the relations between France and England, and the constant
agitation he has kept up, have had these two effects.

Now, this is a course which, in the first place, prevents the
people of this country from attending to their own affairs,
and precludes them from looking narrowly to the observance
of a policy of economy in our expenditure. I do not mean to
say the noble Lord intended that this should be the case, but
there is a passage in a curious work which I have had
brought to my recollection, and which is so completely illustrative of the position which the noble Lord occupies in
relation to this question, that I cannot refrain from reading
it. The passage to which I allude applies immediately and
directly to the point under our notice, and although I do not
suppose the noble Lord has been plotting and acting in the
sense which it describes to attain his ends, yet, by a singular
accident, his line of conduct is most whimsically and amus-
ingly portrayed by Archbishop Whately in a treatise entitled, 'Historical Doubts Relative to Napoleon Bonaparte,'
which contains the extract which I am about to record. The
work is well known; it was written thirty years ago, and
with the view of refuting sceptics by showing that very
good arguments might be advanced to prove that no such
man as Napoleon Bonaparte had ever existed. This is the
passage :—

' Now it must be admitted that Bonaparte was a political bugbear, most
convenient to any Administration :— "If you do not adopt our measures,

and reject those of our opponents, Bonaparte will be sure to prevail over you ;
if you do not submit to the Government, at least under *our* administration,
this formidable enemy will take advantage of your insubordination to conquer
and enslave you. Pay your taxes cheerfully, or the tremendous Bonaparte
will take all from you." Bonaparte, in short, was the burden of every song ;
his terrible name was the charm which always succeeded in unloosing the
purse-strings of the nation.'

Now comes a very apt illustration of the course pursued
by the noble Lord :—

' And let us not be too sure, safe as we now think ourselves, that some
occasion may not occur for again producing on the stage so useful a personage ;
it is not merely to naughty children in the nursery that the threat of being
" given to Bonaparte ", has proved effectual.'

That extract seems to me to completely represent the un-
conscious state of the noble Lord ; and I should like to know
what other ground there is for his popularity with the
country—for he is said to be a popular Minister. When I
come, for instance, to ask a question about the introduction
of a particular measure in this House, the answer I receive
sometimes is, ' Nothing can be done while the noble Lord
is at the head of the Government;' but assuming that he
is as popular as he is said to be, I cannot imagine any other
ground for that popularity than that he is supposed to be
the vigilant guardian of the national safety. Now, you see,
Archbishop Whately is quite correct; there are a good many
' naughty children' behind the Treasury-bench. The noble
Lord has been protecting us against danger to the extent
of 8,000,000*l.* sterling, and the reasons given for his policy,
though not satisfactory to me, are, it seems, very satisfactory
to himself and those around him.

But the noble Lord's fantasy has done more than spend
our money and put reform out of the nation's head ; it has
also prevented an investigation, full and comprehensive, of
the mismanagement going on in both branches of our public
services, especially in the navy. The noble Lord told us that
France was going to surpass us in naval power; that she

was first building one vessel and then another. All the while, however, it seems to me, the country was not made alive to the mismanagement and waste going on in our dockyards, which might have been sufficiently accounted for without referring it to any aggressive designs on the part of France. We have had lately placed in our hands a very valuable pamphlet on this subject, written by Mr. Scott Russell, than whom there can be no better judge of the nature of shipbuilding, and the comparative merits of different kinds of vessels. He tells us that we have during the last thirty years spent 30,000,000*l.* in our dockyards for labour and material in the construction of a class of ships which are now totally useless, there being in our possession only two sea-going vessels which can be said to be really effective. He adds, that he called the attention of the Government to the subject seven years ago ; yet there has been no investigation with respect to it, because this House and the public were diverted with the cry of a French invasion.

Now, a series of articles have appeared in the *Revue des Deux Mondes*, written by M. Xavier Raymond, which I would recommend the noble Lord to read. The writer is, perhaps, one of the most competent authorities on the subject of the English and French navies whom, perhaps, you could find. He enters very much into detail with respect to it, and I hold in my hand an extract from one of his articles which I think very appropriate to the point to which I am referring : it is as follows :—

'The British Admiralty are always wanting in foresight; they do not even know what is going on at their very door. France had seven years previously abandoned the construction of sailing vessels, when in 1851 the House of Commons forced a similar policy on the Admiralty. Four years had elapsed since the French Government had determined not to lay down another screw line-of-battle ship, when all of a sudden, though somewhat late, the British Admiralty, discovering that we had nearly as many vessels as themselves, decided upon what the Queen's Speech in 1859 called the re-construction of the Navy. The moment was, most assuredly, most admirably chosen, seeing that it was notorious to the whole world, that from the year

1855 France had not constructed a screw ship of the line, and that for a year the iron-clad *La Gloire* was visible under her shed at Toulon. Again, it has been necessary to wait till 1861, another seven years, before the Admiralty, conquered again by the House of Commons, renounced the construction of screw ships of the line. If this be not waste and improvidence, where on earth are they to be found !'

Now, that is the judgment pronounced by an eminent writer thoroughly conversant with the question with which he deals, and it is simply a repetition of what has been said by my hon. Friends the Member for Sunderland, the Member for Glasgow, the Member for Finsbury, and other hon. Gentlemen in this House. Yet, notwithstanding all this, nothing has been done to remedy the evils in our dockyards, of which complaint was made, while the country was constantly amused and stunned with the cry of French ambition and French invasion. I shall make only one other quotation from the writer in the *Revue des Deux Mondes*, whose name I have mentioned, but I would again entreat the noble Lord to read the whole of his articles during the recess. M. Xavier Raymond says :—

'Whenever the British Admiralty fall into some fresh scrape, when they find themselves left behind by the superior management in the French dockyards, in order to extricate themselves from their dilemma they resort to an expedient which has never failed them, but which is little calculated to promote mutual goodwill between the two countries. It is an exhibition, certainly, of great cleverness, but cleverness of a very odious nature. Instead of candidly admitting their own shortcomings, they raise the charge of ambition against France, accuse her of plots and conspiracies, and agitate the country with groundless alarms of invasion ; and while thus obtaining the millions of money necessary to repair their blunders, we have, at the same time, the speeches of Lord Palmerston enunciating the singular theory, that to perpetuate the friendship of these two great nations it is necessary to push to the extreme limits the unproductive expenditure on their armaments.'

This, it appears to me, is a very serious question. I do not believe the country or the House is at all aware of its full and extensive bearing on the circumstance, that we are at present without a fleet.

I shall now, with the permission of the House, read an

extract from an American paper, to show what is thought on
the subject on the other side of the Atlantic. This is a
passage from an article in a late number of the *New York
Evening Post*, in which the writer says :—

'But it may be urged that the French and English fleets would open the
ports of the South in spite of our resistance. The answer to this is, that the
experience of our civil war has taught us to despise such fleets as the French
and English Governments have now on foot, so far as attacks on our seaport
town are concerned. It has taught us to resist them by vessels sheathed in
massive plates of iron, mighty engines encased in mail, too heavy for deep-sea
navigation, but well adapted to harbour defence, and of power sufficient to
crush in pieces and send to the bottom, with their crews, the wooden ships on
which England has hitherto prided herself. With these engines we might sink
the transport ships bringing the European armies, as soon as they appeared in
our waters.'

Now, there is not, I think, an intelligent naval man
who will not endorse that doctrine. Admiral Denman, in a
pamphlet which has probably been placed in the hands of
other hon. Members as well as my own, observes :—

'And, again, with respect to the invulnerable ships in which France has
taken and kept the lead, it is equally agreed on all hands, that a fleet built of
wood must be certainly destroyed in a conflict with iron-plated ships. A
French author scarcely overstates the case when he compares an iron-plated
ship among ships of wood to a lion among a flock of sheep.'

[Cheers.] I hear distinguished naval men cheering the sentiment, and therefore I conclude it is unquestioned. If that be
so, what becomes of the responsibility of the Government? I
see before me one of the greatest merchants in England.
Suppose he, or some great wholesale dealer, employs a clerk
to manage a large department of his business, as is constantly
done, and finds some fine spring morning that department
crammed with goods of a perfectly unsaleable character;
suppose, moreover, this clerk or superintendent had ample
opportunity of knowing what description of goods would be
wanting in the market, do you think his employer would
allow him to escape without a reprimand under the circumstances, especially if he were to run up to him and say, 'Oh,

we are quite out of the market. Mr. So-and-So has got suitable goods; we have no chance against him?' Yet this is a parallel to the course which has been pursued by the Government. The Admiralty knew they were without a fleet capable of meeting modern vessels, but instead of coming down to the House, and being filled with remorse at their remissness in the discharge of their duties, they actually bully us, as the noble Lord has repeatedly done. When the noble Lord has said, 'We are very inferior to France,' he thinks he has shown quite sufficient ground for asking for 10,000,000l. or 15,000,000l. more in the Estimates, without giving any explanation of the 30,000,000l. which have already been squandered.

The present Government, not confining itself to the money wasted on our armaments, for which we are partly responsible, is laying the ground for future expenses, the magnitude of which no one can know. And here I must warn my hon. Friends round me, that, unless they detach themselves from this policy, they will, as a party, rot out of existence with such a load of odium, that a Liberal party will never be tolerated, and will stink in the nostrils of the people ever afterwards. Look at the vast expenditure for fortifications. Does anybody doubt that that is entirely the work of the noble Lord? Anybody who has sat and seen the votes upon those Estimates must be convinced that the expenditure on fortifications is solely, individually, and personally the act of the noble Lord. It is the price which we pay for—I suppose I may call it—his obstinacy. But we are very much mistaken if we suppose that the expense of those fortifications will end when the bricks and mortar are done with. During the first debate on the subject, I put under the gallery an artillery officer, well known in this House, who filled the highest posts and a front rank in the war in the Crimea. The next day, on returning to the country, he wrote me a letter, in which he said, in substance,—'I heard the debate the whole evening, and I cannot see any motive for this fortification scheme, but this. It is not to protect us against a foreign enemy, because, if an enemy landed, these fortifications would be an inconvenience and a danger to us. I can make nothing out of them but this,—they are to be a future excuse for keeping 30,000 more men in the country than in time of peace.' I believe that was also the opinion expressed by a gallant officer opposite. All this is done by the Liberal party. That is what we shall have to be responsible for. Why, our very children will shrink from the imputation of having had fathers belonging to so foolish, so extravagant, and so profligate a body.

Take, again, this affair of China. Hon. Members will recollect what was stated by the right hon. Gentleman the Chancellor of the Exchequer when he brought forward his Budget, or, if they do not, I will refresh their memories by reading a short extract. The right hon. Gentleman, in his Budget speech on the 3rd of April, 1862, after having put the charge for China at 7,554,000*l.*, adds this remark, 'which I trust will be the end, strictly speaking, of the charge for the China war.' We have since that gone headlong into an intervention in that country, the ultimate dimensions of which no one can foretell. It is entirely taken from our control, and what I hear in all directions is, that we shall have China upon our hands just as we have India. The *North China Herald*, published at Shanghai, tells us so in plain language:—

'We again warn our countrymen whose good fortune it is to dwell in marble halls in their own native sea-girt island, not to fancy we can pause in this work of redemption. . . . The end may not be very far off; and if any of our readers seek to inquire of us what that end will be, we openly reply, nothing short of the occupation of this rich province by Great Britain. We have no hope of the Imperialists.'

When I saw the vote of the House upon that subject — when I saw that the majority which supported the noble Lord included a great number of the other side of the House, led by the right hon. Gentleman the Member for the University of Cambridge, I could not help exclaiming, ' Where is the Conservatism of this land?' I do not know a more rash or a more reckless proceeding. It is a matter of course for the noble Lord at the head of the Government; but why should Conservatives lend themselves to such proceedings? Do we not see that in this and every other country public opinion from time to time turns round and judges not parties but the governing classes of the State? The time may arrive, as it does once in every twenty or thirty years, when power is thrown into the hands of the great masses of the people, and who can tell that the people will not judge the governing classes by these proceedings? Here is a country to which your exports for the last seven years have not averaged more than 3 per cent., and for that infinitesimal fraction of business you are meddling with the affairs of 400,000,000 of people! You are going into a country eight times as large as that of France, which is in a state of complete revolution, not merely with one rebellion, because your blue-books tell you there are other rebellions besides the Taepings, which the Imperial Government is quite unable to put down. We have got into this entirely because the noble Lord happens to be at the head of affairs. This is one of the evils arising out of the idiosyncrasy of the noble Lord for this kind of intervention, or what, in vulgar phraseology, I might call 'filibustering.' The noble Lord has such a predilection for this kind of sensation policy, that let an admiral or a general commit any act of violence, and he is sure to be backed up by the noble Lord. He acts on that assumption, and he acts wisely, and gets promoted. Let him send home a bulletin of any outrageous act, and I will engage that the noble Lord will back him. In this case of China, the instructions of Earl Russell were most explicit against interfering at all. Your commanders had instructions not to interfere; but when they began these raids and excursions, they knew the noble Lord would back them, and the House, in an incautious moment, and owing very much to the illogical step of the right hon. Member for Cambridge, for whom I have a great respect, and aided by Members opposite, committed us to these rash proceedings.

Who can tell what is the state of our finances at this moment? My right hon. Friend, at the opening of the Session, drew the lines very close. I remember he produced a sensation when he came out with his Budget — ' Expenditure, 70,000,000*l.*; income, 70,000,000*l.*; surplus, 150,000*l.*' I believe it was considered very close shaving. But has he got that 150,000*l.* surplus? He was obliged to assume that the troops in China would come back. They have not come back. It is stated, in a report of a committee, that the Estimates are deranged by that proceeding. Our representatives ordered the troops to go to Shanghai, and there they have remained. They have not come home, and that will more than take away the surplus, which I believe lost a little bit in hops and beer licences. Looking to the state of the revenue—looking to what must happen in the next winter—looking to what must happen to affect our prospects—is it not a most rash and lamentable dilemma into which we have rushed under the leadership of the noble Lord in this affair of China? I do not say that I exonerate his colleagues. But when I am dealing with an army, I like to take the General. When I am dealing with a party, and the chief is near me, I speak to him.

Then, again, the exhibition in Canada is just on a par with it. When my hon. Friend the Member for Birmingham spoke on that subject, I intended to come and speak too, but in the early spring I was denied the use of my voice. I will say a word or two upon it now. I know that country well. I have been along the frontier from St. Lawrence to Lake Michigan. I know both sides. I know the population. I have been there more than once. That, again, was a sensation policy, on a par with the sensation articles of the New York papers. In

November, the noble Lord hears that a vessel has been stopped by an American cruiser. He heard before the middle of December, by the American Minister, that that act was without the instructions or the cognisance of the American Government, and he had full reason to believe that the whole thing would be explained and satisfactorily arranged. Then I will give gentlemen their own way, and say the noble Lord had not full reason to believe that the whole thing would be satisfactorily arranged. It makes no difference in what I am about to state. The frontier of Canada is hermetically closed by ice and snow till the month of March. The noble Lord hurried over 8000 or 10,000 troops to Nova Scotia and New Brunswick, and many, to my knowledge, are there still, and have not reached Canada at all. The noble Lord sent supplies and sledges, which all the horses in Canada could not have drawn, but must have been put on the sledges of the country, so that the sooner they were burnt the better. All these hasty, rash proceedings were done before the noble Lord would wait to hear what the answer was from the American Government. If he had waited until the first week in January, he would still have had three months to send out reinforcements before operations on the lakes and rivers which divide Canada from America were possible. Our troops were not wanted in Canada in the depth of winter; they might as well have been at home. To spend a million of money in that way—money which would have solaced the hearts and homes of the famishing people in Lancashire—was a wanton waste of public treasure. It was part of the policy of the noble Lord, which has always been a ' sensation' policy, the object being to govern the country by constantly diverting its attention from home affairs to matters abroad.

Such are the grounds upon which I think we, as a party, have no reason to congratulate ourselves upon the close of the present Session. But I want to say a word upon the relation of parties in this House—I say the state of parties in this

House—speaking logically, for I do not wish to give offence—
is not an honest state of things. The reason is, that the noble
Lord is not governing the country with the assistance of his
own party. I have no hesitation in telling the noble Lord,
that if the party opposite had at any time during the last six
weeks or two months brought forward a motion of want of
confidence in the Government, there would have been found
Members on this side in sufficient numbers to give them an
opportunity of carrying that motion. Why have the party
opposite not taken that course? I will tell my whole mind
to hon. Gentlemen opposite now. I have spoken plainly to
my own party; often before I have taken the liberty to speak
as plainly to the party opposite, and they have never treated me
the worse for it. I will tell them why they do not propose a
vote of want of confidence in the noble Lord. It is because large
numbers of them have greater confidence in him than they have
in their own chief. What said the right hon. Gentleman the
Member for Cambridge University (Mr. Walpole) on that occasion when he refused to stand to his guns in the premeditated
attack on the Government? The right hon. Gentleman said—
I will merely give the substance—the right hon. Gentleman
said, that Lord Derby, his friend, had stated publicly and privately to his party, that he did not wish to displace the noble
Lord. Have hon. Gentlemen opposite sufficiently appreciated
the full bearing of that? What becomes of government by
party? To whom is the noble Lord responsible if he is to
carry on his Government with the assistance of hon. Gentlemen opposite? I have no hesitation in saying, that the party
on the other side are in power without the responsibilities of
office. Do you think the country will allow such a state of
things to last? I know there are many hon. Gentlemen
opposite who have confidence in the noble Lord, because they
think he is—I will not say as good a Conservative as any of
them, for I regard myself as one of the most conservative
politicians of my age—but as good a Tory as any of them.

If the noble Lord is not responsible to us as a party, but if
hon. Gentlemen opposite keep him in, and enable him to carry
measures against the wishes of a considerable section of those
who sit on this side, he is and must be a sort of despot as long
as that state of things lasts.  But do you imagine it will last
after it becomes known to the country?  It is unnecessary to
mince the matter.  We meet on equal terms in the library
and committee-rooms, and we hear in all directions that the
noble Lord pleases many hon. Gentlemen opposite better than
their own chief.  That is the truth ; and the reason is, that
he has a greater dislike to reform, and spends more money
than the right hon. Gentleman the Member for Bucks.

But don't you think that game is nearly played out?  The
noble Lord has affected to play a popular part, and he has
had what the French call a *claqueur* in the press, who has
done his work very well.  Let us try the noble Lord as a
Liberal Minister by his acts.  How does the noble Lord treat
his own party on questions in which many of them take a
great and conscientious interest?  Take, for instance, the
question of the Ballot.  I am not going to argue the right
or wrong of that question.  I look upon it as far more a
moral than a political question, and I believe the Conservatives are under as great a delusion about the Ballot as they
were about the Corn-laws.  If we had the Ballot for five
years, they would be as loth to give it up as we should be.
Wherever I have seen it in operation, it has thrown an air of
morality over the process of voting.  There has been an
absence of violence, there has been no riot, no drunkenness,
no noisy music ; the whole proceeding has been as quiet and
orderly as going to church.  How, then, does the noble Lord
treat the question of the Ballot?  Whenever it is brought on,
does he not ostentatiously get up and place himself in the
front rank of its opponents, ridiculing and throwing contumely upon the Ballot and those who advocate it?  Then
there is the question of Church-rates.  How has it fared

under the leadership of the noble Lord? Seven years ago, we were in a triumphant majority on the Church-rate question. Mark how our majority has dwindled down under the auspices of the noble Lord. First, it came to a tie, when the question had to be decided by the casting-vote of the Speaker, and then there was a majority of one against us. If, when we had a large majority against the Church-rates, we had had a leader such as the party on this side ought to insist on having, that leader would have taken up the question, and have dealt with it in a becoming manner. Take, again, such questions as the Burials Bill, the Marriage Affinity Bill, and the Grammar School Bill. All those measures, in which many hon. Gentlemen on this side take a deep interest, and which touch the consciences of religious bodies returning Liberal Members, are going back under the leadership of the noble Lord. Why is that? It is because the noble Lord is known to be not very much in earnest about any of these things. The consequence is, that the conduct of the whole party becomes slack, and the principles advocated by the party lose ground. What has been the course of the noble Lord in the case of the Poaching Bill? I think hon. Gentlemen opposite had better not press that measure. I cannot sit here until three o'clock in the morning to vote against them, but I would urge them to take the advice of the Nestor of their party, and to drop the Bill. But what is the conduct of the noble Lord on that subject? The Home Secretary opposes the Bill, moving many amendments, and he gives very good reasons for doing so. There have been innumerable divisions by day and night, but have you ever found the noble Lord voting against the Bill? No; he has given one vote, I believe, to help the Bill to be introduced, but he has not given a single vote against it. Why? Because he knows exactly how to please hon. Gentlemen opposite. He says in effect, 'I do not act along with these low people around me; I sit here, but I am doing your work for you.' I take another question,—the Thames Embankment. I think there never was so audacious an attempt made to sacrifice the interests of the many to the foolish and blind convenience of the few. How did the noble Lord act in that matter? He wanted delay, spoke about what might be done at some future time, but he did not vote for putting an end to the monstrous assumption at once.

How does all this operate? It operates in two ways to serve the party opposite. In the first place, hon. Gentlemen opposite have their own way in everything; and, in the next place, the Liberal party is being destroyed for the future. The longer we sit here and allow ourselves to be treated with contumely through the questions in which we take an interest, the weaker we shall become, and the oftener we shall be defeated by our opponents on the other side. All this comes entirely from the character and conduct of the noble Lord. I have never taken much part in personal politics or change of parties, but I have considered what alternative we have before us. The game is played out; it can't be repeated next spring. I have had communications from hon. Gentlemen which assure me that cannot be repeated. There are many Members gone, as well as many present, who have too much self-respect to allow such a state of things to continue. I may be asked to face the alternative always put by those who sit behind the Treasury-benches—' Would you like to see the Conservatives in power?' Well, I answer that by saying, rather than continue as we are, I would rather see myself in opposition. Let the Liberal party be in opposition, and then you will have the opportunity of uniting and making your influence felt, because you will have popular support, inasmuch as you will be acting up to your principles; but you are only being demoralised while you allow a Session to expire as this has done. I am not creating this state of things; I am only anticipating by a very few days what would explode in the country whenever Members went before their constituents. Such a state of things, I repeat, cannot be allowed to go on. When I came into this House in 1841, I went into opposition, Sir Robert Peel having then a majority of ninety votes. The five years we then passed in opposition were employed in laying the foundations of a public policy and in moulding public opinion to principles which have been in the ascendant ever since, and which have been identified with an augmentation in the prosperity and wealth of the country more than any other measures which were ever passed before. That was the work of the Opposition; and I believe the same work would go on now, if we sat on the benches opposite. I have no hesitation in saying, if you compare the noble Lord with the right hon. Member for Buckinghamshire, the right hon. Gentleman would be quite as desirable for the Liberal party to sit on that (the Treasury) bench as the noble Viscount. Let us be in opposition. But if we go on as we have been, where shall we find ourselves in a short time? Where will be our principles, where our party? Look at the Irish Members. I see with great regret what is going on in Ireland. I am afraid I shall by-and-by find myself in alliance with the Orangemen, and we may reach that lowest step of degradation, of going to a general election with the cry of 'No Popery!' There is no amount of reaction we may not apprehend, if this state of things goes on. Some seem to think that this state of things is attributable to a Conservative reaction in the country. I believe with the noble Lord the Member for Lynn (Stanley), that it is a delusion to talk of reaction. Whoever may be in power, we cannot go on for two successive Sessions with such an Administration as we have had this Session. Therefore,—facing even that worst alternative, that we have no one to lead us, I say, let us get into opposition, and we shall find ourselves rallied to our principles.

I have spoken thus freely because I thought there was a necessity for it. What I have said (if there be in the words

I have used any force of truth and logic) will have influence ;
if not, the words I have spoken will fall as wind.  But, whatever happens, I know I speak in an assembly where there
is a spirit of frankness, liberty, and manliness to hear and
judge what I have said.  I thank the House for the kindness
with which they have listened to me.

# FOREIGN POLICY.

## VII.

### MANCHESTER, OCTOBER 25, 1862.

[The following Speech was delivered before the Manchester Chamber of Commerce. It is well known that at the conclusion of the Crimean war, an attempt was made by general congress of the great Powers to put down privateering. The American Government agreed to the suggestion, provided the Powers assented to the rule, that unarmed vessels should be no longer liable to capture. But public opinion was not ripe for such a change. After the peace of Paris, however, negotiations having the same end were entered upon again, and Lord Palmerston became quite willing to adopt this reform in international law. But for some reason, which it is not difficult to guess at, President Buchanan's Government dropped these negotiations during the year 1860.]

It is now very nearly twenty-four years ago—on the 20th of December, 1838 — that this Chamber met, and after a discussion of two days, which attracted the attention of the whole kingdom, put forth to the world its manifesto in favour of the total repeal of the Corn-laws, and the abolition of all protective duties on manufactured goods. To that proceeding, more than anything else that occurred, may be attributed the struggle which endured so long, which ended in the complete triumph of Free-trade principles in this country, and which will ultimately extend its influence throughout the world. We met then under circumstances of great peril and disaster, in consequence of a failure in the harvest, which inflicted much suffering upon the whole nation. We meet now under circumstances somewhat different, but when I am afraid a still greater calamity threatens your particular district, arising out of the operation of the American commercial blockade. We met, in 1838, to discuss a remedy against famine in the repeal of the Corn-laws; we now meet to devise a remedy for present ills in the consideration of the question of Maritime Laws and Belligerent Rights.

It is deplorable that we are never roused to the consideration of grave errors in legislation until we are suffering under the evils which they entail. It would be well if it were otherwise; but it is useless to quarrel with the constitution of man. We are not mere abstractions; and if the visitation of a calamity such as that which has now befallen us has the effect of leading us to devise a remedy against its recurrence, perhaps that is as much as we have a right to expect from human wisdom and forethought. There are two points of resemblance between the old protective system and that code of maritime law which we are assembled to consider. Both had their origin in barbarous and ignorant ages, and both are so unsuited to the present times, that, if they are once touched in any part, they will crumble to pieces under the hands of the reformer. Upon that account, we ought to be thankful that, in the negotiation of the Treaty of Paris, in 1856, the Plenipotentiaries—I do not know why, for they were not urged at the time to deal with the subject—ventured upon an alteration in the system of international maritime law. You are aware that, at the close of the Crimean war, the Plenipotentiaries, meeting in Congress at Paris, made a most important change in maritime law, as affecting belligerents and neutrals. They decided, that in future, neutral property at sea, during a time of war, should be respected when in an enemy's ship, and that enemy's property should be respected when under a neutral flag; and they also decided that privateering should in future be abolished. These propositions, after being accepted by almost every country in Europe, with the exception, I believe, of Spain, were sent to America, with a request for the adhesion of the American Government. That Government gave in their adhesion to that part of the Declaration which affirmed the rights of neutrals, claiming to have been the first to proclaim those rights; but they also stated, that they preferred to carry out the resolution, which exempted private property from capture by privateers at sea, a little further; and to declare that such property should be exempted from seizure, whether by privateers or by armed Government ships. Now, if this counter-proposal had never been made, I contend that, after the change had been introduced affirming the rights and privileges of neutrals, it would have been the interest of England to follow out the principle to the extent proposed by America. I say so, because an attempt has been made to evade the question by making it appear that the proposal is an American one, and that we are asked to take it at second-hand. But, I repeat, after the Congress of Paris had affirmed the rights and privileges of neutrals, Englishmen had, above all other people in the world, an interest in extending the Declaration so as to include the exemption of private property from capture by armed Government vessels. It has been said that the Americans were not sincere in their proposals, and that their object in submitting a counter-proposition was to evade the fair consideration and acceptance of the Declaration as a whole. Now, it is probably not generally known that the very proposal which the American Government have submitted within the last five years was made by them in the first Treaty with England, after the Declaration of Independence, eighty years ago. It had its origin with that great man, Dr. Franklin, who carried into his diplomacy, as into his philosophy, a high and genial principle of philanthropy. In the *Autobiographical Memoirs of Thomas Jefferson,* I find the following passage:—

'During the negotiations for peace with the British Commissioner, David Hartley (at the close of the War of Independence), our Commissioners proposed, on the suggestion of Dr. Franklin, to insert an article, exempting from capture, by the public or private armed ships of either belligerent, all merchant-vessels and their cargoes employed merely in carrying on the commerce between nations. It was refused by England, and unwisely, in my opinion. For, in the case of a war with us, their superior commerce places them infinitely more at hazard on the ocean than ours; and as hawks abound in proportion

to game, so our privateers would swarm in proportion to the wealth exposed
to their prize, while theirs would be few for want of subjects of capture.'

It is not my intention to dwell further upon the question
respecting the exemption of private property from capture at
sea by armed Government ships. That question has been
dealt with in two addresses, issuing from this Chamber and
the Chamber of Liverpool, and those addresses, published
about two years ago, practically exhaust the subject, leaving
me nothing to say upon it. But, as I have already said, the
whole system of maritime law, when once touched, crumbles
to pieces. When I heard of the intention of the hon. Member
for Liverpool to bring before the House the subject of the exemption of private property from capture at sea, I immediately
observed that he was mooting a question so intimately connected with that of commercial blockades, that the two could
not be kept apart. Mr. Horsfall, who submitted his motion
with considerable ability, was disinclined to embrace in his
proposal any allusion to the system of commercial blockades;
but my experience in the discussion of public affairs teaches
me that it is in vain to attempt to conceal any part of your
subject when it has to go before the public and to be discussed
with intelligent adversaries. If there is any part that you
intend to leave out, and your opponents see that you consider
it a weak point, they are sure to lay hold of it and to press it
against you. So it turned out in the debate on Mr. Horsfall's
motion. He was told, of course, that if you exempt private
property from capture at sea during war, you must also consent to give up the system of commercial blockades. There is
no doubt about it. To exempt a cargo of goods from capture
when it happens to be on the ocean, but to say that it may be
captured when it gets within three miles of a port—or, in
other words, to declare that a cargo may be perfectly free to
roam the sea, when once out of harbour, but may be captured,
if caught, before it gets three miles from land—is to propose
that which cannot be practically carried into effect in negotia-

tions or treaties with other countries.  In addition, therefore, to the question of the exemption of private property, you have to consider the larger question of commercial blockades.  I say it is the larger question, because the capture of private property at sea affects, necessarily, only the merchants and shipowners of the countries which choose to go to war; whereas a commercial blockade affects neutrals as well, and the mischief is not confined to the merchants and shipowners, but is extended to the whole manufacturing population; it may involve the loss of subsistence, and even of health and life, to multitudes of people, and may throw the whole social system into disorder.  It will thus be seen that the question of commercial blockades is one of greater importance to England than that of the capture of private property at sea— which was the principal reason why I ventured to seek an opportunity of speaking to you to-day.

In discussing the subject of commercial blockades, I must again refer to what has taken place in our relations with America.  The American Government were the first to perceive, after they had proposed to Europe to exempt private property from capture at sea, that the proposal involved the question of commercial blockades.  It is no merit on the part of the United States that they have been the first to view the question in the light in which it affects neutrals, nor is it a proof of their disinterestedness.  I do not mention the fact to their praise or blame.  They have been the great neutral Power among nations; they came into existence and acquired an immense trade, while holding themselves aloof from European politics, always acting upon the maxim, from the time of Washington, that they should remain outside the 'balance of power,' and everything that could entangle them in European quarrels.  Hence it happened that, whenever a war occurred in Europe, it was their commerce, as the commerce of neutrals, which suffered most.  They have not shared the enjoyment of the fight, but they have always borne the brunt of the enforcement of the maritime laws affecting neutrals, and therefore they have naturally from the first sought to protect their own legitimate and honest interests by pressing the rights of neutrals in all their negotiations on the subject of international maritime law. It is a curious circumstance, though I wish to guard myself against being supposed to attach undue importance to it, that on the breaking out of the war in Italy, in 1859, between France and Austria, the American Government sent to all their representatives .in Europe a despatch on the subject of international maritime law, in which they, for the first time, broached in a practical form to the European Governments the idea of abolishing altogether the system of commercial blockades. That, I say, is a remarkable circumstance, when viewed in the light of subsequent events; because there is no doubt that if, in 1859, the English Government, followed as it would have been by the other Governments of Europe, had accepted cordially and eagerly, as it was our interest to have accepted it, the proposal or suggestion of the American Government, it would have been possible to avoid all that is now happening in Lancashire; and trade, as far as cotton is concerned, would have been free between Liverpool and New Orleans. For you will bear in mind, that, though it may be said that the war in America is but a rebellion or a civil war, the European Powers recognise the blockade of the Southern ports only as the act of a belligerent. It has been distinctly intimated to the United States Government that we do not recognise their municipal right in the matter; and if they were to proclaim, for example, that Charleston was not to be traded with, and did not keep a sufficient force of ships there, we should go on trading with the port just as if nothing had occurred. It is only upon condition that the blockade shall be effectively maintained, as between belligerents, that the European Powers recognise it at all. Hence, there can be no doubt, that if the proposal of the American Government in 1859 had

been cordially accepted by England, it would have been wel-
comed by the rest of Europe, and have prevented the existing
state of things in this district—a circumstance which shows
the extraordinary and sudden mutations to which the relations
of the various human families are exposed. There can be no
doubt that in that case the American Government would have
been obliged to carry on the war with the Southern States
without imposing a commercial blockade; or, if they had
attempted to establish such a blockade, in violation of their
international engagements, they would have involved themselves in hostilities with the rest of the world—a policy which,
of course, no rational Government would ever dream of entering upon. I mention this as a fact which gives great significance to our meeting, and great opportuneness to the discussion of this question; but I do not insist upon it in the way of
blame to any one. Diplomatic arrangements, especially when
they involve a novelty, are never made in such a way, unless
when an amateur diplomatist interferes, as to warrant us to hope
that in a year or two so great a change—indeed, a revolution in
international maritime law—as the one proposed by the American Government, could have been accomplished. I mention
the circumstance, not by way of blame to any one for the past,
but to draw a most serious inference from it for the future.

We are now suffering from the operation of a commercial
blockade—suffering in a way which could not be matched by
any other calamity conceivable in the course of nature, or the
revolutions of men. I cannot conceive anything that could
have befallen Lancashire so calamitous, so unmanageable, so
utterly beyond the power of remedy or the possibility of being
guarded against, as that which has happened in the case of
the present commercial blockade. You have been trading
fifty or sixty years with a region of the earth which, during
the whole of that time, has been constantly increasing its
production of raw fibre for your use. You have been increasing your investments of capital, training skilled work-

men, preparing in every way for the manufacture of that raw
material. The cotton was intended for you, not for the people
by whom it was grown. You have been making provision
for its use, and now all at once this great stream, which has
been constantly enlarging for a period of more than half a
century, is shut off, and yon are deprived of the means on
which you have been calculating for the employment and
subsistence of your people. Nothing but a commercial
blockade could have produced such a sudden and calamitous
reverse. It has never been expected. We have had, indeed,
our apprehensions of danger, from the fact of our deriving our
cotton from one particular country ; we have speculated as to
the possibility of sterility falling upon a territory so limited in
space; and we have also speculated upon the possibility of a
negro insurrection, that might destroy that social system
upon which we have always regretted that this vast industry
is based; but, if you reflect for a moment, you will find that,
in the nature of things, neither of those events would have
been likely to happen, if left to the operation of natural laws,
with the suddenness of the calamity which has now befallen
us. The slaves might have become free men ; but, generally
speaking, when slaves are emancipated, as in the case of the
West India Islands, if no foreign element is introduced, the
transition from slavery to a state of freedom is accomplished
with comparatively little concussion or violence ; and it is not
likely that from such an event so great and sudden a privation of the raw material of our industry would have arisen.
We might have had some perturbation for a few years, lessen-
ing production and diminishing your supplies to some extent
—a deficiency which would probably have been made up by
the rest of the world, which would have been looking on at
an event that might have been calculated to impair the
powers of that region in the production of cotton. Now, on
the contrary, with the 4,000,000 bales of cotton which may
exist in the Southern States at Christmas, and with the

prevailing uncertainty as to the result of the war, no remedial measure can be applied, inasmuch as people feel a natural disinclination to invest their capital in the production of that article, when the market is threatened with so great a disturbing cause as the sudden release of a vast quantity of cotton in America. Again, as I have said, we might have had to fear sterility in the Southern States of America. We have had blights that have struck particular vegetables. We have had the potato blight, the vine disease, and the mulberry disease, and we have had these visitations of Providence in the form of epidemics—vegetable choleras, as they might be called. It is possible that there might have been some such accidental cause to diminish, for a few years, the production of cotton in America, although hitherto cotton has been singularly exempted from these vicissitudes of nature ; but all that might have been guarded against, just as you find you can get silk in China to supplement a failure in France or Italy. Here, on the contrary, is a case which cannot be dealt with ; it is unmanageable ; it is so grave, so alarming, and presents itself to those who speculate upon what may be the state of things six months hence in such a hideous aspect, that it is apt to beget thoughts of some violent remedy. It is desirable in that frame of mind that we should bear in recollection the facts I have mentioned—viz. that the system of warfare from which we are now suffering so severely is one that we are the chief means of maintaining, in opposition, I believe, to the opinion of the whole mercantile, and indeed civilised world.

With these preliminary remarks, I shall read one short extract from the despatch which, as I have told you, was written on the breaking out of the Italian war by Mr. Cass, then Foreign Minister to the United States Government, and sent to the representatives of the American Government in Europe. An attempt was made in the House of Commons to induce the Government to print and lay that despatch on the table, but the request was refused, on, I think, very insufficient grounds. We have had presented to us lately a large volume of American despatches, which have passed between the Government of Washington and their representatives in all parts of the world, about most of which we have not much concern, and some of which have been rather maliciously printed, because in one case — the case of the Minister at St. Petersburg—the despatch is not creditable to the writer; but the despatch which I hold in my hand, which does refer to an important question deeply affecting our interests, the Government have refused to publish. I have obtained a copy from Washington, where it may be had for a very small sum, and I find that it enters into the subject of international maritime law generally. Apprehending that the war in Italy might extend to other Powers, the American Government, by the hand of Mr. Cass, lay down their views in the following language :—

'The blockade of an enemy's coast, in order to prevent all intercourse with neutrals, even for the most peaceful purpose, is a claim which gains no additional strength by an investigation into the foundation on which it rests, and the evils which have accompanied its exercise call for an efficient remedy. The investment of a place by sea and land, with a view to its reduction, preventing it from receiving supplies of men and material necessary for its defence, is a legitimate mode of prosecuting hostilities, which cannot be objected to so long as war is recognised as an arbiter of national disputes. But the blockade of a coast, or of commercial positions along it, without any regard to ulterior military operations, and with the real design of carrying on a war against trade, and from its very nature against the trade of peaceful and friendly Powers, instead of a war against armed men, is a proceeding which it is difficult to reconcile with reason or the opinions of modern times. To watch every creek, and river, and harbour upon an ocean frontier, in order to seize and confiscate every vessel with its cargo attempting to enter or go out, without any direct effect upon the true objects of war, is a mode of conducting hostilities which would find few advocates, if now first presented for consideration.'

That despatch, dated June 27, 1859, was brought under the notice of the House of Commons on the 18th of February, 1861. I was not present at the time, being in Algiers; but questions were put in the House as to the purport of the despatch, and Lord Russell, who was then, as now, Foreign

Minister, alluded to the fact of the American Minister in London having read the despatch to him. Lord Russell, in describing the contents of the despatch, which he did very accurately, also, unfortunately for our present position, took occasion to give the reasons why he had entirely objected to the proposals of Mr. Cass. He maintained that it was for our interest that commercial blockades should be maintained, adding that he could not entertain a proposal for putting an end to them; and that it was necessary, as a great maritime Power, that we should preserve for ourselves the same belligerent right. That doctrine, coming from the Foreign Office within the last three years and a half, seems to me to have an important bearing, or ought to have an important bearing, upon our attitude at the present time. In the first place, if the system of commercial blockades be maintained, as our Government insists it should be maintained, as a sort of strategical means of defending ourselves—if we are to submit to it because it is necessary for our national defence and honour—then it becomes a serious question whether the particular interests that are from time to time to become the victims of a system over which they have no control, against which they can make no provision, and to which they can apply no remedy, ought not to be considered as fairly entitled to exemption from the whole burden and cost of such a plan of national defence, just as you would indemnify the outskirts of a town for the demolition of houses, with a view to defence against the power of an investing foe. I know no remedy which the parties immediately suffering can apply to such a state of things as this, if you maintain the system of commercial blockades. But I say, if it is necessary for the maintenance of the national honour to adhere to that system, that the cost ought to be borne by the nation at large, and not by any particular section. That will become a serious question if we go on, as we seem likely to do, in this particular district, suffering from the consequences of this system.

But it affects our position in another way, which we can't too carefully bear in mind. Some people say that we must recognise the South, in order to get our cotton. But recognising the South would do nothing towards obtaining the cotton. On the contrary, once recognise the South, and then there is no longer a question of any kind as to the right of the North to blockade its ports. The only question then would be whether the blockade was effective. But what, I fear, is in the hearts of those who are almost bewildered with the calamitous prospect which they think they see before them, is that the recognition of the independence of the South should be followed by some effort to obtain the cotton—in other words, that England and France, or other countries, should go there and obtain the cotton against the will of the party blockading the coast. Well, my own opinion is that, after the statement I have made, after the facts which are on record; if we, when we began to suffer from the application of our doctrines to our own case, were, in the teeth not merely of international law, but of the law of which we are ourselves the chief promoters and maintainers, to resort to violence to procure the cotton, there is no amount of suffering which the American people,—every man and woman of them, supposing them to be the same as their fathers on this side of the water are,—would not endure to resist what in such a case would be regarded as an unmitigated outrage.

But now I will deal with this question generally on its own merits. Is it our interest, the interest of the English nation, to maintain and perpetuate the system of commercial blockades? The particular suggestion of Mr. Cass is this—that in the origin of blockades it was never intended to blockade a whole coast, or to shut out the export and import of articles not contraband of war. Is there, then, any ground for supposing that this country has an interest in maintaining that system by which those blockades are extended to all commercial ports? Mr. Cass argues that it was never intended to be

so extended, and he gives cogent facts and reasons in support
of his assertion that, in its origin, a blockade meant the
investing of fortified places, and their investment by sea and
land at the same time. The American Foreign Minister
does not object to that; he does not object to your investing their arsenals; he does not say that Portsmouth and
Plymouth are not to be liable to investment, but his argument is that the peaceful ports of commerce ought not to be
shut up in time of war. And I ask again, what interest have
we as a nation in opposing that principle? Why, I think it
is easy to show that we, of all people in the world, have the
most interest in establishing it. And bear in mind, that I
am now arguing this matter only as it affects our interests.
I do not come here as a humanitarian or philanthropist,
asking my countrymen to give up a system which is advantageous to them, out of homage to the genius of the
age, or because we are reaching a millennium; but I ask it
because, as an Englishman and as a public man, I have not
and never have had any other criterion to guide me, nor any
other standard by which to form my opinion, but the interests,
the honest interests, of my country, which I believe, with
God's blessing, are the interests of all mankind. Understand
that I don't beg the question, but I challenge discussion upon
its merits, and in the way in which I am now prepared to
treat it. Let us ask ourselves with what country it can be
advantageous for England to maintain the system of commercial blockades, supposing we were at war with that
country.

There are only three nations with which England could
possibly have a maritime war of serious dimensions—viz.,
France, Russia, and the United States. Take France. Why,
since the discovery of the locomotive and the rail, merchandise
intended for the interior of France, which now under ordinary
circumstances goes by way of Marseilles, Havre, and other
ports, could find a way to enter by Rotterdam, Hamburg, and

very soon also, as the lines of rail are completed, by the ports
of Italy and even of Spain, and with little addition to its cost;
certainly without such an addition as would form an insuperable bar to the French people obtaining and enjoying foreign
commodities.    Practically, therefore, a blockade—as an instrument of warfare with France—has lost its force by the
introduction of the locomotive and the rail.

   Now take Russia.   There is no doubt that in regard to that
country, from which we import so heavily of raw materials,
the principle of commercial blockade might still be applied
with considerable force, especially to its southern ports in the
Black Sea.   Therefore, I ask, if you were at war with Russia,
would it be the interest of England to enforce the system of
commercial blockade as a means of coercing that country, and
putting an end to hostilities?   That question is answered by
what was done during the Crimean war.   That war was
declared in March, 1854.   France and England had both had
deficient harvests, and in France, especially, there was a
dearth of food.   What was the course then pursued by
those countries?   Did they instantly avail themselves of the
power of blockading the southern ports of Russia?   No;
though the war was declared in March, 1854, it was not
until March, 1855, that the blockade of the commercial
ports of the Black Sea and the Sea of Azoff was declared.
We purposely left those ports open for a twelvemonth, in
order that England and France might get grain from them;
and England obtained more than half a million quarters of
corn from them to feed our people, while we were at the same
time carrying on the destructive operations of the siege of
Sebastopol.   That is a practical instance in our own day, in
which we applied the principle advocated by Mr. Cass, viz.,
that of besieging a military arsenal, and carrying on simultaneously a peaceful intercourse with the enemy's commercial
ports.   But how was it in the northern ports of Russia?   Bear
in mind that of all the exports from Russia, consisting chiefly

of raw materials—hemp, flax, linseed, tallow, and grain, England takes far more than one half—in the case of some articles she takes even as much as 70 and 80 per cent. Well, if we were at war with Russia, should we enforce a blockade upon her northern ports? Again, we have an illustration of that in the last war. We professed, it is true, to blockade Cronstadt to prevent the export of raw material, such as flax and hemp, by sea to England. By that means we merely diverted that traffic through Prussia; and in one year, 1855, we brought from Prussia tallow to the amount of upwards of 1,500,000*l.* sterling, while in previous years the amount had not been 2000*l.* Well, but the Government knew that those articles were coming from the ports of Prussia in the Baltic, and we had a debate on the subject raised in the House of Commons, where a motion was made in regard to this contraband trade, as it was called, in Russian produce. I suppose that some merchants, anticipating that blockade, had entered into large speculations in Manilla hemp and Indian seeds, and they perhaps thought that they would be cheated of their gains, if Russian commodities were allowed to come into this country in that indirect way. The consequence was, that a vigorous appeal was made to the House, and by deputations to the Government, with a view to stop that contraband trade. The Government were challenged, and were in effect told—' If you will not put down the trade thus carried on under your noses —if you do not enforce some test of origin—you had better abolish the system of blockade altogether, because you are only tempting to their ruin those merchants who have gone to Manilla for hemp.' It was about to go very hard with this Prussian trade, when there appeared another party in the field. The Dundee Chamber of Commerce, taking the alarm, met and sent a memorial to the Government, stating that they viewed with apprehension this attempt to keep out Russian hemp—that the district of Forfar, around Dundee, could not exist without that raw material, and earnestly

begging the Government, therefore, to offer no impediment
to its importation. All this while we were at war with
Russia, and paying for an enormous fleet to blockade her
ports. The result was that nothing was done, and, as I
understand, one or two of the houses connected with the
Manilla hemp trade were ruined in consequence.

Turn now to the third case. Suppose we were at war with
America. Does anybody believe that, if we had been at war
with her last year, we should have gone and blockaded the
Southern ports, and prevented cotton from coming into Lancashire? [Cheers and laughter.] Well, but that is the theory
upon which Lord Russell acts. And my case is this—that,
assuming a theory which we are very careful not to carry out
ourselves, we give to the rest of the world the opportunity
of carrying it out practically and very severely against us.
Nobody supposes that if we were at war with the United
States, we should blockade their ports. I will tell you what
we should do. We should have a blockading squadron there,
and prize-money would flow in great abundance; but you
would never attempt hermetically to seal up that territory.
The cotton would come out, the rate of insurance would rise,
and thus you would get your raw material, but at an increased
price. In 1812 and 1813 we were at war with the United
States. We then imported a considerable amount of cotton
from the Southern States, although it did not, I believe,
amount to one-tenth of the present quantity. But at that
time the very same incidents occurred in the House of Commons which I have narrated in connection with the more
recent case of the Russian war. There was a party in the
City of London interested in Brazilian and Indian cotton,
just as in 1855 there might have been gentlemen in Bristol
interested in Manilla and Indian hemp, and these speculators
prompted their Members to move in the House for the absolute exclusion of American cotton. Motions were made to
that effect, and Lord Castlereagh, then the leader of the

House of Commons, was much embarrassed on the question; indeed, I am not sure whether he was not once placed in a minority upon it. These speculators pressed the Government, saying, 'You know that this cotton is coming, and yet you take no steps to prevent it; you capture a few cargoes, your seamen get their prize-money, but still this American produce enters England.' But, again, there came another party into the field. There were petitions from Manchester, Glasgow, Stockport, and the neighbouring towns, praying the Government to do nothing to exclude American cotton; and the consequence was that nothing was done. American cotton, at a time when the quantity we imported was so small, and when our dependence upon it was so much less than it is now, was allowed to come in, and the blockade was practically inoperative. Recollect that half, at least, of all the exports from America come in ordinary times to this country. But our imports from America do not consist solely of cotton. It would be bad enough to keep out the cotton, to stop your spindles, and throw your workpeople out of employment. But that is not all. You get an article even more important than your cotton from America—your food. In the last session of Parliament, an hon. Member, himself an extensive miller and corn-dealer, moved for a return of the quantity of grain and flour for human food imported into this country from September of last year to June in the present year. His object was to show what would have been the effect on the supplies of food brought to this kingdom if the apprehension of war, in relation to the *Trent* affair, had unhappily been realised. Well, his estimate was, that the food imported from America between September of last year and June of this year was equal to the sustenance of between 3,000,000 and 4,000,000 of people for a whole twelvemonth, and his remark to me was—I quote his own words—that if that food had not been brought from America, all the money in Lombard-street could not have purchased it elsewhere, because elsewhere it did not exist. Well, I would ask whether, in the case of a war with America, anybody would seriously contemplate our enforcing a blockade in order to keep out those commodities? Nobody dreams that we should. And yet we are maintaining a system which hands over to other States, whenever they choose to go to war, the power of starving our people, or depriving them of the raw material of their industry, merely because our antiquated statesmen, who live and dream in the period of 200 or 300 years ago, don't understand the wants and circumstances of the present age.

I hold in my hand two pamphlets, both attributed, and, I believe, truly, to the pen of functionaries employed in the Board of Trade. They both take the largest and most common-sense and liberal views of this question, thereby adding another proof to that afforded in the case of the Corn-laws, that there has always existed in the atmosphere of that department something conducive to the most enlightened and advanced appreciation of our commercial policy. From one of those pamphlets I will read an extract, in which are mentioned the very names of some of the old authorities on international law, which Lord Russell has been quoting in his despatches to America within the last few months. The writer says :—

' The days of Vattel, Grotius, Puffendorf, and Bynkershoek, are not our days ; their doctrines, however applicable to those times, are unfit for these. They may have been suited for an era of war ; they are unsuited to an epoch of peace. They advanced doctrines which in their day it was perhaps possible to maintain in some degree ; but the condition on which their views were framed are changed, and it would now be as easy to revive the dead creed of Protection as to rule the relations between neutrals and belligerents by the antiquated laws of Oléron, the *Costumbres Maritimas* of Barcelona, or the once famed *Consolato del Mare*. It would be as easy to revert in medicine to the doctrines of Galen, and to accept the crude dogmas of Theophilus as the base of modern arts, as to define and govern our international relations by authorities whose dicta have ceased to be in harmony with the feelings of the present time.'

Yet, Gentlemen, it is upon these dogmas that you will continue to be governed, unless you bring some of your practical sense to bear upon the antiquated prepossessions of those who are at the head of affairs. It was so before. We had to fight the battle for Free Trade, in time of peace, with our own governing class; and you will have to fight the battle again for Free Trade, in time of war, with the same class, as the only way of obtaining such a change in maritime law as will put it in harmony with the spirit and the exigencies of our age. Still, we come back to this vague response, ' Oh ! but if you injure yourselves by the system of commercial blockade, you may injure your enemy a great deal more.' I want to know, in the wide range of the world, what conceivable injury you can do to any people that will equal the mischief which must be inflicted upon this region of Lancashire if the present state of things continues for another six months. For, re-collect, that if you blockade the commercial ports of a foreign Power, like America or Russia, you merely prevent them from receiving comparative luxuries into their ports—your manu-factured goods, colonial produce, and the like. People can live tolerably well, as they have lived, without these things. But if you inflict a commercial blockade that stops the exports from, as well as the imports into, those countries, while you are only depriving your enemy of comparative luxuries, you are depriving yourselves both of the raw material of the industry by which your people live, and also of the very food necessary for their subsistence. I have thought much upon this subject, and I can conceive of no case in which, while carrying on war with other Powers, you could inflict upon them the same amount of injury as you would inflict upon yourselves by an effective system of blockade ; and if the blockade is not to be effective, the whole thing falls to the ground as a mere mischievous delusion. But make it effective, and I repeat, there is no great country with which you could be at war, without inflicting fourfold the injury upon your-selves that you could inflict upon your enemy. Is that a right way to strengthen a belligerent Power—to impair its revenue by curtailing its commerce, to deprive its people of the raw material of their industry, and at the same time to starve them by shutting out their food, thus reducing their physical condition, at the very moment when you want their robust arms and muscular vigour to fight their country's battles ? I say, on the contrary, that it is in times of war, above all others, that you ought to have the freest access to the ports of those foreign countries on which you are dependent for your raw materials and your food. I can understand a great manufacturing country like this maintaining a large fleet for the purpose of keeping its doors open for the supply of that food and those raw materials; but by what perversity of reasoning can any statesman be brought to think that it can ever be our interest to employ our fleet to prevent those indispensable commodities from reaching our shores?

There is another point which I do not remember ever seeing discussed, but which is one of very great importance. We should seek to establish it as a principle in the intercourse of nations, that they should not resort to the prohibition of exports as a belligerent act. When I was engaged in arranging the Treaty of Commerce with France, we put in a clause which in its effect interdicted the right of prohibiting the exportation of coal. Now, according to my idea, if our diplomacy is to be carried out in the common-sense interest of these vast communities, we should seek by every means in our power, in the case of war, to prevent belligerent States from stopping the export of articles necessary for the sustenance or the employment of mankind. With the general spread of Free-trade principles — by which I mean nothing but the principle of the division of labour carried over the whole world—one part of the earth must become more and more dependent upon another for the supply of its material and its food. Instead of, as formerly, one county sending its produce to another county, or one nation sending its raw material to another nation, we shall be in the way of having

whole continents engaged in raising the raw material required
for the manufacturing communities of another hemisphere.
It is our interest to prevent, as far as possible, the sudden
interruption of such a state of dependence; and, therefore, I
would suggest it as a most desirable thing to be done in all
cases by our Government, as the ruling and guiding principle
of their policy, that they should seek in their negotiations of
treaties to bind the parties respectively, not, as a belligerent
act, to prevent the exportation of anything, unless we except
certain munitions of war, or armaments. I don't think the
Government should interfere to prevent the merchant from
exporting any article, even if it can be made available for
warlike purposes. The Government has nothing to do with
mercantile operations; it ought not to undertake the surveillance of commerce at all. Of course it should not allow an
enemy to come here and fit out ships or armaments to be used
in fighting against us. But I mean, that for all articles of
legitimate commerce, there ought to be, as far as possible,
freedom in time of war. To what I am urging it may be said,
' But you won't get people to observe these international
obligations, even if they are entered into.' That remark was
made in the House of Commons by a Minister, who, I think,
ought not to have uttered such a prediction. Why are any
international obligations undertaken unless they are to be
observed? We have this guarantee, that the international
rules I am now advocating will be respected; that they are
not contemplated to be merely an article in a Treaty between
any two Powers, but to be fundamental laws regulating the
intercourse of nations, and having the assent of the majority
of, if not all, the maritime Powers in the world. Let us suppose two countries to be at war, and that one of them has
entered into an engagement not to stop the exportation of
grain. Well, we will assume the temptation to be so great,
that, thinking it can starve its opponent, it would wish to
stop this exportation in spite of the Treaty. Why, that would

bring down on them instantly the animosity, indeed the hostility, of all the other Powers who were parties to the system. The nation which has been a party to a general system of international law, becomes an outlaw to all nations, if it breaks its engagement towards any one. And in the case on which I am laying great stress—viz. that of commercial blockade, and the prevention of any stoppage of exports in time of war—I don't rely on the honour of the individual nation making it for observing the law; I rely on its being her interest to keep it, because if she were at war with us, and were to break the law, she would not break it as against us alone, but as against the whole world.

I won't attempt to cover the whole ground over which this question would lead me—I mean the question of the reform of international law, with the view of bringing it into harmony with the present state of things. But this I would say, as a guiding rule of our policy, that as we have adopted Free Trade as our principle in time of peace, so ought we to make trade as free as possible also in time of war. Let that be your object; and whenever you find a restriction upon legitimate commerce, whether in war or in peace, be assured that its removal will do more good to England than it can do to any other country on the globe; and for this simple reason —that we have double the commerce of any other country. Then let this manufacturing district, as it has done before, make its voice heard in order that the enlightened principles which are now finally triumphant in time of peace shall also be applied, as far as they possibly can be, in time of war. I have said — and, after all, this is the practical question — that I don't see how the agitation of this matter can be of any service at this moment in securing a supply of cotton from America, by getting rid of the unfortunate state of things which now exists there. But this I will add, that if there were at the head of the Federal Government men of the grasp of mind of a Franklin, a Jefferson, an Adams, or a Washington,

I can imagine that they would seek to acquire for their country the glory and the lasting fame of inaugurating, even at the present moment, their own principles—for they are their own principles—of the exemption from blockade of the peaceful ports of a whole continental coast. That would reflect great credit on the men engaged in it, while it would also place on a high moral elevation the nation which achieved it. I can imagine that men of the calibre of those I have named, in the circumstances in which they stand, seeing, and being anxious to prevent, the immense and unmerited evil inflicted not only on the capitalists, but on the labourers not merely of England but throughout the civilised world, and seeing, likewise, national safety in such a course, should desire, if practicable—and on its practicability I offer no opinion —to put an end to this state of things in the interests of humanity. But in making that suggestive and hypothetical remark, which I do without wishing for a moment to imply blame or reproach, this I will say, that the only way in which Europe can approach that question with the United States is on the ground of principle which I have laid down, and not by violating the blockade with the view of obtaining their cotton because we now want it, while still retaining that fanciful advantage of applying the principle of blockade to other Powers at some future time. The only possible ground on which Europe can expect from the American Government a disposition to endeavour to remove this great evil, is by the European Powers engaging for the future to adopt the American principle of exempting all commercial ports from blockade, and confining blockades merely to arsenals and fortified places. I know something of the disposition of foreign Governments in both hemispheres, and I tell you again that England has been the great obstacle to such a benignant change of policy as I have indicated. We are, perhaps, not to be blamed for this; we have but followed in one direction, as America has followed in another, the instincts of national self-interest. For nearly a century, England has believed that she has had an interest in maintaining to the utmost degree the rights of belligerents, just as America has believed, and rightly so, that she had an interest in maintaining the rights of neutrals. But the circumstances are now changed. We profess the principle of non-intervention. We no longer intend, I hope, to fight the battles of every one on the Continent, and to make war like a game of ninepins, setting up and knocking down dynasties, as chance or passion may dictate. We avow the principle of non-intervention, which means neutrality, and we have, therefore, made ourselves the great neutral Power of the world. Two great wars have been carried on within the last ten years. One was the war in Italy between France and Austria, and the other is the still more gigantic war in America. During both, England has remained neutral. Our business, therefore, is to shape our policy according to the light of modern events, and I am convinced, that if we look at the matter calmly and impartially, we shall find that our interests are the same as those of the weakest Power in Christendom, seeing that in adopting Free Trade we have renounced the principle of force and coercion.

Allow me to say, in conclusion, that this question is one that ought to engage the serious attention of gentlemen in this district. Where are the young men who have come into active life since the time when their fathers entered upon the great struggle for Free Trade? What are their thoughts upon this subject? They have inherited an enviable state of prosperity from their fathers. For fifteen years there has hardly been a serious check to business—scarcely a necessity for an anxious day or night on the part of the great body of our manufacturing and trading population. But let not the young men of this district think that the possession of such advantages can be enjoyed without exertion, watchfulness, and a due sense of patriotic duty. We must not stand still, or imagine that we can remain stereotyped, like the Chinese ; for, if we ever cease to progress, be assured we shall commence to decline. I would, therefore, exhort the young men, with their great responsibilities and great resources, to take this matter seriously to heart. Something is due, not only to themselves and to those who have gone before them, but likewise to the working population around them, who will expect an effort to be made, if not to put an end to the present state of things, at least to prevent the recurrence of such calamities in future.

# FOREIGN POLICY.

## VIII.

### ROCHDALE, OCTOBER 29, 1862.

[At a public meeting in Rochdale, Mr. Cobden was asked to move the following resolution in favour of Parliamentary and Financial Reform:— 'That this meeting views with dismay the enormous public expenditure of the country, which unnecessarily increases the burdens of the people, is subversive of their best interests, and perilous to Constitutional Government. This meeting is also of opinion that a comprehensive measure of Parliamentary Reform, which would secure a more faithful representation of the people, is absolutely essential; and remembering the pledges with regard to Financial and Parliamentary Reform, given by the present Ministry prior to their accession to power, calls upon them to carry out those pledges, or retire from office.' But before he referred to the resolution, he called attention to the relations between Great Britain and the United States.]

BEFORE I address myself to the general subject involved in the resolution which is now before you, I will, with your permission, say a few words upon that subject which is most near to my feelings, as it must be to every one connected with this borough,—I allude to the present state of distress in this district. I should like, if I could, to state something that might contribute towards making the cause of your sufferings better understood, and which might clear up any impressions that may exist with regard to the position or the attitude of this district amongst our fellow-countrymen in other parts of the kingdom. I should like to say a word

or two with reference, not only to our own interest in this
disaster, but also upon the responsibility and duty arising out
of it, which, I think, fall upon all parts of the kingdom.

You are suffering much in the same manner as you
would be if England were engaged in a foreign war, and
this country were placed in a state of blockade to prevent
the ingress of cotton for your mills.  That would be a state
of things which would be regarded by the whole kingdom
as an affair which concerned the whole community.  All
England, the United Kingdom, would come to your rescue ;
any necessary amount of expenditure would be incurred in
order to rescue you from the danger that assailed you, and
to compensate you, indemnify you for the injuries you might
have sustained.  Well, there is very little difference in principle between such a case and that in which you are now
really involved.  You are suffering, not from a blockade of
Lancashire, you are suffering from a blockade of the Southern
ports of the United States; both arise out of a state of war;
both arise out of a principle recognised in the conduct of
war ; and as our Government and this country are assenting
parties to such a principle of warfare, and as it is an evil
arising out of the war which you cannot provide against,
which you cannot remove, and for which you are not responsible,—I say it must involve the same consequences, that
your sufferings must be shared, and your case relieved by
the efforts of the whole of this community—I mean the
whole of the United Kingdom.  This principle has been to
some extent recognised by the course which has been pursued
to a certain extent in other parts of the kingdom.  There
have been efforts made, and a considerable amount of sympathy manifested, to relieve the distress of this district.  I
do not measure the amount of assistance to be rendered to
you by what has been done : I only say the principle is
recognised, and efforts made in all parts of the kingdom to
support and cheer you in your sufferings and distress.  If

I could only say one word which would tend to remove that misapprehension which parties might have in other and distant parts of the country, in their efforts of humanity, in looking at your case, I should think my time very well employed on the present occasion. There is no doubt there is much apprehension, particularly in the southern portions of the kingdom, with regard to the state of matters here. I am not surprised at this, because I, who was born in the south, and was an emigrant in this region, and again returned to the south, perhaps may be better acquainted than many of you with the ignorance that prevails in the south of England, and even in London, with reference to the state of society in this district.

Now, an attempt has been made to throw blame upon large numbers of parties who are visited by the great calamity in which you are involved. I would not say one word in defence of the capitalists of Lancashire, because they are very well able to defend themselves, were it not that this misapprehension with regard to their conduct had a tendency to check the sympathy and slacken the charity of our fellow-countrymen elsewhere. I am not going to undertake the defence of this class; but an untrue accusation has been made against that class. Men of all classes have their good and bad individuals; fortunately for the world, the good predominate everywhere. But, with reference to the particular fact with which I wish to deal, I may say there seems to be a general forgetfulness, on the part of those bringing these accusations against the capitalists, that the calamity has fallen both upon the capitalists and the working classes, and, if it continues long enough, that it will ruin them both. I will illustrate what I have to say by taking the position of a millowner spinning cotton, and this comparison will be best understood by our fellow-countrymen in the south of England. A millowner who spins cotton is somewhat similar to a flour miller who grinds wheat.

Now, let us suppose a calamity occurred, by which all the

wheat millers of the south of England were deprived of the raw material for their mills—that is, wheat—that the mills everywhere had to be shut up; but suppose, in addition, that these mills were liable to be rated for the relief of the poor, and that the cottages generally owned by the millers, where the workpeople lived, were to pay rent, and were to contribute to the poor-rates. Suppose, simultaneously with such a calamity as that, we had received a cry from this part of the country that these corn millers, whose trade was paralysed, ought, in addition, to keep the workpeople who had been thrown out of work. That would be about as reasonable as much that I have read of the accusations brought against owners of mills in this region. I came last week from Scotland by way of Carlisle, Kendal, Lancaster, Preston, Bolton, to Manchester, and I came through a country where there was a succession—I may say a forest—of smokeless chimneys. Why, for all purposes of productive value, the machinery in these mills might just as well have been in the primitive form of iron, in which they were before they were extracted from the mines. They were utterly valueless as property. And we must bear in mind that, though some millowners are rich in floating capital as well as in fixed capital, yet a great bulk of those who own cotton mills in this county are not rich in floating capital. They are rich in bricks, mortar, and machinery, when they can get cotton to make their looms productive.

Now, take your own borough, and what is its position at the present moment? I have got some authentic facts since I have come into Rochdale—facts applicable to the Rochdale relief district. That district contains ninety-five cotton mills, employing 14,071 persons; of these there are out of work 10,793, and the remaining 3278 are not averaging more than two days a week of work. The relief committee are assisting weekly 10,041, who receive no aid from rates; the guardians are relieving weekly 10,000, making a total of

20,041. The number of the destitute is daily increasing. Bear in mind, I am not speaking to you here, so much as I am speaking to my fellow-countrymen elsewhere, who are less acquainted than I could wish them to be with the actual state of this district; and in speaking thus I am speaking in the interests of you, the working men here present and your families. Now, bear in mind that for all this destitution the whole of the manufacturing capital in this region is liable to be rated. It is not generally known elsewhere that, if the millowner closes his mill, provided that mill be full of machinery, it is still liable to be rated for the relief of the poor. The consequence is that the millowner first loses the whole amount of the interest in his capital, and the depreciation of the capital in suspense. Say his mill is worth 20,000*l.*, and that is a moderate estimate for the average of mills—that is closed, and he immediately loses at the rate of 2000*l.* a year, by the loss of interest and depreciation. But, generally, the mill also has a number of cottages attached to it, in which the workpeople live. These cottages must cease to pay rent when the workpeople cease to receive wages, but the cottages also continue to be rated to the poor. Take, then, the amount which the millowner, with that small mill worth 20,000*l.*,— at least the average mill of 20,000*l.*; take the loss which he is suffering by the loss of interest and depreciation; take also the amount which he is liable to pay for his poor-rate, which may be 5000*l.* or 6000*l.* a year; and that millowner, without going to a central committee in Manchester to put down his name for 100*l.* or 500*l.*, is inevitably, by the very nature of his position, incurring a greater loss by this distress than by any amount contributed by the richest nobleman of this land towards the fund.

It has been said that the millowners and capitalists have not gone to some central meeting, and put down their names for 1000*l.*, along with some of the bankers and merchants or great landowners who have none of these risks and charges attending their property which I have described. But these millowners and manufacturers are generally scattered and dispersed throughout the country ; they have their obligations at their own doors, and they have the apprehension of a very long continuance of this distress which is upon them. I have heard some sagacious men say, since I have been in Manchester,— I hope they have taken a too gloomy view of the situation,— but I have heard some of the longest-headed men with whom I have talked since I have last visited Manchester, say, that they don't believe there will be any more prosperity for the cotton trade for five years to come. I repeat, that I hope they take a too gloomy view of the case; but recollect that, as all is uncertain in the future, and as this fixed property, which constitutes the great wealth of your manufacturers and spinners—this great fixed property in mills and machinery— remains there, always to be rated to the poor, and must be rated to the end, as long as the owner has one shilling of floating capital to pay towards the rates, why, the manufacturer and spinner may well pause and say, ‘ We welcome you, noble lords and gentlemen from a distance, who throw in your mite in the relief of this great calamity ; but, do what you will, and be as bountiful as you please to be’—(and I am sure they will be ; the country will never fail you)—‘ yet still the loss and the suffering and distress to this land must be greater to the millowners and manufacturers than to any other class.’ I know that I am speaking, here, in the presence of a great majority of working men ; and they will not deny the truth of what I say. You have had your own co-operative mills here, and there is intelligence sufficient amongst the operatives of this town to know that in every word I have said I have been speaking the simple truth. But I will not confine myself to the capitalist class. See what the operative is sure to suffer, and the working man is sure to suffer, by this calamity. Take, as an illustration, what is happening at this moment in Rochdale. Again, I take the Rochdale relief distriet, and, from the best information I can get—and I have no doubt it is accurate—I find that the weekly loss by wages, in this district alone, cannot be less than 6000*l.* or 6500*l.* a week. So that the working class of Rochdale alone, at this moment—and you are only at the beginning of your distress —are losing from their income at the rate of upwards of 300,000*l.* a year. I have seen it stated that the relief afforded is about 600*l.* a week. My esteemed friend behind me, Mr. A. H. Heywood, the treasurer of the relief fund, tells me that the contribution which has been made from that fund to the distressed poor of this district is about 600*l.* a week ; and, I am told, that the board of guardians are distributing at the same time 800*l.* a week of relief to the poor—I won't call them paupers, because we won't allow them to be called that name ;—they are the distressed, or they are the bloekaded.

Well, now, 600*l.* a week doled out by the relief committee, and 800*l.* given by the board of guardians, make the total relief to be 1400*l.* a week. Already it is estimated that the working classes of this district have lost 6500*l.* a week in wages, and they are getting relief at the rate of 1400*l.* a week, so that the working classes of this town are receiving from both those sources—the volunteer relief committee and the board of guardians, only about one-fourth of the income which they can earn by the honest industry of their hands in ordinary times. Great praise has been given to the working class of this district for the fine, the magnanimous, the heroic fortitude which they have displayed on this occasion. Well, I sometimes think that there is something rather invidious in the way in which this compliment is paid to you by some parties. It seems as if they had always been assuming that you are a set of savages, without reason or a sense of justice, and that, whatever befell you, your first impulse was to go and destroy something or somebody in revenge. They must have a very curious idea of the people of this district. It reminds me of an anecdote that I remember :— When the late

Dr. Dalton, the eminent philosopher, was presented to King William IV, His Majesty received him with this remark: 'Well, doctor—well, doctor—are you all quiet at Manchester now?'—the idea in His Majesty's head being that in Manchester and the neighbourhood the normal state was one of insurrection or violence. Well, but at least the conduct of this district, of its working population, will stand out all the more honourably before the country when it is known under what circumstances you have borne yourselves so manfully as you have. Where is there another class of the community, —I join with my right hon. Friend Mr. Gladstone heartily in saying that—I am a south countryman, and therefore I shall not share in any praise I give you in this district,—but I don't believe there is any other part of the country where the same number of men would have borne so courageously and manfully the same amount of privation. But still, don't let us make it mere empty compliment—because the people of this country do not care a button for compliments. There is something wanted, and I have no doubt that something more will be had. This is a gigantic evil which has fallen upon this district from no fault of its own, which could not have been foreseen or provided against; and, therefore, the consequences of this great calamity must be borne by the whole country. If they can be borne by voluntary aid from all parts of the kingdom, well; if not, they must be helped by Imperial aid in another form.

But I think, if it is known and fairly understood in all parts of the kingdom what the state of things is, and that a great effort is required, greater than any that has yet been made, I believe that the philanthropy and the generosity of this country will not be found wanting. I would suggest that a systematic plan should be adopted of calling county meetings everywhere by the lord-lieutenants. I have known county meetings called before on much slighter grounds of necessity than this. It is said that there is to be a subscription raised in all the churches. I have no doubt that a large sum will be raised in that way. But it requires that the country should know the necessities of the case, and that the public feeling should not be chilled or distorted by base appeals to their prejudices and their passions. Oh, there is a class of writers in this country,—God knows who they are, who support the vendors of such base commodities ; but there is a class of writers in this country who seem to worship success, and to find no pleasure so great as to jump upon anybody, or any class, that they think is down for the moment, and to trample it still lower in the mire. For myself, I have no doubt whatever that all classes in this country will do their duty. I have heard since I have been in Lancashire of heroic acts of benevolence performed not only by men, but by women, who have shown a bright example in their districts in the devotion they have evinced to relieve the distress of those immediately around them. I have no doubt that the amount of generosity and charity that is going on in private far transcends that which is known to the public, and that the best friends of the poor are very often the poor themselves. I have not the least doubt, I say, that this district will do its duty, and that when this cloud passes away—as I hope it may before a distant day—I have no doubt that there will be a record of bright and generous acts—I won't say such as is creditable exclusively to this community—but such as will reflect honour upon our common humanity.

Now, gentlemen, coupled with this question is another upon which I must say a few words. We are placed in this tremendous embarrassment in consequence of the civil war that is going on in America. . Don't expect me to be going to venture upon ground which other politicians have trodden, with, I think, doubtful success or advantage to themselves— don't think that I am going to predict what is going to happen in America, or that I am going to set myself up as a judge of the Americans. What I wish to do is to say a few words to throw light upon our relations, as a nation, with the American people. I have no doubt whatever that, if I had been an American, I should have been true to my peace principles, and that I should have been amongst, perhaps, a very small number who had voted against, or raised my protest, in some shape or other, against this civil war in America. There is nothing, in the course of this war, that reconciles me to the brutality and the havoc of such a mode of settling human disputes. But the question we have to ask ourselves is this, what is the position which, as a nation, we ought to take with reference to the Americans in this dispute? That is the question which concerns us. It is no use our arguing as to what is the origin of the war, or any use whatever to advise these disputants. From the moment the first shot is fired, or the first blow is struck in a dispute, then farewell to all reason and argument ; you might as well attempt to reason with mad dogs as with men when they have begun to spill each other's blood in mortal combat. I was so convinced of the fact during the Crimean war, which, you know, I opposed, I was so convinced of the utter useless- ness of raising one's voice in opposition to war when it has once begun, that I made up my mind that, as long as I was in political life, should a war again break out between England and a great Power, I would never open my mouth upon the subject from the time the first gun was fired until the peace was made, because, when a war is once commenced, it will only be by the exhaustion of one party that a termi- nation will be arrived at. If you look back at our history, what did eloquence, in the persons of Chatham or Burke, do to prevent a war with our first American colonies ? What did eloquence, in the persons of Fox and his friends, do to prevent the French revolution, or bring it to a close? And there was a man who, at the commencement of the Crimean war, in terms of eloquence, in power, and pathos, and argu- ment equal—in terms, I believe, fit to compare with anything

that fell from the lips of Chatham and Burke—I mean your
distinguished townsman, my friend Mr. Bright—and what was
his success? Why, they burnt him in effigy for his pains.

Well, if we are here powerless as politicians to check a war
at home, how useless and unavailing must it be for me to
presume to affect in the slightest degree the results of the
contest in America! I may say I regret this dreadful and
sanguinary war; we all regret it; but to attempt to scold
them for fighting, to attempt to argue the case with either,
and to reach them with any arguments, while they are
standing in mortal combat, a million of them standing in
arms and fighting to the death; to think that, by any arguments here, we are to influence or be heard by the combatants engaged on the other side of the Atlantic, is utterly
vain. I have travelled twice through almost every free State
in America. I know most of the principals engaged in this
dreadful contest on both sides. I have kept myself pretty well
informed of all that is going on in that country; and yet,
though I think I ought to be as well informed on this subject
as most of my countrymen—Cabinet Ministers included;—
yet, if you were to ask me how this contest is to end, I
confess I should find myself totally at a loss to offer an
opinion worth the slightest attention on the part of my
hearers. But this I will say: If I were put to the torture,
and compelled to offer a guess, I should not make the guess
which Mr. Gladstone and Earl Russell have made on this
subject. I don't believe that, if the war in America is to
be brought to a termination, it will be brought to an end
by the separation of the South and North. There are great
motives at work amongst the large majority of the people
in America, which seem to me to drive them to this dreadful
contest rather than see their country broken into two. Now,
I don't speak of it as having a great interest in it myself.
I speak as to a fact. It may seem Utopian; but I don't
feel sympathy for a great nation, or for those who desire the

greatness of a people by the vast extension of empire. What
I like to see is the growth, development, and elevation of the
individual man. But we have had great empires at all
times—Syria, Persia, and the rest. What trace have they
left of the individual man? Nebuchadnezzar, and the count-
less millions under his sway,—there is no more trace of them
than of herds of buffaloes, or flocks of sheep. But look at
your little States; look at Greece, with its small territories,
some not larger than an English county; Italy, over some
of whose States a man on horseback could ride in a day,—
they have left traces of individual man, where civilisation
has flourished, and humanity been elevated. It may appear
Utopian, but we can never expect the individual elevated
until a practical and better code of moral law prevails among
nations, and until the small States obtain justice at the hands
of the great.

But leaving these matters: What are the facts of the
present day—what appears to be the paramount instinct
amongst the races of men? Certainly not a desire to separate, but a desire to agglomerate, to bring together in greater
concentration the different races speaking the same language,
and professing the same religion. What do you see going on
in Italy,—what stirs now the heart of Germany—that moves
Hungary? Is it not wishing to get together? I find in the
nations of Europe no instinct pervading the mass of mankind
which may lead them to a separation from each other; but
that there is a powerful movement all through Europe for the
agglomeration of races. But is it not very odd that statesmen
here who have a profound sympathy for the movement in
Italy in favour of unity, cannot at least appreciate a statesman
in looking upon the probabilities and the chances of a civil
contest—cannot also duly appreciate the force of that motive
in the present contest in America? Three-fourths of the
white population are contending against disunion; they are
following the instinct which is impelling the Italians, the

Germans, and other populations of Europe; and I have no doubt that one great and dominant motive in the minds of three-fourths of the white people in America is this:—They are afraid, if they become disunited, they will be treated as Italy has been treated when she was disunited — that a foreigner will come and set his intrusive foot upon it, and play off one against another to their degradation, and probably subjection. Without pretending to offer an opinion myself, these are powerful motives, and, if they are operating as they appear to operate, it may lead to a much more protracted contest than has been predicted by some of our statesmen.

But the business we really have here as Englishmen is not to speculate upon what the Americans will do, for they will act totally independent of us. Give them your sympathy as a whole; say, ' Here is a most lamentable calamity that has befallen a great nation in its pride.' Give them your sympathy. Lament over a great misfortune, but don't attempt to scold and worry them, or dictate to them, or even to predict for them what will happen. But what is our duty towards them in this matter? Well, now, we have talked of strict neutrality. But I wish our statesmen, and particularly our Cabinet Ministers, would enforce upon their own tongues a little of that principle of non-intervention which they profess to apply to their diplomacy. We are told very frequently at public meetings that we must recognise the South. Well, but that recognition of the South is always coupled with another object—it is, to obtain the cotton that you want, because, if it was not for the distress brought upon us by the civil war in America, I don't think humanity would induce us to interfere any more than it does in wars going on in other parts of the world.

But, now, let us try to dispel this floating fallacy which is industriously spread over the land,—probably by interested parties. Your recognition of the South would not give you

cotton. The recognition of the South, in the minds of parties
who use that term, is coupled with something more. There
is an idea of going and interfering by force to put an end
to that contest, in order that the cotton may be set free.
If I were President Lincoln, and found myself rather in
difficulty on account of the pressure of taxation, and on
account of the discord of parties in the Federal ranks, and
if I wanted to see the whole population united as one man,
and ready to make me a despot; if I could choose that post,
and not only unite every man but every woman in my support,—then I could wish nothing better than that England
or France, or both together, should come and attempt to interfere by force in this quarrel. You read now of the elections
going on in America. And I look to those elections with
the greatest interest, as the only indications to guide me in
forming a judgment of the future. You see it stated that
in these elections there is some disunion of party. But let
the foreigners attempt to interfere in that quarrel, and all old
lines of demarcation are effaced for ever. You will have one
united population joining together to repel that intrusion.
It was so in France, in their great revolutionary war. What
begat the union there? What caused the Reign of Terror?
What was it that ruined every man who breathed a syllable
of dissent from the despotic and bloody Government en-
throned in Paris—what was it but the cry of alarm that
'the foreigner is invading us,' and the feeling that these were
the betrayers of the country, because they were the friends
of the foreigner? But your interference would not obtain
cotton. Your interference would have, in the present state
of armaments, very little effect upon the combatants there. If
people were generally better acquainted with the geography
of that country and the state of its population, they would
see how much we are apt to exaggerate even our power to
interfere to produce any result in that contest. The policy
to be pursued by the North will be decided by the elections

in the great Western States: I mean the great grain-growing region of the Mississippi valley. If the States of Ohio, Michigan, Indiana, Illinois, Iowa, Wisconsin, and Minnesota—if those States determine to carry on this war—if they say, 'We will never make peace and give up the mouth of the Mississippi, which drains our 10,000 miles of navigable waters into the Gulf of Mexico; we will never make peace while that river is in the hands of a foreign Power,'—why, all the Powers of Europe cannot reach that 'far West' to coerce it. It is 1000 miles inland across the Rocky Mountains, or 1000 miles up the Mississippi, with all its windings, before you get to that vast region—that region which is rich beyond all the rest of the world besides, peopled by ten or twelve millions of souls, doubling in numbers every few years. It is that region which will be the depository in future of the wealth and numbers of that great Continent; and whatever the decision of that region is, New York, and New England, and Pennsylvania will agree with that decision.

Therefore, watch what the determination of that people is; and if they determine to carry on the war, whatever the hideous proportions of that war may be, and however it may affect your interests, be assured that it is idle to talk—idle as the talk of children—as if it were possible for England to pretend, if it would, to carry on hostilities in the West. And, for my part, I think the language which is used sometimes in certain quarters with regard to the power of this country to go and impose its will upon the population in America, is something almost savouring of the ludicrous. When America had but 2,500,000 people, we found it impossible to enforce our will upon that population; but the progress and tendency of modern armaments are such, that where you have to deal with a rich and civilised people, having the same mechanical appliances as you have, and where that people number fifteen or twenty millions, it is next to impossible for any force to be transported across the Atlantic able to coerce that people. I should wish, therefore, that idea of force—and oh ! Englishmen have a terrible tendency to think they can resort to force—should be abandoned on this occasion. The case is utterly unmanageable by force, and interference could only do harm. What good would it do to the population of this country ? You would not get your cotton ; but if you could, what price would you pay for it ? I know something of the way in which money is voted in the House of Commons for warlike armaments, even in time of peace, and I have seen what was done during a year and a half of war. I will venture to say, that it would be cheaper to keep all the population engaged in the cotton manufacture —ay, to keep them upon turtle, champagne, and venison— than to send to America to obtain cotton by force of arms. That would involve you in a war, and six months of that war would cost more money than would be required to maintain this population comfortably for ten years.

No, gentlemen ; what we should endeavour to do, as the result of this war, is to put an end to that system of warfare which brings this calamity home to our doors, by making such alterations in the maritime law of nations which affects the rights of belligerents and neutrals, as will render it impossible, in the future, for innocent non-combatants and neutrals here to be made to suffer, as they now do, almost as much as those who are carrying on the war there. Well, if you can, out of this great disaster, make such a reform as will prevent the recurrence of such another, it is, perhaps, all that you can do in the matter. I won't enter into that subject now, because I have entered at some length into it elsewhere, and I shall have to deal with it again in the House of Commons. All I wish to say is this—that it is in the power of England to adopt. such a system of maritime law, with the ready assent of all the other Powers, as will prevent the possibility of such a state of things being brought upon us in future. And I will say this, that I doubt the wisdom—

I certainly doubt the prudence—of a great body of industrious people allowing themselves to continually live in dependence upon foreign Powers for the supply of food and raw material, knowing that a system of warfare exists by which, at any moment, without notice, without any help on their part or means of prevention, they are liable to have the raw material or the food withdrawn from them—cut off from them suddenly—without any power to resist or hinder it.

Now, that is the only good that I can see that we can do for ourselves in this matter.  Yes; there is one other good thing that we might do.  We have seen a great country, in the very height of its power, feeling itself almost exempt from the ordinary calamities of older nations,—we have seen that country suddenly prostrated, and become a cause of sorrow rather than of envy or admiration to its friends elsewhere; and what should be the monition to us?  Ask ourselves whether there is any great injustice unredressed in this country?  Ask if there is any flaw in our institutions in England requiring an adjustment or correction, one that, if not dealt with in time, may lead to a great disaster like that in America?  It is not by stroking our beards, and turning up our eyes like the Pharisee, and thanking Heaven we are not as other men are that we learn; but it is by studying such a calamity as this; by asking ourselves, is there anything in our dealings with Ireland, is there anything in India, is there anything appertaining to the rights and franchises of the great mass of our own population that requires dealing with?  If so, let what has taken place in America be a warning to us, and let us deal with an evil while it is time, and not allow it to find us out in the hour of distress and adversity.

Now, gentlemen, it was impossible to talk to you to-night without dealing with the subject that is uppermost in all our minds.  But, before I sit down, I will just say a word or two upon the general subject referred to in the resolution that has

been submitted to you. You have been told in the resolution
certain things, which, I am sorry to say, I cannot deny; you
have been told that the Government have not kept their
promises. That is a very common thing. You have been
told that they ought either to keep their promises, or retire
from office; that would be a very uncommon thing. Certainly
they have not kept their promises, if they promised you retrenchment and reform. I was not in England when the new
party combination was made, when there was a compact
entered into at Willis's Rooms. But I think our friend Alderman Livsey has very properly said—I don't feel sure whether
he used the term; if not, I am sure he will excuse me if
I attribute it to him—he said that the Radicals were 'sold'
on that occasion. ['Hear,' from Mr. Ald. Livsey.] You have
had, it is true, a very large addition made to the expenditure
of this country. But why has it been made? How has it
happened? Why, it is nearly all made for the purpose of
warlike defences in a time of peace. There is your great
item of expense. It has been incurred to protect you
against some imaginary danger. Now, what has been the
increase of which I speak? In 1835, when Sir R. Peel and
the Duke of Wellington were at the head of the Government, our military and naval armaments cost under twelve
millions per annum. Well, now, including the money voted
for fortifications, our expenditure last year was nearly three
times that,—nearly thirty millions sterling. Why is that?
Sir R. Peel and the Duke of Wellington certainly could not
be considered rash, unpatriotic men, who had not a full sense
of their responsibility as guardians of the honour and safety
of this realm. How is it, then, that we require pretty nearly
three times as much to defend us now as was required in the
time of Sir R. Peel's Government? Why, there is no doubt
that it has been in consequence, entirely I may say, in consequence of the alleged designs of our next door neighbour;
and there is no doubt, also—there can be no doubt—that the

person who has been prompting all this expenditure, on the ground that we were in danger of an attack from France, has been the present Prime Minister. There is no doubt about that.

Now, I said something about this when I met you twelve months ago here. I was fresh come from France, where I had as good opportunities as anybody had of knowing all about it. I was living eighteen months in France, and everything was open to me or my friends; anybody might go to the dockyard by my applying for an order. I had access to every document, every public paper. I told you this twelve months ago, what I repeat now, that this country had been as much deluded and hoaxed on the subject of the increase of the French navy as ever this country had been hoaxed since the time of Titus Oates. Now, since this last winter, not being able to speak, and not being able to be idle, I employed myself in writing out an exactly detailed account, year by year, of all the expenditure and amount of armaments that were maintained by France and England for their respective navies, —a most elaborate and detailed account, in which I quoted from official authorities at every step; not an anonymous publication, for I published it under my own name. That little work brought heavy indictments against our public men, charging them with the grossest misrepresentation. I stated—I never attribute motives to any man, for there is nothing so unprofitable; and I admit I may have made the statements in ignorance, but — I made the charge against your Prime Minister and others, but against him most prominently, of grossly deluding the public on the subject of the armaments of France, having, first of all, managed to delude himself on the subject. I am not going to give you any of the details or statistics which I brought together in that little publication, but I will give you a summary in two lines. I took great trouble and pains to make out a tabular statement of the amount of money expended in the

French and English dockyards from 1835 every year down to 1859, and I took at the same time a tabular statement of the number of seamen maintained each year by the two countries. The result was as I have already broadly stated—that, so far from the present Government of France having increased its preparations of naval force as compared with our own, it was far less, year by year, in proportion to ours, than it had been from the time of Louis Philippe, when Sir R. Peel was in office. I will give a comparison between the first and last years of the two dates. The expenditure for wages in the English and French dockyards, and the number of seamen in the English and French navies, in 1835, when Sir R. Peel and the Duke of Wellington were in power, and in 1859, the year preceding that in which Lord Palmerston proposed his vast scheme of fortifications, was—in 1835: English expenditure in dockyards, 376,377*l.*; French, 343,032*l.*  In 1859: English expenditure in dockyards, 1,582,112*l.*; French, 772,931*l.*; making the English increase 1,205,735*l.*, and the French, 429,899*l.*; so that the English outlay within the period was nearly three times as great as the French. The number of seamen—for the comparative power of any two naval countries is known by the number of its seamen—the number of British seamen employed in 1855 was 26,041; in 1859, 72,400; the number of French seamen engaged in the same periods, was 16,628 and 38,470 respectively; showing the French increase to have been less than half that of England.

Now, I have told you that the whole of the opinion of this country upon the subject of the naval preparations of France has originated in the misrepresentations of our present Prime Minister, and this brings us to the very part referred to in the resolution before you. There is no doubt that, when the present Government came into power, one of their great claims to the confidence of the Liberal party was that they should keep on friendly terms with France, since the danger was that the Tories would go to war with France. Well, what has been the course pursued ever since the present Prime Minister came into office? Why, for three years, he has hardly attended a public meeting of any kind, whether it has been social, political, charitable, or anything else, but he has somehow contrived to insinuate in it something of an apprehension of an invasion from France. Promising us peace with France, he has been calling out 'invasion' ever since. We ought to advertise, ' Wanted, a Minister, who, whilst promising, *par excellence*, to keep the peace with France, shall give the tax-payers of this country some of the advantages of peace.' The practice of a ruffian that walks your streets is to keep himself from harm by carrying a bludgeon, or perhaps a knife in his pocket. But that is not the mode of preserving peace which respectable people adopt. We want a Minister who, if he has a good understanding with the Government of France, has the skill to employ that good understanding with the Government of France in such a manner as would bring about economy and rational relationships between the two countries by promoting a diminution rather than an increase of forces.

But now, what shall we say of a statesman who, whilst professing to be afraid of an invasion from France, who is constantly telling you that you must be armed—armed, constantly armed and drilled, because you may be attacked any night from the other side of the Channel—but who is, at the very same time, carrying on a most close and intimate system of alliances, even entering into joint expeditions in various parts of the world, and, in fact, going into partnership with a warlike purpose with the very man who at any night might become an invader? Now, I ask you, if you read of Chatham or Sir R. Peel doing such things as that, would they have ever stood out in history as men deserving for one moment the serious esteem of thousands of mankind? Why, it is making statesmanship a joke. It is making a wry face on

one side in the way of a laugh, and on the other side it
is making a profession of solemnity.  It is a mere joke; it
is not serious thought.  But it is more.  If the man is in
earnest when he tells you that he apprehends a danger of an
invasion at any time from the other side of the Channel,
where must be his intelligence, his patriotism, if he enters
into partnership with the very man that he is afraid is
coming to play him such a clandestine trick as that?  If he
believes what he says, he ought to avoid all contact with such
a man, since he was mistaken in his estimate of the man's
character.  If he is not serious, why then he still more betrays
the country that he rules, because he offers to that man
insults; and he is continually giving him and his country an
inducement to play that statesman a scurvy trick, and through
him the people whom such a statesman drags into an alliance.

Now, I have told you, and I tell it you upon my honour,
and could give it you on the most solemn pledge, that I can
give it to my countrymen or my constituents—I tell you that
there is not a shadow of foundation in fact for all that has
been said by the Prime Minister for the last three years upon
the subject of an increase of the French navy in relation to
our own.  For, bear in mind, that cry of invasion would have
done nothing unless it had been backed by something more
practical and substantial to satisfy the practical English mind.
We have been told over and over again—I have heard it
myself—that France was making great preparations to equal
us as a naval Power.  I tell you that there is not the slightest
shadow of foundation in fact for such a statement.  I have
shown you what France spent in her dockyards during the
year 1859; that, while we spent in 1859—the year before
the fortification scheme (upon which I am going to say a
word)—1,582,000*l.* in our dockyards for wages only, for the
wages of artificers, in constructing ships of war, France spent
772,000*l.*, or less than one-half; and as we can build ships
so much cheaper than France, that we can send ships to

France and pay a duty of twenty per cent. upon them—then, I ask you how could France, having spent less than half for wages in her dockyards, where her artisans are acknowledged to be inferior to ours,—how could France, spending half the money we spent, have been in the way of preparing a fleet to rival or to equal our own? When I was in France, and those statements were constantly made, I confess to you I was ashamed of them as an Englishman — placed there to represent, in a certain sense, the Queen and this great country—I was ashamed of those constant statements that were being made by the Prime Minister of this country to the House of Commons; while the Government of France was lost in bewilderment as to the motives of these repeated assertions. My friend M. Chevallier—who is not only my friend, but also the friend of every man who wishes for progress and the enlightenment and prosperity of mankind—he and I spent many an hour over the statistics of the two countries, trying if we could find a shadow of foundation for the statements that were constantly being made in England with a view to excite you to a jealousy and a fear of the French nation; and we could not find the slightest shadow of a ground for anything that had been. said. The Government of France put forward in their organs of the press the most emphatic denial of those statements; but, not merely that, several of our most able practical men in the House of Commons—so astonished and puzzled were they by the constant statements made there by the Prime Minister—actually took the trouble either to go to France themselves, or to send trusty agents. For instance, Mr. Lindsay went to France, and himself consulted the Minister of Marine; Mr. Dalgleish, the Member for Glasgow, who had been appointed on a commission to examine into our dockyards, went to France himself to inquire into the matter; Sir Morton Peto sent a trusted agent, a practical man, who was allowed to go and visit the French dockyards. Others took the same course, and they came back to the House of Commons and stated their convictions of the utter groundlessness of these statements.

Now, what motive, I ask you, could be sufficient to make a public man like myself come before you and advance these statements, if they were not true? What motive could those Members of Parliament of whom I have been speaking—they were not official men—what motive could they have but the best and most patriotic of motives, in going to France to satisfy themselves of the truth of this matter? Well, then, I say there is not a shadow of foundation for the statements that have been made. I will tell you what there is a truth in,—we have spent money, no doubt, in building useless and antiquated vessels; we went on wasting our money upon sailing vessels long after it was known that nothing but steam-vessels would be of any use; we have gone on squandering our money upon wooden vessels long after it was known that iron would supersede wood. Well, but France has not wasted quite so much as we have. I don't give her or any other Government credit for being quite so economical and so wise as it should be in the matter of its expenditure; but France, not having spent her money quite so foolishly as we generally have, has managed to present something that was going to be done a little earlier than we did; and it was because we had wasted our money in useless constructions that we raised the cry of an invasion from France to cover the misdeeds and defalcations of our own Government. Recollect, I am not now leaving this an open question as to whether France had certain designs upon us. I don't rest my case upon any assumed friendliness on the part of any Government. I am speaking as to matters of fact, and I say that you have been grossly, you have been completely deluded. This country has been misled altogether by the statements that have been made from what should have been the highest authorities upon the subject of the preparations of France.

Well, now, it was under this state of things,—I have told you what the comparative strength of the English and French navies in 1859 was,—that the very year following, Lord Palmerston brought forward his gigantic scheme of fortifications for this country, and that is a subject upon which I wish to say a word or two, because it has in one sense a far more important bearing than any other on our military and naval expenditure. In the session of 1860, the Prime Minister himself brought forward a scheme of fortifications for which he proposed to borrow money. The original scheme embraced vast detached forts in the neighbourhood of Portsmouth, going over the South Downs some seven or eight miles—so vast, so extensive, so far inland, that we passed an Act in the House of Commons to abolish an ancient fair, at which cattle were sold on the South Downs, in order that the place might be occupied with these great forts; it embraced a plan for a large fort in the midland counties, on Cannock Chase ; and the whole scheme was devised at an estimated cost of about nine or ten millions sterling, but by those who thought upon the subject — I was in Paris while all this was going on—it was said that it would be more likely to reach twenty or thirty millions than nine or ten, if it were ever allowed to begin. In bringing forward that measure for these fortifications, not one word was said in the speech of the Prime Minister respecting our ability to defend ourselves at sea, though our force was double that of France ; he assumed that an enemy would land and burn our dockyards, and these fortifications were devised in order to protect our fleets. Why, I always used to think our navy was intended to defend us, and that we had not occasion to build forts to defend our navy. You remember the anecdote told of Nelson, when he had an audience of George III, during the great French war, and during the time when there was a talk of invasion. The King said, in his curious repetitive way, ' Well, Admiral, well, Admiral, do you think

the French will come? do you think the French will come?
do you think the French will come?' 'Well,' replied Nelson;
' I can only answer for it that they will not come by sea.'
Well, we seem to have abandoned altogether that confidence
in our navy. I think, after having spent twice as much as
the French for making our navy, and paying for twice as
many sailors to man our navy, that we are cowards if we
are assuming that any enemy is coming to land upon our
shores. But, however, this great scheme of fortifications was
brought in, and it was passed like everything else is in this
House of Commons.

Now, I will tell you what the effect of that will be, and,
perhaps, it has not been sufficiently thought of by the
country. You are borrowing the money to make these fortifications—borrowing it for thirty years. Mark the insidious
process by which you are allowing this grand scheme to
be accomplished. If the Government had to ask every year
for the money in the Estimates to come out of the taxes,
I would engage for it that the 1,200,000*l.* wanted the last
session would not have been voted, because it would have been
needful to lay on fresh taxes, and fresh taxes would not have
been laid on. But they borrowed the money, and so this
expenditure of pretty nearly a million and a quarter is got from
a loan. I will tell you what the consequence will be. You are
going on building fortifications, which, according to the
estimate of Sir Frederick Smith, the Member for Chatham,
who opposed this scheme from beginning to end — and he
is about the highest authority we have in the House of Commons, for he has been a professor of engineering, and is a
man of high and acknowledged talent—according to the estimate of Sir Frederick Smith, those great forts in the neighbourhood of Portsmouth alone will require 30,000 men to
man them, and the other forts will require 60,000 or 70,000
more men to man them. Now, once build those forts, and
you must have an army to keep them, otherwise you must

blow them up again, because nothing can be more unwise,
as everybody will see, than to build forts and leave them
unprotected, to be taken and occupied by an enemy. I will
tell you what this scheme is. I don't say what men's motives
are,—I only tell you what the effect of this scheme will be.
We are just now getting into a discussion with respect to
the policy of keeping an army for the defence of our Colonies.
Very soon that discussion will ripen—as all discussions in
this country are apt in time to do—into a triumph of the
true principle, and the colonists, who are much better able
to do so than we are, will be left to defend themselves, or,
if they call upon us to defend them, will have to contribute towards the expense. We shall be able to withdraw
from the Colonies, nobody can tell how many—it may be
20,000—troops. Here you have a plan—I don't attribute
motives—but, if the design was to prepare a mode by which
the governing class of this country, who, unless they have
been very much maligued, would like excuses for keeping up
our military establishments, could keep them up—here will be
a good excuse furnished them for keeping every man of those
troops at home. You will have the fortifications built, and
you must have an army to put into them, and that will be
just the result of this fortification scheme.

Well, gentlemen, there is no doubt in the world that all
this is the work of one man; it is the work of your Prime
Minister. I don't question the man's sincerity, but he is under
an impression, he is under a delusion, I don't hardly know
what to call it, because I wish to observe the proprieties, but
he is under the delusion that he is living in about 1808, and,
as long as he lives, you will not rescue him from that delusion.
I can make every allowance for one in his position for entertaining such delusions, but what must we say of his colleagues? They are silent. The Prime Minister has to start
up every moment to defend every detail of the plan of fortifications. If the Minister at War gets up to say a word upon

it, it is in such a languid fashion, with such a total absence
evidently of all knowledge on the subject, that it savours
of the burlesque.  Mr. Gladstone has never said one word
in support of this grand scheme.  I need not say that such
men as Mr. Milner Gibson and Mr. Villiers are entirely silent
upon it.  It is wholly the work of one man, and that is
the Prime Minister; and there is not a man in the House
of Commons who, behind the scenes, will not admit that it
would be impossible to carry out such a scheme as that, if it
were not the act of the present Prime Minister.  It is opposed more or less in its details, and denounced by every
authority.  You saw the opposition to it last session, which
was not on the part of the so-called peace men; our friend
Mr. Bright was not present for a great period of it, but
it was opposed by eminent naval and military authorities.  It
was opposed by Sir Frederick Smith, the hon. Member for
Chatham, and by Mr. Bernal Osborne.  It was such men as
these who opposed this scheme, and yet it was carried by
the Prime Minister.

Now, I say, what shall be said of his colleagues?  What
shall be said of the House of Commons?  No doubt these
great monstrosities and excrescences. in our towns, on our
plains, and on our heaths, will be ridiculed by future generations, will be looked at and pointed at as Palmerston's follies.
Well, there may be an excuse for a Minister verging on four-
score, who was brought up in the middle of the wars of the
first French Revolution—there may be an excuse for him.
But what excuse is there for the manhood and intellect of
this country in allowing itself to be dragged into wasteful
extravagance and follies like this, and to be made the laughing-stock of nations, to gratify the whim, the mere whim,
of a Prime Minister?  Are we not become as politicians an
enfeebled generation?  Look at the speeches that are made
everywhere.  What is there in them?  Is there no taste for

anything having good stuff in it,—having, what you call, the weft in it? We seem to have fallen or entered upon our decline, unless some revival or vigorous effort is made to get us out of the terrible trouble in which this district is now involved. How is it that such a state of things as this can exist in Parliament? I'll tell you how it is: we have not an honest state of parties in Parliament. That is the whole thing in a few words. It is a hard truth, but it is the truth, that parties are not on an honest basis in Parliament. You have got a Prime Minister who is at your head, who professes to lead the Liberal party, and—as I have said to his face in the House of Commons — is about the staunchest Tory we have there. The consequence is, that the Tories — particularly the most antiquated and incorrigible Tories—are not the men who intend to be in office; they could not go farther than he does; and so the Tories who sit below the gangway, on the Opposition side, are supporting the present Prime Minister. And why? For a very good reason. He spends far more money to obstruct reform, and that more effectually, than the Tories would, if they were in office. I volunteer my deliberate opinion that he is spending five millions more of the nation's money every year than would be spent if the Tories were in power. We are in this most anomalous position: the High Tories are in power, but not in office. We, the Liberals, are responsible for what is being done, and if we protest against it, our leader calls in the aid of the Opposition, and the Tories enable him to carry his measures in spite of us. There cannot be anything more unfortunate for the country than such a state of parties. There can be nothing so bad in public or private as a man holding a position for which he is not responsible, which is the position the Prime Minister occupies at this moment. He is not responsible to us; he carries on the policy of the Tories, and is supported by them. And there is no remedy for this state of things, that I am aware of, but in the change that shall make the party which is ruling and governing become responsible for the Government.

Now, let us suppose that, instead of our being on the Government side, we were on the Opposition, and let us suppose Mr. Disraeli in power with Lord Derby. You might say it is the practice of the Tory party to spend as much as they can for the military and the naval services. That is true, unless we have very much maligned them all our days. Not that the Tory party has been desirous of engaging in a larger expenditure than the present Ministry has. But bear in mind, that from the moment they got into office other motives came into play. They will make great sacrifices of their own interests in the way of expenditure in order to preserve office, and when they are in power they will immediately begin to carry out works of reform and retrenchment in order to remain there. But, whilst they are in Opposition, as they are now, they are willing enough to see all this extravagance and all this obstruction of reform on the part of a so-called Liberal Government, because it is doing two things : it is giving them an expenditure which they like, while it does not saddle them with the responsibilities of office. But it is doing another thing : it is so damaging the so-called Liberal party, that they know it is only a question of time as to when we shall go out of power, and the more they can tar us with their own brush before we leave, the less we shall have to say in opposition to them when they get there. I don't argue in favour of bringing any party into power, but what I do say is this, that it is dishonouring to us, the so-called Liberals, to sit where we are on the Government side of the House and see everything administered in opposition to, and in downright derision of, our principles. And it must come to this question, ' Will or can this system go on much longer ?' We have two principles at work in our Cabinet, as there are two principles at work in every

individual, and in every body of men—there is the good principle, and there is also the evil principle.  During the first
two years of this Government's existence, the good principle
had some influence and power, and it was manifested in those
great and those conclusive reforms of the tariff carried out by
Mr. Gladstone, in conjunction with the French Treaty.   This
was, to a certain extent, the triumph of the good principle
in the Cabinet.   That occurred in 1861.   There was the com-
pletion of reform in our tariff, so far as protective duties were
concerned, and there was the repeal of the paper duty, both
being great and comprehensive measures.   But during the last
session of Parliament the evil principle of the Cabinet was
wholly predominant, and gave us no compensation whatever
in the form of good measures.

Now, is that to be continued next session?   If it be, well
then, I say, it is quite impossible, if the so-called Liberal
party be true to itself, that they can continue to give their
support to the present Government.   It would be betraying
the people, the constituents that send us to Parliament.   We
sit there, and know what is going on.   We are behind the
scenes, and we see what is vulgarly called in the prize ring
' a cross' being fought between the leader of our party and
the worst part of the party opposite, by which we are victim-
ised and you are betrayed.   But to continue to witness that,
and to connive at it, we betray our trust.   We must separate
ourselves from that state of things if it is to go on any longer.
You cannot expect the constituents to fight the battles of
reform if they see that their chief who represents them in the
House of Commons is in fact handing them over to their
enemies.   Why, how would M'Clellan's troops fight in the
army of the Potomac, if they knew that M'Clellan had a
secret understanding with Jefferson Davis and Beauregard ?
Now that seems to be very much our case, as a Liberal party.

Well, gentlemen, there will be something for us to do next
session.   We shall see.   We shall see whether the good or

the evil principle is predominant in the Cabinet, and the proof will be found in the measures of next session. I can only say for myself, that if the next session is to be anything like the last, and I should not be deprived of my vocal powers by the frosts of the winter, you may depend upon it my voice will be raised in protest against such a state of things. And I will do my best to put an end to it. I will not forget the resolution you have passed—that if the Ministry don't carry out their pledges and their principles, the best thing for them will be to go into Opposition.

I have only a word more to say. We are not merely dealing with financial reform. I am of opinion—and the opinion grows every day, in spite of the apparent apathy that is on the surface—I am more and more of opinion that the true solution of our political difficulties—I mean this state of parties—will only be found in reform of Parliament. I hold to that opinion more and more. I don't see what it is to be, or where it is to go to; but this I know, that the longer you wait for reform the more you will have, because these changes always pay great interest for keeping. For my part, I am moderate—people, when they get grey-haired, always get moderate: I should like something done, and done quickly; but of this I am certain, that you can have no great rectification of this state of parties until you have a reform of Parliament, or, at all events, a party in opposition that is honestly advocating a reform of Parliament. We are frequently asked, 'What would that do?' I am not fond of predictions; but, as that has been thrown out as a challenge—as they frequently say, 'What would you get by a reform of Parliament that you don't get now?'—I will answer that challenge. It is my firm belief that, with a thorough representation of the people of this country, the extravagant expenditure in warlike armaments in time of peace would not be possible. I don't say that the whole people would not go to war sometimes. I should not pretend to say that the English people are altogether certain to keep the peace; but this I do say, that there is something in the self-assurance, and in the dignity, and in the high sense of security which great multitudes of men feel, which would prevent their lending themselves to these delusions, to burden themselves with these enormous expenses, in order to protect themselves against imaginary dangers. The late panics with regard to France never penetrated amongst the mass of the working people—they rested amongst a section of the middle and upper classes. If anybody asks me the question in a spirit of defiance, 'What could you do with a reform of Parliament that you cannot do now?' I assure you,—I do not say it as any more than an opinion, though it is my earnest belief, that if you had a thorough representation in Parliament, you could not persuade the people of this country to spend half the money that is now spent under the pretence of protecting them, but which is really spent in order that certain parties may get some sort of benefit out of it. I am very sorry to have detained you so long. ['Go on.'] You know I never give any peroration to my speeches. When I have finished, I sit down.

I have nothing more to say, but to thank you most cordially for this kind and friendly welcome, sincerely hoping that your stout hearts may bear you manfully through your present difficulties, believing, as I do, that our countrymen will come gladly to your rescue, and assuring you, as I do, that wherever I may be, my humble voice and influence shall not be wanting, in any way, to aid you in your present difficulties.

# FOREIGN POLICY.

## IX.

### ROCHDALE, NOVEMBER 23, 1864.

[The following was the last Speech which Mr. Cobden made. The allusion in the first paragraph was to the loss which Mr. Bright had just sustained in the death of a son.]

BEFORE I commence the few remarks I have to offer, I must be permitted to join in the expression of my profound sympathy with the language of condolence which you have used towards my esteemed friend, and your absent and bereaved neighbour (Mr. Bright). The feeling that has been shown by thousands here to-night is one that will be felt by millions in all parts of the world. May he take consolation by the consciousness of that deep feeling of sympathy and sorrow with which the knowledge of his bereavement will be followed!

Nor can I allow this occasion to pass without noticing a blank in our ranks upon the platform to-night. I have never attended a public meeting at Rochdale which has not been animated by the presence of our departed friend. You will know to whom I allude—Mr. Alderman Livsey. By

his death the most numerous portion of the community of
Rochdale has lost an amiable neighbour, and in many cases
a powerful protector and advocate. And quite sure I am that
all classes and all parties would concur in inscribing this
epitaph upon his monument,—' that he was an honest and
consistent politician, an earnest and true friend.'

Now, gentlemen, when I see this vast assembly before
me—and it is certainly the largest meeting on one floor that
I have ever had the honour of attending—my only regret is
my inability, I fear, to make the whole audience hear what I
would wish to say to them ; but if those upon the outside will
have patience, and if they will practise some of that principle
of non-intervention in the affairs of their neighbours which
our friend Mr. Ashworth has just been so eloqently advocating—I mean, with their elbows and their toes—I will
endeavour in as short time as possible to make myself heard
by those who are present.

It is not much my habit when I come before you, in pursuance of the good custom of a representative paying at least
one annual visit to his constituents, to recapitulate what has
occurred in the preceding session of Parliament. I have
taken it generally for granted that you have been paying
attention' to what has passed, and that you do not require
any retrospective criticism at my hands. But I am disposed
to make the last session an exception to my rule, and I will
offer a few remarks upon what has passed during that session
in order to illustrate and expound that question to which
Mr. Ashworth has alluded,—I mean the question of non-
intervention, and to show you how, in my opinion, the proceedings of the last session of Parliament have necessarily led
to a complete revolution in our foreign policy, and must put
an impassable gulf between the old traditions of our Foreign-
office and that which I hope to see adopted as the foreign
policy of this country.

Now, during the thirty years since I first gave utterance by pen or voice to a sentiment in public, I have always attached the utmost importance to the principle of non-intervention in the affairs of foreigners.  I have looked upon it as a fundamental article in the creed of this country, if we would either secure good government at home, or protect ourselves against endless embarrassments and complications abroad.  You may remember, the last time I had the honour of addressing you here, I was complaining of the incessant violation of this principle ; how I compared the state of a country which is always engaged in looking after the affairs of foreign countries, to what would be the case in Rochdale if your Town Council were engaged in managing the affairs of Leeds or Blackburn, instead of attending to their own business.

Well, we met at the last session of Parliament, and the Queen's Speech announced to us impending negotiations respecting the affairs of Sleswig-Holstein.  From the opening debate on the Queen's Speech, throughout the whole session of Parliament, down to the end of June, which was practically the close of the session, I may say that, without any exception, the whole business of Parliament, so far as the action of the two great parties who contend for power and place in the House was concerned—the whole attention of the House was given to the question of Sleswig-Holstein.  I am not going into the history of that most complicated of all questions further than this : In 1852, by the mischievous activity of our Foreign-office, seven diplomatists were brought round a green table in London to settle the destinies of a million of people in the two provinces of Sleswig and Holstein, without the slightest reference to the wants and wishes or the tendencies or the interests of that people.  The preamble of the treaty which was there and then agreed to stated that what those seven diplomatists were going to do was to maintain the integrity of the Danish monarchy, and to sustain the balance of power in Europe.  Kings, emperors, princes were represented at that meeting, but the people had not the slightest

voice or right in the matter. They settled the treaty, the
object of which was to draw eloser the bonds between those
two provinces and Denmark. The tendeney of the great
majority of the people of those provinces—about a million of
them altogether—was altogether in the direction of Germany.
From that time to this year the treaty was followed by constant agitation and discord; two wars have sprung out of it,
and it has ended in the treaty being torn to pieces by two of
the Governments who were prominent parties to the treaty.
That is the history (I don't intend to go further into it), or a
summary of the whole proceeding.

Now, during the whole of last session the time of the
House of Commons, as I have said, was occupied upon that
question. If you will take those volumes of *Hansard* which
give the report of our proceedings in the last Parliament, and
turn to the index under the head of Sleswig-Holstein, or
under the head of Denmark or Germany, you will find there,
page after page, such questions as these put to the Government:—' When will the blue-books be laid upon the table?'
' When will the conference be called together?' ' When will
the protocols be published?' and ' When will the protocols be
laid before Parliament?' In this way the two great parties
occupied the whole of the last session, because, when they
were not talking upon this subject, they made the want of the
papers or the want of the decision of this conference or the
protocols an excuse for doing nothing else. Now, we had
great debates in the House, and you will find some of the most
prominent among our Members of the House of Commons—
men, I mean, who wage the great party battles in the House—
hardly opening their lips upon anything else but Sleswig-
Holstein. And in the House of Lords they were still more
animated. I have observed, that if ever there is anything connected with an exciting foreign topic, anything that is likely
to lead to an excuse for military or naval expeditions, and
public expenditure, the House of Lords becomes more excited

than even the House of Commons; but you never see the Lords lose their calmness and self-possession upon any domestic question.

Now, there was one noble Peer, who spoke repeatedly on this question, who seems to me to be peculiarly framed for illustrating the fact, that a man may have great oratorical gifts and be quite destitute of common sense or ordinary judgment. That noble Lord, in the early part of the session, in a speech delivered upon this question, assailed the Queen— he attacked her Majesty for having influenced her Ministers in the interests of Germany. But this country is not a republic. The Queen, so long as she accepts a Prime Minister dictated to her by the House of Commons, has no political power, and, therefore, can have no political responsibility. That our present Sovereign accepts her Prime Minister for that reason, and no other, I think we have pretty good reason to know. But what shall we say of the chivalrous assembly which allowed a person to be assailed in her absence—the only person in the country who is defenceless, and that person a lady; for, with the exception of Lord Russell, who spoke in defence of himself rather than of the Crown, there was no one who rose to rebuke that noble Lord—the man that assailed his Sovereign? Later on in the session, we heard more of the noble Lord, who claims the merit of having involved us in the Crimean war, and who has taken the lead in advocating all our fortifications and every abomination of modern times. Having begun the session by attacking the Sovereign, it was only, perhaps, consistent that he should end it by vituperating the people. He said in July, 'I appealed to the higher and nobler feelings of Parliament and of the nation, believing, as I did, that a course which was dictated by generosity was also recommended by policy. Others, with more success, appealed to more common things— to love of ease, to love of repose, to love of quiet, but above all to love of money, which has now become the engrossing

passion of the people of this country.' Now, if I were going
to call a witness to prove that the English people are in pecuniary affairs so chivalronsly generous, almost so foolishly
generous, that they can give an annual allowance to an individual who has certainly no moral claim upon them, who
would in no other country be recognised to have a legal claim
to an allowance which actually amounts to 7700*l.* a year for
life—the individual I would call as my evidence would be this
very peer, the Earl of Ellenborough.

That to which I wish to call the attention of this room, and
of those who will see what we are here saying, is what followed
at the close of those debates.  The newspapers that were in
the interest of the Government were harping in favour of war
to the last moment in large leading articles.  Some announced
the very number of the regiments, the names of the colonels,
the names of the ships, and the commanders that would be
sent to fight this battle for Denmark.  In the House of
Commons there was a general opinion that there was a great
struggle going on in the Cabinet as to whether we should
declare war against Germany.  At the end of June the Prime
Minister announced that he was going to produce the protocols, and to state the decision of the Government upon the
question.  He gave a week's notice of this intention, and
then I witnessed what has convinced me that we have
achieved a revolution in our foreign policy.  The whippers-in
—you know what I mean—those on each side of the House
who undertake to take stock of the number and the opinions
of their followers—the whippers-in during the week were
taking soundings of the inclination of Members of the House
of Commons.  And then came up from the country such a
manifestation of opinion against war, that day after day
during that eventful week Member after Member from the
largest constituencies went to those who acted for the Government in Parliament and told them distinctly that they would
not allow war on any such matters as Sleswig and Holstein.

Then came surging up from all the great seats and centres
of manufacturing and commercial activity one unanimous
veto against war for this matter of Sleswig and Holstein.
The conversation that passed in those gossiping purlieus of
the House of Commons — the library, the tea-room, the
smoking-room, and the rest — was most interesting and
striking. 'Why,' a man representing a great constituency
would be asked,—' How is it that the newspapers are writing
for war?' The newspapers write for war, because the newspapers in London that are in the interest of the Government have been giving out in leading articles that there
was to be war. But they only express their own opinions,
and not the opinions heard on 'Change. By the end of the
week preceding the speech made by the Prime Minister, when
he laid the protocols of the Convention upon the table, and
gave the decision of the Government upon the policy they
would pursue, there came up such an expression and manifestation of opinion, that I was satisfied no Government, whatever the press said, whatever was the opinion in the Cabinet
at the time, could get us into war whilst the Parliament was
sitting. And when the subsequent debate came on, and I
spoke upon the subject, I challenged the House of Commons
to tell me if I was speaking incorrectly, when I said there
were not five men in the House of Commons who would
vote for war on any matter connected with that question.
Nobody contradicted me.

Well, but the feeling out of doors in London was one of
intense anxiety. I never saw the House of Commons—not
even in the time of the Corn-laws—so mobbed by what I
remember a Member called a middle-class mob, as it was
on the night when Lord Palmerston came to make that
final declaration of the decision of the Government on that
occasion. It was evident that the middle classes of London
thought that the question of peace or war was hanging
in the balance, and they seemed rather apprehensive than

otherwise that war would be the decision of the Government.

Well, this places the Parliament and the Government — and, to some extent, the nation represented — in a somewhat ignominious position. And the natural solution, in a case like that, in our constitutional form of government, is this, — the nation must find some vicarious sufferer, who shall be made to pay the penalty of this national blunder. The Opposition in the House of Commons is the proper mechanism by which this necessary constitutional process should be carried out. In ancient times, you know, a Minister that had got the country into a mess would have had his head cut off. Now he is decapitated in another way. He is sent away from Downing-street into the cold shade of the Opposition, on the left-hand side of the Speaker. But on this occasion the Opposition brought forward a motion condemnatory of the Government, which the Opposition had no right to bring forward, because the whole proceedings of Parliament during the session showed that the Opposition was far more to blame for the delusion that had been practised upon the country than the Government itself. The Opposition was constantly stimulating the Government to do something, or making them responsible for not doing something, and putting grave questions to them, keeping their countenances while they did so, and not leading us to suppose it was all a joke; and, therefore, when they had been parties to this waste of the session, on the ground that they thought the Government was responsible for everything done that was being done about Sleswig-Holstein, it was not becoming in them to take the course they did, for they could not very logically or consistently bring forward a motion condemning the Government for what had been done. Mr. Kinglake, who had never been in favour of the proceedings in regard to the Sleswig-Holstein affair, substituted a clause, or passage in the resolution, which did not either absolve the Government or condemn them, but it merely expressed the satisfaction that we had escaped war, and there the matter ended.

Well, but now let me tell the solid, substantial manufacturing and commercial capitalists of this country, that this is not a very honourable position in which to be left. The Government was allowed to go on and commit them—commit them as far as a Government can do, in backing up and encouraging a small Power to fight with a big one. It was very much like a man taking a little fellow and backing him for a prize-fight. He 'draws the scratch,' as they say, across where his toe is to come to, and tells him to stand up to the mark, advises him how to train himself, takes him under his charge, and then, just at the moment when he comes to the place, he moves off and leaves him.

Now, that is the position in which we are left as a nation by what was done last session about Sleswig-Holstein. We were caricatured in every country in Europe. I myself saw German and French caricatures immediately afterwards. There was a French caricature representing Britannia with a cotton nightcap on; there was a German caricature representing the British lion running off as hard as ever he could, with a hare running after him. This is not a satisfactory state of things, because I maintain that to a certain extent we deserved all that;—that is, we did deserve it, unless we show that we did not run away on that occasion, just because it did not suit us to fight, and unless we intend to adopt a different principle in our foreign policy, and say that other countries must not expect us to fight, except for our own business.

The manufacturing and commercial interests of the country were in a state of almost unparalleled expansion. They had entered into vast engagements, expecting that they would be realised and fulfilled in a time of peace; both capitalists and labourers felt that if war had arisen just then, it would have produced enormous calamities, such as no nation ought ever to bring upon itself, unless in defence of its own vital interest and honour. But all that ought to have been foreseen and anticipated, if not by your Governments, which are living in the traditions of fifty years ago, by an active-minded public spirit on the part of your people. You cannot separate yourselves from the honour or dishonour of your Government, or from the acts of those Cabinets and legislators whom you allow to act on your behalf and in your name.

I'll tell you what appears to me to be the result of that week's debate on the Sleswig-Holstein question. Both sides felt that they were parties to such a ridiculous *fiasco,* and were in such an ignominious plight, that as the representatives of this great nation they had so compromised you, that there was a general disposition to take the pledge of non-intervention. But you know when people have got a headache after a debauch, they sometimes take the pledge to be teetotallers for life, but they do not keep it. Now, what I want to do is to prevent a recurrence of that disgraceful proceeding which wasted you the last session of Parliament, and ended by making you as a nation, as far as a Cabinet can make you, ridiculous.

I think we had made some progress, through the general declarations of sentiment in the House of Commons from leading men of all sides. But what did I hear? What do I see? I see the report of a speech made by an honourable and learned Gentleman to a constituency whose good voices and support he is canvassing for the next election—a manufacturing borough that shall be nameless, further than that it is on the banks of the Roche. I read a speech in which this hon. and learned Gentleman, addressing this manufacturing borough, and received with — with immense applause — in which he has a long programme of foreign policy, in pursuance of which, if it is to be carried out and adopted by our manufacturing community, I think we ought to reckon upon being at war every year of our lives; and instead of spending — as we do now, unfortunately — 25,000,000*l.* upon our public services, we ought to begin by spending at least 50,000,000*l.* Amongst other things this honourable and learned Gentleman proposed we should do is this : we should maintain our armaments on a due scale, in order to prevent France from swallowing up Germany.

Well, now, I can only say, for my part, if the French were to perform such a feat as that, they would suffer so terribly from indigestion, after swallowing those forty millions of uncomfortable Teutons, that I think they would be objects of pity rather than terror ever afterwards. Really, you know, when men aspiring to be statesmen come to talk exactly as if they had taken passages from ' Baron Munchausen ' or ' Gulliver's Travels,' how can we possibly say that we have made any great progress? If such sentiments as those can be applauded in a manufacturing borough on the banks of the Roche, what must we expect to hear in agricultural districts in the neighbourhood of Midhurst ?

There has been a speech lately made by my right hon. Friend, Mr. Bouverie, at Kilmarnock, and there seemed to be some baillies, who are generally rather acute folks, on the platform with him, in which he gave utterance to some opinions which rather tended to show that, in spite of what was done in the last session of Parliament, we shall have to do with this foreign policy and this non-intervention just what we did with the Corn question—reiterate and reiterate, and repeat and repeat, until that comes to pass which O'Connell used to say to me, ' I always go on repeating until I find what I have been saying coming back to me in echoes from other people.' Now, my friend, Mr. Bouverie, talks in favour of a foreign policy which should be founded upon a benevolent, senti- mental principle—that is, that we shall do what is right, true, and just to all the world. Well, now, I think, as a corporate body—as a political community—if we can manage to do what is right, and true, and just to each other—if we can manage to carry out that at home, it will be about as much as we can do. I do not think I am responsible for seeing right and truth and justice carried out all over the world. I think, if we had that responsibility, Providence would have invested us with more power than He has. I don't think we can do it, and there's an end of it. But my friend talks as though at some time or other it was the practice in this country to carry out a sentimental policy; and he carried us back, first of all, to the times of Queen Elizabeth. He says that she was a Sovereign who did what was right and true and just, and in the interest of Protestantism, all over the Continent of Europe. Now, I think he could not have made a more unhappy selection than that example he has given; for if ever there was a hard-headed and not a soft-hearted Sovereign it was she; if there ever was a place where there was little of that romantic sentiment of going abroad to do right and justice to other people, I think it was in that Tudor breast of our 'Good Queen Bess,' as we call her. Why, when I read Motley's 'History of the Rise of the Dutch Republic' — an admirable book, which everybody should read—when I read the history of the Netherlands, and when I see how that struggling community, with their whole country desolated by Spanish troops, and every town lighted up daily with the fires of persecution,—when I see the accounts of what passed when the envoys came to Queen Elizabeth and asked for aid, how she is huckstering for money while they are begging for help to their religion,—I declare that, with all my principles of non-intervention, I am almost ashamed of old Queen Bess. And then there were Burleigh, Walsingham, and the rest, who were, if possible, harder and more difficult to deal with than their mistress. Why, they carried out in its unvarnished selfishness a national British policy; they had no other idea of a policy but a national British policy, and they carried it out with a degree of selfishness amounting to downright avarice.

Mr. Bouverie next quotes Chatham. Do you suppose that

Chatham was running about the world protecting and look-ing after other people's affairs? Why, he went abroad in the spirit of a commercial traveller more than any Minister we ever had. Just step into the Guildhall in the metropolis, and read the inscription on the monument erected by the City of London to Lord Chatham. It is stated to be 'as a recognition'—I give you the words—'of the benefits which the City of London received by her ample share in the public prosperity;' and then they go on to describe by what means this great man had made them so prosperous, and they say— I give you again the very words: 'By conquests made by arms and generosity in every part of the globe, and by com-merce for the first time united with and made to flourish by war.' Well, they were living under another dispensation to ours. At that time, Lord Chatham thought, that by making war upon France and seizing the Canadas, he was bringing custom to the English merchants and manufacturers, and he publicly declared that he made those conquests for the very purpose of giving a monopoly of those conquered markets to Englishmen at home; and he said he would not allow the colonists to manufacture a horseshoe for themselves.

Well, that was the old dispensation, when people believed that the only way to prosper in trade was by establishing a monopoly, and that blood and violence would lead to profit. We know differently. We know that that is no longer necessary, and that it is no longer possible. Now, if I take Chatham's great son; if I take the second Pitt, when he entered upon wars, he immediately began the conquest of colonies. When he entered upon war with France in 1793, and for three or four years afterwards, our navy was employed in little else than seizing colonies, the islands of the West Indies, &c., whether they belonged to France, Holland, or Denmark, or other nations, and he believed by that means he could make war profitable. We know that is no longer possible. We know it, and I thank God we live in a time when

it is impossible for Englishmen ever to make a war profitable.
Now, what we want in statesmanship is this—that we should
understand what are the interests of our days, with our better
lights and knowledge, and not be guided by maxims and rules
which appertain to a totally different state of things.    For
no statesman ever was great unless he was carrying out a
policy that was suited to the time in which he lived, and in
which he wrought up to the highest lights of the age in
which he flourished.    That is the only way in which a statesman can ever distinguish himself; and I have no hesitation in saying, that any modern statesman who is trusting for
fame or for future honour to anything he has been doing in
foreign policy for the last twenty or thirty years, is most
miserably mistaken, and that he will be forgotten or only
remembered as an example to be avoided within two years
after his death.

Now, I am going to touch upon a very delicate question.  It
is not enough that our Government should not interfere in
foreign questions ; it is not enough that our Government
should not lecture and talk to foreign countries about what
policy they should pursue.  There is something more required.
Englishmen, through their public speakers and through their
press, must learn to treat foreign questions in a different spirit
to what they have done.  And they must learn to do it as a
point of honour towards foreign countries as well as a matter
of self-respect which is due to themselves.  You will mislead
foreign countries by demonstrations of opinion in this country
which are not to be followed by acts.  Instead of benefiting a
country, instead of benefiting a people abroad, you are very
often injuring them with the very best possible intention.

Of all the public men who have been prominently engaged
in politics, probably there are none who, so much as my
friend Mr. Bright and myself, have always avoided public
demonstrations in favour of some nationality or some people
abroad.  Nothing would have been cheaper from time to time

than for us to get immense applause and popularity by going
down to the Guildhall or somewhere else, to attend a meeting
and make a flaming and declamatory speech about the Poles, or
Hungarians, or some people else a thousand miles away. But
I have always felt that in doing that we were very likely to do
a great deal of harm to the persons with whom we sympathised.
I hope that nobody will suppose that my friend Mr. Bright,
and myself, and those of the Free-trade school who have
acted with us, have less sympathy for other people abroad
than these gentlemen who come either to speak at public
meetings, or to write in the papers in favour of some foreign
nationality. I maintain that if a man is best doing his duty at
home in striving to extend the sphere of liberty—commercial,
literary, political, religious, and in all directions ; for if he is
working for liberty at home, he is working for the advancement of the principles of liberty all over the world. See what
mischief has been done. I have no hesitation in saying—and
I speak with the authority of persons who have been parties
interested and who have been themselves victims of that which
was done in Paris and in London last year upon the subject of
Poland, which has led thousands of the generous youth of
Poland to premature graves, and sent thousands more into
Siberian exile. The manifestations and the instigations in
London and Paris incapacitated that unhappy insurrection—
if it can be called by the name of an insurrection—in Poland
last year. It never had a chance from the beginning. I never
like to speak disrespectfully of any movement of the kind—there
are always, God knows, plenty to decry those who have failed—
but the insurrection never had the slightest chance. The mass
of the people never were with it ; the insurgents were a few
generous enthusiasts, always young men. Out of a population
asserted to be many millions, and said to be interested in this
revolt, you never saw more, even by the most favourable reports,
than 2000 or 3000 engaged in some guerilla warfare at a time.

Now, however, I hear from the very best authority, that

the class of nobles and proprietors in Poland from whom all
the previous efforts at national emancipation have sprung,
have been practically ruined, if not exterminated, by this
last abortive effort; and they themselves—many of the most
intelligent men you see here or in France—tell you it is futile
to expect another effort from that same class; that God, in His
own good time, may probably bring up a class of peasant
proprietors—the serfs are now made peasant proprietors—and
at some future time, either from religious impulse or motives
of patriotism, that this more numerous class may take the field;
but that the class that has always hitherto moved is practically
*hors de combat.* There was a meeting held in the London
Guildhall in favour of that insurrection. There were present
Members of Parliament and noble Lords; and the Lord
Mayor was in the chair. I, who have travelled in those very
countries, know what vast and exaggerated ideas are attached
to a political meeting held in the London Guildhall, with
the Lord Mayor, Members of Parliament, and Peers present.
You may say that by a public meeting like that you only
meant moral support and moral force; but you cannot persuade the poor people abroad but that other consequences
would follow a meeting like that, and that England would
give material aid to this revolution. So of Sleswig-Holstein.
There is no doubt in the world that England and her Government encouraged that small country of Denmark to hopeless
resistance by the false expectation excited from the first that
we should go to its help.

But that is not the only mischief we do. The moment
another nation appears in the field you excite far more resentment, and you stimulate to far greater efforts, the Government which is engaged in putting down an insurrection. I
have no hesitation in saying that the manifestations which
came from England and France respecting Poland, did more
than anything else could have done to consolidate and unite
the power of the Russian empire just at the time when it was

in danger of being thrown into discord and confusion by the emancipation of the serfs. Directly France and England began to address their despatches to the Russian Government, the Russian Government made an appeal to their own people, not so much against the Poles, against whom there was no great resentment, but to resist the attempt of the Western Powers to dictate to Russia; and Russia was enabled by that appeal, not only to call out the patriotic efforts of her own people, but to incur expenses in preparing for a war with Poland, such as she never would have ventured on had it not been for the assumption that she might have gone to war with France and England. A friend of mine who was travelling in Russia was told on very good authority that the Russian Government spent three or four millions of money in consequence of what were understood to be threats held out by France and England, and that was of course available to put down the Poles. These are considerations that ought to make the best-intentioned in the world pause before they join in any demonstrations of this kind. You must not only discourage your Government from taking proceedings, but you must do nothing that is calculated either to mislead the people abroad, or to stimulate the Governments abroad to increased efforts against their own populations. Now, you know, if I would only flatter you, instead of talking these home truths, I really believe I might be Prime Minister. If I would get up and say you are the greatest, the wisest, the best, the happiest people in the world, and keep on repeating that, I don't doubt but what I might be Prime Minister. I have seen Prime Ministers made in my experience precisely by that process. But it has always been my custom to talk irrespective of momentary popularity. You know I always get afterwards, with exorbitant and usurious interest, far more than I deserve.

Now, we English people have a peculiar way of dealing with foreign questions. We are the only people in the world that ever make of a foreign topic a matter of passionate, earnest, and internal politics. You never see in France, or in America, or in Germany, newspapers taking up foreign questions, and attacking one another because they are not of the same opinion. But this is the commonest thing in the world in England. I have had a message from some hon. Gentleman, living in this town, to say that he would not vote for me again, because I did not entertain the same opinions that he did about the American war. Well, I said in reply, that I did not profess at all to dictate to other people what opinions they should have upon a matter of such pure abstraction as that, but I wanted to know who made him my political Pope. Now, when we come to have a proper and due opinion of how little we can really do to effect any change abroad, if we act wisely we shall change our tone with regard to foreign policy, and we shall discuss—if we discuss those questions at all, which everybody will do who is intelligent, and lives in an age of electric telegraphs—we shall discuss these questions calmly and temperately, as I intend to do now just for one or two minutes, upon the subject of the American question.

I am exceedingly tolerant with everybody that differs from me about this dreadful civil war in America. I have intimate friends — some of my dearest friends — who differ totally from me on this question. It never drives me from their doors, or prevents my associating with them in just the same way as if our opinions coincided. Nay, more, I have always said that, while I believe there are many who take a sinister view of that question in America, there are, on the other hand, a great many people who have taken up the side of the South because they are the weaker party — because they are the insurgent party; and also because, looking at the map and looking at the extent of the country, they don't believe it possible that the North can succeed in subduing them, and that therefore it is a hopeless struggle, which ought to be put an end to by separation. Well, all that is very fair and reasonable, and ought to be regarded with perfect tolerance; but at the same time I repeat there are parties in this country, and they have not had the sense to conceal their motives, who want to see America humbled. They have not concealed their sentiments, because we had an explosion in the House of Commons. 'That republican bubble has burst.' They could not contain themselves when the war broke out.

I'll tell you what my opinion is with regard to Republicanism. I think we may have every advantage in this country with an hereditary monarchy that we might have by electing a president every four or six years. That is my theory. But, at the same time, I see a people raising up a Government upon a standard very far in advance of anything that was ever known in the world,—a people who say, 'We rule ourselves by pure reason; there shall be no religious establishment to guide us or control us; there shall be no born rank of any kind, but every honour held, every promotion enjoyed, shall spring from the people, and by selection; we maintain that we can govern ourselves without the institution of any hierarchy or privileged body whatever.' Well, every one will admit that at all events that programme is founded upon an elevated conception of what humanity is capable of. It may be a mistaken estimate,—it may be too soon to form so high an estimate,—it may fail; but don't ask me, who always consult to the best of my ability the interests of the great masses of my kind—don't ask me to wish that it may fail—don't ask me to exult if it seems to fail, because I utterly repudiate the possibility of my partaking in any such sentiment as that.

We have lately seen that country brought into just such a stress and difficulty as we might be thrown into to-morrow. We are governing India. The world never saw such a risk as we run, with 130 or 140 millions near the antipodes, ruling them for the sake of their custom, and nothing else. I defy

you to show that the nation has any interest whatever in that
country, except by the commerce we carry on there.   I say
that is a perilous adventure, quite unconnected with Free
Trade, wholly out of joint with the recent tendency of things,
which is in favour of nationality and not of domination.   You
might have something happen to you there at any time.   You
might have the same in Ireland.

Is it Conservatism to jump up and exult immediately this
great Republic falls into the throes of civil war, from no fault
of anyone who is now living; but, if you may trace it back to
the first cause, rather from the fault of the British nation and
the British Court some 150 years ago?   I ask, is it Conservatism in this country, or amongst the ruling classes in
Europe, that they should have jumped so hastily into a kind of
what I must call partisanship with this insurrection?   Let us
see what it is.   Here you have a great political disruption, in
which the active parties, who are very able men—I know the
leaders on both sides—were aware of what they were doing;
they knew the tremendous consequences they were going to
entail upon this cotton region, for instance.   They meditated
a disruption, by which they were going to throw into convulsion this great and populous district; and many a man
here present is wearing a paler brow than he would have worn
but for this civil war.   What, then, do they do to justify themselves in the eyes of foreign States, that our statesmen and
the ruling classes on the Continent should spring forward to
recognise them immediately as belligerents?

Now, in all other great political convulsions that I remember, the parties who have sought to create a disruption
which tends to shake a community, and by that means to cause
loss and inconvenience abroad, have always put out, in decent
respect to the opinion of the world, a programme of their
grievances.   Where is it here?   Take the case of our civil
war, when Cromwell and his party, who, I always think,
followed on the heels of much better men, committed then

acts of greater violence and greater tyranny than the Stuarts whom they had put down, and left very little trace of good on their own account to posterity. But what was done when Cromwell and his party and the Parliament deposed and decapitated Charles I,—a crime that has been followed by a reaction, as all crimes of blood are, down even to our own time? The Parliament put out a programme of their grievances; they published it in three languages; they circulated it all through Europe, stating to the whole world why they had deposed a king, and why they had established a commonwealth. What happened when James II fled, and William III was invited over? Read the Declaration of Rights with which the Parliament met William III; there was on one hand a narrative of the grievances they had against James II; there was a programme, and a compact of the conditions they required from the succeeding king; there was a justification of what they did. What did the Americans do when they declared their independence in 1776? They put forward a declaration of grievances, and no Englishman can now read it but will admit that they were justified in that rebellion, and in the separation from the mother country. But here you have a civil war of far more gigantic proportions than those I have alluded to—than them all put together; where the parties knew and calculated upon their losses as a means of success—knew they were going to convulse a peaceful district by their insurrection. Have they ever put forth a programme? Have they ever stated a grievance? I know the men, and I know no one more competent to write such a programme than Mr. Jefferson Davis. He could do it as well as Thomas Jefferson did the Declaration of Independence in 1776. But there is none. And why is there none? Because they had but one grievance. They wanted to consolidate, perpetuate, and extend slavery. But, instead of that, what do they constantly say, these eminent men—eminent, I mean, for their intellect—who could so well state their case, if they dared to state the truth? 'Leave us alone; all we

want is to be left alone.' And that is a reason that the Conservative Governments of Europe, and so large a section of
the upper middle-class of England, and almost the whole
aristocracy, have accepted as a sufficient ground on which to
back this insurrection. How would they have liked it, if,
when Essex and Kent had been beaten on the Corn-law question (and we know Essex gave a united and unanimous vote
against us), Kent and Essex had chosen to set up themselves
as an East Anglia right across the mouth of the Thames, as
the Secessionists have done by Louisiana across the mouth of
the Mississippi, and if, when we asked them why they did it,
they should reply, 'We want to be left alone?' Can any
Government be carried on if a portion of the territory, or a
section of the people, can at any time secede when beaten at
the polls in a peaceful election? I again repeat, where is the
Conservatism amongst the governing class of this country?
I come to the conclusion that there is more Conservatism
amongst the Democracy, after all.

Now, we have heard news from America lately which I
confess has struck me as presenting to us one of the most
sublime spectacles in the whole history of the world. You
have twenty-three or twenty-four millions of people spreading
over the territory of some thousands of square miles, exercising on one day the right of suffrage upon a question
about which torrents of blood are flowing. You have seen
the result of that peaceful election given without as much
tumult as I have seen in the dirty little village of Calne, or
the little town of Kidderminster. Well, I say that is a thing
for humanity to be proud of, and not for any particular party
to exult over, or for any party to scowl upon. A people that
can do that, have given to the world a spectacle such as never
was presented before by any other people. And what have
they done? They have decided, mind you, after three years
of war, and after every other household almost has lost an
inmate or a relative by war. The contest that arose was this:

Gen. M'Clellan offers himself as a candidate to put down the war and to restore the Union without making the abolition of slavery a condition of it.  On the other side, Abraham Lincoln says, ' We will put down the war, and we will extirpate slavery.' And, notwithstanding that the appeal was made to the whole people who have been suffering from this war, they have preferred, in the interest of humanity—for that can no longer be questioned now—you can no longer call it pride, it is the lofty motive of humanity that has induced them to risk the longer continuance of the war rather than allow the degrading institution of slavery to continue.  Well, now, let us have no more of the old talk about this not being a war to put down slavery. Everybody now admits, that whatever the issue of this struggle may be, slavery will be abolished by it, and the slaves will be emancipated.

Now, with regard to the issue itself.  I told you here two years ago, that I did not believe I should ever live to see two independent States on the Continent of North America.  I have repeated it since, and I come to confirm that opinion, but with far more emphasis than I ever expressed before. I do not believe that that country will, in our day, ever be separated, for I consider the geographical difficulties in the way of a separation to be absolutely insuperable.  For instance, take the case of the Mississippi River.  There are 20,000 miles of navigable waters through that great western region that fall into the Gulf of Mexico at the mouth of the Mississippi.  In order that the United States might have the mouth of that river in their own keeping,—that they might, so to say, have the key of their own door in their own pocket,— they purchased, with the money of the whole Union, from the first Napoleon, the State of Louisiana for three millions sterling.  And now some two or three hundred thousand who have squatted there—some French, some Spanish, some Irish, some English, some Americans — have taken it into their heads that they will carry off this State of Louisiana, and put the mouth of that great river and the outlet of all these vast tributaries into the hands of a foreign State. I just now illustrated this question by a reference to Essex and Kent, and I say it would be far easier for Essex and Kent to carry off the mouth of the Thames and to set up an East Anglia, than it will be for Louisiana to carry off the mouth of the Mississippi and set itself up as an independent State, and for this reason:—in the case of the Thames there may be a population at some future time, perhaps, of ten millions of people interested in that question in the valley of the Thames, and there will be a few hundred miles of navigable waters; in the case of the Mississippi River, there will be two hundred millions of people, the richest and most prosperous in the world—no doubt of that—living in that Mississippi valley; and therefore it makes it ten times impossible, if the word may be used, that they should ever allow the mouth of the Mississippi River to be blocked. And besides, they can prevent it almost with no expense; a few gunboats patrolling in the Mississippi will keep absolute possession of it; and if they could not in any other way capture Louisiana, why, they might cut the dykes—(as the Dutch did against their enemies the Spaniards)—above New Orleans, and drown the whole State of Louisiana.

Now, I am speaking merely of motives and of forces; I am not speaking my own opinion, not uttering my own wishes in the matter—I am only speaking of what you have to look to when you are estimating the probable future of this struggle. If you think that Mr. Jefferson Davis and his Southern Confederacy would like to have a slave empire merely confined to the cotton States—that he should not be allowed to extend his government across the Mississippi into Texas—why, he would not thank you for anything of the kind. What they are fighting for is to be allowed to carry their slaves not only across the Mississippi into Texas, but into new regions beyond it. And, therefore, when you tell them that they shall not have the Mississippi River, it is giving up the whole question on which their whole cause depends. I say that the chief difficulty, if it had been looked at by our ruling class, by many of those who write in the newspapers, lies in geographical causes, which these writers ought to have considered, for if they had done so they would not have arrived at the conclusion they have as to the success of the Southern cause.

I have spoken of the newspapers. There is a newspaper in London, which, I suppose, is read by almost everybody, and I have marvelled at the ignorance it has displayed on this question. In one leading article, a river of 580 miles internal navigation, to which the largest river in this country is a mere brook or rivulet, was made to run uphill a great number of miles into another river, and then these two rivers united, the waters of which are never blended at all, were made to flow into a third river, into which neither of them pours a drop of water. Now, I think there is a real danger in this ignorance of what I must call for want of a better term the ruling class of this country—in this total ignorance of everything relating to America. These people may get you into a difficulty from their ignorance, which it may cost you much of your national honour to escape from. If I were rich, I really think I would endow a professor's chair at Oxford and Cambridge for teaching modern American geography and modern American history. I will undertake to say —and I speak it advisedly—I will take any undergraduate now at Oxford and Cambridge;—there is a map of the United States there—and I will ask this young gentleman to walk up to that map and put his finger upon the city of Chicago, and I will undertake to say that he will not go within a thousand miles of it. And yet Chicago is a city of 150,000 inhabitants, from which from one to two millions of our people are annually fed. These young gentlemen, I allow, know all about the geography of ancient Greece and Egypt.

Now, I shall be pelted with a heap of Greek and Latin

quotations for what I am going to say.  But I think I have
said it before; therefore I think all the severe things they can
say to me they have said.  When I was at Athens, I sallied
out one summer morning to see the far-famed river, the Ilyssus,
and, after walking for some hundred yards up what appeared
to be the bed of a winter torrent, I came up to a number of
Athenian laundresses, and I found they had dammed up this
far-famed classic river, and that they were using every drop of
water for their linen and such sanitary purposes.  I say, why
should not the young gentlemen who are taught all about
the geography of the Ilyssus know something about the geography of the Mississippi, the Ohio, and the Missouri?
There has been of late a good deal of talk about the advantages or disadvantages of classical education.  I am a
great advocate of culture of every kind; and I say, where
you can find men who, in addition to profound classical learning, like Professor Goldwin Smith, or Professor Rogers, of
Oxford, have a vast knowledge of modern affairs, and who,
as well as scholars, are at the same time thinkers,—these are
men I acknowledge to have a vast superiority over me, and
I bow to those men with reverence for those superior advantages.  But to bring young men from college with no knowledge of the country where the great drama of modern political
and national life is being worked out—who are totally ignorant of countries like America, but who, for good or for evil,
are exercising and will exercise more influence in this country
than any other persons — to take young men, destitute of
knowledge about countries like that—their geography, their
modern history, their population, and their resources, and to
place them in responsible positions in the Government of this
country—I say it is imperilling your best interests, and every
earnest remonstrance that can be made against such a state of
education ought to be made by every public man who values
the future welfare of his country.

You all know my opinion with regard to the future of

America. I want nothing done to enforce my opinions. I should never even have said so much as I have upon American affairs, if there had not been so much said upon the other side. I wanted to trim the scales, to prevent there being an undue preponderance in favour of the other side. I wanted no intervention, I wanted nothing but neutrality; but if we are to have perfect neutrality on this subject, for Heaven's sake let us try also to have a little temper in the discussion of those questions for which we are, happily, not at all responsible. Take up the newspapers and see them assailing each other, or public men, because they have no particular views on foreign questions. It is sheer childishness, when you come to consider that we are not responsible for the facts.

If any one attacks me for my political opinions on home questions, I recognise his perfect right to do it; the more the better. Every public man's language, and his acts, and policy should be well sifted; but to quarrel with each other about a country over which we can exercise no influence whatever, seems to me the most absurd thing in the world. If we were a nation that never went to war, then as a nation we might with justice, perhaps, complain that America is shedding so much blood; but I am mute, I am silenced when I recollect that I have been protesting against the wars of England ever since I came into public life—war in India, China, Russia, New Zealand, Japan, and all over the world—but I never could succeed in this country in preventing bloodshed. We have a fresh war every year, upon an average, with some country or other, and therefore I am mute. I could not say to America, ' Why do you carry on this civil war?' Should I not be subject to the reply, 'Take the beam out of your own eye before you take the mote out of ours?' I should have some ground for using that language as compared with some other people; but I find those who have been the advocates of all these wars against which I have been protesting are now turning up the whites of their eyes, and exclaiming

for all the world as if they had been Quakers from their
birth.

Now, gentlemen, I have done with foreign policy, and I
have only spoken so much to-night upon these subjects in violation of my usual rule, because I say that last session was an
exceptional one ; and if I have spoken upon the subject of non-
intervention, it is because I wish to have less to say about it
in future, and that we may be able to talk upon home affairs
without this eternal meddling abroad to distract our attention,
and prevent our doing anything for our own people. I am
happy to give you, from a very orthodox source, what I consider to be very sound doctrine in few words with regard to
our foreign policy. The *Edinburgh Review* of last month
thus defines the views of foreign policy which have now been
accepted by Parliament, and the majority of the nation, as
to our relations with the Continental Powers of Europe, and
here are the words of the orthodox Whig reviewer. It is
not my language. It was my language some years ago,
but I am very glad to disappear altogether now, and place
before you the much more influential words of the Edinburgh
reviewer :—

'That this country should enter into no official discussion and no public
engagements on affairs remotely concerning herself ; that she will reserve her
power and influence for British purposes ; that she will not pronounce an
opinion unless she is resolved to support it by action ; and that she will throw
on other States the whole responsibility of acts affecting themselves more
directly than they affect us.'

Now, that is unquestionably a wise and sound doctrine. The
only wonder is that ever anybody should have had any
opposite opinions to that, and that they should have now
to pronounce it for the first time. That is taking the pledge,
you know, after the headache in the House of Commons. I
must say I am very glad indeed also to have the opportunity
of quoting the same orthodox publication on another most
important question. The Reviewer speaks of the measures
that still require to be carried out in England in our domestic

policy, for which course we shall have time, when we give up meddling with everybody's affairs on the face of the earth. Now, here are the Reviewer's own words in speaking of the domestic reforms that await our attention :—

'At home, we have still to apply to land and to labour that freedom which has worked such marvels in the case of capital and commerce.'

Bear in mind, that is not my language about free trade in land. But I say 'Amen' to it. If I were five-and-twenty or thirty, instead of, unhappily, twice that number of years, I would take Adam Smith in hand—I would not go beyond him, I would have no politics in it—I would take Adam Smith in hand, and I would have a League for free trade in Land just as we had a League for free trade in Corn. You will find just the same authority in Adam Smith for the one as for the other ; and if it were only taken up as it must be taken up to succeed, not as a political, revolutionary, Radical, Chartist notion, but taken up on politico-economic grounds, the agitation would be certain to succeed ; and if you can apply free trade to land and to labour too – that is, by getting rid of those abominable restrictions in your parish settlements, and the like—then, I say, the men who do that will have done for England probably more than we have been able to do by making free trade in corn.

Now, all that has to be done. Really, the chief embarrassment one has in meeting one's constituents once a year to talk over so many questions is that you cannot logically follow out any subject, but that you are obliged to break off from one to another. As our eloquent friend, unhappily, cannot succeed me, you will excuse me if I take up ten minutes more of your time than I should otherwise have done. Besides the question of Reform in Parliament, which lies at the bottom of most things, there is something for next year which must be done, in the way of our finances ; and it will be done very much as a corollary, as already showing the

. fruits that may be reaped from the adoption of our new foreign policy. You must needs see this reform, if you will only avow the principle that you are not going to fight for anything but your interests and honour—and by honour I mean, not the honour of the barrack-room—for I maintain that the honour of this great Christian country need never, with a wise Government, be dissociated from its interest. But if you will only admit that you will never fight for anything but a direct question of your own honour and interest, I defy you to keep up your present establishment, and spend twenty-five and odd millions a year on your army and navy. There is no pretence for that; and already I see from authoritative quarters that there is to be a reduction next year. I am glad of it; and I am glad of it very much indeed for the sake of Mr. Gladstone, the Chancellor of the Exchequer. Mr. Gladstone is the best Chancellor of the Exchequer England ever had,—and I say that, knowing that he has had amongst his predecessors William Pitt. But I am going to say that Mr. Gladstone has been the most extravagant Chancellor of the Exchequer we have ever had. He has been a master in the adjustment of the burdens of the country; that is, he found the weight placed upon the animal in such a way as rendered it the most difficult to carry his burden. It was tied round his knees, it was fastened to his tail, it was hung over his eyes, it blinded him, and impeded him, and lamed him at every step. Now, Mr. Gladstone took the burdens off these limbs, and he placed them most in-geniously over the softest possible pad upon the animal's shoulders. But the beast is carrying the burden still, and carrying a great deal more than it did before all this beautiful process was commenced. We never before had a Government that extracted from the people ten millions of income in a time of peace. People exclaim against the American expenditure. A friend of mine wrote to me the other day, and told me that the Americans were spending two millions of dollars a day;— what did I think of it? Well, I said—I think it was rather

more, but I took him at his own word—if you take into
account the depreciation of the American currency, and at the
present rate of exchange, the dollar there being worth 20*d.*,
or 2*s.* here, that was as near as I could possibly calculate the
amount Mr. Gladstone in a time of peace was drawing from
this country.  And, mind you, as long as the English people
are given up to that comfortable complacency, that they can go
abroad only to find out objects of pity, they will always be persuaded that they are very clever people, and are doing a great
deal better than other folks.  Why have the Americans astonished everybody?  Why have they laughed to scorn the
predictions of all your City magnates, all your authorities upon
finance, who told them that they could not go on for six months
in their war without coming to Europe for a loan?  How is
it, then, the Americans have so deceived and disappointed the
whole of Europe?  I'll tell you why.  Because the Americans
never spent — never allowed their Government to incur a
war expenditure in time of peace.  That is the whole secret.
They were spending from fifteen to seventeen millions sterling per annum for their Government, for a population
about our own size, at the time the war broke out; and the
saving and accumulation that they were thus making has
enabled them to go through this terrific strain.  You just take
only ten millions of savings for forty years ; add ten millions every year to it for compound interest, and at the end
you will see what a fabulous amount it will come to.  You
will hardly be able to calculate the amount.  That is just
what the Americans were doing.  What are you doing here?
You are committed to a war expenditure in time of peace, and
your people are discontented with the extravagant expenditure, and the consequence is, if you were to go into a war,
you would certainly find yourselves comparatively crippled by
your previous expenditure.

I hope, therefore, that Mr. Gladstone will be enabled, for
the next session, to make a large reduction in the actual

expenditure. I do not want any more of this delusion about the reduction or diminution of particular taxes. I want to look at the whole amount of revenue the Government is getting from us. For instance, here is a very customary piece of deception : we are told how many Customs and Excise duties have been abolished, and how many have been reduced, during the last twenty years. Yes ; but I look at the whole amount now paid, and I find that, this year, it will be about forty millions sterling more than ever we used to pay before these reductions began. Now, I say, the proper way to look at that is to see how the whole amount of the income from the taxpayer is reduced ; and I hope that this next session will not pass without Mr. Gladstone doing justice to himself ; because you must bear in mind that Mr. Gladstone has been telling us repeatedly that he considers the expenditure excessive. It is sailing very near the wind indeed for any Minister to attempt to justify himself in saying, ' I am spending more money than I think I ought to spend ; and do you, the people of England, come and try to prevent it.' But I am constrained to say that Mr. Gladstone, by his immense services in other directions, is the very man who enables the Government to get this money. I am perfectly ready to admit that Mr. Gladstone has, by his skill in dealing with finance, justified himself, up to this time, in remaining in the Cabinet and doing what he has done. But I am sure he will perceive that he has nearly finished his career of manipulating the sources of our taxation. He has removed every protective duty ; he has reduced most of the other duties. And though I am by no means prepared to say that other Chancellors of the Exchequer may not do a great deal more in giving us direct instead of indirect taxation, yet, as regards the question of protection, Mr. Gladstone has finished his work ; and therefore any further services he must render us must be in the reduction of expenditure—in taxing us less. He must remember, too, what we have heard from

the other side.  Lord Stanley intimated, you know, not long
ago, that he could not see his way to sixty millions of expenditure.  I think, when the Chancellor of the Exchequer
sees his opponent on the other side—the most distinguished
member of the Opposition—announcing sixty millions, if I
were Mr. Gladstone I should hurry back to that amount as fast
as I could, for fear of being tripped up by the other side, and
I would recommend him to take advice from that quarter.
He has declared the present expenditure to be profligate—I
think 'profligate expenditure' is the term he used—and I
know Mr. Disraeli talked of bloated armaments ; so that we
have the whole thing condemned all round.  Mr. Gladstone
makes an appeal to the British public.  I do not know how
the British public can interfere in the arrangement of his
Budget in the House of Commons ; but, as there is to be a
general election next year, I advise him to appeal to the
British public at the general election on the question of taxation as the way to give them a chance of expressing their
opinion, and I am very much inclined to think that is the
only way the British public can interfere in the matter.

But I consider the House of Commons to be a great deal
more extravagant than the Government.  That is my experience.  I once stated it in the House.  Since I have been in
the House, we have voted upwards of five hundred millions
sterling for the army and navy services; and I never saw one
item of a single shilling reduced in all that time; though I
have constantly known items increased.  Last session the Government proposed to save 200,000*l.* by not calling out the
yeomanry ; but the country gentlemen went up, and compelled
them to give the money.  The House of Commons is more
extravagant than the Government, and is always urging
them to expenditure.  But if Mr. Gladstone will invite the
British public to speak in the only way in which they can
exercise their voices, at the general election, I am quite sure
they will support him, and not support any other Government

that attempts to oppose him in the reduction of expenditure. What is the obvious remedy for this state of the House of Commons? We all know that the House of Commons wants an infusion of the popular element. I see before me middle-class men, and I see beyond the operatives. Now, you are told, and some of you persuade yourselves, that the middle class govern the House of Commons. It is a great delusion. The middle class element is very small in the House of Commons, and it is getting less and less. We are becoming more and more a rich man's club. That is just it. What you want is a greater infusion of the popular element, and you cannot have that unless you have an enlargement of the political rights of the people. And I would advise the middle class not to allow this to be dealt with as a working man's question. The middle class themselves are interested in having a reform of Parliament, in order that their influence should be felt there, for it is not much felt there now, I assure you; we are a very small ingredient. The world is not standing still, and you must not stand still. A friend of mine the other day said to me, 'I will lay a wager that the blacks in America have votes before the English working-man.' Well, now, I should not like to see that—I don't think that that would be becoming in this country, which has boasted of itself as being in the van of free nations. But of this I am quite sure—and I say it to the middle class here—you cannot with safety exclude the great mass of the working people from a participation in the suffrage; for, recollect, this question never before got into the position it is in now. You have had several successive Governments in their Queen's Speeches recommending a reform of Parliament with the view of increasing the number of voters in this country. But nothing is done, and the mass of the people feel that they are trifled with. There is nothing that breeds such a resentment in the great mass of the people—all history shows it—as a sense of having been betrayed. You will find in all history that the

mass of the people are magnanimous and forgiving for everything else but the conviction—sometimes erroneous—of having
been betrayed.

The working classes are very significantly silent upon
the subject of the suffrage. That is something new; and if
they did not move at all, I should say that that was an additional reason to the middle class why they ought to move in
the matter; because times and circumstances do come—they
always turn up once in twenty or thirty years—when there
must be an appeal to the whole mass of the community; when
the power of the nation really falls into the hands of the mass
of the people, as it always is virtually in their hands, whenever they choose to exercise it. Now, it is not desirable that
you should leave the mass of the people with a grievance, not
a grievance of their own creating, a grievance for which they
can convict you upon your own declarations. It is your
Government, the middle class, it is your Sovereign, speaking
through her Prime Minister, who dictate the public policy;
it is they who have told the working people that they ought
to have the vote, and who have trifled with them for ten or
fifteen years, while nothing is done. I say there is danger in it;
and the shape which the controversy is taking is, to my mind,
very undesirable; it now takes the broad aspect of a question
whether the working classes as a whole should be enfran-
chised, or whether they should not. But it never presented
itself in that way before, because we all know that in olden
times, in the times of the guilds, the working classes were
represented in many forms. You had boroughs, with scot
and lot suffrage; you had in the City of London, for instance,
guilds where every man belonging to a certain business had a
right to exercise his franchise as a freeman. And do you suppose, now, it is possible that, in an age when the principles of
political economy have elevated the working class above the
place they ever filled before, and when that elevation is constantly increased by discoveries and the inventions of machinery,

that you can permanently exclude the whole mass of the
working people from the franchise? You say you must not
give them the whole power. Well, they answer, ' You give
us none.' And I say it is the interest and duty of the ruling
class of this country, and of the middle class who are supposed
to have power, that it is their interest as soon as possible to
solve that question, and that there is danger in allowing it to
go on unsolved.

You know, gentlemen, I never perorate; when I have done
I leave off, and sit down. On this occasion I most cordially
thank you. When I came into this room I confess I felt
daunted, for I did not believe I could have talked so as to be
heard by this whole assembly; but your kindness and your exceeding indulgence has made the task pleasant to me, and I
thank you for the manner in which you have received and
listened to me.

# INDIA.

# INDIA.

## HOUSE OF COMMONS, JUNE 27, 1853.

[On June 3, 1853, Sir Charles Wood introduced his India Bill. Lord Stanley moved an Amendment, the object of which was to delay the measure, but this Amendment was rejected by 182 votes: 322 to 140. Mr. Cobden and Mr. Bright were in the minority.]

I DO not know whether I should have deemed it necessary to address the House myself but for the circumstance of my having served upon the Committee appointed to inquire into the Government of our Indian territories; but, before troubling the House with the few remarks which I feel bound to make, I should wish to offer an observation on the question which has just been asked by my hon. Friend the Member for Ashton-under-Lyne (Mr. Hindley). With regard to the conduct of that Committee, allusion had been made to its proceedings during the last Parliament, and it is allowable to speak of that Parliament as one would speak of the Long Parliament, without offence to the House, since it has passed away and is now matter of history. Now, I feel bound to say, that during that Parliament, the conduct of that Committee was not such as to entitle it to be cited as an authority, or to inspire any very great degree of confidence in its action.

That Committee was appointed to inquire into the important question of the Government of India, and it was divided into eight heads. The first was the question as to the machinery by which the Government of India was carried on. Upon that head the Committee examined eighteen witnesses, every one of whom had been officially in the employment of the Court of Directors or of the Board of Control, or had been in some manner connected with one or other of those services; and, after the examination of those persons, the Committee came to a kind of qualified Resolution approving the conduct of the Government of India. In my opinion, at a future period, if some dusky agitator on the banks of the Ganges should want to find a grievance in the conduct of the British Legislature towards the Hindoo population, he would cite the fact which I have just mentioned, and he would find it potent to raise the indignation of the population, for a more unfair proceeding was never perpetrated by any tribunal calling itself impartial. I will mention, as requested by the hon. Member for Montrose (Mr. Hume), that in that Committee there were two Members who voted against that Resolution.

But, before the Committee in the present Parliament has proceeded to the extent of half their inquiry, it is announced to the House that the Government measure on the subject is prepared. Now, I will confess that from the time that this announcement was made, I have myself never attended that Committee, for although I always try, when serving upon any Committee, to be as assiduous as any member of it, yet I consider that from the moment the Government has taken up this question it has passed from the hands of the Committee. I see no good that we can do in collecting facts and information for the Government of India, seeing that they are generally obtained from persons who come from India, or who have been employed there, and who are more accessible to the Indian authorities. It is my opinion that the whole

case is prejudged, and that a verdict has been brought in
without going through the preliminaries of a trial; and I
must decline, except under the express order of this House,
to attend that Committee for the future, or in any way to
sanction such a course of proceeding.

The question at issue now is—whether the subject shall be
postponed; and, if it be decided that such is to be the course
pursued, I will willingly return to my duties in the Committee, and give my constant attention to the inquiry, which
should, I must say, be one of considerable importance in
deciding the question. The House is now called upon to
decide whether the present Bill shall pass, or whether the
subject shall be postponed for two years, leaving the Government of India, in the interim, just as it is at present. I wish
to state now, once for all, that I do not consider it a party
question. The hon. Member for North Staffordshire (Mr.
Adderley) complains that I and my friends have taken too
material a view of the question, as affecting the interests of
Lancashire and the other manufacturing districts. Now, if
that were true, it cannot be said that we have taken up
the question in a party spirit; but, as far as I am acquainted with the feelings of the people of Lancashire and
Yorkshire, I believe they are generally in favour of postpone-
ment.

In my opinion, the subject is one which calls for further
inquiry, more particularly as regards the Home Government
of India. The problem to solve is, whether a single or a
double government would be most advantageous; and, in
considering that point, I am met by this difficulty—that I
cannot see that the present form of government is a double
government at all. I have endeavoured to find out what are
the powers of the East India Directory, which entitle them
to be called a Government, and I have looked through the
Charter Act to see what controlling power is bestowed upon
them, and, with the exception of the disposal of the patron-

age, there is no power granted to them by Act of Parliament. The Act leaves the whole controlling power to the Board of Commissioners for managing the affairs of India. I, therefore, look upon the Court of Directors, not as a Government, but as nothing besides a screen, behind which the real Government is hid. It is because I wish to get rid of that screen, and that the real Government may stand before the House and the world in its proper character, and take upon its shoulders the responsibility of the misgovernment of India— if there be any—that I want to have this matter simplified, and to do away with the double government, that is, to bring into office the real Government of India.

There has been much misapprehension with regard to this double government. Till the last year or two, I do not believe that anybody understood it at all. Lord Hardinge spoke of it as a mystery, and said it was looked upon as a mystery in India; and he mentioned the instance of an officer of rank in India, who had written an indignant letter to the President of the Board of Control in reference to a communication of the Secret Committee of the Court of Directors, expressing his amazement at the conduct of that Committee; and he was only restrained from sending it by Lord Hardinge telling him that the Secret Committee of the Board of Directors was the President of the Board of Control himself. Many persons whose opinions on the affairs of India are most authoritative, in reality do not know what the double government really is. Mr. Marshman, the conductor of the *Friend of India,* a strong advocate of ‘things as they are,’ when fairly probed and pushed on the subject, shows that he, who was instructing them all, and sending pamphlets to all the Members of the Legislature, has very little fundamental knowledge of what this Government is. Part of the evidence given by this gentleman is so illustrative of this, that I hope the House will permit me to read an extract :—

'In seeking to acquaint yourself with the form of Government for India, you would resort exclusively to the Act of Parliament under which the present Government of India is constituted?—Yes.

'Do you find that by this Act of Parliament any discretionary powers are vested in the Court of Directors, except with reference to the disposal of the patronage?—I should think they are responsible to the Board of Control.

'Admitting that the Court of Directors have no uncontrolled power in the Government of India, how can you make them responsible either to Parliament or to the people of India?—It was the intention of the Act to confer certain powers upon them, and to give a control over the exercise of those powers to the Board of Control.

'You admit that, unless a party has power entrusted to it, it cannot be responsible for the exercise of its power?—No; I can, therefore, only say that they are responsible for the exercise of all the powers given to them in that Act.

'You may still that this Act was intended to vest a certain power in the East India Company?—There must have been some object in view in creating the present Government of the East India Company.

'You say you believe that the intention of Parliament was to give certain powers to the East India Company; having admitted that no such powers exist, except in the disposal of patronage, you would admit that, if Parliament had such an object, it has failed to accomplish it?—That very much depends upon the working of the system. Although Parliament may have exempted nothing from the control of the President of the Board of Control, yet it is certain that the Court of Directors were intended to be a body employed in the administration of the affairs of India.

'To the extent of the disposal of patronage?—Not merely to the extent of the disposal of patronage, because the patronage of the Court of Directors consists only in appointment to service, and not in appointment to office. The great patronage lies in the hands of the Governor-General and the Governors of the various Presidencies. All the patronage which the Court has to dispose of is the appointment to writerships and cadetships.

'Will you explain to the Committee what power the Court of Directors have under this Charter Act beyond the disposal of patronage?—I cannot exactly speak to that, because I have not seen the interior working of the system of either the Court of Directors or the Board of Control.

'I only wish for an answer founded upon this Act of Parliament for the government of India?—All I can say is, if this Act of Parliament was intended to give them no power whatever except the disposal of patronage, it could not be considered an Act for vesting the administration of affairs in the hands of the East India Company.'

This great oracle of the East India Company himself admits that, if there is no power vested in the Court of Directors but that of the patronage, there is really no

government vested in them at all. Now, all this mystery is
productive of the greatest evils. You have been simplifying
the procedure, and getting rid of fictitious forms in your own
Courts of Law recently. You have banished John Doe and
Richard Roe from your Courts; but here you still have John
Doe and Richard Roe in the Government of India. Then
what is the advantage of such a system? Is it for the benefit
either of the people of England or of India? On this subject
I would refer to the evidence of a gentleman, the most remarkable for ability among all the able men who have been
brought before the Committee by the Court of Directors, who
has filled very high offices in India—I mean Mr. Halliday.
This gentleman—speaking in the face of the Court of Directors—in the very presence of his employers and masters—
having stated that the Charter, giving a twenty years' lease
to the East India Company, was considered by the natives
of India as farming them out, was subjected, on account
of the use of this word ' farming,' to a great deal of cross-
examination :—

' You used the expression " farming the Government ;" do you believe the
people of India think the Government of India is farmed to the Company in
the same sense that the taxes were farmed at the period you allude to ?—They
use precisely the same word in speaking of the renewal of the Charter. They
will talk with you as to the probability of the "jarch"or" farm" being renewed ;
and, as far as I know, they have no other term to express it.

' Is not that merely through the infirmity of their language ; have they any
word which signifies " delegation ?"—They may have ; I speak of the fact, and
their use of the term carries with it a corresponding idea.

' How would you translate " delegation " into Hindostanee ; might not
"jarch" be a fair translation of that term ?—It would rather signify " farm" or
" lease."

' You said that, in fact, the Government was that of the Crown, and that
the natives, as they become more enlightened, will more and more understand
it to be so ?—It is the case.

' As they become more and more enlightened, will not the mischief which
you consider arises from their notion of a farm disappear of itself ?—It may be
in that sense, no doubt, and does ; and yet there arises a proportionate weakness to the Government from their seeing that the body held up as their apparent governors are not their real governors. Without wishing to speak irre-
verently, it has somewhat the appearance of a sham.'

Mr. Halliday, in my opinion, disposed of the whole question as regarded the interests of India, and of this country also, if we wish to govern India cheaply and beneficially. He said,—

' If you were to change the system, and to govern India in the name of the Crown, you would immensely add to the reverence which the people of India would have for your Government, and increase the stability of your Empire in the Eastern world.'

Mr. Marshman himself, though he did not speak of carrying on the Government of India under the Crown, distinctly and repeatedly laid it down that the Government of India should be carried on in one office ; that the President of the Board of Control, or whoever was the responsible Minister of India, should sit in the same room with those who constitute the Council, (now the Court of Directors in Leadenhall-street,) and should communicate with them orally, instead of by correspondence, as at present.

But what are the evils of this delusive form of government ? The first and greatest of all is this, that public opinion is diverted from the subject ; that enlightened public opinion is not brought to bear on Indian questions, which would be the case if India were governed in the name of the Crown, in just the same way as the Colonies have been. It might be answered, that if India were governed as the Colonies have been, it would be governed badly ; but if any good has arisen from our government of the Colonies, it has come from enlightened public opinion, emanating from this country, and chiefly brought to bear on our Colonial Minister in this House. If there be any hope for the amelioration of India, it must come from the same source ; and I want the Indian Government to have such a tangible, visible form, that the public opinion of this country may be able to reach it, and that there may be no mask or screen before it as now. With an enlightened public opinion brought to bear more directly on the affairs of India, there will be a better chance of avoiding that source of

all fiscal embarrassment, constant wars, and constant annexation of territory.  In other parts of the world, no Minister of
the Crown would take credit for offering to annex territory
anywhere.  On the west coast of Africa, it might not be less
profitable to extend our territory than in Burmah; yet a
Resolution of a Committee of this House, many years ago,
forbad the extension of our territories in tropical countries.
When an adventurous gentleman, Sir James Brooke, went out
and took possession of some territory on the coast of Borneo,
the enlightened Government of Sir Robert Peel and his colleagues resolutely resisted all attempts to induce them to
occupy any territory there.  Recently, when it was announced
in this House that orders had been given to the admiral on
that station that on no account should any fresh territory be
acquired, the announcement was received with loud cheering.
We had arrived at a point when public opinion in this House
and the country would prevent any such thing; and I believe
the leading statesmen on both sides would resolutely set
themselves against any extension of our territory in tropical
countries.

Then how is it that this goes on constantly in India, to the
loss and dilapidation of its finances?  With a declaration in
the journals of this House, and in an Act of Parliament never
repealed, that the honour and interest of this country were
concerned in not extending its territory in the East, these
continual annexations still go on in India.  Why do these
things happen?  It is because at the present time all the
authority in these matters is left virtually in the hands of the
Governor-General of India.  I say virtually, because I believe
they rest, in point of law, with the President of the Board of
Control.  Nothing can be more conclusive than the distinct-
ness of the avowal of Lord Broughton, that he was responsible
for the war in Affghanistan; and the declaration of Lord
Ellenborough, that when he was President of that Board, he
knew that he governed India.  I am, therefore, astonished,

when I hear the right hon. Gentleman opposite (Mr. Herries) state, that neither he nor his predecessors in office were responsible for the wars in India, but that the Governor-General is responsible for them.

When there exist such differences of opinion on such an important question—a question which involves not only the fate of India but of England—is it not high time to come to some definite understanding on the subject? Is it not right, when such differences of opinion exist between men of the highest authority, that there should be a little delay, in order that we may all come to an understanding on so vital a point? Practically, I believe that these things are carried on in India, where the Governor-General is surrounded by an atmosphere of a warlike tendency — where the mere rumour of war is received with favour by all who constitute public opinion in that country. Even Lord Dalhousie himself has so far given into this spirit as to make a declaration, that—

'In the exercise of a wise and sound policy, the British Government is bound not to put aside such rightful opportunities of acquiring territory or revenue as may from time to time present themselves.'

Yet this is said in the teeth of an Act of Parliament which declares that it is contrary to sound policy to annex any more territory to our dominions in the East. And this declaration of Lord Dalhousie came out before the declaration of the President of the United States, General Pierce, who made a qualified statement that the United States would annex territory by every just and lawful means. We can be very censorious when we hear of such a declaration being made by the President of another State, but we do not attach the same importance to what is said by Lord Dalhousie. How is this? If Lord Dalhousie had been in any responsible position in this House, or had stood in the character of a Colonial Minister, he could have been asked for an explanation, and might have been reminded that such declarations are not in accordance with the views and interests of the nation. It is, however, my firm belief, that nothing will awaken the people of this country to a proper sense of their responsibility and peril in the East, but a due appreciation of the state and prospects of the revenue of that country.   There can be no doubt that in India the extension of our territories is popular among the servants of the Company.   In one of the most influential organs of the Indian Government it is stated,—·

'Every one out of England is now ready to acknowledge that the whole of Asia, from the Indus to the Sea of Ochotzk, is destined to become the patrimony of that race which the Normans thought, six centuries ago, they had finally crushed, but which now stands at the head of European civilisation. We are placed, it is said, by the mysterious but unmistakable designs of Providence, in command of Asia ; and the people of England must not lay the flattering unction to their souls, that they can escape from the responsibility of this lofty and important position, by simply denouncing the means by which England has attained it.'

When asked if Calcutta was a good central station for the metropolis of India, Mr. Marshman, the proprietor of the above newspaper, stated to the Committee that—

'It may not be at present, but it will be a good central station when we extend our dominion eastward.'

This shows the projects which the most influential men in India have in view.

I will now refer to the Secret Committee of the India House.   I should like to have the cross-examination of every Member of that House, and to ask them what they do know of this Secret Committee.   It is composed of three gentlemen from the Board of Directors, to whom all the communications from the Board of Control are made.   It is in the power of the President of the Board of Control to sit down and write an order to annex China, and send that order to these three gentlemen, who form what is called the Secret Committee at the India House ; and they are obliged to send the order to India, for prosecution by the Governor-General.   They may altogether disapprove of the order, but nevertheless they are compelled to send it to India.   Mr. Melvill, Secretary to the

East India Company, stated, that in all cases of declaration of war, it is within the power of the Board of Control to act through the Secret Committee, without the concurrence of the Court of Directors—that orders may be sent out by the President of the Board, through the Secret Committee, to annex the Burman or Chinese Empire to India, without the English people knowing anything about the order. The Court of Directors cannot know it. On the question being asked,—

'How are the English people to know it, if the Court of Directors do not know it?' his reply was—'Till it comes back from India, till it is a *fait accompli*, or the result of the orders is ascertained, they cannot know it.'

Now, what is the practical effect of this state of things? The Court of Directors are often attacked for not making railways and works of irrigation; and I think they deserve the charges brought against them, so long as they submit to the humiliation of their present condition. How can they be expected to make railways and other public works, when they cannot prevent the President of the Board of Control, or the Governor-General, at any time wasting the substance in war which should be applied to these improvements? Suppose that some of the twenty-four Directors should sit down, having 4,000,000*l.* surplus, which the hon. Member for Guildford (Mr. Mangles) spoke of, and a surplus of 2,000,000*l.* a year besides, for the purpose of devising plans of railways, and other works for India? Suppose that they have the maps and plans before them, and that they have called in the assistance of such able engineers as Mr. Locke and Mr. Stephenson? At that very time a letter may come from the office of the President of the Board of Control requiring them to send out an order to Lord Dalhousie to fit out an expedition to Rangoon for the conquest of Burmah; and when that is done, then adieu to the railways and the fabulous 4,000,000*l.* which the hon. Member for Guildford speaks of. But the most ridiculous part of the matter is, that the gentlemen of the Secret

Committee, looking over these surveys, plans, and maps, and knowing the orders sent from the Board of Control, must be perfectly aware that all this is a mere waste of time; and yet they dare not tell their own colleagues, and they must remain in complete ignorance till they learn how the matter stands, by the arrival of the Indian mail.  Under such circumstances, they do not deserve the name of a Government.

And what can be the motive for inducing these twenty-four gentlemen to endure being taunted with the evils of a system under which they are held to be responsible, and yet are not trusted with power?  The reward which they receive for submitting to this humiliation is the patronage of India, and this is another evil arising from the system of double government. Now, it is one of the evils of this system, that the patronage is in a great many instances given to Europeans, where it ought to be given to natives.  But as the Court of Directors are paid by patronage and not by stipends, they, of course, dispose of that patronage to their friends in this country.  I want to see a large number of natives brought into the employment of the Government.  (Hear.)  Yes; but the same thing was promised in 1833, and it was contemplated in the Act of Parliament, but it was never carried out, and it never will be, as long as the patronage is disposed of in its present form. But if we get rid of the double government, and make the Minister for India responsible for the government of India, then public opinion in this country will be brought to bear upon him, and he will be invited to distribute more of his patronage amongst the natives, because the people of this country will not endure that the vast patronage of India shall be in the hands of the Minister of the Crown for distributing amongst his political supporters here.

I have been particularly struck with the overwhelming evidence which is given as to the fitness of the natives of India for high offices and employments.  Nothing comes out clearer before the Committee than this—that the natives are

well fitted to hold the higher class of offices. It was stated
that ninety-seven per cent. of the judicial cases were disposed
of by them. But they are employed to do the humblest work,
at low and insufficient salaries. I wish to see some of the
offices, which are now filled by Europeans, at salaries from
2000*l.* to 3000*l.* a year, filled by natives at half that stipend,
which will be as much to them as double the amount to the
Europeans who receive it. All the great authorities in Indian
matters, Munro, Metcalfe, Malcolm, and Elphinstone, advocate the distribution of patronage to the natives. I was
greatly struck with the answer of Sir G. Clerk to a question
on this point. He says, that the natives are perfectly competent to decide cases and settle differences. Mr. Halliday
also gave evidence to the same effect. But the only way of
ensuring the employment of natives in the higher offices is to
take away the patronage from the Court of Directors.

I will now call the attention of the House to a point of
considerable importance, which was strikingly illustrated by
the facts attending the commencement of the Burmese war in
which we are now engaged. It is another fact, which is a
proof of the precipitancy with which the measure has been
brought forward, and I believe it has not been noticed before
in the course of the debate. I wish to refer to the state of the
relations between the vessels of war in the Indian waters and
the Government of India; and, in illustration of what I mean,
I beg leave to state what has taken place on the breaking out
of this war. In the month of July, 1851, a small British
vessel arrived at Rangoon, the captain of which was charged
with throwing a pilot overboard, and robbing him of 500
rupees. The case was brought before the Governor of Rangoon; and, after undergoing a great many hardships, the
captain was mulcted in the amount of rupees. A month after
this, another English vessel arrived, having on board two
coolies from the Mauritius, who secreted themselves in the
vessel when she left. On their arrival, they said that the

captain had murdered one of the crew during the voyage.
The captain was tried for this, and he was mulcted also. An
application was made to the Governor-General for redress, and
a demand was made on the Burmese authorities to the amount
of 1900*l.* for money extorted, for demurrage of the vessels,
and other injuries inflicted. The Governor-General ordered an
investigation of the case, and he awarded 920*l.* as sufficient.
At this time there was lying in the Hooghly a vessel of war,
commanded by Commodore Lambert, and the Governor-General thought that the presence of this vessel afforded a good
opportunity for obtaining redress. The House should understand that there was no other case to be redressed than these
two; that the parties in them were British subjects, and that
the Governor of Rangoon did not adjudicate between Burmese
subjects and British subjects. Commodore Lambert was
furnished with very precise instructions indeed. He was first
to make inquiry as to the validity of the original claim, and,
if he found that it was well founded, he was to apply to the
Governor of Rangoon for redress; and, in case of a refusal on
his part, he was furnished with a letter from the Governor-
General to the King of Ava, to be sent up by him to the
capital; and he was then to proceed to the Persian Gulf, for
which place he was under orders. He was told not to commit
any act of hostility, if redress was refused, till he had heard
again from the Governor-General. These were very proper
and precise instructions. On the arrival of the Commodore
at Rangoon, he was met by boats filled with British subjects,
who complained of the conduct of the Governor of Rangoon.
If the House wishes for an amusing description of the British
subjects of Rangoon, I would recommend them to read Lord
Ellenborough's sketch of them in a speech which he delivered
in the House of Lords. Rangoon is, it appears, the Alsatia
of Asia, and is filled by all the abandoned characters whom
the other parts of India are too hot to hold. Commodore
Lambert received the complaints of all these people; and he

sent off the letter to the King of Ava at once, which he was
instructed to send only in case redress was refused; and he
made no inquiry with respect to the original cause of the
dispute, and the validity of the claims put forward.  He also
sent a letter from himself to the Prime Minister of the King
of Ava, and demanded an answer in thirty-five days.  The
post took from ten to twelve days to go to Ava, and at the
end of twenty-six days an answer came back from the King
to the Governor-General, and to Commodore Lambert from
the Prime Minister.  It was announced that the Governor of
Rangoon was dismissed, and that a new Governor was appointed, who would be prepared to look into the matter in
dispute, and adjust it.  Commodore Lambert sent off the
King of Ava's letter to the Governor-General, with one from
himself, stating that he had no doubt the King of Ava and
his Government meant to deal fairly by them.  Meantime,
the new Governor of Rangoon came down in great state, and
Commodore Lambert sent three officers on shore with a letter
to him.  The letter was sent at twelve o'clock in the day, and
when they arrived at the house they were refused admittance,
on the plea that the Governor was asleep.  It was specifically
stated that the officers were kept waiting a quarter of an hour
in the sun.  At the end of that quarter of an hour they
returned to the ship, and, without waiting a minute longer,
Commodore Lambert, notwithstanding that he had himself
declared that he had no doubt justice would be done, ordered
the port to be blockaded, having first directed the British
residents to come on board.  During the night, he seized the
only vessel belonging to the King of Ava, which he towed
out to sea.

This brings me to the point to which I am desirous of
calling the attention of the House.  Lord Dalhousie had no
power to give orders to Commodore Lambert in that station;
he could merely request and solicit the co-operation of the
commanders of the Queen's forces, just as we might solicit

the co-operation of a friendly foreign Power. See what the effect of this system is. If Commodore Lambert had been sent out with orders from the First Lord of the Admiralty, he would not have dared to deviate from them in the slightest respect, much less to commence a war. Owing, however, to the anomalous system existing in India, Commodore Lambert felt at liberty to act on his own responsibility; and hence the Burmese war. Why has not this blot been hit upon by the framers of the present Bill? Can there be a stronger proof of the undue precipitancy with which the Government measure has been introduced than this—that it leaves the great defect which I have pointed out—a defect leading to results of immense gravity—uncured? The Government cannot plead ignorance; they cannot allege that their attention had not been directed to the matter. On the 25th of March, Lord Ellenborough referred to the subject in the House of Lords; and on that occasion Lord Broughton, who had just left office, stated that he had received an official communication from Lord Dalhousie relative to the anomalous character of the relations subsisting between the Governor-General and the Queen's commanders, and expressing a hope that the evil would be corrected in the forthcoming Charter Act. But there is nothing on this important subject in the present Bill; and is not this another ground for delay till we have obtained further information?

I have now to say a few words on the subject of the finances of India; and, in speaking on this subject, I cannot separate the finances of India from those of England. If the finances of the Indian Government receive any severe and irreparable check, will not the resources of England be called upon to meet the emergency, and to supply the deficiency? Three times during the present century the Court of Directors has called on the House of Commons to enable them to get rid of the difficulties which pressed upon them. And do you suppose, that if such a case were to occur again, that England

would refuse her aid? Why, the point of honour, if there
were no other reason, would compel us to do so. Do you not
hear it said, that your Indian Empire is concerned in keeping
the Russians out of Constantinople, which is, by the way,
6000 miles distant from Calcutta; and if we are raising
outworks at a distance of 6000 miles, let no man say that the
finances of England are not concerned in the financial condition of India. The hon. Member for Guildford (Mr. Mangles),
referring to this subject on Friday night, spoke.in a tone that
rather surprised me; he taxed those who opposed the measure
with a readiness to swallow anything, and twitted my hon.
Friend (Mr. Bright) with saying that the debt of India, contracted since the last Charter Act, was 20,000,000*l.* The
hon. Gentleman (Mr. Mangles) said it was only 9,000,000*l.*
There has, he said, been 13,000,000*l.* increase of debt, but
that there was 4,000,000*l.* of reserve in the Exchequer. I
will quote the evidence of Mr. Melvill, who signed all the
papers that have come before the Committee on this point.
Mr. Melvill, being asked what the amount of the debt was,
says:—'The amount of the debt is over 20,000,000*l.*' After
this answer of Mr. Melvill, what becomes of the statement
of the hon. Member for Guildford? But I must say that
there is a very great difference in the opinions and statements
of Indian authorities. The evidence of Mr. Prinsep was different from that of the hon. Gentleman (Mr. Mangles); that
of the hon. Gentleman was different from the opinion of the
hon. Member for Honiton (Sir J. Hogg); that of Mr. Melvill
was different from all of them, and Mr. Melvill was sometimes
of a different opinion from his own papers. I want to give
you an opportunity of making up your minds on this subject,
and of correcting the statements that come before you, for
you are to judge of the financial results of your management
of India.

The hon. Baronet the Member for Honiton stated the
deficiency at 15,344,000*l.*; but he has not taken into the

account, as he was bound to do, the sum realised by the commercial assets of the Company. Three or four years subsequently to the renewal of the Charter, in 1833, the Company's
assets, consisting of ships, stock, &c., were sold, and realised
12,661,000*l.* What people want in taking stock, is to know
how much richer or poorer they are as compared with the last
time of striking the balance; and yet these gentlemen kept
out of view a sum of upwards of 12,000,000*l.*, which they
have consumed, exhausted, and spent; and they say that there
is only a deficiency of 15,344,000*l.*, when, in fact, there is a
deficiency of 28,000,000*l.*, as compared with the former period.
The hon. Member for Guildford shakes his head; but I appeal
to the House whether those who are entrusted with the affairs
of the East India Company, and who cannot take stock in
a way to satisfy any Commissioner of Bankruptcy in the case
of the humblest retail trader, are entitled to manage the vast
concerns with which they are now entrusted? The amount,
then, of defalcation, in the last nineteen or twenty years, has
been 28,000,000*l.*; and, if things are to go on in the same
way for the next twenty years, we should have a debt very
nearly approaching 100,000,000*l.* But the worst part of the
case is, that whereas in former instances, when this question
has been discussed, there was something very bad indeed in
the present and the past, yet the House was always told that
there was something in the future to be appealed to which
would compensate for all previous calamities; but now it is a
remarkable circumstance, that, while there is nothing satisfactory in the past, still less is there anything consolatory in
the prospects for the future. The hon. Member for Honiton
has told the House, that, with respect to one essential item
of Indian revenue—that of opium—he considers it in peril.
That hon. Gentleman does not seem to see how he is changing
his tone, and assuming two characters in the course of his
speech, when dealing with the future and the past. The hon.
Gentleman, while answering in an indignant tone the remarks

of the hon. Member for Manchester (Mr. Bright), said, with a view of showing that the 'Constitution had worked well,' that—

'The gross revenue has increased nearly 9,000,000*l.*, yet many taxes have been entirely abolished, and others reduced. Is it not astounding, when the Indian revenue has increased to such an amount, to hear declamation about the misery, the destitution, and the poverty of the country ! The debt shows an increase of 15,344,000*l.*; but what is this compared with the increase which I have shown to have taken place in the revenue ! The revenue has increased in an infinitely greater proportion, so that the increase of the debt is perfectly immaterial.'

Now, what would a person think of a steward who came before him with an account of the condition of his estate, and told him that the debt had increased so much, but, as the rents had increased so much more, it did not signify how the debt had increased ? Yet the steward might have said that he had spent the money in improving the estate, in erecting buildings, and making roads. The Directors of the India Company, however, do not tell the House that they have increased irrigation, or the facilities of communication in India. All this money has been wasted, and is gone, and the people have no compensation for it. The hon. Member for Honiton argues, that it is of no consequence how the India Company got into debt, so long as they have increased the revenue thirty per cent. Is it, then, to such financiers that the fate of India and of England—for the interests of both are connected—is to be entrusted ? But, after giving this glowing description, the hon. Member for Honiton took the other side, when he had another purpose to serve; and then he endeavoured to show that, after all, the state of the Indian finances was not such as to encourage Parliament to assume the possession of them on the part of the Crown. The hon. Gentleman said that—

'The cultivation of opium was, he believed, about to be legalised in China ; and, if that were so, it would have a considerable effect upon the finances of India, and the House ought, under such circumstances, to hesitate before assigning India entirely to the Crown with its liabilities and its debts.'

And then he turned round and said,—

'Will you, with the Burmese war at hand, and with the prospect of losing the opium revenue, take upon yourselves all the responsibilities involved in governing India?'

I am sorry to find the right hon. Gentleman (Sir C. Wood) falling into the same tone :—

'Seeing,' he said, 'into what a debt the East India Company has fallen, do you think it would be a pleasant thing for me to announce to the Chancellor of the Exchequer, that he would have this deficit to provide for in his financial scheme?'

Was there ever anything more utterly indefensible than such a position as that? If we allow the right hon. Gentleman to have another lease, on the plea that the finances have been brought into such a state that it is not desirable for us to assume the management for ourselves, what inducement do we hold out to him to do better in future? I think this House must be very shallow indeed, and the country greatly wanting in that sagacity for which it has credit, if they allowed themselves to be deluded by such a plea as this. The hon. Member for Guildford (Mr. Mangles), in the course of his remarks, took the hon. Member for Manchester (Mr. Bright) to task on the subject of the Punjaub and its expenses. The hon. Member stated, in the jaunty style to which I have alluded, that the acquisition of the Punjaub had not increased our expenses, because the troops there have been pushed forward from the frontier, and, therefore, constitute no addition to our expenditure. I will again quote on this subject from the East India Company's own authority, the statement made by Mr. Kaye in his ' History of the Administration of the East India Company.' Mr. Kaye said,—

'The Punjaub is not yet remunerative. Some little time must elapse before the revenues of the country can be made to exceed the cost of its productive and administrative establishments. The estimated amount of revenue for 1851–2 is 130 lacs of rupees, with about four lacs of additional receipts in the shape of proceeds of confiscated Sikh property and refunded charges. The total expenditure is estimated at about 130 lacs of rupees. This leaves only a surplus of fourteen lacs for the maintenance of the regular troops posted in the Punjaub ; and, as a large reduction of the army might have been, indeed would have been, effected but for the annexation of the Sikh States, it cannot be argued that the military expenditure is not fairly chargeable to the province. It is true, of course, that the possession of the Punjaub has enabled us to withdraw a considerable body of troops from the line of country which constituted our old frontier, and that a deduction on this score of frontier defence must be made from the gross charges of the regular military establishments employed beyond the Sutlej. Still, the cost of the regular troops fairly chargeable to the Punjaub absorbs the estimated surplus, and leaves a balance against the newly-acquired States.'

Mr. Kaye says, there would have been a large reduction of the army, if it had not been for the occupation of the Punjaub. In 1835, the number of troops, European and native, was 184,700 ; in 1851, according to the last return, it was 289,500, being an increase of upwards of 100,000. What was this increase for, unless it were that the new acquisitions required an augmentation of force? During the same period, the European force was increased from 30,800 to 49,000 men ; the ground of this particular increase being, that the Sikhs being a northern nation, could only be kept in awe by Europeans.

Now, if I could treat this question as many persons do; if I could believe that the East India Company is a reality ; if I believed that they could transfer India to the management of some other body, and that England would be no more responsible; that we could have the trade of India, and be under no obligations in reference either to its good government or its future financial state, I should not be the person to come forward and seek a disturbance of that arrangement. Other people may not share in my opinion ; but I am under the impression that, so far as the future is concerned, we cannot leave a more perilous possession to our children than that which we shall leave them in the constantly-increasing territory of India. The English race can never become indigenous in India; we must govern it, if we govern it

at all, by means of a succession of transient visits; and I do
not think it is for the interest of the English people, any
more than of the people of India, that we should govern
permanently 100,000,000 people, 12,000 miles off.  I see
no benefit which can arise to the mass of the English people
from their connection with India, except that which may
arise from honest trade; I do not see how the millions of this
country are to share in the patronage of India, or to derive
any advantage from it, except through the medium of trade;
and, therefore, I say emphatically, that if you can show me
that the East India Company is the reality which many
persons suppose it to be, I shall not be the party to wish
to withdraw their responsible trust, and to place it again
in the hands of a Minister of the British Crown.  But when
I see that this vast territory is now being governed under
a fiction, that the Government is not a real one, but one
which one of the most able and faithful servants of the
Company has declared to be a sham, I say, ' Do not let the
people of this country delude themselves with the idea that
they can escape the responsibility by putting the Government behind a screen.'  I wish, therefore, to look this question fairly in the face; I wish to bring the people of this
country face to face with the difficulties and dangers with
which I think it is beset.  Let it no longer be thought that
a few gentlemen meeting in Leadenhall-street can screen the
people of England from the responsibility with which they
have invested themselves with regard to India.  Since the
granting of the last Charter, more territory has been gained
by conquest than within any similar period before, and the
acquisition of territory has been constantly accompanied with
a proportionate increase of debt.  We have annexed Sattara,
and our own blue-books prove that it is governed at a loss;
we have annexed Scinde, and our own books prove that it, too,
is governed at a loss; we have annexed Pegu, and our own
authorities said that this annexation also will involve a loss.

All these losses must press on the more fertile provinces of Bengal, which are constantly being drained of their resources to make good the deficit. Let me not be told, by-and-by, that the annexation of Pegu and Burmah will be beneficial. What said Lord Dalhousie? He said in his despatch—and the declaration should not be forgotten—that he looked upon the annexation of Pegu as an evil second only to that of war itself; and if we should be obliged to annex Burmah, then farewell to all prospect of amelioration in Indian affairs. Well, then, believing that if this fiction be destroyed—if this mystery be exterminated—the germ of a better state of things in reference to this question will begin to grow; and believing that as yet we are profoundly ignorant of what was wanted for India, I shall vote for the Amendment, that we should wait for two years; and I hope sincerely that the House will agree to it.

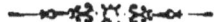

# PEACE.

# PEACE.

## I.

### WREXHAM, NOVEMBER 14, 1850.

[The following was a Speech made at a great meeting in Wales, held under the auspices of the Peace Society.]

Of all the memorable meetings I have ever attended in the United Kingdom, I do not think there has been any which, in some respects, is more significant and surprising than that which I have the honour of addressing. The present would be a large assembly in any town, upon any subject; but when I remember the size of Wrexham, and when I remember that the large assembly before me is not admitted within the precincts of this building without payment, and that a tolerably large payment, I think this part of the United Kingdom must contain a very great number of persons who are, at all events, ready to avail themselves of the opportunity of hearing discussed the subject now submitted to their consideration.

I have heard my own name mentioned here several times, and received with more kindness and partiality than I could

D d 2

possibly have expected to attract from such a meeting.  But
it is my happiness to be half Welsh, and that the better
half.  Though I never before had the honour of addressing
a Welsh audience, I am happy that my first meeting with
you should be on a question second in importance to none
that can be brought before you.  We have met this night
to talk about Peace and the Peace Congress; and let me
once for all say, that when I came here to talk of peace, I did
not mean to treat it as an abstraction.  I came here as a
practical man, to talk, not simply on the question of peace
and war, but to treat another question which is of hardly less
importance—the enormous and burdensome standing armaments which it is the practice of modern Governments to
sustain in time of peace.  For I confess to you, what I have
before avowed again and again, that I have never felt any
alarm about any war in which England should necessarily be
concerned.  I am quite sure it will be our own fault if we
enter into any war, for there is no danger of anybody coming
to molest us.  Still, I find that we are placed in a state of
things hardly different from that of actual war, being, indeed,
subject to the burden of war in time·of peace.

I am not ashamed to avow that I have approached this
question not altogether and exclusively from that point of
view from which Mr. Richard has surveyed it.  I have been
brought to the discussion of the question from another consideration.  In dealing with the practical affairs of the country,
and especially as a politician and Member of Parliament,
whose duty it is to study and control the finances of the
country, I have come to my conclusion, apart from those high
convictions which Mr. Richard and Mr. Sturge have avowed,
and in which I concur, though in their presence I am not
the proper person to dilate upon them.  I gather my conclusion as one desiring to see that the country is governed
with economy, and the people are not burdened with ruinous
taxation; that there is a necessity for the people of this

country to unite in supporting the principles of peace, as the only means of improving their temporal condition.

Now, I say that I deal with this question as a practical man. I have lately been travelling in the rural parts of Wales, and I find that there is a considerable amount of inconvenience among the rural population, among the farming world, who complain of low prices, and the weight of tithe-rent and taxation. We shall have those questions to talk over next session. The whole question of taxation will then come up. Government and Parliament will then have to deal with a Budget of pretty nearly 50,000,000*l.* a year, and they will have to vote money to meet this enormous outlay out of funds raised by taxation on the people. Now, while the great mass of the people are in the enjoyment of a large amount of comfort, probably never exceeded in the centres of industry in former times, I do not conceal that there is also another great mass of the population, and not the least important in a political point of view, who are suffering considerable pecuniary uneasiness; and therefore there will be next session a pressure on Parliament for a remission of taxation. Now, it is in order to be able to deal constitutionally and honestly, and not to take the Government or the country by surprise on any vote, that I now wish to record my opinions, and to prove that no sensible remission of taxation can be made, unless the country comes to the principles of the Peace Society, or, at all events, goes some length towards its objects, and determines to make a very large reduction in the military establishments.

Will any one, then, dare to say that I am making a Utopia of this Peace question, and that I am not a practical man? Can there be any doubt that the Chancellor of the Exchequer, viewing his position in his retirement and during the recess, must have directed his mind to this question, and that he finds dangers and difficulties impending over him in the enormous amount of taxation he is compelled to demand?

There is a Budget of nearly 50,000,000*l.* to vote next session, and has it never entered the minds of Gentlemen present to analyse what it was composed of? In the first place, we have to provide 28,000,000*l.* in round numbers out of the taxation, to meet the interest of the funded and floating debt—that debt of nearly 800,000,000*l.* having been almost every farthing contracted in former wars. Deducting those 28,000,000*l.*, there are left 22,000,000*l.*, about 6,500,000*l.* of which (I still speak in round numbers) are alone required to carry on the civil government, including the expenses of the courts of law, of diplomacy, consular establishments, official salaries, and everything necessary to cover the charge of civil government. After that, we have to vote about 15,500,000*l.* (I speak of what was done last year) for the expenses of the army, navy, and ordnance ; so that out of the 22,000,000*l.* required of you to pay the current expenditure of the State, more than two-thirds are required for military expenses—for these two-thirds, taken from the taxation of the people, are spent on red-coats, blue-jackets, and their appurtenances—and one-third covers all the other expenses. I cannot but think that I should deserve to be scouted if, talking to the people of financial reform, I advocate the principle of Free Trade, that is, of subjecting all classes to the rivalry of the foreigner, and declare that I wish to see the burden of taxation reduced, and yet conceal from you the fact, that out of our current expenditure about two-thirds go to the army, navy, and ordnance.

I therefore declare, that if you wish any remission of the taxation which falls upon the homes of the people of England and Wales, you can only find it by reducing the great military establishments, and diminishing the money paid to fighting-men in time of peace. No doubt the next session of Parliament will open amidst great clamour for the reduction of a great number of taxes ; but we cannot reduce taxation unless we reduce expenditure. If the expenditure is kept up, we must have taxes to pay for it; and therefore taxation can only be reduced by coming to a resolution that we will in some way curtail the expenditure. But how am I, as an individual Member of Parliament, to deal with these questions? Motions were frequently brought forward to repeal obnoxious taxes—such as the window-tax, the taxes on knowledge; and one motion last session was to repeal the tax on attorneys, who, we are told, were very oppressed individuals. One hon. Member wanted half the duty on malt taken off; and another, with more reason, wished to repeal half the duty on tea. These motions are submitted, one after the other, to the House of Commons, which is then called on to vote ' Yes ' or ' No ' upon them; but I cannot vote for taking off taxes that have been rendered necessary by the expenditure which has been voted, and I have said, ' Meet a reduction of taxes by a reduction of expenditure.' But having acted in this way, I have now no hesitation in declaring in these meetings, that if the Government does not do that which the country is told by the organs of military men they are not going to do, if it makes no reduction in military establishments, then, under these circumstances, I shall vote for taking off taxes, and see whether it is possible to pay for the military establishments without money. This, I own, is a clumsy way, and does not recommend itself to my reason; and I would rather go to work as in private matters, and rationally discuss what we can reduce in our expenditure, before taking off taxation; but if I find an unfair, unreasonable resistance to what I believe to be a fair and rational proposition for some reduction, I must adopt the course I have referred to.

I am not liable to the charge of advocating the total and immediate abolition of all our war establishments; but, after such meetings as the present, and after the declarations which I have openly made for many years, I feel I shall be perfectly free next session, with clean hands, and with full consistency and honesty, to vote for the removal of taxation, and

leave the Government to cut the coat according to the cloth.
I have no doubt that in the volume written by Sir F. Head,
the author of ' Bubbles from the Brunnen of Nassau,' which
has been referred to, we may find some statements which run
counter to our principles and reasonings. But I dare say
these ' bubbles ' are just as substantial as the facts in the
volume; for there is something in the antecedents of Sir F.
Head, and his conduct in Canada, which does not recommend
him to me as a good authority in this affair of our finances.
But no doubt I shall be told that we are in great danger
from other countries keeping up large military establishments
and coming to attack us. Now, the answer I give to that is,
that I would rather run the risk of France coming to attack us
than keep up the present establishments in this country. I
have done with reasoning on that subject. I would rather cut
down the expenditure for military establishments to 10,000,000*l*.
and run every danger from France, or any other quarter, than
risk the danger of attempting to keep up the present standard
of taxation and expenditure.

I call those men who write in this way cowards. I am not
accustomed to pay fulsome compliments to the English, by
telling them that they are superior to all the world; but this
I can say, that they do not deserve the name of cowards. The
men who write these books must be cowards; for I know
nothing so preposterous as talking of a number of Frenchmen
coming and taking possession of London. Who is afraid of
them? I believe there never was an instance known in the
history of the world of as many as 50,000 men in military
array being transported across salt water within twelve
months. Napoleon, on going to Egypt, had not so many;
and France, with twelve months' preparation, could not transport across the sea 50,000 men, with all the appliances and
muniments of war. It never has been, and I do not believe
that it could be, done in twelve months. But I repeat, that
I would run any risk, and not listen to those who would

frighten me. I must, however, say that I am not one, because I advocate the reduction of armaments, who would
plead guilty to the charge of being a coward, or who would
submit to injustice. Many people suppose, that because I do
not advocate bullying every nation on the face of the earth,
that, therefore, I would necessarily submit to any one who
might do me an injury. That is not the character of the
Peace Society, nor of the members of the Society of Friends,
who constitute the main force of the Peace Association. Read
history, and see what great courage had been shown by the
Society of Friends, and whether they did not extort from
cruel and intolerant Governments toleration before any other
sect, not by buckling on armour, but by knowing how to
suffer, and by defeating through passive resistance those who
attempted to do them injustice and wrong. And I say that
those people on the Continent, who have a righteous cause,
and wrongs to redress, would do well to imitate the calm
endurance and patient long-suffering of the members of the
Society of Friends. I know more than one community on
the Continent to which this attitude might be adopted —
Lombardy has been mentioned—in which was situated that
town of Brescia, where were perpetrated those enormities by
Haynau, and referred to by Mr. Richard. The population
of that country consists of Italians; and men, women, and
children all joined in opposition and hatred to the Austrian
rule. But what chance had they in conflict with an enemy
who possessed all the fortresses and muniments of war? How
would it be if the Lombards folded their arms, and profited
by the example of the members of the Society of Friends?
Might they not by passive resistance alone set at nought the
power of the strongest Government in Europe? Let me not
be told that I am advocating injustice, and a supine acqui-
escence to wrong; for I have observed, that those who take
up arms to contend against tyranny are not generally remarkable for having any success in the process, and I have a sus-

picion that the people on the Continent will ultimately find
better means of emancipating themselves from their wrongs
than by fighting and soldiering, which too often prove dis-
astrons to the cause of liberty.

The best way for us, as Englishmen, to deal with the
question, is as politicians, and more particularly as looking at
facts from a financial point of view. Everybody can see, and
everybody admits, that the course pursued on the Continent
cannot be continued for five years longer by any Government.
Everybody admits that Austria is bankrupt. When some time
ago I went to the London Tavern, and spoke against the
Austrian loan, and denonnced the Austrians as bankrupts,
there was an attempt to oppose my views; but everybody
now admits that their bankruptcy is inevitable. Well, let us
take France, Prussia, and Russia; and they too, through their
enormous military establishments, are hastening to bankruptcy
and revolution. And it is by peace meetings, by peace congresses at Frankfort and elsewhere, — it is by such means
alone that attention is awakened to the danger of such a
course; and by such means alone,—by public meetings, and
agitation, and public discussion, is any great reform effected in
the affairs of the world.

But when we call attention to these evils, we do not leave
them without suggesting practical remedies. We say to the
Governments of the world, 'Cannot you find some other way
of settling your disputes, and for guaranteeing peace, than by
an array of enormous armaments? Cannot you recognise
between Governments the principle of submitting your disputes to the arbitration of a neutral party?' In France and
England, and other countries, instead of keeping up those
gigantic forces in time of peace, cannot the Governments of
the world, in 1850, devise some other means of providing
something like a guarantee for the continuance of peace?
There is no present quarrel between France and England—no
tender question, and no claim that ought to interrupt the

professions of eternal peace and concord which are made by
both parties. Yet we are told that something might arise
which would cause a war; and, therefore, the country must
prepare for war. But the contingency of a dispute arising
might be prepared for by other means than war; and we, the
advocates of peace, say, Let the Governments refer their disputes to the arbitration of some impartial umpire. I ask
Governments to do in the case of a nation what we always do
in the case of individuals. If a Frenchman living in London
commits a crime, the law—and Englishmen may be proud of
it—allows him to claim to be tried by a jury, half of whom are
foreigners. Now, all I want is, that the nations of England
and France, and other countries, should carry the same principle into operation, and that when they have a dispute—
when they charge a country, as Greece had been, of being in
debt to another, and when that country denies the justice of
the claim (and in the case of Greece subsequent events prove
she is right), then let the matter be referred to arbitrators,
instead of sending out a dozen ships of war, and saying, if
another nation does not take our account of the matter, we
will compel them. Let two arbitrators, one for each nation
disputing, be appointed; and if the two cannot agree, let them
appoint an umpire to settle the dispute according to reason
and the facts of the case. Thus would be avoided the recourse
now had to enormous forces. Is there anything so Utopian in
this? The Peace Congress came to a resolution to recommend
the nations of the world to enter on a system of disarmament.
I have referred to this topic again and again, and I have
learned that the only way to instruct men is to do with them
as with children, and to repeat the lesson.

We have a Treaty with the United States, according to
which only a certain number of ships of war are to be maintained by each nation on the limitary lakes—only one on each
lake. Now, what has been the consequence? Why, from the
moment of the existence of that treaty, both parties have

totally disregarded the maintenance of the force altogether, and there is not at the present moment more than one crazy English hulk on all these lakes, and I do not believe that the Americans have one at all! This occurred from the moment our country showed that she had no desire to run with America that race of national rivalry which Sir F. Head would persuade England to run with France, fitting out a new fleet at Portsmouth, to be followed by an increased French fleet at Cherbourg, and by an augmentation, I suppose, of 100,000 men to the military force of each nation. If England enters with an honest spirit into a treaty with France, similar to that which exists with America, it would, if accepted, be advantageous to the interests of both countries; and if we have not got a Minister for Foreign Affairs who understands his business, and would enter into such an arrangement, then let the English people, who understand their business, advertise for a Foreign Minister, who, instead of following old courses, shall be alive to the spirit of the age, who shall be deemed worthy to have lived in the age of electric telegraphs, railways, and steamboats. It would simplify our foreign policy, if we entered into arrangements with other countries, binding ourselves by previous treaties, in case of dispute and hot blood, not to have recourse to war or violence, but to submit to arbitration. If I could only get the people of England and Wales to feel alive to this question, and to deal with the scorners of the peacemen as they deserved—with that contempt which Englishmen are sure, in the long run, to throw on such offenders,—if I could only get these views implanted into the minds of the people, it would not be long before we should have another Sir Robert Peel to carry them out.

I cannot mention the name of Sir Robert Peel without expressing my deep regret, not for the fame of that statesman, —for, probably, under all the circumstances, he could not have died at a moment more favourable for his fame,—but for the

sake of his country. There are many reasons why we should
regret that we have lost such a man at such a time. I cannot
be expected, of course, to endorse the acts of Sir R. Peel's long
political career. Sir R. Peel was in early life placed, before,
probably, he had the choice of his own career, in a wrong political groove; but that such a man, after forty years' training
in an adverse political school, should at the end of that time
have taken the course he did, entitling himself, as he had done,
by the last act of his political life, to the lasting veneration
of his countrymen, makes me firmly hope that England has
great future benefits to expect from the wise counsels of that
great statesman. On those questions on which I am now
addressing you, and which are agitated by the Peace Congress, I watched Sir R. Peel's course during the last three
years, and, as my friends know, predicted that Sir R. Peel
was preparing gradually to do for his country what he had
done on another question, only secondary in importance to
that advocated by the Peace Congress. It was in 1841 that
Sir R. Peel was the first to recommend that agitation in
which the Peace party and I are now engaged. That statesman then referred to the numerous standing armies, to the
danger caused thereby to the finances, and to the consequent
risk of revolutions incurred by the Governments of Europe;
and he said that those Governments ought to endeavour to
come to terms on the basis of a mutual reduction of the military establishments; and he declared, emphatically, that he
hoped the Governments would take that course; or, if not,
he hoped the different communities of Europe would so spread
their opinions as to force their Governments to adopt that
plan. I have frequently referred to that declaration as being
a direct incentive to the course which is adopted at peace
meetings; and I claim for the peace meetings the sanction
and approval—nay, I claim for them the origination of the
most practical statesman that ever lived.

But this is not all. In the House of Commons, on the 12th

of March, 1850, Sir R. Peel spoke as I will presently read;
and I well remember the feeling of surprise, not unmingled
with a feeling of dissatisfaction, which pervaded that peculiar
assembly when the words were delivered.  I remember, when
they were finished, that half-a-dozen of the Members sitting
round me, congratulated me on having again got Sir R. Peel's
assistance for a movement in favour of reducing expenditure.
The words of Sir Robert Peel, to which I now allude, were
these : —

'For what was said about the comparative lightness of taxation I care
nothing, for there are many taxes pressing on the energies of the country and
diminishing the comforts of the humbler classes; and their repeal, if it could
be effected with good faith and public security, will be of inestimable advantage
to the nation.  Nay, more; I will say, that in time of peace, you must, if you
mean to retrench, incur some risks.  If in time of peace you must have all the
garrisons of our colonial possessions in a state of complete efficiency—if you
must have all our fortifications kept in a state of perfect repair,—I venture to
say that no amount of annual expenditure will be sufficient; and if you adopted
the opinions of military men, who say that they would throw upon you the
whole responsibility in the event of a war breaking out, and some of our
valuable possessions being lost, you would overwhelm this country with taxes
in time of peace.  The Government ought to feel assured that the House of
Commons would support them if they incurred some responsibility with respect
to our distant colonial possessions by running a risk for the purpose of effecting
a saving.  *Bellum para, si pacem velis*, is a maxim generally received, as
if it were impossible to contest it ; yet a maxim that admits of more contra-
diction, or should be accepted with greater reserve, never fell from the lips
of man.'

When Sir R. Peel delivered those words, discrediting the
authority of military men, he spoke in an assembly and especially from a side of the House where the military spirit was
dominant; and he must have felt those sentiments strongly,
or he never could have delivered them in such an assembly
and in such an atmosphere.  And orators should not forget
that statesman's advice, when in after-dinner speeches they
propose 'the Army and Navy,' and declare that to have peace
it was necessary to be prepared for war.  That was not Sir R.
Peel's opinion; and yet I dare say that many of the men
who utter the sentiment about being prepared for war would

have shouted for Sir R. Peel, and would subscribe for a monument to him.

I remember, not long ago, a speech delivered by a sheriff of London at the sheriffs' inaugural dinner. I do not remember the sheriff's name; in fact, very few persons ever remember the names of the sheriffs of London, and as the gentleman I allude to happened to be sheriff and alderman of the City of London,—a very corrupt corporation,—it is not to be wondered at that his name has escaped my recollection, though it has been inserted in the columns of that very best champion of peace—*Punch*, which ought to be seen on the table of everyone, both in wealthy drawing-rooms and humble cottages. This gentleman hiccuped out a great deal of incoherent nonsense about Cobden, and also said that he was in favour of armaments to preserve peace, and called the principles of the Peace Society ' Utopian,' for that is the standard word. Now, what has the Corporation of London lately done? I must say I had not supposed they possessed so much wit—I had not given them credit for having a joke in their whole body.   Why, they have changed the programme of that great children's raree-show on Lord Mayor's-day, and, instead of exhibiting men in armour, they provide in their stead a figure emblematical of Peace, followed by representations of Europe, Asia, Africa, and America.   No doubt that was intended as a sly vote of censure on this talkative alderman and sheriff; but it was too bad that, after eating his dinner, they should have gone away and served him such a scurvy trick as that.   It was said that the peace which the Peace Society was aiming at, and the reduction of armaments, was Utopian and quite impracticable; but, somehow or other, I find that everybody comes before the public with the pretence of being a lover of peace, and endeavours to point out facts in the world with the view of showing that we were going to arrive at peace.   But if it is said, ' Then let us gather these facts together; let us make use of the railways, and visit

different parts, as Paris and Frankfort had been visited, and
let us invite people to talk over the question of peace, and see
if it cannot be forwarded,' then these people turn round, denounce and ridicule the peace-men, and affect a great deal of
scorn for their reasonings, while they very probably desire
peace in their hearts a great deal less than they pretend.

There is a large portion of the community which does not
want peace. War is the profession of some men, and war,
therefore, is the only means for their occupation and promotion in their profession. 15,000,000*l*. sterling are spent
on military establishments. That is a considerable sum of
money spent upon classes who are not very likely to be
favourable to peace. Read the *United Service* and the *Army
and Navy Gazette.* Do you think that these publications are
intended to promote peace? Do they not seek the opportunity of exciting jealousies,—pointing to the ships of war of
foreign countries, and saying, 'There are more guns there,
and, therefore, we must have more?' Do they not endeavour
to produce that rivalry of establishments and armaments
which is always tending of necessity to hostile feelings and
hostile acts? Again, there is a large portion of the continental community which is similarly situated to the portion
of which I have just spoken in this country. Four millions
of men—the flower of Europe—from twenty to thirty-three
years of age, are under arms, living in idleness. There are
often no men in the country parts; the women are doing
their farm work, and toiling up to their knees in manure,
and amidst muck and dirt, at the age of thirty and forty.
They may be constantly seen thus employed, tanned and
haggard, and looking hardly like the fair sex. They do this,
in order that the muscle and strength of the country should
be clothed in military coats, and should carry muskets on
their shoulders—a scandal to a civilised and Christian age.
Thus there is a large body of men who do not desire peace. I
do not believe that peace is their object. I do not know why

they entered the army if they did not want war. That is their employment, and they must be idle if they have not war; and, therefore, it is not unfair to argue that they are not altogether favourable to peace, whatever they may say; and consequently I do not believe that all those men who use these cant phrases about peace care for it.

I have endeavoured to show that I have a practical object in view, and that the members of the Peace Society have some sanction from practical men for what is sought after by this society. What do other men propose—those most opposed to the Peace Society? Do they say that the system which we are opposing will last for ever? Why, every man admits that it cannot last five years. Is there any person prepared to reverse this system of enormous expenditure and ruinous establishments—of waste, bankruptcy, and ultimate revolution? The conduct which the Governments are pursuing is calculated to shake the faith of the mass of the people in the very existence of government—marching and countermarching troops—and all for mere parade and the exhibition of armed men. It seems to me as if there ought to have been a battle long ago on the Continent, and then, I think, there would have been more chance that this turmoil would have been put an end to. For what purpose does this marching and countermarching of troops serve, unless the secret and covert design of bringing the system into disrepute? And it is coming into disrepute. And if we could only prevent the Governments from 'raising the wind' (as Mr. Richard said), we should put an end to it.

I now come to another point of our Peace doctrine, and that is, that we want to prevent people lending money to those bankrupt Governments in order that they may keep soldiers. I said, last August twelvemonths, that the Russian Government, about whose rich and ample resources so much was then uttered, could not make the campaign in Hungary without coming to London or Amsterdam for a loan. I was

laughed at; but the campaign was hardly over before a loan was applied for, under the pretence that it was wanted for a railway. I denounced that loan as an Imperial falsehood. I do not mean to say that the Emperor knew so when he signed the decree, but the Emperor knows that to be the case now, and he ought to repudiate it. It was raised to pay for the atrocities perpetrated in the Hungarian war, not from the savings of Barings or Rothschilds, for they are not the people who lent the money, but from the small capitalists in England, who have small savings, and who wish to get five instead of four per cent. They lent that money, by which they as much cut the throats of the Hungarians and devastated their villages as if they had gone there and done it with their own hands. I was asked whether I, as a Free-trader, was consistent with my principles when I denounced this use of money? I was told that a man had a right to lend his money without inquiring what it was wanted for. But if he knew it was wanted for a vile purpose, had he the right of so lending it? I put this question to a City man:—
'Somebody asks you to lend money to build houses with, and you know it is wanted for the purpose of building infamous houses; would you be justified in lending the money?' He replied, 'I would.' I rejoined, 'Then I am not going to argue with you—you are a man for the police magistrate to look after; for if you would lend money to build infamous houses, you would very likely keep one yourself, if you could get ten per cent. by it.' I say that no man has a right to lend money if he knows it is to be applied to the cutting of throats. The whole of this system of enormous armaments is built on the system of lending money; and thereby there are concentrated into one generation those evils of war, which would not have been suffered except successive generations were called upon to pay for them.

The system is indefensible, both on the principles of humanity and political economy; and I believe the time will

come—it is coming (for I have heard the principle broached
in high intellectual places) — when future generations will
raise the question whether they shall be held responsible for
debts incurred, often for keeping their own country in slavery,
and also for foreign wars, in which they can have no possible
interest.

We have all heard of the disturbances in Sleswig-Holstein;
and I join both with Mr. Sturge and Mr. Richard in the expression of opinion that our Government is heavily responsible
for having meddled in that affair in the way in which it did,
and in joining France, Russia, and Denmark in a hostile
demonstration against Sleswig-Holstein. We have no business to do so; and I could corroborate every word used by
the preceding speakers to the effect, that it had left a
feeling of deep alienation among the whole Protestant community of Germany. I do not use that term with a view of
instituting an invidious comparison in respect to the Roman
Catholics; but the Protestant part of Germany is the most
constitutional; it is the part which has been, and most
naturally, in sympathy with England; but, in consequence
of that proceeding of our Foreign Minister, deep, lasting, if
not ineradicable feelings of alienation and indignation have
been produced against the Government and people of this
country.

But the point to which I wish to refer is this,—Last
year these two parties (the Danes and Sleswig-Holsteiners)
were in collision, and then there ensued a suspension of arms.
In the interval, Denmark raised a loan of 800,000*l.* That
money was spent in preparation for bloody conflicts; and, if
it could not have been raised from the English or Dutch, I
firmly believe that, from the destitution of the resources of
Denmark, peace must necessarily have ensued, and those
hostilities, which have caused so much devastation within the
last few months, could not have been renewed. So with
respect to Russia. We heard of the Emperor dictating to

Germany at Warsaw. I believe that the cost of the visits between Petersburgh and Warsaw has been defrayed out of the money raised from the English; and if that money had not been raised—if those 5,000,000*l.* had not been lent out—if English capitalists had folded their arms, or, better still, had closed their purse-strings — if, too, they had lent no money for perpetrating atrocities in Hungary, and had declared that henceforth no assistance need be expected from them for wars and deeds of violence, then those armaments must have been reduced, and instead of the Czar, in consequence of being full of money, riding backwards and forwards from one city to another, he would have been kept at home, minding the affairs of his own country and not those of Germany, and we should have been saved this turmoil, which will very likely be made an excuse next session for not reducing the army of this country.

Before I sit down, let us prepare for what will be said of this meeting. We shall be called enthusiasts and Utopians, who think the millennium is coming. Now, as the gentlemen who use these phrases are very much at a loss for something new, I will say, once for all, that I am not dreaming of the millennium. I believe that long after my time iron will be used to make the spear, as well as the pruning-hook and the ploughshare. I do not think the coming year is to produce . any sudden change in the existing practice, or that the millennium will be absolutely realised in my time; but I think, if the principles of the Peace Society are true, we are engaged in a work in which conscience, and, I believe, Heaven itself, will find canse for approbation. In that course, therefore, I shall persevere, in spite of sneers and sarcasms. I believe we shall not have long to wait before we shall find from our opponents admissions that they are wrong and we right. I have seen some such things before from the same quarters on another question; and I expect to hear the same things again. Those parties tell us that we must look to Free Trade and to other causes to accelerate the era of Peace—those parties who opposed Free Trade. But when I advocated Free Trade, do you suppose that I did not see its relation to the present question, or that I advocated Free Trade merely because it would give us a little more occupation in this or that pursuit? No; I believed Free Trade would have the tendency to unite mankind in the bonds of peace, and it was that, more than any pecuniary consideration, which sustained and actuated me, as my friends know, in that struggle. And it is because I want to see Free Trade, in its noblest and most humane aspect, have full scope in this world, that I wish to absolve myself from all responsibility for the miseries caused by violence and aggression, and too often perpetrated under the plea of benefiting trade. I may at least be allowed to speak, if not with authority, yet certainly without the imputation of trespassing on ground which I may not reasonably be supposed to understand as well as most people, and to say, when I hear those who advocate warlike establishments or large armaments for the purpose of encouraging our trade in distant parts of the world, that I have no sympathy with them, and that they never shall have my support in carrying out such measures. We have nothing to hope from measures of violence in aid of the promotion of commerce with other countries.

Away with all attempts to coerce any nation, whether civilised or barbarous, by ships of war, into the adoption of those principles of Free Trade, which we ourselves only adopted when we became convinced by the process of reason and argument that they were for our own interest. If we send ships to enforce by treaties this extension of trade, we shall be doing more harm than good to the cause we pretend to aid. Such a policy is calculated to react on the people, by imposing on them great burdens, in order to support those armaments by which it is endeavoured to force our views on other nations. I shall have something to say on another occasion about China and Borneo. I will give some facts, and, before long, I will adopt the most effectual mode which I can, and show the people of this country that they are mistaken, in a pecuniary point of view, when they think that they enforce their interests by ships of war or troops. Therefore, as a Free-trader, I oppose every attempt to enforce a trade with other countries by violence or coercion.

I never thanked the Foreign Minister who came with a Treaty of Commerce from China, or Borneo, or St. Domingo, or Russia, binding them to extend their commerce with this country, and to relax their restrictions, should that Treaty be obtained either by force, chicanery, or fraud ; for, depend on it, a policy so enforced will react, and we shall never make progress in the principles which we advocate until we leave it to other countries to take the course they believe to be best for their own interest, after calm consideration, and until they have seen, by the example England had set, that the Free Trade adopted by her was beneficial to her own interests.

Therefore, on high religious grounds, and on Free-trade grounds, I support the gentlemen who are devoting themselves to the cause of Peace. I think myself that I have done very little in this matter, and I am ashamed when I find myself singled out for obloquy, which I do not deserve, in relation to this cause. I am not ashamed of the title of the " Champion of Peace,"—I only wish I deserved it. I thank the gentlemen who have taken up this cause on all these grounds. I know that they consider no sacrifice too great in order to carry out their conscientious convictions. I thank them for it, and for the opportunity they have afforded me in addressing this meeting, and at the meetings at Frankfort and other places, to address all the countries of Europe, and I entreat them to go on. They are the sons of parents who fought the battle of Catholic Emancipation — (applause) —I meant to have said Slave Emancipation, but the cheer needs not to be recalled, for they were the friends of liberty of every kind, whether to the white man or to the black. Let them not be discouraged by sneers, but let them go on unfalteringly, and, as on the Slave Question, they will bequeath this struggle from father to son, until as glorious a result will be accomplished as any yet recorded on the page of History.

# PEACE.

## II.

MANCHESTER, JANUARY 27, 1853.

[The following is one of the speeches which Mr. Cobden made with the
purpose of disabusing the public of a panic which was common some
years ago. The second Empire had just been established in France.]

I CONFESS I have listened to those letters from our French
correspondents with feelings of shame and humiliation,—
shame, that it should be deemed necessary by our well-
wishers on the other side of the Channel that they should
give us assurances that there is no intention on the part of
France to come and, without provocation, to invade our
shores; and humiliation, that there should have been a considerable number of the people of this country who could
have been deluded by the merest child's cry, the mere baby's
talk that we have been listening to, for the last few months,
and that they should have believed for a moment that anything so absurd and all but impossible was going to happen.

Now, let me just call your attention to the source from
which those assurances come. The outcry that we hear in
this country about an invasion from France is levelled at the

present Government of France. The parties who are addressing us are not the partisans of that Government. We have had a letter from M. Carnot; he is not a friend of the present Government. I have an extract here from the *Journal des Débats*, which is a pacific newspaper, not in the interest of Louis Napoleon, but a decided advocate of peace and free trade; and what is the tone in which that paper speaks of this cry of invasion in this country? It says, that ' whilst the British journals are every day accusing our Government of making large augmentations of its navy, we observe that under this unfounded pretence, England is constantly adding to its fleet and other armaments; and we are led to believe that the English press can have no other object in thus declaiming against the imaginary armaments of France, than to conceal the real preparations that are going on in that country.' Well, you have had a letter from M. Emile de Girardin; he is not a partisan of the present Government; he was an exile after the last revolution, and he is expressing his doubts whether the preparations we are making for ' a disembarkation from France without an object'—for, mind you, with his usual logic, he, in a word, has hit upon the whole point of this absurd outcry,—these preparations, he is rather inclined to think, there must be something else to account for, than the absurd supposition that we are preparing for a descent from France *without an object;* because nobody has ever professed that there is any object; we have had no quarrel; there is no dispute,— no unsettled boundary, no Spanish marriages, no Tahiti question, no Mr. Pritchard; there is no quarrel at all; and, when I ask our invasionist friends what it is the French are coming here for, I never could hear an intelligible answer. Sometimes they say that some five thousand men are coming here to burn down one of our towns, and yet they admit these men will never go back again! I am as much at a loss as M. de Girardin is to see any logical ground for any such attempt as that.

But you may depend upon it that you are apt to under-rate the effect of all this kind of menacing demonstration. The effect will be precisely the contrary of what these alarmists want. Instead of damaging Louis Napoleon, you will unite all parties in France with him as against England. And that is the great evil of such demonstrations as this,—you make every man in France, that has one atom of self-respect, or of French spirit in his blood,—you make him feel indignant that you have lowered him and his country to the rank of savages, in supposing that they are to come here some day, without notice, without declaration of war,—a thing that never happened in any civilised country in the world; that you are assuming that it is going to be done, some day, with-out any fact to warrant it; and that you are making all the preparation which he sees in your ports, in order to receive those savages. And you find people who are still considered fit to be trusted in the management of their business, whom you meet in the streets every day, who will shake their wise heads, and tell you that they believe that there is some danger of a French invasion. Might not I say, 'I think there is some danger of somebody attacking me in the street,'—might not I, with just the same logic, prepare myself with a dreadnought club or life preserver; or, perhaps, a brace of pistols, if I deemed it necessary; might not I make any kind of provision against any such imaginary danger as that? But I should be no more rational in doing it than we are as a nation in making these preparations against France.

I wish I could get some of these public instructors and bring them to the test of how far they are in earnest when they write in the way some of these Manchester papers write about a French invasion. Now, to my knowledge, they have been writing in the same way these last five years; I have had them upon me ever since December, 1847, which is above five years ago. They were writing in the same way

when Louis Philippe was King of the French, and when
M. Guizot was his Prime Minister. I will not let them off
on their protesting that all they want now is to guard us
against a usurper and a despot. I say they raised that cry
as long ago as in 1847, when Louis Philippe was king, as
loudly as they do now. They have been five years in this
state of panic and alarm; and I say it is high time that
such people should take some assurance against the consequences of this invasion, when it comes. Well, now, I am
prepared, not only to give them that assurance on moderate
terms, but I will put their sincerity to the test. Bring me
that public instructor in your town, that has been telling
you for the last five years, and upwards, that this invasion
is so imminent; bring him to me, and I will make a proposal to him. If he will pay one shilling a week to your
Infirmary, as a subscription, I will enter into a legal bond
to pay him down ten thousand pounds when this invasion
takes place. Well, but you sometimes have your public
instructors, who write as though they had some special
sources of information from London.

Now, I tell all those writers in newspapers in the provinces, who have joined in this cry of invasion, that they
are being heartily laughed at by those in London, who are
profiting by the cry. The Government has no belief in any
danger of a sudden invasion. I will prove it to you in a
moment. If an invasion took place without notice, our
Government would be certainly impeached, because they are
allowing our largest concentrated fleet—a fleet more powerful
than the whole American navy;—now, I am speaking deliberately when I say that we have a fleet before which, if
every ship of war which the Americans have were brought,
they could not exist for twenty-four hours; and that fleet
is now lying at Malta, or amusing itself between Malta
and Corfu (with a great expenditure on the part of the
officers for kid gloves for their parties and excursions); and

I say that if Parliament believed what the Government and the instructors of the people are saying, as though it were derived from some special sources of information, that any Government that ever existed in the country, and which was proved, if an invasion or descent on our shores took place, to have suspected it, to have anticipated it, and to have given a hint of it to some of those public instructors in the country, would inevitably be impeached, and deservedly so, for having left our largest fleet 1200 miles off, and at such a distance that it could not be collected in less than a month's time. So I assure gentlemen in the provinces who join in the cry, that they are only being heartily laughed at for their pains, and that the Government, which may profit by the cry, is by no means a sharer in the panic. And that is one of the worst parts of the panic—that Governments do manage to tide over a session, and gain time when thy can find silly people through the country who will occupy their fellow-citizens by such a cry as this, because those who would be better employed in urging forward the Government to do something, are kept trotting about the country to try to prevent the mischief which these alarmists create. Don't you think, now, that I and others on this platform, who form humble units in the political world, might be better engaged, and might perhaps be troublesome to some party in the Government, if we were not kept on trotting about by this cry of an invasion? It is a very clever contrivance, and is the very thing that despotic Governments are always seeking for—something to keep the country always in a state of agitation, from a fear of invasion by any other Power than themselves. That has been the system that has always been adopted from the very beginning of misgovernment; since Governments will always find not only silly people who will believe them and become their dupes, but also people who will perform the part of impostors to those dupes; for there is quite as much knavery as folly at the bottom of this cry.

Now, I think that we are playing very much the part of bullies in this matter. If I have read history to any purpose at all, we have some atonement to offer to the French people. We are not in a position to put our fist constantly in the face of the French, and accuse them of an intention to come and molest us. The last French war arose out of a gross and unprovoked aggression on our part. The last war on the Continent originated with us, from an oligarchical Government, fed from the resources of this great nation, but carried on against the interests of liberty and in the interests of despotism. But, after that war is at an end, I think we might have expected that if there were any complaints, or accusations, or suspicions, they would more naturally have come from the other side of the Channel. I think that, under the circumstances, when we investigate the origin and character of the last great French war with this country, it is surprising that there is not a greater feeling of resentment and indignation on the part of the French nation against the English. But are the English people in a position to begin again to exasperate the French people by accusing them of an intention to invade us, and of entertaining those base intentions against our shores, when the only example in the memory of living man, is one in which we played that part against them? If there should be suspicion in the minds of any, it should be in the breasts of Frenchmen. If we follow the Christian maxim, of doing as we would that others should do unto us, we should try a different tone, and see what a little conciliation towards France would do.

I will tell you what is at the bottom of the whole of this cry in England about a French invasion. It is ignorance in the minds of the great masses of the people, as to what the real condition and circumstances of the French people are. I have told my friends who are met here from different parts of the country, and who are proposing to take steps for a vigorous agitation on behalf of peace, that the first thing they

have to do is to spread four or five lecturers over the face of
the land, to enlighten the public mind as to the state of
feeling in France. We have no danger, it is admitted on all
hands, from any other country. If it was not for this bugbear of France and the French invasion, there would be
lamentation and woe in some clubs in London, for I do not
think they could have any excuse for keeping up so large a
military and naval force. As to America, they do not give
us any excuse for keeping up our navy. If France was out of
the way, and we had only to look to and to be prepared for
competition with America, or even with Austria or Russia,
that would hardly afford us an excuse for keeping up our
present armaments. It is France alone that you are threatened with danger from, and I say that the people of this
country are alarmed with respect to France, simply because
they don't understand the circumstances of that nation; and,
being in ignorance, you may persuade them anything. It
is like blindfolding a man and spinning him round once or
twice. He then does not know where he stands, and you may
persuade him that anything in the world is coming to eat
him up; but unbandage his eyes, and he is not easily frightened. You must go through the country with lecturers,
deluge them with tracts, and show them the actual position
of the French nation. I tell you candidly my firm belief is,
and I am quite prepared to meet the consequences, that if
you will let the people of this country know the whole truth
as to the economical and social condition of the millions of
France, instead of their fearing that the French people are
coming to take anything they possess, they will be themselves possessed of a considerable amount of dissatisfaction
that their own condition, as a mass, is not equal to that of
the French. The French people coming here, like a band of
pirates, to take what the English people have! Why, you
have to deal with 8,000,000 of landed proprietors. A very
worthy friend of ours, who is now travelling in the south of

France, and who is known to most of my friends about me, has written within the last few days to us, that, as the result of his inquiries and investigation, the condition of the rural population of France is very superior to that of the English peasantry. The French peasantry are the proprietors of the land. When the man follows his horse to field there, he is turning up the furrows upon his own soil.

Now, do you think that is exactly the population to run over from their acres and come here on a mere marauding expedition? Our mistake is in judging the French people altogether by our own standard. It is true the French have not yet quite got an appreciation of the representative forms of government according to our machinery, and the habit of association and public meeting, and the freedom of the press which we have; it is because it does not enter into French feeling to appreciate these things. For instance, the French people have no Habeas Corpus Act, as we have in England, to give them the guarantee for their personal liberty. We attach the utmost importance to the inviolability of individual freedom, and I think we are quite right. But the French, though they have had three or four times possession of power in the streets, have never known one of their leaders, when he had absolute possession of their assemblies,—have never seen one of their democratic leaders getting up and inserting a fundamental clause in their Constitution to give them that protection which we have against any arbitrary and undue infringement of our personal liberties. Again, with regard to their habits of association and public meeting, it does not enter into the ideas of the French people to have public meetings such as we have, and discuss such questions as we do. It is not in their habits to do it. No class or party in the country has used it or adopted it with any general success. And, therefore, these things which we prize, the French, up to this time, have not shown that they attach much importance to. Now, the time may come when they may have

precisely the same feelings and views that we have with reference to these questions. The time may come. Recollect
that hitherto they have been about fifty or sixty years in
pretty constant and successive revolutions, so far as the political form of their Government goes. Well, but we had to
go through a century of revolution before we settled down.
From the time of the commencement of the civil war with
Charles I down to the time of our last civil war in '45, this
country passed through a whole century of revolutions. Give
them time, and perhaps at some future period the French
may have your tastes upon those questions to which you
attach so much importance.

And now I'll tell you the lesson I think we ought to learn
from the French having parted, apparently with so little
reluctance, from their representative form of government,
and their freedom of the press ; and the lesson, I say, is this
—that we English ought to learn—not to stroke our beards
and to thank Heaven we are not as other men ; but we ought
to say, 'Let us take care that our newspaper press shall be such
a useful organ, both in the cause of morality, of truth, but,
above all, so useful in the cause of international peace, that
the popular mind shall cling to it as an institution, and never
allow it to be infringed upon ; and let public men, leading
statesmen, be so truthful in their representative capacities ;
and let them show patriotism enough, that the people shall
have confidence in them, and cling to their representative
system, and not abandon it as the French have done, because
probably they have not found those attributes of which I am
speaking.' Now, what the French do, is this. Recollect I am
now, with all submission, indicating what I think is the line
necessary for peace lecturers to take, and whatever it is absolutely necessary to take, if we are to put an end to this howl
of a French invasion. What the French do prize, and we
don't prize much, is equality in social rank. The French
people have abolished and destroyed feudalism for sixty years,

completely. They don't tolerate any arbitrary rank or title, or any entails, or anything which can tend to give social inequality. They carry that principle of equality into their religious concerns; the French people won't tolerate one exclusively endowed religion, even although you had the Church selected that comprises nearly the whole population. All people are treated alike in France. Every religion is put upon a perfect footing of equality. So in the taxation, which is the most equal, fair system of taxation in the world; you could not have in France a probate and legacy duty upon one description of property and not upon another.

Now, I see that France could not have what we have in this country, because public opinion revolts at it. They would not have an hereditary House of Peers. Louis Napoleon would fall instantly—his throne would not be worth twenty-four hours' purchase if he were to attempt anything of the kind. Therefore, they have their tastes, and we have ours. They do not understand our tastes ;—I can vouch for it, from being a good deal among them, that they are very much puzzled at our little regard for this principle of equality which they attach so much importance to; but they discriminate, and they say, ' We envy you your jealousy of personal liberty; we wish we had it; we wish no man might have his personal freedom infringed. But that is not our taste. We have a passion for equality—you have a passion for personal liberty; and we should be better if we perhaps interchange a little and share our respective qualities.'

Well, now, I say, let the English people be told exactly what is the condition of French society. Let them understand, when we are told the French are coming here to rob our banks, that the French have had more silver in the Bank at Paris than we have had of gold and silver in the vaults of the Bank of England at the time that we were treating them as pirates who were coming to rob our Bank. Then we talk of their coming to carry off the various commodities we have in this country. There are more silver forks and spoons in France than in England, a great deal. If you were to go to a roadside public-house in France, you would get a napkin and a silver fork; and we know in all their private families the class of people who live in that style are much more numerous than they are with us; the spirit of equality keeps up a vast mass there who have not similar tastes or aspirations here; and, therefore, when we hear of the French coming to commit a piratical incursion upon our shores, we are dealing with a people who would not be bringing all their worldly wealth in their canoes, like the New Zealanders or the Malays, but with a people that in many respects are considered by the rest of the world more civilised than ourselves. The rest of the world imitates their dress, their language, their amusements, and not ours. We are dealing with a people having more portable property in their country than they would find here. Well, then, I say, to tell us all that of a people that have never molested us within the lifetime of any living being, is absurd. On the contrary, they have a good right to complain of a most aggressive attack upon their shores on the part of our aristocracy sixty years ago. Well, I say we are placing ourselves in the attitude of an insolent, impudent bully that goes about the streets holding up both his fists, and trying to incite peaceable men to attack him. I hope that we shall not separate until we have organised a plan by which we can spread this information, and a good deal more, through the country, in the interest of peace.

Now, something has been said about the financial reformers. I cannot understand what a financial reformer can be thinking of who expects ever to get any reduction of Government expenditure, or any remission of those taxes which are pressing us in so many places, unless he can hope to effect a reduction in our warlike expenditure. Now, take in round numbers—I won't trouble you with figures, but take in round numbers our expenditure: say eight-and-twenty millions

annually go to pay the interest of the debt incurred in past
wars,—I am sorry to say, aggressive wars; well, then, we
have about twenty-four or twenty-five millions more to pay.
Out of that, about sixteen millions go for our present warlike
expenditure.  Well, these invasionists tell us, that cannot be
reduced; and if the interest of the debt must be paid, which
we all admit, there you have twenty-eight millions and
sixteen millions, which make forty-four millions, that must
not be touched.  Then the financial reformers find some five
or six millions more, which make the whole expense of our
civil Government.  Ours is not an expensive Government,
really, for twenty-eight millions of people.  We can find no
fault with these six or eight millions.  But if the financial
reformers join in this great cry for more warlike armaments,
and give way to this red-herring drawn across our path in
the shape of an invasion, then, I think, they ought to close
their books and retire from business, and no longer call themselves financial reformers.

Now, gentlemen, if you can only destroy this wicked delusion, that is spread abroad respecting the conduct of France,
and the intentions of France, there is a very productive mine
still to be worked in this large amount of military and naval
expenditure.  I won't promise you that it shall be quite as
productive as the repeal of the Corn-laws, and yet I really
don't know but what, if you would give me the amount
which, by putting an end to this wicked spirit of animosity
which has crept between France and England, might be
fairly taken from our warlike expenses, and let me deal
with it in the readjustment of taxation, in the reduction
of taxation, I think I could so relieve industry by removing its trammels in the shape of custom-houses and ex-
cisemen, that I verily believe I could give a new lease to
trade, almost as profitable as that derived from the repeal
of the Corn-laws.  And if you tell me that this invasion
cry is founded in common sense and reason, that we must

be prepared with our present armaments and then increase them, I should be guilty of the grossest imposture in the world if I were to tell you that any appreciable diminution could be made in the amount of our Government expenditure. You must, in that case, make up your mind to bear it, and I advise those who advocate this expenditure to do it without grumbling, and without making wry faces over it. I would not, if I believed what these people tell me; I would pay my taxes with right goodwill, and be very glad indeed to pay my money for such security.

Well, now, one word upon that which is of most vital importance in any agitation which may be renewed from this time. We are going to make this a revival, gentlemen; this is to be a new start. Now, you will all remember—I am sure my friend, Mr. Sturge, will — in fact, he has said as much to me this very day himself, and, therefore, I need not appeal to him to confirm what I am going to say,—no taunts ever thrown upon me have ever, to this moment, that I am aware of, led me to open my mouth to say that I disavowed the principles upon which the Peace Society is founded, and that I don't profess to go the lengths which the members of the Peace Society go. I have been told, I confess candidly, by political friends as well as political enemies, that I was doing myself a great deal of harm by allowing it to be thought that I was opposed to all defensive armaments. My answer has been :—If anybody believes that of me, and chooses to make that a reproach to me, I don't suppose that if I disabused him it would do much good, for he would be sure to find something else, to invent something else; and, besides, I add, I have so much respect for those gentlemen who belong to the Peace Society, and see that they are doing so much good, that I don't feel disposed at all to say anything that should appear or be construed to imply anything like a slight or disapproval of their conduct. But it is very well known to my friend Mr. Sturge, and others with whom I have acted,—

and who know me very well, that although I am as anxious as
they are to put an end to war at once and for ever, and see
universal peace, yet that I was not educated in the principles
of the Society of Friends, and it is generally to our education
that we are indebted for our principles. And I have never
avowed—I should be hypocritical if I avowed—that I entertained the opinion, that, if attacked, if molested in an unprovoked manner, I would not defend myself from such an act of
aggression. Nobody, I presume, who wishes to do me justice,
ever dreamed that I would do so. But it was not necessary,
because I found everyone bullying and crying, ' We will remind them of Waterloo ; we will sing " Rule Britannia ;" we
will remind them of Trafalgar and the Nile ;'—it was not
necessary I should join in reminding them of that. But I
hold opinions which are held by the great body of my countrymen, and an unprovoked attack would find, I dare say, as
resolute a resistance from me as from many of those who are
now crying out in a panic, and who, I suspect, would be very
likely to run away from the enemy.

Now, the Peace Society has just as tolerant views towards
me as I have towards them. The Peace Society has never
attempted to coerce me into their principles of non-resistance.
I must say I have never found them attempting to make a
proselyte of me. They perfectly understand what my views
are on this subject,—that I will put an end to war if I can,
but will submit to no injustice if I can prevent it. Now, it
is intended from this time that we shall enlarge the scope
of this movement. We have met this morning, and we have
had a gathering which has reminded me of the good old time
of the League. I have seen at the very outset of this agitation noble-minded men put down their names for a sum of
money which we were glad to wind up with in our League
agitation after a five years' struggle—I have seen 500*l.* put
down to one name this morning ; and it is proposed that
there shall be not a new society, because the Peace Congress

Association forms the common ground on which all men may co-operate. We don't propose to found any new society, but we intend to extend the operations of that body which was founded when we began the Peace Congress which visited the Continent, and also sat in London. We intend that there shall be a more abundant supply of the sinews of war placed in the hands of your committee by the addition of some other names in Manchester and elsewhere; and we hope to set at work, not only with a machinery for inundating the country with printed papers for its information and instruction, but we hope to set four or five lecturers to work in visiting every borough in the country, and see whether we cannot counteract the poison that is being infused into the minds of the people. When I met one of my friends in the streets of Manchester yesterday, he said, ' Why, you have come at a very inopportune time for your Peace meeting; for everybody is in a panic, and thinks you wrong.' I said, ' Why, that is the very reason why we are here; there never was a time yet when it was so necessary for the Peace party to redouble their efforts as at present.' And I venture to predict that the creation of the militia, and the present cry for an increase of our armaments, will give a date for the downfall of this very system which we condemn. This insane and wicked attempt at misleading and exasperating the people will recoil upon its authors—there will be from this time but the beginning of a reaction; and we won't fail to profit by it.

Then our lecturers and our tracts will be directed to disabuse the public mind, in the first place, of the impression which is created with respect to the intentions of France. That is the first thing to be done, because there's where the danger is. Then let them deal with the economical view of the question—I mean the pressure of the enormous burdens on the industry of this country. Let our lecturers go and show what each town pays — why, I heard it stated that

Manchester has to pay 200,000*l.* as its share for our past wars, and for our present preparations. Let them go and show in all our towns and boroughs what are our economical objects. But don't let us lose sight of the still higher motives for peace. I have always been of opinion that the mainspring of this movement must be with those men who look beyond temporary concerns of any kind—who, instead of viewing this as a pounds, shillings, and pence question, or even a question of physical suffering, have an eye to the eternal interests involved in it. I say these are the men who are the mainspring of this movement. If anything be done to destroy the energy, or check the zeal, or to wound the consciences of those men who, from 1815 to the present time, when there was little attention paid to the question, kept the sacred lamp burning in the midst of contempt and contumely—if we do anything to disparage these men, I would not give a button for the prospect of this movement. And, therefore, our lecturers and tracts and publications must not only advocate the cause of peace on the ground of religious duty and the interests of morality, but they must not say one word that shall wound the convictions of those men who conscientiously believe in the inviolability of human life, and who would not resist to the death even to save their own existence.

Now, I know well that our opponents will try to make it appear that it is very inconsistent for men to co-operate together with such different objects, and for those who call themselves members of the Society of Friends to co-operate with others who stop short of their principle. Well, that is a new doctrine, at all events. It was not so when the French war broke out. I find that then the Society of Friends co-operated with Mr. Fox and his colleagues of the Whig party in trying to prevent that most unrighteous and most unhappy war of the French revolution. I find that Mr. Gurney, of Norwich, corresponded constantly with Mr. Fox in the House of Commons, and that Mr. Fox corresponded with Mr. Gurney, entreating him to get up a county meeting in Norfolk, and encouraging him to get up numerous petitions from Norwich; but I certainly never heard anybody among the Whig party saying that Mr. Fox was inconsistent in co-operating with Mr. Gurney to prevent that dreadful war, or saying that Mr. Gurney sacrificed his principles in lending his help to Mr. Fox; although, if they had come together and sought out their points of difference instead of seeking out their points of union, they would have found, very likely, that their principles were quite as opposite, as the principles I hold would be found if compared with those of my friend Mr. Sturge. But we shall not have from the present Ministry, I think, any cavilling—no, nor from their organs of the press either; we shall not, I should think, have any cavilling or criticising as to men co-operating who don't agree on all points.

I recollect that during the debate on the Militia Bill, a certain noble Lord, who is now filling a very important office in the present Government, somehow picked up a pamphlet, written by a gentleman to show the inconsistency of a clergyman joining a rifle club, and the object of the writer was to show that the taking of human life at all, under any circumstances, was inconsistent with a belief of the New Testament; but who, being pushed by his adversary to the logical consequences of his own argument, made sundry admissions which, to those who have not adopted these views, appeared somewhat absurd. Well, this noble Lord, I say, got this pamphlet, and very dexterously turned this pamphlet, written by this gentleman, who, I dare say, was very consistent and very honest in what he wrote—he turned its contents against us who were opposing the militia. Well, that noble Lord is now filling an important office in the Government of Lord Aberdeen. I think I remember, when the Earl of Aberdeen was Foreign Secretary under Sir R. Peel, that that noble

Lord, from 1841 to 1846, employed a vast deal of his time, when in opposition, in criticising and condemning, in no very measured terms, the principles upon which Lord Aberdeen's foreign policy was carried out. But I suppose the noble Lord must now have changed all his views on foreign policy since he took office under Lord Aberdeen; or if he has not, I suppose now that he will contend that it is not impossible for men to co-operate together without having identical views, and without being ready to go to the same extent in their views upon every question. If that be the case, I should hope that the noble Lord will, from the exigencies of his present situation, have learnt toleration for others, and that we shall hear no more of those taunts against men in the House of Commons who advocate the reduction of our armaments, or who resist the increase of those armaments, and who still may no more be identified with all the views of the Society of Friends than the noble Lord would be with all the foreign policy of the Earl of Aberdeen.

Gentlemen, our object here is business. You are here, from all parts of the country; and we have made a beginning in the essential part of our business this morning. At the meeting that has been held since the morning meeting, I think some four or five thousand pounds have been subscribed. It is proposed that it should be made up to ten thousand pounds, and that we go to work at once. Now, let us tell those people who have fancied they have it all their own way, for some time, in calling out for more soldiers, and in threatening us with a French invasion, that we are going to have a good deal to say upon that question, and they may expect to meet us in every borough and town in the kingdom. I presume that our friends who are here will take charge of counties; for instance, suppose my friend Mr. Bowley would take charge of Gloucester,—I was going, almost, as a challenge to him, to take charge of a county myself; but I certainly think that all those who are, as I am, imbued with the conviction that the present is a most critical time in the cause of Peace, should bestir themselves now. I hope they will, and that they will be ready, not only to give their time to it, in all parts of the kingdom, but that they will subscribe the sinews of war; and if it be only known through France that in Manchester, in the centre of the Free-trade agitation, surrounded by the very men who won that battle, there are men here now who are prepared to commit themselves, ay, and to commit liberally of their fortunes, to the agitation of this Peace question, and to the disabusing the minds of the people of this country as to the intentions and as to the condition of the French people,—I believe that if this be known in France, it will have more effect than anything that could possibly be done to counteract the mischievous effects which are being produced by those publications which are now issuing from the press.

# POLICY

## OF THE

# WHIG GOVERNMENT.

# POLICY

OF THE

# WHIG GOVERNMENT.

## MANCHESTER, JANUARY 23, 1851.

[The most important or engrossing public business discussed in the Session
of 1850 was the dispute between the Foreign Office and the kingdom of
Greece in the affair of Pacifico. Towards the end of the year occurred
what was called the Papal Aggression, the Pope having divided England
into dioceses. This act caused great excitement, and a law was passed,
under the name of the 'Ecclesiastical Titles Act,' prohibiting the Roman
Catholic prelates from adopting territorial designations. From the commencement the Act was a dead letter. In the following speech Mr.
Cobden commented on the apathy of the Government of Lord Russell.]

It used to be my practice, when I was agitating with my
friend Bright, to stipulate that I should speak before him,
and I need not tell you why. In entering this room to-night,
I was under the same difficulty that he has expressed. I
was not quite aware of the character of the present meeting;
but when I looked round, upon the countenances of the
gentlemen assembled, I perfectly understood the character
of the meeting. It comprises, I can vouch for it from personal knowledge, the pith and marrow of the Reform and
Free-trade party in South Lancashire. It comprises men
who worthily represent those who cannot be present in this
room,—men without whose co-operation no election can be
carried in South Lancashire, Manchester, or Salford, and
against whose opposition it is equally important to know
that no victory can be won. I appear here to-night as a

spectator and visitor, to be a witness of your reception of those who represent you in Parliament. I am glad to have had the opportunity of beholding the cordial, the kind, and the flattering reception with which you have greeted them. It is right they should be so received by you. They are the men who stand the brunt of abundance of abuse; they have to meet detraction coming from your own city, and professing to express your own sentiments. The shafts of calumny, the mean insinuations of base motives, are continually flung at them—those unfair weapons of political warfare which are never resorted to except when men are either conscious of a bad cause, or acting solely from personal pique and spite. This is the abuse and this is the calumny with which these men have to contend, not only in the arena where they have to fight your battles; but I repeat it, in the very city which they represent, whose best sentiments they express. It is right, when they have to bear the brunt of such attacks, that they should, when they meet you, receive the reward which you bestow upon them. But I, for my part, come here, not to answer to you for my conduct in Parliament, nor to share the tribute of respect and gratitude which you have bestowed upon them; it is as a listener and spectator that I rise here, at half-past ten o'clock, to say a few words; for, after the speeches you have just heard, I should be doing great injustice not only to you but to myself if I were to attempt long to arrest your attention.

This has been called a meeting to talk over all sorts of subjects. Now I am not going to deal in vague generalities. I do not mean to say that anybody who preceded me has done so, for they have been special enough; but I will not range the wide topics of political controversy. I will say, generally, that after we succeeded in the Free-trade controversy, I set myself a certain task in public life. I thought that the natural and collateral consequence of Free Trade was first to endeavour to give the people, along with physical comfort and prosperity, improved intellectual and moral advantages. I thought that the country which had bargained for itself to enter into the lists of competition with the wide world, seeking no favour, but asking only for a fair field and free competition, would set about to economise its resources, and in every way to attempt to mitigate a load of taxation which must impede the career of any nation that is unduly burdened in its competition with more favoured countries. I thought that, when we had said, 'We offer to trade with the whole world, and we invite the whole world to trade with us,' by that very declaration we told the wide world we sought peace and amity with them. Entertaining these views, I set myself the task, as a public man, of endeavouring, by every effort which, in my humble capacity, I could bring to bear, to stand prominently forward as the advocate of education, peace, and retrenchment. I do not come here to enter into a discussion on these questions, each one worthy of an essay by itself; but I will say this, that whilst upon all these subjects we have met with keen opposition, and upon two with obloquy and derision, I see such progress making, and made, as will encourage me to persevere in the advocacy of these principles with renewed and redoubled efforts. I find education assuming a prominence and importance, even by the admission of those who, until lately, have been opposed to it in every form, that I cannot have a doubt in my mind, that public opinion will be brought to bear on that topic with such irresistible force, that, ere long, we shall find a solution for this, which is one of the most difficult problems of our social existence. I find the question of peace, even in the eyes of those who have been attempting to ridicule its advocates, has become a leading topic of the day. Those who have derided us for helping forward the movement in favour of peace, do not hesitate to signalise this as an age which has the pleasing advantage over all preceding ages, of being characterised by symptoms which indicate that we are approaching an era when peace will become the maxim of the whole world. I find that what I told you in the Free Trade Hall, just three years ago,—that we might live to see the time when the expenditure which sufficed for 1835 would suffice again — is in process of being realised. We have already made such progress, that some four or five millions of reduction in our expenditure has taken place. I have no doubt that further retrenchments are going on at this very moment; and I now repeat, not only my conviction that we may return to the expenditure of 1835, but that we shall, ere long, attain that point, and that we shall not stop even there.

As fiscal questions will engage a good deal of attention in the ensuing Parliament, I would have you draw a rigorous distinction between two questions which are very often jumbled together, causing great confusion in the public mind. I mean the difference between a surplus caused by increased revenue, and a surplus occasioned by reduced expenditure. The Government comes forward with a surplus of 2,000,000*l*., arising from an increase in the receipts of the various existing taxes; and the Government is then too apt to take credit to itself for the great merit of having effected the super-abundant revenue. They do not tell you, and you are too apt to forget it, that this surplus is merely the effect of your having given out of your pockets 2,000,000*l*. more into the hands of the Chancellor of the Exchequer in one year than you did in the last year; and then the Chancellor of the Exchequer tells you, 'I have 2,000,000*l*. more than I estimated, I will return it to you.' 'Thank you for nothing,' is all you should ever say for that. But I wish that when the Chancellor of the Exchequer brings forward his Budget, you would look critically to the amount of the reduction of his Estimates for the next year's expenditure as compared with the Estimates of last year. If, in the ensuing session, the Chancellor of the Exchequer does that which he may

do, bring forward a reduction in our establishments, then you
may leave an estimated surplus over the expenditure of next
year of nearer 5,000,000l. than 2,000,000l.  The surplus
that is now being estimated is upon the present year's Estimates.  I want to see the next year's Estimates and the
Budget, that we may judge of the Government by their
Estimates, and not by any revenue they may have reached.
I am not going into any tedious fiscal argument to-night.  I
only want to take this opportunity of saying two words upon
a question which has been already alluded to.  I have not
since the close of Parliament addressed any audience upon
general political topics.  I have addressed peace meetings ;
I have addressed meetings of freehold land societies; I have
addressed education meetings; but I have addressed no
meeting where so wide a range of discussion and observation
has been permitted as is now open to us in this assembly.
I very much regret it, because I should like to say a few
words upon a controversy which has been raging in this
country for two or three months, and to which if I did not
refer I should be guilty of cowardice, seeing it is always my
practice to deal with the prominent topics of the day.  In
these few words I beg to say I speak to you solely as a
politician.  For the last two or three months there has not
been a calm in this country.  We have heard of a great
political calm, but there has been no calm.  On the contrary,
there has been an agitation.  It has, I admit, been mainly
sectional, but it has been widespread, and it has almost exclusively occupied the attention of the leading public prints.

I need not tell you that the question is that which is called
the 'Papal Aggression.'  The remark I wish to make is, that
the discussion of this topic, as a political topic, has overlaid,
arrested, and smothered for a time every other political topic.
It is well known that in this country the public mind entertains but one question at a time ; therefore the first remark
I wish to make is, that the discussion of this topic, as a

political topic, has prevented the public mind from occupying itself with fiscal questions, and questions affecting reform in the representation, and other questions which politicians have had for many years at heart, so that we approach the meeting of Parliament without the opportunity being afforded, or taken, by the country, of signalling to the Government the views we take upon those questions. I wish you to bear in mind that when we meet, ere another fortnight, in Parliament, our time will then, I fear, be very much occupied with the discussion of this same question; for, if we may believe Mr. Hugh Stowell in what he told us at a very large assembly, every political question, whether fiscal, social, or reformatory, must be suspended until this one great question be settled by the House of Commons. What, I want to ask, is this demand? Is this a question that can be settled by politicians? I speak as a politician. I may settle it in my own mind as a Protestant, and as a Protestant I may have my own opinions. I have my own opinions, for it is everybody's duty to have his own opinions, and if he has an aggressive opponent, I doubt if it be not his duty to defend actively the opinion he entertains—always, of course, as an individual. But I want to ask, if there is any reason why religious questions should not be removed out of the domain of politics, just as they are in the United States of America? Lord Carlisle, when he, I will not say descended from his seat in the Cabinet to deliver an address to the Mechanics' Institution of Leeds, but when he honoured himself by coming out of the Cabinet for that purpose, made a remark which, coming at the time it did, I think, expressed more than the ordinary meaning of the words, when he said, ' I confess I do envy the complete toleration which exists in the United States.' I think that was a significant expression, and might be taken, probably, to justify those who believe in the rumour, that the Cabinet is not quite united upon the question of Papal Aggression. In the United States, the Pope may ap-

point bishops whenever he pleases; he may parcel out that
vast Continent into as many dioceses as he pleases, including
even California; he may send as many cardinals as he pleases;
and no matter by what pompous phraseology all that be done,
the United States politicians, and the United States Legislature at Washington, would be perfectly indifferent to it all.
Why cannot we, in this country, as politicians, while giving
the same security to private and individual judgment, leave the
settlement of this question as it is in the United States? Is
it that we are so ignorant, or that we are so liable to be
misled? Then, I say, let us look sharp, and follow the advice
given by Mr. Lawrence, the American Minister, and educate
ourselves.

But I am told that the reason is that we have a State
Church in England. Well, but does a State Church render
the people of this country less able to protect themselves by
their own unaided judgment, knowledge, and sound sense,
from aggression? Are the people less able to protect themselves against error, because they have a State Church? Will
that be the confession? No. But the State Church has
been made the obstacle, or attempted to be made the obstacle,
in every parish, to the promotion of the same liberality that
exists in America, against every proposal with regard to
liberty, whether civil, religious, or commercial. There is no
advance made in the path of freedom of any kind, but we are,
and have been, continually threatened with obstruction by the
cry of 'The Church in danger.' Yet, I must say, that in
every case the partisans of the Church have found their predictions singularly falsified. After the repeal of the Test and
Corporation Act, after the accomplishment of Emancipation,
after the Reform Bill was secured, there was the same cry;
but I believe it will be admitted by both Churchmen and
Dissenters, that the Church never was so active and prosperous, never were so many churches built, and never had the
Establishment greater authority, than after the last of those

great reforms down to the present day.  Where, then, are the grounds for fear, on the part of Churchmen, for the security of the Church ?  But I say here that we will have toleration and religious freedom in this country, cost what it may.  I do not stand here as the advocate of the partisans of the Roman Catholic body.  As a politician, I do not presume to offer my opinions on the faith of any man.  On the polity of that Church, I might possibly be allowed to offer an opinion ; yet at the present moment, when county meetings are held and advertised (partly at the expense of Roman Catholics themselves, who pay rates as well. as Protestants) ; when, I say, so much abuse is lavished upon them, I should be loath to offer any observation upon the polity of that Church.  But I may be allowed to say that I am no friend to the organisation of the Roman Catholic body.  It is too centralising for me ; it is too subduing to the intellect for me ; and if I changed my religion at all, I should be as little likely as any gentleman in this room to go into their chapel, nay, as any one upon the face of the earth.  But, at the same time, let the Roman Catholics living in England judge for themselves, not only of their own faith and motives, but of the mode in which they would constitute the organisation that will always follow religious teaching.  Why should you dictate to the Roman Catholic bishops whether they will govern by a cardinal, an archbishop, or diocese ?  They do not come to me, as a politician, to ask me to give force and validity to their titles, or to give them stipends out of the public purse.  What right have I, then, as a politician, to come before a public meeting, or to get up in the House of Commons, and say a word upon the subject of their faith, or on the polity of the Roman Catholic Church ?

We shall be told pretty often, no doubt, that unless Government interferes, the privileges and prerogatives of the Queen of England will be invaded by the Pope,—not by Cardinal Wiseman.  Cardinal Wiseman is a British subject; he cannot invade the prerogative of the Crown without being guilty of high treason ; and if he is so guilty, let him be tried by the law.   But what prerogatives have been invaded by the conduct of the Pope?   Not the temporal prerogative. Why, the Pope has at this moment in his army a few thousand French and Austrian troops.   And I have it on the best authority, that if these troops were removed, dire would be the dismay and speedy the flight of the whole body, Pope and cardinals.   It is not, then, the army of the Pope that can threaten the temporalities of the Crown.   Are the temporal prerogatives threatened by sea?   You may have a list of the active naval force of the Pope ; it amounts to two gun brigs and a schooner.   Put one quarter of the effective service which is stationed on the coast of Sussex, and it would be quite sufficient to guard the whole island against the Pope's navy.   It is not, then, the temporal sovereignty or the secular privileges of the Queen that can be endangered by the Pope, but her spiritual dominion, we are told, is to be perilled.

Now are we, as politicians, who are called upon fairly enough to vote money for ordnance, and for shot and shells, to meet and repel the aggressive enemy that meets us with spiritual weapons?   Are we to forge the spiritual artillery with which we are to meet the aggression?   If we are, I beg you to consider how capitally we are suited in the House of Commons for that purpose.   I won't say a word to asperse the character of that body, of which I form a humble unit,—I mean the general character of that body, as a religious body. You may say, if you will, and believe, if you please,—I leave you to enjoy the pleasures of your credulity,—that a large majority of that House of Commons are living in an especial odour of sanctity and piety.   You may believe it, if you please ; I offer no opinion on it, for being one of the body, and having to face them in about a fortnight, I hope you will excuse my expressing an opinion on the subject.   But admitting, if you please, — admitting that we are, the great majority of us, eminent for our piety,—how are we constituted? Are we all Churchmen, owning the spiritual authority of the Queen? Why, we are about forty or fifty of us Roman Catholics, and, mark me, you will have a great many more Roman Catholics returned from Ireland at the next election. We have an Independent or two, we have three or four Unitarians, and we have a Quaker, I am happy to say, and I wish we had a good many more; and we have a fair prospect of having a Jew.

Now, is not that a very nice body of men to uphold the Queen's supremacy as the head of England's Church? Why, gentlemen, if you wanted to give us a task in the House of Commons which should last till Doomsday, and that we should therefore put off, as no doubt Mr. Hugh Stowell would require, all reforms, whether fiscal or parliamentary, till that remote day, then give us the task of settling this question of Papal Aggression. I say, give it to politicians to settle, if you want it never to be settled at all. As has been well expressed here by Mr. Bright, politicians have been at the work already for four or five hundred years. They have used every available method. They have tried fire and faggot: that is the most effectual means, I admit—but, then, you must exterminate also those who hold the opinions from which you differ. That was too shocking even for the sixteenth century, and so it was given up—I mean the attempt to exterminate those who professed these opinions. Then came the penal laws, which went every length short of extermination. What has been the tendency of the last century? Constant relaxation—a tendency more and more to religious toleration. What has been the course taken by the leading statesmen of this country? Why, to their honour be it said, the greatest and most illustrious statesmen of the last sixty years were so far in advance of the latent bigotry still existing in this country, that they were ready to sacrifice their fame— I mean such a fame as temporary popularity — they were

willing to forego place, patronage, everything which statesmen
and politicians hold most dear, rather than lend themselves to
the continuance of that system.   But I very much fear there
are men now in the Cabinet, who owe all their distinction
in public life to having been identified with that principle of
toleration to which we are constantly more and more pro-
gressing, but who are now ready to sully their fair fame, and
belie, I had almost said, the whole of their past political
career, on entering into the political session of 1851.   Gentlemen, I entreat you to remove this question of religious
opinions,—remove it out of the domain of politicians, if you
wish not only to make progress in those questions which we
cannot delay, and if you wish to prevent a retrograde policy.
It will not end in a mere return to the paths of religious
monopoly, but will be certain to conduct you into a retrograde track, in questions affecting our temporal interests, and
for which many of those who fancy themselves sincere, are
now lending their voices when they raise this cry for religious
intolerance.   I agree with Mr. Gibson completely, that if this
country permits one step backward, in the career of religious
toleration, you are endangering yourselves on questions in
which you feel most nearly interested.   I never felt the
slightest doubt in the world come across my mind on the
subject of retaining everything we have gained in the way of
social improvement, until I saw the account of a county
meeting in Essex, which has had its counterpart nearly in
every part of England, and at which Sir John Tyrell was one
of the most prominent actors, when he called for three cheers
for Lord John Russell.

Look at the actors throughout the country, in this present
movement against what is called the Papal Aggression.   Who
are they?   Have you seen those men advocating the repeal
of the Corn-laws?   Have you not seen in every case, that
the most prominent actors in these county meetings are the
men who resisted the establishment of that principle of com-

mercial reform? Let me ask you if by any accident,—such
accidents as may happen in our Constitution, which are pre-
cipitated at any moment, — you who entirely agree with
me upon the subject of commercial freedom, and generally
upon questions of liberal policy in secular affairs, let me ask
you to answer me this question: Suppose a general election
were to take place, and those who are prominent in opposing
religious toleration succeeded (and I am not sure that they
would not succeed), in returning to Parliament a majority for
re-enacting the disabilities and restrictions upon Roman Catholics, would not that be a majority that would either tamper
with the Corn-laws, or take care to indemnify themselves for
what has been taken from them? It is so; and those who
are acting have not been so discreet, in this case, as to
conceal their belief in the possibility of retrieving their monopoly. I say to those who have generally been favourable
to commercial freedom, who have been, in fact, friendly to
civil and commercial freedom, and who join in this cry,
and lend themselves to the support of this party who are
in favour of religious restrictions,—I say that they would, in
my opinion, bring back on themselves the commercial monopolies and political monopolies; and I say to them as
inconsistent men,—for I don't address myself to those who
oppose freedom in every shape,—but to those who were generally with us in advocating civil and commercial freedom,
—I say, if they gain the triumph of religious intolerance, and
if they gain along with it a monopoly in food, they richly
merit their fate.

But there is one thing that has been-said by those who
preceded me,—they have alluded to the bigotry, and fanati-
cism, and ignorance, which prevailed fifty years ago amongst
the mass of the people of this country. Now, there is one
symptom, and almost the only symptom, which has consoled
me in this agitation for religious disabilities, and it is this:—
the calm, passive, and, in many respects, contemptuous silence

and indifference with which it has been regarded by the
great mass of the people of this country.  If the same
tumults had occurred fifty or sixty years ago, owing to the
prevailing ignorance and bigotry of the mass of the people of
this country, half the Roman Catholic chapels would have
been in flames, and half their occupants' lives in danger.
And I thank the demonstration only for this : that it has
given me, more than anything else, a conviction of the great
progress that has been made in real intelligence by the
great mass of the people, especially in the north of England.
I will not say so much of the south.  And I cannot say
much for the Corporation of London.  Why, only think of
that Corporation professing to represent the City.  Only think
of it !  Last year it was setting itself up and agitating in a
ferment of enlightened intelligence and patriotism, in favour
of religious liberty to the Jews.  Now it is denouncing the
superstitious ceremonies of the Roman Catholics.  When has
there been such a spectacle, so absurd a spectacle, exhibited as
that which was shown, when the London Corporation took that
great gingerbread coach, the pattern of 200 years ago, and
clothed themselves in that Bartholomew-fair dress of theirs,
and took a man with a fur cap, whose pattern dates back,
I believe, five centuries, with a long sword in his hand, and
all the other paraphernalia of the Corporation of London,
and went down by the railroad to Windsor, in order to
present an address to the Queen, in order to put down—
Popish mummeries !  If you want to see mummeries, go and
see the Lord Mayor's procession.  I have seen the grand
ceremonies in the Vatican at Easter, I have seen the most
gorgeous religious processions the Church of Rome can boast
of, but I never saw anything half so absurd, or half so
offensive to intelligence or common sense, as the mummeries
in which the Corporation of London indulge every year.
Now I am glad to say of the north of England, that the
mass of the people here have not joined in this intolerant

outcry. I only regret that circumstances have prevented this meeting from being held in the Free Trade Hall, that I might have heard the cheer which I should have had from five thousand auditors, in expressing the sentiments I have just enunciated.

Now, gentlemen, only one word more, as a politician again, but not as a party politician, if you please. Something has been said about conduct or misconduct during the last session. I don't come here to answer to you, because I have not the honour of representing many of you. But this I will say, I am exceedingly tolerant of every Member of the House of Commons who strains a point to vote with the Government, provided he has been some fifteen or twenty years longer in the political arena than I have been. I believe my friend Mr. Brotherton, for instance, aims as much at benefiting the mass of the people in this country, in every form by which he can effect it, as I do; but I believe Mr. Brotherton has a stronger sentiment of reliance and sympathy towards the present Government than I have, and it is easily accounted for. Mr. Brotherton entered Parliament after the passing of the Reform Bill, and shared the struggles in obtaining that Bill, which I still regard, notwithstanding what Mr. Dyer said, a great progress in political reform. He shared all the struggles in carrying that Bill, and it is natural that he should have those sympathies. But I will say this in vindication of myself, that I entered somewhat at an advanced time of life for a man who has taken up the discussion of a public question, and I did it resolved to devote my labours to the solution of that question, without reference to the temporary interests or conveniences of any existing political party; and the result of that agitation in the case of the Corn-laws has convinced me that if anything is to be done in this country for the great mass of the people, if you are to succeed in establishing any reform of magnitude, it can only be done by the people out of doors, and in the House resolving to do that one thing, and totally disregarding the existing political parties in that House.

I desire to see something accomplished. I have set myself the task of accomplishing certain things, and amongst them that which is most dear to my heart is the advocacy of a more peaceful and conciliatory policy in the intercourse of nations, or, as I would especially say, in the intercourse between this country and weaker nations. If you want to wound my principles most acutely, it will be to show me England violating the principle of a conciliatory and humane policy when it has to deal with a weak Power, which is like a child in its grasp. I look upon inhumanity, rudeness, or violence, on the part of England towards a powerless state like Greece, with additional resentment, just as I should regard that man as a coward as well as a despot who molested and ill-used a child. Feeling, then, that my principles were violated in the case of Lord Palmerston, in the Greek affair, I voted against him on that occasion, and I should do so again, if ten thousand seats in Parliament depended on the issue of my vote.

Now, gentlemen, let me give one word of advice to those who are in Manchester or elsewhere, and take up a hasty conclusion against some of our Members, with whom you generally agree, and in whose judgment and sagacity you have some confidence, to beware how you take a side against them, merely because you see a certain line of policy argued in certain public prints. Give them credit for being wary : they have a better opportunity of sifting public men than you have. A man must be a fool, if he does not, after being in Parliament seven or eight years, and sitting in Committees with nearly all the Members, discover the motives of Governments when they are disclosed, not on the public arena, but where they are chatted over by friends in private. Depend upon it your Members will have rather better opportunities than you will have of judging the conduct of public men. And if you happen to think that Lord Palmerston, although

he did try to maintain a fixed duty long after Lord Aberdeen
had become the advocate of total repeal and untaxed bread,—
if, notwithstanding certain other symptoms I could mention,
which prove that Lord Palmerston is not the champion for
liberty that you suppose,—if, I say, notwithstanding you have
an impression in favour of Lord Palmerston, your Members
come to a different conclusion, why, give them credit for the
same honesty of purpose and intelligence with yourselves ;
and bear in mind, that they have the better opportunity of
forming an opinion than yourselves. I have no desire to
stand out singularly in my vote. As was well expressed
by Mr. Bright, it is a very unpleasant thing to do so ; it
would be far more agreeable to make companionship with
those men on the Treasury-benches, instead of treading on
their toes, and poking them in the ribs, and making them
uncomfortable. Is it any satisfaction to me, do you think,
that Lord Palmerston's organ, the *Globe*, has denounced me,
over and over again, as a disappointed demagogue, and hurled
language at me which no other journal, the *Times*, for instance,
has ever levelled at me ?   I know perfectly well that on the
Manchester Exchange, and the Leeds Exchange, and the Liverpool Exchange, where the *Globe* paper is taken, and is understood to be a Whig paper, when persons see it speak in such
terms of the Member for the West Riding, they are apt to
think there must be a great deal in it, and that the Member
must be making himself especially ridiculous in the House
of Commons.   I am not a disappointed demagogue ; if ever
there was anybody who ought to be satisfied with his public
career, it is I. I thank you for giving me the only response
which could relieve me from the imputation of great egotism
in saying so.

Well, as I said before, my position is not the same as that
of Mr. Brotherton. I cannot see the line of demarcation
between Whig and Tory which he sees. I cannot see what
principle the Whigs advocate which the Tories do not ad-

vocate. I find in Lord John Russell, in the House of Commons, not simply great impatience but petulance, and I had almost said great insolence, in his dealings, particularly in the remarks he has made to our friend, Mr. Bright. He, I am sure, is very indifferent to the remarks themselves, but they are sufficiently important as indicating the tone of the man who is supposed to be the leader of our party. I must confess that, in regard to fiscal matters, I am bound to say, I believe the Opposition party would do quite as much in the way of retrenchment as the Whigs; I am not sure that they would not do more. I believe Sir James Graham, for instance, would show less subserviency to the Duke of Wellington, in military arrangements, than Lord J. Russell or Lord Palmerston. I believe in Colonial policy, whilst Sir R. Peel resolutely refused to add another acre to our tropical possessions, the present Government are taking possession in Asia, as well as Africa, of tracts of tropical territory, which, I believe, notwithstanding anything that may be said to the contrary by the Manchester Association, are only calculated to entail additional expense upon us, instead of benefiting us, as a free-trading community ; and I fear that next session we shall be placed in a still worse dilemma. If we are to believe the reports that Lord J. Russell, instead of being the champion of religious liberty, is going to embark in a crusade against religious freedom, I shall then find myself still further alienated from the present party. But this I say: if I do not see that I have at least the liberty of voting in the House of Commons for something different to that which now exists,—if I cannot hope to see some change and some reform,—at least if I am not allowed the free advocacy of my own opinions for some distinct principle different from that which is now the rule of conduct with Whig and Tory,—why am I to be sitting up till twelve o'clock every night in the House of Commons? This disappointed demagogue wants no public employment; if he did, he might have had it before now.

I want no favour, and, as my friend Bright says, no title. I
want nothing that any Government or any party can give me;
and if I am in the House of Commons at all, it is to give my
feeble aid to the advancement of certain questions on which
I have strong convictions. Deprive me of that power; tell
me I am not to do this, because it is likely to destroy a
Government with which at the present moment I can have
no sympathy; then, I say, the sooner I return to printing
calicoes, or something more profitable than sitting up in the
House of Commons night after night in that way, the better
both for me and my friends. I have come here, then, merely
to renew personal acquaintances,—or rather, anxious by a
short sojourn in this neighbourhood and in Yorkshire, not
to lose old acquaintances which I highly prize and value. I
come, moreover, in order to have an opportunity of testing
the current of public opinion a little, and sounding its depth,
to see whether it be an unusual tide, or a steady, permanent
stream. I think this meeting has demonstrated to me, that
whatever exists in other parts of the country, here at least
there is no reaction; and that, remembering what are our
recorded opinions, you in Lancashire, and I hope my friends
in Yorkshire, will always be found true to the principles of
liberty and toleration.

# PARLIAMENTARY REFORM.

# PARLIAMENTARY REFORM.

## I.

### HOUSE OF COMMONS, JULY 6, 1848.

[On June 20, 1848, Mr. Hume moved the following resolution:—'That this House, as at present constituted, does not fairly represent the population, the property, or the industry of the country; whence have arisen great and increasing discontent in the minds of a large portion of the people; and it is therefore expedient, with a view to amend the National Representation, that the elective franchise shall be so extended as to include all house-holders, that votes shall be taken by Ballot, that the duration of Parliaments shall not exceed three years, and that the apportionment of Members to population shall be made more equal.' On July 6, the motion was rejected by 267 (321 to 84).]

I RISE under great disadvantages to address this House, after the hon. and learned Gentleman (Serjeant Talfourd) who has just sat down; and the difficulty of my position would be very much increased if I were called upon to address myself to this question in the manner, and with the eloquence and fancy, by which his speech has been distinguished; but I make no pretence to follow in such a track. I can only help observing, that the hon. and learned Gentleman has not given us any facts as the groundwork of his reasoning. There is one statement, however, made by the hon. and learned Gentleman, which is not a fact, but on which the opponents of my hon. Friend the Member for Montrose (Mr. Hume) seem very much to rely. The statement to which I allude is to this effect,—

н h 2

that the wishes of the country are not in favour of the change which my hon. Friend proposes. That assertion, as we all know, was made by the noble Lord the Member for London.

Now, it must be generally felt that this statement is of more importance than any other that has been uttered upon this subject.  On other subjects connected with the Government and Constitution of this country there may be much diversity of opinion; but I ask, is there any great diversity of opinion, at this moment, amongst the great class, who are now excluded from the franchise?  I put it to the noble Lord to say, does he, or do his friends, mean to say, or do they not, that the masses of the unrepresented population in this country have no desire to possess political power and privileges? Will any one utter such a libel on the people of England? Will any one say that they are so abject, so base, so servile, as not to desire to possess the rights of citizens and freemen? I have not believed, and I do not believe, that such are the sentiments of my fellow-countrymen.  I should entertain a very poor opinion indeed of the people of this country if I were to give a vote in favour of such a proposition; but yet it forms an important element in the reasonings of the Gentlemen who oppose my hon. Friend the Member for Montrose. If you admit the most evident truth that can come under the notice of any man, you must admit that at least six-sevenths of the male population of this United Kingdom are earnestly pressing for and claiming the rights which you are denying them.  I will go further, and tell the House that a very large proportion of the middle class regret that so many belonging to a humbler order of society than themselves should have been included amongst the unrepresented portion of the community.  They express a sincere desire that the franchise should be extended; they look with great interest to the result of this night's division; and I undertake to say, that you will find those Members of this House who represent large and independent constituencies, comprising, for the most

part, persons belonging to the middle class, you will find such Members voting with my hon. Friend—they are the men who will go into the lobby in favour of his motion. It is thus that the strongest and most useful appeal will be responded to by the great mass of the middle orders, and thus, I think, it will be shown, that the middle class entertain no such feeling of hostility against the admission of working men to political power as they are said to indulge. In proportion as the middle class are free and independent, in so far do they desire the freedom and independence of the rank nearest to themselves, in that proportion do they desire to open the portals of the Constitution to the poor man. Some hon. Members in this House have contended against this truth; but I take the liberty of saying, that I have for a long time been accustomed to watch the progress of opinion on this subject out of doors; and this I tell the hon. and learned Gentleman, and I can prove it, even to his satisfaction, that I have had better opportunities than he possesses of estimating the state of opinion out of doors upon this matter; and I beg to inform him, that this opinion in favour of my hon. Friend's motion has arisen spontaneously — that there has been no organisation; and the best proof of this assertion that I can offer is to be found in the fact, that the number of public meetings to consider, discuss, and petition upon this subject, has been no fewer than 130. I find it so recorded in the *Daily News,* and I repeat that this is a purely spontaneous movement. I have no hesitation in frankly acknowledging that we were five years agitating for a repeal of the Corn-laws, before we reached so advanced a point as that which the friends of the present question now occupy. Respecting the repeal of the Corn-laws, the mass of the people were said, truly enough, perhaps, to have been galvanized from a centre. But, with regard to the motion of my hon. Friend the Member for Montrose, the practice has been reversed; and whatever manifestations of opinion have been displayed out

SPEECHES OF RICHARD COBDEN.

of doors, they have arisen without any exertion of central
influence.

I do not say that all men are agreed upon this subject—
that there are no diversities of opinion ; but I say there is
much less of this than those who resist my hon. Friend's
motion at all like to see. We have had petitions from those
who favour the Charter, and from those who desire universal
suffrage, and very many in favour of the particular plan upon
which we are now speedily to divide. I have not anything
to say against those petitions in favour of the Charter, or in
favour of universal suffrage. I am not contending against
the right of a man, as a man, to the franchise—I mean the
right that a man ought to enjoy apart from the possession of
property ; but I feel I should not be justified in taking the
line of argument adopted by the hon. and learned Gentleman,
and by the noble Lord the First Minister of State, who
addressed himself to the advocates of universal suffrage, and
seemed to argue that they were more right than the advocates
of household suffrage. If he intends to vote for universal
suffrage, I can understand the force of that argument; but
as I am not going to oppose universal suffrage, and as I do
not stand here to support it, I leave him in the hands of the
advocates of universal suffrage, and, judging by what has
been done, they seem disposed to make the most of the argument which has been put into their hands.

I will not occupy the time of the House in discussing this
point further, but rather prefer to direct attention to this circumstance,—that the hon. and learned Gentleman did not
display his usual legal skill and knowledge in dealing with
the question of household suffrage, for it certainly is not
surrounded with the difficulties which the right hon. and
learned Gentleman has imagined. To judge from his speech,
it would seem to be the law, that no one except the landlord
and occupier of a house enjoys a vote in right of that house.
Surely the hon. and learned Gentleman ought to have known

that the Court of Common Pleas has decided that lodgers paying more than 10*l.* annually, and rated to the poor-rates, are entitled to be placed on the list of voters—that is to say, in cases where the landlord does not live on the premises. That is the state of the law as established by the Reform Act, and my hon. Friend seeks only to extend that privilege a little; it therefore can scarcely be considered a matter difficult of arrangement. The mere extension of the existing rule gets rid of all difficulty, and gives the franchise to prudent young men—too prudent to marry and take houses with insufficient means; to them, being lodgers, and paying a rent exceeding 10*l.*, the plan of my hon. Friend gives the franchise. The law of the land already goes very near to this.

The allusion which the hon. and learned Gentleman made to the case of Cooper must be fresh in the recollection of the House. I am sorry he alluded to that part of Cooper's career, who, I believe, greatly regrets those events, and would be glad to forget the part that he took in the affair at the Staffordshire Potteries. I again say, I am sorry that the subject was introduced here, for we want no additional examples to prove to us that a very good poet may be a very bad politician. The object of the motion of the hon. Member for Montrose is, that he may bring in a bill for the purpose, among other things, of giving votes to householders; that is to say, that parties not only paying taxes to the country, but rates to the poor, should have a voice in the election of Members to this House. In advocating this principle, we are really acting on the theory that exists as to the franchise of this country; for we say that the people of this country elect the Members of this House. Is that sham, or is it reality?

Now, if there is one thing more than another that the people do not like, it is sham. The people like realities. The theory of this country is, that the people like political power; and there is nobody responsible, as the hon. and learned

Gentleman in his poetical flight seemed to imagine, for the
education of the people and the preparation of them for the
political franchise. If there had been any such responsible
parties, the thing would have been done long ago. But, I
ask, what danger is there in giving the franchise to householders? They are the fathers of families; they constitute
the laborious and industrious population. What would be
endangered by giving this class the franchise? When our
institutions are talked of, I always hear it said that they live
in the affections of the country, and that the Queen sits en-
throned in the hearts of the people; and I have no fear of
danger from any such wide extension of the suffrage as we
now contemplate. I do not believe that it would lead to any
change in the form of our government. I say, God forbid
that it should. I sincerely hope, if there is to be a revolution
in this country in consequence of which the monarchical form
of government shall give way to any other form, that that
revolution may happen when I shall be no longer here to witness it, for the generation that makes such a revolution will
not be the generation to reap the fruits of it. I do not believe that the people of this country have any desire to change
the form of their government, no do I join with those who
think that the wide extension of the suffrage, of which we
now speak, would either altogether or generally affect a
change in the class of persons chosen as representatives. I do
not think that there would be any great change in that respect. The people would continue, as at present, to choose
their representatives from the easy class,—among the men of
fortune; but I believe this extension of the suffrage would
tend to bring not only the legislation of this House, but the
proceedings of the Executive Government, more in harmony
with the wants, wishes, and interests of the people. I believe
that the householders, to whom the present proposition would
give votes, would advocate a severe economy in the Government. I do not mean to say that a wide extension of the

suffrage might not be accompanied by mistakes on some
matters in the case of some of the voters; such mistakes
will always occur; but I have a firm conviction that they
will make no mistake in the matter of economy and retrenchment. I have a firm conviction, that, if proper political power were given to the people, the taxation necessary
for the expenditure of the State would be more equitably
levied.

What are the two things most wanted? What would the
wisest political economists, or the gravest philosophers, if they
sat down to consider the circumstances of this country, describe as the two most pressing necessities of our condition?
What but greater economy, and a more equitable apportionment of the taxation of the country? I mean, that you
should have taxation largely removed from the indirect
sources from which it is at present levied, and more largely
imposed on realised property. This retrenchment and due
apportionment of taxation constitute the thing most wanted
at present for the safety of the country; and this the people,
if they had the franchise now proposed, would, from the
very instinct of selfishness, enable you to accomplish. Let
me not be mistaken. I do not wish to lay all the taxation
on property. I would not do injustice to any one class
for the advantage of another; but I wish to see reduced,
in respect to consumable articles, those obstructions which are
offered by the Customs and Excise duties. You ought to
diminish the duties on tea and wine, and you ought to remove
every exciseman from the land, if you can; and I believe that
the selfish instinct—to call it by no other name—of the great
body of the people, if they had the power to bring their will
to bear on this House, would accomplish these objects, so
desirable to be effected in this country.

Then where is the danger of giving the people practically
their theoretical share of political power? We shall be told
that we cannot settle the question by household suffrage; and I

admit that by no legislation in this House in 1848 can you settle any question. You cannot tell what another generation or Parliament may do. But, if you enfranchise the householders in this country, making the number of voters 3,000,000 or 4,000,000, whereas at present they are only about 800,000, will any one deny that by so doing you will conciliate the great mass of the people to the institutions of the country, and that, whatever disaffection might arise from any remaining exclusion (and I differ from the hon. and learned Gentleman, who thought that more disaffection would thereby be created), your institutions will be rendered stronger by being garrisoned by 3,000,000 or 4,000,000 of voters in place of 800,000?

The hon. and learned Gentleman has expended a great deal of his eloquence on the question of electoral districts. Now, when you approach a subject like this, with a disposition to treat it in the cavilling spirit of a special pleader, dealing with chance expressions of your opponents, rather than looking at the matter in a broad point of view, it is easy to raise an outcry and a prejudice on a political question. But, as I understand the object of the hon. Member for Montrose, it is this,—he wishes for a fairer apportionment of the representation of the people. He said that he did not want the country marked out into parallelograms or squares, or to separate unnecessarily the people from their neighbours; and I quite agree with the hon. Member for Montrose, that his object can be attained without the disruption of such ties. The hon. and learned Gentleman dealt with this question as if we were going to cut up some of the ancient landmarks of the country, as the Reform Act cut up some counties in two, and laid out new boundaries. But I will undertake to do all that the hon. Member for Montrose proposes to do without removing the boundary of a single county or parish; and, if I do not divide parishes or split counties, you will admit that I am preserving sufficiently the old ties. I must say that I consider this question of the reapportionment of Members to be one of very great importance.

When you talk to me of the franchise, and ask me whether I will have a man to vote who is twenty-one years of age, and has been resident for six or twelve months, whether a householder or lodger, there is no principle I can fall back upon in order to be sure that I am right in any one of those matters. I concur with those who say that they do not stand on any natural right at all. I know no natural right to elect a Member to this House. I have a legal right, enabling me to do so, while six-sevenths of my fellow-countrymen want it. I do not see why they should not have the same right as myself; but I claim no natural right; and, if I wished to cavil with the advocates for universal suffrage, I should deal with them as I once good-humouredly dealt with a gentleman who was engaged in drawing up the Charter. He asked me to support universal suffrage on the ground of principle; and I said, ' If it is a principle that a man should have a vote because he pays taxes, why should not, also, a widow who pays taxes, and is liable to serve as churchwarden and overseer, have a vote for Members of Parliament ? ' The gentleman replied that he agreed with me, and that on this point, in drawing up the Charter, he had been outvoted; and I observed that he then acted as I did,—he gave up the question of principle, and adopted expediency.

I say that, with respect to the franchise, I do not understand natural right ; but with respect to the apportionment of Members, there is a principle, and the representation ought to be fairly apportioned according to the same principle. What is the principle you select? I will not take the principle of population, because I do not advocate universal suffrage; but I take the ground of property. How have you apportioned the representation according to property ? The thing is monstrous. When you look into the affair, you will see how property is misrepresented in this House ; and I defy any one to stand up and say a word in defence of the present system. The hon. Member for Buckinghamshire alluded the other night to the representation of Manchester and Buckinghamshire, and made a mockery of the idea of Manchester having seven representatives. Now, judging from the quality of the Members already sent to this House by Manchester, I should wish to have not only seven such Members, but seventy times seven such. I will take the hon. Member's own favourite county of Buckingham for the sake of illustration, and compare it with Manchester. The borough of Manchester is assessed to the poor on an annual rental of 1,200,000*l.*, while Buckinghamshire is assessed on an annual rental only of 760,000*l.* The population of Buckinghamshire is 170,000, and of Manchester 240,000; and yet Buckinghamshire has eleven Members, and Manchester only two. The property I have mentioned in respect to Manchester does not include the value of the machinery; and, though I will grant that the annual value of land will represent a larger real value of capital than the annual value of houses, yet, when you bear in mind that the machinery in Manchester, and an enormous amount of accumulated personal property, which goes to sustain the commerce of the country, is not included in the valuation I have given, I think I am not wrong in stating that Manchester, with double the value of real property, has only two Members, while Buckinghamshire has eleven. At the same time, the labourers in Buckinghamshire receive only 9*s.* or 10*s.* a week, while the skilled operatives of Manchester are getting double the sum, and are, consequently, enabled to expend more towards the taxation of the country.

If this were merely a question between the people of Buckinghamshire and Manchester,—if it were merely a question whether the former should have more political power than the latter, the evil would in some degree be mitigated, if the power really resided with the middle and industrious classes; but, on looking into the state of the representation of the darling

county of the hon. Member, I find that the Members are not
the representatives of the middle and industrious classes, for I
find that eight borough Members are so distributed as, by an
ingenious contrivance, to give power to certain landowners to
send Members to Parliament.   I will undertake to show that
there is not more than one Member in Buckinghamshire
returned by popular election, and also that three individuals
in Buckinghamshire nominate a majority of the Members.
If called on, I can name them.   What justice is there in, not
Buckinghamshire, but two or three landowners there, having
the power to send Members to this House to tax the people of
Manchester ?   When this matter was alluded to on a former
occasion, the hon. Member for Buckinghamshire treated the
subject lightly and jocosely, as regarded the right of Manchester to send its fair proportion of Members to this House, and
that jocularity was cheered with something like frantic delight
in this House; but I think this is the last time such an argument will be so received.   I maintain that Manchester has
a right to its fair proportion of representatives, and I ask
for no more.

I will now refer to the case of the West Riding of Yorkshire.   That contains a population of 1,154,000; and Wilts
contains a population of 260,000.   The West Riding is rated
to the poor on an annual rental of 3,576,000*l.*, and Wilts on
an annual rental of 1,242,000*l.*, yet each returns eighteen
Members; and when I refer to Wilts, I find six of its boroughs down in *Dod's Parliamentary Companion* as openly,
avowedly, and notoriously under the influence of certain pa-
trons, who nominate the Members.   I hold in my hand a list
of ten boroughs, each returning two Members to Parliament,
making in all twenty Members; and I have also a list of ten
towns in the West Riding of Yorkshire which do not return
any Member; yet the smallest place in the latter list is larger
than the largest of the ten boroughs having two Members
each.   Is there any right or reason in that?   According to a

plan which I have seen made out, if the representation were fairly apportioned, the West Riding of Yorkshire should have thirty Members, whereas it now has eighteen only.   We do not wish to disfranchise any body of the people,—we want to enfranchise largely; but what we would give the people should be a reality, and they should not be mocked by such boroughs as Great Marlow, where an hon. Gentleman returns himself and his cousin; as High Wycombe, Buckingham, and Aylesbury; but there should be a free constituency, protected by the ballot.

With respect to Middlesex, the assessment to the poor is on an annual rental of 7,584,000*l.*; and the assessment of Dorsetshire is on an annual rental of 799,000*l.* Yet they both have fourteen Members, while the amount of the money levied for the poor in one year in Middlesex is as large within 6*l.* as the whole amount of the property assessed to the poor in Dorsetshire.   The assessment to the poor in Marylebone is on an annual rental of 1,666,000*l.*, being more than the annual rental of two counties returning thirty Members.   Why should not the metropolis have a fair representation according to its property?   I believe that the noble Lord at the head of the Government did intimate a suspicion of the danger of giving so large a number of Members to the metropolis as would be the result of a proportional arrangement.   I am surprised at the noble Lord holding such an opinion, as he is himself an eminent example and proof, that the people of the metropolis might be entrusted safely with such a power.   I observed, that in the plan for the representation in Austria, it was proposed to give Vienna a larger than a mere proportional share in the representation, because it was assumed that the metropolis was more enlightened than the other parts of the country.

Now, notwithstanding all that may be said to the contrary, I maintain that the inhabitants of your large cities—and of a metropolis especially—are better qualified to exercise the right of voting than the people of any other part of the empire; for they are generally the most intelligent, the most wealthy, and the most industrious. I believe that the people of this metropolis are the hardest-working people in England. But where is the difficulty ? An hon. Gentleman has objected to large constituencies, on the ground that Members would then be returned by great mobs. Now, my idea is, that you make a mob at a London election by having too large a constituency. Some of your constituencies are too large, while others are too small. Take Marylebone, or Finsbury, with a population of between 200,000 and 300,000; the people there cannot confer with their neighbours as to the election of representatives. But you may give a fair proportion of representatives to the metropolis; and you may lay out the metropolis in wards, as you do for the purpose of civic elections. I do not undertake to say what number of electors should be apportioned to each ward, that is a matter of detail; but if the subject were approached honestly, it would not be difficult to come to a satisfactory conclusion. I believe that if the metropolis were laid out in districts for the election of Members of Parliament, the people would make a better choice of representatives than any other part of the kingdom. Do not be alarmed by supposing that they would send violent Radicals to Parliament. You would have some of your rich squares, and of your wealthy districts, sending aristocrats; while other parts of the metropolis would return more democratic Members. It is a chimera to suppose that the character of the representation would be materially changed; the matter only requires to be looked into to satisfy any one that it is a chimera. I tell you that you cannot govern this country peaceably, while it is notorious that the great body of the people, here in London and elsewhere, are excluded from their fair share of representation in this House. I do not say that you should have an increased number of representatives. I think we have quite as many representatives in this House as we ought to

have; but if yon continne the present number of representatives, you must give a larger proportion to those communities
which possess the largest amount of property, and diminish
the number of Members for those parts of the country which
have now an undue number of representatives. You cannot
deal with the subject in any other way; and you cannot prevent the growing conviction in the public mind, that whatever franchise you may adopt—whether a honsehold or a 10*l.*
franchise—you must have a more fair apportionment of Members of this House. Do not suppose that this is a mere question of mathematical nicety. No; where the power is, to that
power the Government will gravitate. The power is now in
the hands of persons who nominate the Members of this
House,—of large proprietors, and of individuals who come
here representing small constituencies. It is they who rule
the country; to them the Government are bonnd to bow.
But let the great mass of the householders, let the intelligence
of the people be heard in this House, and the Prime Minister
may carry on his Government with more security to himself,
and with more security to the country, than he can do with
the factitious power he now possesses.

Upon the ballot I will say but a few words; and for this
reason — because it stands at the head of those questions
which are likely to be carried in this House. I mean, that
it has the most strength in this Houso and in the country
among the middle classes, and particularly among the
farmers, and among persons living in the counties. Some
hon. Gentlemen say, 'Oh!' They are not farmers who say
' Oh, oh !' they are landlords. The farmers are in favour
of the ballot. I will take the highest farming county—
Lincolnshire. Will any one tell me that the farmers of
Lincolnshire are not in favour of the ballot? I say this
question stands first; it will be carried. Why, no argument is attempted to be urged against it, except the most
ridiculous of all arguments, that it is un-English. I main-

tain that, so far from the ballot being un-English, there is more voting by ballot in England than in all the countries in Europe. And why? Because you are a country of associations and clubs,—of literary, scientific, and charitable societies,—of infirmaries and hospitals,—of great joint-stock companies,—of popularly governed institutions; and you are always voting by ballot in these institutions. Will any hon. Member come down fresh from the Carlton Club, where the ballot-box is ringing every week, to say that the ballot is un-English? Will gentlemen who resort to the ballot to shield themselves from the passing frown of a neighbour whom they meet every day, use this sophistical argument, and deny the tenant the ballot, that he may protect himself not only against the frowns but against the vengeance of his land-lord?

As to triennial Parliaments, I need not say much on that subject. This, also, will be carried. We do not appoint people to be our stewards in private life for seven years; we do not give people seven years' control over our property. Let me remind the House that railway directors are elected every year. Something has been said by the Prime Minister as to the preference of annual to triennial Parliaments. I think I can suggest a mode of avoiding all difficulty on this point. Might it not be possible to adopt the system pursued at municipal elections—that one-third of the members should go out every year? I mention this only as a plan for which we have a precedent. If one-third of the Members of this House went out every year, you would have an opportunity of testing the opinion of the country, and avoiding the shocks and convulsions so much dreaded by some hon. Gentlemen.

I will only say one word, in conclusion, as to a subject which has been referred to by the hon. and learned Member for Reading (Mr. Serjeant Talfourd) and the hon. Member for Buckinghamshire (Mr. Disraeli). They complain that

leagues and associations were formed out of doors, and yet
in the same breath they claim credit for the country that it
has made great advances and reforms.  You glorify yourselves that you have abolished the slave-trade and slavery.
The hon. and learned Gentleman has referred, with the
warmth and glow of humanity by which he is distinguished,
to the exertions which have been made to abolish the punishment of death.  Whatever you have done to break down any
abomination or barbarism in this country has been done by
associations and leagues out of this House; and why?  Because, since Manchester cannot have its fair representation
in this House, it was obliged to organise a League, that it
might raise an agitation through the length and breadth of
the land, and in this indirect manner might make itself felt
in this House.  Well, do you want to get rid of this system
of agitation?  Do you want to prevent these leagues and
associations out of doors?  Then you must bring this House
into harmony with the opinions of the people.  Give the
means to the people of making themselves felt in this House.
Are you afraid of losing anything by it?  Why, the very
triumphs you have spoken of—the triumphs achieved out of
doors—by reformers, have been the salvation of this country.
They are your glory and exultation at the present moment.
But is this not a most cumbrous machine? — a House of
Commons, by a fiction said to be the representatives of the
people, meeting here and professing to do the people's work,
while the people out of doors are obliged to organise themselves into leagues and associations to compel you to do that
work?  Now, take the most absurd illustration of this fact
which is occurring at the present moment.  There is a confederation, a league, an association, or a society,—I declare I
don't know by what fresh name it may have been christened,
formed in Liverpool, a national confederation, at the head of
which, I believe, is the brother of the right hon. Member
for the University of Oxford, Mr. Gladstone, a gentleman

certainly of sufficiently Conservative habits not to rush into anything of this kind, if he did not think it necessary. And what is the object of this association? To effect a reform of our financial system, and to accomplish a reduction of the national expenditure. Why, these are the very things for which this House assembles. This House is, *par excellence,* the guardian of the people's purse; it is their duty to levy taxes justly, and to administer the revenue frugally; but they discharge this duty so negligently, that there is an assembly in Liverpool associated in order to compel them to perform it, and that assembly is headed by a Conservative.

It is not with a view of overturning our institutions that I advocate these reforms in our representative system. It is because I believe that we may carry out those reforms from time to time, by discussions in this House, that I take my part in advocating them in this legitimate manner. They must be effected in this mode, or they must be effected, as has been the case on the Continent, by bayonets, by muskets, and in the streets. I am no advocate for such proceedings. I conceive that any men of political standing in this country —any Members of this House, for instance—who join in advocating the extension of the suffrage at this moment, are the real conservators of peace. So long as the great mass of the people of this country see that there are men in earnest who are advocating a great reform like this, they will wait, and wait patiently. They may want more; but so long as they believe that men are honestly and resolutely striving for reform, and will not be satisfied until they get it, the peace and safety of this country—which I value as much as any Conservative—are guaranteed. My object in supporting this Motion is, that I may bring to bear upon the legislation of this House those virtues and that talent which have characterised the middle and industrious classes of this country. If you talk of your aristocracy and your traditions, and compel me to talk of the middle and industrious classes,

I say it is to them that the glory of this country is owing.
You have had your government of aristocracy and tradition ;
and the worst thing that ever befel this country has been its
government for the last century-and-a-half.    All that has
been done to elevate the country has been the work of the
middle and industrious classes ; and it is because I wish to
bring such virtue, such intelligence, such industry, such
frugality, such economy into this House, that I support the
Motion of the hon. Member for Montrose.

# PARLIAMENTARY REFORM.

## II.

[The object of the meeting held at the London Tavern, and of which Mr. Samuel Morley, now Member for Bristol, was Chairman, was to advocate the scheme of the Metropolitan and National Freehold Land Association. Mr. Cobden's Speech introduced the following resolution :—' That this meeting is of opinion, that the Freehold Land movement, adapted, as it is, to the varied position and circumstances of all classes of the people, is calculated to improve the parliamentary representation of the country.']

If I understand the character of this meeting, it is assembled solely for business purposes. We are the members and friends of the Metropolitan and National Freehold Land Society, and we meet here to promote the objects of that society. It is an association framed for the purpose of enabling individuals, by means of small monthly contributions, to create a fund by which they may be enabled, in the best and cheapest way, to possess themselves of the county franchise. You will see, then, that this society has a double object in view: it is a deposit for savings, and a means of obtaining a vote. Now we don't meet here to-day, as a part or branch of the Birmingham Society, which was formed a few days ago, and called the Birmingham Freeholders' Union. That is a society composed of individuals, from all parts of the kingdom, who choose to subscribe to it, for the purpose

of enabling a committee in Birmingham to stimulate
throughout the country by lectures, and by means of a
periodical journal called the *Freeholder*, to be published on
the first of next month, the formation of freehold land
societies. We do not meet as part of an agitating body,
but merely to promote the objects of the Metropolitan and
National Freehold Land Society. The plan of that society is,
to purchase large estates—large, comparatively speaking, and
to divide them amongst the members of the association at
cost price. In that explanation consists the main force and
value of this association. The principle, you will see in a
moment, is calculated to give great advantages to those who
wish to join associations of this kind. I know that some
gentlemen, who have given their attention to building societies, will say that this is not a building society. Why, the
building societies, as they are called, are none of them, strictly
speaking, building societies. They may be properly called
mutual benefit security societies ; but this Freehold Land Association is enrolled under the Building Society Act, and certi-
fied by Mr. Tidd Pratt, the revising barrister ; and the object
is, that members of the association shall have all the benefits
the Act of Parliament can give them, and all the security it
confers ; and we propose to give them some other additional
advantages. It has been said by those who look closely into
the rules of this association, ' You have no power under the
Building Act to purchase estates and divide them.' That is
perfectly true. We have no such powers; but the directors
will, at the risk of the parties who buy the estates, undertake
to purchase land, and to give the members of this association
the refusal of that land. So that our object is to give you all
the benefits of the Building Societies Act, and also the refusal
of portions of the estates which have been bought at the risk
of others.

I need not tell you, that a great deal of the success of all
associations of this kind depends, first, on correct calculations

being made in framing the society; and next, and, perhaps,
most of all, on the character and stability of those who have
the responsible management.  Now, with regard to the calculations on which this society is founded, I should be very
sorry to allow this opportunity to pass, without coming to a
perfectly clear understanding with all who are concerned in
the association, as to what I propose, as a member of the
board of directors, to undertake to do towards the share-
holders.   It has been stated that we undertake to find a
freehold qualification for a county at a certain sum, say 30*l.*
I believe that, in the first prospectus, that sum was stated ;
but, when I heard of it, I stipulated that it should be withdrawn, for I will be no party to any stipulation of the kind.
I do not appear here, having myself land to sell.   All I
promise you is, that, while I remain for twelve months as a
responsible director, all the property bought shall be divided
without profit, and that the members of the association shall
have its refusal at cost price.   But, whether it cost 20*l.*, or
30*l.*, or 40*l.*, or 50*l.*, is a matter to which I do not undertake
to pledge myself, because it is a matter which I cannot
control.   It has happened, at Birmingham, that many persons
obtained as much land as gave them a qualification for as
little as 20*l.*, but that may be a lucky accident.   I will not
be a party to any pledge that we shall procure land for others
on equally favourable terms.

Well, having cleared the ground, so that there may be no
misunderstanding, I next come to the consideration of the
character of those who have the direction of the affairs of the
society.   I am very happy to see our chairman (Mr. S.
Morley) here on this occasion.   He is one of the trustees,
and I need not tell you that he stands very well in Lombard
Street.   The other trustees are responsible men ; not merely
responsible in point of pecuniary circumstances, but men, any
one of whom I should be happy, were I making my will
to-morrow, to leave as trustees for my children, of every

farthing I had in the world. This is the only test you can, with safety, apply. If you have not men, whose private characters will bear such a test as that, you had better have nothing at all to do with them in public matters. Besides the trustees, you have the board of directors. I have attended every meeting of the board of directors when in town, and there is not one of the gentlemen I have found at the board whom I should not be happy to meet in private life, and to call my friend. I believe, therefore, leaving myself, if you please, out of the question, that the affairs of the association are in truly responsible and honourable hands. And here I beg not to be misunderstood. We do not come here to puff ourselves off at the expense of other associations. There are other societies formed, or forming, and, no doubt, their directors are as trustworthy as those of our association. We are not so badly off in England that we cannot find honour and honesty enough for every situation in life. You will get the strictest integrity for 20s. a week, and as much as you wish to hire.

It has been objected (and I confess there was some difficulty in my mind on the subject) that, in working an association of this kind, you may not be able to find freehold property, in convenient situations, or of convenient size, to carry out the movement. There may be that difficulty; but there are difficulties in every useful undertaking in this world, and there always will be. Those who make it their business to turn a green eye on our proceedings, will, no doubt, find plenty of difficulties; but, from every inquiry I have made, since my connection with the board of directors, I believe that there will be no insurmountable obstacle in working out our plan. It is perfectly true that, in seeking property, you may not find it at your own doors. If you live in a street in this metropolis, you may not be able to buy building-land in the immediate neighbourhood of your own residence, but you must be content to go farther from home, just as you would in other investments. One man buys Spanish bonds, and another Russian and Austrian bonds. Others, again, buy railway shares, which are running all over the country, and some of them running away. But give me a freehold investment in the earth, which never does run away, and it does not matter whether it is in my own parish or not, so that I have good title-deeds, and receive my rent by the penny post. I need not care, then, whether I see it or not. With that proviso, that you cannot always get land at your own doors, I do not see any difficulty in qualifying a person in the county in which he resides, with a freehold franchise. Many people think, that the only object for which they should buy land is, to build a house upon it; but there are other ways of disposing of it. Gardens, for instance, than which nothing is more sure of a rent; for if you buy land in the neighbourhood of any town, that land is always increasing in value; since, whatever the Corn-laws may have done to the agriculturist, you may depend upon it that, if food be cheap, population will be increasing in towns, and land, in the neighbourhood of towns, will increase in value. Whatever the foreigner may send us in the shape of wheat, he cannot send us garden-ground.

Now, for the purpose of illustration, I will take the case of Surrey. Many of you, I have no doubt, come from the other side of the river. I will suppose, then, that our friend Mr. Russell, the indefatigable solicitor of this association, whom I have had the pleasure of knowing and co-operating with for many years, has heard that there is a bit of land to be sold in the neighbourhood of Guildford. I will suppose that there is a farm, or one hundred acres of land to be sold, within a mile or two of that town, and that Mr. Russell goes, with one of the directors, to look at it. They get a valuer to examine it; and, having learned the price at which this farm can be bought, they buy it; and then, instead of letting the hundred acres to one farmer, they determine to cut it up into plots of one or two acres. Now, if the shopkeepers and mechanics of the town were told that this land was to be let, I will venture to say that there is not one of the plots which would not let at the rate of 40*s*. an acre.

I know the avidity with which the peasantry in our towns and villages take half an acre or an acre of land. It is an article which is in greater demand than any other. I could find land in Wiltshire, which is, I am sorry to say, let to the peasantry at the rate of 7*l*. or 8*l*. an acre. I am supposing that a person wished to buy as much land as would give him a county vote, but, living in a borough, did not require land for his own purposes. Such a person might let his acre of land for 40*s*., in the form of garden allotments, without any difficulty.

And here I wish much to guard myself against being supposed to countenance a very popular, but, in my opinion, a most pernicious delusion. I would not have it imagined that I am a party to the plan of transferring people from their employments in towns to live on an acre or two of land. If a person leaves a workshop, a foundry, or a factory, and tries to live on even two or three acres of land, why, all I can say is, that he will be very glad to get back to his former occupation. No, no; we have no such scheme as that. If a man has followed a particular pursuit, whatever it may be, up to the age of five-and-twenty, and if he is still receiving wages or profit from that pursuit, that man had better, as a general rule, follow his business than go to any other. In ninety-nine cases out of a hundred he will succeed better in that pursuit than in any other to which he can turn his hand. But what we say is this, that it is a very good thing for a man who is receiving weekly wages to have a plot of land in addition. Nothing can be more advantageous to people living in the country than to have, besides their weekly wages, a plot of ground, on which they can employ themselves with the spade, when they have not other employment. With the proviso which I have mentioned—guarding myself against being supposed to be a party to the delusion to which I have alluded—I say, that if you have a freehold qualification in the neighbourhood of an agricultural town at a distance from you, but in the same county, even in that case the security will be good, the rent will be received, and the value of your plot of land will always be increasing instead of diminishing. If your object be to get a vote, and to have along with that vote a freehold property, even at the worst, if you cannot get a bit of garden-ground near the metropolis, you can always get it in the county. The freehold being in the county, you can claim to vote in any part of that division of the county. If the property be situated at one end, you can poll at the other. I have looked at this matter with some care, and, I will confess, with some suspicion; and I must say that I see no difficulty in the way of everybody qualifying, and obtaining good security for his money.

I have explained practically what is the object of this association; suppose I go a little more widely into the question. Leaving our immediate practical object to others who will follow me, and who will answer any questions that may be put to them, let us look at this matter generally. Now, here we are, standing in the ancient ways of our Constitution. Nobody can say that we are red republicans or revolutionists. Here we are, trying to bring back the people to the enjoyment of some of their ancient privileges. Why, we have dug into the depths of four centuries, at least, to find the origin of this 40s. freehold qualification. But now, as to the practicability of our plan, as a means of effecting great changes in the depository of political power in this country. That is the question. Can you by this means effect a great change in the depository of political power? Because I avow to you that I want, by constitutional and legal means, to place, as far as I can, political power in this country in the hands of the middle and industrious classes ; in other words, the people. When I speak of the middle and industrious classes, I regard them, as I ever did, as inseparable in interest. You cannot separate them. 'I defy any person to draw the line where the one ends and the other begins. We are governed in this country—I have said this again and again, and I repeat it here to-night—we are governed, in tranquil and ordinary times, not by the will of the middle and industrious classes, but by classes and interests which are insignificant in numbers and in importance in comparison with the great mass of the people. Every session of Parliament, every six months that I spend in the House of Commons, convinces me more and more that we waste our time there—I mean the seventy or eighty men with whom I have been accustomed to vote in the House of Commons, and to whom your chairman has alluded in terms of so much kindness—I say, we waste our time in the House of Commons, if we do not, in the recess, come to the people, and tell them candidly that it depends upon them, and upon them alone, whether any essential amelioration or reform shall be effected in Parliament. I repeat, that in ordinary times we are governed by classes and interests, which are insignificant, in real importance, as regards the welfare of the country; and if we did not occasionally check them—if we did not, from time to time, by the upheaving of the mass of the people, turn them from their folly and their selfishness,—they would long ago have plunged this country in as great a state of confusion as has been witnessed in any country on the Continent. Take the class of men who are ordinarily returned by the agricultural counties of this country. What would they do, if you let them alone? Nay, what are they trying to do at this moment? Why, at the very time, when even the Austrian Government is proposing to abandon the principle of high restrictive tariffs; when the Government of Russia has in hand a reduction of duties ; when America has participated in the spirit of the times; when Spain, which some wicked wag has called the

'beginning of Africa,' has imitated the example set by Sir R.
Peel three years ago; these county Members and Members
for agricultural districts are thinking of nothing but how
they may restore protection.  Surely such people must be the
descendants of those inquisitors who put Galileo into prison!
Galileo was imprisoned because he maintained that the physical world turned upon its axis, whereas these men insist
that the moral world shall stand still; and, if left to themselves, they would soon reduce England to the state in which
Austria is now.  But is it a wholesome state of things, that
nothing can be done in this country except by means of great
congregations of the people forcing the so-called representatives of the people to something like justice and common sense
in their legislation?  Nothing of importance is ever done by
Parliament until after a seven-years' stand-up fight between
the people on the one side, and those who call themselves the
people's representatives on the other.  Now, I say that this
is an absurd state of things, and that, by constitutional and
moral means, we must try to alter it; and I believe that we
have now before us a means by which such an alteration can
be effected.

I am here speaking on a subject to which I have given
much attention for many years.  It is more than six years
since it was attempted to secure the repeal of the Corn-laws
by means of the 40s. franchise, as part of the tactics of the
Anti-Corn-Law League.  I should be sorry to claim to myself
exclusively the merit of first suggesting it.  I rather think
that Mr. Charles Walker, of Rochdale, recommended it before
I announced it publicly.  But from the moment that the plan
devised was put forth at a great meeting in Manchester, I
never doubted of the ultimate repeal of the Corn-laws; although until then I could never conscientiously say that I
saw a method by which we could legally and constitutionally
secure their abolition.  I will give you the result of our labours
at that time in two or three counties.  You know that the

West Riding of Yorkshire is considered the great index of public opinion in this country. In that great division, at present containing 37,000 voters, Lord Morpeth was, as you are aware, defeated on the question of Free Trade, and two Protectionists were returned. I went into the West Riding with this 40s. freehold plan. I stated in every borough and district that we must have 5000 qualifications made in two years. They were made. The silly people who opposed us raised the cry that the Anti-Corn-Law League had bought the qualifications. Such a cry was ridiculous. The truth was, that men qualified themselves, with a view of helping the League to obtain the repeal of the Corn-laws; and you are aware that, in consequence of this movement, Lord Morpeth walked over the course at the next election. We followed the same plan in South Lancashire, and with a similar result. Our friends walked over the course at the next election, although at the previous one we had not a chance. My friend, the Member for East Surrey (Mr. Locke King), joined us in carrying out our plan in his division; and its adoption was there also attended with success. I am not sure that it would not have been better in some respects if the Corn-laws had not been repealed so soon—though of course I should like to have had them suspended for three or four years; for in that case we should have carried half the counties of England. Now, when I came back from the Continent, after the repeal of the Corn-laws, I told my friends — (I have never disguised my feelings from that day to this)—as the result of constant reflection for several years, ' If you want to take another step, constitutionally and legally, you must do it through the 40s. freehold; by no other process will you succeed.'

Let us talk this matter over, as men of common sense. Ask yourselves how do you purpose to obtain reforms? Do you intend to try violence and fighting? No, no; you see the result of that everywhere that it has been tried. Violence does no good to those who resort to it. I do not mean to blame those in other countries, who have not the right of meeting in assemblies like this, if they do not pursue the same course that we do. I do not blame them, because, being without experience, and not being permitted to gain experience, they do not succeed, when they make a bold and sudden trial of constitutional forms. No; I leave those to blame them, who will blame us equally, for adopting constitutional means. The very same parties who are now so intolerant, with regard to the failure of Hungarians, and Italians, and Germans, were the constant assailants of my friends and myself, at the early stage of the League agitation. Every species of abuse, every sort of misrepresentation, every kind of suppression, was resorted to by them, until we became strong; and when we were both strong and fashionable, we were beslavered with their praise; and I confess I liked it less than their abuse. No; we do not come here to censure other countries. England is under no necessity for resorting to force or violence. Our ancestors did all that for us, and they were obliged to do it. During the greater part of the seventeenth century, England presented a scene of commotion almost as great as that which has been witnessed in Hungary, Germany, and Italy; and to the great sacrifices then made, we owe almost all the liberties we possess at present. But to go back to the kind of warfare pursued in the seventeenth century, would be to descend from the high position, which, at the expense of so many sufferings, our ancestors obtained for us.

But as everybody admits that we must not go into the streets to fight, let me ask my friends what other step they intend to take? Petition Parliament! Petition Parliament to reform itself! Why, no; the clubs would not like that; it would not suit their cards. Nobody thinks of getting a reform of Parliament by petitioning. Well, then, how are you to get it? I find that every person is brought to the same dead lock, as regards substantial reform or real retrenchment, that I was in

when, in 1843, I sat down to think of the freehold movement.
You must aim at the accomplishment of your object, through
the plan which the Constitution has left open to you. Men
of common sense, when they have a certain thing to do, look
round for instruments for effecting their purpose. In other
countries, men who resort to physical force, always adopt
that plan. They adapt their tactics to the physical features
of the country. If the people of Switzerland have to fight
for their liberties, they retire to the mountains, and there
defend them; in Hungary, the army of the people, retreat-
ing beyond barren heaths, puts two rivers between itself
and the enemy; while the patriots of Holland in former days
cut their dykes and let in the water to drown their enemies.
These are the means adopted by parties who have to use
physical force. What are we to do, who have to fight with
moral force? Why, here is a door open, which is so expan-
sive that it will admit all who have the means of qualifying
themselves through 40s. freeholds. These are our tactics—
these are our mountains—these our sandy plains—these our
dykes. We must fight the enemy by means of the 40s.
freehold.

Now, what chance have we of succeeding? I have paid a
great deal of attention to this subject, and I shall proceed to
trouble you with a very few figures, from which you will be
astonished to find how little you have to do. We have as
near as possible at this moment a million of registered electors for the whole kingdom. According to a valuable return
made on the motion of Mr. Williams, the late Member for
Coventry, the total number of county votes on the register
in 1847 was 512,300. What proportion of them do you suppose are the votes of occupying tenants? 108,790. All that
boasted array of force, which constitutes the basis of landlord
power in this country, and about which we have frightened
ourselves so much, amounts only to 108,790 tenants-at-will
in the fifty-two counties of England and Wales. Why, half

the money spent in gin in one year would buy as many
county freeholds as would counterpoise these 108,790 tenant-
farmers. What resources have we to aid us in the process
of qualifying for these counties? I shall surprise you again,
when I inform you how very few people there are who are
qualified for the counties. I will take, for illustration, three
or four of the counties at random. There is Hampshire :
there are in Hampshire, according to the last census, 93,908
males above twenty years old. The registered electors in the
same county amount to 9223; so that only one-tenth of the
adult males are upon the register, and 84,685 are not upon it.
In Sussex, there are of males above twenty years old, 76,676 ;
of registered electors only 9211, or one-eighth of the entire
number of adult males : 67,466 adult males are not voters.
Take the purely agricultural county of Berkshire, which has
43,126 males above twenty years old ; 5241, or one-eighth,
was the number of registered electors ; 37,885 are not voters
for the county. In Middlesex, the numbers I find are as
follows :—males above twenty years old, 434,181 ; registered
electors, 13,781, or one-seventeenth ; 420,400 not being
voters. In Surrey, the males amount to 154,633 ; of these,
9800, or one-sixteenth, is the proportion of registered electors ; and thus 144,833 are not voters. Why, if only one in
ten of the men who are not qualified to vote in London
and Southwark, would purchase votes in the neighbouring
counties, it would almost suffice to carry every good measure
that you and I desire. In round numbers, there are sixteen millions of people in England and Wales; there are four millions
of adult males above twenty years of age. There are 512,000
county electors in the fifty-two counties of England and
Wales ; so that at this moment there is but one in eight of
the adult males of England and Wales who is upon the
county register, and seven-eighths of them have no votes.
That is our ground of hope for the future. We must

induce as many as we possibly can of these unenfranchised people to join this association, or some other association; or by some means endeavour to possess themselves of a vote.

I do not disguise it from you, there is a class in this country that has not the means of finding money to purchase a vote. The great bulk of the agricultural peasantry, earning 8*s.*, 9*s.*, 10*s.* a week—it is impossible that you can expect that any considerable portion of that class can possess a vote; but when I speak of the mechanics and artisans of our great towns, I will say, there is not one of them that, if he resolutely set to the work, may not possess the county franchise in a few years; and, having the county franchise, who will not be in a position to help his poorer and humbler neighbour.

I am perfectly well aware that this is work that cannot be done in a day; and, if it could be done in a day, it would not be worth doing. I have no faith in anything that is done suddenly. My opinion is, that no very great change in the policy or the representation of this country will be effected in less than seven years. Many great struggles have lasted seven years. The great war of independence in America took seven years; the civil war, in which our ancestors were engaged against prerogative, in the reign of Charles I, lasted seven years; the Anti-Corn-law contest lasted seven years. I think we might assert of these great public questions, that the danger is, that when you have effected your object suddenly, you do not know how to value it, and have not the conviction that it is valuable and worth preserving. That is the great advantage of having to struggle some time for a great object; and I tell you candidly, when I enter on this 40*s.* movement, it is with the idea that it will be a long and arduous struggle. I am prepared, if health and strength are given to me, to give some portion of every working day for the next seven years to the advancement of this question. I do not propose this in exclusion of other reforms ; I do not propose this as an obstacle to any other plan which other persons may have in view. If anybody thinks he can carry reform in Parliament by any other plan than this, I hope he will show us how he would do it; I do not see any other way. Let no one who has any other popular object or great reform to carry in this country—if he does not co-operate with us, let him not look disparagingly at our efforts; for I tell him, that in proportion as this 40*s.* freehold qualification movement makes progress, just in that proportion will he find that the votes of the House of Commons on all liberal questions, will also make progress. And when I say that it may be necessary to work for seven years to accomplish this object—that is, to effect a great change in the depository of public power in this country (for this is the object, and I avow it), although it may be necessary, that for these seven years there should be continuous work in this matter, it does not follow you will not reap the fruits long before the seven years are expired. They are wise people in their generation whom we wish to influence. They gave up the Corn-laws, for they saw the question was settled when we carried South Lancashire, the West Riding, East Surrey, and Middlesex. I always said, if we can carry these counties, they will give up the Corn-laws.

In proportion as you exert yourselves for this great movement, you will become powerful. Every class of men that sets itself vigorously to work, by means of the 40*s.* qualification, to place as many as possible of that class on the register, will find itself elevated, politically and socially, by the position it has given itself. Take the mechanical class. Nothing could so elevate them in the eyes of their countrymen as to know they had a voice in the representation of the country— that the knights of the shire were partly indebted to them for their election. Take the class of Dissenters. Their very existence is ignored by the County Members; the most moderate measure of justice they ask is the removal of church-rates.    I do not believe that there are ten County Members who would vote for that moderate instalment of justice— [from the meeting, ' Not five !']—perhaps not five ; but I have heard the most insulting language from County Members towards Dissenters on that very question.   Why is it? Because this numerous and really influential body of men have not had self-respect enough to guard themselves, by the possession of the franchise, so as to be in a position to protect their religious liberties, by the exercise of the dearest privileges of free men.   Throughout the country you will find great bodies of Dissenters, who are religious men, moral men, and, which always is the consequence of morality, men who keep themselves from those excesses which produce poverty and degradation; and these are the very men who ought to possess the franchise.   We tell them to place themselves on the county list.   We do not wish to give them complete dominion and power in the country.   I say to no class, come and gain exclusive power or influence in the country; I am against class legislation, whether from below or above; but I say, if you wish to have your interests consulted—your legitimate rights respected ; if you wish no longer to have your very existence ignored in the counties ; then come forward, and join such a movement as this, and by every possible means promote the extension of the 40s. freehold qualification.

In conclusion, let nobody misunderstand me.   I do not come here to seek this or that organic change, without having practical objects in view, which I believe to be essential for the interests of this country.   I believe our national finances to be in a perilous state.   I say that the extravagant expenditure of the Government is utterly inconsistent with the prudent, cautious, economical habits, which the great body of this people are obliged to follow.   I want to infuse the common sense which pervades the bulk of the people into the principles of the Government, and I declare I see no other way of doing it but by increasing the number of voters, and no other way of doing so, independent of the House of Commons, but by joining yourselves to this movement, and possessing the 40*s.* freehold.

# PARLIAMENTARY REFORM.

## III.

### MANCHESTER, DECEMBER 4, 1851.

[The subject of Parliamentary Reform occupied the attention of the House of
Commons for a short time during the session of 1851, for Mr. Locke King
carried the first reading of a bill to reduce the county franchise, on Feb. 20,
an occurrence which was followed by a Ministerial crisis. In the country,
however, the feeling in favour of Reform grew till it was arrested by the
Russian war, and the circumstances which followed that war.]

I FEEL too much commiseration for you to delay you more
than a very few minutes with any remarks upon this important question. I have been sitting on a comfortable chair
with a back to it, and have been surveying the scene before
me, and I have felt my heart melt at the position in which
you must be placed. And after all, gentlemen, there is
nothing new to discuss about the matter that is before us.
There have been four propositions, as old as the hills almost,
that have been now submitted to this meeting. We have
had a discussion in a Conference this morning for five hours ;
this Conference resulted simply in declaring itself in favour
of those four points, which Mr. Hume has for four successive
years been bringing before the House of Commons,—household
suffrage, with a right to lodgers to claim to be rated and to
be upon the rate-books,—triennial Parliaments,—a re-distri-

bution of electoral power, and the ballot. Why, gentlemen, these four points have been subjected to a discussion, within the House and out of it, which I am sure renders it impossible for any one to say anything new upon the subject here. There may be persons who think that this programme of Mr. Hume, who is as honest, and sincere, and disinterested, as any man in this assembly or out of it, does not go far enough to satisfy the demands of all. On the other hand, I have no doubt there will be many people who will laugh at us, and treat with scorn a demand which they will consider so unreasonable, because so great.

Well, now, household suffrage is the old recognised Saxon franchise of this country. The whole community in ancient times were considered to be comprised in the householders. The head of the family represented the family; the heads of all the families represented the whole community. With the addition of a clause which shall give to those who are not themselves householders, but who may become so, the right to claim to be rated, I think the rate-book of this country may be taken now for as good a register as it could have been in the time of our Saxon ancestors. When you have a re-distribution of the franchise proposed, no one would suppose that you could continue to give Manchester and Harwich the same number of representatives. It does not require an argument; the figures that the chairman gave you are sufficient to settle the point. There is not an argument that can be used to enhance the force of those figures. We don't propose—Mr. Hume never proposed — that you should cut the country into parallelograms in a new fashion; he has always said in the House of Commons,—we have always said in the country,—that we will take the ancient landmarks and respect them as far as we can. Keep to the bounds of your counties; group boroughs together where they are too small to have a representative of their own, that by such means you may get an equalisation of political power, a fair distribution of the franchise, which alone can give anything like a fair representation to the whole country.

Well, we come to triennial Parliaments. Many people say it ought to be annual; in America they say biennial; some people say triennial; we had friends at the Conference who were for quinquennial Parliaments. I think we have precedents for three years' Parliaments in the old custom of the country; but as there is a ground of union sought on that question, I think there can be very little difference about reformers who are in earnest agreeing to the extent at least of triennial Parliaments.

Well, now, I come to another question, to which I confess I attach great importance—I mean the ballot. Give us the franchise extended, with the other points alluded to, and yet they will be comparatively worthless unless you have the ballot. The ballot in other countries has been adopted as necessary to the protection of the voter. You have never had, I believe, a large representative system anywhere without the adoption of the ballot; but it is perfectly necessary that you should have the ballot in this country, because in no country in the world where constitutional government exists, is there so great an inequality of fortune as in this country, and so great an amount of influence brought to bear upon the poorer class of votes. And I don't confine my advocacy of the ballot merely to protecting the farmers or the agriculturists; give me the ballot also to protect the voter in the manufacturing districts; for you may depend upon it that you have quite as glaring an evil arising from the influence of great wealth and station, in your electoral proceedings in Lancashire and Yorkshire, as you have in any purely agricultural district.

Now, go into any borough like Stockport, or Bolton, or any other neighbouring borough; give me the names of the large employers of labourers, and I will tell you the politics of the men employed by these capitalists, by knowing the politics of the capitalists themselves. Nine-tenths of them in ordinary circumstances vote with their masters. Why is that? Is there any mesmerism, or any mysterious affinity which should make men think the same as those who happen to pay them their wages? No; it is from an influence, seen or unseen, occult or visible, I don't care which, but it is an influence which operates upon the mind of the labouring class. But they have a right to a vote without any such restriction, or any such coercion. I want the ballot to protect everybody in their votes from the influence of everybody else. I want it as a protection against landlords, manufacturers, millowners, priests, or customers; and I for one would look upon any Reform Bill—I don't hesitate here to declare it— as nothing than delusive, that does not comprise the ballot; and I don't call myself, and never will own myself, as a member of any political party, the heads of which set themselves absolutely in opposition to the ballot.

Now, other questions admit of modification, and other difficulties also admit of being surmounted by electoral bodies themselves, and their representatives, without going to Parliament at all. For instance, though the Parliament won't give a vote to a man, there's a way by which some men may get a vote without going to Parliament to pray for it. Though you don't get triennial Parliaments, there's a way by which constituents can arrange with their representatives, as is often done, and make a bargain with them that they will come every year to give an account of themselves, and to receive their re-election. . So with the question of the redistribution of the franchise. Well, we all know that that is a question, after all, so vague, that a greater or a less degree of adjustment may be pleaded as meeting our demands, and I don't see how you can lay hold of any defined principle by which you can secure a fair and equal re-adjustment of the representation; but when I come to the ballot, it is something ay or no; you have the whole thing, or you have nothing;

and you cannot get it without an Act of Parliament. And I
say, I take my stand upon the ballot as a test of the sincerity
of those who profess to lead what is called the Liberal party in
this country.

Now I, once for all, beg to state that, according to my
opinion, settled now for three or four years, ever since the
passing of the repeal of the Corn-laws, when parties were all
broken up, I have never considered that we had a political
party in this country, nor a Whig or a Liberal party: we
have had a Free-trade party to fight for and maintain the
Free-trade victory ; that party is as much a Sir Robert Peel
party as a Whig party; but I have always thought that the
necessities of parties, and the difficulties of carrying on
business in the House of Commons, for want of a party
organisation, is no longer to be rendered necessary, and that
as the time must come, and come speedily, when everybody
would admit that Free Trade was a matter of history, and no
longer to be made a bugbear for maintaining this or that party
in the ascendant ; so the time must come when there must be
a reconstruction of parties, and that there should be now a
bid made to the country, by which there could be a reconstruction of what is called the Liberal party. Well, now,
I once for all state that, not recognising the bonds of party
in any way, since the time of the passing of the Corn Law
Bill,—feeling that I as much belonged to Sir James Graham's
party as I did to Lord John Russell's party from that
moment, I wanted to see where there would be a flag hung out
that would warrant me in ranging myself under that organisation, without adding the gross imposture of pretending to
belong to a party, when I knew there was no bond of union
or sympathy existing between us.

Now, I say, I take the ballot as one test, and it is the smallest
test I will accept, of the identity of any political party with
myself and my opinions. And I say more, that if any body
of statesmen attempt to carry a Reform measure, and launch

it on the country with the idea of raising such an amount of enthusiasm as shall enable them to pass such a measure; and if they think that the constituencies will allow that Ministry to leave the ballot out of it, they are under a very gross delusion, and don't know what they're about. In fact, it is more palpable every day and every hour, that what the people have fixed their minds upon as one of the points in the new Reform Bill, is the ballot. Why, listen with what acclamation the very word was mentioned here;—there was a perfect unanimity in the Conference this morning, amongst the men who met from all parts of Lancashire and Yorkshire, upon the subject; and I venture to say, that if you take what is called the Liberal party in this country,—that party which is reckoned upon by your Reform Ministry as a support to them in carrying any measure of reform in the House of Commons, I have no hesitation in saying, that nine-tenths of that party are in favour of the ballot; and that being the case, there being a greater unanimity out of doors amongst the Liberal party upon the ballot than on any other question, I say it would be the most absurd, and most inconceivably unreasonable thing on the part of the leaders of that so-called Liberal party, to think that that which constitutes the greatest bond of union amongst the party, should be left out in the programme of their Reform Bill.

I can understand that people should have their doubts about the efficiency of the ballot. I am not intolerant at all with people who tell me that we are deceived with respect to the ballot; who say, ' I don't think it would cure this drunkenness or demoralisation, or that coercion or intimidation would cease; I don't believe that it would prevent many of these evils;'—I can fully understand that there may be a difference of opinion about it; but I never can understand how a person calling himself a reformer, should set himself up resolutely to oppose the ballot; that he should make a point at all times to speak against it, and to quarrel with those who advocate the ballot ; that I can't understand ; and I must confess, that so far as I am concerned, I can have no party sympathy with any leaders who do take that course in repudiating and opposing the ballot.

Now, gentlemen, I have only to say in conclusion, that I have seen to-day a meeting at the Conference this morning which has exceedingly gratified me, because I there met men from all parts of these great counties, and other parts of the kingdom, among whom were some whom I saw thirteen years ago this very month, when we began another struggle, which, after seven years, was successful, for the repeal of the Corn-laws.    I have seen great numbers of those men to-day, meeting in Manchester, some of them more mature in age, I am sorry to say, for the thirteen years that have elapsed, but as earnest and resolute in giving their adhesion to what they believe to be the interest of the great mass of the people, as ever they were in the contest for free trade in corn.    Yes, it is a good augury when you find men who possess the sinews of war, as these men do, joining the rank and file of the people in their efforts to obtain political justice.    And don't let anybody persuade you, the working classes, for a moment, that you can carry out any great measure of political reform, unless you are united with a large section of the middle and capitalist classes ; and don't let anybody persuade you, either, that you have an especial quarrel with those rich millowners and manufacturers down here.    For I will tell you, the result of my observations and experience is this : that of all the rich men in the country, the most liberal men are those that you have among you in these two counties.    It is not to be expected that a man who has a large balance at his banker's, and perhaps 100,000*l*. capital in his business, should rush at every proposal for change quite as readily as a man who is not so fortunately situated; because the natural selfish instinct occurs to him,—'What have *I* to gain by change? I have got the suffrage ; I don't want political power ; I don't want the protection of the ballot;' and, therefore, you must make allowances for all such men ; but, also, you must value them the more when you catch them.  And I can assure you, if you go to Lombard Street, or any other quarter where rich men are to be seen, you will find much fewer liberal politicians, fewer men that will ever join together, pulling shoulder to shoulder with the working classes for great political reforms, than in Lancashire and Yorkshire; and I was glad to find, this morning, the hearty concurrence with which these men joined in advocating the ballot.  Let it not be said by the great landowners, or any people elsewhere, that the manufacturers and millowners of this part of the world, those, at least, with whom I have ever been accustomed to associate, are afraid of giving to the working classes political power, and ensuring them in the full exercise of that power. The experience of this morning has redounded to the honour of those men ; and if the union which I perceive to have arisen between the working classes, and a large portion of those who should be their natural leaders in these struggles, be cemented and continued, nothing can prevent you, be assured, from obtaining those political rights which you seek.

Now, since I have been in Manchester, we have heard news from France, which probably some of our opponents will think ought to be turned in argument against us, as discouraging further political change.  We have heard that one branch of the Government of France at Paris has shut up the shop of the other branch.  And the latest accounts are, that he and his soldiers together have carried off some hundreds of the representatives of the people, and locked them up. Will it be pretended that that is an argument against our advancing in the course in which we now propose to advance ? I tell you what I find it an argument for,—for doing away with some of these soldiers, like those that are doing the work for the President over there.  Is it not a nice illustration of the beautiful system of governing by 350,000 or 400,000 bayonets? The Assembly meets, votes the army estimates without any discussion at all; it would be quite heretical to think of opposing a vote for the maintenance of this army. As soon as they have got their pay the President sends for them, and says: 'I intend to-morrow to shut up that Assembly; and you shall assist me by occupying all the streets, and I will declare Paris in a state of siege, and you shall enable me to do it.' Now, I hope one of the lessons learnt from such proceedings as this will be, that no constitutional Government, at all events, is likely to be served by basing itself on the power of the bayonet. But what other lesson do I find in this state of things in France? Why, this, that the French people have not learnt to do what Englishmen have done—to make timely repairs in their institutions; not to pull them down, not to root them up, but to repair them. The French, instead of building upon old foundations, expect the house to stand without foundations at all. They expect the tree to grow without the roots in the ground. The English people have been in the habit of repairing and improving their institutions, and widening the base of their Constitution, as we are going to do now. It is by widening the base that we intend to render the structure more permanent. And when I look at France, and see what a terrible evil it is that men have not confidence in each other, and that there is such a separation of classes, and such a want of cohesion in parties, that there scarcely exists a public man who can be said now to possess the confidence of the people, or whose loss, if carried off to Vincennes, will ever be felt in the hearts of the people; therefore do I rejoice again for the safety and security of my country, that I have witnessed to-day such an instance of the union and confidence that exists among the people of this country.

I entreat all classes to cherish this union for the common benefit of all; for there is no other security for you. I remember, quite well, that, at the time of the passing of the Reform Bill, I was then living in London. Just before the Reform Bill passed, as you will recollect, the Duke of Wellington was for a few days called to power, and there was a momentary belief and apprehension in the country, that the King, aided by the military, was going to resist the passing of the Reform Bill; you know the awful state of perturbation in which the country was placed; you know how you sent off, in a carriage and four, your petition from Manchester, and petitions were carried up with it from all along the line of road; you know what a dreadful state of excitement the country was in. I remember, at that time, one of your largest calico-printers in Manchester called upon me, in my warehouse in London. He employed between 700 and 800 men, and was a very rich man, but had never formed any decided political principles. In our conversation, I spoke to him of the crisis then impending in the north of England. He was deeply anxious, and he said :—' Yes, I expect every day that the cauldron will boil over, and that we shall be in a state of social anarchy.' I said, ' If such is the state of affairs, what do you intend to do in this emergency?' He said, ' I'll go home this very night by the coach, and I'll put myself at the head of my men, and I'll stand or fall by my men ; for that is the only security I have, to join with my men, and to be with them.' Now, I tell all the manufacturers, and the capitalists, and the men of station in the country, that, whether it be a time of crisis or a time of tranquillity, the only safety for them is to be at the head of the great masses of the people. I therefore do rejoice at the proceedings of this day, which have given so favourable a prospect of that union, in which there is not only strength but safety.

# PARLIAMENTARY REFORM.

## IV.

### ROCHDALE, AUGUST 17, 1859.

[Mr. Cobden was elected to Parliament for the borough of Rochdale at the General Election, in April, 1859. He was at that time absent in America. On June 17, the Derby Ministry resigned, and Lord Palmerston succeeded to office. He offered the Presidency of the Board of Trade to Mr. Cobden, who, however, declined a place in the Administration. The following Speech was delivered to the electors of Rochdale on Mr. Cobden's return.]

I AM rather out of practice, for I think it is now two years and a half since I addressed a public meeting out of Parliament, and I am afraid that, with the disadvantage of being under canvas, I may fail to make myself heard by every one of you who are here present, unless you indulge me with silence during the short time I shall occupy your attention. And first, gentlemen, let me tender to you my too-long deferred personal homage for the kindness you showed me, when I was four thousand miles distant from you, in having returned me for your constituency, which I make no secret of telling you is an honour I coveted beyond that of representing any other constituency. For having returned me voluntarily, I may say almost without solicitation, I return you, one and all, my

hearty thanks for the honour and kindness you have shown
me. I thank those gentlemen here present who took the
leading part in my committee; I thank those gentlemen at
a distance, some of whose letters caught my eye, who tendered
substantial support in my cause; and I will venture—if I am
not travelling beyond the bounds of strict party discipline—
also to express my acknowledgments to our opponents, who
on this occasion sheathed their sword, and granted me an
armistice, and which I hope—at all events it will not be my
fault if it should not be so — may ripen into a permanent
peace. And now, when I read and hear of the transactions
at the last general election, I think my acknowledgments are
still more due to you for having thought of me during my
long and remote absence; for, if I gathered correctly the tenor
of the last general election, it was this, that there was a more
than usual avidity to obtain seats in Parliament; there were
more contests than usual to achieve that honour; and, unless
I am greatly misinformed, some of the aspirants for that
honour did not confine themselves within the strict rules of
propriety or decorum.

Now, I do not think it out of place here, at our first meeting, to say a word or two upon that subject, whilst it is fresh
upon our memories. We have had presented to Parliament
upwards of forty petitions praying for inquiry into the proceedings at so many different elections. But I am informed,
that if all those had petitioned who had proofs that corrupt
practices had been resorted to, the number of election petitions
would have been double what they are. Now, I am going to
say something which I am afraid, in these days, when we are
very fond of soft phrases, will be considered to be unchari-
table, and yet, Heaven forgive me if I am not telling the
truth when I say that I do not believe that Parliament is in
earnest in its attempts to reform this system, or it would have
accomplished the intention long ago. For what do these election petitions mean, after all? Let us say a word or two

about them while one is fresh from the scene of their operations.

What is the meaning of an election petition? Why, in the first place, when the petitioner has been unduly deprived of his seat by the improper and corrupt proceedings of his opponent, he has to appeal to a tribunal for justice,—to a tribunal which is the most inaccessible and the most costly in the civilised world. For I will venture to say, that a man who presents an election petition to the House of Commons, goes before a tribunal the expense of which makes the equity which is administered at the Court of Chancery dirt cheap indeed. In fact, the principal obstacle to a petition at all is that the party paying for redress of this grievance—I mean the grievance of having been deprived of a fair chance of being elected by the free and unbought suffrages of his fellow-countrymen — that the petition is so costly that no man can tell him beforehand how much it may cost. The election petition may cost a man 500*l.*, or it may cost him 5000*l.*; and no Parliamentary lawyer who had one shred of conscience would ever venture to say that he could guarantee him against the larger amount. The consequence is, that very few men have the courage to present a petition, and to undergo the risk and expense of following it out before a Committee of the House of Commons. But supposing he does so—and this is my great grievance and charge against the proceedings of the House of Commons—what does it end in? He proves corrupt proceedings on the part of his opponent, he proves corruption on the part of the constituency, and the result may be that his opponent is declared unseated. But that does not give him the seat; it merely says that there shall be another election in the same borough, that he may go again, and, if he likes, incur the same expense with the same prospect of an election petition, and that those very men who have been shown to have sold their votes before, may have the privilege of selling them again; another election in such a case being nothing more nor less than a fresh harvest to those corrupt voters who make merchandise of their privileges as free citizens.    Such being the case, what wonder is it that not one-half of those who lose their elections venture to petition for a redress of grievances?    A friend of mine lost his contest for a very large borough in one of the Eastern counties, and he told me that he had a clear case against his opponent for bribery, but he did not intend to petition, and for this reason—he petitioned once before, and his expenses cost him 500*l.* a day, and if he went into a Committee again, he had no guarantee that it would not cost him as much, and therefore he abstained from prosecuting his petition at all.

Well, now, this is the state of things; and I may be asked, What is the remedy for it?    Well, I repeat, if the House of Commons was in earnest to put down this system, a remedy would be found.    In the first place, make this inquiry cheaper and more accessible.    If you cannot have a tribunal on the spot to inquire into these proceedings, at all events spare the aggrieved party this enormous expenditure; and where he has a case, and where he is proved to have had a case—I would not say where you have frivolous and vexatious petitions, but where there is a good case for a petitioner—let the expenses be borne by somebody else than by him.    If the country has an interest in putting down this system, if the very foundations of our representative system depend upon purity at their source, why then, who so interested as the great body of the community in not allowing those forty or fifty boroughs, that are now going scot free, to go unpunished?    But who are the parties that should so properly pay the expense as those communities themselves where those transactions are permitted, or by the whole country at large, if it should be thought more expedient?    Well, I say, let the inquiry be carried on in such a way that it shall not be the punishment and probably the ruin of the petitioner.    But beyond that, let there be some punishment inflicted upon those who are detected as the guilty parties in these transactions.

Now, I will venture to say that if, when a case of bribery is clearly detected, the House of Commons would order in every such case that the parties detected in the act of bribery should be prosecuted criminally by the Attorney-General—I venture to say that that would very soon put down bribery and corruption, more than anything else that the House of Commons could resort to.   Formerly, you know, the system of corruption and undue influence in our constituencies was confined very much to a privileged class in this country.   One noble family contested a county against another noble family, and they spent a hundred thousand pounds apiece, and all the world knew it; it was agreed that they should all resort to the same habit of expenditure, and it was considered, in fact, the legitimate exercise of their wealth and their power.   In the same way, if a contest took place in a borough, it was some leading landed proprietor or some influential family of the neighbourhood who contested with another individual having the same pretensions as himself, and they fought the battle of some borough during fourteen or twenty days of saturnalia, extravagance, and corruption; and there again it was considered so much a matter of course in this country, seeing that the system was patronised by the titled and the great, that those things were passed over with very little notice.   But now, gentlemen, we have another class of aspirants for Parliament altogether.   During the last general election, I have seen a new element in our system of electoral corruption.   We have had a number of gentlemen come over from Australia, where, I suppose, they have been successful at the diggings; they have brought over great nuggets, and they administer them in the shape of 50*l.* notes.   They have gone to some of our boroughs and there fought their battles and bribed just as their betters did fifty years ago.   Now, I have great hopes, when this system is resorted to in that unblushing way by parties who have none of the prestige of our ancient nobility about them, that very likely it will be treated differently by public opinion and by Parliament, and that some plan may be resorted to to put it down.

I remember when duelling in this country was so regular a mode of meeting a certain description of insult, that if a man holding a certain position in society received an affront at the hands of his equal, he was obliged to meet him in deadly combat, as a consequence, or he would have been banished from the social life of his equals. Well, I remember that some linendrapers' assistants took it into their heads to go down one Sunday morning (I think it was to Wormwood Scrubs, or somewhere where the nobility used to carry on that pastime), and they began fighting duels; and that as soon as the linendrapers' assistants took to duelling, it became very infamous in the eyes of the upper classes. The consequence was that some of these young gentlemen were sent to New-gate; and now nothing would be so ridiculous as any noble-man or gentleman thinking of resenting an insult by going out and fighting a duel about it. Now, I am very much in hopes that since this system of bribery and corruption has fallen into hands such as I have described,—that is, since gentlemen coming home from the Australian diggings, or from their broad acres and pastures and their flocks and herds of those regions, have begun to rush into the market of electoral corruption here, and offer to buy their seats by the expenditure of 400*l.* or 5000*l.* for a little dirty borough in the west of England—I have very strong hopes that the system won't be as fashionable as it has been, and that very likely we may succeed in having those parties prosecuted criminally. I say criminally—let them be indicted criminally, and let the consequence of their conviction be a few months at New-gate, or in the House of Correction; and if they are ex-M.P.'s, and they wear the prison dress and have their heads shaved, there cannot be the least doubt in the world it would do very much to put an end to this bribery and corruption.

And now, gentlemen, this is a much wider question than that. I do not mean to say that it is the only way in which our electoral system is to be reformed. I shall have something more to say of that to-morrow evening, when, I believe, I am to meet the whole body of my constituents, who will attend here with free access, and to whom a greater development of that system would properly belong; but this I may say, that I look upon all the present attempts and pretended measures for putting an end to this system of corruption as insincere on the part of the House of Commons. There is a rule resorted to when bribery has been proved, in certain cases, of ordering commissioners to proceed to a town and inquire into these proceedings. Now, I will tell you what that amounts to. Your Select Committees that sit in the House of Commons produce a pile of blue-books after every general election. About five years ago I took the trouble to measure and weigh this pile of blue-books, and it was just four feet high, and it weighed rather over a hundredweight, and I will undertake to say that these blue-books, recording the misdeeds of all the delinquent boroughs, were never read by half-a-dozen people in one of them. I will tell you another device of the House of Commons. They pretend to send out commissioners to inquire into these proceedings at particular boroughs, where they have reason to suppose the corruption is more than usually vile. What does that amount to? Why, two or three young barristers are sent down to a city like Gloucester, and there they pass a few months in summer-time very pleasantly, hearing stories from Jack, Tom, and Harry. They prepare a large blue-book, much larger than the blue-book that comes from the House of Commons, and then in six or twelve months that is presented to Parliament. The report is more voluminous than the one we had before, and if six men read the report from the House of Commons, when there were some people still feeling an interest in it, why, not three people would ever open the big blue-book that comes out when other things occupy the people's attention. The consequence is, you are put to an enormous expense for these commissions, and no result comes from them, and no result is intended to come from them.

Now, I myself voted the other day in Parliament against the issue of a commission in the case of Gloucester, and nobody will suppose that I so voted because I wished to screen that city from inquiry; but I knew the futility, the utter valuelessness of the inquiry, and, therefore, would not lend myself to what I knew would be the perpetuation of a delusion. I say that any man, who will resort only to the existing means of putting down corruption, must have a larger credulity than I possess. I have no faith in any existing means, and I will not lend myself to the delusion that is willing to practise them any longer.

What you want, besides such plans as I have spoken of, is honesty enough in your Parliament to at least try the experiment of the ballot. I do not speak of the ballot as a cure for all these evils; I do not speak of the ballot as a political measure, mixed up with other questions of organic change; I speak now only of the ballot as a means of preventing, to a large extent, the exercise of this gross corruption, and as a moral instrument to check the growth of that rottenness which is sapping the foundations of our electoral system. You have all observed, I dare say, in the accounts that have been published of the recent Election Committees, that when there has been the existence of bribery, particularly in the smaller boroughs, the price of votes has risen just in proportion as the day has advanced; that whilst the polling has been going on, a vote has been worth probably 5*l.* at ten o'clock, 10*l.* at twelve o'clock, 20*l.* at two o'clock, 50*l.* at three o'clock, 100*l.* at half-past three o'clock, and in some cases 250*l.* five minutes before the clock strikes. Again, you have seen, that whenever you have had ruffianism and rowdyism, if I may use an American phrase—whenever you have had the party whom we call the roughs at an election called into requisition—it has been to hustle and jostle the electors just at the critical time of the poll, when probably the scale might be turned by the forced absence of one or two electors. Why, we have seen a trial the other day of a gallant admiral who tried to record his vote in a borough in the west of England, and who was seized by the roughs, not knowing that he was a valiant servant of the Crown, wearing Her Majesty's livery, and who was carried off and prevented from voting at the poll.

Well, now, let us, whilst these pictures are fresh in our observation, see their bearings upon the question of the ballot. If you voted by the ballot, the state of the poll would never be known until the voting was over, and you would have none of this tumult and excitement. The great merit and the great recommendation of the ballot is this—that it would promote order, decorum, and morality in taking the poll. I am by no means certain—and I tell it in all frankness—that the ballot would have a very decisive effect in forwarding any one of the particular parties interested in the poll. I am not prepared to say that my views with regard to public questions would be likely to be more represented in the ballot-box than they are now by open voting. I think it very likely that the political party that most dreads the ballot would sometimes the most profit by it. But this I say, that nobody who has inquired as to the proceedings in elections in America, in Switzerland, in France, in Spain, or anywhere, and compared them with the proceedings, the tumults, the violence, the bloodshed, the disgusting and odious corruption witnessed at our elections — that nobody can doubt that as a moral engine, as a means of repressing these excesses, the ballot is the best resource, the best expedient that can be resorted to.

I will mention one illustrative fact which I acquired in America upon this subject. Now, understand, I am not going to quote America as a country where you should go for imitation in everything regarding their political institutions; theirs are as unfitted for us in many respects, as ours would be unfitted for them. But this I may say, in passing, that the white men of the United States have a theory of government, and they have laid down a theory of government in their Constitution, which, if the human instrument be equal to the political machine, means to deal justly and fairly by every man in their community. But now I confine myself to one fact that was given to me during my travels in America. I was speaking to a gentleman—whose letter I might read, for it is but a few words—whose name, Mr. Randall, is known to some of our statesmen here, for I remember he gave evidence before a Committee of the House of Commons, upon which I sat, to inquire into the mode of proceeding of our Houses of Parliament, in order to furnish information as to the results of proceedings in the Congress of the United States; he is a man standing high, both socially and politically—who mentioned this fact in conversation with me, and wishing that I should have the full benefit of it under his own signature, wrote me a letter after I had left Philadelphia, where this gentleman lives, which letter I will take care to have published. The letter was addressed to me at Washington, and it contains these lines:—' I have been for fifty years connected with political and party movements in Philadelphia, and I never knew a vote bought or sold.' Philadelphia is one of the largest cities in America, and contains one of the largest populations of mechanics and working-men; for Philadelphia has changed its character from being, as it formerly was, a leading seaport, and it has become almost entirely a manufacturing city, containing now 600,000 or 700,000 inhabitants. Now, this gentleman would not have told me, I am sure, that elections in America were pure in every respect, that there are not a great deal of manœuvring and party management, that there are not very often the same liabilities as here to personation, to double votes and the like; and he would not have told me that, without exception, all their elections were carried on peaceably and tranquilly; but he mentioned the fact that the ballot presented such an obstacle to bribery, that nobody cared to buy a vote, and pay for it, when they did not know that they got value received.

Well, I will say no more with regard to my experience in America at present; for, to confess the honest truth, I was so kindly treated there, and I felt that I was treated so kindly from my connection with a great question of cosmopolitan interest—and I felt, in all humility, that I was so treated as the representative of those who had the same claim as myself to receive the kind civilities of that people, and who, if they had presented themselves there, would have been received with the same hospitalities as myself—I confess, I was so kindly treated in America, that I feel I am not an impartial witness in the case, and that I ought to say as little as I possibly can about them.

It is important that we should see that the source of our electoral system is pure, inasmuch as it is quite evident that, for weal or for woe, public opinion in this country, as manifested at the polling-booth, must become more and more powerful in the government of this country. And not merely in our own domestic government, but—and it is a question, too, which at the present moment we may well refer to— public opinion in this country is becoming more and more potent in matters of foreign as well as domestic policy. We have seen lately, and I have seen it with very great satisfaction—it was during my absence that it occurred—that the public voice of this country was raised in opposition to any interference by force of arms in the dreadful war which has raged on the Continent since I left England. I was glad to see that outburst of public opinion in this country in favour

of non-intervention ; and I congratulate you all, and I
congratulate this country, that we have for the first time,
almost, in our modern history, seen great armies march and
great battles take place on the Continent without England
having taken any part in the strife.

And now, shall we take stock just at the present moment—
to use a homely but expressive phrase—shall we take stock,
and ask ourselves whether all the old musty predictions and
traditions of our diplomacy have been proved to be true on
this occasion ?  They told us that if we did not mingle in
European wars we should lose our prestige with the world ;
that we should become isolated; that we should lose our
power.  Well, now, I ask you, whilst the thing is fresh
upon our memory and observation, have we lost prestige or
power by having abstained from the late war in Italy ?  On
the contrary, do we not know that now the great Powers
on the Continent, feeling that England is powerful,—more
powerful than ever, in her neutrality — are anxious, are
clamorous, are most solicitous, that we should go and take
a part in the peaceful conferences that are to take place with
a view of securing peace ?

Well, gentlemen, we have prevented intervention by force
of arms.  I say, let public opinion manifest itself, as I believe
it has manifested itself, against any intervention by diplomacy, unless it can be upon principles and with objects of
which England may be proud to approve; but do not let us
have any more Congresses of Vienna, where we are parties to
treaties that partition off Europe, and apportion the people to
different rulers, just with the same indifference to their wishes
and their instincts as though they were mere flocks of sheep.
Now, I think Lord John Russell in the House of Commons
laid down certain conditions, upon which alone the Government would be disposed to go into a Continental Congress, in
order, if possible, to arrange and perpetuate the terms of
peace ; and he made conditions which I thought were good,

though I think they are not very likely to be acted upon or
accepted by the great Powers of the Continent.    But what I
wish now to express, and I am sure I cannot utter any words
that will be more likely to express your sentiments; they are
these—that if England takes any part in the Congress that is
to be held by the great Powers on the Continent, our object,
and the sole condition on which they should go into that Congress should be,—that the Italians should be left free to
manage their own affairs; that they should be as secure from
intervention—that they should enjoy the privilege of non-
intervention in the management of their own affairs, just
as entirely and as sacredly as the great Powers themselves.
I know what is the excuse that is made by those great Powers
for interfering in the affairs of Italy and the smaller States ;
they do it under the pretence of preserving order,—the hypocritical pretence, I have no hesitation in calling it.    Do the
great Powers preserve order themselves?    Have we had perfect order reigning in the Austrian empire or in the French
empire for the last twenty years?    Do they preserve the earth
from bloodshed ?    Have not those two great Powers, Austria
and France, during the last six months, shed more blood in
their mad quarrels than has been shed by all the smaller
States of Europe for the last fifty years?    And shall these
great Powers, for the purpose of interfering, and sending their
armed bands to coerce the free instincts of the people of Italy,
be allowed to set up the pretence that they want to preserve
order and prevent bloodshed ?    I will face the chance of disorder.
I say that if the Italians cannot settle their own affairs without falling into discord, why should not they be allowed even
to carry on civil and domestic tumult, or even war itself,
without any other Power pretending to take the advantage
and entering their territory ?    How did we act in the case of
France, when she fell into her almost red republic ten years
ago?    Was not our Government most eager at once to proclaim that, whatever happened in France, we would never

interfere with her internal affairs, but would leave her free to
choose any government she pleased ?

Well, I say, that which you allow to the great Powers,
allow to the smaller Powers; and I say this, not merely in
the interest of those Powers themselves, but of humanity,
for I say there can be no peace in Europe, there can be
no chance of peace, and no prospect of any abatement
of those vast military efforts that prevent the people from
enjoying the fruits of their industry, until you have the principle of non-intervention recognised as applicable to every
small State as sacredly as to a large one. I say, therefore,
and I do not say wrongly when I express my conviction that I
rightly interpret your views on the subject—I say that one
condition, and almost the sole condition on which our Government should be prepared to take any part in any Continental
Congress with reference to the affairs of Italy, should be by
laying down and insisting upon the fundamental maxim that
Italy should manage her own affairs, without the interference,
by force of arms, of Austria, or Russia, or any other Power
whatever.

I confess that I do speak with some strong sympathies on
this question. I have had the opportunity of mingling much
with the Italians. I have travelled in all parts of their country. I have watched, with the greatest interest, the proceedings of their late elections. I have seen, with admiration,
the orderly moderation in which they have carried on the
elections, though plunged suddenly, as it were, into the fur-
nace of revolution, and with all their old landmarks and all
their old politics disappearing. And I have been very much
struck with this fact, and I mention it not merely for this
meeting, but because our proceedings will be heard and read
elsewhere; I say that I have observed that both in Tuscany
and in the Legations of the Pope, as well as in other parts of
Italy with which I am acquainted, the people have elected
not only the very ablest men, but they have elected the men

who, by their wealth and their position, represent the wealth and property of the country.   There are men elected—I have seen their names in the papers—as their representatives, who are as fairly entitled to be taken as representing the great wealth and influence of the country as Lord Derby would be, or Lord John Russell, or Lord Lansdowne, or any of our great names of historic family fame in this country.

Well, the Italians having done this, having shown themselves capable of maintaining order amongst themselves, are entitled, at least, to the forbearance of those countries which surround them.   But we all know that if the more powerful nations choose to send secret emissaries, and spend money in corrupting or debasing the least instructed part of the community, it will be very easy to produce disorders in those countries; or it will be very easy to make it difficult for those eminent men who have been elected as the representatives of the people, to carry on a Government with moderation or success.   But, I say, if they should fall into disorder by such means, or because they have not within themselves for the moment the elements of self-government (and, God knows, it must be difficult to find them, with so little experience as they have had in such matters), that is no reason—it is a hypocritical pretence, it is no reason — why the stronger Powers of the Continent should go and interfere in their concerns.

What would have become of this great nation, if, when we were in the cauldron of revolution,—if, during the hundred years that elapsed from 1645 or 1650 down to 1745, when the last battle was fought in favour of the Stuart dynasty,— what would have been the effect on this great nation if, instead of allowing us free opportunity to fight out our own redemption, to turn away first one king and then another, and to overturn one Ministry after another,—what would have become of us as a nation, if some great Power from the Continent, immediately that we fell into civil war or commotion, had planted a large permanent army on our shores, and had insisted on taking the power out of the hands of the people—the power to remove their grievances—the power to rescue themselves from disorder? What would have been the fate of this country? Could it have grown up with that stamina, and power, and force, and wisdom, and experience that we have enjoyed? Why, what we went through during that century was a process of fermentation, which, in the moral as in the physical world, is necessary to throw off impurities and attain objects which it is desirable to secure. What gives strength to nations or individuals but battling with difficulties? Where would have been our maxims of self-government if that century of commotion of which I spoke had been blotted out from our annals,—if, instead of those contests to which I have alluded, we had had a French army, or a Spanish army, or the two united, placed in the city of London to control our operations, to dictate to both parties? They might have preserved peace, but where would have been our liberties?

Now, I contend, and Heaven knows I shall not be charged with being one who looks with anything like sympathy, or anything like toleration, on violence or bloodshed as a process of attaining any human good in this country; but I stand here to maintain the right of every people, however weak, on the Continent, having the same opportunity of going through the same process which we went through; and (if it cannot be had by any other means) attaining to the maxims of self-government which we have attained to, by that dreary and melancholy, but, in such a case, probably inevitable process of civil commotion and strife.

Now, gentlemen, I have said that I am in favour of non-intervention in the affairs of Italy; but it may be said, Where would Italy have been at this present moment if there had not been the intervention of the Emperor Napoleon? Well, I am not going to be so unreasonable, as, I fear, some of us have been, as first to have a quarrel with the Emperor Napoleon for having gone to Italy, and then having a quarrel with him for coming away from Italy.  He has removed the Austrians from Lombardy; he has left them in Venetia; and I quite agree with Mr. Gladstone, that he has done as much good for Austria in removing her from that perilous position, as he has done for Italy in getting rid of her hated masters; and I will add one word more, and say, that I do not think Austria could do a wiser thing than make an arrangement with the population of Venice and those provinces that are called Venetia, for abdicating her sovereignty altogether, and, for a consideration, such as that a fair proportion of her national debt should be borne by those provinces—and they are rich enough to bear a very considerable pecuniary fine for the blessing of independence—I say, that Austria could not do a wiser thing than to emancipate the rest of Italy, and remove herself into territory where she will be tolerated and probably loved, which she never will be so long as she remains in Italy. I have said, if she were wise; but Governments never are wise; they are never wise in time, and the least wise of all the Governments of Europe is the Government of Austria.  It seems to me that this Austrian Government is living in so happy a state of blessed ignorance, that she has no more notion of what public opinion is thinking of her Government, than if she were in the middle ages.  She might have avoided all this bloodshed and all her present disasters—she might have left Lombardy, and she might have received, no doubt, a very much larger payment for the independence of Lombardy— nay, she might have avoided this collision with France—if she had only undertaken to have abstained from interfering with the States of Italy, other than those which have belonged to her by the Treaty of Vienna.  But she loves no terms—she listened to none—and was mad enough to commence the encounter by crossing into her neighbour's territory; and I say that from such a stupid Government as that,

—for it is the stupidest Government in all creation,—it is useless to expect any wisdom; and, therefore, I do not think it is worth our while to say anything upon the subject of what she ought to do with the remainder of her territory in Italy. I said I did not blame Louis Napoleon for going to Italy, and I did not presume to judge his motives for going there; it was no business of mine. I did not blame him for coming from Italy, because, as he did not go there to do my business or my bidding, I do not think I had any reason for calling in question his motives for coming back. But I must say that we Englishmen have quite a due notion of our own import- ance and power of undertaking to judge people for what they do and what they do not do, and without any reference exactly to our rights or pretensions in the matter.

Now, we have an interest, apart from the question of Italy, in these questions of foreign policy. I may say that our Budget is framed with reference to our foreign policy, not to our domestic policy. It is not what we want to spend at home that oppresses the people, and troubles them with taxes: it is what we want to spend with reference to proceedings abroad; and it is on these accounts that I talk to you of foreign policy now, because I see no progress (and I will say a word about it directly)—I see no chance of progress in these fiscal reforms to which the resolution which has been read to-night refers, unless we can bring our relations with foreign countries into a different position to that in which they are. I do not come here to advocate, and I never have advocated, a principle of defence- lessness—of total disarmament; that we should trust any man on the face of the earth, and not be prepared to defend ourselves, like rational beings, against all probable contin- gencies. But what I do stand up for is this—that which I heard the late Sir R. Peel declare in connection with the question of our finances, that for England to pretend to take precautions so that every mile of her coasts, and every mile of the coasts of her colonies, shall be safe from aggression, that is a hopeless and a ruinous policy; and he used these words : 'We must be prepared to take some risks; and the wisest statesman is he who will face some risks rather than undertake these ruinous precautions.'

Now, that is my principle and my policy with regard to our foreign policy. Gentlemen, what would you say if I were to tell you,—and I do it as the result of a little calculation,—that if you take the amount of money which we annually spend in this country as a means of defence and precaution against possible warlike aggression from France, as I will take it, at the very lowest possible amount—six millions sterling,—and I believe it is nearer twelve millions,—if you assume that we spend six millions sterling per annum as a means of protecting ourselves against the possible aggression of France, beyond the ordinary amount which we should sustain with reference to the preparations for war with the rest of the world,—and if I were to tell you that that sum of money represents far more than the whole of our trade with France,—that, as a consequence, as a politico-economical maxim, I can say that it would be for the benefit of England if France did not exist; and assuming that France's preparations against us are in the same way, and on the same scale, that England's are against her, then I say it would be equally an economical truth that it would be better for France if England were at the bottom of the sea.

Well, now, I ask you one question as a corollary to that. Is that man who calls himself a politician, and does he then aspire to the rank of a statesman—is he deserving of the name of Utopian, is he to be considered as living only on dream-land, and to be incapable of giving counsel to practical men like Englishmen—if he asks whether there is no possible remedy to such a state of things as that? Is it so hideously unnatural that 36,000,000 of people in France and 28,000,000 of people in England, separated by only twenty

miles of sea, that they, in 1859, are so incapable through
their Governments of placing themselves on any footing of
real security and of trust towards each other, and so unable
to believe the professions and protestations and engagements
of each other, that they must keep themselves prepared in this
deadly attitude for mutual attack and defence—I say, is it
too Utopian to ask whether diplomacy and statesmanship
cannot devise some scheme to spare the age in which we live
such frightful scandal as this? I need not trouble you at
length upon the whole question; you will say I am harping
upon the old string; but I am bound to say that we ourselves have much to answer for under this unnatural and
most unprofitable state of things. I know I shall be called
to account by those organs of public opinion which claim the
right to think for us, to speak for us, to predict for us, to
guard us, and which expect that we shall allow them to do
all that they say, and which, if we attempt to say a word for
ourselves, immediately chide us as a very intolerant and very
troublesome people; but I venture to say that a large part of
the newspaper press of this country, and a good many of the
politicians, themselves weak vessels who follow and are easily
led by a popular cry, have had much to answer for this state
of things in which we are now placed with regard to France;
for I hesitate not to say, as an observer of this matter for the
last ten or twenty years, and as a close observer of it, that
the increase of the army of France, and their preparations in
their dockyards, and their other naval and military preparations, so far as they relate to England, have been quite as
much provoked by this country as our preparations have been
provoked by theirs.

Now, probably in this matter we should be more inclined
to take the opinion of a native of another country. I confess
to you that most of the good feeling and all the high respect
which I found in the United States was entertained towards
this country—the high respect of the offspring towards their

parents, and of offspring proud of their parents, and parents proud of their offspring, and I believe and feel that they have a very good cause for their pride,—arose from the fact that they were ever most ready and willing to admit that everything that is worth possessing in maxims of liberty and freedom they owe to that parent.   Yet one thing which I saw in the papers of the United States always struck me with shame and humiliation, and that was the ridicule which they cast upon us for this constant cry in England about a French invasion.   We were again and again the laughing-stock of the newspaper press of America.   I will just read you an extract from the *New York Times*, a paper not unfriendly to England, and one which evidences great knowledge of European affairs ; I will read one extract, and no more :—

‘ There was a time in English history when the “ inviolate island” laughed all foreign threats to scorn, and met even the terrible peril of the great Armada of Spain with a front of haughty defiance.   But that time seems to have passed by.   The press and the orators of England have now no capital stock so rich in sure returns of interest and excitement, as the chronic terror of invasion which seems to have fixed itself in the British mind.   On the slightest disturbance of the continental relations of the great Powers ; on the least appearance of unusual activity in the dockyards of France ; on the merest rumour of a new combination between one or more States of Europe, not commonly united in their policy, England at once sets up her outcry of distress.   Her leading journals thunder alarm over the land ; her parliamentary candidates make the hustings ring with the “ dreadful notes of war ;” her captains take down the sword of Wellington, and her poets-laureate take up the lyre of Tyrtæus.   If England were consciously the weakest or the wickedest of Powers, her conduct in this respect would be perfectly reasonable.   If she knew herself to have fairly earned the hatred of all the world, and felt herself unequal to resist the onslaught of avenging justice, one might attribute her propensity for panics to causes that would be rational, at least, if not respectable.’

Now, I repeat, that it is not pleasant for an Englishman travelling in a foreign country to read paragraphs such as that—and that is the mildest part of the whole article.   There is scarcely a post that has not brought me some newspapers from some part of France, and particularly from a seaport, from Havre, and the centres of commerce in France, in which they do not speak with a pity and charity which you would show to a child of the outcry by the English newspapers about a French invasion: the Americans call this outcry the 'craze'—'the English craze.' Well, now, is it too much—I don't want our newspapers to abstain from expressing their opinion—I don't want to say one word then; I don't wish to curtail their privileges to criticise the world. They may say just what they please of Louis Napoleon or any other arbitrary sovereign on the face of the earth; and I tell these sovereigns, that if they cannot bear the criticism of the English newspapers amidst all their other triumphs, they must be difficult to please, and that, if they will only sift it, they will find a great deal more good than bad treatment in this world, and they ought to be content to bear it. I don't want to curtail the liberty of the press, so don't let them get up a screech against me, and say I want to put down the liberty of the press. But I ask these newspapers, in lending themselves to all this absurd scream about a French invasion, not to make me and the rest of my countrymen ridiculous in continuing this tone hereafter. Is that an unreasonable request to make of them? Well, if you will only strike—will only treat these outcries with the ridicule these panics deserve, we shall be able to put an end to them.

Now, what are the facts? When I came home, I looked into a blue-book that had been presented to Parliament. I found—I don't believe anybody else looked into it, because it did not just answer the cries of the moment, it was not the pabulum that these papers wanted for the moment—I found that there was a paper presented to Parliament which had been drawn up by the late Government, giving us an account of the condition of the French and English navies. I read the account in the House of Commons. It has never been contradicted. And recollect that this was the state of our navy and the French navy in 1848, before our present increase. I read these figures in the House of Commons, and they have never been controverted. They showed that for every vessel that France has increased in number in her navy during seven years—the time when all this extension of our navy was going on—that for every vessel she (France) has added to her fleet, we have added ten; and that whilst our writers and those public speakers who seem to pander to this panic, want to make money out of it in some direction or other, while they were giving you merely the statistics of the line-of-battle ships and the frigates that were building and in preparation, they ignored and kept out of view altogether the rest of our naval preparations, and which preparations, I venture to say, the scientific and nautical men of this day declare to be the most perfect preparations you could bring against aggression by a foreign foe; because you have in all one hundred and sixty steam-gunboats lying in the creeks and harbours of our coasts, which have been pronounced by the highest scientific nautical men in Europe and America to be, in the event of an aggressive war against this country, the most desirable means for the defence of the country of any you could possess. And for this reason. In the present state of the improvement of our cannon; in the deadly nature of the missiles which can now be projected from our cannon; and in the enormous distances at which we can strike an object, either with solid shot or hollow shell — the most scientific nautical men say that, to put a thousand in a line-of-battle ship — I repeat the words I made use of in the House of Commons—with thirty or forty thousand tons of gunpowder in her hold, and to place her to be shot at with an Armstrong gun, which striking the vessel would blow it to atoms, is a piece of suicide, and has earned for such vessels the *sobriquet* of ' slaughter-houses.'

Now mark what I tell you. We had at the end of 1848, when this panic began, when the French accused us of making excessive preparations, two hundred more steam-vessels of all sizes than the French had; and I tell you that we had increased tenfold in the number of vessels, sailing and steam, as compared with the French increase, since 1852. Now, what has been the consequence of this panic outcry? You have added 4,000,000*l.* or 5,000,000*l.* yearly to the taxation and expenditure of the country. Bearing in mind the rule laid down before, I have no hesitation in saying that this has been a perfect waste, and that we were as safe before from any aggression as now, with all the additional expenditure. Well, but what would that money have done—that is the point which I want to refer to—if left in the hands of the Chancellor of the Exchequer? It would have given him 5,000,000*l.* of revenue to deal with. Instead of voting that money by acclamation, as many do for these useless and senseless preparations, give him that 5,000,000*l.* of money to deal with in the modification of taxes, in the reduction of the customs duties—in relieving us from excise incumbrances and interferences,—give him that money and see what can be done with it,—see how he could remove the incumbrances and obstructions to commerce; see how he could reduce those high duties which check our intercourse with France itself. Give him that money to deal with by reducing the duty on French commodities, and this would be the most effective bond of peace between this country and France. Far more will be done by that means than will be accomplished by any preparations for war, for France is a country which we cannot terrify by preparations; though you may provoke them into antagonistic rivalry, you cannot coerce them into peace by mere shows of superiority of naval strength.

Let me remind you, that while we have heard from France —I don't pretend to know with what truth—a proposition for the reduction of her navy, our trusty advisers are telling us that we must not diminish for a moment our preparations. I will tell you in all soberness what the consequences will be. If you show yourself with ten or twelve line-of-battle ships sailing up and down the Mediterranean—the Mediterranean which belongs as much to France as to us—I say no French Government will dare to disarm or reduce its navy while you make such a display on the French coast. For bear in mind that France has a sea-coast second only in extent to England, and her commerce is next in importance to our own. Would a proud nation like ourselves be content to see a vastly superior force at the entrance of her seaports? But it is said that France has no occasion to be afraid of England, that we have no intention of invading her; but if we consult history, we find that whenever there has been invasion between England and France, it has always been an invasion of France by England, and not an invasion of England by France. Bear in mind that the French children read in their schoolbooks of our carrying armies into France, and our taking their great seaports. When they read this, they form a different opinion of us to that which we entertain ourselves, and they don't believe us to be a nation of Quakers, whatever some of us may fancy.

Now, gentlemen, I am not sure that the experience of the last six months may not have had a tendency to incline the great Powers of the Continent to peaceful counsels, if this country should do its best to promote those views. I think the experience of the last six months must have shown the two great military Powers of the Continent that war is too serious a pastime in our day to be resorted to lightly and at very short intervals. It is a very serious thing, with our immense power of locomotion, with our tremendous preparations of the means of destruction, to bring 500,000 or 600,000 men in array against each other; for a few days will now do what would have taken months to do at the beginning of last century; we now bring these mighty hosts into instant collision with means of destruction such as the imaginations of our forefathers would never have conceived. Well, that has been found out, and I think something more has been found out—that public opinion in Europe is not in

favour of these wars. I have never presumed, since I have
spoken in public on the question of the ruler of France, to
offer one word of censure or praise on that individual, and for
this reason. The Emperor of the French was elected by the
whole people of France, and I believe freely elected, inasmuch
as he received more than two-thirds of the whole votes of the
country for President when the ballot-boxes were in the hands
of his rival, Cavaignac. When I take that as a proof that
the feeling of the people was in favour of Louis Napoleon,
I take it for granted that they voted for him as Emperor as
freely as they voted for him as President.

Well, now, such being the case, what may have been the
motives of 6,000,000 of people in the election of their chief, it
is not my business, and I have no right, to inquire. I bow
to their decision. Supposing they have acted from impulse ;
that may have been very right in them, though it might not
be right in us. I have had the impression the last seven or
eight years that the ruler of France has a perception of the
altered times in which we live, and that his career was not
to be the career of one who bore his name before ; and this I
will say, that if he or any other ruler on the Continent should
so far mistake the spirit and requirements of the age as to
dream of repeating the career of war, of annexation, and of
conquest which Napoleon the First achieved, then he will
find that public opinion, which was impotent sixty years ago,
will be sufficiently powerful now to avenge itself against the
man, whoever he may be, who may attempt to trouble the
industry, commerce, and agriculture of the present world,
and deprive the populations of Europe of their just expectations of reaping the benefits of those improvements and those
inventions which characterise the present age. I say, if such
a man should attempt to convert the inventions and discoveries of the commerce of our day into such purposes—if he
should attempt to convert the steamboat, and telegraph, and
railroad, merely to purposes of warlike accommodation—I say

then that he will have the prayers and aspirations of nineteen-twentieths of the honest, industrious men of Europe in favour of his dethronement and downfall.   And where nineteen-twentieths, where such a majority proclaims its voice now, its power, sooner or later, will make itself felt.   And such an individual, in mistaking the character of the age in which he lives, will realise very soon in his own person the truth of that Divine precept, 'They who take the sword shall perish by the sword.'

As I am going to have the pleasure of saying a few words in this place to-morrow, I will not now trespass at further length ; but I find I am expected here to offer an explanation with regard to an incident that occurred some little time ago. If it should be thought that, even at this distance of time, it is becoming in me to say a few words to you on the subject—(I should have thought it presumptuous to say anything on the subject to anyone else)—but if I understand from your chiefs on the platform that such is your wish, I, of course, must obey.   Gentlemen, I need not tell you that on my arrival in England, on finding myself your representative, I received a communication from Lord Palmerston, and also another from Lord John Russell.   In Lord Palmerston's letter, he was kind enough to urge many reasons, frankly expressed, why I should accept a seat in his Cabinet, as President of the Board of Trade.   Now, I will not affect any modesty in this matter : I will say that if I was fit for any office in the Cabinet, I should be fit for the office of President of the Board of Trade.   I think, probably, if other cir-cumstances had not intervened, my being in that place would have been really putting a square peg in a square hole. But, gentlemen, my reasons, if you will have them, for de-clining to accept the honour which was offered to me were as follows.   The honour, I beg to assure you, I did not con-sider a matter of indifference, it was probably peculiarly in-viting to me, if I had been one of an ambitious character, because, taking it for all in all, it would have been the first instance of a man springing immediately from amongst you, literally a man of business,—being offered a seat in the Cabinet at all. I was not indifferent to the honour; none of the concomitants of office could have been a matter of indifference to me; but in that case I felt that it was a matter calling for my conscientious action; the more so in proportion to the inducements that were held out to take a particular course. Well, gentlemen, I went to London, and before calling on any one, or receiving any one, I thought it best to call upon Lord Palmerston, and to express to him exactly my views in the matter; and I may tell you just as frankly as I have told him what passed between us. I stated to my Lord Palmerston my case thus: I have been for ten or fifteen years the systematic assailant of what I believe to be your foreign policy. I thought it warlike,—not calculated to promote peace or harmony between this country and other countries. I explained to him exactly what my feelings had been, in those words; and I said to him, it is quite possible that I may have been mistaken in all this; when a man takes an idea and pursues it for ten or twelve years, it is very likely that he takes an exaggerated view of his first impressions; but I put it to Lord Palmerston, and now I put it to you, whether, having regard to those opinions, it was fit and becoming in me to step from an American steamer into his Cabinet, and there and then, for the first time, after having received at his hands a post of high honour and great emolument, to discover that I had undergone a change in my opinions; and whether I should not be open to great misconstruction by the public at large if I took such a course; and I candidly confess that it was inconsistent with my own self-respect.

Now, gentlemen, I do not intend to dwell upon this subject, because it would be egotistical to do it. And I do not intend to claim for myself more humility in the matter than belongs to me, and I do not wish that my abnegation should be considered to in any way reflect upon others who take a different course.   I must explain to you candidly the course which I took had reference solely to my own conviction in the matter.   I told the gentlemen at Liverpool who did me the honour to meet me at my landing there, that it was a question which I alone could decide; and I tell you that I alone could decide it, because I alone was conversant with the extent of my convictions with respect to Lord Palmerston's policy ; and I was bound to be faithful to my own convictions, and especially was I bound to be so when under the temptation which his very magnanimous offer presented to me.   I am bound to say, at the same time, that whilst my own feelings and convictions prevented my taking that step which many of you here wished, and which so many of my friends in Liverpool and Lancashire pressed upon me, — though I could not take that course myself, I was very glad to find that my friend Mr. Gibson found himself in a position to be able to accept office in Lord Palmerston's Government.   And I confess to you that I was glad to find that my friend Charles Gilpin has taken a subordinate office, where there is plenty of work if he chooses to do it ; for I will avow to you candidly that I like to see a man cropping up from the lowest stratum,—one who has worked as hard as any man here present,—and step into a public office from the very ranks of the people ; because what we want is to show that you need not be born in certain regions to be able to serve the Queen.

Now, gentlemen, I need not, I hope, add—and it is all I have to add—that I had no personal feeling whatever in the course I took with regard to Lord Palmerston's offer.   If I had had any feeling of personal hostility, which I never had, towards him, for he is of that happy nature which cannot create a personal enemy, his kind and manly offer would have instantly disarmed me; I think I am made of very yielding materials when anything in the way of conciliation presents itself to me. But I had no such feeling. I should be sorry if it were thought so ; and, as I told him, I tell you, if, in my attacks upon his foreign policy, I ever said one word that was offensive to himself or any public man, I am very sorry for it. I told him the motives which actuated me in the course I have taken. I claim no merit whatever for doing more than any other public man in my situation would have done. I can only justify myself by falling back, as I do, upon my own strong feelings and convictions in the matter ; and I will only now say to you, that I trust to your kind and indulgent interpretation of the course which I have thought it my duty to pursue.

# PARLIAMENTARY REFORM.

## V.

ROCHDALE, AUGUST 18, 1859.

[This second Speech was delivered to the whole body of inhabitants at Rochdale.]

I AM more distressed and disappointed than I can express to you to find myself so hoarse to-night from the effects of our last night's meeting, that I am almost afraid I shall not be able to make myself heard by this meeting; but I will, at all events, reserve so much of my voice, that if there should be anything which I shall omit to say that may be interesting to any one here present, whether elector or non-elector, I shall be happy, as your Mayor has intimated to you, to answer any questions, and consider myself here now in the position which I should have been if I could have been present when you so generously elected me without having the opportunity of questioning me as to my views on any particular topic; and I shall be gratified if any gentleman present, who feels any inclination to elicit information which I have it in my power to give, would give me the opportunity of imparting it.

Gentlemen, I have heard it announced that this is to be considered rather a non-electors' than an electors' meeting, though I believe this assemblage comprises both classes in Rochdale. You are fortunate in this borough in having less of that jealousy and discord of classes than are unfortunately to be found in other places; and the very fact of my finding myself here to-night, at a meeting presided over by the Mayor of the borough, shows, at all events, that in the eyes of the first magistrate of the borough the non-electors hold the same rank in the social scale, at least in a political capacity, as any other class of the community.

Now, gentlemen, I feel that I have a fair right to consider myself at home in addressing a body of non-electors, for I can conscientiously say—and I do not say it in the way of boast, because there are many politicians who are just as sincere in that respect as myself—but I can conscientiously say that I have never entertained a political view, or cherished a principle in connection with politics, that has not embraced the well-being of the great mass of the community as the fundamental rule and maxim of my politics. And I need not hesitate to say, that I do this not from any exclusive regard for any particular class of the community, but from this view, that I hold it to be quite impossible that you can promote the permanent well-being and prosperity of any part of the community, unless you carry with you in that career of advancement and prosperity the great mass of the people who form the working class in the community. And I will go still further and say, that any policy which has for its effect to promote the prosperity of the great mass of the people, cannot fail in the end also to benefit every class who are above them in the social scale. Therefore, with these doctrines, which I conscientiously hold, I always feel myself as much at home, and as fairly entitled to the confidence and the friendly regard of the working class, as I do to those of any other class of the community.

Now, we have on this occasion promised ourselves that we will discuss that question, which I believe is of most interest to the non-electors of this borough—I mean the question of Parliamentary Reform. It is a good sign to find so many of the working class, the non-electors of this borough, taking an interest in this question; for I should despair of my country, I should think that there was little chance, at least, of our preserving those institutions which we prize so much, unless the great bulk of the people, who are now unfortunately deprived of the electoral franchise, were pressing forward, and anxious to elevate themselves to the dignity of free citizens. Now I will, in the first place, say a few words to you upon the subject which I consider to lie at the foundation of all questions of organic change—I mean the suffrage. I am inclined to think that we Reformers have probably erred in times past in having dealt with the question of reform rather as a compound than as a simple or separate question. I mean this—and I take to myself the full blame of any mistake that may have been committed in it—we have always lumped three or four things together, and advocated them all as one measure, or one bill, when I think it would have been wiser if we had dealt with them separately, and had begun with the franchise as the thing which must carry with it, and as a consequence establish, the other points of our Reform Bill. I once heard Mr. O'Connell, in his humorous way, illustrate this policy, which I think we have erroneously followed, in this fashion. He said, 'If you want to get through a gateway with a waggon, where there is hardly room for one horse to go, it isn't wise to put on four horses abreast, because it will be still more difficult to get through.' I have come to the conclusion that in any future measure of reform the wisest way would be to deal with the question separately, to have one bill for the extension of the franchise, to make the ballot another measure, to make the shortening of Parliaments another,—that, I believe, would be the wisest course to pursue;

and my opinion is, that the franchise being that upon which all the rest depends, ought to be dealt with first. My opinions on the franchise have for the last twenty years been pretty generally given. I do not think I have gone as far as everybody in this assembly; I have gone a great deal farther than many of those with whom I have found myself acting in the House of Commons. I always voted for household suffrage. I know you have many partisans of that amount of the franchise, and you have also friends of manhood suffrage in this borough. My idea is this, that whether you get manhood suffrage, or whether you get household suffrage, or whether you get something different from either,—which we are very likely to get before we get the other two,—my idea is this, that some step in advance in the franchise will render future steps in the direction of the franchise and other measures of reform far easier than the first step will be. We have got to a dead-lock now, when the question of the franchise must be dealt with, for parties in the House of Commons have come to that pass, that, whilst all of them have agreed to some measure of reform, there seems to be hardly power in either side of the House to carry any efficient measure; and therefore I say, in the interest of parliamentary government, as well as for the benefit of the people at large, it is most important that this question of the franchise should be dealt with speedily, and I hope it will be dealt with largely and generously.

Now, I have told you what my advocacy has been; I have also named what others in this borough to a large extent, I believe, advocate; but I will not disguise from you, who are non-electors, that, in dealing with this question, we have to argue it before a tribunal which already possesses the franchise, and it would not be human nature if we did not find that the class that already possess the electoral power are a little bit jealous, and a little bit reluctant to diffuse their power over a greater number of voters, and thereby lessen the intrinsic value of the franchise itself. It is very much like somebody having a glass of pretty strong wine-and-water, letting somebody come and water it for him and make it weaker. There is no doubt an idea amongst the electors that the extension of the franchise to a large body of the working classes would weaken their own power, and probably endanger their influence; and therefore it is only human nature to expect a reluctance on the part of those who have the franchise to grant it to those who have not got it. Now you know I was always a practical man; even in advocating the repeal of the Corn-laws, I never found that I could make any progress until I began to take up the landlord's and the farmer's view of the question, and try to reconcile both to the change, and show both that they were not going to get any harm from it.

Well, now, in advocating the extension of the franchise, on your behalf, I should always present myself before the present body of electors with such arguments as I could find to show them that they would not derive any injury from a large extension of electoral rights to those outside of the electoral pale. My first question to the electors would be this, ' What interest have you of the middle class that the people of the working class have not also got?' You cannot separate the interest of the one from the other. The question then will be, ' Are we sure that if we let in a large number of voters from another class, the working class, that they will see their own interest in the same way as we see ours?' Well, I think people are generally very quick-sighted as to their interests; and fortunately there is this in the constitution of society, and of all earthly things, that if a man does not pursue his interest, if he does what is wrong, he is very soon reminded of it by the damage he does to himself as well as to others. I therefore do not think there is much danger that a large proportion of the working class, by following merely their own instincts, will not take a wise view of their own interest. But

I would ask the middle class, if I may call them so, who have now got the franchise, whether they may not incur some difficulties and dangers themselves if they keep out of the electoral pale the vast majority of the community who have now no interest in the suffrage? The working class, and those who are not entitled now to vote, I believe amount to five millions of persons. Well, I say to those who have the vote, 'Take into partnership with you a portion of those who are now excluded from the right of voting, and do it, if you have no other motive, from the selfish motive of being secure in the possession of the power you have.' For your electoral system is standing now upon so narrow a foundation that it is hardly safe to reckon upon its standing at all in case of some certain contingencies arising, which we can imagine may some day arise. Why, what have we seen abroad? I remember quite well when Louis Philippe, the last king of France, was strongly urged by the reformers in France to double the electoral body in that country. They then had only about 250,000 voters. He was urged to double the number of votes. He refused; he continued to govern the country through this small minority of voters; and one evening when we were sitting in the House of Commons, the telegraph flashed the news from Paris that the Government of Louis Philippe had been overthrown, and a Republic proclaimed in its place. And I remember quite well when the buzz of the conversation ran round the House as this piece of news was passed from Member to Member, I remember saying to the late Mr. Joseph Hume, who sat beside me, 'Go across to Sir Robert Peel, and tell him the news.' Sir Robert Peel was sitting then just on the front seat on the other side of the House, having been repudiated by his large party, which he had lost by having previously repealed the Corn-laws. I remember Mr. Hume going and sitting by the side of Sir R. Peel, and whispering the news to him, and his immediate answer was this: 'This comes of trying to govern the country through a narrow

representation in Parliament, without regarding the wishes
of those outside.   It is what this party behind me wanted me
to do in the matter of the Corn-laws, and I would not do it.'
We stand here upon a different basis; instead of 250,000
voters, we have about a million; but recollect this, that whilst
France had been only a constitutional country, at that time,
about twenty-five years, we have been governed under constitutional maxims for centuries.   Recollect that it is our
boast that the people here do rule, and that they have ruled
for centuries; and I do say that, taking into account our
great pretensions in regard to the freedom of the subject in
this country, and comparing our present state, when we have
but a million of voters, I declare that our state is less defensible
than the case of Louis Philippe was in the time of which I
speak, because, compared with our pretensions, our system of
representation is no doubt an enormous sham; and there is
no security in shams at any time, because they are very liable
to be upset by any sudden reality such as that which occurred
in the streets of Paris at the time of which I speak.

Now, I can imagine such a thing as our hearing some day
within the next five years of some hurricane of revolution
passing over the Continent of Europe, and we know what
the effect of that was upon this country in 1830; and I can
imagine such a state of things as that we should be in such
a position at some time, owing, for instance, to some circumstance that has happened in India or elsewhere—for we are not
without our outlying dangers — I can imagine ourselves in
such a state of things at that moment that there may be
very great excitement in this country, and probably very
great discontent and suffering and consequent disaffection;
and I can imagine this great change, coming like a thunder-
clap from the Continent, might rouse up elements in this
country which might produce changes far greater than anything which is now contemplated in this country, and which
would make those men who then had to deal with this

question look back with regret to those tranquil times in which we now live, and lament that they did not, like wise statesmen, deal with this question as they ought to deal with it, in a time of prosperity and of political calm. I am therefore using the most homely and the most common-sense counsels when I advise the class in this country which has the possession of political power, to deal with this question now, when the people are in a good temper, and when we are in a prosperous state. Besides, we have seen another change on the Continent. We have seen the great mass of the people sometimes throw themselves into the scale in favour of some one great man, or some great party; and although it is not a thing that is very likely to happen in this country, yet I can imagine in any country that, if you exclude five-sixths of the male adult population from electoral rights,—I can imagine a state of things when, if they have been proscribed for generation after generation, that they might be disposed to avenge themselves upon a privileged class by turning the scale in favour of some other party in the community, who might be in favour of oppressing those whom they may consider to have been their oppressors. I think these are not whimsical fancies, but they are chances which ought to be considered by every thoughtful and prudent man, and they should be a motive, even though drawn from the instincts of selfishness, why the middle class of this country should seek to deal with this question of the franchise at the present moment.

Well, but still we have the bugbear, that the working class of this country are not to be trusted with the franchise; the saying is that the people would injure themselves if you gave them the franchise; that they cannot take care of themselves. Now, in answer to that, I will put another question which has often occurred to me in my travels in distant countries: ' If the people are not fit to take care of themselves, who are to be trusted to take care of them?' That is the question which I have asked myself in many countries. I have asked it of myself where they are governed as they are in Russia, I have asked it where they are governed as they are in Austria, where they are ruled as they now are in France— I have asked myself this question : Where will you find a resting-place—how will you ever establish a system by which the people can be governed unless you come to this, that they must be left to govern themselves ? Why, we do not profess to go to any of those countries for a rule and system of Government. Well, there is another remedy for this difficulty of ignorance. [A Voice : 'Go to America.'] A friend says, 'Go to America.' Well, I have been to America. But we must deal with this as an English question, and we must deal with it in a practical way; we cannot deal with it as an American question ; but I have no objection to illustrate what I am going to say by a reference to America.

Now, in America they have generally universal suffrage, but not everywhere; until lately, the suffrage was not so widely extended as it is now. I saw it lately stated, in a New York paper, that, thirty years ago, the franchise in the State of New York was not more popular than it is in England now. In the various States of the American Union they have a great variety of franchises. In some parts, it is universal suffrage; in others, it is a tax-paying suffrage ; in some, it is a kind of household suffrage ; and in others, it is a property qualification. But the tendency, everywhere and always, is constantly to widen the possession of the franchise, constantly to increase the number of voters; and the principle is now everywhere admitted, that they must come to manhood suffrage for the whole of the white population. And this is the point that I was coming to as an illustration of my argument with reference to the alleged ignorance of the people. I have found in America that everywhere the question of education lies at the foundation of every political question. I mean this: that in America the influential classes, as you may call them, the richer people, everywhere advocate education for the people, as a means of enabling the people to govern themselves. Their maxim is this : the people govern for themselves ; they govern us as well as themselves ; and, unless we educate the people, our free institutions cannot possibly work. Their maxim is everywhere, 'educate or we perish ;' and the consequence is that the influential classes in America devote themselves to the education of the whole people, in a manner and to an extent of which no country in Europe can have any idea. Wherever I have been on my travels there I have found—and I have visited in some places where, when I was in America twenty-four years ago, the Red Indians were still encamped, and where, twenty-four years afterwards, I have found flourishing towns—I have found that everywhere in these new communities the schoolhouses were the largest and most conspicuous buildings, and that, even whilst the streets were unpaved, and whilst most of the citizens were still dwelling in wooden houses, there were large brick or stone buildings run up, containing eight, ten, or twelve long rooms, and every room, from the floor to the roof, was filled with children, receiving, without one farthing fee or charge, as good an education as you could give to the sons of the middle classes in this country.

Now, I have no hesitation in saying that the system of education in America has gone hand in hand with the extension of the electoral franchise to the people, and that the one great strong pervading motive of the people of America to educate their sons is that they may be enabled to exercise the power which they possess for the benefit of themselves and the whole country. One of the advantages which I expect to see derived from the wide extension of the franchise in this country is that there will be increased attention paid by those who are in influential places to the promotion of national education. And if it has the effect of drawing the different classes together, and inciting them to a common effort to raise the intellectual and moral condition of the great mass of the people, I know of no better effect which could be produced by any measure than that which will come from an extension of the franchise.

Well, there are questions connected with our taxation which some people think could hardly be safely left to be dealt with by a largely and widely-extended constituency. Now, I am of opinion that the country will gain in the question of taxation; that it will have a chance of reforms, which, under existing circumstances, there seems to be little, or only a very remote prospect of effecting. Everybody is, or ought to be, interested in a sound and just system of taxation, because nothing cripples people more than unjust or excessive taxation. But having already expressed my belief that the extension of the franchise will tend to the extension of education in the country, I say, in reference to the taxation of which some people are afraid, that I think that the tendency of legislation in our fiscal affairs, as the result of a widely-extended franchise, would, in my opinion, go very far to promote the prosperity of our commercial system.

Now, what is it that people are afraid of? They say, 'If you give a vote to the people they will tax property, and they will relieve themselves of taxes.' Well, now, although I cannot follow the subject into all its details, I am not at all alarmed at this threat. I believe that even if all that is predicted in that direction should be fulfilled—I am not quite sure that it would be, but assuming that the effect of an extension of the franchise was that the votes of the people removed, to a large extent, taxes which now press upon articles of consumption, such as tea and sugar, paper, and other articles taxed at our custom-houses and excise-offices— I say that if it had that effect I do not believe that would prove injurious to the country. I believe that if the instinct of the people—the working people who would be thrown in as an addition to our electoral list—if their instinct led them to substitute for a large portion of our indirect taxes, taxes upon property, or taxes upon incomes, I believe that it would have a beneficial effect upon the commerce of this country; and that, though urged by their natural instincts, their selfishness, you may say, they would, in fact, be carrying out the most enlightened principles of political economy.

Now, I do not know anything that could come from an extension of the franchise that would be more likely to benefit the upper classes as well as the lower, if I may use the term, than a change in our fiscal system, which very largely removed those taxes and duties that are now paid in the consumption of the working classes, and transferring that revenue to income and to property. I therefore see in that fear of ignorance the greatest chance of an improvement in the education of the people. In the tendency of an extension of the suffrage, in regard to taxation, I cannot see that the working classes can possibly do that which could prove injurious to other classes of the community. But I am sometimes told that the working classes, if they had the power, would be very likely to deal with their power after the manner of a trades' union, and attempt to force measures through Parliament that would benefit particular classes. Well, I am not afraid of that. We have had classes before who have had possession of the power of legislation, and who have used it for their own advantage. We had the Corn-laws passed by the landowners, the Navigation-laws passed for the benefit of the shipowners, we had the timber duties passed for the benefit of the timber merchants, and we had the sugar monopolies established for the benefit of the West Indies. We have had classes in this country who have usurped political power, and have applied it for their own purposes; but the progress of enlightenment and the continued discussion of these questions have shown that this process of selfish legislation is found only suicidal to those who follow it, and that the best interests

of all are consulted by those measures which deal fairly with
the interests of all. And I do not think that if the matter
came fairly to be discussed between those of the working
classes who are possessed of the franchise and those who
are above the working classes in the social scale,—I do not
think they would be likely to come to any conclusion, respecting these questions, which would prove inimical to the
rest of the community. For bear in mind that I always
fall back upon this: when we have taken into partnership
a larger section of the working classes as electors, we shall
all be interested in seeing that they get all the information we can possibly give them on these subjects. The law
of self-preservation will be immediately at work, and we
shall, through the newspapers, through our addresses, and
through our schools, be constantly trying to bring up the
intelligence of the working classes—if that be necessary,—so
as to enable them to fulfil their duties as electors, without
any of those dangers of which some people are—but I am
not—afraid.

Well, now, with regard to the probable measure itself, with
which we shall have to deal—I am sorry to say it, because
it may have the effect of damping some of your spirits, but
I do not think the country or the House of Commons is in a
mood for a very considerable measure of parliamentary reform.
I do not know who is to blame—the House of Commons or
the country. I rather think there is quite as much agitation
about parliamentary reform in the House of Commons as
in the country. It has got into the House of Commons, and
they don't know what to do with it. It is bandied about
from side to side, and all parties are professing to be reformers; everybody is in favour of an extension of the suffrage; and, upon my honour, I think in my heart that no one
likes it much, and that they don't care much about it. Well,
then, I must deal frankly—because I like to speak my mind
fairly; and, though it may not excite cheers or be very

acceptable, it is the best way to tell the honest truth, and I
am sure a Rochdale audience will always approve of the
truth being told them—I must say that there has not been
very much stir in this country in the cause of parliamentary reform. When I was travelling in America, my friend
Mr. Bright was making some of the most eloquent speeches
that have ever been delivered by any human being in this
country in favour of a large measure of parliamentary reform;
but I did not gather from the newspapers which fell under
my eye in America that there was much spontaneous com-
bustion in the country to help him in his efforts. I will
tell you what an American friend of mine said in the course of
conversation about it. He was a great admirer of Mr. Bright's
eloquence, but he said, 'Ah, you made a great mistake, you
and Mr. Bright; if you are going to be political reformers,
you should have gone for the reform of Parliament before
you repealed the Corn-laws; because now the people are well
fed, and have plenty of work and wages, and they have all
turned Tories.' Well, I don't go so far as that; but in
looking back to the last forty years, over which my memory
unfortunately extends, I must say I have found that in almost
all cases of great political excitement—when reform was most
popular with the masses,—I must say that it was always at
a time of great manufacturing distress, when provisions were
dear and labour was scarce, and the people were discontented
with everybody and everything about them. On the contrary,
there is no doubt that by the measures that have been passed,
and with which I hope that, without vanity, 1 may say
Mr. Bright's name and my own, and the names of many
other gentlemen here present, are associated, we have put
an end to those periodical seasons of starvation. People are
not driven now to eat garbage, or to subsist upon cabbage-
stalks. There is generally plenty to eat; but I should be
sorry to find that my American friend was so far correct
that the people of this country, because they are well fed,

and because they are generally getting fair wages, are therefore indifferent to their political rights.  I hope to find it
otherwise; but it must be admitted there has been rather an
unusual quiescence in regard to this question of parliamentary
reform.  I may tell you candidly, that those who advocate reform in Parliament, find it very difficult to get admission to
the electoral pale for those outside, unless these outsiders
are knocking for admission, and knocking pretty loud.  You
know it is not easy to get those who are inside the privileged
apartment to open the door, unless those outside manifest
some desire to get in.  But still, I say, this is the time when
we ought to deal with this question effectually, for all parties
now agree that in the next session we must have a measure
of parliamentary reform that shall carry us over at least the next
twenty years.  Lord John Russell has given notice of his
view.  He has pledged himself to a measure, as I understand
—I was not present at the time, and have not referred back
to his speech—of a 6*l.* rental for boroughs, and a 10*l.* franchise for the counties.

Well, I suppose a 6*l.* rental in a borough like Rochdale
would make a very large addition to your electoral list; because,
owing to the high rents paid in a town like this, a 6*l.* rental
would include a very large proportion of the working class.
But if you go to smaller places in the rural districts, into
the farming villages and small towns generally, a 6*l.* rental
would not add largely to the constituency; and I believe
that in Scotland and Ireland it would have a very slight
effect.  Altogether, this 6*l.* rental would not, I believe, double
the present constituency.  I have not had an opportunity
to investigate it, and perhaps it would not be easy to ascertain
it, but I am told, that if we had a franchise extended to a
6*l.* rental, it would not add a million to the present million
of votes.  I have heard some people say it would not add
more than five or six hundred thousand.  I hear a voice say,
'Not so much.'  Well, I have heard, but I cannot quite

believe it, that amongst some of the statesmen, Lord John
Russell's colleagues, there is contemplated a resistance even
to this measure of a 6l. rental franchise; but I would ask
those Lords and right hon. Gentlemen, whether it is worth
disturbing the franchise at all, if they do not go as far as
that at the least? Let us see—it will be thirty years next
year since we had the last Reform Bill. That Reform Bill
gave us about a million of voters. We wait thirty years,
and now it is considered an extreme measure if we add one
million more to our voting list; but, as I understand it,
there are six millions of adult males in this country, five
millions of whom at present have no votes. Well, if we take
in a million next year, after thirty years' waiting, and if
we are to go on no faster than that for the future, it will then
take four times thirty years to bring in the other four millions
of voters; and, in fact, it will take 150 years before the whole
of the adult males are entitled to vote in this country. I
apprehend that nobody would think we were travelling too
fast at that rate.

I do not say that it is necessary that we should do everything at once. There are young men now growing up who
will have better capacity than their fathers to agitate and
work and argue for their own franchises. I have no objection
that the measure which I look for shall not come all at once,
but gradually, and as soon as we can get it; but this I do
say, that if the present Government really falter in that
measure which Lord John Russell has proposed, it will be
the most unwise and suicidal thing that the privileged class
of this country, who really have the executive power in their
hands, could possibly accomplish. Assuming, at all events,
that the franchise will be dealt with, there is another question
to which I attach the utmost importance,—I mean the
question of the ballot. Now, I consider, myself, that the
ballot is sure to follow an extension of the franchise. There
are about 230 men now in the House of Commons, who are

pledged to the ballot. One election under a Reform Bill would inevitably carry the ballot. And, therefore, I consider that an extension of the franchise necessarily leads to the ballot. I am for keeping the questions separate. There is a society in London organised for the purpose of advocating the ballot. I have advised them always to keep their society separate from all others. They have, I believe, some supporters in Rochdale. That society is worthy of your support, and will, I hope, go on advocating the ballot, and adducing, as it is adducing, the best possible arguments to show its morality and its efficiency.

Well, now, since I have been home, I have been asked a dozen times what the people think of the ballot in America. It is a very remarkable thing that I never heard anybody say anything about it in America. It is a thing that nobody thinks of discussing. It is so perfectly understood by ninety-nine hundredths of that community to be the best way of taking votes, that they no more think of discussing it than they do as to whether it is better to button their waistcoats in front rather than button them behind; or whether it is better to mount a horse on the left side instead of getting awkwardly on on the right. It is not a subject that ever forms matter of discussion there. There are not two sides of it. Nobody questions it; it is the last thing you ever hear. discussed in America; and the reason is this, that everybody admits, wherever the ballot has been tried, that it is the most convenient, the most peaceful, the most moral, the most tranquil, and therefore the most desirable mode of taking votes of any that was ever devised. In an ordinary case, their votings in their large towns go on with as much tranquillity as your proceedings on a Sunday do, when people walk quietly off to their different places of worship. A man goes to one of the different polling-places; he deposits his vote; nobody is there to shout at him or ask him questions; nobody expects to know how he is going to vote; nobody cares to inquire; it is assumed that no one has a right to interfere with another man's right of voting as he pleases; and when that is once assumed and once conceded, there is nobody that has any interest in opposing the ballot.

I last night alluded to a communication I had received from a gentleman in America—in Philadelphia. I had not the letter in my pocket then, but I have it now. When I was in Philadelphia, a large manufacturing city of more than half a million of inhabitants, I met a gentleman who had been previously very well known to me, and who is in the highest social and political circles in that city, and he was talking to me about the ballot; and after I left Philadelphia, and reached Washington, he sent me this letter, which I have no doubt he intended that I might publish, and therefore I will read it to you :—

'Philadelphia, April 29, 1859.

'Dear Sir,—I called upon you yesterday, a few minutes before twelve o'clock, and found that there had been a mistake about your time of departure. I desired to have had some conversation with you upon the subject of vote by ballot, and to repeat what I had verbally stated before, and now subjoin in writing. During fifty years' close intimacy with the machinery of parties, and in active participation in conducting our elections, I have never seen a vote bought or sold, nor one which I had any reason to believe had been bought or sold.—Hoping to see you once more before you leave our country,

'I remain, yours truly,

'JOSIAH RANDALL.'

Now, that was written to me by a gentleman who is at the head of that party in America, which is considered to include in its body the largest portion of the working classes of that community,—I mean the democratic party; and that gentleman had never seen a vote bought or sold. Now the reason, no doubt, was partly this,—that their constituencies are so large in most cases that it would be quite futile to attempt to carry an election by bribery, just as it would be impossible to carry one by bribery in Manchester or Leeds; and consequently you hear much less of bribery in the large constituencies than in the smaller ones. But I would ask whether, considering that we are twenty-eight millions of people, ought we not to have, as a rule, all our constituencies much larger than they are? I know not how you are to keep your House of Commons within its present numbers, unless you are to enlarge all your constituencies, and thereby secure to a fair proportion of the population their right of representation.

And this brings me to the question of the redistribution of the franchise; and I would say, gentlemen, I have a very strong opinion that where you have to give, as you would have to give in any new Reform Bill, a considerable number of new Members to your large cities,—as, for instance, Manchester, Liverpool, and the like,—and Rochdale will, of course, be included in the number,—it would be the most convenient and the fairest plan, if you apportioned your large towns into wards, and gave one representative for each ward. I mean that, instead of lumping two or four Members together, and letting them be the representatives of a whole town or city, I would divide the place into four wards, and I would let each ward send one Member. I think there is a fairness and convenience about that plan which ought to recommend it to Lord John Russell, and to everyone who has to handle a new Reform Bill. For instance, you will find in a town, generally, that what is called the aristocracy of the town live in one part, and the working classes live in another. Now, I say, if, in dividing a town into three or four wards, it should happen that one of the districts where the working class predominates should have the opportunity of sending a Member which that class may consider will most fairly represent their views, and if in another part of the town another class, living there, choose a Member that more completely represents theirs, I do not see why the different classes or parties in the community should not have that opportunity of giving expression to their opinions. I think it would be much better than having two or four Members for one borough; for I have observed, in watching the progress of elections in England, that where you have one Member representing a borough, as in the case of Rochdale, there is a tendency to maintain a higher degree of public spirit—there is a more decided line of demarcation in parties; and men are more earnest in their political views, than where they have two Members to a borough; for I have frequently seen, as in the case of Liverpool, Blackburn, and many other towns that I could name, that the people begin to get tired of contests, and acquiesce in a division of the town. They say, let us vote one-and-one, and do not let us have any more political contests. That is a very bad state of things; because, if a country is to maintain its free institutions, it must constantly have political discussions and contests.

Well, I do not say anything about the shortening of Parliaments; at present, we seem to have Parliaments very short, and I think that we are likely to have a recurrence of elections until, at all events, our Legislature deals with this question of parliamentary reform, and puts us on a footing by which some one party or other can have a preponderance in the House. But I have always advocated, at the same time, the ballot and household suffrage, and a return to triennial Parliaments. I think that a short lease and frequent reckonings are likely to maintain the character both of the representatives and of their constituents; and the oftener they meet, within moderation as to time, to renew the lease of the confidence of their constituents, the better it will be for the working of our free institutions.

Gentlemen, I could enlarge upon these subjects, if my time and yours would permit; but I am to be followed by other gentlemen — one, in particular, who has more peculiarly identified himself with this question, and to whom, if we get any measure of reform, the country will be largely indebted for succeeding in it. I am to be followed, also, by a gentleman —Mr. Sharman Crawford—who was formerly your representative.  I say yours, for the working men and the non-electors never had a more honest representative than Mr. Sharman Crawford.  I cannot too much, I cannot too heartily, express my gratitude to him, coming, as he has, across the stormy Channel, to pay us a visit here to-night.  I cannot forget, either, that when I was in America, and my name was proposed to this borough, he volunteered to come across from Ireland to represent me at the hustings, if there was any need.  I tender him my warmest gratitude for his kindness to me.  There are other gentlemen here present who will also address you.  I reserve what little voice I have left to answer any questions that may be put to me by any gentleman here present.  I invite discussion now, just as if I were going to be elected by you to-morrow.  And thanking you all for the kind support you gave me at the late expected contest, knowing, as I do, that I owe my election to the enthusiasm of the working classes in my favour, as well as to the favour of those of their employers who sympathise with my views, I cordially repeat my thanks to you all for your kindness to me in my absence, and for the warm and generous reception which I have met with on this occasion.

# EDUCATION.

# EDUCATION.

## I.

MANCHESTER, JANUARY 22, 1851.

[The National Public School Association, the objects of which were nearly the same as those advocated at present by the Education League, held an annual meeting at Manchester, at which Mr. Cobden moved the following resolution :— 'That the present aspect of the Educational Question gives high testimony to the value of the efforts of this association, and promises a complete and speedy triumph.']

THE aspect of this room certainly affords encouragement to the friends of Education. The very numerous and influential body of gentlemen that I see before me is a proof of the growing interest taken in this important question; and I see around me many gentlemen,—I see many of the old familiar faces with whom I was associated in a former struggle; and if continuous courage and perseverance, and an undeviating adherence to principle under trying circumstances can warrant success, then, I think, the past experience which those gentlemen have given to the world, augurs a triumph for the cause we have now in hand. But, gentlemen, I don't disguise from myself,—and you will not for a moment conceal from your minds, that we are indebted for this meeting, in some degree, to a recent movement that has taken place in this city by gentlemen who have hitherto not taken a prominent part in the cause of national education.

Now I join most unfeignedly in the expression of congratulation upon the fact, that those gentlemen have come forward to avow, to a great extent, their adhesion to the principles of this association. They have given the sanction of their approval to the main features of this association, as has been well observed, — they have adopted the principles of local rating; and I will further say, they have, by one of the provisions of that scheme which has been published to the world, given in their adhesion to the principle of secular education, inasmuch as they leave to the parents of children the power of demanding for their children an exemption from that doctrinal instruction, which has been hitherto held by every party an indispensable requisite of education. Now, I must confess, I have always been so impressed with the difficulties of this question, that if a proposal had been made by which it was intended to give an improved education to the people, coupled with conditions ten times as objectionable as those we have lately had proposed to us, I do not think I could have found it in my heart to have offered any very strong opposition. I have really passed beyond the time in which I can offer any opposition to any scheme whatever, come from whatever party it may, which proposes to give the mass of the people of this country a better education than they now receive. I will say more, — that in joining the secular system of education, I have not taken up the plan from any original love for a system of education which either separates itself from religion, or which sets up some peculiar and novel model of a system which shall be different from anything which has preceded it in this country. I confess that for fifteen years my efforts in education, and my hopes of success in establishing a system of national education, have always been associated with the idea of coupling the education of this country with the religious communities which exist. But I have found, after trying it,

as I think, in every possible shape, such insuperable difficulties
in consequence of the religious discordances of this country,—
that I have taken refuge in this, which has been called the
remote haven of refuge for the Educationists,—the secular
system,—in sheer despair of carrying out any system in connection with religion.   I should, therefore, be a hypocrite, if
I were to say I have any particular repugnance to a system
of education coupled with religious instruction.   But there
is no one in this room, or in the country, that can have a
stronger conviction than I have of the utter hopelessness of
ever attempting to unite the religious bodies of this country
in any system of education ; so that I can hardly bring
myself even to give a serious consideration to the plan that
has been now brought forward by gentlemen in this city, and
who have brought it forward, no doubt, with the best possible
intentions, and who have only to persevere in order to find
what I have found, for the last fifteen years,—the hopelessness
of the task.   For what is it those gentlemen have now proposed to do?   Is there any novelty in it?   Why, it is precisely
what Parliament, and the Government, and the Committee of
Privy Council, have been attempting to do now for a great
number of years,—that is, to give a system of education to the
country which shall comprise religious instruction, and which
shall call upon the people of this country to subscribe, through
taxation or rates, for the general religious as well as secular
education of the country.

There is no novelty in the plan now brought forward ; it is
merely a proposal to transfer to Manchester, as the theatre of
contest, what has been hitherto just going on in the House of
Commons and the Government.   It is, in fact, a proposal by
which everybody shall be called upon to pay for the religious
teaching of everybody else.   Now, this is precisely what has
been objected to by a great portion of this community, and
what has prevented the present system, administered through
the Minutes of Council, from being successful.   There is this

novelty, certainly,—that for the first time a body of Churchmen have themselves come forward, and recommended that
all religious denominations should be allowed to receive public
money for the teaching of their catechisms and creeds.  Now,
that is a novelty, because hitherto although the Church body
have themselves been in favour of endowment for one particular sect,—if I may be allowed to call it so,—yet the
Church has not hitherto been an active promoter of any
system which shall recognise the right of other religious sects
to receive public money to teach their catechisms.  So far,
then, we have a difference in the quarter from which this
proposal has come; but does this alter the character of the
opposition we may expect from those who have hitherto
opposed the Minutes of Council and the parliamentary grants
for education ?  It is precisely the same thing over again,—
the same thing, whether you ask the religious voluntaries of
this country to receive and pay public money for religious
teaching through a local rate in Manchester, or through the
Minutes in Council voted by Parliament in the annual grants.
There is no difference in the two proposals, except that one is
done by rates levied in Manchester, and the other by a vote
in the House of Commons.  How then are we to escape those
difficulties in the religious question which we have hitherto encountered?  If the members of the dissenting bodies have been
sincere in their opposition hitherto to the national system of
education, as administered through the Minutes of the Committee of Privy Council, there is not the slightest hope of that
proposal, which has now emanated from the Church party in
Manchester, being acceptable to this city.  But I am not
sure we are dealing with any well-considered or matured
proposition from any particular religious body.  We probably
have the plan of an individual rather than the manifesto of a
party.  I am not sure that any party in this city, any religious
body as a body, or any committee as a committee, has yet
endorsed the proposal submitted to us; and I do not think

the gentlemen who have so far given in their adhesion to this proposal, as to assemble together and discuss it, have considered the ultimate bearing and scope of the proposal that has been put forward. It is based upon the principle of voting public money for the teaching of the religious creeds of every religious denomination in the country. If it does not recognise that principle, it is an unjust proposal. There are but two principles on which you can carry on an education system in this country, or in any other, with the slightest approximation to justice. The one is, if you will have a religion, to form your plan so as to pay for the teaching of all religions; the other is, to adopt the secular system, and leave religion to voluntary effort.

Now, I must say, I doubt if the gentlemen who have so far joined this new association as to attend in person to hear it mooted, — I question if they fully understand the ultimate scope of what must be their proposal, if carried out with fairness; for it amounts to this, that you should pay from the public rates of this city the money for educating children in the Church schools, where, independent of the secular education which they shall have secured to them, they shall be taught the Church Catechism; and to the Independents, the Baptists, and the Unitarians and Wesleyans, the same system would be applied, in which, besides the secular instruction which should be enforced, they must be allowed to teach their various creeds or catechisms. But there is a large body in Manchester and Salford lying at the very lowest stratum of society, whose education must be embraced in any plan, or that plan must be worse than a mere pretence, fraught with downright injustice and negligence, and negligence of the most necessitous portion of the people. I speak of the Roman Catholics,—that portion of the people which was described by Dr. Kay, now Sir James Shuttleworth, in his pamphlet written here, some fourteen years ago,—that portion of the population which he has described, comprising 60,000 or

80,000 of the Irish, or immediate descendants of the Irish, being all Roman Catholics, and who import into this city a great deal of that barbarism which has, unfortunately, characterised the country from which they came. Any system which does not embrace that part of the population, cannot be entertained for a moment as a system.

Well, then, the proposal of the Church party must mean, that the schooling of all of those Roman Catholic children shall be paid out of the public rates, and that, besides the secular instruction they may receive, they shall be taught their catechism, and be permitted to observe their other religious ceremonies, precisely in the same way that the Church of England and the dissenting schools are allowed to do. Have those gentlemen made up their minds that they will pay rates for the purpose of the religious training of the Roman Catholic children? Now, I say, I should be a hypocrite if I expressed any great repugnance myself to that which would give these poor children an education, coupled with that sort of instruction which I am here to advocate. But have the gentlemen who put forward this proposal fully considered the scope of their own plan? Have they made up their minds that the whole of the Roman Catholic children in Manchester shall be taught their religion at the expense of the ratepayers of Manchester? Have they made up their minds, when they talk of enforcing the reading of the Bible—have they made up their minds what version of the Bible they mean in all this? Has that subject been discussed among them,—has it been settled? Do they mean that the Douay version of the Bible shall be taught in these Roman Catholic schools? Because, if they do not mean that, when they make the Bible the condition of receiving any schooling, it is at once shutting the door most effectually to the instruction of the great mass of the Roman Catholic children in this town. Do not let any one suppose I am interposing these objections as my objections. They are what I have encountered here for the last fifteen years. I remember so long ago as 1836, when Mr. Wyse, himself a Roman Catholic, and Mr. Simpson, of Edinburgh, and others, came down here to enlighten us on the subject of education — I remember having in my counting-house in Mosley Street, the ministers of religion of every denomination, and trying to bring them to some sort of agreement on the system of education we were then anxious to advocate. I believe the insuperable difficulties that then existed have even increased now, and have not been in the slightest degree modified; and I believe those gentlemen who, with the best intentions, have brought forward this plan now, will find, before they have pursued it to one-twentieth part of the time and trouble gentlemen here have given to the Education question, that they have attempted an impossibility, and will be compelled to turn aside from what they are attempting to do. And if they view education at all as of that paramount importance I trust they do, the effect of this well-meant effort will be to bring many of those gentlemen to our ranks, if, as I sincerely hope and trust will be the case, we do nothing in the meantime to repel them from joining us.

The difficulties I spoke of have been encountered in two other countries, the most resembling us in the state of their civilisation and religion—the United States and Holland. They have both gone through the very same ordeal. In the United States, the education was once religious. When the Pilgrim Fathers landed in New England, the system of education then commenced embraced religious teaching; everybody was taught the Catechism, and there was no objection made to it. But when the number of sects multiplied, this religious education became a bone of contention; a great struggle ensued, and the Americans have had to go through the same difficulty that we have now; and it has ended, as it will end in this case, in the fundamental principle laid down in the Massachusetts statute for erecting

common schools, which says that no book shall be admitted
in the schools, and nothing taught, which favours the peculiar
doctrines of any particular religious sect.   In Holland, they
have come to precisely the same conclusion.   There they have
adopted a system of secular education, because they have found
it impracticable to unite the religious bodies in any system of
combined religious instruction.

Well, now, if ever there was a time when it was desirable,
more than another, to try and separate religious from secular
instruction, it is the present time.   And why?   Because we
have arrived at that period when all the world is agreed that
secular instruction is a good thing for society.   There are no
dissentients now, or, if there be, they dare not avow themselves.
We are agreed that it is good that English boys and girls
shall be taught to read, and write, and spell, and should get as
much grammar and geography as they can possibly imbibe.
There is no difference of opinion about putting the elements of
knowledge into the minds of every child in the land, if it can
be done.   But while we are all united on that, can any one
who moves in society conceal from himself that we are also
arrived at a time when we have probably more religious
discord impending over us than at any period of our history?
I do not allude to the dissensions between Roman Catholics and
Protestants ; I do not allude to them, excepting so far as they
may lead to schisms and controversies in the internal state
of other religious bodies.   But I think there is at the present
moment looming in the distance, and not in the very remote
distance, a schism of the Church of England itself.   I think
you have two parties, one probably more strong than the
other in numbers, but the other far more strong in intellect
and logic, which are going to divide the Church.   I see the
Wesleyan body torn asunder by a schism, which, I think, the
most sanguine can hardly hope to see healed ; and I think
there are several other religious bodies, not perfectly tranquil
in their religious organisation.

Now, while we have the prospect of these great internal dissensions in religious bodies,—while we are all agreed that secular education is a good thing,—is it desirable, if it can be avoided—would it be desirable, if it were practicable, which it is not, I think,—that our national education should be one which is united and bound up with the religious organisations, when schisms may prevail in the churches, and must be necessarily transferred with increased virulence to the schools? For bear in mind that what you see now pervading the churches in Scotland, where you have an irreconcilable dispute with regard to the appointment of the masters of the parochial schools—a dispute between the Old Kirk and the Free Church —recollect, if what I say be correct, that you have an impending schism in the Anglican Church, that then you will have precisely the same difficulty in the appointment of masters in the national schools. You will have High and Low Church contending for the appointment of masters; in one parish, High Church predominating, the masters will be dwelling on the necessity of the old forms of the Church, and enforcing the ritual and observances prescribed by the Liturgy and Canons; and in another you will have the Low Church, on the other hand, dwelling on what they regard as the more vital essence of religion, and discountenancing those forms which the High Church regard; and you will have the same discords pervading your schools; and the consequence will be, decreased efficiency of the masters, and, in some cases, a divided school, a disruption of the school along with the congregation; and you will have to fight the battle again, to reconcile the different bodies; and in the end, I believe in my conscience, it will come as in America and Holland to this,— you will be obliged, after a great waste of time, to return to the secular system which they have adopted, and which we are met here to advocate.

Since I addressed you here last, I have been visiting many places—Birmingham, Leeds, Huddersfield, Bolton, and elsewhere,—and I have sought private interviews with numerous bodies of gentlemen interested in the question. I have especially sought private interviews with those who have been supposed to differ from us, but have been thought usually as ardent advocates of education as ourselves,—those connected with the dissenting bodies in different parts of the kingdom. I have endeavoured to meet them privately, and to have a full and free discussion of the question, because I thought that such a cause would be more likely to put them in possession of the real objects of this association, which have been so much misunderstood. I thought it better to do so in a private conference, rather than to enter on an antagonistic discussion with them in the public arena, where they might be committed to views which I hope and trust, when they have fully considered our plan, they may be induced to modify and even to change. One of the objections made to our plan has been alluded to by my friend Mr. Schwabe; and it is that we propose by our plan to supersede all existing schools, and render all existing school-rooms valueless. Now, it seems to me, that the plan put forward by the Church party here, seems rather to insinuate that they have caught us tripping, when they offer to avail themselves of school-rooms already in existence, and assume that we contemplate doing nothing of the kind. I have mentioned a dozen times, it is my firm belief, if a system of education such as we propose were adopted, you would have no difficulty in getting an Act of Parliament for a local rate in Manchester, and in doing what your Corporation does with the waterworks, taking power to use, either by purchase or renting, existing school-rooms. I do not conceal the fact from our friends, that I believe, if we have a system of rating for free schools, the effect will be to supersede all other schools, which are now partly supported upon the eleemosynary principle, that is, by charitable contributions. I do not conceal from others, —I cannot conceal from myself,—that if you establish free schools in every parish, you will ultimately close all those schools that now call upon the poor children to pay 3*d*. or 4*d*. a week, and in which the difference of expense is now made up by the contributions of the congregations. If they did not have this effect, they would be unworthy of the name of national schools. But I have never considered that the school-rooms in connection with existing places of worship, or otherwise, would be rendered useless, for I have always considered they might be rented or purchased in precisely the same way as Mr. Schwabe has suggested; they might be rented for the week-time, and left on the Sunday in the hands of the congregations. This is merely a matter of detail; but we should be taking a rash leap if we had contemplated closing all existing schools, and wasting the vast capital invested in bricks and mortar for the erection of them.

Another strong objection which I have heard from our dissenting friends has been, that the secular system of education is adverse to religious teaching. I cannot tell how to account for it, but there seems to be a pertinacious resolution to maintain that the teaching the people reading, writing, arithmetic, geography, grammar, and the rest, is inimical to religion. Now, I have found the most curious refutation of this doctrine, where I have been, in the practice of the very parties who have objected to us. I remember at Birmingham, I found there a preparatory school built by a joint-stock association, by men of every religious denomination —I heard of a clergyman sending his son to that school. No religion is taught there—the building would never have been erected, unless by a compromise, which agreed that no religion should be taught in that school; and yet, the very parties that object to us for not proposing to give religion with secular education, send their sons to schools where secular education is separated, avowedly, from religious teaching. Again, in Yorkshire, I was present at a meeting where a gentleman stontly maintained it was impossible to separate religious from secular instruction. It was in Huddersfield.

And another gentleman said, ' How can you possibly maintain that doctrine ? You know the Huddersfield College here could not exist a day, unless we consented altogether and totally to separate religious from secular teaching ; and you know you send your son to the college, and that he never received any religious instruction there !' I must say that gentleman was silent for the rest of the evening. But I also found that at Huddersfield, they have, in connection with their Mechanics' Institution, a very excellent school for young children (not for adults), where they may go and enjoy the benefits of this institution for a week, by subscribing 3½d. They give the smallest doses of instruction, because they see the ginshops and such places offer to their customers a twopenny or three-penny taste ; and so they let the children come in for a week for 3½d., in hopes that they will be tempted to repeat the dose,—I think a very wise regulation. I find there are hundreds of the children in this admirable school ; but that excludes all religious teaching. I do not know whether the Bible exists in the institution library ; but they never touch it in the schools, and never use it as a school-book for teaching religion. And this applies to the schools generally connected with the mechanics' institutions in Yorkshire, of the union of which my friend, Mr. Baines, is president ; in those schools there is no religion taught or professed to be taught. And, therefore, in my travels, I have found that gentlemen offered in their own practice the best example of the success of our principle, and the best refutation of their own theories.

I have heard it said, the voluntary principle is succeeding very well, and that has been said by men for whose judgment in other matters I have great respect ; but I am glad, among the other advantages afforded by our friends, the Church Society in this town, that we have got a corroboration of the doctrine with which we started, that the existing system of schooling is very defective. The Church party tell us, what we were aware of before, that we have a multitude of schoolhouses, but they are badly attended, and the instruction is not sufficiently good to attract children. The great fallacy we have hitherto had in the statistics of education is this, —we have taken school-houses for schooling, and mistaken bricks and mortar for good masters. I never doubted we have had vast efforts made in building schools; nothing is so easy as to galvanise an effort in a congregation or a district for raising a school, or to persuade men that when they have done that they have provided for education. What do bricks and mortar do for education? The gentlemen of this Church system have told us—these schools are in many cases standing idle, and the children do not come to them. I have heard mentioned, wherever I have been, that you have plenty of schools, and the people will not attend the schools until you adopt some system of compulsion, some coercive system, and compel people to send their children to school; it is of no use building schools, for the children will not attend them. I have heard this compulsory system of attendance at schools advocated in private meetings, in friends' houses, wherever I have been—where gentlemen have spoken, probably, with less reserve than they would in public; and I have found, to my astonishment, everywhere a strong opinion in favour of a compulsory attendance in schools.

Now, I beg my friends will understand that I did not bring that principle with me to Manchester. We have stopped short of that yet; and we say, before you call on us to do that, you must show us first that people will not send their children to school. You have two things to do: firstly, to establish free schools in Manchester, to receive all the children of those who may choose to send them there; and, in the next place, to have good schoolmasters. I am firmly convinced, as I have told my friends everywhere, that if you set up good schools, and have good schoolmasters, you will have no difficulty in filling your schools. I have never yet found a good schoolmaster that did not fill his school, even when the

children had to pay 2*d.* or 3*d.* a week for the schooling.
And if, after you had established a free school, and given
every one the opportunity of attending gratis, and given
them good masters, you find the people will not send their
children to the schools, but bring them up in idleness and
ignorance, I don't know that, under such circumstances, I
should see that it would be any great infringement of the
liberty of the subject, if you did adopt some plan; first,
perhaps, to seduce or bribe them to send their children to
school, and, if that would not do, to try a little compulsion.
I don't see any objection in principle to that; but I say to
our friends, before you do that, try every inducement to make
them come; and I should not be squeamish about any outcry
there might be of the liberty of the subject, and so on ;—there
is just as much liberty in Switzerland as in England, and in
Switzerland they do punish parents who do not send their
children to the free school, unless they can show they are
giving them an education elsewhere.

These are some of the objections I have heard our friends of
the dissenting bodies urge to this plan in the last few weeks.
They have objected, on the ground of principle, that they
cannot separate the secular from the religious education.
Well, I must say we have endeavoured to be very accommodating to these gentlemen, and have found it very difficult
to please them. When the attempt was for many years to
have an education combined with religion, then these same
gentlemen told us it was contrary to their consciences, either
to receive or pay money raised by taxation, for teaching religion. When we offer to separate it, we are told by these
same gentlemen, that it is contrary to their conscientious convictions to separate religious from secular teaching. I do
think such a course, if persevered in, will go very far to
alienate the feelings of the great mass of the working community, who, I am very much afraid (speaking of the sur-
rounding district), are not in communion with either Dissent

or Church ; it will do very much, I fear, to alienate the great
mass of the people from those who take an impracticable
course, which stops the avenues of education to the working
classes, by setting up obstacles which it is impossible for any
rational man either to obviate or remove.

Now, have those gentlemen a due appreciation of the value
of the education which they are opposing, apart from religious
instruction ? I believe they must have an adequate idea of the
value of secular knowledge. I put it to them, do they not
value it in their own cases and in their own families ? I put
it to a gentleman I met with, one of my strongest opponents,
—a minister of religion,—and he told me, in a party of religious men, that ' he valued secular knowledge so much, he
would not give his secular knowledge, apart from all religion,
in exchange for all the world.' Well, and if he would not
put himself on a par with the unenlightened peasant for the
whole world, is he carrying out the Christian principle of
doing to others as he would be done by, if he lightly inter-
poses obstacles to the acquisition of some portion of that
knowledge which he values so highly, by the great mass of
his poorer fellow-countrymen ? I want to ask the gentlemen,
who interpose at all times the question of religion as an
obstacle to secular teaching, do they or do they not consider that knowledge is in itself a good ? I will say, apart
from religion altogether, do they consider that Seneca or
Cicero were better for their knowledge than the common
gladiator or peasant of their day ? But even as a matter
of religious import, I would ask those gentlemen, do they not
think they will have a better chance of gaining over the mass
of the people of this country to some kind of religious influence, if they begin by offering to their children, and tempting
their children to acquire, some kind of secular knowledge ? It
seems to me, that to argue otherwise would contend for this,
—that ignorance and barbarism, and vice, drunkenness, and
misery, are conducive to Christianity, and the opposite qualities

contrary to it. I feel we are in danger of alienating the great mass of the people in these manufacturing districts from every religious communion, and even estranging their minds from every principle of Christianity, if we allow this unseemly exhibition to go on—of men squabbling for their distinctive tenets of religion, and making that a bone of contention, and a means of depriving the great mass of the people of the knowledge that is necessary for them to gain their daily bread, or to preserve themselves in respectability. Why, what a spectacle do we present to the world? Where is our boasted common sense, which we think enables us to steer our way through social and political difficulties, when we vaunt ourselves with our superiority to Frenchmen, Germans, Danes, and Italians? Where is our boasted superiority, when the American Minister can come to our Town Hall here, and taunt us with the ignorance of our people, and when nobody dares to rise up and say, we have done as much for education as they have in America? Is it not true (as Mr. Lawrence properly said), that we can show a great accumulation of wealth, that we are exporting more largely than any other nation, but there is something more wanted; and I agree with him, there is danger so long as it is wanted; and that there is no time to be lost—not a day, not an hour to be lost. I do not boast of the country we live in, so long as the mass of the people are uneducated and ignorant. Our friend, our worthy president (Mr. A. Henry, M.P.), whom I met at Leeds—and who, allow me to say, most manfully maintains your principles wherever he goes — told them at the Mechanics' Institution meeting at Leeds:—'They say we are a great nation—that is true, we are a great nation, if paying an enormous taxation, and keeping up an enormous navy, and exporting a large amount of goods, constitute greatness, we are a mighty nation; but so long as we have an ignorant people, we have not much reason to boast of our greatness.'

I have nothing more to say than to exhort you, now you have encouraging symptoms of progress, to continue and agitate in the same way you have hitherto done. I have seen nothing since I joined your ranks to make me doubt you have got hold of the right principle. I don't think any other can possibly succeed in this country, that is, provided what I have heard from religious bodies for the last fifteen years be truth,—if they have been shamming, and telling us they have qualms of conscience while they have none at all,—if they have been telling us they are voluntaries, when they are looking and sighing for endowment,—then, I say, the parties who have taken up another principle may succeed, and we may fail, and I can only say I am sorry they allowed me to lose time in trying to make them take up with this. But I do not think it possible that any plan of this kind can succeed. I want you to base it on the American experience; they have gone through this ordeal, and adopted the very plan we want. I call for the American system. I do not want to have my Bible read in the schools; because, if so, the children of 60,000 people here must go uneducated. I am neither an advocate for the Bible as a school-book, nor for its exclusion as a school-book; I am for the American system precisely as it stands. And I say, now is the time for you to continue the agitation of this question, and more actively than ever. The very fact of the attention paid to what is going on in Manchester, by the press of the whole kingdom, shows to what a degree the whole kingdom looks to Manchester to solve this great and difficult question. You have had the honour of commencing this agitation; you are now met with another agitation, which is far from being an enemy or a rival, and will ultimately be an assistant. I will say,—go on—quarrel with nobody—invite their concurrence. If you will appoint me to the Conference, I shall be happy and proud to be one of a deputation to their body, to seek an interview, and ask a private and confidential conversation with the gentlemen taking the lead in this scheme. I say, don't go in opposition to anybody, but keep your own course. I believe you have got the right principle, and, if you have—I know you of old—I believe you are the right men to succeed in it.

# EDUCATION.

## II.

### HOUSE OF COMMONS, MAY 22, 1851.

[On May 22, 1851, Mr. Fox, M.P. for Oldham, brought forward the following motion,—'That it is expedient to promote the Education of the People of England and Wales, by the establishment of Free Schools for secular instruction, to be supported by local rates, and managed by Committees, elected specially for that purpose by the ratepayers.' The motion was supported by Mr. Adderley. It was rejected by 90: 139 to 49.]

IF some stranger had entered the House during the speech of my hon. and learned Friend (Sir D. Dundas), he would suppose that the motion of my hon. Friend the Member for Oldham (Mr. Fox) is not a proposition for voting an additional sum of money to remedy a defect in education, the existence of which we are all ready to admit, but he would rather imagine it to be a proposal to withdraw the funds already applied to the instruction of the people in general, or that my hon. Friend intends to abolish the National Church, and to withdraw the 5,000,000*l.* or 6,000,000*l.*, which is its present endowment; and that the moment he should succeed in carrying his motion, all the present voluntary contributions of the dissenting bodies would entirely cease. That would be the conviction of any one who entered the House during the speech of my hon. and learned Friend. When my hon. and

learned Friend charged the hon. Member for North Staffordshire (Mr. Adderley) with fallacy, I thought that his (the
Solicitor-General's) speech had been founded on fallacy from
beginning to end.    And I think the hon. and learned Gentleman has misunderstood and misapplied the argument of the
hon. Member for North Staffordshire; for he went upon the
assumption that the hon. Gentleman supported two kinds of
education—an education of a secular, and an education of a
religious kind, both out of the public funds.    I understood
the hon. Gentleman to say, that there is an ample provision
for religious, but that there is no sufficient provision for
secular education, and that he would agree to a system of
secular education, rather than have none at all.    The hon. and
learned Gentleman the Solicitor-General said this question
was impracticable ; but the hon. and learned Gentleman
forgets that his own plan has been tried for fifteen years in
this country, and has been brought to a dead-lock; and the
right hon. Baronet the Secretary for the Home Department
(Sir G. Grey) has informed us that a deputation has come
from Manchester, and informed him that the scheme which
has originated and has been attempted to be carried out by
the men of Manchester has failed ; and that, he contended,
was an argument against the proposition of the hon. Member
for Oldham.

Now, before the House decides upon the subject, it is, in my
opinion, right that we should examine the statistics which are
before us.    Let us, in particular, look to the amount of money
which we have granted for educational purposes.    For the
last five years we have had a grant of 125,000*l.* a year, while
there has been but a very trifling increase on the population,
and scarcely any to the persons who have received education
in consequence of the State grant.    And why?    Because it is
a subject that the Government dare not touch in this House ;
because the present system is so unsatisfactory, that, in spite
of two large blue-books of correspondence and minutes, and

an expenditure of 125,000*l*. per annum, the little education we do get in this country is owing to the efforts of the Committee of Privy Council; and I do not blame them for those efforts; but I honour them for trying to do that which cannot be done in this House. No one knows better than Government does that it dares not stir the question with a view of getting a grant commensurate with the wants of the country, in order to carry out the system which at present exists. And now what is it that Government is falling back upon? A local scheme in Manchester, which has already failed in precisely the same way as the Government plan has failed on these religious difficulties. The gentlemen who came to town from Manchester did me also the honour of calling upon me; and I rejoiced to see them endeavouring to overcome the difficulties of realising a system of education. They told me, as they told the right hon. Gentleman the Home Secretary, that they had the concurrence of all the religious sects—that the Roman Catholics had joined them as well as the Dissenters; but I received a letter from them, after their return to Manchester, that, to their surprise and regret, they had to tell me that not two of the Roman Catholic clergy, as the hon. and learned Gentleman had stated, but eighteen, virtually the whole body of the Roman Catholic clergy in that town, had seceded from that plan of education. And why? Simply because the Committee that met in Manchester made it a fundamental principle of their scheme, that in all schools erected at the public expense in Manchester, the authorised version of the Bible should be read; and that being a condition which the Roman Catholics could not comply with, that, of course, separated them altogether from this plan of education.

Now, I ask any one in this House, if any plan of public education can be satisfactory in the boroughs of Manchester and Salford combined, which excludes the poorest of the poor classes? There are in Manchester and Salford at least

100,000 Roman Catholics. They are the poorest of the
population; and, if ignorance be an evil, they are the most
dangerous part of the population to be left in ignorance.
And yet this is a plan on which the right hon. Gentleman the
Home Secretary relies, in order to relieve him from the diffi-
culty he was in. They are in precisely the same difficulty in
Manchester that we are in this House; for I maintain that
the little good that is done was done surreptitiously by the
Educational Committee of the Privy Council, and not by a
vote in this House. What are the Minutes of the Privy
Council? Do you suppose they represent the debates in this
House any more than they do the motion of my hon. Friend
(Mr. W. J. Fox)? Bring forward a vote for the maintenance
of Roman Catholic colleges, in which they will be allowed to
carry on in their own peculiar way their own doctrines and
worship, and do you think that such a vote will pass this
House? There is a fundamental evasion and fallacy about
the whole of this educational vote. I ask you, when you talk
so much of religious education, if this 125,000l. is for religious
teaching?—because I understood, when we were passing an
educational vote, it was not for religious education. When
the vote was first agreed to, in 1834, it was called school-
money; it was 10,000l. or 20,000l. to begin with. Afterwards it was changed to a vote for education; but you did not
vote the money for religious education. Could you vote any
sum in this House, if it were asked fairly for religious instruction? No, it could not be done; and it could not be done for
many years past, and never more shall we vote any money
in this House as an endowment for religion; and, therefore,
when you talk to me about voting for religious education,
I say it is not an accurate description of what we vote
it for.

The hon. and learned Gentleman the Solicitor-General has
talked as if there were some great conspiracy in the country,
—as if there were some parties aiming to deprive the country

of its religious faith; and he seems to assume that, if we allow schools to be established without religious teaching, they would practically be establishing schools to teach infidelity; and he also says, that by establishing schools for secular education without religion, we are, in fact, divorcing morality and religion from education. Now, when the hon. and learned Gentleman rung the changes about advancing the attributes of our nature, and of promoting the intellectual qualities at the expense of the religious and moral, he might surely give us credit for knowing that it was practically impossible to do anything of the kind. We know that religion is a part of moral training as well as the hon. and learned Gentleman does; but what we say is, that there is ample provision in this country already for religious training. There is twice as much spent in this country for religious training that there is in any other country in the world. Then how can it be said that we should exclude religion from education? I want to do nothing of the kind.

Again; we have been taunted with the use of the word ' secular.' Well, I do not know any other word we could use. I say once for all, I consider there is provision made for religious training, but not for secular training, and therefore I wish to provide for secular education. I want people to be able to read and write—to be able to write their names when they sign a contract, or register the birth of their children; I want people to be trained in habits of thought and forethought; and I do not know any other term than ' secular ' for this kind of education    But why ring the changes upon secular education? I say, once for all, that I am not opposed to the Bible, or any other religious book being read in schools.

What I want is, to have the same system of education in England that they have in Massachusetts, in the United States of America. I will not go to Louisiana or Georgia, but my system is that of Massachusetts; and I challenge hon.

Gentlemen to test that system by the experience of that State, and the good it has effected there. That State is not open to the argument that it was a thinly-peopled country: it is an old country, and one which sends forth vast numbers of emigrants; the people are of our own race, and have our own habits; and I want to know why we cannot adopt the same plan in England that they have adopted with success in Massachusetts? We have just now a competition with all the world in the production of that which ministers to the comforts of mankind. If we see the result of ingenuity in any part of the world, we plume ourselves that we can imitate it. If we go to the Great Exhibition, and find a machine there, however cunningly it may be contrived, we shall find men say that what is done in Boston, in America, we can do in England. But if we adopt the Massachusetts system of education, you say it will make the people an irreligious people. I will meet you on that ground. I have been in Massachusetts, and, testing them by any test you may wish—by the number of their churches, by the number of attendants at their churches, by the amount paid for the teaching of religion, by the attendance at Sunday-schools, by the observance of the Sabbath, by the respect paid to religious teachers, by any one test with regard to religion,—I can challenge a comparison between Massachusetts and any part of England.

Well, then, the system of education adopted in Massachusetts is a secular system; and do they prevent the children from reading the Bible? Why, I venture to say, that in the report which I hold in my hand of the Board of Education in Massachusetts, there is not a single word about religion from beginning to end; and yet, probably, there is not one in a hundred of these schools where the Bible is not read. I have no objection to a parish having local management having the Bible in its schools as well as any other book; but what they do in Massachusetts we should do here, by saying, as a fundamental principle, no book shall be admitted into the common school which favours the peculiar doctrines of any Christian sect. Well, now, with a people so jealous of their religious independence as the people of Massachusetts are, what they had been able to do surely we can do in England. They had the same battle to go through there that we have. In Massachusetts, originally, they taught the Catechism in their schools, which had been taken there by the Pilgrim Fathers when they left England, and who carried with them as much intolerance almost as they left behind; but another system now prevails, and with the greatest possible advantage.

Practically, I believe that system will work as well in this country as it does in Massachusetts; and if the system proposed by my hon. Friend the Member for Oldham were carried out, I am persuaded that in ninety-nine out of a hundred of the parishes of England, nobody would object to the Bible being read in the schools, provided it were read without note or comment. In a vast proportion of these parishes there are no Roman Catholics; but I have that opinion of the good sense and rational conduct of men, that, if there were a very small minority — if there were a few families of Roman Catholics who objected to the reading of the Bible — the reading of it could be so adapted to particular times as not to interfere with any one's religious conviction, and in a way that would exclude nobody.

I believe that when the system of free schools is adopted, such will be the estimation in which education will be held by the mass of the people, that it will not be easy to keep children from the schools. Where is the difficulty of our doing what has been done in Massachusetts? I will not be driven from that ground. Give me the Massachusetts plan. I declare my belief, that the mass of the people in Massachusetts are as superior in intelligence to the population of Kent, as the latter are to the people of Naples. I say this advisedly. I ask, then, why we cannot have this system in England? Will you tell me it is on account of the Established Church?

Why, surely, having an Established Church with a very rich
endowment, which supplies a clergyman to every parish, and
the means of religious instruction to the mass of the people—
for the mass of the people has religious instruction without
paying a farthing for it in the rural parishes—will you tell
me, having this advantage, you could not maintain your
ground against another people, who have left religion to voluntary effort, and who have endowed their secular schools?

Now, there has been an objection made that this scheme is intended to supersede existing school-rooms; it has been assumed
that the plan of my hon. Friend (Mr. W. J. Fox) must necessarily throw to waste all existing schools belonging to places
of worship.  I see no necessity for that at all.  I consider that
we may make use of the existing school-rooms, as well for this
system as for any other, and I never contemplated such a
waste as to render useless existing school-rooms.  The hon.
and learned Gentleman the Solicitor-General has told us, and
the right hon. Gentleman the Secretary of State for Home
Affairs is of the same opinion, that if we adopt this plan of
secular education we shall shut up all the other schools.  That
is an admission, by the way, that we are going to establish
something better than the old system.  But they went further,
and said, when we shut up the schools we shall deprive the
people of religious education, because the great bulk of the
people get no religious instruction now, except what they get
in their schools.

When my hon. Friend the Member for Tavistock (Mr.
Trelawny) ejaculated, 'What are the clergy doing?' I
thought that was a natural exclamation.  We pay 5,000,000l.
or 6,000,000l. a year to the clergy, and it is rather a bold
thing for a devotee of the Church to say, if the children do
not get religious training in the schools, they will get no
religious training at all.  The hon. and learned Gentleman
the Solicitor-General, when he answered that ejaculation of
the hon. Member for Tavistock, turned immediately to the

manufacturing hives, where, from increase of population, he says, there is much ignorance. I beg the hon. and learned Gentleman's pardon; but the great mass of ignorance is not in the manufacturing towns but in the rural districts. I admit, indeed, that there is much ignorance in the manufacturing districts, but it is because the surplus population of the agricultural districts go to the manufacturing districts. I do not blame the clergy for being the cause of that ignorance in secular matters, although I think there is a great deal to be said as to the duty of the clergy to see that all persons in their parishes can read, inasmuch as I cannot see how a person can be a Protestant at all, who cannot read; yet I do not attempt to fasten upon the clergy all the responsibility for the ignorance that exists in the country parishes. I know that in many districts they have undertaken more than any one else for the cause of education, and I know that they find great difficulty in maintaining their schools by voluntary efforts in some places. In many rural parishes, three-fourths of the land is owned by absentees, and the clergy have very little chance of getting support from absentee landed proprietors.

How, then, are we to raise the funds to maintain the schools? I want a plan by which, for the purposes of secular education, a parish would be able to rate property. Let property be rated, and each proprietor, whether he were an absentee or resident, would contribute towards the education of the people. I am firmly convinced that money cannot be better applied in any of the small rural parishes than in providing good secular education. By such an education, the people will gain self-reliance and self-respect. Let them be taught a little geography; let them learn what is going on in other parts of the world—what, for example, is the rate of wages in the Colonies—and they will not then rot in parishes where they are a burden on the poor-rates. 80*l.* or 100*l.* a year laid out on education in a rural parish will do more to keep down the poor-rates, and to prevent crime, than the same amount expended in any other way.

I cannot help expressing the great gratification which I feel at the difference between the tone of the discussion this evening, and the tone of the debate last year. For my own part, I must say that there is no other subject on which I feel so tolerant towards everybody as I do on this subject of education. If I see the Government doing something—I care not how—I am grateful for it. If I see hon. Gentlemen opposite—whether High Church or Low Church—trying to secure for the people a better education, I thank them. I see the enormous difficulty of taking any combined step, owing to the religious element, which always stands in the way. If ever there be a time, however, when it is necessary for parties to combine in a system of secular education, apart from religious sects, the present is such a time; for no one can deny that never before was there so much strife and disunion amongst different religious bodies. The hon. Member for Stockport (Mr. Heald) belongs to a religious community which is torn in twain. Is there to be one set of schools for the reformed, and another for the old Wesleyans? As a matter of economy —as a matter of charity, goodwill, and kindness—let us all try to get on neutral ground; let us try to do so, not only on account of the good which will thus be done to the mass of the people of this country, who will never be educated under any other system, but in order that we may have an opportunity of meeting, as it were, out of the pale of those religious strifes which are now more threatening than ever.

# EDUCATION.

## III.

### MANCHESTER, DECEMBER 1, 1851.

[In 1851, two schemes, called respectively the National Public School Association, and the Manchester and Salford Scheme of Education, were recommended to the public, the latter being antagonistic to the former, and
projected in rivalry of it. Mr. Cobden gave in his adhesion to the former
plan, under which, in the face of religious differences, it was advised that
rate-supported schools should not be denominational.]

We are hardly arrived at that point in this great struggle
in which we can venture to say that we will define what the
particular kind of secular education shall be which shall be
enjoyed in the schools which are to be erected or to be maintained out of the public rates. But when that time shall
come, I am quite sure that a great deal of that knowledge
appertaining to our own nature, and to our own design and
object in this world, as described by our friend Mr. Combe,
will undoubtedly form a part of the secular education of this
country—as a part, and only a part of that education—combined, as it will be, with the religious instruction. But,
gentlemen, we have yet to settle this question,—'Shall we
have any education at all in this country, such as is enjoyed
in almost every other civilised country,—I mean an education
supported by all, and free to all?' Now, that is the question.

I hold anything else but that to be short of the real end and object of this controversy. Shall there be a system of education supported by all, and common to all? Well, you are going to settle that question, as you have settled so many other important topics, in Manchester. For I don't conceal from myself, that upon the local contest in which you are now engaged, will depend the kind of education which is likely to be adopted in this country.

The application which is about to be made to Parliament for a private bill embodying a scheme for giving to Manchester and Salford a local system of education, a system confined to those two boroughs, will, if it be adopted, I have no doubt in the world, be made a model for the adoption of all other localities similarly circumstanced—I mean, manufacturing districts and our great commercial centres; and whatever may be adopted as the Act of Parliament for Manchester, will, as in the Municipal Corporations Act, become a general Act, under which other places may put themselves, just as they now apply for the benefit of a charter under the Municipal Corporations Act. I have no doubt of that; and therefore you are engaged in a struggle of vast importance, not only to yourselves, but to the whole community. Scotland, as Mr. Combe says, has its eyes upon you. The rest of the country is equally interested in what you are now doing.

I do not want the National Public School Association to think that at present their important duties lie elsewhere. Their duties lie here at home; and my opinion is, that if their exertions are not centred here, in Manchester and Salford, we shall fail to do our duty in this crisis of this controversy. Now, what is the question at issue between the National Public School Association, which would apply their scheme to Manchester and Salford, and the Manchester and Salford Association, which applies merely for a local bill? Why, I think the whole difference between you may be traced to that

long-standing and almost sole difficulty in the way of a
national system of education in this country—I mean the
religious difficulty.  The real question which you are now
disputing is this—shall the education be one in which the
secular shall be separate from the religious element, or shall
it be one where the teacher in your schools shall be paid out
of a public rate to teach all kinds of religion, at the expense
of all sorts of people?  That is the sole difference—I mean,
that is the source of all your differences; because, if you removed the religious difficulty, I do not think that people in
Manchester would be at all disputing as to whether there
should be more or less of self-government in your scheme.  I
believe that the members of the Manchester and Salford
Scheme Association would be just as much inclined to preserve the municipal self-government of Manchester as you
would be; but they remove a part of the administration, and
control, and discretion, in their school business to London,
simply and solely because they think by that they are going
to escape the religious difficulty which lies in their way.  And
it is not a question of whether the school-rooms that are
now in existence shall be used for giving both secular and
religious instruction, because by the plan which has been
adopted by this society at a Conference which met this
morning, it is now the rule of this society,—it is a plan which
we propose to adopt as a part of our bill for Parliament, that
all schools belonging to separate churches or chapels which
may be disposed to give education, subject to inspection, in-
suring that the secular instruction shall be good in quality,
may receive payment per head for all the scholars educated in
those schools, just in the same way as it is proposed in the
Manchester and Salford plan, only there is a stipulation,
there is a safeguard, that there shall be no payment made
to those teachers for religious instruction; that the religious instruction shall be given apart, and at separate
times; and that it be distinctly understood, that out of the

public rates there shall be no payment made for instruction in religion.

Well, then, let it no longer be said that, by the plan which we propose, we are going to sacrifice the existing schools. We propose to take authority for buying existing schools, or for renting existing schools; and we now propose, in addition, by the resolution of this morning, to do precisely what the Manchester and Salford Society proposes to do,—that is, to pay for the instruction of children in secular knowledge, in all schools belonging to the churches or chapels where they may be disposed to give us the guarantee by inspection that they are giving a proper secular education. The question between this association and the rival association is simply reduced to this:—they insist that in all schools religious education shall be given at the expense of the whole community. That involves one or two difficulties and objections, which I think are insuperable. In the first place, what a reflection it is upon the office of religious teacher;—they say, 'We will make schoolmasters the teachers of religion.' Do they propose that schoolmasters shall graduate in a course of divinity in order to be qualified for that instruction? Why, how they discount and degrade their own profession, in making a schoolmaster, who is never taught divinity at all, on equality with clergymen, and calling upon him to give religious instruction! But it involves a greater difficulty than that; and here is my objection to the principle which requires absolutely and without exception that religious instruction is to be given in the school. It involves this grand and insuperable difficulty and injustice,—that by these means you exclude from those schools many of those whose parents have been rated to the maintenance of those schools.

Now, in the first place, I find in the local bill, as drawn up here, that in all schools which are to be built out of the rate levied upon all the property of this borough, the reading of the Holy Scriptures in the authorised version shall be a part of the daily instruction of the scholars. Everybody will remember that I took my stand against the exclusion of the Bible from any schools, when we were settling our points of faith as a secular association. I said, 'I never will be a party to any scheme that attempts to lay down in an Act of Parliament this monstrous, arrogant, and dictatorial doctrine—that a parish or community shall not, if it please, introduce the Bible into its schools.' I made my stand against that, and said I never would put my hand to any such doctrine; but at the same time, I am just as prepared to take my stand against any system which levies taxes upon Jews and Roman Catholics, which sends the tax-gatherer round to their houses, and calls upon them to contribute to the school-rate, and then insert a clause like that which says they and their children shall enjoy no advantage from those schools.

Now, I ask those gentlemen, have they any scheme by which they propose to exempt these parties from paying the taxes, whom they exclude by this clause in their bill? Well, then, I ask them if they are prepared to carry us back, not only into a worse state of intolerance and bigotry than any that exists on the Continent of Europe at the present time in any Protestant country, but actually to the times when, in towns like Frankfort in olden times, Jews were shut up and set apart in the town, and made to live in certain streets, and be locked up at home at night long before Christians were required to be in their domiciles! Why, it is a worse treatment to the Jews than they received in those countries where they were thus persecuted. You educate Christians out of Jewish money, and you deny them the right of having education themselves for their own children. What would be said,—now just put a parallel case,—if, after levying a rate for lighting the town and supplying it with water, you compelled the Jews to live in some street by themselves, where there was neither a gas-lamp nor yet a water-pipe carried? And I won't say merely the Jews, but the Roman Catholics;

because you absolutely prohibit the Roman Catholic from entering those schools, if you mean what you say in the clause of this bill. You say, 'the authorised version of the Bible,' nine hundred and ninety-nine thousand parts of which are verbatim the same as in the Roman Catholic version; but it contains two or three passages, in which I never yet could perceive any very material difference of meaning, and by retaining those passages, by making that the test, and thereby striking at a point of conscience in those who object to that version of the Bible, you prohibit them as much as though you put a policeman at the door, and said, 'No Roman Catholic shall enter here.' Well, I say it is impossible that such a thing as that can continue permanently to be a recognised state of things in a country that asserts in the slightest degree that it is under the government of just principles.

And now, where is the difficulty of our opponents agreeing to our own terms? Where's the difficulty of the friends of the other society joining in the principle which is now enunciated by this society? They insist upon making the schools doctrinal and denominational, but at the same time they have so far receded from the stand which the Church formerly made, that they will allow a scholar to enter other schools and be exempted from the doctrinal teaching of those schools, provided he carries a written request from his parents to be so exempt. So far, they go a great way towards recognising our principle, that secular education may be given apart from religious instruction, inasmuch as those children who are allowed to carry in their pockets a pass by which they are exempt from this religious teaching, at all events are placed very nearly in the position in which we would place all our schools; and therefore, in point of fact, they recognise the principle which we advocate, with this exception, that they require absolutely that the Bible—the authorised version of the Bible—shall be read daily in all their schools. Now, I do hope that the authors of the Manchester and Salford School

Society will address themselves to-morrow to that question, and see whether they cannot move one step farther, and abstain from the attempt to inflict injustice and wrong upon a large section, and that the most necessitous part of the community, by attempting to make them read that which, if they did read, they could only do it with hypocrisy; and, therefore, by practising that hypocrisy for the sake of getting education, certainly could not, in the eyes of any rational being in the world, become more just or more moral by the process.

Well, gentlemen, there's the position in which we stand, or, rather, you stand, in Manchester. I have stated the amount of difference between your two schemes, which will next session come before Parliament. Were I now living in Manchester, I should address myself solely to the question, for the present, at least, as it affects these localities; because, I repeat to you, whatever is done in Parliament the next session will, in my opinion, act very much as a model for a great part of the kingdom; and, therefore, it is your business. We shall have only that strength in Parliament to deal with these two topics which you give us by your support out of doors. It is for you to decide which of these two plans shall be adopted; but sorry I am to see that a great portion of those who I thought were, above all others, vitally concerned in this question,—I mean the dissenting bodies,—have stood aloof from this controversy under the most vain and delusive ideas that ever possessed human beings,—that this was not a question solely as to one or another scheme, but because they are under the impression that there is a possibility in this country of going back to no scheme at all. How men moving in society can be at all under the delusion that there is a doubt about such a subject, I cannot imagine. If there is one point upon which this great community, I think, has more made up its mind than another, it is in adopting some system of combined action for public education, under the sanction of Government, through local rates and local management, as far as possible.

There's no doubt but that is determined on by the great mass of the community ; and however any body in sincerity, which is so involved in this question as the dissenting body is, can be moving about the country and trying to advocate or plead for that impossible cause—no public education at all—passes my comprehension. I believe them to be sincere, I cannot doubt they are sincere; but if they were really aiming at playing the game of that party which they have always considered inimical to their religious interests and their religious freedom, they could not have taken a more effectual course than they have been during the last twelvemonth, by ignoring the existence, almost, of this National School Society, and detaching themselves from that side of the question in which I should have thought, at all events, looking upon their principles as they avow them themselves, they were more interested than any part of the community.

Now, I speak with some degree of feeling on this subject, because I have taken to this secular school association simply and purely, as I have avowed again and again, because I thought there was a great act of injustice perpetrated upon Dissenters. I thought they were going to be wronged by another system which they regarded as a system of endowments. I have again and again said, that as one who every Sunday take my children to a parish church, and therefore am living, as it were, upon endowments, I could not plead for myself that I had those conscientious scruples which I was told and believed the Dissenters had. ·I took up this secular system, because I thought, while it did no injustice to the Church, that it did injustice to Dissenters. I find the great body of Dissenters not only holding aloof, but some of them,— Dr. Halley, for instance, and his friends, and the great organ of their party, the *Banner*,—stating that if driven to take one or the other, they will take the Church system. Do they understand their own principles? Have I done right in believing what they have told me of their principles,—that they shnn the system of endowments? I was advocating the American system of education, because I knew there, in America, it was applied to the satisfaction of those descendants of the Nonconformists who have not forgotten their principles, and where we know the system works without injury to the rights of conscience of any individual in the country. I speak thus emphatically upon this subject, because I don't hesitate to say, I am for the edncation of the people. I believe the great mass of the people take less interest in this sectarian squabbling than many others of us are apt to imagine. The great mass of the people want education for their children; they are sick to death of these obstacles you throw in their way. I believe that when our extended franchise throws more power into the hands of the multitude, you will see that what I say is true,—that there's a feeling for national edncation which will sweep away all these cobwebs with which you attempt to blind the great mass of the people; and feeling this, and having done my best to do justice to all parties in the matter, I say now, emphatically, ' I vote for education ; I'll support edncation ; I'll do the best I can for Dissenters ;' bnt I'll never oppose a system of education, which promises to give to the mass of the people an opportunity of raising themselves in life, and benefiting their children, by having a share in its advantages, which, as Mr. Combe says, those alone above them have hitherto enjoyed. I don't, therefore, profess to come here to oppose the local plan. I believe, if that plan be adopted, it won't remain where it is.

I believe, if we once get a system of free schools, the spirit of a free-school system will very soon possess itself of the minds of the people; that it will be found here, what it has been found in Ireland, under a far severer pressure and test than it ever can have in this country : it is superior in its strength to almost all other influences ; and I believe, if we once establish a system of free schools supported by rates in this country, it won't be long that you who pay rates here in Manchester will allow either Roman Catholics or Jews to be excluded from the benefits of those rates.

I won't go into the question of how far the people of this country want education. Go and inquire amongst the people themselves. Go and ask the agricultural labourer at his plough; test the amount of thought and capacity that that man has had by instruction imparted to him; ask him where the guano he's dealing with as a manure, day after day, comes from: he has no idea. He never heard such a subject suggested. Ask him whose land it is he's working upon. He can tell you the farmer's name, because the farmer pays his wages; but ask him who his landlord is;—ten to one he has never thought of it, because in England, from want of education, and training the mind to thought and reflection, such men don't learn to note causes of any kind. Ask him the geography of the next parish. As for the geography of the world, he can't tell you whether America is in France or in Spain. It is unquestionably true, and cannot be denied by any one that has travelled, that we are the worst educated people of any Protestant country in any part of the earth. Mr. Combe has borne witness to this; Mr. Baines has borne witness; and I challenge denial on personal investigation. Is that a safe state of things to be left in? They tell us that voluntaryism has worked well. I say we are the only people that have had voluntaryism, and we are behind all the world. What do they say in America? Hear what Mr. Daniel Webster said, in a speech delivered at an open-air meeting the other day, in Washington :—

'The population of the United States is 23,000 000. Now take the map of the Continent of Europe, and spread it out before you. Take your scale and your dividers, and lay off any one area in any shape you please, a triangle, a circle, a parallelogram, or a trapezoid, and of an extent that shall contain 150,000,000 of people, and there will be found within the United States more persons who do habitually read and write than can be embraced within the lines of your demarcation.'

But in the United States they don't trust to voluntaryism. They make use of their parochial and their municipal organisation to secure a system of schools free to all, paid for by all, and not a system of schools merely for that class of destitute people to whom Mr. Baines has alluded. The New England schools have so grown and improved, that they have taken in by degrees from one class to another, from one grade to another, till now, in many parts of New England, you find no private schools at all. All classes are educated at the common public schools.

It is my firm belief that, in this country, a system of schools once established, paid for by all, would very soon here —as, in fact, we have seen in the case of the King's Sombourn school, conducted so admirably by the Rev. Mr. Dawes— be found to go on so, that, by degrees, the small farmer's son would be sitting by the labourer's son; and as you improved still more in your system of education, the small farmer's son would be coming and taking his seat by the side of the rich farmer's son. I have no doubt in the world that would be the case, because by combination— by co-operation—you would have a better system of schools than you could have anywhere else; and therefore I don't look to a system of free schools as one of charity for the great mass of the people,—I mean for the poorest people. One of the benefits we should derive from common schools would be, that it would cause that greater intermixture and blending of society that would arise from the middle and working classes sending their children to one common school, where they would become more familiarised in their common views, and tastes, and habits, and the boys would be brought up in genial sympathies and more intercourse than that which prevails at present in this country. I do not argue with those gentlemen who tell us that the voluntary system has answered; I don't argue with them. I say, 'Go into the highways and byways, and inquire for yourselves if it answers.'

I don't think it is safe for us as a nation to be the most ignorant Protestant people on the face of the earth. This is a period in the world's history when the very security, the trade, and the progress of a nation, depend, not so much on the contest of arms, as on the rivalry in science and the arts, which must spring from education. Even lately, we have been inviting all the world to a great competition. Did any reflecting man walk through the Great Exhibition without feeling that we were apt to be a little under a delusion as to the quality of men in other parts of the world, and their capacity to create those articles of utility of which we are apt to think sometimes we possess a monopoly of production in this country? Did nobody feel somewhat struck at the vast superiority of the French in articles of taste and delicate manipulation ; and were we not equally struck to find ourselves so closely trod on the heels in everything that relates to the more rude utilities of life, in American productions, where we found ourselves beaten in shipbuilding, in locks, pistols, and many other things we had to show? Did it not make Englishmen feel that they had to look about them? And how will you be able to rally, how will you attain to further improvement in arts and manufactures but by improving the education of your people? I don't think we can wait. And this is a reason why I am tired to death of this sectarian quarrel, which is preventing the people from being educated : year after year is passing away, and the time we are losing is not to be recalled. Why, it has been stated in public, it has been stated in our public records, that the poor people don't send their children to school, upon an average, more than two or three years, and in some cases not more than ten months.

Well, we have passed over two or three years in this sectarian strife, in which we prevent the people from having education as they have in America, by a system of common schools, and whilst we are doing so a generation, a section of the community, passes into mature life without any educa-

tion at all.   One great wave of humanity passes on, and we
never get a reflux of the tide, we never have a chance of
giving these people an education.   We cannot wait!   I hope
the people of Manchester will rouse themselves to a consideration of the danger and difficulty of this matter.    I
hope you, who have gained so many victories in other things,
will find yourselves called upon to exert yourselves, not only
for your own benefit, but for the benefit of the people at
large.   I augur well from the large meeting I see here to-
night; I augur from it that you take an interest in this
question.   I am told that a still larger meeting is to take
place to-morrow, on this subject.   All this augurs well of the
interest you take in this question.   If Manchester men will
direct their minds to this question perseveringly and energeti-
cally, and if you consider that in this case, as in a former
struggle, you are fighting the battle, not only for England,
but, in some degree, for the whole civilised world, I have
no doubt you will present such a case to the House of Commons next session, that we shall be relieved from any doubt
or difficulty as to the course we shall have to pursue.   Send
up your petitions for what you conceive to be the right
measure for Manchester and Salford; give us your support,
and your Members, I have no doubt, will do their duty in
this matter, and most happy I shall be to be found alongside
of them in that which is found to be necessary.

# EDUCATION.

## IV.

BARNSLEY, OCTOBER 25, 1853.

[Mr. Cobden made the following Speech in the Hall of the Mechanics' Institute at Barnsley. During the time that he sat for the West Riding, it was his custom to deliver addresses at the principal towns within that division of the county.]

THE details we have heard of the early difficulties and infant struggles of this association are only just those trials which we are all liable to encounter in every good and great work which we undertake; and I should not consider a good worth possessing, unless it were deserving of those efforts which are required to make such an institution as this prosper. I remember the time when the first mechanics' institutions were launched under the auspices of Dr. Birkbeck—a man whose name can never be held in too high reverence for disinterestedness and truly Christian patriotism, and his honoured colleagues, Lord Brougham and others. I remember when they launched the first mechanics' institutions. They were intended not so much as schools in themselves, but as something to supply the defects of early education to that class which in former times had not had an opportunity of receiving such

education ; for you must remember that Dr. Birkbeck and
others were the strenuous advocates of a better system of
education for the young, and the mechanics' institutions were,
to a large extent, something devised as a resource for those
who had not had any opportunities for early education.  Such
being the case, in order to carry out the object of the founders
of these institutions, it is not enough for you to draw together
a large number of members in your lecture-room or your
library, or to collect books in your library ; these things could
have been obtained, probably, in a less convenient way before
mechanics' institutions were created ; but one of the primary
objects of mechanics' institutions was to enable young men,
feeling themselves deficient in some particular branch of
knowledge, to join a society where they could have the opportunity of repairing such a deficiency.   For this purpose it has
been customary, in all good mechanics' institutions, to
establish classes — classes for different branches of study,
which young men, or men of middle age, or even old men,
could join, and find that particular knowledge they were in
quest of.  Now, I believe your institution has not such classes.
I don't mean to mention it as a reproach, because you have
had so many difficulties to fight against, that I did not expect
you could get over all these things at once ; but, having surmounted so many difficulties, and placed your institution, as I
cannot but hope, on a firm basis,—for an institution which
has grown under so many difficulties must have a firm basis,
—you must determine that it shall be—what all mechanics'
institutions were intended to be—a means of instruction to
the neglected adult population.   I think, too, you must have
classes—classes for teaching arithmetic, geography, drawing ;
and even chemistry is not too much to aspire to.   You must
have also—and I hope you will—a class for French.

   Now, there has been an allusion to one branch of study
which particularly interests the manufacturers of this district
—I mean drawing and designing.   I think I have heard the

gentleman who last spoke say that there was no drawing-master in Barnsley; that you must have an itinerant drawing-master, who, located at Sheffield, must have his circuit, radiating from that town, and who must pay occasional visits to Barnsley. If I were a Barnsley manufacturer, and dealt in figured damask linens, I should beg and entreat the reporter not to let that fact get out; don't let the world know that Dunfermline has got all the designs. I am told, for I am very curious in inquiring anything about the art of design, inasmuch as my own business was very much connected with that art,—I have been told, I say, in consequence of inquiries I have made since I arrived here, that your damask linens—the patterns of those damask linens which we all so much admire, are made by the weavers themselves; that the patterns are designed by the labourer who weaves the cloth; and that he, so far from having had any instruction in the art of designing, has been living in a town where there is no drawing-master. Now, I take it as a proof that you have a talent for drawing among you; that you have had a body of men brought up as weavers, who have been able to make patterns for you; but I say to the capitalists, ' You are not doing justice to that mechanic, if you are only going to give him a ninth or a tenth part of a drawing-master.' You must let it go forth from this moment—and I hope my friend on the left (Mr. Harvey), who is interested in the matter, will rise before the conclusion of these proceedings and declare it—that another month shall not elapse before steps are taken to insure the presence of a drawing-master in Barnsley; and that all those ingenious young weavers who are able to put together a damask pattern shall be so circumstanced as to be able to learn something of the art of design from a practical teacher before we meet here again.

I say, then, that one of your classes must be a drawing-class; and in this respect you will be aided by the Government in a way which I think it is perfectly legitimate for a

Government to aid—I mean this, you will be supplied by the Board of Trade with the best possible models, both of sculpture and drawing.  I am an advocate so far for centralisation, that I will at all times sanction and applaud a Government which draws to one centre the best designs and models for drawing and sculpture, and then multiplies those designs and models in the cheapest possible way, with a view to their diffusion among the general public.  I rather think you have already been to the Board of Trade, and got something in the way of models, or something of that kind; and, if you have, I suppose you are going to make some use of them; but you can't make any use of them unless you have got classes; and I will undertake, on behalf of this meeting and the intelligent manufacturers of Barnsley, to say, that it is intended to connect with this institution a drawing-class, and that a drawing-master shall be appointed who will be capable of giving efficient instruction.

With regard to other branches—take, for instance, a class for arithmetic—I would ask, how many young men are there who may be sitting at their looms with the best of heads upon their shoulders — phrenologically speaking — but who, from some circumstances not under their control, had no opportunity of cultivating those heads when children ?  And yet such young men feel within them a capacity to fill any station of life, if they had only had the necessary education to enable them to rise in society.  The first thing such young men require, if they are to do anything in the way of business, is to learn something of arithmetic; but in your institution how is a young man to learn the rule of three, or obtain any knowledge of arithmetic ?  It is necessary, therefore, that you should have a master.  I don't mean a stipendiary master, for I hope you will find independent, public-spirited men enough in Barnsley who will begin and initiate the necessary classes in connection with your institutions; and that you will not only have drawing and arithmetic classes, but also a French class ;

for, now that French is very generally spoken, a knowledge
of it is necessary to enable you to enter into communication
with a large portion of the public, and there is no reason
why you in Barnsley should not be able to do this as well as
others. It is the object of mechanics' institutions to bring
those branches of knowledge within the reach of adult mechanics and labouring men in all the towns of the kingdom.
Now, Barnsley is of such a size, that it ought to be able to
maintain a mechanics' institution of such a magnitude as to
support all these classes. I am aware it is difficult in a small
town to do this; but here you have a population of from
14,000 to 15,000 in Barnsley and the neighbourhood, and I
must say that 250 members are not enough for a population
of such magnitude. You must double that before we have
another anniversary. Let every member try to find another
member, and then the thing is done. Your terms are 10*s*.
a year. How in the world can anybody buy amusement, or
gratification, or enlightenment, cheaper than at 10*s*. a year?
And I would say to the members who already belong to the
institution, you have a particular motive in trying to add to
your numbers. You have a large lecture theatre, a reading-
room, and library; and I venture to say, if you double your
numbers, you may still comfortably accommodate yourselves
in your lecture-hall, reading-room, and library, while your
fixed expenses remain the same. If your income at the present
is 130*l*. a year, your fixed charges will be from 70*l*. to 80*l*.,
leaving you not more than 50*l*. for the purposes of lectures,
purchasing newspapers, and such-like things. Your current
expenses must be going on, whether you have few or many
members; and, therefore, by increasing your numbers, the
additional subscriptions you get will be so much gain in the
way of providing education, and increased attraction in your
institution.

I think you ought also to try to establish a school in connection with this institution. That is one of the most useful

of the adjuncts of the Huddersfield and other mechanics' institutions.    I would recommend you to endeavour to connect
a school with this institution, as a feeder to it, for it is by
means of schools that you are to get members.    If, in consequence of the advice given by our friend, Mr. Wilderspin,
twenty years ago, there had been an infant-school established
in every village, you would not have wanted customers for
your mechanics' institutions; they would have grown up
around you.    And this brings me to the question—leaving
for a moment this institution—what were these institutions
established for?    Not as a system of education, but to supplement the want of education, and we want the education
still which we wanted when these institutions were founded.
I know that it is made a vexed question, and to some extent
a party question.    I never regarded it as a party question.    I
don't care through what it comes.    Give me voluntary education, or State education—but education I want.    I cannot
accept statistics to prove the number of people who attend
schools—to prove that the people are educated, because I cannot shut my eyes to what is evident to my senses,—that the
people are not educated,—that they are not being educated.
I was talking only yesterday with a merchant in Manchester,
who told me that he had attended at the swearing-in of the
militia in one of the largest manufacturing towns of England,
and that not one-half of those sworn in could read, and not
one-third could sign their names.    Now, without wishing to
utter any fanatical opinion with regard to the Peace question,
I must say, with all sincerity, I think it would have been much
better to hand these young men over to the schoolmaster
rather than to the drill-sergeant; for I think the safety of this
country would be more promoted by teaching them to read and
write than by teaching them to face-about-right rightly.

I was talking this subject over to an old friend of mine
at Preston, and he said, 'I attended the coroner one day
last week at an inquest.    There were thirteen jurymen;

five signed their names, and eight made their mark.' Can I
shut my eyes to what is going on around us? I cannot; and,
therefore, I say, we are not an educated people; and I say it is
our duty, and our safety calls upon us, to see that the people
are educated; and I know of no place more fitting to discuss
this subject than in such a meeting as this, because I take it
for granted you are all interested in it. You all admit the
deficiency of juvenile instruction, or you would not have
attended to the defective adult education. We are not an
educated people, and I have no hesitation in asserting that, in
point of school learning, the mass of the English people are
the least instructed of any Protestant community in the
world. I say that deliberately. I remember quite well, at
the time of the Hungarian emigration into this country after
the revolution, a very distinguished minister or religious
teacher of Hungary was talking to me on the subject of our
education, and I told him a large portion of our people could
neither read nor write. He could not believe it, and said,
' If it is true a large proportion of your people can neither
read nor write, how do you maintain your constitutional
franchises and your political liberties? Why, it is evident to
me that your institutions are rather ahead of your people, and
that this self-government is only a habit with you.' It is a
habit, and we will cling to it and hold it; but I want a safer
foundation. I want to have our self-government a habit of
appreciation—something our people will be proud of, not
simply a habit; and there is no security unless it is based
upon a wider intelligence of the people than we meet with at
the present moment. It meets us at every turn—you can't
do anything in social reform but you are met with the question of education. Take the question of sanitary reform.
Why do people live in bad cellars, surrounded by filth and
disease? You may say it is their poverty, but their poverty
comes as much from their ignorance as their vices; and their
vices often spring from their ignorance. The great mass of

the people don't know what the sanitary laws are; they don't know that ventilation is good for health; they don't know that the miasma of an unscavenged street or impure alley is productive of cholera and disease. If they did know these things, people would take care they inhabited better houses; and if people were only more careful in their habits than they are, and husbanded their means, they might get into better houses. And when I hear persons advocate temperance, which I, as one of the most temperate men in the world, always like to hear advocated, I say the best way is to afford them some other occupation or recreation than that which is derived only through their senses—the best way is to give them education. If the working man is deprived of those recreations which consist of the intellectual and moral enjoyments that education and good training give, he naturally falls into the excitement of sensual indulgence, because excitement all human beings must have. Therefore, when you wish to make them more temperate, and secure moral and sanitary and social improvements among the working classes, education, depend upon it, must be at the bottom of it all.

Gentlemen, I see in different parts of the country a great social quarrel going on between different classes of the community. For instance, in the town of Preston, you have 20,000 to 30,000 persons out of work; and there is in that place not a chimney but is cold and cheerless—neither smoke nor steam cheering your eyes. Look at the destitution and misery caused by laying a town in this state for a month or six weeks. Why is this? I answer, it springs from ignorance. Not ignorance confined to one party in the dispute. It is ignorance on both sides, and deplorable is its result. But do you suppose that when the world becomes more enlightened, you will have such a scene as this,—of a whole community stopping its labours for a month or six weeks, and creating misery, immorality, and destitution, that may not be removed for five or six years to come? When masters and men understand the principles upon which the rate of wages and profits depend, they will settle their matters and arrange their differences in a less bungling way than that which now brings so much misery upon all parties to the quarrel. Even now, however, we see great progress in this respect. I remember the time when the cessation of labour by 25,000 persons would have led to riot and disturbance, and the calling out of the military. This is not to be seen now. We see passive resistance and firmness to an extent which, if they had policy and propriety at their back, would be highly desirable and most commendable. But we shall probably live to see the time when another step will be taken onward. You will live to see the time when men will settle these matters, not by resorting to blind passion, by vituperation, and counter-vituperation—when the question of wages will be left to the master and man to arrange according to their own interest—when the whole question of wages and the rate of wages will be settled just as quietly as you now see the price of any article fixed in the public market. I am not saying one word of the merits of either side upon this question. Both parties think themselves right, and both are, no doubt, right in attempting to get the best price they can, the one for his labour, and the other for his capital; but if there were more intelligence upon this question—if the laws were better understood which decide finally and inexorably the relative value of labour as well as everything else, these matters would be settled without that hideous amount of suffering which I deplore to see accompanying these strikes and troubles in the manufacturing districts. And when I say, gentlemen, that intelligence will put an end to these things, I am only saying that will be done here which has already been done in America. You cannot point to an instance in America, where people have more education than they have here, of the total cessation from labour of a whole community, of an entire town given over as a prey to destitution. You cannot point out such an instance in America; neither will you see it in England, when that intelligence and enlightenment which these institutions are intended to promote shall be spread throughout our country.

Well, this brings me back again to the point that we want schools—schools to teach people these principles—schools to teach people from their youth to take a calm and reasoning view of the things which affect their interest, and so to educate them, that they shall not allow others to lead them away by appeals to their passions. We shall never be safe as a manufacturing and mining community until a school invariably grows up along with every manufactory and at the mouth of every pit and mine in the kingdom. Now, I must here again allude to America. When I came through Manchester the other day, I found many of the most influential manufacturing capitalists talking very gravely upon a report which had reached them from a gentleman who was selected by the Government to go out to America, to make a report upon the Great Exhibition in New York. That gentleman was one of the most eminent of the mechanicians and machine-makers of Manchester, employing a very large number of workpeople, renowned for the quality of his productions, and known in the scientific world, and whose scientific attainments were appreciated from the astronomer-royal downwards. He has been over to New York to report upon the progress of mechanics and mechanical arts in the United States. Well, he has returned. No report from him to the Government has, as yet, been published, and what he has to say specifically upon the subject will not be known until that report has been so made and published to the country. But it has oozed out in Manchester among his neighbours, that he has found in America a degree of intelligence among the manufacturing operatives, and a state of things in the mechanical arts, which have convinced him that, if we are to hold our own—if we are not to fall back in the rear in the race of nations—we must educate our people, so as to put them upon a level with the more educated artisans of the United States. We shall all have an opportunity of judging of this matter when that report is issued; but sufficient has already oozed out among his neighbours to excite a great interest, and, I may say, some alarm. Well, I am delighted to find an intelligent man has been selected for this duty, for all the world will approve of the selection made, because the gentleman alluded to was fully competent to the task; and he has come back to tell us it is necessary to educate the people.

I went to that country twenty years ago, and I published a record of my opinions. That was written in 1835, and I stated that England would be brought to the consciousness that it was to that country she would have to look with apprehension as to manufacturing rivalry; and now I am delighted that it should turn out as I have stated, that it has come from a quarter—from a person so well qualified to procure correct information, that no one will question the truth of his report when it comes out. I say I am delighted, because I want England to know her danger, if there is one. Napoleon used to say to those in communication with him, ' If you have any bad news to tell me, awake me at any hour of the night, for good news will keep, but bad news I cannot know too soon.' I say, then, I am delighted with this, for let but Englishmen know of a danger to face, and of a difficulty to surmount, and there is nothing within the compass of human capacity which they will not accomplish; but the great misfortune is, that Englishmen are too much given up to and incrusted with their insular pride and prejudice,—a sort of Chinese notion of superiority,—that they will not awaken up and use their eyes as to what is going on in other countries until it is too late. I am glad, therefore, that this question is to be brought forward; but why should America be better educated than England? Do you think that a new country, which has the wilderness to cultivate, primeval forests to level, roads to make, and every bridge

and church to erect,—do you think that such a country is in
a position to rival an old country, if that country will only do
its duty to its people? No; an old country has greater advantages and facilities at command than a new one; and if
you find a new country beating an old one in this matter,
depend upon it, it is because of some fault in the old one. We
don't read in ancient Greece, when she sent forth her colonies,
that they became the teachers of the mother country. No;
Athens always remained the teacher of the whole world. And
it is a shame if a new people, sent out from us only yesterday,
is to be held up for our admiration and example, and this, too,
in the matter of education.

Now, I hope that it won't be said that there is anything in
these remarks which is out of place in an assembly such as
this. We are all here, at all events, presumed to feel an
interest in the subject of education, and therefore anxious to
promote it. And I don't despair even now. I should not
despair of this country, if the people of this country would
only resolve to do it, surpassing all the world in education in
a generation or two. But we must not refuse to adopt the
improved machinery of other countries. We must not be like
the Chinese with their junks, who refuse to build their ships
after our improved model; we must not refuse to adopt what
we see in other countries if better than our own. If we see the
Americans beating us in their spinning-jennies and in their
sailing-boats, we adopt their improvements; if they send over
a yacht which beats ours, we send over and build one which
will beat them; if a man comes over and picks our locks, we
may wonder how it is he makes better locks than we do, but
we buy them; and so it is in other matters of this kind. But,
on the question of education, they have in the United States
adopted a system which we in this country have not adopted,
except in Scotland to some extent; and what is so natural as
that we should follow the same rule in this matter as we do
in the manufacture of our machines for spinning cotton, and

in the construction of our ships? I take it that, the result being in favour of American education, it proves that they have adopted better means than we have; and, if we would rival them, we must not be ashamed to adopt their plan, if better than our own   There is not any party, I believe, now opposed to education; none who do not think that there is more danger from ignorance in our present artificial state than in education. Whatever our political predilections, there is not one who will not say—whatever we are doomed to undergo, whether proceeding from a straitening of circumstances, from a decline of our commerce, or from difficulties of a strictly political character—whatever there may be in store for us of troubles and distresses—there is nobody but will say we had better have an educated people to meet them than have to encounter them with masses of ignorance and untrained passion; for, after all, the masses of the people do govern in this country—they are called on in the last resort. Everyone must admit it is better to have an arbitrator who is trained to discuss reasons and to deduce facts from evidence— it is better to have minds of this sort to settle great national questions, than to refer such mighty interests to the arbitrament of ignorance and passion.

Now, ladies and gentlemen, if I have said too much on this subject to you, and to those elsewhere who may read what we are now saying, I must tell you that I feel so strongly upon it, that, when among a body of men met together in favour of education, I will not be responsible for withholding my opinions in reference to the want of juvenile education, for it is not possible to compensate for the want of juvenile education by means of such institutions as this. We may by such means improve the education of the people, but we cannot have a really educated and safe community, unless we begin at the beginning by training the young. I can only say, whether you look at this question of education in the interest of morality or religion, as affecting the happiness, interest, or the welfare of society—in whatever way you regard this question, you may depend upon it the very highest interests, the dignity, honour, and happiness of the people, are bound up with it.

# INDEX.

## U.